D0604355

THEO TAN AND THE IRON FAN

THEO TAN
AND IRON FAN
THE

JESSE Q. SUTANTO

FEIWEL AND FRIENDS
NEW YORK

A Feiwel and Friends Book
An imprint of Macmillan Publishing Group, LLC
120 Broadway, New York, NY 10271 • mackids.com

Our books may be purchased in bulk for promotional, educational, or
business use. Please contact your local bookseller or the Macmillan
Corporate and Premium Sales Department at (800) 221-7945 ext. 5442 or
by email at MacmillanSpecialMarkets@macmillan.com.

Library of Congress Cataloging-in-Publication Data
Names: Sutanto, Jesse Q., author.
Title: Theo Tan and the iron fan / Jesse Q. Sutanto.
Description: First edition. | New York : Feiwel and Friends, 2023. |
    Series: Theo Tan ; 2 | Audience: Ages 8–12. | Audience: Grades 4–6. |
    Summary: After learning that his brother's spirit is trapped in Diyu,
    twelve-year-old Theo and his snarky fox spirit, Kai, encounter demons,
    Kings of Hell, and Princess Iron Fan as they try to reach Jamie's spirit
    before it faces judgment on the solstice.
Identifiers: LCCN 2022046355 | ISBN 9781250794369 (hardcover)
Subjects: CYAC: Spirits—Fiction. | Supernatural—Fiction. | Brothers—
    Fiction. | Chinese Americans—Fiction. | LCGFT: Paranormal fiction. |
    Novels.
Classification: LCC PZ7.1.S8823 Tj 2023 | DDC [Fic]—dc23
LC record available at https://lccn.loc.gov/2022046355

First edition, 2023
Book design by Mallory Grigg
Feiwel and Friends logo designed by Filomena Tuosto
Printed in the United States by Lakeside Book Company, Harrisonburg, Virginia

ISBN 978-1-250-79436-9
10 9 8 7 6 5 4 3 2 1

To my husband, Mike, who is the fan that every author deserves. Thank you for seeing this one through.

KAI

1

The shopkeeper yawns. I yawn as well. I wish I could nod at the pimply kid and say, *Yeah, it's mind-numbing stuff, innit, watching over a shop like this?* But alas, I'm here undercover, so I am unable to say anything to him for fear of giving myself away.

When I say "undercover," I mean it in a very real way; I am currently under the folds of a burlap sack filled with—ugh—dried bright-purple beetles. I've changed into a purple beetle myself just to fit in, though of course I lack the desiccated, blank appearance the other beetles in the sack have.[1]

At four minutes to closing time, one last customer hobbles in. The customer base of the health shops on Stockton Street are always hobbling, given they're all ancient with gray hair, gently bowed backs, and missing teeth. The one who's just come in is a sweet old granny with cloudy eyes who shuffles ever so slowly while peering at all the containers of rare and not-so-rare medicinal herbs and lizards and various animal parts. A stark contrast from Theo, who I catch a glimpse of pacing outside, a worried frown dug into his face. Normally, I have nothing but the utmost respect for elderly humans, but right now, I'm practically boiling with impatience. I mean, come on, coming into a shop four

---

1 I can't help but be fabulous in every form I take—you must know this by now.

minutes before closing is such a Karen move. I scratch my chitin irritably with my front legs.

The shopkeeper speaks in fluent Mandarin, greeting the customer without any trace of irritation.

"Two hundred fifty grams of yínxìng, please," the old lady warbles.

The shopkeeper nods and takes out a tin from the back of the counter. "We're also having a special on fortune-telling here," she says, gesturing at a poster behind her. The poster says: THE PAST, EXPLAINED! THE FUTURE, REVEALED! JUST $5.99!

Ugh, charlatan. There's nothing I despise more than those who claim that they can see the future, because no one can predict it. I make a face at the shopkeeper, but of course she doesn't see it.

As the shopkeeper doles out the dried herb, the old lady asks for a hundred grams of dried léi gōng téng. "It's for my arthritis," she explains. "I'm brewing a spell to prepare for the autumn weather."

Uh-oh. Arthritis medicine usually requires some . . .

"Oh, I have just the thing for that!" the shopkeeper says. Argh, what is this kid's problem? All they have to do is get the lady's order and be done with it, but nooo. They have to go above and beyond. "Powdered beetles."

"Oh, I don't know about that. I don't like the bitter taste of insects . . ." The old lady grimaces.

"You really can't taste it at all," the shopkeeper says. Maybe she's paid on commission. "We powder them right here in the shop for you, and you just sprinkle a pinch over your food or drink and voila! My grandmother swears by it. A miracle cure, she calls it."

The old woman peers suspiciously at the shopkeeper, who smiles and says, "Tell you what: I'll give you two ounces for free, okay? You can tell me if it works or not."

No, not okay!

But the old lady is smiling. "Oh, what a polite child you are. So kind to your elders."

"It's nothing," the shopkeeper laughs, walking over toward the section with rows of burlap sacks.

Uh, what to do, what to do . . . I should skedaddle out of here. But then she might see me and try to, I don't know, crush me with a shoe or something.[2] Instead, I burrow deeper into the sack, scuttling past hundreds of dead beetles, their hard, shiny carapaces clicking crisply around me. Not my finest hour, I must say. Now that I'm buried under dozens of layers of beetles, I'm probably safe. Safe-ish.

But instead of scooping up the top few beetles, the shopkeeper plunges her metal scoop deep, deep into the sack. I catch a glimpse of dull metal and have scant time to say, "Uh-oh," before the scoop turns my world into a tornado. I'm yanked into a wave of beetles stirred everywhere in a mad jumble. I scurry, fluttering my wings, desperate to get away from the chaos, but as a tiny beetle, I'm no match for the brute strength of a teenage human, even a pimply one. Then the stirring stops, and I feel a sudden sense of weightlessness. Light blinds me for a second before my

---

2 You humans are barbaric like that.

little beetly eyes adjust. AH! I'm at the top of the pile of scooped beetles! This is bad.

And the shopkeeper is moving swiftly toward a horrible rectangular contraption with metal teeth inside it. She flicks a switch and the machine clunks to life, the metal gears grinding with the most horrific noise. Okay, the time for subtlety is over. I rush off the pile of dead beetles.

"Aiya! One of them is alive!" the old woman screeches.

The shopkeeper looks down and spots me. She moves fast, without any hesitation, and her hand closes over me. Ack! I focus my qì and change into a tarantula. She must have felt my bristly fur because she goes, "Huh?" and opens her hand. I wave a furry leg at her and grin, flashing my fangs meaningfully.

She throws her hands up and shrieks. Beetles rain down on us as the two humans dance around the shop, screaming. I scuttle away as fast as I can, but tarantulas aren't known for their speed, and the shopkeeper has recovered from her initial shock and grabbed a broom. *Thump!* The broom crashes down less than an inch away from me. Now it's my turn to shriek. I zigzag as fast as I can, shouting, "Spiders are your friends! We eat flies! Everybody hates flies! They eat poop, you know!" But it comes out as a spidery squeak, too high-pitched for lousy human ears to catch. I run into the wall. Trapped. No cracks to slip into, no burlap sacks to hide in.

I've got two options.

1. Change back into fox form and tell off these humans for almost killing me, a venerable almost-goddess. Downside:

They might not know what an impressive creature I am and treat me as a demon and make a huge fuss.

2. Stay in character. Downside: I will get squished by the broom, which is probably quite injurious to my health.

I close my eyes.[3]

But before I can do anything, the front door swings open and someone rushes in and shouts, "HI! HELLO!"

We all pause, mouths agape. Theo stands at the entrance, his eyes wild with panic, his mouth frozen in a terrified grin. "Um, HI!" he shouts again. "I AM HERE . . . to, uh, buy ingredients for, um . . . one potion."

As the shopkeeper/spider-murderer and the old lady stare at Theo, I quickly change into a fly and zip away into the air. Theo watches me for a second before realizing that would give away my position, and he tears his eyes away from me. I land in the farthest corner of the room and wipe my brow. That was way too close for comfort. If only I could leave this place now, but no, a fox spirit's work is never done. I rub my two front legs together and watch as Theo babbles on about needing to brew this and that for a summer project.

The shopkeeper grits her teeth and glances at the spot where I was. Seeing it spiderless, she sighs and turns to Theo. "Kid, there's like thousands of ingredients here. The number of potions you can make is practically endless. You need to come back when you

---

3 Okay, so technically spiders don't have eyelids, but I'm used to having them so let's just say I am closing the windows to my soul—look, it's really hard to explain and you're interrupting an action scene, Bertha.

know exactly what you need, okay? Shop's closed." She ushers him out impatiently before turning back to the gruesome task of crushing dead beetles for the old lady. Far, far in my corner, I stay as still as I can, watching as the shopkeeper gives the old lady her order and locks up for the night.

As soon as the lights go out, plunging the shop into darkness, I buzz around the room, checking for any alarms. I spot one at the front—a lizard perched above the front door, its eyes red as it scans the room for any warmth that might indicate life. Another lizard guards the back door. Okay, not a problem for me, especially since in my current form I'm way too small to register any body heat. But just to be safe, I give the lizards wide berth in case one of them decides to have me as a late-night snack.

I scan the room, my bulbous fly eyes roaming over the numerous sacks and containers of ingredients. Various insects, roots, and herbs. Rolls of silvery spun moonlight, golden sunlight, and cottony clouds. I buzz to the back of the counter, where there's a glass cabinet. Inside are vials of rarer stuff—shimmering dragon tears, a single phoenix feather, flames gently licking from it inside its vial, the curved toenail of a xièzhì, and—success!—a vial of spirit-world river water. I rub my two front legs together again, grinning with excitement.[4]

Now how do I get to it without these lizards catching me? I think for a moment, then wave my front legs around and form an Illusion. The next moment, the shop is filled with juicy, fat flies

---

4 Yes, I know flies can't grin, but I'm grinning inside, okay? Look, we've been over this, Bertha. Don't get so hung up on the technical details. Now shh, you're going to alert those lizard spirits, and then we'll really be in trouble.

buzzing around. The lizards jump up, their red eyes widening, their tails ramrod straight. Their forked tongues flop out of their mouths as they look at the dozens of tantalizing flies around them. While they're distracted, I quickly zip to the cabinet. I change into a tiny monkey, open up the cabinet, wrap my tail around the vial of river water, and jump out.

In my mammalian form, the lizards should detect my body heat, but they're still too busy chasing the flies, getting increasingly confused when they throw out their tongues and catch nothing but thin air. No time to lose. I run to a side window that we've left propped open with a stick earlier in the day. But as I climb up the wall, my long tail swishes a little too wide and brushes against a display case of dried bat wings. The ropey monkey's tail takes a while to get used to; I'm more accustomed to my usual soft, bushy fox tails.

The vial in my tail tinkles against the glass case. A soft sound. If the shop were open, with customers bustling about, no one would have heard. But now the little noise slices through the silence with painful clarity. The lizards' heads snap round, and their beady eyes lock on me. Fear jolts through my limbs. I scrabble for the window as the lizards open their mouths. A small, sickly green flame forms between their lips.[5] I catch hold of the windowsill and pull myself up. Too slow. With a pop, the lizards blow jets of green fire at me. I leap away just in time, the fur on my back singeing as the flames just barely miss it. These lizards are not playing around. Unfortunately, my tail knocks against

---

5 No, I don't know if lizards technically have lips, Bertha. It's so not the time to be asking such questions.

the window, and the stick propping it open falls down and the window slams shut, trapping me inside.

Panic sizzles deep in my gut. I'm going to have to break something to be able to escape out of here, and doing so would mean that I'm committing a bad deed. Of course, stealing a vial of river water is also considered a bad deed, but we've got an idea on how to circumvent that little detail. Breaking and entering, on the other hand . . . I've been down the whole turning-into-a-demon route before, and I have no interest in going down that same path. It's not a good path, trust me. But I don't see any other ways out of here.

There is the sound of breaking glass as a stone crashes through the small window. The lizards jump and open their mouths, emitting a piercing squeal.

"Kai!" Theo's voice calls from outside.

I summon the last of my strength and make a giant leap through the hole he's made for me, the jagged glass around the window frame scratching my fur as I fly. I land right in Theo's arms, and he flings a coin purse through the window and shouts, "Sorry! But I hope that pays for the window and the water!" before dashing away with me clutched tight in his arms.

Despite the wailing alarm, I let my breath out in a small sigh, relieved to be reunited with my human companion.

THEO
2

My heart is still racing even after we've turned several corners and arrived at a deserted alleyway. No one's pursued us. We're okay, I keep telling myself. But still . . .

I take a deep breath and look down at Kai, who's turned back into her original fox form.

"Are you okay?" The words tumble out in a rush as I check her snout, her eyes, her teeth for signs of demonic corruption. "Do you feel any—uh, I don't know—demonic stirrings?"

She licks her front paw and scratches her ear with her hind leg. "Nope, just the usual amount of demonic activity." She sees my expression and quickly adds, "I'm just kidding! I'm fine, really."

My muscles unclench. "You can't joke about that, Kai. I mean, after what happened last month—"

"When you made me turn into a demon, yeah, I remember. But we were careful this time. Technically, I was already in the shop when it closed, so it doesn't count as breaking and entering." Kai grins and swishes her two tails. "And *you* broke the window, so that bad deed's on you. And then you paid for the river water and the broken window, so technically it wasn't shoplifting."

I wince. "I'm pretty sure the shopkeeper, and the law, wouldn't agree with you on that. If we got caught, we'd definitely be in trouble. And I hate doing this—all this skulking around, stealing stuff."

Kai's smile fades, her little fox eyes turning somber. "I know, but we don't have a choice."

I nod. "Yeah."

After Niu Mo Wang told us that Jamie's soul is stuck in Diyu, I told Namita, Danny, and Xiaohua about it. The five of us put our heads together to try and think of a way to rescue Jamie, and the best we could come up with was to find some spirit-world river water, which would allow us to travel from the human world to Diyu.

But spirit-world river water is such a dangerous item they only sell it to authorized people. There's no way I would be able to get permission from the Bureau of Magic Safety or from my parents, so I've been reduced to stealing, which leaves me feeling slimy and awful. But I would do anything to save Jamie. The thought of him in Diyu is a knife buried in my side. Kai says Jamie is technically not in hell; he's in hell's waiting room, but that doesn't sound that great, either, to be honest.

"How much did you put in that purse you threw into the shop?" Kai says.

"Half of everything I saved up."

Kai whistles. "That's more than enough to cover the cost of the river water and the broken window. Stop beating yourself up over it."

I manage a small smile. "Thanks, Kai."

"I should be thanking you for getting me out of there." She rubs her fuzzy head against my chest, and I feel a million times better. Then she uncurls one of her tails and drops a small vial into the palm of my hand. "There you are."

It's as though my insides have caught fire. Just the sight of it brings a tremor to my hands. Here it is: the key to saving my brother's soul. I lift it up, as though in a trance, and open it.

The smell hits me right away. Summertime, pools, laughing kids.

"Chlorine?" I say.

"What?!" Kai snatches the vial from me and sniffs it. She groans. "This isn't river water from Spirit World—it's water from the local pool. It's a fake. Curses! I should have known that charlatan would sell nothing but fakes. She's also a part-time fortune teller, you know. I saw a poster in the shop. Didn't I tell you fortune tellers are the worst? Anyone could tell your fortune—all they'd have to do is make stuff up from thin air!" Her tirade over, Kai's face sags; even her large pointy ears droop. "All that trouble we went to, and for nothing."

It feels as though the strength has completely leached out of me. I slump to the ground, not at all caring that it's dirty, and bury my face in my hands. Kai nuzzles her snout into the crook of my neck, and we're silent for a while, both of us lost in thoughts of Jamie.

—※—

It feels like ages later that we finally gather enough strength to start walking to the meeting place. Along the way, I practice using my qì to cast minor spells. It's become a habit, ever since the Know Your Roots program at Reapling, to continue learning how to use my qì. I didn't even want to get a replacement cirth pod, but I had to for school. But outside of school, I rely instead on my inner power to cast spells. The cool thing about using qì to cast spells is that unlike cirth pods, qì is never depleted. I do get tired if I cast too many complicated spells, but a hearty meal and a good night's sleep are all it takes to refresh me. I'm now adept at most of the simple ones, like lifting small objects or heating up dinner, and I can even do some of the more moderate spells, like retrieving objects from a faraway distance.

Kai is no longer as snarky when I run into difficulties with it, which honestly helps a lot. I didn't think her encouragement would mean so much to me, but it really, really does. Kai knows all the spells I've been learning to cast with my qì. Well, almost all. There's one that I haven't told her about, because I'm sure she would—well, actually, I don't know how she'd react, and I'm too scared to find out. It's taken a lot of energy for me to keep it locked away in the deepest, darkest part of my mind, well away from the mind link that Kai and I share. Fortunately, there are limitations to our mind link; we can still choose to keep some things secret from each other, which is probably for the best. I'm hoping against all hope that we can convince the kings of Diyu to let Jamie come home, but in case that doesn't work, I'm going to cast this spell. It'll put everything right. I'm just not sure that Kai would agree with me. Or maybe she might, and that would somehow be even worse.

Namita spots us before I see her, jumping up from the bench she was sitting on and waving madly at us. "Here, guys!"

"Shh, you'll wake the whole neighborhood," Danny says.

Namita continues waving and calls out in a hushed whisper, "Here, guys!"

Although I'm down about our lack of success, the sight of Namita, Danny, and Xiaohua warms my chest. They've been so involved in my quest to rescue Jamie. I know firsthand the difference between taking something huge on all by myself versus doing it with trusted friends, and I definitely prefer the latter.

"Any luck?" Namita says.

I shake my head and let out a frustrated sigh.

"And have you figured out the right chant to take us to Diyu?" Namita says, adding salt to the wound.

I tighten my mouth into a line.

"If you drank the river water without chanting the right spell, it would just take you to Spirit World," Namita says. "You need the right words to take you to Diyu, or as close to it as possible."

Honestly, she's been just a tad insufferable ever since she decided to take on Chinese mythology in preparation for our journey. If we ever figure out how to get to Diyu, that is. I glance at Kai, hoping she'll have some bright suggestion, and see that she's staring pointedly at Xiaohua. I realize that Namita is also staring at Xiaohua expectantly. Then it dawns on me. Xiaohua is well-versed in all things related to mysticism. If anyone knows the right spell to go to Diyu, it would be her!

Xiaohua shifts on Danny's shoulders, her eyes narrowing as she frowns. "Why is everybody staring at me?"

"Um, I think they're hoping you'd know a chant to take us to Diyu," Danny says.

A puff of smoke releases from Xiaohua's nostrils as she grunts. "Unlikely. First of all, as a dragon, I am a divine being, I have no need of ever going to hell."

Kai gasps. "Are you a divine being? Goodness, I would never have guessed. It's not like you've mentioned it fifteen times in the last two hours."

Namita and I exchange a look and bite back our smiles. I hate to admit it, but Xiaohua does use the word "divine" quite a lot.

"Second of all," Xiaohua says loudly, "you shouldn't go to Diyu, Master. It's full of dangers."

Now we all look at Danny, who shifts awkwardly before looking down at his feet. "Um, yeah. About that. I . . . I want to go."

Xiaohua rears back, her golden eyes widening and her nostrils flaring. "What do you mean?"

"I want to help find Theo's brother," Danny blurts out.

Gratefulness nearly overwhelms me. "Thank you."

"And to be honest, I also want to go for myself." He looks up and gives us a hesitant smile. "Ever since Kai attacked me, I've been having nightmares. I'm scared of shadows. Heck, I'm even scared of my own shadow now."

My stomach turns into a knot of writhing snakes. "I'm so sorry—"

"It's fine. I mean, it's not fine, but you've apologized enough and made up for it already. I just—I need to do this for myself." He straightens up, his jaw squaring with determination. "I want to face my fears."

Xiaohua closes her eyes and hugs Danny tight, pain and worry and affection clear on her face.

"What about when Xiuling sent you guys to Diyu?" Namita says. "Did you hear what spell she used?"

"No," I say, "and plus, that sent us straight to Niu Mo Wang's lair. I don't think that's quite where we want to go."

"Maybe you could ask Niu Mo Wang?" Namita says. "He's still stuck in that cage, right? So maybe you could ask him to tell you in exchange for you letting him go?"

Kai and I grimace. It's true that Niu Mo Wang is still trapped in a small cage. I keep him in a corner of my room and give him plenty of food and water each day. But we haven't told the others how, even now, the bull-demon king still begins each day with a fierce, albeit tiny, roar and swears vengeance on us all. It's why Kai and I have yet to figure out how to release Niu Mo Wang back to Diyu in a way that wouldn't endanger us.

"I don't think he's in any sort of mood to help us," Kai says. "More likely he'd tell us a fake chant to entrap us somewhere and get us killed in the most horrific way."

"Yes," Xiaohua mutters with a pointed look at Kai, "we all know better by now than to trust demons."

Kai narrows her eyes but doesn't bother replying. For a moment, we're quiet, all of us out of ideas. I look out at the view around us. Standing near the Exploratorium gives us an amazing view of San Francisco, with the twinkling lights of the city sprawled out above us like a million fireflies. Once in a while, when the wind blows in the right direction, I catch snatches of music and laughter and squeals from Pier 39. I can see the Ferris wheel lights turning in the distance, and I'm suddenly filled with a dull ache as I remember Jamie taking me there just a couple of years ago for my birthday. Well, to be fair, Mama and Baba took us, but they didn't do much with us, just walked to the end of the pier and looked out onto the vast, heaving ocean below. They gave me and Jamie ten dollars each, and we spent half of it on rides and the rest on saltwater taffies and silly charms. Jamie got a charm that made his farts smell like doughnuts—but of course, the charm was a mere trinket and made his farts smell like, well, fart doughnuts. I bought a charm to ward off bad dreams. The charm worked well until Jamie died, then nothing could ward off those nightmares.

Namita puts a hand on my shoulder to reassure me. "I'm sorry, Theo," she says. "I know how much this means to you."

Somehow, I manage to muster up a smile for her. "Yeah. It's just—gosh, it feels like there's an obstacle every single step of the way, you know?"

"That's just how anything worth fighting for is," Namita says. She gazes out across the bay at the impressive hulking form of the Bay Bridge. There are thousands of lights all over it, and it's one of the most beautiful sights the city has to offer. "But we're here for you. Let's go home and sleep on it, and maybe an idea will come tomorrow."

I frown.

Namita sighs. "I know. Trust me—I'd like to stay and think about this some more, but sometimes, sleeping on a problem is the best way of solving it."

"No, it's not that. When you said sleep on it, I thought of something . . ." I gnaw on my lower lip and try to grab the fleeting thought I'd just had. Then it comes to me. "The slumber party!" I shout. I turn to Danny, who flinches slightly. "Danny, you remember that night? When Xiuling basically drugged us and got us to go to the spirit world?"

"Um, yeah?" he says cautiously. "But like you just said, we went to the spirit world, not to Diyu."

"You all did, but I didn't!" I cry. "I mispronounced the chant and ended up in the Doorway. Kai, you found me in the Doorway, remember?"

Kai flicks her two tails and licks her front paws. "Not your finest moment, mind you. You were drugged out of your mind."

"What's the Doorway?" Namita says.

"It's the place that connects Spirit World to Diyu," I say. "I think it's got doors leading to hells from different cultures."

"That's right," Kai says merrily. "It's got a door to Diyu, a door to Naraka, a door to Hades, a door to . . ."

"We get it," Danny says, looking markedly uneasy. "Doesn't sound like a great place."

"No." I shudder, recalling the trees with snakelike roots and the boiling sky. And of course, the Yāoguài that had hunted us like prey. "But it's probably our best route to Diyu."

"Sounds awesome!" Namita says, as though I've just told her about Disneyland and not an actual doorway to hell. "Tell us the chant!"

I wince. "I don't know it." At everyone's look of dismay, I quickly add, "I was drugged, remember? I could barely recall my own name. But I know how we can find out!"

"How?" Namita says.

Kai guesses what I'm about to say before I open my mouth, and I feel her muscles tighten, her tails bristling.

"We've got to go back to Reapling, haven't we?" she says.

I meet her eyes and nod. "Yes. We're going back to Reapling."

KAI

3

Reapling is a mere shell of what it used to be. I'd thought that the sight of the ruin of this evil corporation would make me happy, and it does, in a petty human way, but it also elicits a surprising stab of sorrow deep inside me. Because I remember seeing it for the first time with Jamie. I remember sharing his excitement at the magnificence of the grounds, his pride in the program he'd helped design. And I remember, too, all the fun we had flying around the place, zipping over and under the floating islands, splashing through the floating waterfalls, and laughing as we got soaked.

Now Reapling is completely silent, almost pitch-dark, the only light available the weak silver light of the stars and the full moon above us. The kids were chattering merrily as they flew on Xiaohua's back, but when she lands in the middle of the ruined grounds, we all fall silent. It's like landing in the center of a graveyard.

And it is a graveyard, a place of death and mourning. In the darkness, the empty buildings around us resemble the carcasses of some great beasts, broken and crumbling. Many of them have smashed windows and doors hanging off their hinges. The police combed through this place with ruthless efficiency, gathering everything that might be useful as evidence. The angry mob did the rest. As soon as the police were done with their search, the people of San Francisco, horrified and enraged by the news of what had been going on in the company, gathered and stormed the place, breaking everything that remained.

I have such mixed feelings being back here. I mean, aside from the awful ambiance, there's also a worry that's been niggling at the back of my mind. See, I'm not actually sure what's going to happen when Jamie comes back. I'm already spirit-bonded to Theo, but I'm pretty sure I still retain my old bond with Jamie. Which means . . . when he does come back, whose companion spirit would I be? As usual, I shove the thought to the back of my mind. I'll deal with that part when it comes.

"Wow," Namita whispers. "This is really different from what I remember."

"Yeah," Theo whispers back.

Times like these, I would've usually come up with some witty repartee, but even I'm rattled. I walk ahead of Theo, sniffing the air, trying to detect any signs of danger. Xiaohua apparently feels as cautious as I do because she doesn't bother shrinking back down. She remains in full size, staying close to Danny as she surveys our surroundings with a low growl.

"I do not like this," she grumbles.

"Fair," I say, "but have you ever liked anything?"

She shoots me a look. "I like plenty of things, fox. Funny though, I can't think of a single one that involves you."

Ouch. Okay, maybe I deserved that zinger. A flash of light catches my eye, and I quickly hiss to everyone to be quiet. We crouch low, and in the distance, I spot a uniformed guard walking across the grounds, waving a wand idly. Gah, it's just like Reapling to still be employing guards to haunt their ruined grounds. We wait until the guard is safely out of sight, then breathe a sigh of relief.

"So what are we looking for, exactly?" Danny says in a hushed voice. His eyes are wide, his mouth slightly open, a scream probably ready to leap out at any moment. It's a testament to my kind and gracious nature that I haven't taken the chance to shift into something horrific that would shock the boy. Okay, that and the fact that Xiaohua would probably immolate me. Also, as much as I hate to admit it, things have been rather awkward between me and Danny since the Know Your Roots program. I mean, did I kidnap him and then leave him cursed for a bit? Yes. But I've been cleansed. You'd think he'd be over it by now. "This place looks like it's got nothing to offer us," he says.

"I hate to say it, but I agree with Danny," Namita says. "The police have probably taken every scrap of evidence. Whatever's left was probably looted or destroyed."

We all look at Theo. I'm ready to comfort him and tell him not to feel too bad for failing to come up with an actual viable idea, but he's wearing a weirdly eager expression. "What have you got up your sleeve?" I muse.

Theo gives me an apologetic grin. "Um, I've got a wacky idea . . . a one-in-a-million chance. It probably won't work, but it's worth a try?"

"What is it?" Namita says impatiently.

"Well, we know that Eyes are most often trained to hide so that they're subtle. Chances are the cops might have missed a couple of Eyes. We could try luring them out." His grin has turned into a full-on grimace. "Do you guys remember my fight with Creighton Ward?"

The name alone is enough to make my hackles rise. I can't stop my upper lip from curling up and revealing my fangs. Creighton Ward was a fox spirit in disguise. Over the years, his evil deeds had turned him almost fully demonic, and he nearly killed Theo.

"Well, during the fight, an Eye flew toward us. I was trying to get it to help me, but it was completely loyal to him. I think they're all taught to view him as their master. So maybe if we make them think that Creighton Ward is here, any remaining Eyes around might come out of hiding?" Theo chews his lip and gives me an apologetic look.

"What?" I say, taking a small step backward. Everyone is now looking at me. "Oh no. No. Definitely not."

"Please? Just for a minute," Theo says.

I groan. "You can't possibly know what it's like to take the form of that greasy human! Well, fox. But he might as well be a human; he was so repulsive. No offense to you humans, of course."

"Has anyone ever told you that saying 'no offense' doesn't actually make the thing you say inoffensive?" Namita says.

I shoot her a look.

"Come on, Kai," Theo says. "Please?"

"Please?" Namita says.

Even Danny and Xiaohua are looking at me expectantly. And so, yet again, the fate of our quest rests on my delicate, graceful shoulders. With a dramatic sigh, I focus my qì and conjure up the image of Creighton Ward in my mind. I feel my form changing—

my limbs lengthening, my fine, sharp features turning blunt, my beautiful glossy fur melting into rubbery human skin. Ugh, definitely a downgrade. When I open my eyes, the others shrink back from me ever so slightly.

"You look disturbingly like him," Namita says.

Danny nods and gulps audibly.

"Yes, well. Ask, and you shall receive." I stretch out my arms, testing the weight of them. I'll never get used to the heavy, cumbersome weight of human arms. The next moment, I realize that I'm being strangled. Argh, not this again! This time, I identify the culprit immediately and wrench the cursed tie from my neck. "Why do human males love to wear a noose around their necks?"

"It's fashion," Namita says, like that explains anything.

"Oh, that makes it all right then," I say snarkily.

"Kai, you forgot your tails again," Theo groans.

"I didn't forget—it's just really hard to shift them."

Namita takes off her hairband and uses it to tie up my tails. I stuff them down the back of my pants. We all survey the results dubiously.

"It looks like you have a very . . . ah, ample behind," Namita says, grinning at me.

"Eh, I can carry it off.[6] Right, now what?"

"Now we—" But Theo doesn't get a chance to finish whatever he's about to say, because a tiny whisper pipes up from a distance, getting louder by the second.

"Behind me!" Xiaohua hisses, circling her great scaled body

---

6 What can I NOT carry off? That's the question.

around the kids and turning to face the source of the sound with teeth bared.[7] I ball my hands into fists and raise them, though what I'm about to do with these clawless things, I have no idea.

The thing finally comes into sight. It's a small orb zooming toward us with an angry hiss.

"It's an Eye!" Theo says. "It worked!"

Sure enough, the Eye screeches to a halt right in front of me. The orb cracks open, revealing the tiny imp inside, who leaps out and flings itself straight into my chest.

"Master!" it cries. "O Great Venerable Master of mine, thou art back!"

"Uh . . . " I look up at Theo, who nods and gestures at me to keep up the ruse. "Uh . . . affirmative, aye, aye. But let's be quiet, yes?"

"Oh, a great tragedy has befallen us all, Master! But Pea Green was smart, Master! Pea Green hid far, far away when the bad people came to take all of Pea Green's comrades away."

I raise a hand and lightly pat the small imp on the head with the very tips of my fingers. "Er . . . good job, Pea Green. Jolly good. Could you speak in a whisper, perhaps? Good, thank you." I'm painfully aware of the guards, though I'm not sure how many there are and how far apart they are stationed. If any of them were alerted and saw me in Creighton Ward's form, things are not going to end well.

Pea Green sniffs. "Ha, and to think, everyone used to make fun

---

7 I can't help but notice that she's left me out of the circle. Do you think it was intentional? A bit mean of her, really, don't you think?

of Pea Green! 'Pea Green is so weird,' they used to say. You used to say it, too, Master, but it's okay when you say it."

I widen my eyes again at the others. Really now. I didn't think I could possibly hate Creighton Ward any more than I did before, but the man's awfulness knows no bounds. "Uh . . . I . . . apologize?"

"Oh, Master, no!" Pea Green shout-whispers. "No, thou shalt not debase thyself by apologizing to a lowly creature such as myself!"

"Er, well, it sounds like I was a right bully, and that wasn't very nice, so I'm sorry."

Pea Green gasps, his eyes turning glassy with unshed tears. "They said to me, they said, 'Pea Green, that master of yours is a bad-news bear. He will never appreciate you.' But I said, 'NO, he holds me in the highest esteem! Despite all the insults he throws my way, and the occasional kick, I know he regards me well.' And now I have been proven right. Look at that! An apology!"

"Right, yes, I apologize," I say, to sobs of happiness from Pea Green. "Jolly good. Er, listen, Pea Green, I need to ask you for a favor."

Pea Green gasps. "A favor? But of course, Venerable Master, you do not need to ask—merely command me as befits an all-powerful being."

"Oh? Oh, right. Of course, yes." I clear my throat and tug at my collar, belatedly recalling that I've thrown away my tie in a fit. "Well, ah, I would like to see a recording of the Chinese children at the Know Your Roots program. Specifically the night of the slumber party, where they—ah, we—got the children to drink a potion and chant a rhyme to take them to Spirit World."

"Right away!" Pea Green says, and he taps on his small wrinkled head for a second. When he blinks, his eyes cast an eerie green glow, which flows over all of us. As the light touches us, it swallows us into the imp's memory.

Around me are the kids, being led by Xiuling into a circle. The sight of Xiuling makes my breath catch. She's still missing, still out there somewhere, doing gods know what, and the anger and hatred that I feel toward her is overwhelming. My stumpy human fingernails stretch back into claws as I watch her walking into the center of the circle.

A glance at Theo tells me it's just as difficult for him to look at her as it is for me. Next to Theo, Danny is staring, wide-eyed, at the illusion of himself. Past-Danny dismisses Xiaohua, and Danny winces, wrapping an arm tightly around Xiaohua. "I shouldn't have done that," he mutters. Belatedly, I recall that this was the same night that I attacked Danny to take his vial of river water. Guilt lances through my belly, hot and sharp. I try to shoot Danny an apologetic look, but he's studiously avoiding looking in my direction.

Xiuling tells the kids that they're going to play a game. My ears prick up. This is it. She teaches the kids the rhyme, and I move closer to Past-Theo to hear exactly what he says. Theo does the same, advancing to the other side of Past-Theo.

As the children start chanting, I pick out Past-Theo's voice, slurring from the potion and stumbling with his trademark hesitation when it comes to speaking Mandarin. He mispronounces at least a third of the words. I spot the bits that sent him to the outer reaches of Spirit World instead of where the other kids were going, and I smile to myself. That's it. We got the chant, and I know exactly how we need to modify it to make sure we end up in the Doorway.

"Very good, thank you, Pea Green," I say.

Pea Green closes his eyes, and the memory dissipates. When he opens his eyes again, he's frowning at me. "You thanked me."

"Er, yes?" Belatedly, I realize that Creighton Ward probably never bothered to thank the Eyes. With a small sigh, I lift my chin haughtily and snap, "Don't get used to it."

The frown melts away from Pea Green's face. "I won't, O Fabulous One!"

"Good, well, you're dismissed. Toodles!" I wave at him and turn excitedly to face the gang.

"What's that?" Pea Green says.

"What's what—oh." Namita's hairband must have snapped under the strain of my bushy tails, and now one of the tails has flopped out of the back of my pants.

"Is that a fox's tail?" he says with open shock and horror.[8]

"I have this condition . . ." I struggle to think of what possible condition might explain the presence of a bushy flame-orange tail. "It's called, ah, tailitis."

He gasps. "You're a fraud! A lowly fox spirit who has stolen the venerated form of the great Mr. Creighton Ward!"

"Okay, first of all, fox spirits are hardly lowly. And second of all,

---

8 I mean, really now, is there a need for such rudeness?

speaking of Creighton Ward, boy do I have news for you. Incidentally, did you know that he was also a fox—"

"What he means to say is," Theo hurriedly says, jumping between me and Pea Green, "we were sent here by Creighton himself."

"Yeah, we had to retrieve some information for Creighton Ward," Namita pipes up. "And you've been such a great help. We'll totally mention that you were the one who helped us out."

"LIES!" the imp shouts in a shockingly loud voice for someone so little. "I can smell the stink of your lies! How dare you come here in his beautiful form and desecrate these hallowed grounds?"

"It's a corporation, dude, geez," Namita mutters.

"Please, please lower your voice—" Theo says.

"I shall rain down such havoc upon you!" Pea Green screams, zipping around us.

Xiaohua draws herself up, lifting her great big dragony face toward Pea Green. Smoke curls from her nostrils, and in her deepest voice, she says, "Are you threatening us, little one?"

"You bully!" Pea Green shouts. "You will be sorry, all of you! You will pay dearly for this!" Then he shoots up into the sky, emitting an ear-splitting wail as he does so.

Shouts erupt from around us. The guards!

"Climb up!" Xiaohua roars. The kids and I clamber up onto her back, and as the first guard comes into sight and aims his wand at us, Xiaohua soars into the night sky. Bolts of attack spells fly toward us, but Xiaohua avoids them with infuriating ease. Such a show-off.

She doesn't stop flying until we're well away from Reapling, back in the heart of San Francisco. She alights at the Golden Gate Park, and the kids slide off.

I clear my throat, breaking the silence. Looking around at the visibly shaken faces around me, I say the only thing I can think of. "Right! I think that went well, don't you?"

THEO
4

It takes a while for my heart rate to go back down to normal, but when it finally does, I feel the first stirrings of excitement coursing through me. We did it. I can hardly believe it, but we really did! We got the chant to take us as close to Diyu as possible, and now we've only got to . . .

Get some spirit-world river water. Right.

As though reading my mind, Kai says, "Well, now that all we need is the river water, I think it's high time for somebody to step up, don't you?"

We all look blankly at her.

"What do you mean?" I say.

Kai swishes her tails and studies her front claws. "You know who can spot fakes?"

"Ma says she can spot fake Gucci," I mutter with a wry smile.

"And a very useful skill that is," Kai says. "But I'm talking about fake potions, like fake river water. Know who can spot them?" She doesn't wait for a reply. "Divine beings. Like phoenixes, xièzhì, and . . . dragons."

Danny, Namita, and I all gasp and whirl around to face Xiaohua, who's rearing up with indignation.

"Excuse me?" Xiaohua half gasps, half rumbles, drawing up to her full intimidating height. She stares down at us with obvious disapproval, and when a fire dragon stares at you with disapproval, there's a definite sense of *Uh-oh, am I about to be fried to a crisp?* Kind of like having Ma glare at you. "You want me to—to *steal* for you?" The word "steal" actually comes out with a small spark and a puff of smoke.

Kai groans. "We've been over this, Xiaohua. This is about saving someone's soul! How could you be so selfish, you narrow-minded little—"

"Xiaohua, we don't need you to steal," I say quickly. "We just need you to spot a real vial of spirit-world river water. You don't have to take it. We'll do the rest."

"Yeah," Namita pipes up. "And it's not technically stealing—we'd leave some money behind as payment."

Warmth floods my chest. Namita knows I don't have much money left, but she's willing to chip in her own allowance so we can do this. I truly do not deserve her friendship. I give her a smile, and she winks and gives me a look that says, *I got your back.*

Xiaohua turns away, her scales flashing in the moonlight. It's a warm night, but Xiaohua's foul mood turns the atmosphere cold. "This is base," she rumbles.

"I didn't think you cared about being basic," Namita says.

"Basic?" Xiaohua says.

"You know, being predictable, mainstream."

Xiaohua sighs. "I meant base as in dishonorable."

Namita shoots a look at Danny, who clears his throat and finally says, "Um, I wouldn't go that far, Xiaohua. I mean, like Namita said, we'd pay for it. We just need to make sure it's true river water. And it's for a good cause. We're trying to save some-one's soul, so. Pretty good reason, right?"

I grin at Danny. It's nearly impossible to describe how it feels to have two friends who have your back, and it's even stranger and better when one of those friends is Danny, of all people. I think back to how much we disliked each other when we first met, and the fact that we're now good friends feels like noth-ing short of a miracle. It's too bad that he still harbors a strong mistrust toward Kai. Not that I blame Danny; she did put him through a traumatic event, so I'm not one to judge him for not fully forgiving her.

A stream of smoke hisses out of Xiaohua's nostrils as she mut-ters about how we're all a bad influence on Danny. "Fine. But I want no part of the actual stealing."

I sigh with relief. We make plans to retire for the night and reconvene the next afternoon after school. Still grumbling, Xiao-hua lowers herself and tilts her head, gesturing at us to climb up onto her back. Danny jumps up with practiced ease. It takes Namita and me more effort as we grunt and climb, clutching at Xiaohua's brilliant red mane to pull ourselves up. Kai wraps her-self around my shoulders, her two bushy tails swishing down my back.

"This is so overrated," she mutters.

I settle down behind Namita, grabbing a tight hold of Xiao-hua's mane. Danny sits at the very front, patting Xiaohua's irides-cent scales. He turns around, beaming, and says, "Ready?"

I nod eagerly. The scales under my legs flash, the muscles underneath them bunching up, and I whoop as Xiaohua takes a giant leap into the sky. Wind whistles in my ears, blowing my hair back as Xiaohua slices smoothly through the air, and it's the best feeling in the world. If I were Danny, I would beg Xiaohua to just fly round and round the bay every single day. In front of me, Namita is rigid.

"You okay?" I call out to her.

She glances back at me with a terrified grin.

"Still afraid of heights?" I shout, to be heard above the wind.

"Of course not!"

"Looks like you are."

Namita shakes her head. "I'm still afraid of falling!"

I can't help but laugh at that.

We fly to South San Francisco, to Namita's neighborhood. Xiaohua hovers outside of Namita's window, and Namita clambers inside. "Oh, thank gods, solid ground." She rests her hands on her knees and breathes out. "No offense, Xiaohua, but that was terrible."

"None taken."

"See you guys tomorrow!" Namita waves at us from her bedroom, and Xiaohua flies off once more, this time heading back to Chinatown to deposit me and Kai. By the time I climb through my window back into my bedroom, I'm so tired I barely remember waving goodbye at Xiaohua and Danny before collapsing into my bed in an exhausted heap. I vaguely feel Kai next to me, turning in a circle as she does every night before curling up, the warmth of her soft, furry body a comforting presence. I want to tell her good job tonight, but already I'm drifting off. And when I next open my eyes, sunlight is piercing through the window and

Ma is shouting, "THEO! WAKE UP NOW OR YOU GONNA BE LATE!"

The weeks after Jamie died, we were all subdued, quietly puttering about, lost in our respective fogs of grief. But the past couple of weeks or so, Mama has gone from her grave sadness to loud anger. Baba, meanwhile, has retreated even further into himself. The only constant has been Nainai, who is her sweet old self, although I do sometimes see her weeping gently when she thinks no one's looking.

With a groan, I push myself out of the bed. "Okay, Ma," I call out before she can shout at me again. Kai stretches and starts grooming herself while I go to the bathroom to wash and dress. By the time Kai and I come down, Ma is muttering to herself.

"Why you can't wake up by yourself? At your age, Jamie wake up at dawn to study!"

Ma's nagging doesn't make me angry anymore. It doesn't even irritate me. All it does is make me even sadder. And her comparing me to Jamie just cements why I've learned the spell I plan to cast when I finally get to Jamie.

"Sorry, Ma," I mumble. I no longer have it in me to talk back to my parents.

Baba, who is sipping glumly at his congee, glances up. He looks like he's about to say something to Ma, but he changes his mind and goes back to eating. He barely notices me there. Nainai is still in her bedroom. She's been staying in there longer and longer every day. Kai leaps up and settles herself around my shoulders, nuzzling the top of her head into my cheek. She senses my sorrow at my parents' reception, but I'm used to it by now. I really, really am. Totally.

"Have you finish your homework?" Ma snaps.

I nod.

"With Jamie, I never have to remind—"

"Enough." Baba doesn't shout it, but there is a sharp edge in his voice that slices through the room. Mama immediately falls silent before marching into the kitchen. Baba doesn't even look up from his bowl.

Tears sting my eyes. I'd foolishly thought that me going to the Know Your Roots program would've helped somehow, but of course nothing is ever going to fill the Jamie-shaped void that's seared itself into our lives. It's my responsibility to make sure that void is filled, no matter the cost. I can just imagine Mama and Baba's relief once Jamie is back here with them. All my life, my parents have been telling me tales of familial duty, and it's only now that I think I fully understand what it means.

Once I'm done eating, I go to the kitchen, where I find Ma stirring a pot with furious energy. When she spots me, she turns away, swipes a hand across her eyes, and says in a stern, albeit slightly wobbly voice, "Pay attention in school today."

"Yes, Ma." Before I can stop myself, I give her a quick, awkward hug; then I scamper away. Back in the dining room, I consider giving Baba a quick hug as well, but I swear it's like his grief has basically turned into full-body armor, and something about it just repels me. I have no idea how he'd react to me hugging him, and so I simply say, "See you, Baba." Then I call out, "See you,

Nainai!" And with Kai still on my shoulders, I grab my backpack and leave the claustrophobic dark sadness of my house.

Outside, I take a moment to exhale and breathe in the fresh air. The atmosphere at home is so thick and heavy it's like breathing in soup. I hate it, and I hate that it's what my home has become. Kai pats the back of my head with a paw.

"You okay?" she murmurs.

"Yeah," I sigh. There's not much else to say. I don't blame my parents for being so fully wrapped up in their grief. I mean, I'm the one who's roped my friends into a quest to hell, so I'm not one to talk about how to handle grief in a healthy way. Kai gets it. She doesn't ask me any other questions, but her presence is comfort enough. When we spot the bus puttering and panting through the sky toward us, Kai changes into a hamster and slips into my pocket.

Ever since I presented Kai to the rest of my class, school's become just about bearable. Skinner and Co. wisely keep their distance from me, and I've even started having conversations with a handful of my classmates. I wouldn't say we're friends, but we're definitely friendly. The only thing I'm meh about with school is the fact that all the magic we're taught is, of course, still cirth-based, and after what we learned at Reapling Corp. over the summer, Namita, Danny, and I all feel kind of icky using cirth for anything. I've tried asking my teachers if I could rely on my qì instead of cirth, but all they did was stare at me with confusion and irritation before telling me that I could only use qì outside of school grounds.

As usual, I scrape through my lessons, half-heartedly casting cirth-based spells and poring over Jamie's notebook whenever my teachers aren't paying attention to me. I've perfected quite a few of his spells, though the pronunciation is still kind of tricky. Currently, I'm practicing a spell called Skin like Petal to Metal, which, according to Kai, should turn soft human skin into metal for a few minutes. When I first started, all I did was give myself a poison ivy–like rash, but after a couple days of practicing, I've managed to turn my skin into something more like leather.

Once the school bell rings, my spirits lift. For the first time that day, I feel like I'm finally coming alive. I'm on my way to meet up with my friends—actual friends!—to work on our quest to save Jamie. It's the only thing keeping me going these days, and I'm so grateful to have Danny and Namita by my side. We take the bus to Chinatown and there, at the top of Stockton, are Danny, Namita, and Xiaohua, waving at us.

"Hey, we just got here a minute ago," Namita says. "Good timing."

I grin at them. There are no words to describe that amazing sensation of seeing your friends after a long, hard day.

"Ready?" Danny says.

Xiaohua shrinks down until she's merely the length of my arm, then drapes herself around Danny's shoulders and exhales a puff of smoke grumpily. "We may begin," she rumbles.

"Aww," Namita sighs, "I wish I had a companion spirit I could wear as a scarf, too. My neck looks so bare compared to the two of you."

Danny and I stare at each other, both of us wearing our companions round our necks like the world's strangest scarves. There's a tiny moment of awkwardness as Danny meets Kai's eyes, and he quickly looks away before Kai can say a word. Kai unwraps herself from my neck and leaps onto Namita's shoulders, making Namita giggle.

"Ah, your hair smells much nicer than Theo's," Kai says, settling down around Namita's shoulders. I roll my eyes at her.

"Let us not waste any more time," Xiaohua says. "I'd rather get this dreadful task over and done with."

We walk down the street and into the shops as a group, and each time, Xiaohua lifts her head and regards the shop balefully before giving us a small shake of the head. Twenty minutes and seven shops later, I'm starting to despair. She's even rejected Mr. Huang's Emporium—the biggest, fanciest shop on the street, the one I would've bet had real magical stuff in it.

"Are you sure?" I say, when she shakes her head.

I immediately regret asking that when Xiaohua's eyes flick to mine. The pupils of her eyes are as sharp as a cat's, and the whites are a shimmering gold. When they look at me, I feel as though she can see straight into my innermost thoughts.

"Little human," she rumbles, "are you questioning my judgment as a five-hundred-year-old dragon, or are you questioning my honesty as a divine being?"

"Uh . . ." My insides turn to water.

"My guess would be neither," Kai interjects. "It's quite common human behavior to ask one another if they're sure because they so rarely are." She grins so widely that we can all see her sharp teeth. My chest expands. Kai's words are flippant, but I know she's just trying to ease the tension and take Xiaohua's intimidating attention from me.

Xiaohua grunts, releasing a puff of smoke. "Do not presume to question me again, child."

I nod hurriedly. "Yeah, no, of course."

Namita shoots me a look with wide eyes, and onward we go, though by now, I no longer have as much hope of locating real spirit-world river water on Stockton Street.

KAI

5

Ugh, dragons, I tell you. They're all such hams. *Oh, look at me—I'm a Venerable One! I'm a divine being! Ooh, worship me!* I mean, really, have you ever come across another living thing quite as melodramatic and attention-hungry as a dragon? I think NOT.

I'm having to focus hard to keep my hackles from rising as Xiaohua milks every possible drop of attention while locating river water. Each twitch of her long whiskers, each sweep of her otherworldly gaze, everything she does sets my teeth on edge. Twice now I've had to consciously remind myself to not peel my lips back to reveal my fangs.[9]

After we fail to find true spirit-world river water for the umpteenth time, we trudge down a side street glumly. "Excuse me for asking the obvious question," I mutter, "but why are we going this way?"

"I sense something," Xiaohua says.

"Care to be a bit more specific?" Dragons, I tell you. *Ooh, I'm so mysterious.* What she senses is probably an exceptionally pungent fart.[10]

Xiaohua shoots me a sharp look. "It would be a waste of

_____

9 Just as an aside, did you know that foxes are descended from the mighty wolf, while dragons are descended from the lowly worm? It's true! Just ask your biology teacher.

10 It is possible that I may just be a tad cranky.

time explaining my superior instincts to a lowly being such as yourself."

The audacity! I'm about to shoot back with a cutting retort, but then we arrive at a little shop.

I scoff. No way this little hole-in-the-wall could have such a thing as true spirit-world river water. Xiaohua says nothing as the wizened old woman behind the counter gives us a genial smile and asks if we need help. The kids shake their heads and out we go, not at all looking suspicious.

Outside, we go farther down the alleyway until we're out of earshot, then Xiaohua rumbles, "This shop has it. True water from the winding river of the spirit world." See what I mean about being a ham? She couldn't have just said *They got the stuff* like normal beings do.

"Are you sure?" I snap.

Xiaohua ignores me. "It's in the locked glass cabinet behind the counter, next to the vial of vampire bile."

"Ah." Namita nods wisely. "It's always the little hole-in-the-wall shops that have the biggest treasures."

"Really?" Theo says.

Namita grins. "How would I know, knucklehead? I've never had to look for hidden treasures before."

"Nice one," I say, and Namita beams at me. "So shall I just go in and get it, then?" I summon my qì and turn into a Guatemalan bearded lizard, one of the rarest lizards left in the world. Admittedly not the most subtle of forms, but I might have been trying to show off a little here, just to remind everyone that Xiaohua isn't the only impressive being here.

"Wait, how are you going to get into the locked cabinet?" Namita says.

"Easy peasy." I concentrate hard and turn my tail into a key. I really shouldn't have; the change into an inanimate object saps a lot of my energy, and by the time I switch it back to a lizard's tail, I'm slightly winded. Still, it's worth it just to see the wide-eyed looks of appreciation from the kids. Xiaohua rolls her eyes, and if you've never seen a dragon roll its eyes before, count yourself lucky.

We discuss the plan. It's pretty simple, as far as plans go. Within minutes, Theo and Namita are headed back to the shop. I'm tucked into Theo's backpack. As soon as they get inside, I peek out.

"Ah, you're back," the old lady says in Cantonese. "Are you going to buy something this time?" She's a tiny woman, her hair almost fully white, her face as wrinkled as a walnut. Her eyes are a light watery gray, somehow more piercing than they should be.

Something in her voice tweaks at my nerves, and I scratch my hard, smooth head thoughtfully. I don't have time to dwell on it, though. When I'm sure she's looking at Theo's face and not his shoes, I scurry out of the backpack and scuttle quickly across the grimy floor.

"Uh . . . I'm here to . . . uh . . . ," Theo says in mangled Cantonese, before giving up and switching to English. "I was wondering if you had the ingredients to make the, uh, the Clear of Mind, Bright are the Eyes potion?"

We've agreed that he would ask for that specific potion because it's complicated enough for the old woman to have to check some guidebook for it, but not so obscure that it would make her suspicious.

"I do," she says flatly. "In fact, I have the potion ready-made, so you don't have to bother with preparing the ingredients. Some of them are quite dangerous for children, you know," she chides.

"Oh," Theo says. "Uh."

Luckily, Namita is quicker on her feet. "We don't need the actual potion itself. It's for our school project—um, we just need to take photos of the ingredients. If you don't mind, that is. We'd pay you for your time, obviously."

The old woman peers at Namita, who returns the suspicious look with her best I'm-a-goody-two-shoes smile. With a grunt, the old woman starts taking various things out from the old medicine drawers behind her. "Here's huánghuāhāo, and this is shānyao." She pauses, muttering to herself, "And then you'd need the shell of a quánxiē. It's in the back room." She narrows her eyes at them. "Stay here and do not touch anything."

Namita and Theo nod vigorously. The old lady shuffles out from behind the counter, and I swear we all collectively hold our breaths as she makes her way slowly to the back room. Once she's out of sight, I sneak out from where I've been hiding and climb up to the locked glass cabinet. I peer into the keyhole, make my best guess at what kind of key it requires, and shift my tail. But the change saps me of energy, and I find that I can barely move my tail up to insert it into the keyhole.

"Theo, you're going to have to move me," I croak.

Quickly, Theo slips behind the counter and lifts my body up, grimacing as he puts his hands around my midsection. "Ugh, you're so scaly."

"That typically comes with being a lizard, yes." I wince as he stabs my tail into the keyhole and twists. I can feel the pins inside the lock shifting, but the fit isn't perfect, and it refuses to unlock. Theo wiggles me back and forth, and I wince at the ache as the imperfect fit bites into my tail.

"It's not fitting," I say. "Pull me out—we'll try something else."

"Okay." Theo pulls my tail out.

Or tries to, anyway.

It's stuck fast. Uh-oh. Theo wiggles me again and tugs, both of us getting increasingly worried, but I swear there's even less wiggle room now, as though the keyhole has tightened around my tail, which is impossible. Right? I try to shift my tail back, but it stays firmly as a key.

"Kai, what's going on?" Theo whispers.

"I—uh, I might be a little bit stuck," I squeak.

"Just shift into something else and get unstuck," Theo hisses.

"Oh, brilliant suggestion, that. Bravo! Why didn't I think of that sooner?" Okay, so I might be a little bit snarky, but it's kind of challenging to not snap when you're in a position as awkward as I'm in.

"She's coming back!" Namita whispers.

"I'll have to figure out something later!" Theo hurries round the counter.

I jerk my tail back with all my might, and pain shoots up my tail to my entire body. It feels like if I yank too hard, I might just leave my tail behind, which would be very unfortunate.

"And here's the quánxiē," the old woman says, coming back into the shop. She glances at Theo and Namita, whose eyes are wide with horror. "Something wrong? You didn't touch anything, did you?"

They both shake their heads wordlessly. Just five feet away from the old lady, I'm stuck to the glass cabinet like a giant limpet.

"Good," she says simply.

"Um, not that we did," Namita says, "but if we were to touch something without your permission, what would happen?"

"Oh, the shop would eat you up," the old woman says quite jovially. "Now, I think all we're missing is the zhūshā. Hmm, that should be—"

"Uh, eat us up? You don't really mean that, do you?" Namita says with a nervous laugh.

"Well, yes. It's been in my family for ages, so lots of ancestral spirits and all that in these walls. They're—well, I suppose you could say they're trapped in the walls and are somewhat angry. The only thing that appeases them is eating. They eat all sorts of things—they're not picky."

Theo is looking markedly pale. "Um, we should—um." Thanks to our mind link, I know he's shuffling through all the spells he's learned, trying to come up with a spell that might get us all out of here. He raises a hand and casts a spell to beseech ancestors. "Ancestors of old, if we may be so bold—"

"We will be having none of that!" the old woman snaps, waving her hand almost lazily and casting away Theo's spell. "What in the world are you trying to do, boy?" She narrows her eyes and follows his gaze, and I feel her eyes land on me like a thousand needles. I widen my mouth into a sheepish grin. "Ah, what have we here?" the old woman asks.

"I'm so sorry!" Theo bursts out. "It's all my fault—please just let my companion go, please. We'll get out of here; we'll give you all our money; we don't mean any harm, please!"

But the old woman is smiling. "Oh my, it's one of those shape-shifters, isn't it?" She bends over and peers at me closely. "Let's see, are you a snake spirit, my dear?"

"Obviously not!" I cry before I can help myself. Oops.

"Oh? We have some of those around, you know. You'd be in fine company." She waves a hand at one of the medicine drawers, which slides smoothly open to reveal a jar of coiled white snakes suspended in green liquid. My insides churn. Namita and Theo start, their faces draining of blood.

"Um—" Namita says, but the old woman waves her off before grinning at me, showing a mouth full of yellowed teeth.

"Perhaps a minor Yāoguài, then?"

I don't answer. Theo is still begging the old woman to let us go, even though it's clear there's no chance in Diyu that she'll ever do that. As she reaches out to me with a crooked, gnarly hand, the sight of her pointed nails sends a jolt of panic searing through me. Instinctively, I make a switch. A sparrow, something that can fly the heck out of her reach.

Or, at least, I try to. But it's as though something is blocking my qì; I can't even grow a single feather. It seems I'm stuck in lizard form.[11] Unfortunate, that. The old woman's fingers curve around

---

11 The only form worse would be a huma—uh, never mind. I don't want to be cruel.

me like the bars of a cell, and the stink of demonic presence envelopes me. All too late, I finally sense that the shopkeeper isn't human, not even close.

The thought of my human companion in the clutches of this demon is too much to bear. I can't lose another bonded master. "Run!" I scream at Theo and Namita.

My shout jolts them into action. Namita grabs Theo and mutters a spell; I vaguely recognize it as a spell to travel instantaneously, and indeed, the two of them turn into a blur, but in the next moment, they fall back with a cry.

The shopkeeper cackles. "Silly children, you didn't think I was going to let you leave so soon, did you? Don't bother wasting your energy on more escape spells, little girl—you're no match for me." She grips me tight and waves her free hand at the kids. Ropes snake out of nowhere and begin to wrap themselves around Namita and Theo. "Now, let's get comfortable, shall we, and let's give the ancestors a nice little treat."

There's a tremendous roar and blinding light, as though the little shop has just been struck by lightning. The front windows shatter, glass jars explode, and it feels like the world is breaking apart. The old woman cries out and snatches her hand away from me. The ropes shrivel up and fall from Namita and Theo. I writhe helplessly, my tail still stuck in the awful magical keyhole. Xiaohua storms through the front door, reducing the wood and glass into splintered wreckage.

"Demon!" she booms in her deepest, most dragonliest voice. "Unhand these humans and release the fox spirit immediately."

I turn to look at the old woman and startle. Xiaohua's divine light has melted away her harmless old-lady disguise, showing the evil spirit underneath. She's shockingly thin, her bones sticking out painfully, and her skin is bleach-white, her hair gray and so long that it pools on the floor. Her eyes are bloodshot, and when she grins, her teeth are small but horribly pointed. She's a guǐ pó— the spirit of friendly old women, mostly helpers of rich families before death. They're usually friendly, albeit slightly naggy, but on rare occasions, there are evil ones. This is one such occasion.

The guǐ pó shies away from the brilliant light emanating from Xiaohua. When Xiaohua had come into the store earlier, she had made herself small, muting her aura to avoid attracting too much attention. But now, she's grown back to her full size, nearly filling the little shop with her scaly body. To humans and good spirits like myself, she is impressive. To demons like the guǐ pó, Xiaohua's unbridled divine aura would be painful.

Sure enough, the guǐ pó shrieks and claws at the air in front of her. "Get out of my shop, dragon!"

In answer, Xiaohua's tail scythes through the air and crashes into the glass cabinet mere inches above me. "Watch it, you brute!" I cry. Then I realize she's setting me free. Oops. The glass shatters, the wooden frame splinters, and the unforgiving grip on my tail loosens. With a joyous shout, I yank my tail free and quickly shift into a sparrow hawk. Xiaohua coils around Theo and Namita and snarls at the guǐ pó as the kids clamber up her back, little licks of flame appearing between her fangs. "Do not try anything, demon," Xiaohua growls.

I fly up, grab the vial of spirit-world river water in my claws from the cabinet, and beat my wings frantically.

The guǐ pó screams again, her voice jagged with rage, and reaches a gnarled hand toward me. Her cracked, sharp fingernails graze the ends of my feathers, and I flinch and beat my wings even harder. And somehow, I manage to dodge her.

Once I'm safely out of reach of the guǐ pó, Xiaohua unfurls her magnificent length and together, we smash out of what remains of the front of the store and soar into the sky. Behind us, the guǐ pó screams. "My meal!"

I glance back long enough to see her rushing out of the store, her movements wrong and alien, her limbs moving like spider legs. A strange sensation unfurls inside me, like a weight dragging me down. It's the realization that just one month ago, I very nearly turned into a full demon. If not for Theo's sacrifice, I would've been like the guǐ pó, hungry for human flesh and trapping fellow spirits in jars. I shudder at the jagged memory and beat my wings faster, eager to leave all traces of the demon behind.

THEO
6

Flying on Xiaohua's back is one of the best feelings in the world. Not that I would ever tell that to Kai. I know she feels intimidated by Xiaohua. She hasn't admitted that, of course, but I can sense her prickliness whenever Xiaohua is around. And when Xiaohua expands to her full form, I can feel Kai's hackles rising and her eagerness to prove that she's every bit as good as Xiaohua. I get the rivalry and the fear that you're just not good enough, and I wish I could convey to Kai that she's the best companion spirit around and that I wouldn't trade her for any dragon, not even a water dragon—and those are really cool because they allow you to breathe underwater when you're on their backs, so you could dive to the deepest parts of the ocean and look at the sprawling underwater kingdoms. But I would still choose Kai over that.

As we fly over the bustling streets of Chinatown, I turn to look at Kai and give her a reassuring smile, but she doesn't see because she's too busy flapping her wings hard, probably trying to outfly Xiaohua. I sigh and shake my head, smiling slightly. When Kai is being this prideful, I can't decide if I want to roll my eyes or hug her.

We land at the top of the Exploratorium, where Danny has apparently been deposited by Xiaohua, well out of any potential danger, and he's been waiting for us with growing impatience. As soon as Xiaohua lands on the roof of the building, Danny rushes to us and fires question after question.

I turn back to look for Kai as Namita fills Danny in, and moments later, she arrives looking winded, her feathers ruffled and her eyes dull. I hold out my arm and she lands on it, her talons wrapping gently around my limb so she doesn't break skin. She drops the vial of river water from her beak into my hand and shifts back into fox form before wrapping herself up around my shoulders and nuzzling my neck. I laugh when her cold, damp nose presses into my skin. "So glad you're safe," I say, stroking her bushy tails.

"Don't be so melodramatic," she sighs. "I had it all under control."

I grin. "Of course you did."

Xiaohua snorts. She's reduced her size and, like Kai, has twined herself round her master's shoulders. "Under control? As I recall, you were trapped by a simple demon's spell and about to be crushed."

Danny looks at us, wide-eyed. "So it's true? There was a demon? Right in the heart of Chinatown?" He looks so worried that it makes my chest tighten. The old Danny had been a jerk and a bully, but the new Danny, hesitant and overly cautious, makes me feel so guilty. He's only this way because Kai attacked him when she was halfway demonic, which was my fault. Guilt sits in my stomach like a lump of hot coal as I remember how I had been the one who asked Kai to cheat, which turned her demonic.

"I had it all under control," Kai grumbles. She gives Danny

what's probably meant to be a reassuring smile, though it only ends up showing off her pointy canines. Danny shrinks back.

"Do not speak to my master," Xiaohua rumbles.

"Just trying to break the ice, sheesh," Kai says. "And to answer your question, yes, the old woman was a demon and also a shopkeeper. Women are always having to juggle multiple roles, aren't we?"

"Ignore the fox spirit," Xiaohua says. "I daresay the guǐ pó probably minded her own business most of the time. She only attacked when she realized that a mischievous spirit was trying to break into her precious glass cabinet to shoplift."

"I resent that statement." Kai straightens up, her two tails standing upright. "Though yes, you probably have a point. Still, does it count as shoplifting if you're taking from an actual demon?"

"Yes," Xiaohua snaps. "Do not debase me with your sly logic, húlíjīng."

"This is the problem with dragons," Kai mutters. "They think of logic as sly, which is why they are so often illogical."

Xiaohua shifts her long, scaly body to glare at Kai, and Namita hurriedly says, "Anyway, we've got the spell and the river water now! So what's the next step? Do we just drink it and start chanting?" She beams at us, and I'm almost overcome by an urge to give her a huge hug. From the beginning, back at the Know Your Roots program, Namita has always been so enthusiastic about helping me. Even after she found out about how I snuck into the program and that Kai turned into a demon, she still chose to stick by us. And now, she's ready to leap into hell to help me save my brother's soul. She's definitely set the bar for friendship really high.

"Pretty much, yeah," Danny says. "Um, except our parents might get angry if we went to Diyu all of a sudden? So I think we should do a bit of prep work, decide on what we're going to tell our parents, and then maybe do it over a weekend?"

"Ah," Namita says, "so we don't miss out on school. Good point."

It's kind of making my head spin how casually these two are talking about traveling to Diyu, as though it were a weekend trip to LA instead. "Great," I say, swallowing the lump in my throat.

"Okay, how about we gather at my place on Saturday morning?" Danny says.

We all nod at one another, our faces wearing excited/terrified grins. I guess it's agreed that this weekend, we'll embark on our journey to hell.

─═✱═─

On Saturday, Kai and I rise at the crack of dawn, which is strange; Kai has been known to lie in until well past noon. Mama and Baba have called us both lazy bums way too many times for me to count. But neither of us could sleep much at all the night before, not after everything that's happened. As we tossed and turned in bed last night, I could sense the anticipation crackling like electricity in the air around us. After weeks of futile searching, last night we made a giant leap toward getting closer to our goal of saving Jamie. And both Kai and I are ready to go, burning with the need to rush to wherever Jamie's soul is entrapped and save him at all costs.

As soon as the darkness melts away into gentle light, I bound out of bed and grab my backpack off the floor. My room is no longer as messy as it was before Kai became my spirit companion, but Kai still complains that being here is like staying in a rat's nest.

I have no idea what to bring to Diyu. What does one take with them on a journey to hell? In the end, I shove a collection of random things inside my bag—a bottle of water, a protein bar, a pack of Band-Aids. When I can't think of anything else to put inside it, I approach the farthest, darkest corner of my room, where Niu Mo Wang's cage is. I've put a blanket over it because Niu Mo Wang hates the light. I pick up the cage carefully and pull the blanket up. Niu Mo Wang, still locked up tight in the little cage, lifts his head and eyes me balefully.

"Why have you woken me?" he snarls.

"Um, hi, Niu Mo Wang. We're going on a journey."

For a second, Niu Mo Wang doesn't say anything. Then he snorts. "I smell the stink of fear, human."

"I think that's just morning breath," Kai says mid-yawn from the bed.

"Do not speak to me, fox," Niu Mo Wang growls. Over the past few weeks, despite not having much to do in his cage, Niu Mo Wang has resisted all our efforts to talk. He's just as angry and vengeful as the day we put him in the cage. He also looks exactly the same as the day we put him in there; if anything, his muscles seem to have swollen a bit more. Kai says that Niu Mo Wang spends most nights working out inside the cage, snorting noisily as he does thousands of pull-ups. Apparently, he said he wanted to be in top health when he takes revenge on all of us, which is not at all reassuring. I have no idea how we can safely return him to Diyu.

Kai's face falls. "Oh no! You don't want to talk to me? What should I do? Where else can I find someone as dour and aggressively uninteresting to talk to?"

"Kai," I sigh. You'd think that given Kai's a two-hundred-year-old spirit and Niu Mo Wang is, well, probably thousands of years old, they would be too mature to bicker like this. But nope. I swear they fight more often than toddlers do.

"When my Iron Wife finds you, you will rue all the times you have disrespected me!"

"Ooh, I'm so scared," Kai yawns.

"Okay, I'm just going to put you very gently into my bag . . ." I carry Niu Mo Wang's cage gingerly, careful not to make the mistake of putting my fingers through the bars. He's been known to bite.

"Where are you taking me?"

Some strange instinct tells me I should try to keep Niu Mo Wang in the dark for as long as I can. "Just for a bit of a walk." I give him what I hope is a reassuring smile and put the cage inside my bag before layering a hoodie over it to muffle the angry hisses coming from within.

"Phew, good to have that out of the way," Kai says extra loudly, no doubt to annoy Niu Mo Wang even more. Sure enough, curses stream out of my bag.

"Don't provoke him," I scold her. "Is his 'Iron Wife' Princess Iron Fan?"

"Someone's been brushing up on Chinese mythology! Yes, that would be Princess Iron Fan, and yes, she is fearsome. Her fan is probably the deadliest weapon there is. But we don't have to worry about her. She lives in Bajia Cave, and there's no reason for our paths to cross. None!"

"Okay, if you're sure." I shrug and take Jamie's notebook. There. I'm packed and ready to go.

I take a deep breath at my reflection. Grief has left a permanent imprint on me. I see traces of it in the way I carry myself, the slightly haunted look in my eyes, the way I always have my hands stuffed into my hoodie's pockets now. Kai springs up onto my shoulders and gently nips at my right ear, and despite my anxiety and fear and sadness and everything, the knot in my chest loosens.

"We'll get Jamie back," she says.

"Can we actually do that, though?" I can't help but voice my deepest fears now, before we're about to embark on our trip. "He—he died, so chances are they're not going to let us have him back, are they?"

Kai's ears twitch in the way that they do when she's unsure about something. "Well, technically, he didn't die. His soul was snatched out of his body—"

"Yeah, then his car crashed and his body . . ." I can't finish my sentence. I don't want to think of my poor brother's body being destroyed in that accident.

"It's a gray area," Kai says quickly. I don't know who she's trying to convince: me or herself. "Surely even the old geezers in Diyu can see that it's such a grave injustice. And I'm sure there are things they could do. They are deities, so if they wanted to, they could very definitely bring him back to life."

I ignore the uncertainty in her voice and cling instead to the hope, no matter how slim, that yes, what happened to Jamie was a grave injustice and that surely the kings of Diyu would want to put things right. We'll never know unless we try.

"I'm ready." I wouldn't be able to do this without Kai or the others. It's so weird to think that only a few months ago, I was basically friendless and companionless. Now I can't imagine a life without Kai, and I can't imagine even trying to go on this journey without Namita, Danny, and Xiaohua.

Kai walks quickly ahead of me out of the bedroom and down the stairs, her movements fluid and graceful. Downstairs is empty. I guess for once I'm the first one awake. But then I see movement in the shadows and almost shriek out loud. It's Baba, gazing out the window.

"Oh, Theo," he mumbles, getting up. "You're up early."

My heart is still galloping, and I quickly turn the lights on. "Baba, why are you sitting alone?"

He shrugs forlornly. "Just thinking."

Guilt and sorrow stab at me. My poor dad. There is so much sadness in him now, an entire ocean of it filling up every fold of his soul. But I'm about to fix it, I remind myself. I take a breath and say, "Okay, Baba. I'm, uh—I'm off to Danny's. I told you guys that I'll be staying at his place this weekend?" The lie flops out easily, which makes me feel even worse.

"Oh?" Baba hesitates, then nods. "Yes, you did mention it, didn't you? Sorry, Theo, I am always forgetting things these days. But I think Nainai made some almond cookies for you to give to Danny's parents. They are on the dining table."

Tears burn my eyes as I turn and see that, yes, there is a container of cookies on the dining table. I grab it and stuff it into my backpack, clearing my throat and swallowing the giant lump that's in it. "See you later, Ba," I say hoarsely. Before I can second-guess myself, I throw my arms around him and hug. He stiffens up, unused to the close physical contact, but then his muscles relax and he returns the hug.

"Have fun, son."

"I will. Thanks, Ba."

Blinking my tears away, I hurry out of the house into the heavy chill of a San Franciscan dawn with Kai in front of me.

It's been a while since I walked through my neighborhood, deep in the heart of Chinatown, at dawn. The sights and smells hurt; they remind me so much of that morning when Jamie took me to the meat freezer to try and warn me about Reapling. I'd been so grumpy about being woken up early, and then, thinking it was a prank devised by Kai, I hadn't bothered to listen to Jamie.

"Watch it!" Kai hisses at a companion spirit in the shape of a blackbird flying low enough to almost crash into my head. The blackbird swoops up with a muttered curse, and Kai snarls at it before continuing to walk.

With a start, I realize she's walking a step ahead of me to help clear me a path. I watch as she growls and snaps at anyone in our way. She must sense how raw I feel going through the hustle and bustle of Chinatown, how deeply mired I am in the memory of Jamie, and she wants to make the walk as comfortable as possible for me. Her bristly attentiveness makes me smile despite myself. The last time I walked through this part of the city at this time of day, I had to duck so many times to avoid a flying beetle spirit or swooshing monkey spirit that I could barely catch a breath.

At the base of Stockton Street, we catch a tram toward Nob Hill, which is where Danny lives, because of course he lives in one of the most prestigious areas of San Francisco. Not that I'm jealous or anything, obviously.

The tram's wings flap and it flies up the hill a bit shakily, teetering as it does a turn. I grip the pole tightly, gulping as my backpack becomes weightless with the momentum of the tram. There's only one other passenger on the tram, and he's an old man who seems half asleep, barely reacting as he slides across the seat. I wish for flying shoes or a flying bike or one of those incredibly cool flying skateboards you always see kids whizzing around on downtown.

Although Nob Hill isn't technically far away from Chinatown, it feels like it's a whole different world. Like Chinatown, all the houses are smooshed together so they all share walls with their neighbors. But that's where the similarities end. These houses look like mini palaces, decorated elaborately, and all the owners must have cast cleaning spells on their properties because they are all meticulous, down to the perfectly pruned trees lining the sidewalks.

Kai sniffs. "If you ask me, I find this street quite characterless."

I bite back a smile. "Are you maybe ever so slightly jealous that Xiaohua's house is so much nicer than ours?"

"Moi? Jealous of that tomato-colored worm?" She throws her head back and swishes her two tails with indignation. "Never!"

But Danny's house is so tall that we have to tilt our heads way back to take it all in, and even though we've been here several times now, the sight of it never fails to impress. I ring the door-bell with slight trepidation, and it slides back to reveal a small imp.

"Name?" it says in a surprisingly deep voice.

"Oh. Er, Theo." Every time we come here, the door imp insists on asking us our names. Every. Single. Time. It's humiliating.

"And the fox?"

Kai rolls her eyes. "Aren't you tired of playing this game, imp? You know who we are."

"Name?" the imp hisses.

Kai's chest puffs out. "I am the honorable fox spirit Kai, of Clan Shi, from the Yellow Flower Mountain Province of the—"

"We're here to see Danny," I say quickly, then shoot Kai an apologetic look.

"Wait, please." The imp shuts the doorbell and through the door, I hear it say in its deep, somber voice, "Master Daniel, you have a visitor. A male human child named Theo and a rather bedraggled-looking fox spirit named Yellow Flower Mountain."

Danny says something, and the door swings open. "You may come inside," the imp says, looking very grave, like it's disap-pointed that we're actually being allowed in.

"I'll show you bedraggled," Kai growls as we walk past the imp, but I grab her and hold her tight before she can do anything.

"We're in the kitchen!" Namita calls out.

The kitchen is gorgeous—a huge island, brass pots and pans hanging on the walls, a large pizza oven on one side over which Xiaohua is draped, probably to savor the heat from it. On the other side of the room are big bay windows, which let in plenty of light. And on the kitchen island is what seems like an entire feast: pizzas dripping with gooey cheese, stacks of pastries glistening with syrup glaze, colorful swirly cupcakes, a mountain of donuts, and even a stack of caramel waffles.

"You might think that we've ordered this from the magic oven," Namita announces, "but no! Young master Danny here cooked everything—can you believe it? Look, he's even made gulab jamun." She points to a bowl of golden sticky, sweet balls drowning in thick syrup. "How amazing is that? Here, have one." She waves at the bowl and one of the balls lifts, dripping with syrup, and flies right into my face.

"Wait, I—oof!" The rest of the sentence is cut short as the ball shoots into my mouth. I chew, and delicious rose syrup oozes out of the dough ball. For a moment, all I can do is savor the sweetness. "That's delicious," I say, after I can finally swallow.

Danny gives me a small smile. "I, uh—I cook when I'm anxious, and I guess our impending journey has made me, uh, somewhat nervous. You might as well help yourselves—my dad is going to freak out when he sees how much I've cooked."

Namita, who's in the process of taking a huge bite out of a cheese naan, nods eagerly. "Hey, we need lots of energy for where we're about to go. And plus, unlike you guys, I don't have a spirit companion to rely on—yes, I've said that before, and yes, I might be just a tad jealous—okay, a lot jealous. Anyway, all this is to say that I need nutrition." With that, she continues chomping. Danny and I start eating, and I'm surprised at how amazing everything tastes.

"Geez, Danny, this is really good," I say, my mouth filled with the most delicious waffles.

Danny smiles at me. "The waffles are rose-flavored. Took me months to perfect them."

I finish the triangle of waffle and dig into the pizza next, which tastes mind-blowing. Who would've thought? We all eat until we can no longer sit comfortably; then Kai says, "Now that you're all done stuffing your faces, can we get a move on?"

From on top of the pizza oven, Xiaohua cracks one eye open and snorts, letting out a small puff of smoke. "I remain dubious about this foolhardy quest you are insisting on dragging my master along on."

Kai opens her mouth, no doubt about to say something rude, but before she can, Danny says, "I know you're worried, but it's for a good cause." He turns back to the rest of us and stands. "Anyway, I've got everything ready. Follow me." He leads us up the stairs to his bedroom, which is just as impressive as everything else in the house and kept as neat as something out of a home magazine. "I bought these safety charms we can put in our pockets," he says, handing out small packets of what feels like sand. I put mine up to my nose and smell a mix of sage, smoke, and some other scents I can't identify.

"These little trinkets are hardly going to save you from a demon in Diyu," Kai says.

With a shrug, Namita, Danny, and I stuff our charms into our pants pockets. Better to have something than nothing, even if that something is next to useless.

"Spellbooks, um, cirth pendants—I've got extra pendants here in case anyone needs them," Danny says.

Before the Know Your Roots program, such a show of wealth—I mean, excess cirth? Whoever heard of that?—would've made me so jealous. But now, I just say thanks and take one, though I don't expect that I'll need it. It's been weeks since I used any cirth. I've been getting by using old Chinese magic, and every day I'm getting better at it.

"Gosh, I haven't used these in a while," Namita says, echoing my thoughts.

"Yeah, me neither." Danny shrugs. "But in case we get too tired to use our qì or mana, it's always good to have backup."

"What did you bring, Theo?" Namita asks.

I gesture at my backpack. "I've got Niu Mo Wang inside—"

"I love how you so casually said that," Namita laughs nervously. "Oh yeah, I've just got a demon king in my backpack, no big deal."

I give a weak smile. When she puts it that way, it does sound ridiculous.

"Anyway, I've also got, uh." Danny clears his throat. "My bow and arrow with me."

We all groan. As it turns out, Danny is really into archery, and it's kind of obnoxious because of course it's dreadfully expensive and it feels like he mentions it a lot. Xiaohua gently pats Danny's shoulder. "You do realize that your bow and arrow won't do anything against the kinds of monsters we'll be going up against?"

"You never know!" Danny argues. "Every adventure needs an archer. Think about all the books we've read and movies we've watched. It's always the archer who saves the day."

"Gods save us," Namita moans, "the boy thinks he's Katniss Everdeen."

Danny's cheeks and ears are turning red. Time for a subject change. "Anyway," I say, "let's go over the plan again. We're going to chant the spell to get to the Doorway. From there, we'll find the entrance to the First Court of Diyu."

"That would be King Qinguang's court, where souls undergo review and are given judgment," Xiaohua says.

"The old man's tough, but fair," Kai adds. "If we explain things to him, there is a good chance he'll let Jamie go back with us."

Xiaohua gives Kai an odd look, which I can't quite decipher, and it makes a shiver run down my spine because there seems to be sadness in it.

"What is it?" I say.

Xiaohua turns her gaze to me. It's impossible not to see the ancient well of wisdom within her, calm and endlessly deep. "You are both blinded by desperate hope. It is very rare that King Qinguang lets those who have died return to life."

Kai visibly bristles, her vibrant orange fur standing like a thousand needles. When she speaks, her voice is brittle, at the edge of breaking. "Well, technically, Jamie didn't die. His soul was stolen—"

"Kai," I interrupt, pulling her close. The last thing I want is for Kai and Xiaohua to get into yet another fight.

But instead of retaliating like she usually does, Xiaohua bows her head, her eyes still filled with sadness. "Little fox, it is not my wish to keep your previous master in Diyu. I am merely pointing out that perhaps it is best to temper your expectations."

"I don't need advice from you," Kai snaps, turning abruptly away.

There's a painfully awkward pause, then Namita says, "Anyway, we're all good to go, right? I've told my parents I'm staying at my friend Anju's house. She's vouching for me. And you guys?"

"I told mine I'm staying here," I say.

Danny nods. "And I told mine I'm staying at yours." We all look at one another and nod.

"We're ready," I say.

We file downstairs and out to the backyard, where Xiaohua grows to her full size so we can all climb up onto her back. We've all agreed that we'll fly to Muir Woods and chant the spell to get to Diyu there, just to avoid any unwanted attention. I can't help gripping tight to her scales as she ascends to the skies, my insides tangling with anticipation and not a small amount of fear, especially when I recall what Xiaohua said about tempering our expectations. But Kai is right. Jamie rightfully belongs to us. King Qinguang will see that and release him back to the human world—and if not, I have my backup plan.

KAI

7

Xiaohua's impertinence has already put me in a bad mood, and when we arrive at Muir Woods, it darkens even more. It's such an unpleasant atmosphere: the smell of everything, the heavy, damp scent of redwood trees and the way the air here feels thick, like a cold soup matting up my fur. The smell takes me back to that horrible time at the Know Your Roots program. So many painful memories resurface as I breathe in. The secret research facility that Reapling owned had been located here, though it has since disappeared, swallowed into a tiny black hole that Reapling conjured up to try and hide evidence of wrongdoing. This was where I was nearly turned into a full demon, and Theo was nearly killed by Creighton the fox. And is it just me or can I sense the many ghosts of wrongdoing here? The research facility had had a dungeon where Reapling employees were slicing into spirits, and the memory of that evil place makes me shudder. The aura here is all off, as though all the misery and cruelty performed here have seeped into the ground, tainting it forever with darkness.

Xiaohua lets us off in a small clearing. Theo takes out three little paper cups and pours out a small amount of spirit-world river water into each one. I wrap myself around Theo's shoulders, and Xiaohua does the same with Danny. The kids go over the rhyme a couple more times, then there's nothing left to prepare. They look at one another, and even Namita looks uncertain.

"Last chance to bail," Theo says with a weak laugh.

"And leave you to have the coolest adventure of the year? I don't think so!" Namita says.

"I think you meant the worst, most dangerous adventure of the year," Danny says. "But I'm with Namita. We're going."

Theo's smile grows. "Okay, let's do it. Ready?"

They nod and lift the cups to their lips. At the count of three, they drink it; then they hold hands and begin chanting the rhyme. A soft breeze picks up, swirling around us, causing my fur to bristle. Electricity sparks in the air, and there is a sort of heaviness, like the wind around us has turned into a blanket, thick with magic from the chant. As a fox spirit, I can see how the spell is tearing open a hole between two worlds and beseeching the powers that be to allow safe passage from one to the other. The spirit-world river water acts as a catalyst to help untether the body from the human world, but the rest depends on the chant and the will of the caster. I open my mouth, about to ask them to stop, to find a different way, but just then, the spell takes effect.

It's as though a huge hand has caught hold of our feet and yanked. For a moment, I feel our bodies elongating, like spaghetti;[12] then my powers kick in and I spring back into shape. Theo and the kids stay spaghettified a few more moments, long

---

12 As a side note, did you know that "spaghettification" is an actual scientific term to describe what happens to your squishy human body if you were to get sucked into a black hole? Yeah, the smartest, most educated people got together to discuss this and the best they could come up with was "Haha, sounds like a noodle. Oh, how about 'spaghettification'?" Now you know why I hold humans in such low regard.

enough for me to start worrying. What if they remain spaghettified? How would they ever find clothes to fit into? The next moment, we land with a thud that slams all breath out of our lungs. I scramble up quickly and inspect the kids, finding to my relief that they're back in normal shape. Not that their usual selves are worth crowing about, mind you, but it's admittedly somewhat better than a string of spaghetti. Theo looks like he's half in shock, his hair standing up like a stiff broom, but when I lick his cheek, he manages to give me a shaky smile.

I hide my relief by swishing my tails casually and saying, "All right, then? Arrived safely, did you?"

He nods and turns to check on Namita, but she's already bounced back onto her feet. "That was awesome!" she says, grinning wide.

This girl has issues.

Xiaohua is fussing over Danny like the naggy auntie she is. "Are you hurt in any way, Master?" she says, her voice sharp with concern.

"You know, if you keep babying him, he'll never learn," I say helpfully.

Xiaohua snarls at me, baring her obnoxious fangs in my face. "And whose fault is it that he's so damaged?"

"Damaged?" Danny says, frowning. He pushes her away and stands up, brushing himself off.

"I did not mean it in that way," Xiaohua says. "I meant . . . you know, touched by a demon."

"Wow, please, continue digging that hole," I mutter.

"Stop that, Kai," Theo says, tugging me back.

"Yeah, this isn't the time to argue," Namita says. "Let's just focus on—uh, wow, this place is . . . whoa."

It seems as though the children have just registered where we are because they all stop talking and look around, eyes wide, at the Doorway. Theo's been here before, of course, but I guess his mind had been addled by Xiuling's potion, and plus we were sort of in a hurry, being chased by a skeleton demon and all. I can't help but notice that Xiaohua's eyes have widened as well, and it strikes me that she's never been here before, because as she likes to remind anyone who will listen, she's a divine spirit, yada yada.

I take a deep breath. I shouldn't be as anxious as I was the last time I was here. For one thing, this time I'm not tainted by the corruption of turning demonic. For another, I no longer have the fear of Ox Head and Horse Face coming after me. Ox Head and Horse Face are two of Diyu's most well-known guards. A month ago, while hot in the pursuit of justice for Jamie, I very nearly turned myself demonic. The change alerted Ox Head and Horse Face, who took it upon themselves to capture and banish me to Diyu. It was only through Theo's sacrifice that I was able to be cleansed and escape Ox Head and Horse Face's wrath.

Everything will be okay, I remind myself. And with that, I conjure up a bright-blue hat with the words KAI'S AMAZING TOUR ADVENTURES, a checkered scarf, a bright-blue flag, and a loudspeaker. Then I belatedly realize that we shouldn't be making loud noises in here because of Yāoguài,[13] etc., so with some

---

13 Remember those deadly monkey Yāoguài that time we went to the Doorway? You know, the ones

regret, I shift the loudspeaker away. I clear my throat. Everyone looks at me and frowns when they see my new outfit. Not quite what I was looking for, but never mind.

"Hello and welcome to Kai's Amazing Tour Adventures!" I say. The effect is somewhat diminished because I'm having to say everything in a whisper rather than the loud, booming voice it deserves. "I'm Kai, your tour guide. Please follow all of my instructions to the letter and keep your hands to yourselves because if you fling them around, there's no telling what might bite them off." Everyone is looking at me with horrified expressions. I laugh nervously. "Everyone ready to go?"

They nod hesitantly, except for Xiaohua, who rolls her golden eyes and sighs another puff of smoke out of her stupidly huge nostrils.

"Right then, off we go!" I wave the flag above my head and trudge forward, hiding my trepidation. "You may notice the trees around us. Frightful sight, aren't they? Nothing but dead, crooked branches and twisted roots. Fun fact—the roots drink human blood, so they are very attracted to your scent right now. As we move, you might notice that the roots are starting to seek you out and perhaps even twine around your legs to break your bones and absorb your blood. So ha ha, um, arms and legs inside—well, close to your bodies—at all times, okay? Okay."

With a start, the kids realize that the roots are slithering slowly, like thick coils of snakes, becoming ever more restless as we pass.

"Oh gods, not again," Theo mutters. "This time, I'm not as

---

with needle-sharp teeth? Well, never mind. There are worse ones here. Like Xiaohua, for example. You didn't hear that from me.

helpless." He raises a hand and mutters a spell called Cast a Small Light to Dispel the Dark Blight. His palm shines bright and he aims it down at the roots, which shrink away from the light.

Encouraged, Danny does the same while Namita casts a different spell that makes her feet shine, so the roots are repelled wherever she steps.[14]

"Ah, wonderful job, tourists!" I say, waving my flag enthusiastically. "You did much better than expected. I thought for sure we'd lose one of you."

"She thought 'for sure' she'd lose one of us?" Danny mutters.

Xiaohua sighs a tired rumble. "I would never let anything bad happen to you, you know that."

"And I would never let anything bad happen to me," Namita says.

"So that leaves you, Theo, as the most vulnerable member of the group!" I say in what I hope is a comforting way.

Theo frowns. "Hardly! I've been practicing a lot of defensive spells."

"And don't forget my bow and arrows," Danny says, pointing at his quiver.

"Oh dear," I sigh. "Look, they're not going to do you much good against those trees."

Danny's shoulders sag. "I know—I just hate feeling helpless."

And somehow, despite myself, I actually feel bad for the kid.

"Well, don't worry—I'm sure Kai won't let anything bad happen to us, right?" Theo says.

---

14 Have I mentioned yet how much I love this girl?

He stares at me. I stare back.

"Right?" he says again.

"If it's between you and Namita, there's no question about it. I'm saving her."

Namita whoops. "All right, Kai!"

Theo narrows his eyes at both of us, though he is smiling a little. "Okay, I see how it is."

"Anyway, let's keep moving, and don't forget to watch for other flesh-eating demons!" I throw the flag up and catch it with my tails before advancing rapidly across the tangle of bloodthirsty tree roots, desperate to keep my tone light to keep them from seeing just how scared I am in this place. The roots shift restlessly, shrinking away with horrible rustles as the kids' lights shine on them, and before long, we're out of the forest of dead trees. Phew. Not that I would let them know, but I'm so relieved I nearly pee myself.[15]

"Jolly good, gang!" I cheer. The group give me half-hearted smiles, like they're not altogether that impressed at how masterfully I've led them through the forest. I'm about to give them a piece of my mind when a splash catches my attention. "Ah, here is the Kunlun River, which flows from Spirit World all the way to hell, going through the Doorway in between. Looks nice and refreshing, doesn't it?"

The kids walk to the riverbank and crouch down. Theo starts to reach into the water, but I blow a whistle (quietly) and say, "Please do not touch the water, for it is sometimes pure acid."

---

15 It's hard maintaining a calm, controlled demeanor when you're the only one who knows just how dangerous everything here is, but that's me. Brave. Selfless. Courageous.

Theo snatches his hand back, his mouth dropping open.

"Sometimes it's pure acid?" Namita, who's always faster on the uptake, says. "What is it at other times?"

I shrug. "It depends on its mood. Sometimes it's the most delicious elixir, which will grant you immortality and godlike powers. Other times it's molten lava. Other times it's mountain dew."

"Like the soft drink?" Theo says.

"No, like real dew from the mountains. Why would it be the soft drink? Anyway, the moral of the story is 'don't touch anything here.' Come, we shall follow the river down to the entrance to Diyu."

As we start down the path along the riverside, a chittering noise catches my attention. I frown back at the forest of dead trees. Something—or rather, some things—are moving, flitting from the branches toward us. Lightning flashes across the boiling bruise-colored skies, revealing the threat. I'd been expecting the macaque demons that Theo and I had come across on our last visit here, but this time, the demons have taken the form of bats. It's a battle keeping my voice light as I announce, "Ah, for the next part of Kai's Amazing Tour Adventures, we seem to be hunted by flesh-eating bat demons!"

The group jumps, and everyone raises their hands at the advancing cloud of bats. Xiaohua rears up, drawing in a great breath and shooting up into the sky. She dives into the mass and sprays a jet of blinding fire out of her mouth. We all gasp at the sight. It's hard not to; it's magnificent and terrifying in equal parts, and I realize that Xiaohua has been holding back the true magnitude of her powers in the human world. Dozens of black shapes plummet from the sky, burning as they fall, but even more bat demons appear, joining the fray. Xiaohua twists this way and that, roaring and blowing fire as she flies, while hundreds of bat demons fall like flaming marshmallows. Fleetingly, I wonder if I should help her, but even as I consider what shape to shift into to deal with an infestation of bats—an owl, perhaps? Or a hawk?—the bat demons decide that they've lost enough of their numbers. There is a high-pitched squeak and as one, they all disperse, melting into the turbulent sky the way that a fog clears up in the sun.

The kids whoop and clap and cheer as Xiaohua spirals back down to the ground. She's breathing hard, but her eyes are aglow and her scales burn an even more vivid red than before. She's just undergone a literal glow up. The children crowd around her, chattering excitedly.

"That was amazing!" Danny cries, and he almost hugs her, but she rears back.

"Don't touch me, Master! I'm burning hot." True enough, she's still sizzling, and from where I stand two paces away, I can feel the heat radiating off her glowing scales. I guess Danny was just overcome with excitement.

"Well, that was so, so cool!" Namita says.

"Yeah, you saved us," Theo says.

"I mean, technically I saved you by guiding us all to Diyu," I mutter, "but whatever."

Xiaohua bows her head in an effort to seem humble.[16] "It was

_____

16 But you're not fooled by that, are you? ARE YOU?

nothing," she murmurs. "It is my honor to be able to protect my chosen master."

"Gosh, with you around, nothing here can touch us!" Theo says.

I snap round at him, glaring, and he at least has the presence of mind to look guilty. "I mean, with both of you around, nothing here can touch us."

"Harrumph," I snort. "Well, now that the bats are taken care of, let's commence to the next part of the journey." I wave the flag rather aggressively and lead the group down the river until we reach the mouth of a cave with an intricately carved bronze door. "Aha! Here we are: the entrance to Diyu, as promised."

"Oh, Kai, you did it!" Namita cries, throwing her arms around my neck. "You wonderful little creature."

"Yes, well, this sort of world-class treatment is the least you can expect from my tour company, obviously."

"You did great, Kai," Theo says, holding out a fist for me to bump. I do so, gingerly, before shooting Xiaohua a smug smile. She may be the brute of the group, but I have proven myself to be the brains, which is surely far more worthy.

"Well, let's go in!" I open the door with a flourish. Noise spills out of the cave. Prominent barks thunder out, along with screams. I jump back and slam the door shut.

"What's wrong?" Theo says.

I smile at the group sheepishly. "Wrong door. That was Tartarus and the barking pup Cerberus. Heh-heh, honest mistake, really—anyone could've made it."

"Did the Greek symbols on the door not give it away?" Xiaohua says lazily.

I glare at her. "You could've mentioned it."

"And give away the surprise? Unlikely."

"I thought such petty behavior was beyond divine beings like yourself," I say.

"ANYWAY," Theo says loudly, "where should we go?"

I sniff and straighten my tour-guide hat before waving the flag, albeit a little bit less enthusiastically now. "It should be straight down this way."

We follow the river once more, and before long, we come to another cave mouth. This time, I don't miss the Sanskrit words carved into the stone door.

"Let me guess—that's Naraka?" Namita says.

"Right you are! The next door should be the way to . . . ah, yes!" I stop in front of a wooden door with Chinese characters cut into it. "Here we are."

The group takes a collective breath, everyone looking more serious than before. Even Xiaohua is looking somewhat less smug, which I didn't think she was capable of. Theo turns to Namita and Danny and casts a minor protection spell on them; then Xiaohua breathes over the children to bless them with divine energy.[17] With all that done, there is nothing to do but open the door and step through to the First Court of Hell.

---

17 Sounds rather unhygienic, if you ask me. That's how airborne viruses spread, don't you know?

THEO
8

Whoa, so this is what hell looks like. Honestly, I was expecting more fire and brimstone, a cave filled with ghosts and monsters, with pits here and there spitting out flames, but the First Court of Hell is nothing like that. In fact, it's actually really amazing. It looks like the entrance to the Forbidden City in Beijing, but unlike the Forbidden City, this one has a multi-story pavilion that stretches up as high as I can see. Everything looks clean and orderly and everyone is shuffling along quietly, no screaming, tortured ghosts to be seen. Though we're underground and I can sense the weight of the stone ceiling above us, I can't actually see the ceiling. The cavern just stretches on for miles until it disappears into the dark. All of us, even Kai, are awed to hushed silence as we make our way across the stone courtyard. Red lanterns hang above us, glowing gently in the darkness.

The courtyard is deserted, but at the gateway to the pavilion is a man in an elaborate floor-length tunic. Before the Know Your Roots program, I would've seen it and thought, *Traditional Chinese outfit*. But ever since the program, I've been immersing myself in Chinese studies, and now I recognize his clothes as a Ming-dynasty court official's hanfu, with a large flowing black coat tied carelessly at the waist. The coat is partially open and shows off a skinny chest, and the man flaps a bamboo fan lazily as he leans against the doorway.

"Wei," he calls out to us as we near, greeting us in casual Mandarin. "What have we here? Oh my, quite a young group of people to be crossing into the courts of Diyu. Let me guess: school bus accident? Tragic." Despite the sympathetic words, his face remains impassive, his eyes barely resting on us before rolling upward to the endless ceiling.

"Honorable Wuchang Shifu," Xiaohua rumbles, "I apologize for disturbing your rest."

The man throws his head back and laughs. "Oh my. Wuchang Shifu?" He laughs again. "It's been so long since I've come across a dragon that I've forgotten how archaic you creatures are. Please, let's not bother with formalities. Call me what I am: Wuchang Gui."

"What's going on?" Namita whispers.

"Um, he wants us to call him Ghost Wuchang instead of Master Wuchang," I whisper back.

"That's because it's what I am," Wuchang Gui booms, suddenly appearing between me and Namita.

We startle, jumping away, and he grins slyly at us. "Oh? Have you not heard of me? I am the Ghost of Impermanence—my role is to lead spirits to King Yanluo for judgment. Though sometimes I can mete out judgment myself, if you like."

"With all due respect, Honorable Wuchang Shi—er, Gui," Xiaohua says, "we would like to see King Qinguang for a specific matter. I hope this does not cause offense to you or King Yanluo."

"I'm so confused right now," Namita whispers. "I thought the one who gives out judgment is King Qinguang."

"Little girl, I have excellent hearing, you know," Wuchang Gui says. He snorts and spits to one side. "Yes, technically King Qinguang is the ruler of the First Court, the one who decides whether souls have to go through the Ten Courts of Hell or get reincarnated. But King Yanluo also has the right to judge whether souls are to be punished—and between you and me, King Yanluo is the wiser of the two. He lived as Bao Zheng in the human world. You know Bao Zheng? The world-famous judge? Very honest, upright, all that wonderful stuff."

Even I've heard of Bao Zheng, a famous judge from the Song Dynasty who was celebrated for being fair and fearless, going so far as to impeach a member of the royal family. Jamie had been a huge fan of his. There are endless TV series about Bao Zheng, most of them called Bao Qing Tian, and Jamie watched all of them, some of them twice over. His favorite Bao Zheng story was one where Bao Zheng had been injured by a poisoned arrow and had to have the poison carved out of his arm. He'd refused all forms of anesthesia during the surgery and even chose to play chess while the doctor carved his arm to the bone. Jamie had dubbed him "China's biggest badass."

Xiaohua says again that we have urgent need to see King Qinguang, but I can see that Wuchang Gui is getting increasingly annoyed by this request.

"I simply don't understand why you are rejecting this generous offer. King Qinguang is far more strict—I can assure you." His easygoing expression is gone, his face turning an alarming shade of red, and I'm sure he's increasing in size.

My anxiety doubles, then triples, until finally my mouth opens of its own accord. "I want to see King Yanluo! I mean, I would love to. My brother was such a huge fan of his, but that's why we're here. We're here to see my brother, and he's at King Qinguang's Court."

There is a shocked silence. Kai shifts uneasily, and I sense through our mind link that she thinks I've made a mistake revealing our true purpose here. I grimace inwardly. Oh no, have I really sabotaged our quest so early in the journey?

Wuchang Gui's eyes narrow. "What do you mean, you're here to 'see' your brother? Are you not souls requiring judgment?"

We all look at one another, panic written clearly on our faces. Danny looks like he's almost ready to faint. I'm also incredibly nervous for another reason: Niu Mo Wang. I wonder if Wuchang Gui would be able to sense Niu Mo Wang's aura inside my backpack and what he would do if he does. He'd definitely freak out, and who could blame him then?

"Oh, rest assured—we are souls seeking judgment," Kai says.

Wuchang Gui glares at her, then at Xiaohua, then back at Kai again. It seems he can't sense Niu Mo Wang's aura. My heart rate slows down a little. I guess the cage is doing its thing and muting the aura of whoever's trapped inside it.

"A fox spirit and a dragon traveling together," Wuchang Gui muses. "Strange company you keep, divine dragon."

Xiaohua's whiskers twitch, though she keeps her face straight. "This particular fox spirit has shown herself to be unlike the rest of her kind. It is an honor for me to travel with her."

"Hmm," Wuchang Gui mutters, still eyeing us suspiciously. He reaches into his black tunic and pulls out a tattered scroll. Unrolling it, he scans the scroll before looking back at us. "I see no dragon or fox spirit scheduled to arrive here today. I don't like this."

My stomach falls. We're being denied right at the front gate of Diyu, so close to Jamie.

"You're right," Namita says suddenly. "We're not exactly planned visitors, but don't you think it's more fun that way?"

We all stare at her.

"What are you doing?" I whisper.

"Trust me on this. My mom is a bureaucrat. Her job is to make sure that the admin work in the government runs smoothly. And you know what she hates most? Unexpected applicants. They interrupt the flow of everything. She's got a whole system, right? And unexpected applicants turn up and the system grinds to a halt."

"You're kind of arguing against us here," I mutter.

But Namita's eyes shine with excitement as she says, "Think of how annoyed King Qinguang would be when we show up at his court! You said it yourself, Mr. Wuchang: Not only are we not on the list, but we're also a very unlikely group. A dragon and a fox spirit and human kids—not to mention, in case you haven't noticed, I'm not Chinese. I'm not Buddhist or Taoist; I'm Hindu. What am I even doing in Chinese hell? Can you imagine how confused King Qinguang would be?"

A new expression melts across Wuchang Gui's face, changing it completely. He'd been glaring at us so intently just moments ago, but now, the lines on his face have rearranged themselves into an almost smile.

But Namita isn't done. "Now," she adds, "think of how angry King Yanluo would be if you led a group as problematic as us to his court."

And there it is: her final blow. The wicked joy on Wuchang Gui's face is replaced by a look of horror as he envisions his boss's displeasure. Bao Zheng was known to be fair, but in the TV shows I've watched, he also had a temper.

Wuchang Gui quails visibly before he manages to control his emotions. He draws himself up, standing straight and lifting his chin. He makes a show of studying the scroll once more. He sniffs. I have barely drawn a single breath since Namita last spoke. Finally, Wuchang Gui clears his throat. "Due to the unnatural circumstances of your presence here, I do not recommend you to His Royal Majesty King Yanluo's court. You may proceed to His Majesty King Qinguang's court. Please follow me."

We all release our breaths. I feel as though I could melt into the stone floor. I look at Namita, my eyes shining with gratitude, unable to speak for the massive lump in my throat.

"Namita," I croak at last. "Thank you."

Namita rolls her eyes. "Of course, dum-dum. Aren't you glad I came along?"

I laugh then, and we all follow Wuchang Gui through the grand gate and into King Qinguang's Court.

≈ ⚜ ≈

The First Court of Hell is basically a giant courtroom, with rows and rows of benches filled with waiting souls and a massive table at the front. It is one of the most beautiful halls I have ever been in, and the grandness of it makes me even more nervous.

My insides quail at the size of the courtroom. There are hundreds of souls in here, all of them seated quietly. Pop culture has got it right: They're blue in color and slightly see-through. It's a really weird feeling, seeing them. They're both familiar and yet strange. I've seen enough movies to know that ghosts and souls are often portrayed that way, but seeing them in person is an entirely different thing. Each soul is in their own little world; no one talks to anyone else, and I just have this feeling that if I were to reach out and try to touch one of them, my fingers would go right through.

As though reading my mind, Kai says, "Don't disturb them. Everyone here is on a slightly different plane to maintain order. Can't have human souls talking to one another, plotting to undermine the justice system."

Which is sort of exactly what we're here to do. I gulp as Wuchang Gui leads us to a side table with a box the size of a watermelon on it. "New soul," he says to the box. It whirrs and spits out a small piece of paper. Wuchang Gui rips off the piece of paper and hands it to Namita. "Here's your number. Take a seat and do not speak to anyone until it's called."

I'm so scared that I might mess something up that I can only jerk my head into a small nod.

"You guys have automated service down here?" Danny says, sounding as confused as I feel.

Wuchang Gui looks insulted. "It's the twenty-first century. What did you expect us to have: stone tablets?"

Danny blanches and shoves his hands into his pockets, shuffling his feet as he mutters, "Sorry. I didn't mean to be rude."

Despite myself, I feel an overwhelming need to defend him. "We just didn't expect to find human inventions here, that's all."

"Human inventions?" Wuchang Gui cries, his eyes widening before he bends over and starts cackling. "Where do you think humans get ideas for machines in the first place?" He taps on his temple with a skinny finger. "Divine intervention, obviously!" With that, he turns and walks off.

A deep gong reverberates throughout the large hall, and we all turn to look at the source of the sound. At the front is a huge paper screen with volcanoes spitting fire painted across it. I can see shadows moving around behind it and a huge silhouette of someone sitting in the middle. I guess that must be King Qinguang. A soul moves forward and goes behind the screen. Murmurs rise from the hidden stage, strangely muted. I try to swallow, but my throat sticks. I can't believe that right at this moment, someone—an actual soul—is receiving his end-of-life judgment.

The number on the screen says 98124.

I reach over for our piece of paper. It says 98276.

It seems like we're in for a bit of a wait. I scan the large hall and spot a sign that says SPECIAL CASES. My heart leaps into my throat. Could that be where Jamie is? So close to me, and yet still hidden from sight? As though the sight of the sign has pushed me into a trance, I stand, barely aware of what I'm doing. My eyes are riveted on the sign and what's behind it. Vaguely, I sense myself walking toward it. The others are asking where I'm going, but I take no notice of them. Kai lands on my shoulders.

"Kid, what are you doing?" she whispers.

I nod at the sign without slowing down, and Kai abruptly falls silent. She gets it, too. How close we are to Jamie. And I sense her need to see him, as fierce and hot as mine. Together, we make our way down the aisle, walking past rows of waiting souls and down a dark corridor. At the end of the corridor is a door that's labeled WAITING ROOM.

I feel as though I've forgotten how to breathe. How to walk, how to control any part of my body, because my consciousness has just floated out and I'm watching everything unfold before me. I'm about to see Jamie. This is it. Oh my gods, I can't wait. My insides are a mess of exploding fireworks. I feel like I could scream and cry and laugh all at once. Jamie is right there, waiting for me behind that door.

And now that we're both finally about to be reunited with Jamie, what's going to happen?

As soon as I think that, I chide myself for my selfishness. Of course I would insist that Kai be Jamie's spirit companion once more. I'll summon another spirit companion, a less argumentative one. Maybe a water dragon, if I could somehow save enough money for it? Kai would hate living under the same roof with a water dragon. The thought of Kai playing pranks on a water dragon makes me smile. Anyway, it might not even matter, because . . . well, we'll see.

I take a deep breath, place my hand on the door, and push it open.

THEO
9

There are no words to describe the emotions surging through me as I push open the door. My heart, my blood, it all thumps to one single rhythm: *Jamie, Jamie, Jamie.*

And there he is, sitting quietly, alone in the middle of a vast room. He glances up, his expression empty, then at once, his eyes widen and his mouth falls open. He stands slowly, as though in a dream, and the way he moves is so familiar that it cracks something open inside me and I shout out.

"Jamie!"

"Theo?"

We dash toward each other and, oh my gods, I can't believe that after everything, my brother is here, and he's okay, and I'm hugging him, I really am. I know it's impossible because he's a soul, and souls probably don't have any smells, but I swear I can almost smell the old Jamie—a wholesome combination of warm, clean sweat and that sweet hoisin sauce he loved so much.

"Jamie!" Kai shrieks, and leaps from my shoulders and wraps herself fiercely around his head, yipping and growling, overcome with emotion.

"Kai!"

Kai is so excited that she can't keep still, climbing all over Jamie's head and sniffing him, her two tails practically wagging.

The sight of her overwhelming joy is amazing to see and yet also slightly painful in a way I can't quite explain. I tighten my arms around Jamie's broad chest.

"You're here," I whisper. "I found you."

"You did. You guys—I don't even know—I—how?!"

"You're not going to believe it."

Jamie grins at me, then raises his eyebrows. "Hang on, you two worked out your differences long enough to come here together?" he says in wonderment.

Guilt lances through my gut. I haven't even thought of how he might feel, knowing that Kai is now my spirit companion. "Yeah, long story."

Kai is still in a frenzy, scolding Jamie one second, hugging him the next. "Why didn't you tell me what you found at Reapling? Oh gods, I could kill you! Sorry, that was in bad taste. But I really could! Oh, I'm so happy you're here—this is the best day ever!"

Jamie laughs as Kai climbs all over his shoulders, her tails wagging this way and that. "I can't believe you both are down here. How—is this real? Are you two really here? I mean, how?"

I squeeze Jamie's hands before wiping the tears from my cheeks. "We're really, really here. We had some help from our friends." I turn my head and see Namita, Danny, and Xiaohua a few paces behind us. As Jamie gapes at them, Danny waves and gives a shy smile. Namita waves more enthusiastically, and when I gesture at them to come forward, she runs toward us, grinning.

"Hey, Jamie. I'm Namita. It's really good to finally meet you." She holds out a fist to Jamie.

Jamie laughs and bumps her fist, then does the same with

Danny before nodding at Xiaohua. "I can't believe this," he breathes out.

"We all got to know each other at Know Your Roots, and they decided to come down here to help me get you out of Diyu."

"Know Your Roots?" Jamie says. "Wait, you actually enrolled in the program? After I told you to go to the police?" There's a hint of anger in his voice.

"I thought you wanted me to! You left me that notebook with all these clues, and I thought you wanted me to solve them."

"Theo!" Jamie pinches the bridge of his nose and grinds his teeth. "I wanted you to take the notebook and go to the cops. Remember? I said if you found a quest that's too difficult to do on your own, you should report it to the game master. I can't believe you joined the program instead. That's so dangerous. Know Your Roots was being run by bad people. Anything could've happened to you." With a pained expression on his face, he pulls me into a fierce hug. "I can't believe I put you in so much danger, Didi."

It's the term Didi, little brother, that does it. Something cracks open inside me then, and I don't even try to hold back as the tears wash over me. Huge, ugly sobs rip out of me. I didn't know, didn't want to admit to myself or to anyone, how much I've missed being a didi. My whole life, that's been such a huge part of my identity that without it, I was lost. I needed my gege, my big brother. I still do. I cling to Jamie and cry and cry and cry.

"Thank you," Jamie whispers. "I can't believe you put yourself through all that for me."

After what seems like an eternity, I manage to get the crying under control and say, "I had a lot of help. Kai—she was, um, there was a sort of mix-up, and she became my spirit companion." I look guiltily at Jamie. I have no idea how he's going to react. "But of course, if you want her back, she's all yours. I mean, if you want to be Jamie's spirit companion, that is, Kai."

Kai snorts and shrugs. I can't tell what she's thinking.

Jamie grins. "Kai? You guys are spirit companions? Whaaat?" He laughs. "I can't even—how many times have you two tried to kill each other?"

"Only about a million times," Namita pipes up. "You should've seen them at the Know Your Roots program. They were constantly arguing. It was unbearable."

Jamie chortles and pulls me and Kai into another hug. "I can't believe this."

"Me neither," I murmur. I look at him through my tears, still not quite believing that we're here, and I'm touching Jamie. Well, Jamie's soul, that is. "Are you—have you been tortured or anything?"

Jamie shakes his head. "No. It's been pretty dull, actually. I don't even really know what happened. When I woke up, I was down here, with a number, and then they called my number and King Qinguang was like, 'Aiya, not another complicated case! Take him to the waiting room. I don't have the energy to deal with this today.'"

I exchange a glance with the others.

"So I've just been at the waiting room for . . . I don't know—how long has it been?"

My throat closes up again. The thought of Jamie sitting in that room, alone, listening to Muzak over and over, not even knowing how much time has passed, is awful. I'm relieved that he hasn't been tortured, but waiting without an end is a form of torture in itself.

"Well, it doesn't matter, because you're coming home with us," I say.

Xiaohua lowers her head. "Little human," she says gently, "I think we need to discuss the actual process before doing anything brash because the last thing we want to do is offend King Qinguang by taking a deceased person back to the human world without his consent."

"Tch," Kai snorts, "always with the rules. Don't you get tired of—"

"Hang on," Jamie says. He stares at us in confusion. "What do you mean 'deceased person'?"

We all stare back at him. No words come out of my mouth.

"Theo? Kai," Jamie says softly, "I don't understand. What happened to my body?"

I can't bear to look at his expectant face. He doesn't know, I realize, and the realization hits like a giant hammer. He doesn't know that after his soul was ripped away, his physical foot remained on the gas pedal of his car. He doesn't know that the car veered off the freeway and crashed horribly. He doesn't know that he did, in fact, die that day.

I see the moment that my brother realizes what has happened back in the human world. I see the painful, excruciating moment of horror dawning on his face, and I wish I could wipe it away. Just like that, I'm enraged at Reapling all over again. How could they do this to him? He was only seventeen; he was about to graduate high school and go off and do amazing stuff. He would've been a doctor, the best one ever, yanking people from the gates of Diyu.

How do I explain this to him? "Jamie," I croak. "I'm so sorry."

Sorrow overwhelms Jamie's features, his face crumpling like paper. Kai and I hug him so tightly, as though we're trying to absorb as much of his sadness as we can. The whole time, I say, "I'm sorry. I'm sorry," as though it could help, as though it makes a difference.

But before I can say another word, a loud alarm blares through the waiting room. We all start and look up to see a screen flashing with numbers: JAMIE TAN: NUMBER 98280

"What?" Jamie says.

We all gape at the screen, then at one another.

"I think . . . ," Xiaohua ventures, "it is time for you to join the queue."

"Is that a good thing?" I say, my voice wavering. I turn to the others, anticipation roiling inside me. "It is, right? We need to present his case to King Qinguang, so this is a good thing, right?"

After a long pause, Namita says, "I don't think we have a choice. The best thing we can do right now is join the queue, and when we get to Jamie's turn, we'll explain everything to King Qinguang."

"I'm sure he'll see reason," Danny says, but he looks as uncertain as I feel.

Jamie looks down at me, sees my stricken gaze, and makes himself smile. My chest twists with pain. He's always a big brother, even now. Always taking care of me, making sure I'm okay. "Hey, I'm sure it'll be okay."

How ridiculous that even now, when what's at stake is his soul, he's the one comforting me? I force a smile onto my face. "Yeah, totally." I know it will turn out okay for Jamie.

We walk out of the waiting room in silence, me clutching Jamie's hand like a little kid. I'm never letting go of my big brother's hand, not ever again.

KAI
10

We're all silent as we shuffle out to join the queue in the main hall. Well, outwardly I am quiet, but inside my head is a full-on chorus singing at the top of its lungs: *JAMIE IS HEEERE!* I am over two hundred years old, with a vocabulary that would've made Shakespeare cry with envy, but at this moment, I quite simply do not have the words to describe how I feel. I keep glancing over at Jamie and touching him to make sure he's really there, not a figment of my cruel imagination. My paws jump nimbly from Jamie's left shoulder to his right, to the top of his head, then around his neck, and he laughs and says, "Oh, Kai," which makes my heart seize up with every emotion in the world. I'm so overcome by Jamie's presence that I can hardly sense Theo's thoughts in our mind link. With a flash of guilt, I look at Theo. He seems to be in as much of an emotional turmoil as I am, which makes me feel even more—well, turmoiled.

The number on the screen says 98129. So I suppose there will still be a bit of a wait before it's Jamie's turn. We make our way past the paper volcano screen, find an empty bench and slide in wordlessly, all of us too tense to say much.

I look at the front of the courtroom, where King Qinguang has stood up to pass his judgment on a soul, and something close to fear electrifies my fur, making it stand on end.[18] Xiaohua is always yammering on and on about being a divine being, and technically she is, but there are minor divine beings like her, and there are actual Divine Beings like a king of Diyu. It's like looking directly at the sun. King Qinguang's qì is so powerful that I feel my skin crackling, my insides slowly melting like they're trying to merge with his magnificent qì. Next to me, Xiaohua bows her head and averts her eyes; I guess his brilliance is also too much for her to bear.

Fortunately, human eyes aren't as sensitive as ours, so the kids have no trouble looking straight at King Qinguang. Even though they're unable to see the blinding glow of his aura, King Qinguang still makes a half-amazing, half-terrifying sight. For one thing, he's twice as large as a normal adult human, and he sits upon a large dais so he towers over all of us like a small mountain. For another . . . well, the whole ginormous thing is enough, is it not? But in case it isn't, for another, he's staring down at the soul in front of him with a very stern expression, his bushy eyebrows in the shape of a V. And being a judge of human souls, he's had all of eternity to practice looking stern.

The soul falls to his knees; it's instinctive for you humans. The muscles in your legs turn to water and your bowels churn and your primitive lizard brains[19] yell, *KNEEL!*

---

18 Sort of like when you get goose bumps, except when I do, it actually does something: It makes me look bigger and more threatening. I'm not sure what your goose bumps achieve, aside from making you bumpy.

19 Well, you have a lizard brain. Mine's a honed, cultured fox brain.

"Yangruo, you used your precious time in the human world to do nothing but bad deeds," King Qinguang booms, his voice thunderous and deep, like the grinding of the earth as land masses crash into one another. "Your company exploited its employees and dumped tons of toxic waste into the rivers, poisoning the drinking water for thousands of people. What do you have to say for yourself?"

The soul is visibly trembling. "Please, Your Honor, I didn't know—"

"You claim ignorance? I can see straight into your heart. I know you were perfectly aware of what you were doing." To my surprise, a tinge of sadness enters King Qinguang's voice then. "Yangruo, I do not give out my sentences lightly. But your sins are grave, and you have a valuable lesson to learn. Guards, take him to King Biancheng's court."

Next to Theo, Namita utters a small gasp.

"What is it?" Theo whispers.

"King Biancheng rules the Sixth Court of Hell," Namita whispers. "It's where those who have broken laws are punished . . . by, uh, being thrown onto a tree of spikes."

Theo looks ill.

The soul screams as two demon guards march him away. "Please, Your Honor, I can pay you! Any amount of money you want!"

King Qinguang laughs, not a pleasant sound. "Do you know why King Yanluo was demoted to the Fifth Court of Hell?"

The demon guards halt, and the soul stares expectantly at King Qinguang.

"It was because the Jade Emperor thought he was too merciful. He has a soft spot for mortals, you see. I have no such soft spot; therefore, I am able to judge well. With fairness, not with mercy."

The number on the screen changes. "Next!" an announcer shouts out.

"Well, settle in," I mutter. "We've got quite a long wait—"

Just then, a side door opens and figures march out of it. Though no one else takes notice of them, something about them draws my attention. The courtroom is too dimly lit for me to make out the figures. One of them speaks. "Do you see her?"

The voice curdles my essence and makes my guts tighten. The voice of my forever nemesis. And if that voice is here, then the other will surely follow. Sure enough, as I think that, another voice booms: "Can you spot her?"

"I already said that, brother," the first speaker grumbles.

"Two is more effective than one, brother," the second speaker argues.

And finally, they step into the light, wearing smug grins on their stupid, hateful bovine faces. My lips curl back on their own accord, revealing my fangs, for before me stand my tormentors, the two beings hell-bent on my destruction. Ox Head and Horse Face.

"I smell her—there!"

I leap up, all of my muscles tense, but there's no time to hide as they march straight toward us. The other souls glance up, but as soon as they see the horrible sight of Ox Head and Horse Face, they quickly lower their heads. It's obvious that these two are not anyone you want to mess with.

"What's happening?" Jamie says.

As Ox Head and Horse Face approach us, the kids bunch up together, quailing from their frightful, brutish forms. My tails flick up and I force myself to make them flap casually as I say, "Oh hello, Ox Head, Horse Face. Fancy meeting you here."

"I told you not to call me that!" Horse Face growls.

"It's your name," I mutter. Maybe it's unwise to be so flippant in King Qinguang's courtroom, but there's just something[20] about these two that make me want to irritate the heck out of them.

"Yes, but you're saying it like an insult!" Horse Face snaps.

Something flies around Horse Face and Ox Head, whizzing like an overeager fly. It stops next to Horse Face. It's a small imp. With a start, I realize it's Pea Green.

"There they are!" Pea Green chitters. "I told you they'd be here! That one, that was the one that took the form of the great Creighton Ward to trick me!"

My mouth drops open as realization sets in.

"Oh my gods, it's the Eye from Reapling," Danny gasps.

"Yeah, that's me, all right. I told you you'd be sorry," Pea Green says with a smug look.

"Pea Green," I gasp. "What have you done?"

Pea Green blows a raspberry at me. "What you deserved, lowly fox spirit! I found these two intrepid guards of hell"—Ox Head and Horse Face snort and stand up straighter—"and I alerted them of your duplicitous, sneaky, underhanded plan of coming to Diyu!"

---

20 That "something" is probably the fact that they're so obsessed with, you know, killing me.

My lips peel back to reveal a snarl. How dare this little upstart betray me like this? I mean, yes, I may have taken advantage of his affection for Creighton Ward, but still! "Oh, you little . . ."

"You don't scare me!" Pea Green sneers, and makes a rude gesture. "And now, my job is done and I shall take my leave. Enjoy being tortured in hell, fox demon!" With one last obnoxious hoot, Pea Green shoots up and disappears with a small pop.

"Now," Horse Face says, grinning evilly, "we're going to enjoy torturing you for all eternity, fox demon."

Theo turns to me, and his eyes are wild with fear. His thoughts surge into my consciousness. *Kai, they can't get you. I can't lose you, too.*

His fear is contagious, filling all of my senses, overtaking my whole body, down to the tips of my tails. *You won't lose me.* I try to soothe him, but my own mind is shivering. Can we ask King Qinguang for help? But how could we, when Ox Head and Horse Face are his guards? Who's he going to believe: his own guards or a ragtag bunch that doesn't even belong here? What if my conflict with Ox Head and Horse Face angers King Qinguang and ends up ruining Jamie's case?

Theo must have read my mind because he says, *King Qinguang said it himself: He doesn't rule with mercy. Kai, you have to run.*

YOU HAVE TO RUN.

He flings the last thought at me with so much force that it comes as a physical blow. I stumble back, all rational thought pushed out of my mind, my survival instincts taking over. All of my thoughts shaved down to primal instinct. Theo's right. I need to run. I make a change into a giant eagle and spread my wings.

Ox Head jumps up, raising his trident. It catches the light of the flames, glinting horribly as he throws it straight at me. Except I'm already moving, no longer where the trident is flying toward. Danny, who was directly behind me, is now in its path.

"No!" I don't know who shouted it, me or Xiaohua. The next instant, she's in front of Danny, but Danny is no longer there because I have him in my claws, and I'm flying—flying as he shrieks, as everyone shouts, as Ox Head's trident pierces through dragonscale, the unforgiving blades biting into dragonflesh, as Xiaohua's roar rends the cavern. Danny cries out, arching in my claws as though he, too, had been stabbed. I don't stop to think. I cast about for an exit and find a door. Horse Face is galloping straight toward us, but I don't hesitate. I fly through the door and slam it shut right before Horse Face crashes into it.

THEO

11

The moment that the door slams shut, cutting my spirit companion from me, I freeze. It's as though I've lost one of my limbs. My surroundings gain an unreal quality, like I'm watching them from afar, their voices muted: on one side, Xiaohua keening with pain—on the other, a few paces away, Ox Head and Horse Face hammering on the door, shouting to be let in. And in front of us, the great and terrible King Qinguang, eyes glowing red, shouting commands at various demon guards, who come flying in. It all seems to be happening in slow motion around me, like we're underwater. Maybe I'm dreaming. Maybe—

Something shoves me roughly, jolting me out of my shocked stupor.

"Theo!" Namita cries, slapping my chest hard enough to smart.

I blink at her. Noise rushes back in, everything in chaos, everyone shouting and running and flying everywhere. On the stage, King Qinguang roars, "What is happening? Who dares to cause such disorder in my court?"

Ox Head and Horse Face scramble down the aisle toward the dais, bowing every few steps. "Your Honor, my brother and I were trying to apprehend a fox demon," Horse Face calls out.

"A fox demon in my court?" King Qinguang thunders.

"Yes," Ox Head says, "we have been pursuing her for months

now." He continues to give his version of his run-ins with Kai, and the frown on King Qinguang's face deepens as Ox Head talks.

"Oh gods, this is bad," I whisper. King Qinguang doesn't seem like he's going to be in any mood to listen to our explanations.

"Come on, we've got to go!" Namita snaps. "We need to—I don't know, we need to come up with a new plan."

I turn to Xiaohua. "We can't leave her."

"I know." Namita puts her arm around the dragon. I flinch at the sight of the broken scales and stab wounds still oozing blood. The blood is gold in color, beautiful and horrible to behold. Xiaohua twists with obvious pain. "Xiaohua, shrink down! We'll carry you out of here," Namita says.

With a nod, Xiaohua closes her eyes and shrinks down until she's about as thick as my arm. Namita and I pick her up, trying to be gentle but also in too much of a rush to be very gentle, and Xiaohua flinches. Gritting my teeth, I place her round my shoulders, shuddering as the scalding hot gold blood drips down my back.

"Come on, Jamie," I say, but Jamie shakes his head.

"I can't leave the queue," he says. "Souls are not permitted to leave the First Court until they receive their judgment. You guys need to go ahead without me."

"No—" The idea of leaving my brother now, mere moments after we've been reunited, is inconceivable.

"You don't have a choice," Jamie hisses. "Go now! You have to find Kai. I can't sense her—can you, Theo? She's in trouble. Go. I'll be here."

I glance up at the queue number. "But what if your number's called before we come back? You barely remember what happened back in the human world. You need us here to explain your case."

"I'll be fine. I have faith in you. You'll come back before my number's called." And with that, Jamie pulls me into a fierce hug.

I choke back my tears and hug him back, hard. "I'll come back soon," I promise. Then I break away and run off before I can change my mind.

"Let's go!" Namita calls out, already a few steps ahead of us.

I run toward her and to my surprise, I overtake her immediately. But there's no time for me to pause and wonder about that, because something shouts, "Brother, didn't the fox demon come here with human children?"

The back of my neck prickles.

"Yes, why?"

"The humans are trying to escape!" Horse Face says.

I grab Namita's arm and run even faster, and before I finish taking a single breath, we're right in front of another door. I shove it open, yank Namita through, and slam it shut. Namita and I both lean against the door with all our weight, even though we would never be able to hold off Ox Head. The door shuts, and a heavy lock automatically falls into place. Sure enough, though we wait for a few moments behind the door, there are no sounds from the other side, not even faint noises or knocks or anything. It's as though we've entered into a whole other world.

I breathe a sigh of relief and close my eyes, feeling like I might just curl up and bawl. How in the world did things go so wrong? We were so close to getting Jamie back, and then that Eye . . .

"You okay?" Namita says, placing her hand on my shoulder.

I open my eyes and try to muster up a smile, but it feels like a wince instead. "I could be better. You?"

"A little bit shaken, but that is to be expected from a journey through hell, I think." Namita gives me a brave smile, and in that moment, I'm so grateful that she and I became friends. I don't know what I would've done if I'd been here alone. Well, I would've been captured, for one.

"How're you doing, Xiaohua?" Namita says.

I look down at my right shoulder, where Xiaohua's head is resting. Her eyes are still closed, but she cracks one open and rumbles, "I have seen better days. I will heal, but it will take some time. What's more important is to find Danny. Please, find my master—ensure his safety."

"Yeah, of course we will," I say hurriedly. The sight of Xiaohua looking so weak and helpless is so wrong. I know Kai dislikes Xiaohua's self-importance and grandness and power, but I would give up a lot to see Xiaohua recovered, back to her usual confident self.

"And try not to get in more trouble," she mutters.

"Oof, tough one. We are in hell, you know," Namita says, patting Xiaohua gently. I can tell Namita's trying to be brave for our sake, and I reach out and squeeze her hand. She smiles at me, some of the tension leaving her shoulders. "We'll be okay."

I nod, even though it feels like we're about as far from "okay" as anyone can physically be.

"Hey, how did you run so fast back there?"

"Huh?"

"Back at King Qinguang's court, when all hell—ha-ha, all hell—back when all hell broke loose, you ran so fast. I swear you were, like, faster than an Olympic sprinter."

"Oh yeah. That was weird, wasn't it?"

Xiaohua lifts her head a little from my shoulder. "That would be the effects of my blood. Haven't you heard all those stories about humans seeking the blood or tears or sweat of dragons?"

I scour my memories for childhood stories I've heard, and I nod. "Yeah, for eternal life?"

The corners of Xiaohua's mouth lift into a wry smile. "Only the first-generation water dragons can grant eternal life." The smile dims. "Which is why they have been hunted to near extinction. My kind cannot give such things, but our blood does enhance your physical abilities. Namita, you may take some."

With wide eyes, Namita gingerly pats Xiaohua, getting some of the spilled golden blood all over her hands. "Thanks, Xiaohua." She holds up her hands, staring at them. "Whoa. That was like a really intense shot of caffeine. I feel so energized. This is amazing, Xiaohua!"

"Use it wisely, for I am unable to grow back to my true size and fly you out of here while I am injured," Xiaohua says gravely.

I gnaw on my lower lip, anxiety clawing at my chest. Instead of answering, I turn around and study our surroundings. We're inside a dark cave, but there's plenty of light coming from the other end. "Let's go." Namita and I start walking toward the light. "I'm sure we'll be fine. We just need to—"

Oh. No.

The rest of the sentence dies in my throat as we reach the

mouth of the cave and stop short. Namita's breath comes out in a low whistle. "How in the Ten Courts of Hell are we going to get out of here?" she whispers.

I can't bring myself to say anything.

Because we are right at the very top of a mountain. Light glints off the surface in a thousand different angles. Because the mountain is not made of soil. It's made of hundreds and thousands and maybe even millions of knives, all sorts of knives—daggers, cleavers, katanas, all of them shining evilly, their edges sharpened to unforgiving thinness.

"We're at the top of Dao Shan," Namita mutters.

"Dao Shan?" I translate this quickly in my head. "Does it mean 'Mountain of Knives'?"

"Yes, actually. It means exactly that."

"Doesn't leave much room for misinterpretation."

Namita nods weakly. "I've read so many books about the Ten Courts of Hell in preparation for our journey. I knew about Dao Shan, but seeing it in person is—uh—something else."

All I can say is "Yeah." Because it's true. I'm staring down the peak of an actual mountain and seeing its magnitude and the way the light from the braziers around us catch on the multitude of blades, and there is no way that any book could have shown the overwhelming horror of it. The sight turns my stomach. Just as I'm standing there, frozen to the spot, a voice booms from somewhere above us.

"Yanshi, for being a ruthless, greedy loan shark, you are sentenced to fall down Dao Shan!" it announces.

One second later, there is a terrified shriek, and a gleaming blue figure is dropped from the black sky. Namita and I gasp as the figure plummets straight onto the summit of Dao Shan. My mind recoils from the sight. Yanshi's soul is see-through, so surely these knives wouldn't hurt him? Right? RIGHT?

But Yanshi roars with pain as he lands on the blades, and he continues screaming as he rolls down the mountain, though there is no blood, no wound, that we can see.

"I feel sick," I moan.

Namita, always faster on the uptake than I am, has wisely closed her eyes and covered her ears. "Is it over yet?"

I peer down. He's about halfway down, still shrieking as he rolls. I quickly lean back. "Um, it's almost over."

Namita gingerly removes her fingers from her ears. "Whose court is this?"

Between the shouting and the gruesome mountain, it takes a moment for my rattled mind to focus on the question. "I think it's King Yanluo's Court."

Namita frowns. "Isn't he supposed to be the merciful one? The one who got demoted because he was so nice to humans?"

Oh gods. She's right. That was what King Qinguang had said. We both stare down the mountain once more. To my horror, there are little bits and pieces of gleaming blue blobs stuck on the knife blades. Pieces of Yanshi's soul, I realize with a shudder.

"Looks like he no longer has that problem," I say.

"Or he's over-corrected and now he's super unmerciful to prove that he should be promoted back to Court One?"

I shrug helplessly. Either way, King Yanluo doesn't strike me as the kind of king who would take kindly to two kids and a dragon stealing into his court. "We should get out of here."

"Yeah, obviously, Sherlock. But how?"

For the next few minutes, Namita and I are both quiet as we think of spells that might help us down the mountain. I keep glancing over at Xiaohua, concern gnawing at me. She's dozed off now, probably exhausted and hurting from her wounds. The sight of Xiaohua—who's normally so powerful—reduced to this helpless state is horrible. Doom sits on my chest, squeezing the air from it.

I sort through the list of spells I've learned and decide on the most appropriate one. Before casting it, I take a few deep breaths, forcing myself to calm down. I've been working hard on correcting my Chinese pronunciation, but when I get anxious, all my newly learned lessons fly out the window and I revert back to my wonky pronunciations. The last thing I want to do here is cast the wrong spell.

Holding out my palms, I swish my right hand in a figure eight and cast a spell called It's Not Asked Often, Please for Once Soften. The spell darts out of my right palm in a perfect, confident line. I've pronounced the words flawlessly, thanks to weeks of practice. But as soon as it hits Dao Shan, it dissolves into the murky air with a sad fizzle.

"Let me try," Namita says. She touches the tips of her middle fingers to her thumbs, then her index fingers, and does a complicated motion before casting a spell in Hindi. A bolt of bright green light shoots from her fingertips. But like mine, the spell dies as soon as it hits the first knife. Namita's shoulders droop. "That wasn't supposed to happen."

"What was the spell for?"

Namita frowns. "Turning metal to water."

"That would've been useful."

"Yeah."

I straighten up and take a deep breath. Maybe it just wasn't the right spell. I sift through the list of spells again and decide on another: Sure as the Hammer's Pat, You Shall Become Flat. I focus so hard on getting the spell right—the pronunciation, the will behind it, the focusing of my qì—that when it does leave my hands, I have no doubt that it'll work. The spell is beautiful, a bright blue-tinged ball that flies in a confident arc . . . only to melt into nothing when it hits the mountain. I groan.

Namita raises her hands again, a focused frown on her face, but before she can cast another spell, a small voice squeaks, "My goodness me, you lot are slow learners, ain't you?"

We look around us, gaping. Even Xiaohua has opened her eyes a little to look for the source of the voice.

"Who's there?" I call out. My voice comes out wobbly with fear. What if it's one of King Yanluo's guards? Or maybe one of the falling human souls doomed to be punished here? Or . . . I don't know, there are too many possibilities, and none of them is a good one.

"Down here, woodhead!" the high-pitched voice squeals.

"Woodhead?" Namita raises one brow.

"It's the Chinese version of 'bonehead.'"

Carefully, Namita and I peer over the edge of the cave mouth. I don't see anything beyond the awful mountain at first.

"Heeere!"

Then I spot it: a tiny blue blob waving at us from the foot of the mountain. We're too far away to see the soul and gauge whether it's a child or an old person. Hesitantly, we wave back at it.

"How did you see us from all the way down there?" Namita shouts down.

"When you die, your senses are no longer impeded by the limitations of your fleshly body, that's how. Now stop trying to cast spells on the mountain itself, numpties," it calls out. "It's spell-proof."

"Oh." My shoulders sag. It feels like all the energy has suddenly left my body. Dejected, I slump down onto the floor of the cavern, and Namita sits down next to me with a sigh. "I guess we're stuck here. For all eternity."

"Or until the door we came through unlocks again and we get arrested by King Qinguang." Namita gives me a terrified grin.

"Or that."

"Hellooo? You still there?" the blob shouts up.

"Yeah, we're still here." Namita pops her head out and waves at it again.

"Do the spells on yourself!"

"Oh. OH!" Namita cries. "Oh my gods, how did we not think of that?"

We scramble back to our feet, looking at each other with a spark of hope. "Okay, we need to work together. Let's not waste any more energy. Can you . . ." I pause, trying to come up with the best combination of spells that would get us down the mountain safely. After a moment, I snap my fingers. "Got it! How big can you make your feet?"

Namita grins with obvious pride. "I've been practicing, and I can get them to the size of a surfboard now."

"Awesome!"

"But Theo, I don't really want us to surf down the mountain on my feet. They'll be torn to ribbons."

Now it's my turn to smile. "You're not the only one who's been practicing." Focusing hard, I wave my hands at Namita's feet and cast a spell called Strengthen the Skin, Even Harder than Tin. The spell, a soft green ball, lobs itself from my palms and lands on Namita's feet, where it melts into her skin, leaving it with a green tinge. "How does it feel?"

Namita raises her feet slowly. "Heavy." Before I can say anything, she conjures up a knife and stabs it into her foot.

The words *Oh my gods what are you doing* are on their way out of my mouth when the blade bounces off her foot with a loud ping.

I gape at Namita. "That's so dangerous! Why would you do that?"

She laughs. "Because I could feel that my feet have turned to metal, silly. See?" She raps on one foot with her knuckles, and it gives a dull metallic sound.

I take a few deep breaths, still shaken, as Namita casts the spell to enlarge her feet. True to her words, her feet soon swell up to the size of surfboards, which is a really weird sight to see. She lifts her left foot and wiggles it. The movement makes her upper body sway. "Whoa, it's so heavy," she says, laughing, pinwheeling her arms to regain her balance.

"Are you sure you're going to be okay riding down the mountain?" What I really want to say is *Are you sure you're not going to tip over while going down the mountain, because falling means we'll both be DEAD.*

"Pfft, no biggie. Look, I'm used to them already!" She does a little hop, and when her giant feet land, it makes the entire cave shake. "I'm an amazing skier, Theo. I eat black-diamond slopes for breakfast. This is just like skiing."

"Okay . . ." I'm still not convinced, but what choice do I have? I look down at Xiaohua with concern. She's asleep, her body rising and falling gently with each warm breath. If only I could be unconscious, too, so I wouldn't have to actually experience the horrors of what's about to happen.

"Hop on!" Namita says merrily.

With no other choice, I step onto Namita's feet. I grit my teeth, expecting the squish of skin and flesh, but my spell has worked well, and it feels like stepping on solid rock. I stand in front of Namita, and she wraps her arms around my waist, which makes me nervous in an entirely different way. I clear my throat and adjust Xiaohua round my neck, making sure she's secure.

"Ready?" Namita says.

"Uh, considering we're about to surf down a mountain of knives on your bare feet—no?"

"Great!" With that, Namita lunges out of the cave and together, we soar through the sky before landing onto a thousand hungry blades.

KAI
12

I'd forgotten how heavy human children can be, and as I grab hold of Danny's arms in my clawed feet, his solid weight almost prevents me from soaring to the sky. Almost. I furiously beat my newly grown wings, and we fly through the side door just in time to avoid Ox Head and Horse Face catching us. The door slams shut with a thunderous final click, cutting off all the noise and confusion behind it.

"Let me go!" Danny bellows, thrashing wildly. One of his fists catches me in the stomach.

"Oof!" I squawk, my breath knocked out of me, my balance lost. I flap my wings, but my flight arc's broken and I can't stop us from crashing unceremoniously to the ground. We roll over and under and over again, limbs flying wildly. I got a shoe in my beak, and I'm pretty sure my head was knocked into Danny's bum at some point, which is something I am not in any rush to repeat, let me tell you. Finally, we roll to a stop and we both lie there, gasping for breath, trying to stop the world from spinning. When I can finally draw in a full breath, I sit up and glare at Danny. "What in the world are you playing at, hitting me while I'm flying? We could've been killed!"

Danny drags an arm across his brow, his chest still heaving

as he sits up. When he finally meets my eye, I take a step back because there isn't just rage written all over his face; there's also an animalistic fear that's nearly tipping over into hysteria. "What am I playing at?" Danny says shrilly. "What are you playing at, catching me in your claws like that? Did you turn demonic again? Do you know what it feels like to be snatched up into the air by a giant demon bird?" His voice breaks, and still he carries on talking, his eyes bright with tears. "Do you know how many nightmares I've had about that night? About being flung up into the air by you? And you were laughing the whole time, just throwing me about like a ball. At any moment, you could've just decided to drop me and let me fall to my death, and there was no one to save me, because you made me dismiss my companion!" He shouts the last word in a voice raw with emotion, and with that, Danny crumples over and covers his face.

Guilt floods my chest, and instead of the indignant tirade I was prepared to unleash on him, all that comes out is a small guilt-ridden "I see." After a while, I push myself to say, "Um, that's understandable. You're still working through your trauma. Which I caused. Yes, um. So. Well. I apologize." And I do. I really, really do, even though it's completely against my nature to admit any wrongdoing. But the sight of Danny's anguish, no longer covered by fear or politeness or whatever it is that's been hiding it all this time, is painful to see. "I'm sorry, Danny. There is no excuse for what I did to you. Is there any way that I can make up for it?"

It takes a while for Danny to reply. He stares at me with distrust. "Well, you did just separate me again from my companion."

The mention of Xiaohua causes pain to flash across his face. "She was injured. I felt that trident stabbing into her."

I wince. I'd seen it, too, and the sight of those spikes shattering Xiaohua's scales and stabbing into her flesh was sickening, almost unbearable. "Is she—can you sense her?"

Danny sighs. "Yeah. She's still alive. In pain, but alive. And . . . I don't think she's in the First Court anymore. I need to get to her."

"I know. I can sense that Theo isn't in King Qinguang's court anymore. They've escaped . . . somewhere." I close my eyes and try to find the thread linking me and Theo to each other, but it seems that down in Diyu, there is a lot of interference, because I can only sense enough to know that Theo is still alive, but nothing more concrete than that. Danny's right: We do need to get to them somehow. "They're probably in one of the other courts. All the courts are linked to one another. We just have to find out which court they're in and locate the right door."

For a second, Danny stares at me in that disconcerting way again. Then he narrows his eyes and says, "Fine. Sounds good. But could you please change out of bird form? It's—I hate seeing you as a bird."

My instinctive reaction is to tell him to stop looking at me, but I realize that he does have a point. With a nod, I change back to my fox form.

"Thanks." Then Danny glances over my shoulder and gasps. "Wow. This is . . . not what I was expecting to find in hell." Danny is right—this court is actually very pleasant for a court of hell. We've walked into a beautiful garden in front of a majestic palace. The palace itself looks like it's carved from pure jade, its walls glittering a deep, rich green with veins of gold. The garden is filled with trees of various shades of red and has a river snaking through it, and the river isn't even blood or anything. It's plain water, and below the surface I spot colorful koi glittering like jewels as they swim happily.

We walk slowly across the garden, marveling at the abundant fat fruits hanging heavily from the trees. All the trees and plants have been arranged in harmony, all of them trimmed into very neat, deliberate shapes. "I hope I don't have to tell you not to eat anything here," I whisper, though admittedly, my own mouth is watering at the sight of all this food. When was the last time I ate?

"Tch, of course I wouldn't," Danny snaps, just as his stomach grumbles. His face reddens to match the leaves around us. "I've read enough folktales and mythology to know not to eat anything in hell."

"And if you did eat something, it better be something good, not just fruit. Can you believe Persephone gave up all that to eat six pomegranate seeds? I mean, really now. She could've had a beautiful wagyu steak, but nooo."

Danny cracks a smile. "Yeah, I've always thought that was a bad trade."

We round a corner and find ourselves at the front of the palace. In the middle of the massive stone steps leading into the palace is a giant millstone the size of a studio apartment in Manhattan.[21] We stop short and stare at the contraption. It's a typical ancient rotary stone mill, complete with a crank and connecting rod,

---

21 That is to say, inhumanly small for a living space, but very large for a millstone.

except of course in this case, the rod is way too large to be meant for human hands.

"That's a large mill."

I nod. "Indeed."

"That's, um, it seems over-the-top for something that's used to grind wheat." Danny looks down at me with a smile that looks more like a grimace. "Right?"

"Yes, I would agree with that. It does seem rather excessive for wheat. So perhaps it's not meant for grinding wheat, but for grinding something much larger." I really hope this boy isn't going to make me say it.

"Like what?"

I sigh. He is going to make me say it. I open my mouth, wondering how best to break the news, but just then a loud voice booms from the sky.

"Jiasheng, for being a murderer, you are sentenced to be ground to a paste."

This is followed by a shriek as a bright blue human soul is dropped through the sky and straight onto the grindstone. A giant spectral ox appears, a yoke connecting it to the millstone's rod, and as the soul struggles to escape, the ox begins to walk. The ox's hefty muscles ripple and bunch as it strains against the yoke, and the massive stone begins to rotate.

I jump up onto Danny's shoulders and put my paws over his ears and my tails over his eyes. The poor kid isn't going to recover if he witnesses what's about to happen. I stay in that position as the soul screams, and luckily Danny must have realized I'm protecting him from a lifetime of therapy because he doesn't resist.

A few excruciating minutes later, there is silence, deafening after all the screaming. I gingerly lift my tails and my paws, and Danny blinks.

He looks around, wide-eyed. "Where's the soul?"

I grimace and point to one side of the millstone, where a wooden pail sits, collecting what the stone has ground. Danny steps carefully toward the pail.[22]

"What are you doing? Don't look. It's not the kind of pot that you find at a rainbow's end. Nothing good can come of this," I hiss.

But he doesn't listen, so with a reluctant huff, I follow. We look down at the pail and, ugh, I feel sick. It's filled with a glowing blue goop. I clear my throat. "Well. That's that, then. Come, let's skedaddle out of here, shall we?" I put my front paws up against his back and push.

"You don't have to tell me twice." He starts walking briskly, and I fall into step beside him. "I didn't think I would ever say this, but I—"

I follow Danny's gaze to see why he's stopped talking. Uh-oh. Towering right in front of us is the giant ox that had been yoked to the millstone, and its gaze is far too intelligent for my liking. Drat! Why had I assumed that the ox was a mere dumb, harmless beast? Ox Head should have been a clue or a warning that oxen down here are not to be trusted! But this one's walking on all four legs, unlike Ox Head, and she's not carrying any weapons or wearing any armor, and she let herself be tied to

_____

22 What is it with you humans and your morbid curiosity? Clearly there's nothing good to be found in the pail, but for some unknown reason, your kind always feels compelled to look.

the millstone! I don't see Ox Head letting himself be strapped to a millstone any time soon. So maybe this particular ox is harmless.

"Oh, hello, all right then? Looking well. Nice, glossy hide and I see you keep your horns well oiled. Very good, yes. Right, we won't take up too much of your time—we're just going to step around you and . . ." I forget what I was about to say when the ox turns into a beautiful maiden wearing an emerald-green silk hanfu with gold ribbons. Her face is a perfect heart shape, with smooth porcelain skin and pursed cherry lips, and her hair is done up in the most intricate braids and stabbed through with elaborate flower ornaments. She gives me the kind of smile that would stop most people dead in their tracks.

"Hello, little fox, little man." Her voice is like poetry, soft and melodic.

A glance at Danny tells me he's fallen for her spell. His eyes are all glazed over, his mouth parted into a half-gaping smile. He looks as though if she were to tell him to climb into the grindstone, he would do so quite happily. I roll my eyes. Really, now. Why must you humans make it so easy to dupe you? But it's not a problem; I'm a fox spirit. We basically came up with the whole shape-shifting-into-a-beautiful-maiden trick. And this upstart of a cow thinks she can fool me with this old trick?

"Lady, we just saw you as a cow, so don't even try that whole 'Oh, I am but a helpless maiden' act with me, okay?" I snap, while at the same time poking Danny vigorously in the leg.

Danny starts and blinks down at me before frowning at the maiden. "She's the ox?"

"The one who just used the millstone to grind a soul into liquid? Yep, that's her."

Danny pales. Poor kid. But at least he's no longer buying into the ox maiden's little act.

The ox maiden smirks. "Unlike your evil Illusions, fox, this is my true form."

"Oh, right, I toootally believe you."

She laughs. "Well, no matter if you do. You are both coming with me."

"Yes, see, we're actually not. We've got a very important meeting with the CEO of hell. Very much above your pay grade, so we'll just be off now." I stand on my hind legs and push Danny along again. He's still staring openmouthed at the lady. I'm sure she's cast some sort of spell to bewitch human men. So predictable.

The woman sighs. "I had hoped you would come peacefully. We don't have any time to waste." With a snap of her fingers, the gold ribbon that was tied around her slim waist uncurls like a snake and whips toward us with shocking speed. I don't even have a chance to take a single step before it's around our necks.

"Whoa!" Danny cries, stumbling back. The ribbon wraps around our necks several times, not tight enough to choke us, but tight enough to focus all our senses on it. He reaches up for his silly bow and arrows.

"Uh-uh, none of that barbaric human weaponry," the maiden says, plucking the bow and arrows from Danny's hands. She gives an effortless squeeze of her hand, and the weapons disintegrate into dust. Danny's mouth falls open in silent distress. "If you continue struggling, I will snap your necks," she says, as pleasantly as though she's asking what kind of tea we would like. "Come, come." She turns toward the palace, and the ribbon tugs us forward like a leash.

"So much for your bow and arrows," I mutter. Of course, I am too smart not to be formulating an escape plan as I walk. I would change into a big bird again, slice up this cursed ribbon with my sharp beak, and then grab Danny and fly away. But then I remember Danny's fear of me in bird form. I'd just promised that I wouldn't change back into bird form. Gah! Well, never mind, I'm sure I'll think of something equally brilliant soon enough.

Danny and I stagger along. He keeps throwing me panicked looks, and I try my best to return a calming look, but it's rather a challenge with a ribbon half choking me. My tongue flops out quite unattractively, and I am soon out of breath as we climb the stone steps.

The lady throws open the massive doors to the palace, and Danny and I stop and stare. The place is indescribably grand, all its walls adorned with intricate paintings or statues, its huge pillars dripping with gold. Courtiers mill about, whispering to one another, though these courtiers are unlike anyone in the human world. Like human courtiers, they're dressed in elaborate court outfits—lots of smooth silk and heavy brocade and gold thread. But that's where the similarities end, for these courtiers are all demons. There are two-headed demons—one head arguing with the other—and one with a pig's head atop a human's body and another with a face on its belly. They're all whispering in low voices, their monstrous features contorted into frowns. Something's off in this court.

"Come," the lady snaps. The ribbon yanks us forward, straight into the throng of demons.

One by one, as they notice our entrance, the demons fall silent, their stares a heavy, terrifying weight.[23] Danny's breath is coming in and out in rapid, wheezing gasps. He looks like he's about ready to faint dead away. Poor kid.

"Don't worry," I whisper to him. "Just look down at the floor—don't look at them. Focus on my voice. We're going to be okay."

He does as I say, dropping his gaze to the lacquered floor. I continue whispering encouragements to him as we walk through the sea of bloodthirsty demons. Each one looks like it could eat Danny up in one gulp. As I comfort Danny, I look about the room, noting the numerous exits available to us, and I try to formulate an escape plan. Oh, if only I could change into a bird! But even as I think this, I notice that quite a few of the demons we pass by have wings—bat wings, swan wings, leathery wings I don't recognize. Even if Danny didn't have a bird phobia, flying out of here is not going to be as easy as I'd hoped.

The lady leads us all the way to the center of the room, in front of an enormous golden throne. On the throne sits the king, his chin resting on one hand, his expression thunderous. Beside him is a slightly smaller throne on which a woman, who is presumably the queen, sits. The ox lady kneels down and bows her head.

"Venerable King Wuguan, núcái has brought Your Majesty a gift."

I roll my eyes. "Núcái" means lackey, a term that ancient

---

23 Not that I'm scared, of course. Hm? I look terrified, you say? That's all just an act, Bertha, gosh. Everything I do is just an act. For example, I act like I like you, but do I really?

courtiers used to refer to themselves when addressing the royal family. It's so outdated. That tells me we're dealing with an old-fashioned king.

"I tire of gifts," the king grumbles.

The ox lady bows her head even lower. "Núcái apologizes, but these are special gifts. One is a living human boy, and the other a living fox spirit."

There is a pause. I glance at Danny, who's gone even paler than before. "Kid, look at me. Don't worry—we'll get out of this."

King Wuguan lifts his head and stares at us with red-rimmed eyes. He takes a deep breath. "A living human. I haven't come across one in a long time."

"Perhaps we could grind him up so you might drink him, Husband?" the queen says. There's a brittle quality to her voice that speaks of desperation. "Maybe that might help."

Danny trembles visibly. The king grunts. "Perhaps. Let it be done."

"No!" I shout.

All their gazes snap at once to me.

"How dare you, unworthy fox?" the queen hisses. "You dare defy the king?"

"The millstone works on fox spirits, too," the ox lady says.

"Uh . . ." Think, Kai! Think fast! I glance from the pallid, lined face of the king to the tight, worried face of the queen, to the ox lady and the rest of the courtiers, who are all looking stressed out, and finally, again to King Wuguan. He seems . . . unhealthy. Pale and frowny, with a slightly clammy look about him. I struggle to recall what I know about the kings of Diyu. Part of my preparation for our journey had been to listen to every piece of gossip I could pick out about the kings of Diyu. Now I recall a conversation I had eavesdropped on between two companion spirits. Something about King Wuguan being in a foul mood and having even fouler breath. "If I may, Your Majesty, I sense a . . . something is off with your court, am I right?"

"Preposterous!" the queen cries. "King Wuguan's court is running as smoothly as ever. Our millstone is as clean and strong as the day it was carved. How dare you suggest anything otherwise? I should punish you myself for slander."

I bow my head, putting my front paws together in a gesture of apology. "I am so sorry to offend. Your stone mill is great and wonderful indeed. But if I may, I sense that perhaps King Wuguan is feeling under the weather?"

A sudden deathful hush tells me I've just put my paw on it. Well, no turning back now. My mind races ahead, putting two and two together. "If I had to venture a guess, would it be because he's been on a steady diet of ground-up human souls for the last, uh, ten thousand years?"

No one dares to speak. Everyone's eyes dart back and forth between me and King Wuguan. Finally, when the tension becomes unbearable, King Wuguan groans. "Oh, what's the use of hiding it? Yes, fox spirit, I am suffering from constipation. It has been a century since I was last able to go."

Danny's mouth drops open. He looks at me. *To go?* he mouths.

"He means to poop. He's been unable to poop for the last century."

"Oh!" Danny looks up at the king. "Your Majesty, I can help!

My parents are all about healthy bowel movements. I know exactly what you need."

The queen snorts. "You? A little human child? Husband, do not waste your time listening to these charlatans. I say we grind their bones up and cook up a nice meat stew for you, yes?"

"No, that's exactly what you don't want," Danny says. "Trust me, my grandmother is a nutritionist. She lives and breathes this stuff."

"We have tried a lot of your remedies," King Wuguan grumbles to the queen. "None of them have worked." He pauses to consider us. "Fine, you have one hour to come up with a solution for me."

"That's great—thank you so much, Your Majesty." Danny grins at me with hope.

"If it doesn't work, then I shall grind you into a paste myself," King Wuguan continues.

I side-eye Danny. His grin has shifted into a terrified grimace. Great. What could possibly go wrong?

THEO
13

Namita's giant steel feet land on the mountain with a horrible, teeth-grinding crunch of metal on metal. "Wahoo!" she shouts as we start sliding down, slowly at first, but quickly gaining more speed.

I don't know how she can be so happy when we're honest to gods sliding down a mountain of knives on her naked feet. We're close enough that I can see each blade clearly before it zips past, and they're all cruelly sharp. The awful crunching metal sound follows us as hundreds of knives bend and break under Namita's feet, and wind whips into my face, making my eyes water. I try not to look at the many blue forms we're passing by, slumped lifelessly on the mountain.

A spear sticks out above the rest ahead of us, and before I can second-guess myself, my hand shoots up and a flash of magic leaps from it, morphing into a small but heavy shield. I hold it at an angle and the spear glances off it, making us swerve left. A blue soul lies straight ahead. I raise my hands and scream out another spell, but it comes out garbled, my pronunciation thrown off, and instead of helping us swerve (zhuǎn), a dollar bill suddenly appears (zhuàn) before flying away in the wind. Screaming, we slice right through the blue blob and it's like being swallowed by a freezing, talking cloud. I catch snippets of the soul's voice. It sounds angry, vengeful.

"Sorry!" I manage as we pass through. Thank gods Xiaohua is still unconscious. Somehow, I doubt she'd be impressed with us skiing through a human soul.

"That was hideous. Ugh, I feel sick. I think I got some soul in my mouth." Namita retches behind me and wobbles.

"Whoa! Focus on your balance!" A terrifying image of Namita losing control and all of us falling sideways onto the waiting knives flashes through my mind.

But the soul's thrown her off, and I can feel her giant feet tilting. My stomach turns along with us, a sickening feeling of vertigo followed by a surge of dread. My backpack swings hard, and I hear Niu Mo Wang's muffled voice saying, "What's going on?"

We're going to fall. We're going to tip right over onto the knives, and at the speed we're going, the blades will shred us into ribbons. No! I can't let that happen. With a cry, I swing my arms and aim my palms down. I shout out the same spell I'd cast on Namita just minutes ago, turning my hands into steel. Somehow, against all odds, I manage to get the spell out just right. And as we fall, I push down with my hands. My palms hit the sharp blades with a teeth-gritting crunch. The knives crumple like paper. My spell worked! I keep pushing until Namita regains her balance once more, and it's only then that we both release our breath.

"Thanks, Theo." Namita's voice is shaken.

I manage to croak out, "No worries." That had been way too close for comfort.

After what seems like an eternity, we finally hit the bottom. With a whoop, Namita leans her weight to one side and slides to a stop. We tumble in a mess of limbs, half giggling, half in tears, both of us babbling excitedly.

"I can't believe you did it!" I shout.

"That was AWESOME! Better than a roller coaster!" Namita lets out another whoop before focusing on her feet and casting a spell to shrink them back down to normal size.

"That's a shame—I was getting used to you having giant feet."

She groans. "That's such a Kai thing to say, Theo. You two share, like, a mind or something."

The mention of Kai takes away a bit of the effervescent joy I'm feeling, replacing it with worry.

Namita must have seen the concern on my face, because she pats me on the shoulder. "Don't worry. Kai will be okay. She's got more tricks up her sleeve than all of us combined."

"Yeah." I pull open my backpack to check on Niu Mo Wang. He blinks up at me when I pull off the hoodie covering his cage, and his lips curl back, revealing his teeth.

"Where are we? This place smells familiar," he snarls.

I gulp and hurriedly put the hoodie back. I zip up the bag and nod at Namita. "He seems to be okay."

"Good." She steps closer to me and peers somewhere below my face, her expression turning somber. "Hey, Xiaohua, how're you doing, girl?"

I look down, and Xiaohua blinks, yawning, and raises her head slowly.

"I must say, I was not expecting you kids to make it down that mountain in one piece," she murmurs.

"Geez, have more faith in us, lady." Namita frowns playfully, but her eyes remain concerned as she inspects Xiaohua. "How are you holding up? That ride wasn't the smoothest one. It can't have been good for your wounds."

A huff of hot dragonbreath blankets my arm as Xiaohua exhales. "Dragons heal faster than humans do. I should be almost healed by now."

The frown on Namita's face deepens as she peers closer. I try to see what she's looking at, but with Xiaohua around my neck, it's kind of a challenge to find the wound marks. "Um, I hate to break it to you, but I don't think that wound is almost healed. It looks the same as before."

"Who did that to the poor dragon?" someone says.

"Ox Head," I sigh.

"Ooh, that's a mighty brute, that is. I wouldn't want to be on the business end of that trident. I've seen him skewer three souls at the same time. He likes to show off, you know."

"Yeah." From the number of rants that Kai has gone on about Ox Head, that sounds about right. Then I startle and turn around to find the source of the voice.

"Down here."

Namita, Xiaohua, and I look down, and there, glowing an unearthly blue and slightly see-through, standing all of twelve inches tall, is a small, rotund pig.

"Aww, hi cutie!" Namita crouches down and beams at it.

The pig snorts. "Please, don't patronize me, child. I may be small and undoubtedly adorable, but I'm also two hundred years old. Respect your elders."

"Oh, I'm sorry." Namita nods. "You're right—that was really patronizing of me." She holds out a hand. "I'm Namita, and that's Theo, and the dragon round his neck is Xiaohua."

The pig holds up a see-through trotter and places it in Namita's outstretched hand. To Namita's credit, she doesn't flinch, even though the touch can't be at all pleasant. "Greetings. I am Fragrant Sausage."

Namita and I exchange a look, and it's a struggle to keep from laughing. I fight to keep my face and my voice solemn as I say, "Fragrant Sausage?"

Fragrant Sausage narrows her eyes. "Yes, do you have a problem with my name?"

"No, no, of course not! It's just . . . somewhat unusual."

"My name in life was Number Four. It was stamped on my back. See?" She turns and gives us a view of her butt, on which indeed the number four is stamped in bright-red paint. "Fragrant Sausage was the fate that befell me. I keep the name as a reminder of what you evil humans did to me back in life."

"Oh, er." Wow, this turned dark very quickly. "I—I'm sorry." My insides twist with guilt as I recall the number of times that Mama cooked up some delicious, aromatic Chinese sausages for dinner.

Fragrant Sausage grunts. "Yes, you should be. Pigs are very intelligent creatures. You shouldn't be eating us. But never mind that, I've spent a lovely two hundred years in here, watching you humans get thrown down this majestic mountain or flung into the lava pits—have you seen the lava pits, by the way? Do you like the redesign? I came up with the idea, you know."

Namita and I stare blankly at Fragrant Sausage. After a while, Namita shakes her head and manages to say, "Um, no, we haven't."

"Oh? Well, that's okay—I can take you there. I know this place like the back of my trotter. I'm very special, in case you haven't figured that out. Most animals, when they die, just go to the First Court and get reincarnated. But not I! When King Qinguang was about to get me reincarnated, I said, 'NO! I'm not ready to be reborn yet.' I wanted to remain down here and enjoy my time, watch the various tortures in effect. King Qinguang was so impressed by my intelligence that he said I could roam Diyu for as long as I liked. SO. Shall we go to see the lava pits? There's a very cunning ledge I'm especially proud of, and—"

"Actually, we were hoping to get back to the First Court," I say quickly.

Fragrant Sausage's eyes narrow again until they're practically closed. I have no idea how she can see through them, but then again, I'm not one to argue about the semantics of a ghost pig. "Why do you want to go back to the First Court so badly? Most people I meet want to—well, usually most people I meet are too busy screaming about the spikes going through their heads or the lava melting their—"

"Okay, yes, we get it. Most souls you come across are too busy being tortured." I hesitate before continuing. What have we got to lose? "But we're not actually dead. We traveled here to save my brother's soul, which was stolen by a demon back in the human world."

"Oh?" Fragrant Sausage's eyes open wide. "Wait, you're not . . . dead?" She steps closer to us and sniffs. "Oh my, you're right. Mmm, the smell of life. I'd forgotten what that smells like. Mmm, human blood, warmth, sunshine . . ." She takes a deep inhale, her eyes fluttering closed.

"Er, so as Theo was saying, we need to get back to the First Court?" Namita says loudly.

Fragrant Sausage snaps back to attention.

"Can you help us, Fragrant Sausage? Please?" I say.

Fragrant Sausage purses her lips, which is a strange expression to see on a pig. "I don't know—it's not really in my nature to help humans. I did tell you what your kind did to me, yes?"

I nod. "And I'm so sorry about that. Really."

"Harrumph." She side-eyes Xiaohua. "Hey, dragonface, what do you say? Should I help these miserable souls?"

Xiaohua lifts her head weakly. "Please do, little pig. I do not have much love for humans in general, but these children are purehearted and courageous. They deserve your help."

Fragrant Sausage groans out loud, and when a pig groans, she does so with her full body, from the tip of her curly tail up to her snout. It's a very rattly, very deep groan. "Oh, fine," she says. "You know what? Your scent has reminded me of earthly pleasures: wallowing in mud, stuffing myself silly with freshly picked apples . . . all right. I have made a decision. I would like to go back to the human world. But I don't want to be reincarnated. I'd lose all my memories; I'd be in a different body—ew, I might even be reborn as one of you, gods forbid. No, I'll have to follow you kids out of here. Right." She stands to attention. "Follow me. And try not to attract any attention—there are lots of creatures here that love nothing more than human flesh. Fresh human tenderloin is such a rarity down here, you know . . ." Fragrant Sausage trails off meaningfully.

As we walk around the Mountain of Knives, Fragrant Sausage keeps up a steady chatter about all the things she's missed in the human world. The adrenaline rush from sliding down the mountain leaves my body, and I feel spent but also really grateful. I glance at Namita and seeing her warms me, like a cozy blanket being wrapped around my shoulders. I'm so thankful that she's here with me. Without her, I would still be stuck up there, despairing at the sight of a million knives at my feet. Heck, I wouldn't even have made it to Diyu in the first place.

As if she can feel my gaze on her, Namita turns to me and raises her eyebrows. "Stare much?" she says with a slight smile.

I'm about to turn away and say I was just looking at our surroundings, but then I stop myself. Why not be honest? "We wouldn't have made it down here without you. So, um, thanks."

Namita's mouth spreads into a bashful smile. "Aw, Theo. To be fair, without YOU, we would've tipped over and been shredded, so thank you." She hesitates, then says, "How're you doing?"

"What do you mean?"

"Well, it must be horrible to have come all the way to Diyu and been reunited with Jamie . . . and then have to be parted from him like that. You okay?"

That makes me pause. "You know what? I—I am, actually.

I mean, it's not great, but for months now, I've felt so helpless. I had no idea how to save Jamie, how to get down here, how to—anything, really. And now we're here, and it really sucks that nothing is straightforward, but I feel like we're at least doing something."

Namita nods. "Yeah, that makes sense. And we'll get to him in time."

We will. I have to believe that with everything I have—believe that everything will work out in the end, and we'll all make it out of here in one piece.

KAI

14

"Are you sure about this?" I mutter from the corner of my mouth as Danny stands atop a ladder to reach the top of the millstone.

"Trust."

"Yeah, you keep saying that, but it doesn't actually have the desired effect unless it's backed by logic and reason to support why this would work."

Danny ignores me and sits down on the edge of the millstone before asking one of the court's handmaids to pass him one of the baskets he's prepared. The basket is filled with bunches of kale and spinach. He stuffs the vegetables into the hole in the middle of the top stone and nods at the ox lady to start walking. The millstone is so big and the ox lady so strong that Danny sitting on top of it doesn't seem to affect anything. With a loud grinding noise, it starts to revolve, and the pile of kale and spinach is ground into a paste. Bright green juice flows down the spout into a glass. Danny adds more vegetables to the mix—broccoli, cabbage, and beetroot. When the huge glass at the bottom is nearly full, he tells the ox to stop and hops off the millstone.

"That looks ghastly," I say helpfully as Danny lifts the glass—in his hands, it's so big that it looks more like a pail than a drinking glass—and peers at the contents. The vegetable juice is the color of a dark bruise, thanks to the beetroot, and it's the pulpiest glass of juice I have ever had the misfortune of seeing.

"It's the best drink you could ask for." Danny smiles primly. "It's got all the perfect nutrients and vitamins your body needs—plus, we didn't throw out the pulp, so it's got plenty of fiber, which will help with digestion."

"I refuse to believe that a glass of juice is what it'll take to save our lives."

Danny gives me a look. "Do you have any better ideas?"

"Yes, we could fly out of here."

The ox lady cocks her head to one side and regards me with narrowed eyes. "Try it, little fox," she says. "Let's see which one of us is faster."

I narrow my eyes back at her but manage to keep myself from retorting. The ox shape-shifts into the beautiful court maiden and takes the glass from Danny. I expect her to give it to the king, but instead, she thrusts it in my direction.

"Drink," she commands.

"You have got to be kidding me. I am not drinking that foul concoction. No way, nuh-uh."

She stares at me. "You refuse the drink? Is that because it's poisonous? Are you two trying to kill the king? Because that will certainly land you in hot water. Literally."

"What? No!" I cry.

"Then drink it." Again, she thrusts the glass at me, and this time, I have no choice but to accept it.

I sniff at the vile contents delicately, and I swear my nose practically crawls all the way to the back of my head.

"Come on, Kai," Danny says. "It's just vegetable juice."

I shut my eyes and take a gulp before pushing the glass into Danny's hands and flinging myself to the ground. "Oh gods!" I cry.

"I knew it—it's poisoned, isn't it?" the ox lady says.

Danny looks like he's about to faint from fear. "No, please believe me; there's no poison in it."

"Argh, it tastes like a lawn!" I spit, trying to get rid of the grassy taste. It takes a few moments for me to realize something.

1. I'm not about to perish from revulsion.
2. I actually feel kind of . . . refreshed?

"Huh," I say, sitting up and scratching my ear sheepishly with my hind leg. "I'm okay. In fact, I feel better."

Danny is practically glowing. His smirk has taken up half his face. "See? It's all that kale and beetroot and spinach. So many vitamins and nutrients. It'll wake you up faster than coffee would—that's what my grandmother says!"

The ox lady narrows her eyes at me, inspecting me from multiple angles, before sniffing. She seems disappointed that I haven't just keeled over, dead from poison. She takes the glass from Danny and puts it on a golden tray before sashaying to King Wuguan, who's sitting a few paces away next to the queen under the shade of a silk umbrella. The ox maiden kneels down and presents the glass of juice to the king with head bowed.

"Your Majesty, if it pleases you, here is the concoction that the human boy has come up with."

"Husband, it looks like filth," the queen says. I don't blame her, honestly.

King Wuguan grunts. "Call forth the boy."

The ox maiden glances over her shoulder and raises her eyebrows at us. Danny and I come forward reluctantly.

"Boy, do you swear by this elixir?" King Wuguan says, stroking his beard.

"I—er, well, it's not an 'elixir.' It's just vegetable juice . . ."

The queen wrinkles her nose. "An eternity we have spent, feasting on juicy human bodies, and now you expect him to drink this?"

Danny must have caught the shadow of displeasure that crosses the king's face because he quickly adds, "I swear by it. It's the best thing you can take for your . . . ah, condition."

King Wuguan narrows his eyes at the drink. "Because of all the masticated vegetable flesh?"

"Er, I wouldn't call it—"

I cut in quickly. "Precisely because of all the vegetable flesh, and the vegetable blood is also particularly nourishing. This single glass contains the blood of no fewer than half a dozen different vegetables. It's a drink fit for the most fearsome tyrant."

"I suppose there's no harm in trying." With one last frown, King Wuguan lifts the massive glass to his lips and drinks the whole lot in five hefty gulps. When he's done, he wipes his beard with the back of an arm and belches loud enough to make my ears ring. "That wasn't half bad!" he roars with a smile.

We all watch him expectantly. The queen leans closer to him. "Husband, how do you feel?"

King Wuguan waves away a court maiden who's dabbing at his beard with a silk handkerchief. "Refreshed. That was an interesting taste. Clean. Not as much iron as human juice. It's—oh—"

We all hear it then. A wet rumble coming from deep in King Wuguan's belly.

"Husband, is that you?" the queen says, leaning away from him.

"I—er, well, that was embarrassing—" The king starts visibly as another growl comes from his gut, like the sound of a drain burping. Then he staggers to his feet, says, "Excuse me!" and waddles away quickly, both hands clapped on his buttocks. The queen hurries away with him.

We all stare at his retreating back.

"I . . . didn't think the juice would work so quickly," Danny stammers.

"Well, he's had nothing but human souls to drink for the past few thousand years, so who's to say how long it should take for vegetables to take effect on his system?" I scratch the back of my ear and swish my two tails. "Deities and gods, most of them are so unhealthy. Just because they're immortal, they think they don't need to watch their diets. I bet Niu Mo Wang's backed up, too—that's why he's always in such a foul mood." The thought of Niu Mo Wang reminds me of Theo, stuck in Diyu with Namita, an injured dragon, and an even-angrier-than-usual Niu Mo Wang. I wonder how they're doing. I hope they're managing without us.

Danny looks at me with a world of hope in his eyes. "But this is a good sign, right? I mean, this is exactly what he wanted, to be able to, like . . . go. So . . ."

Just as he says that, the queen reappears before us with a loud thunderclap. Danny yelps and falls onto his backside. The queen looks down her nose at us. Then, as suddenly as she entered, a small smile appears on her flawless face.

"Good work, human. It appears that your concoction has worked. My husband is very happy."

"Is he still, ah—occupied?" I venture.

The queen nods. "Better that we stay out here, I think."

We all smile tensely at one another for a moment, then I straighten up. "Well, I'm glad we were able to help. We'll just be off then, shall we? Toodles!"

The queen makes a small gesture with her hand, and the ox maiden, standing behind us, claps one hand around Danny's wrist and another around my paw.

"What the—" I don't have time to finish the sentence before manacles appear under the ox maiden's hands. With a small *snick*, the manacles snap shut. Chains tinkle into existence, one link appearing after another from our manacles, all the way to the millstone. I yank at my paw, but the chain holds fast. "Uh, Your Majesty, there seems to be a slight misunderstanding—"

The queen smiles, revealing all her pearly white teeth. "Oh, this isn't a misunderstanding, little fox."

"But you said my concoction worked!" Danny cries.

Still smiling, the queen reaches out and pats him lightly on the head. "Yes, it did. What a smart little human you are. We'd like you to extend your stay with us and share more of your cunning recipes with us. Put the millstone to good use, yes?"

"No, wait," Danny pleads, "you don't understand. We need to get back to the First Court."

The queen wrinkles her nose. "To that stuffy old court? Whyever for?" But before either of us can reply, she holds up her hand. "Don't answer—I don't care. You are now honored to be our esteemed guests."

"For how long?" Danny says.

"What a curious question." The queen cocks her head, as though in confusion. "For eternity, of course." And with that, she nods at the ox maiden and the two of them stroll away, leaving Danny and me chained up to the giant stone mill.

THEO
15

Namita, Xiaohua, Fragrant Sausage, and I dash through the door to the next court and manage to slam it closed before the hellhound chasing us can make it through. Looking around, we find ourselves in yet another dark cave. From behind the door come the growls and barks of the hellhound. The door rattles in its frame as the hound pounces on it over and over, and the sound of its razor-sharp nails scraping the wood makes my skin crawl. I hurry away from it as fast as I can, but before we can come out of the cave, Namita stops us. She crouches low, putting her face in front of Fragrant Sausage's snout.

"Okay, Fragrant Sausage, we're gonna have a heart-to-heart. A real girl talk."

Fragrant Sausage's face brightens up. "Ooh, that sounds fun. Will we be doing mud masks, too? I love mud masks. Did you know that we pigs came up with that particular beauty treatment?"

A wry smile appears on Namita's face. "The mud masks will have to wait. But I need you to be real with me, okay? What are we going to find out there?"

"Well . . . I think it's best if you see for yourself."

Namita's eyes laser into Fragrant Sausage's eyes. "And this isn't a trap, right? We're not about to walk out and fall straight into a vat of boiling oil or anything like that?"

"Or a pit of lava," I add helpfully.

"Or a pit of snakes."

"Or a pit of spiders."

Fragrant Sausage frowns at us over her snout. "Geez, you kids are twisted. No, it's nothing like that. I'm trying to help you."

At that moment, the door behind us gives a particularly loud shudder as the hound crashes into it again.

"Let's risk whatever's out there," I say. Namita nods. I adjust Xiaohua around my neck and we walk out of the cave. "Oh no," I whisper, immediately wishing we'd stayed inside.

Deep in a valley below us is the biggest tree I have ever laid eyes on. It's as tall as the Empire State Building, its branches stretching on for what seems like miles. But that's not the worst of it. The most awful thing about it, the thing that turns my stomach, is that the branches are covered with spikes as tall as any grown-up.

Demons run around the tree, their bodies human but their faces wrong—some of them have emerald-green faces, others have velvet blue ones; some have fangs, and others have yellow cat eyes. They run like animals, on all fours, lithe and graceful and terrifyingly fast.

"Welcome to the Sixth Court," Fragrant Sausage says. "King Biancheng is very into efficiency. He's all about increasing the number of souls he processes, so he's not too hung up on accuracy. Anything that moves and isn't a demon is scooped up and thrown onto the tree. So I would try to be, you know, more subtle around here."

"Are you serious?" I hiss. "You said this wasn't a trap!"

Fragrant Sausage looks back at me innocently. "It's not! The only other door out of King Yanluo's Court would've led you straight into a vat of boiling oil. This one at least gives you a chance of survival. A very slim chance."

Namita puts a hand over her eyes and groans. "Right, well. How do we make it out of here?"

Xiaohua shifts, exhaling a puff of hot air against my skin. "I am healing, somewhat. Perhaps I would be able to fly us out."

Hope blooms in my chest, but when I look down at her, I see that gold-colored blood is still seeping out of her wounds. The thought of her exerting more energy to try and get us out of here makes me uneasy. It would definitely make her injuries worse. I can't agree to that. There has to be a different way out.

I turn to Fragrant Sausage. "Where's the other door? There are usually multiple ways in and out of each court, right?"

"There's one on the trunk of the tree."

I squeeze my eyes shut. That's probably the worst answer I could've gotten. The trunk is right in the middle of the crowd of demons. How in Diyu would we get to that door? And just as I think that, I catch a short connection to Kai, like an echo flitting by in the wind. Everything inside me seizes. Because that echo I caught was full of distress. Kai is in real trouble. I turn to Namita, desperation boiling inside me. "Namita, didn't you say one of the spells you were learning at Reapling was to make things heavy? Can you cast that spell on one of the souls?"

Understanding dawns on Namita's face. "Ooh. The soul would be so heavy that none of the demons would be able to move it. That's a great distraction. I can do that."

"And you'll run for the door while they're busy trying to move the soul?" Fragrant Sausage says. She rubs her chin and studies us. "I mean, it's a rather risky plan, don't you think?"

"We don't have a choice. Can you think of anything else? We really need to get to our friends," I say.

Fragrant Sausage sighs. "Okay, but just for the record, I do not like this idea."

I look down at the valley of demons and cringe, hating that such a big part of me agrees with Fragrant Sausage. I don't like this idea, either. "I've got a spell to make us run faster, and coupled with the effects of Xiaohua's blood making us faster than usual, I think this will work." I don't actually know if it'll work, but I decide not to think of the million ways that it could—and probably will—fail.

We take a few steps forward. I glance at Namita and she nods. Raising her hand, she points a finger at a soul that's just landed on the ground and starts chanting. The soul twitches, quivering for a few seconds, before becoming very still. While we wait for the demons to notice the super-heavy soul, I take a few deep breaths, calming myself before I cast a spell on us.

Namita glances down at her hands, which glow with a soft yellow light for a second. "What did you just cast?"

"It's a spell for introverts called I'm Too Shy to Say Goodbye. It doesn't make us invisible or anything quite so dramatic— invisibility spells are too complicated for me—but it'll mute our presence so we're less likely to be noticed."

"That's useful." Namita grins at me. "Great job, partner."

I return the smile, and for the millionth time, I consider just how grateful I am to have Namita here with me.

"This is going way too slowly," Fragrant Sausage moans, and before we can stop her, she trots downhill and goes straight to the soul that Namita has magicked. A handful of demons lift their heads and look at her.

"Fragrant Sausage!" I hiss, not wanting to shout for fear of attracting any attention.

She ignores me and hops on top of the soul. She clears her throat dramatically, then opens her mouth and hollers, "HEY, DEMONS. Hullooo! Demonface, yes, you with the horns, I'm talking to you. And you, yes, with the third eye and—oh, is that a third nostril? Very unique. C'mere!" She waves them all over, and they approach warily, their pitchforks held in front of them as though Fragrant Sausage were a large dragon and not a little plump pig. When she's gathered a large enough crowd, she gestures at the soul beneath her. "You guys, I bet that none of you is strong enough to lift this lump."

There is a wave of laughter and one of the demons, a tall one with skin the color of a fire hydrant and fangs that reach all the way below his chin, steps forward. "Little pig, I will move this soul and then I shall skewer you and have you for lunch."

Fragrant Sausage wrinkles her snout. "Goodness me, is that how you treat a wonder such as myself? I'm a talking pig—I promise you I am exceedingly rare. Not that it matters, because you're so weak that you won't be able to move this soul." She glances our way and winks at us.

"She really reminds me of Kai," Namita whispers.

Despite the extremely stressful situation, I laugh a little. *She really does remind me of Kai.* The thought of Kai makes my smile wane. I'm so worried about her. *She's probably doing much better than you are. She's a wise, cunning fox spirit. She'll do just fine.* I keep reminding myself of this over and over again, but I can't quite convince myself of it.

As though reading my mind, Namita gives my hand a squeeze. "I'm sure they're okay. Kai is more than capable of looking after the both of them."

Xiaohua snorts. "I wouldn't be so sure. The thought of my master left alone in hell with that mercurial fox is a thorn in my side."

"Kai will make sure no harm comes to Danny," I say firmly.

Below us, the large demon pushes his pitchfork under the soul. Or tries to, anyway. He can't get even the tips of the pitchfork under the soul. His eyes widen in obvious surprise, and the other demons burst into laughter.

"See? Feeble," Fragrant Sausage says. She points at another demon. "You, the one with the—what is that? Oh, it's an ear on your forehead. Very original. I like. Come, have a go."

As the second, then third demon tries to pry the soul off the ground, the group gets louder, attracting more and more demons into the fray. Soon, all the demons in the court are gathered around the soul, booing and shouting and cheering at the attempts to raise it. They completely ignore their surroundings. Fragrant Sausage waves her trotter at us.

"Now," I say, and Namita and I sprint down the hill. I try to run as gently as possible to avoid jostling Xiaohua too much, but it's a tricky journey as we keep having to dodge falling souls, and our new speed is hard to get used to. It's as though my legs have some sort of mechanical pistons in them, jerking them to move faster than ever before, and it takes all of my focus to concentrate on not falling over. We weave our way toward the tree, ducking behind rocks and bushes now and again. Occasionally, one or two demons would look around, but thanks to my spell for increased subtlety, none of them detects us.

In no time, we're almost at the tree. I peer around a large boulder. We're so close that I can see knots on the tree bark and the outline of a door in its massive trunk. "Ready for the final stretch?" I ask Namita.

She nods. We take another deep breath, go around the boulder, and break into a run. But just then, a soul drops right in front of me. With a yelp, I jerk out of the way. It grazes my arm as it drops to the ground, and I shudder at its slimy, cold touch. It's like being licked by a frog. I step around it, but it wraps a hand around my ankle. I gasp. Its grip is ice-cold, the chill spreading with unnatural speed up my leg, then my thigh. "L-let go!" Already I'm shivering so hard that my words are coming out all stuttery.

"So warm," the soul whispers. "Human flesh."

Now my hips are freezing, my movements slowing. It feels as though my blood has solidified into jelly. I might as well be moving underwater. "Namita—"

But she's a few paces away from me. She hasn't noticed that I'm not right beside her. Oh gods, I'm going to freeze to death down here, so close to the tree of spikes.

"Warm," the soul rasps again, but I can't help him—I can't even help myself. My teeth are chattering so hard that I feel as though they might break. *Please let go of me,* I want to say to the soul, but nothing comes out of my mouth.

Just before the chill reaches my heart, Xiaohua slithers around my neck, opens her mouth, and breathes out a stream of fire at the soul. It cries out and releases its icy grip. Warmth floods back to my limbs. I stumble forward, gasping for breath, my nose running.

"You saved me," I babble at Xiaohua. But my relief is short-lived. The fire has broken my spell of subtlety. It's like a blanket that's been covering me and Namita is suddenly thrown off. A demon with a lizard's head twitches, sensing my presence. His red eyes cut into my skin as he straightens up and peels away from the group, his long leathery tail swishing back and forth. A forked tongue darts out as he approaches. "Oh no." But before the demon can come for me, he's distracted by something else.

Namita.

Dread claws into my belly. She's too far away from me. As though she senses something, she stops and turns around at that moment, her eyes widening when she realizes I'm not with her.

"Theo?"

"Watch out!" I shout, but it's too late. The demon rushes forward, closing the gap between him and Namita with frightening speed. He grabs her arm. He's so huge that his fist covers the entirety of Namita's forearm.

"Let go!" She struggles, but she might as well be fighting a stone pillar.

I run toward her and stumble; my legs haven't quite recovered from the freezing, and anyway, even if I could run at full speed,

I'd still be too slow. I need to do something else. But what? No spell comes to mind. I cast one anyway, a spell to make an arm go noodly. It glances off the demon without any effect. Namita shouts a spell of her own at the demon, but it does nothing.

More demons lift their heads from the heavy soul, maybe losing interest in it, maybe distracted by our shouts. Their mouths stretch into grins, revealing fangs and tusks and broken shards of teeth. I run, stumble, stagger, and continue running toward Namita, but I'm so slow, and the demons are as strong and fast as cheetahs. I'm barely halfway toward her when the first one reaches me and catches me in a painfully tight grip. Another one grabs Xiaohua, and the one who has Namita drags her toward us. We're trapped. More and more demons crowd around us, the stink of their bodies overwhelming, a heavy feral scent of wild animal. Fragrant Sausage is screaming at the top of her lungs.

"Hey! You guys haven't lifted this soul yet! Let those kids go—they're so boring, aren't they?"

But no one takes any notice of her. The demon holding Xiaohua finally speaks, and his voice is unlike anything I have heard, growly and guttural, like a beast. "Human flesh."

The words, and the obvious hunger behind them, make my skin crawl.

"Fire," the one holding me growls back. "Roast."

The one holding Namita shakes his head. "Oil. Fry."

"That's really disgusting!" Fragrant Sausage hollers. "Human flesh is really gross! It's all juicy and tender and savory!"

"You're not helping," Namita snaps.

"Wow, very ungrateful." Fragrant Sausage hops around angrily on top of the soul. "But hey, demons! Seriously, don't eat them. They're so bony—look at them!"

"Oil," another demon growls.

"Oil."

"Yes, oil."

Namita meets my eye. I don't know how to begin describing the look in her eyes. Fear is there, obviously, and sorrow, but behind that is determination. We can't die here, not like this.

"Remember Niu Mo Wang?" Namita says.

Understanding passes between us. We know exactly what to do. She raises a hand and casts a spell, making it swell to ten times its size. She points it at Fragrant Sausage. I point at Namita's hand and shout out the words for the Path of the Pig Be Big. The spell hits Namita's palm and she guides it to hit Fragrant Sausage. It strikes the little pig with a dazzling green light, but Fragrant Sausage is so deep into her rant that she barely notices anything.

"—because I'm a small pig, is that it? That's why none of you are listening to me? That's pigist, you know!" she says angrily as she balloons up, and still none of the demons pay her any attention. She shakes a trotter at them, then pauses, looking at it. Her little piggy eyes widen. "Hey, guys? Is it just me or do I seem a bit bloated to you?"

"Help us!" Namita shouts, before the demons fling us over their shoulders and start walking, still grunting the word "oil."

By now, Fragrant Sausage is the size of an elephant. "Oh wow, you guys are tiny. I could just—" She gallops over to us, lowers her head, catches one of the demons with her snout, and casually tosses him up into the air. She looks at us with huge eyes, and even then, she's still growing. Slowly, a smile stretches across her face. "I could get used to this." She catches another demon in her massive mouth and flings him away like a Frisbee. "MWA-HAHA! I have ascended to my final form!"

"Are we going to regret making her so powerful?" Namita mutters, as Fragrant Sausage tosses demons left and right while doing her massive evil laugh.

"It's the lesser of two evils?" Though having said that, I'm not actually sure that Fragrant Sausage is the lesser of two evils. Still, she's on our side, so that's gotta be better than being cooked alive by demons.

Fragrant Sausage has just removed the last demon from us when there's a noise that sounds like the sky is cracking apart. And that's because it is. The ceiling of the cave rips apart, making everything shake. Even the giant tree trembles, its spikes shuddering. Rocks rain down on us, and Namita and I crouch underneath Fragrant Sausage for cover.

"What's going on?" Namita shouts.

I shake my head. I have no idea, aside from that it seems like the entire place is about to come crashing down on us.

Just then, a thunderous voice booms from above us. "Why aren't the souls being processed fast enough? Who's holding up my court?" An angry face peers through the rip in the ceiling, so big that I can only make out a single eyeball. The eye immediately sees us and flashes with anger. "Intruders! How dare you come here and interrupt the smooth procedure I have put in place! You must have been sent by King Dushi. He's been eyeing my position for centuries."

I have time to say, "Wait, no—" before the eye blinks, and in that instant, the spell on Fragrant Sausage is canceled by the eye. Fragrant Sausage shrinks down to her normal size, and we find ourselves seized by an invisible hand.

"You are now my prisoners. We'll show King Dushi how we deal with intruders."

Somehow, I think that maybe being boiled in oil might have been a better fate than the one King Biancheng has in store for us.

KAI

16

"Huh. Did you mean to transform into a worm?"

I lift my head and give Danny a look. Of course, earthworms aren't the best at giving baleful looks, so it flies completely over his head.

"The manacles transform along with you," Danny adds, stating the obvious.

"I see that." Or rather, I feel that. I'd cunningly thought that shape-shifting to an earthworm would allow me to be free of the cursed things, but instead, they've shrunk down with me. "On the other hand, if they're this small, they should be easier to break . . ." I gesture at Danny to come over.[24] "Try to pry it apart. Or break it, or something."

He crouches down and grimaces as he puts his hands around me. "Gross," he mutters.

"Rude! I can hear you, you know."

"Sorry, you're just so . . . wormy."

If only I had eyes I could roll. "Believe it or not, I am aware. Now, break the manacle off my sleek body—ow! Be gentle."

Danny fiddles with the manacle, turning it—and me—this way and that. "It's hard. You're so wriggly and slippery, and this

---

24 Very challenging to do in worm form. It basically involves me wiggling back and forth until he realizes I'm not just wiggling back and forth for fun.

thing is way too strong for me to pry open." He puts me down and looks around the courtyard thoughtfully. "Maybe I could try breaking it open by . . ." He picks up a rock.

"What? Crushing it? Have you forgotten I'm in a rather vulnerable position here?"

With a sigh, Danny tosses the rock away. "Okay, got any bright ideas?"

"Maybe if I just change very quickly to something big, the manacles will break."

Danny shrugs. "Worth a try."

I focus my qì and make the fastest change into a silverback gorilla. The wormy rings around me expand into creases on my leathery skin. Fur sprouts all over me as I grow and swell and—

Nope. I'm still a worm. I can practically taste the gorilla scent, but despite my mind shrieking at the rest of my body to switch to gorilla form, it refuses to listen. Or it can't. This is not good. Of all the forms to be stuck in . . .

"What are you waiting for?" Danny says. "I thought you said you wanted to change into something big."

"Obviously I've just discovered that I can't do it, haven't I?" I snap.

"It wasn't obvious," Danny mutters. "You're just lying there, not moving."

"Yeah, because I'M A WORM."

"I SEE THAT."

"DO YOU?!" Okay, so maybe the both of us aren't coping so well with, you know, being chained up and enslaved for eternity in hell. The only way this could get any worse is if Ox Head and

Horse Face were here to witness my humiliating form. Well, they would do more than witness it; they'd take the chance to capture me for themselves. Thank the gods for small mercies, eh?

Danny sits down, his head slumped over. "Told you we needed my good-luck charm."

I frown at him. "Do you really believe in those things? They're just as bad as fortune tellers, you know. Nothing but a bunch of fakes."

He releases a long sigh. "I don't know. I guess ever since my mom passed away, and then being kidnapped and cursed by you, I've started believing more in such things. They're like an extra form of security."

Oh gods. I didn't think I could feel any worse than I already do, being stuck in worm form and all, but I'm feeling so ashamed now that I could just about crawl out of my skin.[25] "I'm sorry."

"You don't have to keep apologizing." Danny glances at me, and surprisingly, the corners of his mouth are turned up, his face warm. "It hasn't been as bad as I thought it would be, being stuck down here with you. I mean, okay, it's pretty bad because we're chained up and all, but you know. I'm glad you're here. I mean, I would much rather have Xiaohua here, of course, but you know."

"Yeah, yeah, stop adding qualifiers—you're ruining the moment." I pause, realizing that I feel the same way. I miss Theo and every bit of me aches to know if he's okay, but being stuck with Danny hasn't been as unbearable as I thought it would be. "Yeah, you haven't been as ghastly as I thought you would be."

---

25 Come to think of it, if I could actually crawl out of my skin, it would help us get out of this mess.

"Thanks," he laughs, then hesitates. "Um, and thanks for not changing into a bird form. I know it seems ridiculous to want you to not change into bird form down here, but . . ."

"It's not ridiculous."

Danny smiles at me.

"Aiya, will the two of you please be quiet?" The ox maiden strides toward us, her expression stern, her hands on her hips. "You're disrupting everybody. We've got so much to do: feasts to prepare, souls to torture . . ."

"Of course, wouldn't want to get in the way of torture," I mumble.

"We've got a backlog of souls now, thanks to you two." She glares down at Danny and me, reminding me a bit of Theo's mother whenever she scolds him. Except with Theo's mom, there was never the possibility of her shoving us into a giant millstone and then crushing us into a pulp—so there's that. "We've had to switch to the mortar and pestle since you are chained to the millstone."

"Sorry about that—pounding souls instead of milling them must be such a bother," I say.

The ox maiden frowns at me. "What happened to you? Why're you an earthworm?"

I wriggle in shame. "Oh, no reason. Just thought I'd fertilize the soil a bit. Earthworm poop is gardener's gold, you know."

A slow, wicked smile spreads across the ox maiden's face. "You were trying to escape, weren't you? Did you try to shape-shift because you thought the manacles wouldn't shift with you?" She throws her head back and laughs.[26] "Oh, this is too good. And now you're stuck in worm form. Well, as delightful as it is to see you crawling in the dirt, unfortunately, I do have to change you back into a more useful form." With that, she snaps her fingers and I feel my muscles stretching, my gaze going farther from the soil beneath me. In the next instant, I find myself as a fox once again.

"Oh thank gods," I gasp, kissing my beautiful paws and swishing my two tails with delight.

"You're welcome," the ox maiden says with a flip of her hair. "Now, get to work. You two have a feast to prepare."

Danny's eyes bug out. "A feast? Hang on—"

"Yes, we have a very important guest coming for dinner, and the king and queen want to impress her. That means none of the usual fare that she would be used to—human eyeballs, human blood, etc. We want innovation, creativity."

Danny and I look at each other, then at the millstone, and back to each other. "Um, apologies, my lady, but preparing such a feast requires a lot more than just a millstone." Danny scratches the back of his head apologetically.

The ox maiden sighs with obvious impatience. "What else do you need?"

Danny gestures wildly. "I don't know, so many things! A stove, an oven, ingredients? You can probably find them in the kitchen."

It strikes me what he's doing; he's trying to get her to agree to

---

26 See, this is how you know someone's a villain. Only villains throw their heads back to laugh. What about heroes, you say? Well, usually heroes have some tragic backstory, so they don't make a habit of laughing. Remember that, Bertha. Laughing is a sure sign of villainy.

let us into the kitchen, so she'd have to unchain us. And as soon as she does, I'm changing into something and getting us out of here. Good plan, Danny! I side-eye him and wiggle my eyebrows to let him know I've got the message.

The ox maiden snorts. "I rather like you two being chained up to the millstone. But yes, I see your point." She waves her hand languidly and next to the millstone appear a woodstove, a stone oven, and a large table laden with meats and vegetables. "Will this suffice?"

Danny looks at me helplessly. "Y-yes, thank you. This is good."

"Get to work." With one last pointed look at me, the ox maiden leaves, whistling a tuneless song.

"Well, I hope you cook just as well down here as you do in the human world," I grumble.

Danny sighs and sifts through the ingredients on the table. "Shii-take, chanterelle, portobello . . . wow, and I think these are mat-sutake mushrooms!" Despite our situation, he seems to be getting excited as he goes through the food. "Gosh, look how big the black fungus is. That's amazing." He must have caught the expression on my face because he sobers up a bit.

"I have to say, you didn't strike me as someone who likes to cook. I'm impressed."

He shrugs. "A little. My dad works a lot. Especially ever since my mom died. He's rarely home. The only time we're together is, like, once a week, at dinner. So I like to surprise him with a good meal."

I think of Danny and Xiaohua sitting in a large dining room, Danny eating and missing his mother, and my chest gives a funny twinge. "You know, you could always come eat at Theo's house. And I suppose you might as well bring Xiaohua with you."

A corner of Danny's mouth quirks up into a hesitant smile. "Yeah, that would be nice."

How strange that only yesterday, the thought of inviting Danny and Xiaohua over for dinner would've made me snort. But now, I find myself looking forward to it, wanting to fill Theo's house with noise and laughter once more. I know Theo's parents would love Danny, and they would certainly be impressed with Xiaohua.

For the next few hours, Danny cooks and I follow his instructions, chopping this and stirring that. He makes a surprisingly good head chef, confident but not bossy, and I could swear that once he gets into the swing of things, he forgets that we're trapped in hell. He even hums as he fries up the lotus root with ginger and scallions and plenty of chilies. It's so weird seeing Danny as neither a bully nor a cowering mess, but someone who is in his element, happy and secure.

Finally, Danny plates the last dish, and the two of us stand back and survey our work. It's truly an impressive feast that we've managed to scrounge up. There's a chicken stuffed with Chinese sausages and glutinous rice, wrapped in lotus leaves, and baked until it's so tender that the meat is sagging off the bone. There are wonton noodles swimming in fragrant, rich broth, and fat buns stuffed with barbecued pork.

"Here, have some chicken." Danny hands me a bowl filled with a baked chicken leg. The smell is so fragrant that I practically swallow the entire thing, bones and all, in one gulp. "Wow, okay, you must be really hungry, huh?" Danny says in between bites of food.

My mouth is so full that I can only nod in reply. Just like the vegetable juice, the chicken is fortifying, reviving my energy and making me feel more sure, like I know exactly how to get out of this place. Which I don't. But I feel like I could.

I lick my lips and look at the rest of the food on the table. In addition to the Chinese dishes, Danny's also prepared some Western ones: a wild mushroom risotto, a garlic-and-herb loaf, and a pizza with plenty of cheese.

"The ox lady did say they're looking for something different," Danny says, when he sees my skeptical expression.

As though the mention of her has summoned her, the ox maiden appears at that moment. "Everything better be ready," she says by way of greeting. When she surveys the table of food, her mouth parts a little. "Well, this looks . . . different. Whose idea was it to make this—what is this?" She pokes at the risotto with a spoon.

"It's sort of like . . . Italian congee," Danny offers up.

The ox maiden shoots him a sharp look. "Italian congee? I don't know if this will please the king and queen."

"You did say they wanted something different to serve their special guest," I say snidely. Danny gives me a grateful look.

The ox maiden sniffs. "We shall see." With a wave of her hand, the dishes float up into the air and fly toward the palace. She glances at us and shows her teeth in an unfriendly smile. "Wait here."

"Wait? What for?" I growl.

"Well, if they dislike the food, which is more than likely, then you will be punished. Maybe you'll be ground up in the mill-stone or pounded in the mortar and pestle, whichever."

I refuse to let this obnoxious ox demon rile me up. "And if they like it?"

"Unlikely!" she laughs. "But if they do, then you probably won't hear from them. You'll live to cook another day. Isn't that a nice thing to look forward to?" With another cackle, she strolls away.

Danny slumps down to the ground, looking exhausted. The poor kid. I settle down next to him, curling up into the shape of a comma, my bushy tails flicking now and again. I feel drained as well and ready to sleep for a month.

"Here," Danny says, handing me a bowl. "I saved some risotto for us. Or should I say, Italian congee?"

We both smile at that, and despite the circumstances, we manage to have a somewhat pleasant chat as we eat the surprisingly delicious risotto. At some point, exhaustion overtakes us both and we must doze off because next thing I know, I'm shaken awake roughly. I blink, sitting up, and am faced with half a dozen demon guards, each one uglier than the last. Danny is gaping up at them with silent terror, his eyes wide and his whole body trembling.

"What is it?" he warbles. He looks at me with desperation and fear. "Kai, they must've hated the food. Oh no, I knew it—I shouldn't have taken the risk of cooking Italian food for them!"

"Calm down." I pat his shoulder gently, but inside, my mind is a turmoil. Danny's probably right. King Wuguan must have really disliked the unfamiliar dishes and ordered us to be tortured. Even as I think that, the nearest demon guard grabs me in an unforgiving grip. They unlock the chain from the millstone and tug at the chain so that Danny and I stumble forward. We have no choice but to follow the group of demons as they yank us toward the palace.

"It'll be okay," I whisper to Danny.[27]

He seems to be too frozen with fear to respond, which is just as well. With an increasing sense of doom, we trudge up the steps into the palace, crossing the massive front hall. There is a handful of demons in there, whispering to one another. They all fall silent as we pass by, watching us carefully with an expression I can't decipher.[28] We are led through a golden sliding door into a grand dining hall. The hall is stunning, with towering golden pillars and beautiful Chinese calligraphy adorning the walls. In the middle is a huge circular dining table, around which sit King Wuguan, the queen, and people who are presumably members of the royal family. My eye is immediately drawn to the woman sitting on King Wuguan's right.

She's beautiful, with flawless features. Ornate beaten-gold combs in the shape of curling flames are tucked into her shiny black hair. Her dress is of the finest vivid green silk with gold trimmings. Her eyes are lined, her lips painted a perfect cherry red. But her appearance isn't what makes my breath catch in my

---

27 This is what's called a "white lie." White lies are trivial lies, usually told with good intentions (i.e., telling your companion that everything will be all right when, in actuality, you're both about to be ground like soybeans into tofu).

28 To be fair, it's hard to guess what your average demon is thinking. The horns, fangs, and fur tend to get in the way of their faces.

throat. It's the large banana leaf she holds. It's the magical banana-leaf fan, the only thing strong enough to put out the raging eternal fires of Huoyanshan, the Flaming Mountains. The only thing strong enough to defeat even Sun Wukong, the near-invincible Monkey King.

King Wuguan's guest of honor is Princess Iron Fan. And she happens to be married to none other than Theo's prisoner, Niu Mo Wang.

I gulp. Princess Iron Fan might be the key to getting out of King Wuguan's court alive. But if I play this wrong, she will kill us without a second's hesitation.

THEO
17

At the very top of the enormous tree of spikes is a sort of tree-house, though calling it a treehouse fails to capture just how incredible of a structure it is. It basically looks like a little palace built right into the tree. Namita, Fragrant Sausage, Xiaohua, and I are whisked inside the tree palace. The clawed hands holding us hostage disappear, and we stumble to our knees, breathless. The inside is even more impressive than the outside: impossibly huge, a hall that defies all logic and laws of physics, with the tree going through its center, spreading its branches all the way throughout the room. All over the walls are alcoves, where souls are sorted and judged by King Biancheng and his minions. The souls moan with fear, the demons chitter excitedly, and every few seconds, King Biancheng waves his hand and a soul is pushed off a ledge, where it falls onto the horrible tree.

King Biancheng's booming voice made me think he would be a huge monster, but when we finally come face-to-face with him, he's a slender man with a meticulously neat beard and round spectacles. He looks more like a neurosurgeon than one of the kings of Diyu. He sits on a throne in the middle of the great hall, scribbling onto an endlessly long scroll with a delicate pen. He looks up at us and frowns before he motions at us to come closer. Two demons at our backs shove us forward.

When we get to within ten paces of the king, one of the demons barks, "That's close enough!" Something hits the backs of my legs, and I yelp and stumble onto my knees. "Kneel, humans!"

"Um, excuse me, but as you can see, I am very far from human. I am in fact a—ow!" Fragrant Sausage squeals when one of the demons whips her across the rump.

"Silence!" the demon shouts.

We all fall silent. I have no idea where to look; I'm so fearful. This is the end of the road for us—I know it. We've been caught stealing into a court of hell—a literal court of hell—and I don't know what's about to happen to us, but I know it can't be good.

King Biancheng narrows his eyes at us. "Names." It's a demand, not a question, and impossible to resist.

"Theodore Tan." The words fly out of my mouth without even consulting my brain.

Namita, too, doesn't hesitate. "Namita Singh."

"Fragrant Sausage."

"Xiaohua of the Red Rock Mountain."

We all stare in mute fear as King Biancheng gazes down at his endless scroll. A few seconds tick by with painful slowness, and when he next looks up, he's wearing a frown. "I can find none of your names in my guest list. You were not sent here by King Qinguang."

I open my mouth, but no answer comes out. I don't know what to say to that. Should I lie and say that we were sent here by King Qinguang? But then that would mean that we're supposed to be thrown onto the spikes, which is definitely something we want to avoid. Should I say that we snuck in? But he looks so annoyed already. If we told him we snuck in here, that's going to make him even angrier.

"Answer!" he snaps, and again, the single word reaches straight into the depths of my mind, knocking over whatever restraints I have, and rips the answer out of my mouth. It makes me think of Creighton Ward casting Bagbott's Tongue Loosener on me back at Reapling, forcing me to give up information that didn't belong to him. I'm so tired of feeling helpless, always being pushed around by others.

"We stole in here!" I blurt out. "We were escaping the Fifth Court, and we were in there because we ran away from the First Court, because we're not souls—we're alive. Well, Fragrant Sausage is a soul."

"Darn right I am," Fragrant Sausage says, wiggling her curly tail. "I've had enough of being a fleshly being, thank you very much."

King Biancheng leans forward, and I feel his gaze boring inside me, seeking truth. "Interesting. You evaded King Qinguang of the First Court."

"Yes," I say, and I can't keep the anger out of my voice.

A demon aide standing next to King Biancheng laughs nastily. "No doubt they think they have good reason to steal into Diyu, probably on a fool's errand to save some loved one."

King Biancheng gives a slow nod, then says, "True, though it's usually one individual barging his way in here, not an entire group like this."

The demon aide shrugs. "Your Majesty, we must have order around here. Each time one of them obstinate humans comes rushing in here, it disrupts our workflow. Such a distraction. Unacceptable. We must make it clear that this kind of interruption will not be tolerated. Throw them onto the tree—that's what I think. Except the fire dragon. Can we keep the fire dragon, Your Majesty? It would look grand down here."

I feel as though the entirety of Diyu has just crushed me. Thrown onto the tree of spikes. What have I gotten Namita into? And poor Xiaohua. And Fragrant Sausage. I've doomed us all, and it's all my fault. We have to escape somehow, but how? There is no way out. We're deep in King Biancheng's court, surrounded by demons atop a tree of death. Even if we were somehow able to rush out of here, where would we rush to?

"Oh no," Fragrant Sausage wails. "Is this where my magnificence ends? Surely not!" She turns to Namita and her face softens a little. "I'm sorry. It was my fault, wasn't it?"

"It's nobody's fault," Namita says, holding out her arms. Fragrant Sausage jumps into them, and Namita hugs the little pig tightly. The expression on Namita's face is so sad that it tears me apart. I'm used to Namita looking confident and smug and badass even in the face of the worst obstacle. But now, she looks dumbstruck, her face pale, her mouth slightly open. It's my fault; I was the one who dragged her into this.

"You can't do this to us!" I shout. "We've been through so much. It's all my fault. You should punish me. Leave them alone. All they did was try to help me, and now Namita's stuck here and Xiaohua's injured, and—"

King Biancheng raises a hand. "Xiaohua?" He leans forward

and pushes his glasses up his nose. "Ah, the dragon. How quaint. I didn't notice before."

Before I can react, King Biancheng raises his hand and warm light emanates from his palm, engulfing Xiaohua. She groans and unfurls from around my neck, and I open my mouth—I have no idea what's going on—but the next moment, Xiaohua flies up, stretching her serpentine body, before swooping back down in a graceful arc. She lowers her head to the floor in front of King Biancheng.

"Your Majesty, thank you for your kindness," she says.

"Xiaohua, are you okay?" Namita cries, rushing forward.

"I am. King Biancheng has healed me."

We all crowd around her, gaping at her scales. They're all intact now. I look up at King Biancheng in wonder. I don't know what I had been expecting from him, but given he is a king of hell, the last thing I would have expected was kindness.

And yet that is exactly what I see in his face. He regards us solemnly, patiently, like a slightly distant grandfather. Leaning back in his chair, he says, "Now, tell me why you are here."

And though his voice is powerful, I sense a note of gentleness in it, which gives me hope. I tell him everything, starting from Jamie's death to our ordeal at Reapling and how we've all come to Diyu to rescue Jamie. At the end of it, King Biancheng looks thoughtful.

"Interesting. So King Qinguang will have to decide on your brother's fate. And yours, of course. And you are now separated from your companion spirit."

"Yes." My voice comes out cracked with emotion at the thought of Kai.

"Well." King Biancheng sits back, twirling his pen. "It would be interesting to see how Qinguang will handle this case. I, and a few others, have always thought that Yanluo should be ruling the First Court. This case might just tip the balance in Yanluo's favor." He studies us a bit longer before nodding. "I'm not unreasonable. I can see that your hearts are pure and unsuited for Diyu. And you do have a compelling case. You may go back to the First Court."

Fragrant Sausage squeals with excitement, but Namita and I stand there, frozen. Then I gulp and say, "Thank you so much, Your Majesty—but, um, before you let us go back to the First Court, would it be possible to reunite us with Danny and Kai?"

"Ah, indeed." King Biancheng's gaze unfocuses for a moment, as though he's looking at something far away. Then his top lip curls and he sneers. "I see them. They are at Wuguan's court. I can open a door to his court, but I won't be setting foot in it. This will be where we part ways."

"Thank you, Your Majesty!" I cry.

"Do not thank me yet. I warn you: Wuguan is unpredictable and unjust. He is unfit to rule as a king of Diyu. If he or his demons catch you, I cannot guarantee what the outcome will be."

Namita and I look at each other. Her expression is firm, her mouth stretched into a thin, determined line. She looks as resolute as I feel. There is no choice. Leaving Danny and Kai behind is not an option. We nod, and Namita says, "We understand, and we are willing to take that risk."

"Then go, and good fortune with you. I will keep an eye out on the First Court to see if you make it back there alive."

And with that, King Biancheng waves his hand, and a door appears next to us. With one last look at the king, I open the door and step through it.

KAI
18

"Princess Iron Fan," King Wuguan booms, smiling and rubbing his belly, "I present to you my chefs for this evening's feast, er . . ." His eyes narrow, and he leans forward and says in a loud whisper, "I've just realized that I never asked for your names."

Danny jumps to attention. "It's—"

King Wuguan roars with laughter and waves a big meaty hand at Danny. "I don't care, boy! Your name might as well be Human Boy, and your name shall be Fox."

"How very inventive," I say, but I say it so quietly that the king won't be able to hear.[29]

"Show some manners to our honored guest," tuts the queen at Danny and me.

We hurriedly bow our heads. "Princess Iron Fan," Danny says, "it's a great honor to be presented to you."

Fleetingly, I wonder how Danny knows who Princess Iron Fan is. Then I recall how obnoxious he had been at the Know Your Roots program and what a hard time he'd given Theo for not knowing anything about Chinese mythology. Okay, so he probably knows who she is. I need to somehow convey to him my plan to convince Princess Iron Fan to get us out of here.

---

29 It's called survival instincts.

Princess Iron Fan is leaning languidly back in her chair and studying her fingers, which are covered in long, golden tapers. She spares us a lazy smile. "You cooked well. There were some dishes I have never seen before tonight, and they were a pleasant surprise."

Danny sags with relief. "Thank you, Princess."

"It's very quaint, a human boy and a fox spirit cooking together. That's not a sight you see every day, is it?"

I'm not sure who the question is aimed at, but just to be safe, I bow lower and say, "The circumstances which brought us here are most uncommon, Princess."

"Oh? Sounds like the makings of a good story." She leans forward, her eyes glittering. "Tell me: How did you end up here in King Wuguan's court?" She pauses, sniffing, and says, "Oh my. The two of you are alive, aren't you? That's fresh human flesh."

To my consternation, she swallows then, like she just caught herself starting to drool despite the huge feast that Danny and I had made them.

Luckily, King Wuguan seems to have caught on to the drooling, and he frowns at her. "It would cause me much displeasure if you ate my cooks, Princess Iron Fan."

"Of course," she laughs. "I was just teasing."

We all look at her with disbelief, and she coughs delicately and says, "So tell me then, how did a delici—a healthy, fresh human boy and a fox spirit end up as cooks for one of the kings of Diyu?"

"Funny story, that," I pipe up. My heart is racing, my whiskers twitching with excitement. This is our chance to tell her about Niu Mo Wang and convince her to get us out of here. "We actually came to Diyu voluntarily, to save someone who is being wrongly held here."

Princess Iron Fan covers her mouth and laughs. It sounds like "Ho ho ho!" but one that comes from an evil Santa. "Oh, I love stories that involve foolish humans coming down to hell to save another human. Wasn't there one that Hades loves to tell over and over? What's the lad's name? He had a harp."

"Orpheus," the queen says, rolling her eyes. "My gods, the number of times he told that story. That's why we stopped inviting him over for game night."

"I know, right?" Princess Iron Fan says. "The worst. And that Persephone, leaving smears of pomegranate juice everywhere she goes. Uncouth."

"I like Hades," King Wuguan says grumpily. "We always have a good time coming up with new ways to torture souls."

"All of the methods you two come up with after a few rounds of báijiǔ are untenable," snaps the queen. "Messy, require too much demonpower, unfeasible. Waste of time."

The king pouts at her balefully.

Princess Iron Fan redirects her attention back to Danny and me. "Continue. So you two came down here because for some strange reason, you thought you could outsmart the age-old system in Diyu?"

"Not outsmart," Danny says. "Just . . . we thought we'd be able to reason with King Qinguang."

Groans rise from around the table. "That tiresome old fool," the queen says.

"He can barely keep up with the day-to-day workings of his

court," King Wuguan says. "He really shouldn't be the king of the First Court."

Princess Iron Fan laughs and directs her question at us. "Let me guess: You talked to King Qinguang, and he got so confused that he randomly threw you to this court to avoid having to deal with you?"

"Not quite," I pipe up. This is it. I have to approach this carefully. Our lives depend on it. "You see, we didn't come here on our own. We had our friends with us, but we were attacked by Ox Head and Horse Face in the First Court, and we got separated. They ran through one door; we ran through another . . ."

Princess Iron Fan giggles, her eyes glinting evilly. "How fun! So your friends are scurrying about the other courts as well? Assuming they haven't been caught and killed, that is."

I feel a twist of anxiety and anger at how casually she talks about our friends' possible demise. I soldier on. "Yes, it's a real shame, too, because we didn't just come here to rescue a human soul. We came here to return a king. A king who was stolen from here."

The laughter dries up. Princess Iron Fan's gaze sharpens like a needle, her smile fading. "What do you mean, a king that was stolen from here?"

I swish my tails with discomfort and take a deep breath. "Some time ago, some humans figured out a way to summon mythological creatures to the human world in order to suck out their qì for profit."

"That is a very human thing to do," King Wuguan murmurs. Everyone else in the room nods.

"They started by summoning Peng," I say.

The murmurs rise up in volume, becoming angry. "Yes, I heard of that," the queen says. "The audacity."

"My human companion was the one who found Peng and set him free, with the help of the rest of our friends," I quickly add.

There's silence as they all regard me. The queen stares for a while, reading my mind, then turns to the others and says, "The fox spirit isn't lying." She nods at me. "Go on."

"The same people who kidnapped Peng decided to kidnap another mythical creature. A demon king this time, just to deter anyone from trying to save him." I falter when I see the way that Princess Iron Fan is gripping her magical banana-leaf fan so tightly that her knuckles have turned a shocking white. "Uh . . . well, as you might have guessed, uh—"

"They kidnapped my husband?" she hisses. "Lowly, pathetic mortals?"

I open and close my mouth a couple of times. Finally, I say, "Uh, forgive me, my lady, but did you only just now notice that your husband has been missing for a month?"

Now King Wuguan and the queen are both side-eyeing Princess Iron Fan, who turns red. "I don't keep tabs on where Niu Mo Wang goes. He likes to go on very long trips, and so do I—we have an understanding to be flexible with each other. I assumed he was off visiting our son, Red Boy." She returns her full attention to me, her eyes filled with rage. "But now you have come here and told me that he isn't on one of his trips—he's been kidnapped."

I can't stop my whiskers from quivering under that iron gaze.

"Yes, this is true. But like I mentioned before, we came here to return him to Diyu safely."

"Why didn't you just free him in the human world?"

"Forgive us, my lady," Danny squeaks. "But he was wreaking havoc in the human world. Destroying entire neighborhoods, attacking humans. He had almost destroyed the Golden Gate Bridge in San Francisco before we—uh, before he was subdued."

Princess Iron Fan exchanges a look with the queen. "That does sound like my husband." She sighs. "Right, give him back to me now, and we shall hear no more of it."

"Er, yep, we would love nothing more than to reunite you two lovebirds, but there's a slight problem," I say. "He's currently with our friends. But we can lead you to them!"

"This is a trap," King Wuguan growls. "They're just trying to trick you into letting them go."

"No, I promise you." I turn to the queen. "Read my mind again! You'll know I'm not lying." But as soon as I see the queen's expression, I know I've miscalculated everything. Because the queen doesn't want to lose Danny and me. When she looks at us, it's with a possessive expression, the way one would look at a well-filled piggy bank. I can practically see her mind whirring, considering how to keep Princess Iron Fan from taking us.

The queen barely spares me a glance before she says, "The fox spirit cannot help but lie. It is her nature to do so. You know their kind."

Princess Iron Fan's mouth curls into a scowl. "You dare waste our time, fox spirit? I will show you what I do to liars." With a single fluid leap, she bounds from her chair, landing right in front of me. Before I can react, she places a foot on the back of my neck and shoves down. I fall onto the ground, my muzzle smashing painfully against the stone floor.

"Kai!" Danny cries, scrambling up.

"Don't move," Princess Iron Fan says, lifting her hand. Danny is slammed back down by an invisible force. She lowers her face toward mine, shifting her weight so her foot grinds heavily into my neck, cutting off my breath. "Did you have fun spinning your little lies, fox?"

"Not—lies," I gasp. I can hardly breathe. I'm running out of time. This is my last chance. I desperately grasp for a solution, anything that might prove to her that I'm telling the truth. "He— he calls you his Iron Wife!" The pressure from my neck eases, just a tad. Just enough for me to draw in a breath and add, "He said you're the strongest person he knows and there's nothing you can't take on." It's a risk, saying that, but it's also a hint. A suggestion for Princess Iron Fan.

There's a moment of silence, then Princess Iron Fan says, "I'm going to need to borrow your cooks."

"How dare you?" the queen says. "We invited you to our house for dinner, and you demand our cooks from us?"

"I'm not demanding—I'm asking."

"Preposterous!" King Wuguan roars. "You are known for your haughty nature, Princess Iron Fan, but know your place. This is our house; you are in our court—you must follow our rules."

Princess Iron Fan lifts her foot from my neck and gives a huge, exaggerated yawn, lifting her hands over her head. Then she says, "Haven't you heard, my dear king? Rules are meant to be broken." Quick as lightning, she grabs her banana-leaf fan and sweeps it in the direction of King Wuguan and the queen. The king, queen, and their consorts and guards are blown away like dust. Their enraged shrieks and alarmed wails are cut short as they slam into the opposite wall. Princess Iron Fan doesn't wait for them to retaliate before she picks me and Danny up easily by the scruff of our necks, as though we weigh nothing at all.

She flies out of the dining hall and into the main hall, where all the demon guards jump to attention. They look at us in confusion, and that one moment of hesitation is enough for Princess Iron Fan. She gives another swipe of the fan, and the demon guards are blown away. A moment later, we're out in the courtyard. The sight of the legendary iron fan in action is overwhelming. I've heard so many tales about it, but nothing could prepare me for its incredible strength.

"Stop!" King Wuguan thunders. He flies out of the palace with the queen and the ox maiden flanking him. He carries a staff, a tall bronze one with a carved dragon curling around it and a jade ball at the end. It vibrates with so much power that just the sight of it makes my fur bristle. He aims it at us, and I quickly shift so I'm between Danny and the staff, just in time for King Wuguan to shoot a flash of blue lightning from it. Welp, this is it. This is how I die. Fried to a crisp by a lightning bolt sent from a king of hell.

But with a snort, Princess Iron Fan flaps her banana-leaf fan behind her, and the bolt is blown back toward the king. The king's and queen's eyes widen, and they jerk away out of the path of the lightning bolt just in time. It shoots into the front door of the palace, and the grand wooden door immediately catches fire. Princess Iron Fan aims her fan at the door and waves it once more, this time with a different movement. The gust of wind that comes out of the fan is slower. Gentler. And hotter. Belatedly, I recall that the fan can be used in many different ways. It's well known for summoning great winds, but in the hands of a master like Princess Iron Fan, it can also summon fire or lightning or very subtle, focused darts of wind.

The flames licking the door burst into a giant wall of roaring fire, quickly spreading to the rest of the wall. Within seconds, the whole front of the palace is covered in a horrific curtain of flames.

"My palace!" shouts King Wuguan.

Princess Iron Fan does that evil "Ho ho ho" laugh again and calls out, "Next time, think twice before you dare attack me, peon." With that, she turns to Danny and me and says, "Time to make our exit, don't you think? I don't like to overstay my welcome."

By now, the whole place is so full of black smoke that I can barely talk. I cough, managing a nod, wondering just what in all Ten Courts of Hell Danny and I have stumbled into. But as Princess Iron Fan prepares to fly us out of there, the outline of a door appears in the courtyard. The next second, the door opens and out tumble Namita and Theo, with Xiaohua twined around his neck.

Namita's mouth turns into an O. Theo cries out, "Kai!"

"Theo!" His name wrenches out of me and I shoot forward, barreling straight into his chest. I can't describe how good it is to be reunited with my human companion. It feels like the other half of my soul has finally returned and sewn itself back into one whole piece. Next to us, Danny and Xiaohua are similarly twined in a tight hug, both of them sobbing each other's names out loud.

"This is him, then?" Princess Iron Fan says. "The human child who has my husband?"

Thinking fast, I say, "Yes, but let's get out of here first before King Wuguan brings out the big spells, eh?"

Princess Iron Fan narrows her eyes at Theo. "Child, you'd better have treated my husband with the respect he deserves; otherwise, you'll wish you never set foot here."

Theo gulps. Princess Iron Fan waves her fan gently, lifting us all up. I cling tightly to Theo the whole time, determined to never be parted from him again, and try to squash down the sensation of dread gnawing at my stomach. Everything that's happened so far has shown me just how ruthless and impulsive Princess Iron Fan is. I don't want to know what will happen when she finds out that we've put Niu Mo Wang inside a cage.

KAI
19

The journey seems to take hours with the tornado of death and lightning herding us to an unknown destination. Princess Iron Fan flies ahead of us, waving the banana-leaf fan behind her in a consistent motion. I'm so overwhelmed by this turn of events, so overcome with joy over being reunited with Theo and yet anxious about the plans that Princess Iron Fan has in store for us, that I don't even bother making a joke about how Xiaohua the great and amazing dragon is being herded like sheep.[30]

"Are you okay?" I ask Theo again and again.

Theo gives me a tired smile. "Yes, Kai. Are you guys okay?"

I nod.

"Where do you think she's taking us?" Namita says.

The little blue pig lying down next to her raises its head. "I reckon it would be Bajia Cave. That's Princess Iron Fan's home." It notices me watching it closely and says, "What're you looking at?" rather rudely.

I shrug. "Nothing. Just . . . well, it's not every day that you come across a . . . what are you, exactly? The ghost of a pig? Do animals even go through Diyu? I thought they just get reincarnated in the First Court."

---

30 Okay, I did crack that joke, but my heart wasn't in it.

The pig grunts. "Obviously I'm a special sort, aren't I? I've got leave from King Qinguang himself to roam the courts of Diyu to my heart's desire. The name's Fragrant Sausage, in case you missed it."

"And she's been so, so helpful," Namita says, picking Fragrant Sausage up and giving her an affectionate squeeze.

I look again at Fragrant Sausage and try not to think about how delicious her rotund body looks. "Well, the pig—"

"Fragrant Sausage."

"Right, Fragrant Sausage is right. In all likelihood, we're being herded to Bajia Cave. But that's not a problem—all we have to do is find a way to escape once we get there." I give them an encouraging grin.[31]

Instead of looking uplifted by my inspirational speech, they all stare back at me glumly.

"And how are we going to escape, exactly?" Fragrant Sausage asks.

I have to fight not to snarl at her. I'm not used to food talking back at me.

"I hate to say it, Kai," Namita says gently, "but I don't see how we can possibly escape Princess Iron Fan's clutches. I mean, she trapped us all with just one wave of her fan."

"Yeah, even Sun Wukong was unable to defeat her," Danny adds, as though I'm not aware of that obvious fact.

"Ugh, you're all such downers." I flounce to one side before remembering that there's nowhere to flounce to. I opt to sit down in a huff instead.

---

31 See what a team player I am?

And thus, in gloomy silence, we travel until the tornado disperses and we find ourselves in the mouth of a giant cave. The walls of the cave are glimmering, shot through with veins of rainbow-colored minerals. It's like swimming through the Milky Way. We all look around with mouths agape at the constantly glittering walls and ceilings and startle when Princess Iron Fan appears. She strides to Theo and glares down at him. "Well? Where is my husband?"

Theo licks his lips and bows his head before unzipping his backpack. "Um, Princess Iron Fan, I have to explain—"

"Ugh," Princess Iron Fan grunts. Her hand shoots out and she grabs hold of his backpack, ripping it open in one fluid motion. She dips inside and brings out the cage. "Oh, for gods' sakes. You put him in a cage?" she hisses.

"Wife!" Tiny Niu Mo Wang calls out. "Finally. Let me out."

Princess Iron Fan waves her hand, and the cage clicks open. Oh no. Niu Mo Wang starts growing even before he's fully out. It happens so fast it's like a trick of the eye; one moment he's the size of a hamster, the next, he's out of the cage and back to his terrifyingly huge size.

Princess Iron Fan links her arm through his. Niu Mo Wang is now easily over ten feet tall, and he's a ferocious sight to behold—a hulking, fearsome demon king who could swallow men in one gulp. His gaze slides from left to right, his eyes lighting up with cruel glee as he surveys us.

"I have dreamed of this moment for quite some time," he says, his voice a deep rumble that shivers through my bones. "Revenge will be had and, oh, how sweet it shall be."

"Please, Mr. Niu Mo Wang, sir," Theo says, "we didn't mean to—"

"Do you kids like how I've decorated our humble abode?" Princess Iron Fan says.

For a moment, we all stare at her in confusion. Why is she asking about interior design?

Then Danny the butt-kisser says, "It's very pretty. I love what you've done with the walls." I roll my eyes at him, and he narrows his eyes at me.

Princess Iron Fan smirks. "Come in here—you all can admire it better from the living room." Then she clicks her fingers and the cave expands.

Or rather, it just seems like the cave is expanding because we're shrinking, the room spinning as my eye level goes down and down, and before I can react, we're flying through the air in a single line. My legs flail about and I try to twist my body to break the arc of my flight, but it's useless trying to resist it. One by one, we are flung into the golden cage. I land on top of Theo, and moments later, Fragrant Sausage lands on top of me, followed by Namita, Danny, and Xiaohua. We all scramble up, but the cage door slams shut before we can even get near it.

Niu Mo Wang approaches, and in my miniature size, I can feel every tremor from the cave floor as he stomps toward us. He bends over the cage and peers through the bars, one massive eyeball blinking at us. It's bigger than my entire body. It takes everything inside me not to quail at the sight.

He grins, showing molars the size of my skull. "Well, well," he booms. "How the tables have turned. I did warn you, didn't I? That I would have special treatment in store for you."

I can't help it. Snorting, I say, "Well, it's not really you who did this, is it? It's Princess Iron Fan."

"She's my wife!" Niu Mo Wang snorts. "Her achievements are my achievements, too!"

I roll my eyes. "If you say so."

"Kai!" Theo hisses at me. "Don't make him angry."

"Or rather, don't make him angrier than he already is," Namita adds. Then she says, "We're very sorry, Niu Mo Wang."

He grunts and does that bull headshake snort. "Have a pleasant wait while I decide how exactly I will punish all of you." With that, he stomps off.

I sigh inwardly. The thing these kids can't seem to grasp is that it's good to make your opponents angry, because angry people make mistakes. Honestly, I don't know which is a worse enemy to have: Niu Mo Wang, or Ox Head and Horse Face? Niu Mo Wang is more ruthless, but Ox Head and Horse Face are more determined. It's a toss-up.

As soon as Niu Mo Wang is out of earshot, I go around the cage, sniffing at the bars, looking for any weaknesses. The others have come to the same conclusion I have, all of them studying the cage closely. All of them except for Xiaohua, who's closed her eyes and is frowning hard.

"Ugh," I say, "if you need to go, please do so in that far corner, not in the middle of the cage."

"Oh, ew," Fragrant Sausage squeals. "I hate to say it, but the fox is right. Can we all just agree on which corner is the toilet?"

I side-eye Fragrant Sausage. Despite myself, I'm starting to like the little pig.

Xiaohua cracks open an eyelid and glares at us. "I'm not about to relieve myself. I'm trying to expand to my full size."

Typical. I wish I wore glasses and had fingers so I could use them to take off my glasses and pinch the bridge of my nose.[32] "Right, let me spell out the obvious for you: This cage was used to trap Peng. Remember him? A demigod? The size of Japan? After that, it was used to trap Niu Mo Wang, an actual demon king from hell. Neither of them could grow to their full size while they were in the cage, but you, a common fire dragon, think you might be able to do it, because . . . ?"

"Because we have to try everything in our power to get out of this!" Xiaohua snarls. "Now leave me alone—do not bother me with your inane chatter."

I'm about to snarl at her, but Theo puts an arm around me and pulls me away.

"Kai, leave her alone. Stop, like, poking everyone and everything. I know you're scared, but we have to stick together." He looks so earnest that I can't bear to snap at him.

And he's right. I am lashing out because I'm scared. And guilty. My mind keeps jumping to the awful tortures that Niu Mo Wang and Princess Iron Fan are concocting for us, even now, and I can't bear the thought of losing Theo. Not when we've just found our way back to each other. How in Diyu did we land ourselves into this mess? And it's all my fault. I should've known that this journey

32 Teachers do this a LOT. It's a sign to mean that they LOVE their students and can't have enough of them.

would be too dangerous for us to go on. I mean, this is Diyu, for crying out loud! It's HELL, literally! And I'm such a terrible companion that I allowed my human master, who is a CHILD, to gather his other CHILD friends to come down here in the hopes of saving Jamie. When I look at it that way, it's beyond stupid and well into irresponsible. I have failed him and Namita and Danny, and now look what's about to happen to us all.

Namita is hugging Fragrant Sausage the way a little kid would hold a well-loved soft toy, and though Fragrant Sausage is grumbling softly about it, I get the feeling that she secretly enjoys the comfort and attention. Danny is leaning against Xiaohua, murmuring softly to each other in worried tones.

I curl up against Theo, tucking my nose into the crook of his arm, and close my eyes. I wish I wasn't here. Theo hugs me tight and buries his face in my fur. My shame wraps thickly around me like a wool blanket, and I wish I could hide from it all. Hide from the world.

Hide from the world . . .

The kernel of an idea forms, and I lift my head so fast that I bump it into Theo's chin. "Ow!" we both cry.

I leap out of his arms. "I . . . I think I might have an idea."

Theo rubs his chin and looks at me. "Yeah?"

"Well, Niu Mo Wang and Peng tried to grow back to their full sizes and couldn't do it because the cage must have been imbued with spells to stop things inside from expanding." I pace about excitedly. "But maybe the cage won't stop me from . . . shrinking."

By now, the others have stopped what they're doing and are all staring at me.

"I'll try to shift into something small and find a way to open the cage!" I say.

They look at one another, their expressions ranging from skeptical (Xiaohua) to hopeful (Danny and Theo) to excited (Namita and Fragrant Sausage). Before I can second-guess myself, I focus my qì and switch into a bee. There's a flash of light, and when I open my eyes, I look down at my paws. Except my paws aren't there anymore. I now have thin insect legs instead.

"It worked!" I shout. My voice comes out all tinny and small. I look up and everyone else is a giant compared to me. "And I don't even feel tired at all."

"Must be all that veggie juice and nutritious food I made for you," Danny says.

"I hate to admit it, but you might be onto something there." I fly up excitedly and go around fist-bumping everyone except for Xiaohua, who's still frowning at me, probably bitter that she can't be of any use to anyone. Then I scurry over to the edge of the cage. Here goes nothing. The cage might also be imbued with spells to prevent anything small from flying through the bars, in which case trying to fly through would probably result in me turning into a deep-fried blackened husk of a bee. I rub my two front legs together and take a deep breath. Here goes. I fly up, my little wings buzzing madly, and hover in front of the bars. I glance back at Theo, who's looking at me with huge, terrified eyes. He must've caught some of my fear through our mind link and realized how dangerous this potentially is.

"Wait, Kai—" he begins to say. Uh-oh. I can't let him stop me.

I close my eyes and buzz through the bars of the cage. I'm

expecting a spell to take effect and strike me. In fact, I'm expecting it so fully, with all of my being, that I half smell the sizzle of my body as the spell burns me.

But nothing happens. My wings continue to beat. I continue flying. I open my eyes. I'm alive.

And I'm out. I'm out! I can hardly believe it! I fly round and round the cage, buzzing excitedly while everyone inside it hugs one another and cheers softly. Oh my gods, it worked. And thus we have proven, once again, that I am the superior companion! Or, um, yay it worked—now I can save everyone. Priorities, am I right?

I alight in front of the cage door, and everyone rushes to it.

"Kai, you did it!" Theo says, his face splitting into a huge grin. "You're amazing!"

"Of course, I knew that already, but I'm glad the rest of you realize it now."

"Less talking, more opening of cage doors, please," Namita says.

"Right, yes, of course." I clear my throat and survey the cage lock. "Er, I don't know how to open this. Any ideas?"

"Is there a keyhole?" Danny says.

"If you think I'm going to stick one of my limbs into a keyhole in hell, you've got another think coming. Remember how I did that back at that shop and almost ended up eaten by a building?" I pause. "How did we get Peng out of the cage?"

The kids look at one another for a second, then Theo says, "Oh yeah, I cast a spell to make him big, remember? The Path of the Pig Be Big spell. I guess the cage allowed people outside of it to cast spells on things that are inside. Maybe this one works the same way? So you can cast the spell on us!"

Right. I grimace at them. "I can't cast spells like that, I'm afraid. The only spells I can cast on others are Illusions."

Xiaohua snorts. "That's because your kind is all about tricking others."

I studiously ignore her. "Maybe I could shift into something really strong, like a gorilla, and smash the cage open?"

"That's too dangerous," Namita says. "You might crush us."

"True," I say. "I keep forgetting how squishy you humans are."

We stare at one another through the bars of the cage, our initial excitement quickly fizzling out the longer it takes. My mind is scrambling, looking with increasing desperation for solutions, but I find none.

Then comes the worst sound in the world. From the other room, Niu Mo Wang bellows, "The torture device is almost ready! The boy who put me in a cage for so long shall be the first one to go on it." A loud laugh follows. "Oh, how I shall enjoy listening to his cries."

The thought of losing another master is soul-ripping. I can't do it. It would kill me. I would rather die. I would sacrifice myself a thousand times over if it means saving Theo.

I'm about to shift into a large animal and go rampaging toward them, even though I know it wouldn't do any good. All that would happen is that Princess Iron Fan will lazily flap her cursed fan at me, and I would be rendered useless. Somehow, I'm able to subdue my rage and panic long enough to stop myself from charging in.

Think, Kai! What can you do? There must be a way out of this; there's always a way, especially when you've got nothing else to lose!

Nothing else to lose. Right. I would willingly sacrifice myself to save Theo. I would.

The realization jolts me forward. As Niu Mo Wang and Princess Iron Fan laugh their way to the living room, I fly back toward the cage.

"I have an idea, but you'll all need to buy me some time," I say quickly. "Distract them!"

Namita and Danny nod quickly, their faces tight with horror. Namita shouts out, "Hey! YO, NIU MO WANG!"

"HEY, COW!" Danny shouts.

The laughter from the other end of the cave stops, and Niu Mo Wang says, "Who dares call my name in such an insolent way?"

Danny grimaces but says in a slightly trembling voice, "Uh, that would be me. Um, I just—I was wondering if you'd be so kind as to explain the mechanics of your torture device to me?"

I don't waste any more time. I fly up, switch into a hummingbird for more speed, and zip out of Bajia Cave. Outside, I look around until I find what I'm searching for: a door. I rush forward and open it. It opens out to the Second Court. I pop my head in and shout out, "Hey, it's me, Kai. Ox Head, Horse Face, you there? I'm at Bajia Cave. Any of you demon guards want me? I'm alive! So are my friends. You won't get any fresher meat than this! And in case you're listening, King Chujiang, I am a live fox spirit! Fresh meat. Yum, yum, don't let this offer pass you by before others catch me." I leave the door open and fly back, looking around the vast cavern for another. Once I spot one, tucked into the far wall, I zip there and open it. I don't even bother checking which court it leads to before I shout out the same thing. By the time I find the third door, demons are already streaming through the first door, led by a thunderous King Chujiang from the Second Court. I shout through the third door, then I quickly fly back up to the mouth of Bajia Cave.

There, I focus all of my qì, not to shift into something else, but this time to expand my aura as much as I can. I concentrate on my essence, my scent, and my voice, and I make it swell until it fills up the cavern, then I fling it out as far as it will go. *Ox Head, Horse Face,* I call out, *I'm here. Come get me.*

I open my eyes and zip off just in time before the first of King Chujiang's demons arrive at the front of the cave.

I don't know if you've ever had the misfortune of coming face-to-face with royalty. But I can tell you this: Royals are sooo overrated. First of all, they've got the biggest egos. Second of all, they've got the biggest egos. It's just what happens when you're told that you're special and meant to rule your kingdom from the day you were born.

The kings of Diyu are no different; each one is more arrogant than the last. Each one thinks he's meant to rule the others. Each one resents his post in the Ten Circles and believes he should be promoted by the Jade Emperor to the highest order.

So when two of them walk through their respective doors and find each other, they both take a sharp inhale, puff up their chests, and glare at each other in a most predictable show of toxic masculinity.[33]

"What is the meaning of this?" King Chujiang says.

"Who dares summon the great King Wuguan here?" King Wuguan says.

"In the name of where we live, are you still referring to yourself in the third person?" King Chujiang says.

King Wuguan's face turns red as the demons around them snort with laughter. He takes a step forward, raising his hands slightly, and King Chujiang and his demon guards immediately tense, raising their weapons. This isn't good. I don't want them fighting one another. I want them to fight Princess Iron Fan and Niu Mo Wang.

I quickly shift back into fox form and call out, "I invited you here because you all lost a few human souls today, didn't you? Actually, they weren't just human souls; they were live, fresh humans. Very fleshy and all that."

"It's you!" King Wuguan shouts, stating the obvious.

It's a testament to my self-restraint that I don't roll my eyes at him. I mean, of course it's me—who else would it be? Now I know why everyone says King Wuguan is the absolute worst king. I wave a paw at him. "Yep, hello, it's me: your precious chef. I was kidnapped by Princess Iron Fan, so if you want me back, you'll have to fight her."

---

33 Toxic masculinity: The belief that human males are superior when, really, foxes are much more superior than—oh, that's not what it means? Oh, you know better, do you, Bertha? Would you like to tell the story, then?

King Wuguan looks confused. "But you're right there. I could take you back with me right now."

"Oh, right. My mistake. Let me just go back in the cage . . ." Then, as the kings stare on with mouths agape, I switch back into a bee. And just in time, too, for right at that moment, one of the doors crashes open and Ox Head and Horse Face come charging in, their nostrils flaring, their weapons flashing in the light. "Oh, hello! Just in time. Come catch me, Cow Face!" I call out, before quickly flying back into the darkness of Bajia Cave.

Behind me, there comes an ear-splitting roar and the sound of stampeding feet. I put on a burst of speed and zip straight back. I shift into fox form just as I enter the cage, and I wrap myself around Theo's neck, breathless.

"Kai! Are you okay?" Theo says.

"I am, but be prepared. Things are about to get interesting."

As I say it, Princess Iron Fan and Niu Mo Wang, attracted by the noise, come rushing out from the other side of the cave and almost crash right into the kings' armies.

"What is the meaning of this?" Niu Mo Wang booms.

"You have my chefs!" King Wuguan screams.

There's a pause as Niu Mo Wang gapes at him. "Your chefs?" Niu Mo Wang asks from the side of his mouth.

"Long story," King Wuguan snaps.

"He made us cook for him to cure his constipation," I call out helpfully from inside the cage.

There are a few snorts. "Constipation?" Niu Mo Wang says, not even bothering to hide his grin.

King Wuguan clears his throat. "Yes, well. Human souls aren't very fibrous, are they?"

Niu Mo Wang roars with laughter, but Ox Head grunts and says, "Do not be distracted by the fox! She is the most cunning, most devious liar." He launches into a litany of my past sins, which sort of gives me another idea.

I slink behind Theo and change back into a bee.

"What are you doing?" Theo whispers.

"Trust me." I don't wait for a reply before buzzing out of the cage and flying toward the crowd of kings.

"She tricked us," Ox Head is saying.

Horse Face nods. "Yes, she did. She fooled us."

"That's what I just said," Ox Head snaps. I buzz closer as quietly as I can.

"No, you didn't. You said she tricked us, and I said she fooled us."

"It's the same thing."

"Enough talking!" Niu Mo Wang says. "I want all of you out of my house!" I'm so close now that I can see Niu Mo Wang's nostrils flaring, see the way his pupils have dilated.

"Not without my chefs," King Wuguan says.

"They are not your chefs," Niu Mo Wang roars. "They are my prisoners."

Princess Iron Fan sighs. "I tire of all the noise." With that, she lifts her fan.

Now's my chance!

In an instant, I leap at the fan. As I do so, I shift back into fox form, turning into my magnificent self in midair. My jaws snap around the stem of the fan, one of my fangs catching Princess Iron Fan's hand, and I bite down. She shrieks, and I try to yank the fan out of her grip. But she's had thousands of years of practice keeping the fan safe from thieves, and despite her shock and pain, she doesn't let go of the fan. If anything, she only grabs it harder.

But the distraction gives the others enough of a chance. I don't know who strikes first, but the next moment, the fighting starts. Swords are swung out of their scabbards, double-headed axes are thrown, and spears are flung. Shouts drown the cave. I keep my jaws clenched around the stem of the fan, clinging with dear life as Princess Iron Fan flails at me and tries to shake me off. As the fan is shaken about, abrupt gusts of wind lurch from it, whirling through the cavern and making everything around us shake. Stones rain down on us.

"Stop shaking it!" someone cries. "You're going to make the cave collapse!"

Princess Iron Fan hesitates, and that's when I take my chance. I twist my body and yank the fan out of her grip. And suddenly, I have it. I have one of the most coveted, most valuable magical weapons in the entirety of Chinese mythology. The others must realize this as well because there is a sharp intake of breath before they all pounce at me.

I run with all my might, dodging grabbing hands. A spear thuds into the ground where I was a split second ago. I zigzag and very nearly smash into a bolt of fire. I leap out of the way, my nose filling with the smell of burned fur. I don't stop running, don't pause to look behind me. I sprint until I'm in front of the cage.

The kids crowd to the front of it, their little hands grasping the bars, their eyes wide.

"Stand back," I say. I shift into a monkey and adjust my grip on the stem. The kings are going to be here any second; the only reason they haven't caught up is because they're attacking one another as they fight their way to me.

I aim the fan at the cage.

"You have to do it right, or you might kill us all," Xiaohua says.

"I know that," I snap. I take a deep breath and point the fan at the cage. I focus my mind on opening it. On twisting the bars far enough for the kids to slip through. I focus on the image so hard that I can practically see it already happening. Then I wave the fan gently, throwing the image in my mind across the fan, letting the wind carry it toward the cage.

A warm wind flows from the fan and envelops the cage. It whirls, twirling around the bars, and suddenly, as though they were made of silk, the bars twist and fold.

"I did it!" I shout, hopping up and down.

Instead of jumping with joy, Theo's eyes widen. "Kai, watch out!"

I barely have time to react before a massive hand wraps around my neck and lifts me clean off the ground.

"Got you," Ox Head says.

THEO

20

When Ox Head catches hold of Kai, it's as though he's wrapped his massive hand around my own neck. "Kai!" The word rips out of my mouth and I rush forward, but I'm too far, and Ox Head is too strong, too fast. He doesn't even spare me a glance before turning away, still carrying Kai easily with one hand.

Horse Face arrives next to him and Ox Head gives his brother the fan, but before they can leave, one of the demon warriors throws a swallowtail knife at them. It strikes Horse Face's arm, and he cries out, dropping the banana-leaf fan.

"The fan!"

"Leave it," Ox Head says, and with that, the two of them fly out of Bajia Cave with Kai.

I run out of the cage and stumble. "What—" The ground is falling away under me. It takes a moment to realize that now that I'm no longer in the magical confines of the cave, my legs are growing back to their full length. The others are startled by the same effect, staggering everywhere the moment they spill out of the cage. The last one to come out is Xiaohua, and as she slithers out, she jerks and twitches, and then she begins to expand—first to the size of a garden snake, then to her full size.

Princess Iron Fan rushes toward us and grabs her fan with vicious strength. "I can't believe I almost lost this. How dare you all come here, disrespecting our property, and make us lose one prisoner!"

King Wuguan clears his throat and tugs at his beard uneasily. "Yes, well, that's a bit unfortunate. But never mind—bygones, eh? I'll just take my chef—my other chef—and get out of your hair."

"Like Diyu you will!" Princess Iron Fan hisses. "The humans are all mine."

"You can have the humans," King Chujiang says. "I came here for fresh, live fox, but I see she is in rather high demand, so I'll just take the fresh, live dragon. Makes for a fine pet, doesn't she?"

Xiaohua snarls and wraps herself around all of us, shielding us from them.

"They're mine!" King Wuguan shouts.

"We can't just stand here and wait for them to come to an agreement over who gets to take us," Namita whispers.

"You're right," I say. But if we tried to get Xiaohua to fly us out of here, no doubt the horde would follow. Worse, they might strike at us with lightning and fire bolts. I need to first create a distraction. I rack my mind, trying to come up with a good idea. Then it hits me. I don't need to lure the kings' attention away; I should take advantage of their enmity toward each other. I need to—ah, I'll cast a spell called Add Oil to the Fire and Make It Boil. They'll get so caught up in their argument with each other that we'll be able to sneak out of here.

But even as I cast the spell, I find out, too late, that I'm too frazzled to get it right. I should've known better than to try casting a Chinese spell this minute, moments after Kai's been snatched away in front of my eyes. I should've known my nerves are too shot for me to focus properly on the spell. And the moment I realize this, I drop my hand, hoping to stop the spell, but that only changes the direction of the spell. Next thing I know, there's a sudden blinding flash and the acrid, nose-wrinkling smell of burning plastic. When the smoke subsides, there's a small, sad lump on the ground.

"Fragrant Sausage!" Namita screams.

Horror slams into me with unforgiving force.

"Namita! We have to go," Danny cries.

She ignores him, grabbing Fragrant Sausage and cradling her in her arms. Her face scrunches up with grief. "She's not breathing."

"Do souls even breathe?" Danny says.

I can only stare at Fragrant Sausage's lifeless form. I hadn't meant for the spell to hit her! My mind is scrambling at the words I'd said. What did I mispronounce? What had I said wrong? I have no idea, but there's no time to think about that because the kings and Princess Iron Fan and Niu Mo Wang are coming for us.

"Come on, Namita," Danny says softly.

"I can't just leave her like this," she says, her voice wobbling. "I have to do something, and I have to do it now, before it's too late."

"We haven't got time!" Danny gestures frantically at the horde.

Once upon a time, I would've left. I would've turned and run and hid myself. But I'm not that person anymore. And it's all my fault, my lousy grasp of the Chinese language that has harmed an innocent soul. I unfreeze and run to Namita. A moment later, Danny follows me, and Xiaohua curls up around us and snarls at the incoming horde.

"Do whatever it is you have to do," I tell Namita as I raise my hands. "Danny, cast a protection spell and I'll back you up."

It's a testament to how far we've come that Danny doesn't argue or second-guess me. He immediately raises up his hands and casts Let This Armory Protect You from Injury. I focus on Danny and will my qì to flow in his direction.

The spell flows outward in a bright white light, creating a dome around us to shield us from incoming attacks. Used against the average human spellcaster, it's pretty effective. Used against beings like Niu Mo Wang, Princess Iron Fan, and the kings of Diyu, the dome might as well be a soap bubble. But it's better than standing here and doing nothing.

Behind me, Namita has closed her eyes and is murmuring a spell I don't know into Fragrant Sausage's limp form. Her eyebrows are knitted with sadness and concentration, and her murmurings get faster and louder.

"Get ready," Xiaohua snarls, moments before the first demon warrior gets to us. Xiaohua takes a deep breath and when she breathes out, a fearsome jet of fire shoots out of her mouth. The demon warrior dodges, pressing his blue-colored body to the ground, and Xiaohua aims the fire at him. He rolls away, though the flame gets close enough that his blue skin turns tomato-red and he screams in agony. As Xiaohua pauses to draw breath, another demon warrior pounces, holding an evil-looking scythe in his hands. I focus all my will on keeping the shield up, even though my stomach is curdling and everything inside me is screaming to duck and run. The demon crashes against the shield dome and bounces off. I feel the force of it reverberating through the shield. I can't believe it held. But if a mere demon underling can cause it to judder like that, a single blow from one of the kings would break it completely.

Just as I think that, the first king—King Wuguan—gets to us. Xiaohua blows another jet of fire at him. King Wuguan sneers and waves his hand, almost lazily, and the flames curve around him like a river going round a bend. He raises a palm at us, his eyes meeting mine, and I truly understand in that moment just how hopeless the entire situation is. Despite the disdain that King Chujiang and everyone else in Diyu seem to have for King Wuguan, at the end of the day, he is still a king of Diyu. In his eyes lies eternity; he's existed for an impossibly long time, has lived through the birth and death of entire nations, and cultivated wisdom and power for so long. Whereas I am a twelve-year-old kid. I should give up now. I should drop to my knees and beg for mercy.

But somehow, I keep my hands up, and I focus all of my energy on maintaining the shield. A corner of King Wuguan's mouth quirks up into a smirk. He turns his palm to face up, and a ball of light appears above it. I try to swallow, but my mouth is a desert.

"Oh gods," Danny whimpers. But still he remains behind me, casting the spell. None of us are giving up.

"Namita, hurry," I whisper, even though I know there's no time. Even if she were to finish her spell now, we're already doomed.

The ball of lightning in King Wuguan's hand grows to the size of a basketball, turning and flashing with an awful green light. He throws it at us.

Right before it hits, Namita shouts out the final word of her spell. The lightning ball hits us, and the world explodes into a bright white light.

$$\sim \!\! * \!\! \sim$$

I blink and lift my head from the ground. It takes a moment to realize that I'm still here, in my mortal human body. I'm not dead. I'm not a soul. I'm not even injured. I lift my arms, and there's not a single scratch on them. "What? How?" I whisper. Then reality rushes back, and I quickly get to my feet and look around for the others.

Namita is a few paces away and looking just as stunned as I feel. Danny has thrown his arms around Xiaohua, who's checking him for wounds.

"Wowee, my head doesn't half hurt!" someone squeals.

"Fragrant Sausage!" Namita shouts, picking up the little pig and squeezing her tight.

Fragrant Sausage wriggles for a while before abruptly stopping and peering at Namita with a curious expression. "Did I just— did you—was I . . . dead?"

Namita nods, her eyes shining with tears.

"And you brought me back?"

Namita nods again, looking at Fragrant Sausage with obvious affection.

"But . . . why?" Fragrant Sausage says. "Why do you care?"

"Don't be silly—of course I care because you're obviously the MVP of us all," Namita says, planting a big kiss on Fragrant Sausage's head. Fragrant Sausage looks pensive, like she's thinking of pushing Namita away, but then she relaxes into the hug, nuzzling her snout into Namita's cheek.

I turn back to face King Wuguan and startle. He's lying prone on the ground, surrounded by the rest of the horde. King Chujiang pokes King Wuguan with his trident, and King Wuguan groans.

"This reminds me of the morning after that party we had at the First Court during the Spring Festival," Niu Mo Wang says.

Princess Iron Fan rolls her eyes. "You mean when you all drank too much báijiǔ and basically destroyed the entire ballroom?"

Niu Mo Wang looks down at his feet guiltily before recovering and saying in a gruff voice, "Well, looks like Wuguan is all right, so now I shall claim my prisoners." He stomps toward us and I'm out of ideas, out of options. We can only stand there helplessly as Niu Mo Wang reaches out to catch us in his massive grip, smiling evilly. His hand blocks out the light and closes around my neck. There's another blinding flash, and the next thing I know, Niu Mo Wang is lying down a few paces away from King Wuguan. King Wuguan sits up slowly, rubbing his head. He sees Niu Mo Wang next to him and shakes his head.

"Figures the silly cow would try the same thing when it obviously doesn't work. Oof, that was an interesting experience." King Wuguan gets back to his feet and brushes dirt off his magnificent robes. He looks at me with narrowed eyes. "What spell was that, boy?"

It takes everything inside me not to cower from that ageless gaze. "It was just a minor spell of protection. We learned it from a farmer's almanac that my brother left me."

King Chujiang frowns. "That's a minor human spell. Not even the biggest, most complicated human spell ever concocted could stop a king of Diyu."

"Husband, get up, you big oaf," Princess Iron Fan snaps, nudging Niu Mo Wang with her sandaled foot. Niu Mo Wang groans and pushes himself off the ground.

"What happened?"

"We're still trying to figure it out," King Chujiang says.

As one, they all approach us, their gazes riveted on us as though properly seeing us for the first time. As their heavy footsteps near, we shrink closer to one another. Namita hugs Fragrant Sausage tight in her arms. The ghost pig grumbles something under her breath.

Fragrant Sausage, who I swear was dead moments ago. Well, whatever "dead" means for a spirit, that is. But she was definitely . . . gone, and now she's back and just as grumpy as before. Because Namita did something, cast a spell to bring her back.

"What spell did you cast on her?" I say to Namita.

"What?"

I'm so excited that my words come out in a rush. "You did something to bring Fragrant Sausage back. What was it?"

"Oh, uh. I remembered what you did to cleanse Kai's soul. You said you gave her some of your qì? I did something similar."

Fragrant Sausage stares up at her. "You gave some of your life to revive me?"

"Yeah. I thought—I don't know—you've had a hard life, Fragrant Sausage." Namita gives Fragrant Sausage a sad smile. "And you've been stuck in here for so long, and I just didn't want you to end like that."

"You sacrificed some of your life to save hers," I mutter in wonderment. And the answer clicks into place with the finality of the last puzzle piece. "Self-sacrifice!" I shout at the horde. "I read about it in some of the old texts I was researching. To give up part of yourself, to be completely selfless all for the sake of someone else, that's the purest thing you could ever do in life."

The kings look taken aback. Princess Iron Fan, who's apparently faster on the uptake, is the first to get it. She grits her teeth and takes a deep, frustrated breath. "A curse be upon you humans," she hisses.

"What is it, Wife?" Niu Mo Wang says, still rubbing his head.

"Haven't you all been listening to the human boy?" she snaps. "The human girl has—for some inconceivable reason—sacrificed some of her own life to save that—that blobby thing."

"A magnificent pig, which is me," Fragrant Sausage pipes up.

"And in doing so, she's ensured that she can't be touched by any of us. Because she doesn't belong in hell. She's quite literally too good for us."

King Wuguan grunts. "Well, that may be so, but what about the other humans? We should still be able to touch them."

He's right. Why can't they touch me? I didn't give up any of my life to save anyone. In fact, I knew without a doubt that the flimsy shield Danny had thrown up, even with my help, wasn't going to do much good against the kings. It was a futile effort, and—oh.

The answer fills me in a rush, and I can't help but laugh. Everyone turns to stare at me, and still I can't stop laughing.

"He's finally lost it, has he?" Fragrant Sausage mutters.

"Theo, what is it?" Namita says.

"It's that pathetic, flimsy shield spell," I manage to gasp out in between laughs.

"The one that was about as strong as a piece of paper?" Danny says. "What about it?"

I turn to face him. "You and I knew it wouldn't work. We could both feel how weak it was."

"Right . . ."

"But we stayed on. We stood our ground. Why?"

Danny shakes his head. "I don't know."

"Because we couldn't leave Namita. We stayed on to protect her while she protected Fragrant Sausage. We were prepared to sacrifice ourselves for her. We did it, too—we sacrificed ourselves."

Danny's jaw drops. So do Namita's and the kings' and Niu Mo Wang's.

Niu Mo Wang is the first to recover. His eyes turn red with rage and he shouts, "WHAT?"

It's so loud and so filled with burning anger it's nearly impossible not to quail from it. Nearly. I remind myself that he can't touch me, that he can't hurt me or anyone I care about here, and I stand straight and lift my chin at him.

"How long does this infernal protection last?" Niu Mo Wang demands.

The kings look in bewilderment at one another. "Funny, that. I have no idea," one of them says. "I'm quite sure it's not forever."

"It must wear out after a while." King Wuguan scratches his beard. "We could try to wait until it fades."

Princess Iron Fan snorts and looks up to the ceiling with obvious impatience. "It could take years!"

"You have to let us go." The words feel so powerful coming out of my mouth.

"NEVER!" Niu Mo Wang bellows.

Xiaohua raises herself to her full height. "According to the divine laws from the Jade Emperor, innocent souls do not have a place in hell. You must return us to the First Court, where King Qinguang will review our case."

As Niu Mo Wang and the kings grow even redder with anger, I smile at them, feeling free for the first time in a long while. We're not theirs to judge or punish or keep as pets. We're free to go.

KAI
21

You know what's worse than being presented to a frowning king of hell for crimes you've committed in the human world? It's being presented to a frowning king of hell while being held captive by two sweaty, smelly, snorting brutes. Ox Head and Horse Face are standing on either side of me, which is bad enough, but of course they have to make it a million times worse by standing right up against me.[34]

"Do you mind?" I snap as Horse Face's stinky tail flaps against me for the millionth time. Or rather, I try to say. I can't actually say anything, unfortunately, because they've very cunningly cast a spell on me to make it impossible for me to speak. My words come out as, "Mmm mm MMM?" and Horse Face snorts at my obvious frustration.

"Now serving soul number 98214," King Qinguang's assistant calls out.

But before soul number 98214 can step forward, Ox Head and Horse Face stampede to the front of the hall and shove the poor soul out of the way.

"Hey! No cutting lines," calls out the assistant, a demon with three yellow eyes and the world's most unusual spectacles.

---

34 And you can bet that these two oafs have never heard of deodorant. Phew!

"Quiet, Chicken!" Horse Face snaps.

"It's Chiqen and you know it," the assistant grumbles.

"We're here on important business," Ox Head says.

We are led around the huge screen, where I finally lay eyes on the famous King Qinguang. He looms behind a beautiful lacquered table, tall and regal, with a thick black beard and bushy eyebrows half hidden under the tassels of his crown.[35] He's dressed in a Qing-dynasty robe, an intricately designed court ceremonial dress, and coupled with King Qinguang's regalness, it makes him almost as impressive as the sun.

Ox Head shoves me forward, and he and Horse Face bow their heads. "Your Majesty, we present to you the most evil, cunning, disrespectful fox demon that ever left the spirit world."

Half a dozen retorts are bubbling their way up my throat, each one ruder than the last, but the spell holds tight and I am unable to say a word as King Qinguang leans forward to peer at me. "What has she done?"

"She helped her human master cheat during a test," Ox Head intones, holding up one finger. "Thus leading her human master down a path of corruption." He holds up another finger. "She helped her human master tell multiple lies."

"Thus leading her human master even deeper down the path of corruption," Horse Face adds.

Ox Head gives him a look. "I think the king gets the gist."

"I'm just saying."

---

35 The king, not the table.

King Qinguang sighs. "Is that all? I'm very busy. Do speed it up."

"Of course, Your Majesty," Ox Head says hurriedly. "The worst thing she has done is . . ." He lowers his voice conspiratorially and leans forward. The king leans forward, too. Everybody wants to hear tea being spilled, I guess. "While she was in the human world, she . . . kidnapped a human child."

King Qinguang's eyebrows shoot up.

"Harming a human!" Horse Face crows. "The most wicked of deeds, one that violates the rule that the Jade Emperor has imposed upon us!"

"Only demons are allowed to harm humans, and only because it's in their nature, Your Majesty," Ox Head says. "We ask that you turn this fox spirit into a demon, as that clearly suits her nature, and sentence her to spend eternity in Diyu, where all demons reside so as to keep them from harming humans."

My insides are twisting tight and tearing apart at the vile thing that Ox Head is suggesting. Turning me into a demon would mean that I can no longer be Theo's companion, that I would be, as Ox Head says, stuck in Diyu because that is where demons belong. I would be assigned to one of the ten kings of hell and forced to serve him for eternity, torturing human souls on his behalf. The thought of it is unbearable. I shriek with all my might, begging for mercy, but the spell holds tight.

"These are most serious charges," King Qinguang says, stroking his beard. "Do you have anything to say for yourself, fox spirit?"

I do!

My eyes fill with tears at the effort I'm making to create a single sound. My body trembles all over, my fur standing on end.

"Your Majesty, this is the most arrogant spirit we have come across," Ox Head says. "Look how she refuses to even acknowledge your question. She thinks she's too good to speak to any of us."

What? NO. That's not why! Oh gods, Ox Head has been a dimwitted brute for as long as I've known him, and now he decides to get all cunning? I have to hand it to him—it's actually a pretty brilliant ruse.

King Qinguang's eyebrows knit together, and we all shrink away from his obvious displeasure. His aura is overpowering, and though he hasn't said or done anything, his anger thickens it, turning the air around him as heavy and hot as boiling lava.

"You dare disrespect me, the first king of Diyu?" His voice booms as loudly as a thunderclap.

I shake my head vigorously, my eyes wide with fear and bright with tears.

"I sentence you, proud fox spirit, to an eternity as a dem—"

"WAIT!" a voice cries out.

I turn around and look at the sea of souls, a glimmer of hope springing inside me.

"Quick, Your Majesty," Ox Head says. "Finish the sentence!"

But King Qinguang, too, is searching the sea of souls before him. "Who dares interrupt me?" he growls.

Then, from high in the sky, swoops a bright red streak. Xiaohua! Never before have I felt so glad to see the obnoxious dragon. I could've hugged her and cried, honestly. On her back are Theo,

Danny, Namita, and Fragrant Sausage, all of them waving at us and shouting, "Wait!" Behind them, inexplicably, is an army of kings and demons.

Xiaohua lands in front of me, twitches her enormous head at Ox Head and Horse Face, and snorts. Smoke streams out of her nostrils, and Ox Head and Horse Face stumble back. Theo slides down from Xiaohua's back and sprints toward me. He catches me in a fierce hug, burying his face in my fur.

"Kai! I'm so glad you're still here."

Danny throws his arms around us. "I never thought I would be happy to see you, but gosh, I really, really am."

The horde that's flown in behind them alight as well, and all at once, the kings start shouting.

"These are my chefs!" King Wuguan says. "I demand—"

"How dare you demand anything from King Qinguang?" King Chujiang snaps.

King Wuguan rolls his eyes. "Still sucking up to King Qinguang, I see."

"Order in my court!" King Qinguang roars, slamming his gavel down. We all jump and everyone goes silent.[36] "What is the meaning of this?"

For a long moment, no one speaks. Then King Wuguan raises his hand. "If I may, that fox spirit and that boy—" He points to Danny, who shrinks back. "Are my rightful chefs. I have sentenced them to serve me for all eternity."

"We're not under your jurisdiction!" Theo shouts. "None of us

---

36 Well, I mean, I've been silent this whole time due to Ox Head's hateful spell, but who's keeping track?

are. We're not even dead. Kai, tell them." He nods at me encouragingly. I gesture madly at my mouth, widening my eyes meaningfully, and Theo snaps round to glare at Ox Head. "What have you done to her? Why can't she speak?"

"She's not speaking because she's too arrogant to talk to any of us," Ox Head says.

"That's a lie," Theo spits. He turns to King Qinguang and bows his head. "Your Majesty, I think Ox Head has cast a spell on my spirit companion to make her unable to speak. Could you possibly undo it, please?"

King Qinguang crooks a finger at me, and I'm yanked toward him like a fish caught on a hook. When I'm a mere foot away from him, his frown suddenly deepens and he mutters a counterspell. Immediately, I feel the pressure around my muzzle lifting, and I sag with relief. "Thank you so much, Your Majesty."

But King Qinguang isn't paying any attention to me. He's glaring at Ox Head and Horse Face, who have inched away to hide behind King Wuguan. When King Qinguang next speaks, his voice is soft and poisonous. "You two—my own personal guards—tried to deceive me, your lord and master?"

King Wuguan, noticing Ox Head and Horse Face cowering behind his robes, catches them by the scruff of their necks and shoves them forward. "The worst thing you can do is hide," he says. "Own up to your crimes."

"Please, Your Majesty," Ox Head cries, flinging himself to the floor. "It was all his idea!"

Horse Face gives a scandalized gasp. "Brother! How could you?"

"Silence!" roars King Qinguang. "Explain yourselves: Why did you not want the fox spirit to speak?"

"She is a wily one, Your Majesty," Ox Head sobs. "We merely wanted to make the process expedient and straightforward and—"

"Enough," King Qinguang says, moving one hand in a slicing motion. He turns his attention to me. "These two brought up very serious charges against you. Charges which, under normal circumstances, are unforgivable. But now I see that I shouldn't take their word for it. So I am asking you, fox spirit: Are the charges they have listed true? Did you really kidnap a human child?"

Even though I'm no longer bound by Ox Head's spell, I suddenly find it next to impossible to speak. Everyone's eyes are on me, their gazes heavy with expectation. I take a deep breath. "Yes, Your Majesty. It's true. I did kidnap a human child, and worse than that, I harmed him." I look at Danny and he gives me a small sad smile. "And I regret it every day."

King Qinguang frowns. "Then if the charges are true, why did they bother to silence you?"

"Because my human master gave up years of his own life to cleanse my soul." I smile at Theo, and he reaches out to grasp my paw. "Look into my eyes, and you can see that there are no traces of demonic energy. Theo has made the ultimate sacrifice for me."

"Your Majesty," Danny calls out, "this is true. She did kidnap me and unwittingly put a curse on me, but I am vouching for her now. She is completely changed. While she and I have been stuck here, Kai has done nothing but try to keep me out of harm's way, even if it was sometimes to her own detriment."

I give Danny a wink and he smiles.

King Qinguang's gaze drills into my eyes, and I can sense him rifling around my head, searching everywhere. After a moment, he leans back and nods. "The fox spirit is right," he announces to everyone. "She is cleansed." He turns to Ox Head and Horse Face. "Which makes your betrayal even more serious. You would've had me sentence an innocent spirit to eternal damnation."

Ox Head and Horse Face fall to their hands and knees. "She is no innocent spirit!" Ox Head cries. "It's only a matter of time before she succumbs to her evil side!"

"Then it is her choice to do so!" King Qinguang shouts. "We do not punish for crimes that haven't been committed. Ox Head, Horse Face, you have not only abused your positions, but you have also made me lose face in front of all the other kings. You are hereby sentenced to go through all ten courts of Diyu. I daresay the other kings will enjoy putting you through their signature tortures."

"It's not every day that we get to work with non-human souls," King Chujiang says, wiping his glasses eagerly.

"Mercy!" Ox Head cries.

"Mercy, please!" Horse Face sobs.

"Take them away," King Qinguang orders, and a flock of demon bats pour down from somewhere in the ceiling and surround the wailing forms of Ox Head and Horse Face. The bats lift the two of them up and fly them out of the way.

As strange as it sounds, the sight of my two nemeses being carried to the bowels of hell doesn't spark as much joy as I thought it would. Before I can think better of it, I raise my paw and clear my throat. "Your Majesty? I was wondering—um, I know it's probably a lot to ask of you, but would it be possible to not give Ox Head and Horse Face this punishment?"

"Kai, what are you doing?" Theo whispers.

I ignore him. "It's just that, you see, while it's true that they violated your trust, they did so because they're so passionate about their jobs. I mean, if anything, it shows what good, eager employees they are. Hard to find such driven workers nowadays, am I right?" I stretch my mouth into a hesitant grin. King Qinguang, with his constantly frowning expression, is not exactly the easiest audience to have.

"They would've gladly doomed you into eternal suffering," King Qinguang says.

"Yeah, but . . ." I hesitate, trying to explain to him what I don't quite understand myself. But then I look at Theo, at the love and respect between the two of us. And I look at Danny, at the bond we've managed to forge through our awful adventure down here, and I get it. I gesture at Danny. "This is the human child I kidnapped and harmed. For days after I kidnapped him, he suffered because of my demonic touch. And even after I was cleansed by my master, Danny was still traumatized. I mean, can't blame him, really. But then Danny and I had to go through Diyu together, and there were all these moments where he had to fully trust me, which must've been really hard for him." Danny gives me a wobbly smile. "And vice versa. It was hard on me because trusting a human is, like, the worst thing you can do—am I right? Just kidding! Um, anyway, my point is . . . Danny forgave me. I think? Wait, do you forgive me? It's totally fine if you don't. I didn't mean to put you on the spot like that—"

"Kai," Danny says, laughing. "Yes, I do. I forgive you."

I grin and turn back to King Qinguang. "See?"

"No. I don't see. What's your point?" he rumbles, frowning.

I resist sighing. I mean, really, for a king whose job it is to judge souls, he's not very perceptive. "My point is, if Danny can forgive me for doing something so horrible to him, I think . . . I can forgive Ox Head and Horse Face for trying to trap me for eternity. Maybe instead of having to be punished by getting tortured in every court of hell, they could be sentenced to serve as King Wuguan's chefs for a few years?" Heh-heh, Ox Head and Horse Face would soon find out that working for King Wuguan is no walk in the park.

"Er . . . ," King Wuguan says.

"Do you have a problem with that?" King Qinguang says, his aura growing thick once again.

"No, no, that's . . . great. Thank you for your wise judgment." King Wuguan bows and steps backward, mumbling, "Do those oafs even know how to cook?"

"Right, if everything's resolved, I'd like everyone to clear out of my court."

"Um, Your Majesty?" Theo says. "We actually came down here to plead with you for a favor." He takes a deep breath. "My brother's soul was stolen from his body back in the human world." His voice wobbles with raw emotion, but somehow, he manages to keep going. "And we would like his soul to please be returned to his body?"

The frown on King Qinguang's face grows deeper. "A most unusual request." He strokes his beard thoughtfully. "I shall hear the case. Summon his brother's soul."

A shocked gasp flies out of Theo's and my mouth. For a moment, all we can do is stare at each other, our hearts racing as one. Because—could it be? After all this time, we're finally going to present Jamie's case.

THEO
22

The assistant gestures at us to wait. "He's with the other souls, in a separate antechamber after all the chaos that happened earlier. I will go and retrieve him."

As the assistant shuffles down the dais toward the waiting room, I raise my hand. "Your Majesty, permission to follow your assistant to the waiting room?"

King Qinguang shrugs and waves me away. I follow the assistant, my heart thundering a staccato rhythm. To my surprise, Kai, Danny, Namita, Xiaohua, and Fragrant Sausage all follow me.

"What are you guys doing?"

"Obviously I can't just wait there in the main hall," Kai says.

"Well, yeah. You, I understand. But what about the rest of you?" I look at the rest of the group, who shrug.

"I mean, we did come all the way down here for Jamie," Namita says.

"And I didn't want to be left alone with the kings," Danny mumbles. "King Wuguan has been staring at me with a very weird intensity. I think he's still trying to figure out a way of stealing me back to his court to cook for him."

"And where you go, I follow," Xiaohua says with grave solemnity. Danny reaches out and places a hand gently on her scales, and the two of them smile at each other.

"I just want to see what all the fuss is about," Fragrant Sausage says primly.

I can't help but smile at them. Together, we make the most ridiculous ragtag team, but somehow, we did it. Everyone here has gone through hell for my sake, and I know I can never repay them. We're led into a hallway filled with waiting rooms.

"Have you thought about what you're going to tell him?" Namita says as we walk.

"Only about a million times." I recall the shock on Jamie's face when he learned that he had died back in the human world, and I wince. "And I still don't know what I'm going to say." My voice cracks with emotion, and I try to cover it up by clearing my throat.

Kai jumps up to my shoulders and wraps herself around me. "I'm sure you all expect some brilliant wit from yours truly, but I must admit that I find myself somewhat at a loss for words as well."

"Well, I know what I'm going to say to him," Fragrant Sausage pipes up. We all look down at her.

Kai narrows her eyes at the little pig. "Er . . ."

"I'm going to march right up to him, poke him in the chest—"

"You won't be able to reach up to his chest," Xiaohua points out.

Fragrant Sausage huffs. "Well, I will march right up to him and say, 'Greetings, human, pick me up, please.' And when he's picked me up, I shall poke him in the chest and say, 'You have no idea the amount of trouble I have gone to in order to come and save you. You may thank me by serving me for—whoa!' Hey, stop that!"

Namita has scooped the tiny pig up and is hugging her like a soft toy. "Fragrant Sausage, you are ridiculous, you know that?"

"What? Me, ridiculous? Who got you down the Mountain of Knives?"

"Technically," Namita says, "we did. Although you did give us some really good advice, so there's that."

"See?" Fragrant Sausage says, wriggling out of Namita's arms and climbing up Namita's shoulders and neck to perch on top of her head. "And did I not lead you kids to safety from the tree of spikes?"

"Uh . . . ," Namita says dubiously.

Fragrant Sausage stands straight and proud atop Namita's head and says, "Well, I'm glad we all agree—like you said, I am the MVP of this group and I should be allowed to claim this Jamie as my pet."

Kai and I exchange a glance, then as one, we both burst into laughter. After a moment, Namita and Danny join in, and we laugh so hard that tears spring to our eyes. Somehow, the heavy tension breaks and the snakes in my gut stop twisting into painful knots. I know that no matter what, everything will be okay once we're reunited with Jamie.

King Qinguang's assistant clears his throat meaningfully, and we all quiet down.

"We have arrived," he says primly, gesturing at a large nondescript wooden door. But before the assistant can slide the door open all the way, it explodes into smithereens.

"What the—"

A huge shape bursts out of the room with so much force that

we're all thrown back. I thump into the opposite wall and fall to the ground. What's happening? I don't understand anything; nothing makes sense. Somehow, I retain enough consciousness to lift my head. Blinking up, I catch sight of the large, dark shape that had barreled into us like a cannonball. It's Niu Mo Wang, arm in arm with Princess Iron Fan, who is using her magical banana-leaf fan to propel them out of the corridor. Then I glimpse the bright blue figure, slumped over and unconscious in Niu Mo Wang's clutches, and my heart stops.

Niu Mo Wang's promise to take revenge on us by torturing Jamie's soul echoes in my mind, and blood roars in my ears as the awful reality sinks in. Because the figure caught in his unforgiving grip is Jamie.

KAI
23

My anguish at the sight of Jamie's soul caught in Niu Mo Wang's meaty fist is overwhelming. With a roar, I leap at the bull-demon king. Every muscle in my body pushes me forward. My jaws are open, my fangs gleaming. He will soon feel my wrath.

Princess Iron Fan turns and, in one fluid motion, waves her fan. The gust of wind is impossible to fight. It's so strong that it feels like a physical blow, like I've been punched in the face. It rams into my open mouth and pushes back against my breath, making me choke and cough even as I tumble back uselessly. I slam into Xiaohua's great scaly hide and thump to the floor.

"Jamie!" I croak, scrambling back up. Niu Mo Wang and Princess Iron Fan are running away at full speed. The tightness of the hallway stops them from using the fan to fly, but it doesn't matter how slow they run as long as they can keep blowing us back.

We all get up and start to run forward again, but it's futile. All it will take is another blow from the cursed fan, and we'll be back right where we started.

"Kai, what do we do?" Theo cries, his voice breaking with emotion. "I can't lose him again!"

My chest cracks at the sorrow and fear in Theo's face. It feels like my heart is actually breaking in two. "I know, I can't lose him again, either. I—" I scour my mind, looking for a solution. Any solution.

What's the fastest thing I can change into? A bird? A cheetah? They would all be thrown back without a fight.

Something smaller, maybe? Something slim and small that won't be so easily blown away by the fan. A hummingbird? No, it needs to be even smaller than that. Some sort of insect? I can't think of an insect fast enough to catch up with them.

Think, Kai! I need to think outside the box. A memory surfaces of Jamie encouraging me to turn into various objects. An inanimate object! That's it! A spear? No, a spear won't go far enough.

The answer comes to me in a horrible rush of cold realization. A bow and arrow. If someone shoots the arrow, it should get there before Princess Iron Fan can wave her fan. But this is a dangerous, potentially fatal, move. Turning my whole soul into two separate objects and then separating them—I might tear myself apart.[37] There would be no coming back from that. My essence would rip, and I would simply cease to exist. No going through King Qinguang's judgment, not even a journey through Diyu.

But even as I stand there hesitating, the distance between us and Niu Mo Wang grows. Soon, it'll be too late to do anything. I swallow, my mouth painfully dry, my gaze bouncing between Niu Mo Wang's hastily retreating back and Theo. Theo's face is unbearable to look at. There's so much pain written on it. Pain that I share and understand more than I want to.

Between Jamie's safety and my own, there is no competition. I

---

37 Literally. Not like when a bard sings a ballad about how a heartbreak is tearing him in two. What do you mean you don't have bards? What uncouth era are we living in?!

have failed to protect him once; I won't fail again. I would give up everything I have to save him. I make my decision.

"Get ready," I say to Danny.

He goggles at me. "To do what?"

"What you've been dying to do this entire time." I focus my qì. I try not to think of the ridiculousness of my plan, the myriad ways it could fail. Turning into an inanimate object takes up so much more of my energy and concentration. I think of the blood flowing through my veins and my flexible muscles and soft fur, and I imagine each one solidifying, crystallizing into something hard.

"Kai? What's happening?" Theo says, fear apparent in his voice.

When I finally open my eyes,[38] I'm an orange-colored bow and arrow. The tip of the arrowhead splits into two, and I squeak to Danny, "Shoot me!"

"What?" Danny pales. "I—I don't know—"

"Shoot me! You've been trying to show off your archery skills at every turn. Now do it!" I shout. Then it hits me what I need to say to him. "I trust you completely."

Danny's breath catches in a gasp, and he gulps. He picks me up gingerly and slowly, then he nocks the arrow to the bow. As he pulls the string, he gives a hesitant smile and says, "Told you guys every adventure group needs an archer."

Namita rolls her eyes. Xiaohua glides through the air and stands next to me.

---

38 No, I don't technically have eyes. Yes, I can still see. Did you not read the first book, Bertha? Just go with it, okay? It's magic.

"Are you sure about this?" she murmurs, and for the first time ever, her voice is gentle with me, tinged with sadness. She knows the risk I'm about to take. She knows this might kill me.

Theo must have detected the sadness in Xiaohua's voice because he grabs Danny's arm and looks at Xiaohua. "Wait, why do you sound like that?"

"There's no time!" I look straight into Danny's eyes. "Danny, we've gone through literal hell together and we did it by trusting each other. Trust me to have faith in you. DO IT NOW."

The urgency of my words sinks in, and Danny lifts me up again. This time, his arms do not waver. His fingers grip me with confidence, and he draws me back until the string of the bow hums with tightness. Then he lets go.

I fly through the air with deadly speed, so fast I can practically feel the sharp point of my head slicing through air molecules. Princess Iron Fan glances back, and her mouth parts slightly. She lifts her fan, but I'm too fast. I'm a speeding bullet, a flying point of death. Before she can wave the fan, I hit my mark.

Straight in the center of Niu Mo Wang's muscled back.

There is a thick *thump* as I bury into his flesh. The muscles around my arrowhead bunch up, and Niu Mo Wang jumps with a huge, earth-shattering bellow. I feel a hand grappling all over his back, trying to grab my shaft, and I wiggle this way and that to avoid it. My movements cause him to roar with pain. I don't blame him. Imagine being impaled by an arrow that then starts wiggling to and fro.

"Ignore it!" Princess Iron Fan shouts. "We need to keep going!"

Easy for her to say—she's not the one with an arrow piercing her flesh.

Niu Mo Wang roars so hard that the entire length of my shaft shudders, all the way to the tips of the fletching. "Pull it out!"

"Just ignore the pain! Oh gods, why are you men such babies?" She pulls at his arm and tries to tug him forward.

"It's the fox spirit," Niu Mo Wang hisses. "She's—she's turned herself into a bow and arrow." His words are punctuated with gasps of pain.

"So what? We'll pull her out once we're safe."

"We can't," he pants. "The bow is back with those kids. It's part of her body. If we keep going, and we get too far away from it . . ."

Understanding must have dawned because there is a sharp intake of breath. Princess Iron Fan says, "She'll rip apart."

"Yep," I call out, though my voice is rather heavily muffled. "And the ripping apart of souls isn't known for being a gentle process."

Niu Mo Wang stops moving, stops trying to catch hold of me. I'm sure that at this very moment, he's imagining me exploding while I'm imbedded in his back. It's a rather sobering image for everyone involved, really. Unfortunately, as humorous as it might be, I am not in a position to enjoy it.

"It's a lie," Princess Iron Fan says. "The fox spirit is bluffing. There is no way that a fox spirit would sacrifice her life to save a human's soul. It's just a human, for crying out loud! What's all the fuss about? Surely he can't be worth your life, fox."

I think of Jamie, still captured in Niu Mo Wang's huge hand,

and I think of all the things Jamie and I have been through. I think of all the lessons he's taught me and Theo, the ways he's made me grow. When he first summoned me, I'd been a typical fox spirit: filled with disdain for all humans and preoccupied with silly, flimsy things like fame and power. All I cared about was climbing the hierarchy of spirits, of gaining another tail, and another, until I finally have nine and become the most powerful fox spirit around. Now, those concerns seem so childish. I can hardly remember why in the world they would matter to anyone. Jamie and Theo have taught me love and forgiveness and kindness and courage, intangible things that are worth more than any amount of gold or power.

When I do answer, my voice is solemn, without a trace of irony or wit. "He is worth all of our lives combined, and more."

"Then maybe I should just kill him now and be done with it!" Niu Mo Wang hisses.

I twist with fright at the thought of Niu Mo Wang crushing Jamie. "If you do, I will break apart with sorrow."

"That's fine with—"

"I will break apart into tiny, sharp pieces, all of them buried inside your flesh. You will never again be able to move without excruciating pain. You'll have to sleep on your stomach. I swear this to you, Niu Mo Wang: I will not leave your flesh, not without a fight that will leave you scarred and broken."

There is no reply, but around me, I can sense Niu Mo Wang's blood pounding as he digests my awful threat.

With a frustrated groan, Princess Iron Fan hurries to his back. "Fine, I'll pull the thing out."

Uh-oh. I wriggle as hard as I can, bending my shaft in crazy directions. Niu Mo Wang bellows again. "It hurts!" he wails.

"Stop being such a baby!" Princess Iron Fan snaps. She makes a grab for me, but I bend in a different way. She tries to smack me down but ends up slapping Niu Mo Wang's shoulder instead. He roars and she smacks him once more, telling him to stand still. Then her fingers close around my shaft, and with a cry of triumph, she says, "Got it!"

I'm wrenched out of Niu Mo Wang's flesh just in time to see Xiaohua flying toward us at full speed, the kids riding on her back. Her enormous jaws are open, her razor-sharp teeth flashing in the light. Princess Iron Fan drops me and reaches for her fan, but it's too late. With a loud chomp, Xiaohua buries her teeth in Niu Mo Wang's back.

THEO
24

"Hang on!" I shout. Or try to, anyway, because right at that moment, Niu Mo Wang leaps up with a giant cry and Xiaohua is jerked up with him. The words get caught in my mouth and come out as an "oof" instead. I clutch Xiaohua's scaly body as hard as I can, wrapping my arms around her so tight that I can hardly feel my hands. Behind me, I hear Fragrant Sausage going, "Whee!" as Xiaohua bucks wildly, her teeth still determinedly buried in Niu Mo Wang's back. It's like being on one of those mechanical bull rides. My head is whipped left and right and up and down, and I can hardly draw a single breath in, but somehow, I manage to cling on. Namita and Danny sit in front of me, and both of them maintain their grip on Xiaohua with a fierce intensity. I don't know how much longer we can hold on.

"Oh, for—" Princess Iron Fan snaps. She lifts her fan.

"No—" Niu Mo Wang says.

With one last murderous look at us, Princess Iron Fan flicks the banana-leaf fan. The air slams into us with the strength of a tsunami. All of us, including the impossibly large Niu Mo Wang, are whipped away, our shouts cut off by the unforgiving wind. I think I'm yelling—I don't know. The world is tumbling round and round, and I can't tell which is the right way up or where we're headed, but somehow, I manage to hold on to Xiaohua.

We burst out of the suffocating corridor into sudden bright light. There is a stomach-turning sense of weightlessness before we plummet to the floor. We land with a horrific crash, the force of it reverberating through my bones and making my teeth clack painfully. I'm flung off Xiaohua like a pebble and collapse on the floor heavily. Agony sears through my body at the force. It feels like I just got hit by a truck.

The last thing I want to do is move, but even through the fog of pain, I retain enough consciousness to know that I can't just lie here. I need to get moving. I wiggle my toes and fingers, and finding nothing broken, I lift my head. The room swims around me, but the dizziness fades away as I sit up. Namita and Danny are a few paces away. I call out to them, and relief floods me as they push themselves off the floor. They look dazed but otherwise uninjured. Where's Jamie? I look around frantically for him, but I can't see him. I—

"Mmf mff!" squeals a voice from underneath Xiaohua. Xiaohua grunts and lifts the front half of her body off the floor, revealing a significantly flatter Fragrant Sausage. "Geroff me, you big oaf!" Fragrant Sausage says. She plugs her trotter into her snout and blows, reinflating herself like a balloon.

Before Xiaohua can move, there is a shout and I turn to see Niu Mo Wang a few paces away, getting back to his feet. The blood drains from my head. Xiaohua no longer has a hold of him. And Kai—

Princess Iron Fan holds the arrow in her hand with a cruel smile. The arrow that is Kai. She grasps it with both hands and holds it up high before bringing it to her knee, about to break it.

"No!" I cry out. I'm too slow, too far away. I can't get there in time to save Kai. I'm about to witness her being broken into two. I—

Right before the arrow makes contact with Princess Iron Fan's knee, it disappears. In Princess Iron Fan's hands is a lizard, rearing its head to bite Princess Iron Fan's hand. With a squawk, she flings the lizard away from her. Something smacks the back of my shoulder, and I realize that the bow Danny's carrying has turned into a wriggling, thrashing lizard tail with two points. For a second, all I can do is stare at the squirming thing. Then I realize it's Kai, and she's broken in two, one half scurrying around Princess Iron Fan, the other half with Danny. Danny holds out the tail and I grab it.

"Kai, over here!" I cry out, but she doesn't seem to hear me. She scampers this way and that, seemingly confused. It strikes me then, Xiaohua's concern when Kai decided to turn herself into a bow and arrow. Breaking herself into two parts like this must have disoriented her. I need to get the pieces back together, and fast.

I point at Kai, my chest squeezing at her confused, frantic jumps, and I shout out a retrieval spell. I feel the force leaving my hand, like an extension of it, and I will it to wrap around Kai's thrashing body. She freezes for a second, then starts to struggle wildly, throwing herself this way and that. I tighten my grip, not wanting to lose her, but it's a challenge because I also don't want to accidentally squish her. Somehow, while still hanging on to Kai, I manage to reach deep into my mind, seeking out the link I have with her.

It's okay, I murmur into our connection. *It's me, Theo. I'm here. It's okay, I've got you. You're going to be okay.*

The lizard's muscles stiffen, then it goes limp in my grip. I will the invisible hand to bring Kai back to me, not daring to draw even a single breath as Kai is pulled closer. When she's within reach, I hold out my arms and catch her, hugging her tight. I grab the forked lizard tail and press it against her body, and to my immense relief, the two halves stitch themselves back together. A light enters Kai's eyes, and she stops twitching, her body relaxing. The next moment, she changes into her fox form and sags against me.

"What happened?" she mutters.

"You changed into a bow and arrow and nearly lost your mind," Xiaohua grumbles, slithering next to us.

"Did it work? Did I stop them?" Kai scrambles up my shoulders, still panting slightly.

Jamie! I look around the large cavern and catch sight of Niu Mo Wang getting to his feet, rubbing his back and snorting angrily. Somehow, in the chaos, Niu Mo Wang has lost his grip on Jamie. And now I see him in Princess Iron Fan's clutches. In her other hand, she holds the nearly invincible banana-leaf fan. My stomach sinks. Never before have I felt such dread, such helplessness.

There are shouts, and from the other end of the cavern, the kings of Diyu rush in, flanked by scores of demon guards.

"Stop them!" King Qinguang shouts, pointing at Niu Mo Wang. "He's stolen one of my souls—this is outrageous!"

The demon guards rush ahead, some of them running on all

fours like cheetahs, their muscles rippling fluidly, their mouths drawn back in fearsome snarls. Princess Iron Fan's mouth curls up into a sneer and she says, "Oh, I can't be bothered with you lot." With that, she waves her banana-leaf fan, and she flies up with Jamie in tow. The demon guards who have wings on their backs fly up as well, and Princess Iron Fan waves her fan at them, flinging them away. Even as the guards are blown away, more appear, launching themselves at Princess Iron Fan, who slashes the air, fighting the waves of demon guards back. Meanwhile, on the ground, more demon guards have swarmed around Niu Mo Wang, who is roaring and charging at them, flinging them this way and that.

"Theo, what do we do?" Danny says, rubbing his arm wearily.

Kai looks at me, and I feel her trying not to panic, the same way I'm trying to quell my own rising panic. We both have too much to lose, and yet we are powerless. Sure, we might have the protection that our sacrifices have lent us, but that's not going to do much at all. We're just a bunch of kids. If the kings of Diyu can't defeat Princess Iron Fan, what can we do?

"It's that freaking fan; it's so overpowered," Namita says, echoing my thoughts.

"Undefeatable," Fragrant Sausage says. "It's made Princess Iron Fan quite unbearable. I mean, who calls themselves Princess Iron Fan? What even is her real name? She's got no identity beyond that fan—is that a strong female role model? I think not!"

"I think you're missing the point," Namita says gently.

"I'm just saying," Fragrant Sausage grumbles. "She's not even that powerful—it's all down to the fan."

All down to the fan. If we could just get our hands on it . . .

Something tweaks in my memory. "Hang on, in *The Journey to the West*, Sun Wukong managed to get ahold of the fan! He tricked Princess Iron Fan into giving it to him. He did that by—uh . . ." My voice falters as the mythology comes back to me, and I look at Kai apologetically.

She sighs and says in a flat voice, "By shape-shifting into Niu Mo Wang and asking to borrow her fan. Yeah, I don't think that's going to work here. For one thing, the real Niu Mo Wang is right there? And even if we somehow manage to switch him out with an improved version of him, i.e., me, why would he ask to borrow the fan?"

She's right, and I hate it—I hate everything. I hate how overpowered everyone is here; I hate how fragile and useless we are.

At that moment, Princess Iron Fan must decide she's had enough fighting with the demon guards. "I tire of all of you," she shouts, waving away another attack with a bored expression. "Come, husband! Stop playing with them."

There's no time to waste. I turn to Kai. "You have to trust me—change into him!"

For a split second, doubt crosses her face, but then her expression becomes resolved, and she nods. "This had better work," she says, her orange fur melting away, becoming short and brown and stiff. She grows larger and larger, her sharp snout blunting into a bull's muzzle, two large horns sprouting from the top of her head. In a few heartbeats, Kai has been replaced by a replica of Niu Mo Wang. She looks so much like the real version that we all shrink back for a second.

"Go, Kai," I say. "You gotta get in there. Stand right next to Niu Mo Wang so Princess Iron Fan won't be able to tell which is the real you."

With one last grimace, Kai nods and charges right into Niu Mo Wang and the writhing mass of demon guards swarming all over him, and I raise my voice and shout, "Princess Iron Fan, Niu Mo Wang is in trouble!"

THEO
25

Princess Iron Fan freezes, a frown crossing her flawless face. She looks down at the fray of demon guards fighting two Niu Mo Wangs. She narrows her eyes. "Oh for Diyu's sake, husband. Stop playing with them, I say, and come here!"

In answer, both Niu Mo Wangs shake off the demon guards before catching sight of each other and pausing.

"Who are you?" one of the Niu Mo Wangs says.

"Niu Mo Wang. Who are you?"

"I'm Niu Mo Wang!"

"Oh for . . ." Princess Iron Fan groans. "Not again."

"It's me, wifey!" one of the Niu Mo Wangs says. "Er . . . I love eating grass and drinking beer, and I end every meal with a cave-shaking belch!"

"Well, you're not wrong . . ."

Niu Mo Wang takes a step toward her. "I leave the toilet seat up all the time!"

I pull Danny and Namita close and whisper to them. Their eyes shine, and they nod eagerly.

"Let's do it," Namita says.

"Yes, let's end this," Danny says, looking as resolute as I've ever seen him look.

Clasping her palms together, Namita closes her eyes and mutters a spell. Within moments, her right arm and hand expand until her arm is the size of a surfboard, and her hand as large as the hood of a car. She holds it out, palm up, and I step gingerly onto it, afraid that even though it's so huge, I might still somehow end up hurting her.

Both Niu Mo Wangs are getting close to Princess Iron Fan. "Remember that time during the Spring Festival? You wore that dress—"

"Darling, you can't possibly be falling for it!" Niu Mo Wang bellows. "He's obviously a fake!"

"Quiet!" Princess Iron Fan says. "How would he know about the Spring Festival if he's a fake?"

I can't believe that Kai is managing to trick Princess Iron Fan into believing her, if only for a while. This is exactly what she was complaining about when it comes to fortune tellers, I realize. Gods, she's going to be unbearable when we go home. If we go home.

My shoes sink into the fleshy surface of Namita's palm, and I grimace. "Does this hurt?"

"Are you kidding?" she laughs. "It feels like having a hamster walk across my hand."

We look at Danny, who nods and turns his attention to Namita's hand. He points at it, frowning in concentration, and says the words to magnify its strength. A vibration goes through Namita's skin, and as it travels up my feet, I feel energized, reinvigorated. Like I could totally sprint a full mile if I wanted to.

"Ready!" Namita says.

Kai is now only about ten paces away from Princess Iron Fan.

"Do it," I say.

Even though I know what's about to happen, when Namita lifts her giant arm up, and me along with it, I still feel like I'm about to throw up. It's like the world's worst roller coaster ride, and even scarier because I know what's about to happen, and it doesn't involve seat belts. What if she misjudges the distance? Does she even know how to throw a ball? I mean, not because she's a girl, but because like me and Danny, Namita is a huge nerd. I should've cast a spell of accuracy on her. I should have—

With one huge burst of magnified strength, Namita throws me like a baseball, and all my thoughts screech into one terrified scream.

It's as though time has stopped. Everyone is moving in slow motion. My life flashes before me, then flashes again because I'm somehow still flying, flying past all the kings and their demon warriors, who are also watching me with open mouths.

Then the upward trajectory ends and, horribly, I feel the weightless, stomach-turning sensation of gravity staking its claim. I begin to fall. Princess Iron Fan is right in front of me. I stretch my arms out toward her, see her eyes turning into shocked circles, and I open my own mouth to scream, but the shout is cut short as I crash straight into her.

"OOF!"

No idea who shouts what. Before we even touch the ground, I'm clawing for her fan. We smack onto the ground painfully, but I have the element of surprise; I was expecting the force, and she wasn't, and I'm driven by pure animal desperation. I tear blindly at anything and everything, and the world is shaven down to its core—an all-out fight with fists and kicks and teeth. There is no room or time for magic—I'm not giving her the chance to wave her fan.

Her fan. One of my flailing hands closes around something, and inexplicably, it's the smooth, silky leaf of her fan. I crush it and yank, and in her surprise, she lets go of it. I scramble back, grasping its stem, panting.

"No!" she shrieks, making a grab for it. Instinct takes over, and I flap the fan. Just one flap, and Princess Iron Fan is blown away like a piece of tissue, wailing as she flies up.

"Theo!" Kai cries, and I turn just in time to see that Kai's magic has worn off and she's back in her fox form. Then Niu Mo Wang's meaty hand shoots out and catches Kai round her slim, fox neck.

I raise the fan, but Niu Mo Wang only smiles a bitter smile. "You can wave that fan, boy, but I'm not letting go of this one. Not before I break her neck."

KAI
26

Okay, let's rewind a bit, shall we? Because I feel the need to explain myself, to make it clear how I, a brilliant and brave fox spirit, managed to land myself in such a compromising position.

So here I am, cunningly disguised as Niu Mo Wang. My form is so exquisitely done, down to the smallest detail like the little nick in his left ear, that even Niu Mo Wang himself is confused.[39] Uncertainty crosses his features when he catches sight of me, like his tiny cow brain is going "Wha? There's two of me?"

And the things I throw out there to convince Princess Iron Fan that I'm the real Niu Mo Wang! It's a challenge to keep a straight face. How would I know about the Spring Festival? I know nothing about it. But I've seen enough charlatans to know exactly what to say. The truth is most people would be wearing something special and new for the Spring Festival. And Princess Iron Fan, who's obviously into fashion, would pounce on any chance to wear a new dress. So it was a safe bet to bring it up.

So far, so good. The problem came when I actually got close to Niu Mo Wang. I may be an exceptionally intelligent being, but even I would be loath to claim that I could best Niu Mo Wang in a melee. I mean, have you seen those bullish shoulders and

---

39 Not that it's hard to confuse someone as thick as Niu Mo Wang.

the size of those arms? They would make even Dwayne Johnson jealous.

Technically, while wearing his form, I have the same muscles, but there's just something about shape-shifted muscles that's somehow less solid, less strong than the real deal.

But I have the element of surprise, and I'm not letting that go to waste. When Theo is flung through the air like a little pebble, I take my chance. I squeeze my large hand into a fist and smash it into Niu Mo Wang's muzzle. It was a great punch, one of those punches that totally deserves to be turned into slow motion to show the sheer force of it. It also serves to remind me that I am not, in fact, used to throwing punches. Throwing barbed comments, yes. But punches? Nope.

The pain is excruciating. It shoots up my fist, all the way up my arm, to my shoulder, until even the hair on my head hurts. I yowl.

"For crying out loud! What is your jaw made of?"

Niu Mo Wang shakes his head once, twice, and then spits to one side, which is just another reminder of how unhygienic demon kings are in general. "You're going to pay for that," he rumbles, stepping toward me. His massive shape looms in front of me, and even though we are the exact same size and shape, I know there is no defeating him, not like this. I'm not used to this body the same way he is. He squeezes his free hand into a fist and pulls it back.

In a flash, I change into a flea and hop up onto his muzzle. Ignoring all of my survival instincts, which are screaming, *Ew, ew, ew, noooo!* I jump into one nostril.

It's about as pleasant as you might expect, which is to say not at all. "Ugh, it looks like you have a sinus infection," I call out. "Have you tried Claritin?"

In answer, Niu Mo Wang roars so hard that the walls of his nostrils shake around me, and my tiny insect body is rattled from head to bum.

"Yeah," I mutter, "I'm more of a Sudafed girl myself." Cringing, I make myself hop deeper up his nostril. Do I have a plan? No, no I don't. But just as I consider turning around and going back out, a ginormous finger flies up and stuffs itself into the nostril. "Ack!" I cry, scrambling farther up his nose. The finger digs deeper, almost squashing me.

"Why are you standing there digging your nose?" a high-pitched voice says from somewhere outside. I recognize the very judgmental, acerbic tone as that of Fragrant Sausage.

"That cursed fox spirit is up my nose!" Niu Mo Wang shouts.

"Still. It's so unbecoming. Your wife's in a bit of a bind, in case you haven't noticed, and you're just standing around with a finger up your nose."

Despite the unsavory circumstances I'm in, I stifle a laugh. That little pig's growing on me.

Unfortunately, my mirth is cut short by a shiver that curls through Niu Mo Wang's nasal passage. I freeze, unsure of what's happening, then it hits me: He's going to SNEEZE. With a gasp, I hop to a nearby nose hair[40] and wrap all of my little insect legs around it.[41]

---

40 Ew.

41 Ew, ew, ew.

The sneeze is an overwhelming explosion of noise and a force so strong that I'm ripped off the nose hair in a second. I fly, screaming, out of the tunnel and back into bright lights, and the shock wave must have scrubbed me of my flea form because I land on the ground as my magnificent true self. Well, maybe less magnificent than usual because my beautiful orange fur is covered with a slimy layer of snot.

"Oh, I think I'm going to be sick," Fragrant Sausage moans.

She's going to be sick?

Before I can reply, a large hand closes around my throat and lifts me bodily from the ground. "Theo!" I gurgle.

"Got you," Niu Mo Wang growls.

My eyes meet Theo's. He's got the fan. But what good is that going to do us now?

As if reading my thoughts, Niu Mo Wang says, "You can wave that fan, boy, but I'm not letting go of this one. Not before I break her neck."

I shut my eyes and try to shift into something else, anything. But Niu Mo Wang only laughs and says, "Oh no you don't." He gives me a little shake, his hand squeezing slightly tighter. He's blocking me from shape-shifting somehow. I guess that's one of the many perks of being a demon king.

Wave the fan, I want to say to Theo, but Niu Mo Wang's squeezing too tight, and I can't say a single word. I can only look on as Niu Mo Wang lifts his other hand up. My heart twists, contracts, thumping painfully.

Jamie.

He's awake. He stares with open shock at me. "Kai?" he says, right before Niu Mo Wang starts squeezing him, too. His eyes bulge out, and his voice turns into a squeak.

NO! I scream silently. Tears drip down my slimy fur.

"You've all been a thorn in my side," Niu Mo Wang roars. "Now watch as I kill you all, starting with this human soul!"

My eyes are riveted on Jamie, on the awful excruciating expression on his face. I can't believe I'm about to fail him another time and watch as his soul is extinguished, for the final time. If we are both about to end, then I want my final vision to be of Jamie.

THEO
27

Something tightens around my neck, and I realize it's my mind link with Kai. I'm feeling what she's feeling, and it is awful—the airflow restricted, panic rising inside me like a wave.

I look down at the fan in my hands. I don't know how to use Princess Iron Fan's fan. I don't. I've never even held it before, and it's so strange in my hands, light and yet somehow with the echoes of heaviness. It thrums with power, its surface silky smooth and inviting to the touch, as though it wants to be picked up. It longs to be waved, to exert its incredible power over everything in its way.

I have blown mountains away, it whispers. *Whole mountain ranges reduced to dust with a single wave. I have put out raging volcano fires, and I have created tsunami waves so large they swallowed entire countries. Wave me. Let's see what destruction we can wreak.*

"How dare you!" someone behind me cries.

Princess Iron Fan! I jump, ready to wave the fan at her, but I don't need to do so because without the fan, her powers are greatly reduced. Xiaohua has flown over to her and twined her great, scaly length around Princess Iron Fan, pinning her to one spot.

"Let go of me!" she snaps, but Xiaohua ignores her.

"Do something, Theo!" Namita shouts.

I don't know what to do! I want to shout at them. I don't know how to control this fan! What if I waved it at them and caused a wind so great that it made the entire cavern collapse onto us?

Then Niu Mo Wang lifts Jamie, and I see that Jamie's conscious now, his eyes blinking slowly. Warmth floods my chest. My brother's awake. He's there, in front of me, so near and yet also unreachable. Unless I do something.

Niu Mo Wang starts squeezing Jamie at the same time he squeezes Kai. No. I can't let this happen. I will bring this whole place crashing down on all of us if I have to.

I raise the fan. It trembles with anticipation, its power radiating through my hand, down my arm. *Wave me,* it whispers. *Let us destroy everything. Bring down Diyu itself.*

I'm about to do exactly that. I can almost hear the cracks in the walls and the ceilings, feel the destruction as giant chunks of rock rain down on us. But what would be the point of that? Nothing but revenge, and for whom? I need to save my brother and my spirit companion. I need to let go of my anger. I've brought my friends down here with me to save them. I can't destroy this place. I can't put everyone I love in so much danger.

The moment I realize this, it becomes clear how to use the fan. I can't quite describe it—there isn't a single thought of *Oh, okay, this is how it's done.* But somehow, the magic flowing from the fan, seeping through my skin, twining around my muscles, tendons, and bone, carries with it the instructions for the fan. It can be used for mass destruction, yes, but it can also be used with frightening accuracy. My blood knows this.

I raise the fan, pointing it straight at Niu Mo Wang's heart. His grin widens. "If you think a bit of wind is going to make me drop them, you have another think coming, boy! Humans can't wield the fan well enough."

Before doubt can stop me, I swallow, take a deep inhale, and release it through my mouth. I can hear my own heartbeat, steady in the face of everything. I see nothing but Kai and Jamie. Jamie and Kai. The two souls I love most in every world. I don't wave the fan; I turn it.

A jolt of fire shoots out of the tip of the banana-leaf fan, so hot that it's electric-blue in color. It zips out of the fan with a loud crackle. There's only time for Niu Mo Wang's smile to freeze, and then the firebolt hits him in the middle of his chest.

It hits like a thunderclap, deafening, shocking, earthshaking. Niu Mo Wang is flung back like a paper doll, Jamie and Kai thrown from his clutches. I'm already running before they land.

With every step, my heart thumps the same harried rhythm: *Jamie, Jamie, Jamie.*

By the time I reach him, my face is wet with tears, every part of my body shaking. I stumble once, twice, my legs wobbling. I practically pounce on him once I get within reach. He's lying down on the ground, his soul slightly see-through and glowing weakly.

"Jamie?" I say softly. I hold out a trembling hand and, taking a deep breath, place it on his arm. I give it a gentle shake, then another more vigorous one. "Jamie, oh gods, please be okay." I can't lose him again, not like this.

His eyes open, and he blinks dazedly at me. "Theo?"

"Jamie!"

He pushes himself upright and hugs me, and I close my eyes and sob because somehow, we've made it through literal hell and here I am with him once more.

A huge commotion starts up behind us. I startle and swing round, expecting to see Niu Mo Wang charging at us, but it's the kings of Diyu and their demon warriors rushing toward us. Niu Mo Wang is a few paces away, lying prone, his large body gently steaming, and Princess Iron Fan is still in Xiaohua's clutches.

"Arrest the two of them!" King Qinguang orders. "We'll present them to the Jade Emperor for judgment."

I hurry over to Kai, who's already lifting her head, her two tails swishing slowly. But I've barely reached her side when she gets to her feet, blinks, and zips past me. Straight into Jamie's arms.

"Jamie! Jamie!" she shouts over and over again.

I would be lying if I said that didn't sting, just the slightest bit, but I'm too overwhelmed by happiness to mind anything much at all. My brother is here, and he's okay, and the people who were out to hurt him are being put in chains. It's true; the kings of Diyu have conjured up the thickest, longest sets of chains I have ever seen. Each chain link is as thick as a full-grown man. With a wave, the chains wrap themselves round and round until Niu Mo Wang and Princess Iron Fan resemble pigs in a blanket, but where the blanket is made out of chains and not dough.

Jamie hugs Kai tight, both of them laughing and crying.

I run to them and am engulfed in a tight hug, and I'm in the midst of swearing to myself that I will never let go when a deep voice says, "Come, all of you. It is time for JUDGMENT."

KAI
28

If there's one thing the kings of Diyu have mastered, it's *drama*. I rather think that King Qinguang got his position as the first king of Diyu by being the best at delivering Oscar-worthy performances. Don't believe me? Only hours ago, when we first saw him, he had been dressed in normal robes. But now, he's magicked himself a new set of robes, much grander than the last, all because he's about to handle a special case. This set of robes is made of gold silk and embroidered with a fearsome black dragon that twines itself round and round the torso. He's also wearing a larger hat than before, with longer tassels. I swear even his beard has grown thicker.[42]

He towers before us, flanked by the other kings—all of whom have refreshed their outfits—and glares down with all the fierceness and majesty of that purple guy in *Avengers: Endgame*.[43] He holds out one massive hand toward Theo. "Boy, hand me that fan now. It is much too dangerous to remain in the hands of a human."

Theo gulps and glances at Jamie, who nods at him. With obvi-

---

42 Why are humans so obsessed with chin fur? Why not go the extra step and aim to grow a full body's worth of fur and make it bright orange like yours truly?

43 The one who had the right idea to get rid of half the human population. Wait, what do you mean it's not just humans, but all species? Even foxes? *Gasp.* And here I was rooting for you, Thanos!

ous reluctance, Theo places the banana-leaf fan in King Qin-guang's palm. King Qinguang closes his fist, and as he does so, the fan shrinks down to the size of a playing card. He tucks it into his silk robes and straightens up. "Now, it is time."

The words are said with such somber finality that the kids visibly cower.

The kids and I exchange looks with one another. Only Xiao-hua looks unruffled, probably because she feels like she's too divine for this place, etc. But I can't even pretend to be flippant; whatever's coming, it doesn't sound good. I try to imagine these aloof, fearsome kings delivering good news, and I can't. They're kings of hell, after all, not heaven. My anxiety mounts as we shuffle after the kings, herded on all sides by demon guards bearing tridents and spears. Oh, if I could only shift into something big enough to fly everyone out of here! But after my battle with Niu Mo Wang, my energy is spent, and I know there's no use trying to escape.

We walk into King Qinguang's courtroom. All of the viewers' seats are full of souls, and the sidelines are filled to bursting with demon guards. As soon as we enter, every head turns to face us, and the demons start howling and jeering while the souls whisper to one another, their voices rising in a susurration that makes my fur stand up on end.

"Silence!" King Qinguang bellows. He strides behind his desk, picks up his gavel, and slams it down. The noise in the room is cut with sudden finality. He narrows his eyes at the audience, as if daring them to defy him, and after a few seconds of utter and complete silence, he nods at us. "Kneel," he orders.

There's no defying that voice. It's as though it reaches straight into our bodies, bypassing our minds, and takes control of our limbs. I find myself hopping forward and bending my legs before I know it, like an obedient Labrador retriever. The others do the same, hurrying forward and kneeling beside me. Even Xiaohua slithers up and curls herself so that her front half is bowed low.[44]

King Qinguang side-eyes an assistant demon, who hits a huge brass gong with flourish. "Court is in session!" the demon cries. "Court in sessssssionnnn!"

King Qinguang narrows his eyes, and the demon hurriedly silences the gong. "All bow to the venerable, the wise, the just King Qinguang!"

The souls and demons behind us bow their heads, and at a stern look from the demon assistant, we quickly do the same. Since we're already kneeling, this means we end up touching our foreheads to the floor.[45]

King Qinguang clears his throat and picks up his scroll. When he speaks, he's using his solemn, growly voice. "We are here to review the case of Jamie Tan, aged 17, of 52 Ferry Alley, San Francisco, California. Jamie Tan, identify yourself."

My breath catches in my throat as Jamie lifts his head and raises a hand. He looks so vulnerable in the midst of all this pomp. "That's me."

---

44 Gosh, I really need to learn how to use this voice. Imagine the fun I'd have with Xiaohua. I'd be like, *Sit, giant worm! Fetch, giant worm! Roll over, giant worm!*

45 See what I mean when I say these kings live for drama?

"Address His Majesty with the proper title, human!" the demon assistant snaps.

"Sorry. That's me, Your Majesty."

King Qinguang grunts, reviewing the scroll in front of him. I wonder what in the world it's telling him. The silence stretches on, curiosity and anxiety boiling inside me until I can no longer stand it. "If it's okay with you, Your Majesty—" I begin.

"Silence!" the demon assistant crows, obviously enjoying his role way too much.

King Qinguang looks at me with displeasure for way longer than necessary. Even Mrs. Tan would've been like, *Okay, that's enough drama.*

Finally, he says, "Jamie Tan. Like all other humans, you have done many misdeeds in your lifetime. You have lied to your parents many times, telling them you were practicing violin when you were really out carousing with other humans. You have looked the other way when your little brother and your spirit companion fought with each other. It seems that your kind can't help but be deceitful and selfish."

My fur stands on end. Technically, what King Qinguang is saying is true. Jamie did often err in his lifetime. But it's a bit rich coming from King Qinguang after all the shenanigans the other kings have pulled. "If I may, Your Majesty," I say again, speaking quickly this time so the over-enthusiastic demon assistant can't interrupt me. "It's not quite like you've described."

"Oh? Is that so?" There is a dangerous tone in King Qinguang's voice. "Am I to trust the wily fox spirit over my scroll, which is literally called the Scroll of Ultimate and Unflinching Truth?"

"Admittedly, your scroll sounds like quite the reliable witness." My mind knits itself into a tortured knot trying to think up a good counterpoint. "But I think your scroll might be a bit too on the nose? It's missing a not insignificant amount of subtlety. In which I am a bit of an expert, in case you couldn't tell." I swish my vibrant tails and muster up a winning grin. "You see, for example, did Jamie lie to his parents about practicing the violin? Yes, he did. But he only did so because he had taken on so many other responsibilities like extracurricular activities and lots of AP classes. As Peppa Pig would say, he is 'a clever clogs.'"

"'A clever clogs.'"

This guy has a very annoying way of asking questions in such a way that they come out as statements. "Never mind the clogs. It just means he's clever. And he had all those responsibilities to shoulder at such a young age, and don't most kids lie to their parents at one point or another?"

"So you're saying he doesn't know how to manage his time, and it's okay to lie to his parents because all humans, as I said before, are deceitful."

Theo, Jamie, Namita, Danny, Fragrant Sausage, and Xiaohua are all staring at me with "What the heck, Kai??" expressions.

"I'm saying you should look at the context," I warble. "And that other thing you said, about me and Theo fighting—that's not on Jamie, is it? That's just Theo and me being ourselves."

King Qinguang raises his hand. "I've had enough out of you, fox. Not another word, or I shall be truly angry."

I grit my teeth and swallow the rest of my words.

One corner of King Qinguang's mouth curls up as he consults

his silly scroll. "My scroll continues on to tell me that though Jamie Tan is guilty of all these transgressions, he also possesses a spirit of uncommon courage."

I gasp. "Your Majesty! I didn't think I would be recognized in such a way, but yes, that is very accurate. Thank you, Scroll of Honesty and Thingamajig!"

King Qinguang narrows his eyes at me. "I'm talking about Jamie's spirit."

"Yes, that's me, his spirit companion. Or rather, his old spirit companion."

"I meant his character."

"Ah." I cast my eyes down and mumble, "Could've clarified earlier."

"Kai, shush," Theo hisses.

I snap my mouth shut. I know I should've just kept quiet, but seriously now, I couldn't just stand back and let some scroll slander Jamie like that.[46]

"It says here," King Qinguang continues, "that you risked your own life to save that of Peng's. Huh," he grunts then, and looks, really looks, at Jamie for the first time. His gaze is sharp, unflinching. Even I, kneeling next to Jamie, can feel the heat of it drilling into Jamie's core. "Why did you do that?"

Jamie swallows visibly, which is weird because do souls even produce saliva?[47] "I—I don't know, Your Majesty. I just thought

---

46 Okay, so maybe it might have something to do with me turning into a bit of a blabbermouth when I'm nervous. Maybe.

47 Stick with me, kid, and this is the sort of educational, insightful, and pertinent question you will find from me.

it was wrong, what Reapling was doing to Peng. I was allowed to watch the summoning. I guess they thought I would be really into it. I saw him soaring free in the sky, and then the summoning caught hold and it was horrible. They caught him and caged him and then—" His voice breaks. "It got worse. They were torturing him. Sticking these giant needles into him, sucking out his qì. They were going to do it until they killed him, this deity who's older than all of us at Reapling combined. I couldn't let them do it."

I take a deep breath because I'm filled with so many emotions right now. When I look at Jamie, I'm overcome by love and pride at how selfless he was.

So I do the only sensible thing. I smack him over the head and yell, "Argh, how could you do that? You know how dangerous that was? You could've died! You did die! You know how irresponsible it is to get yourself killed like that?"

"Ow, jeez, I'm sorry. Peng really needed help."

I'm in full Mrs. Tan mode now. I put my front paws on my hips and glare at Jamie. "Ooh, and you, a lone kid, was what this deity needed to save him from an evil corporation? You could've gone to the police!"

"I couldn't, because of the MNDA I signed, remember? I wasn't able to report it to the police!"

"You could've told me," Theo interrupts. "I would've helped."

Jamie looks at him with obvious anguish on his face. "And put you in danger? No way in Diyu would I have done that."

"Instead, you left me brotherless!" Theo half shouts, his voice raw with emotion. Tears flow freely down his cheeks. "I would've rather died helping you than go through life without my big brother."

Jamie's face screws up and his eyes fill with tears, too. "I know, and that's why I couldn't ask you." He turns to me. "Or you. I couldn't drag both of you into danger, too."

Theo and I are silent, both of our chests rising up and down rapidly. Through our mind link, I can sense that Theo is going through the same exact emotions I am. Love and respect intertwined with intense frustration. We both want to hug and hit Jamie.

"Selflessness," King Qinguang says, breaking the moment. "Sacrifice." For the first time, the stern frown melts completely from his face, turning it young and fresh. "These are qualities we so rarely see down here."

Hope flutters in my chest. Somehow, despite all of my raging emotions, I feel buoyant. Oh gods, this is it. It's going to happen. Jamie is coming back to us.

"You do not belong here, not in Diyu," King Qinguang continues. "You are a good soul; it's a pity you died so young."

Fear clutches at the fluttering hope, and I jump up. "He didn't die, Your Majesty!"

King Qinguang frowns at me. "Clearly he did, because his soul is right in front of me."

Here we go, diving right into the gray area. This is the time for me to make my case. "No, he—his soul was taken from his body by a demon and thrown into Diyu. He didn't die in the traditional sense; his body wasn't dead when his soul left it." I'm rambling—I know I am, but I can't seem to stop myself.

Against all odds, King Qinguang hesitates, combing his fingers through his beard as he mulls over what I just said. "Right . . . So his body isn't dead? Is it preserved at a hospital? Connected to tubes, which continue to support his organs? Shrouded in a time-stop spell to prevent cellular death while you kids set out to retrieve his soul? It is most unconventional, of course, but it has been known to happen, and I like to be open-minded."

"Not quite. But we were hoping, perhaps, that you might be able to, ah, revive it?"

King Qinguang frowns. "And ignore the laws of physics and time and space? Doing so would wreak so much havoc on the precarious balance of nature. All of the kings and queens from every hell and every heaven would have my head. No, it doesn't work that way."

Disappointment crashes down on me, almost crushing my spirit. But still, I rally on. "Then maybe you could find another vessel to put his soul into?"

A shake of the head. "Such things can only happen when there is a thread binding the soul to the body. I will not put his soul into a random body; the conflict it would cause between body and soul would destroy him."

And there, I cease talking. Because I understand completely now what I've been too afraid to consider. What I've been hoping against hope for is utterly impossible. I glance at Theo and Jamie, and sorrow plunges into my heart like a knife. I look away abruptly, my eyes stinging with tears. I can't tell them. I won't be the one who tells them that Jamie is dead, and there is no bringing him back.

THEO
29

I see the look of immense and utter sorrow etched onto Kai's face. And when I look at Jamie, I see him thinking of his broken body, and I hear King Qinguang's words, rejecting all of Kai's solutions, and I can't stand it any longer.

"It's okay!" I cry out. They all look at me like I've finally lost it. Maybe I have. I train my gaze on Jamie's because now that the time has come, I find myself shaking. With fear, with grief, and a lot of reluctance, if I were to be honest with myself. I will do it—there's no question about it, but that doesn't mean I'm not scared to death at the thought. Ha, to death. Pretty appropriate saying, given the circumstances. I swallow, moistening my throat, and carry on. "It's okay, Jamie. Because I know how to make it right."

"Theo, what are you saying?" Namita murmurs, a touch of concern tingeing her voice. She's always been faster on the uptake than everyone else.

"I've been learning this spell," I say, taking Jamie's hand in mine. It's larger than mine is, but it's also translucent and weightless and cold. I can see my own palm beneath his, and it's just wrong. His hand should be solid, made of bone and flesh and blood. It shouldn't be like this. Holding it shouldn't feel like holding mist. Kai shifts uneasily, her ears pricking, and I barrel forward. Because I'd known back home, when Kai had talked about making King Qinguang see what a grave injustice Jamie's death was, that it was a long shot. Horrible, untimely, unjustified deaths happen all the time, and none of them are resolved with the victims coming back to life. So why should we be the exception to the rule? I had known even then that it was up to me to think of an alternate solution, and I did. I knew all along that it would come down to this: me or Jamie.

"How to transfer souls into a different body." Realization hits Kai the same moment I start chanting the spell.

"No—" she cries.

I feel it taking hold as I say the words out loud. An old spell—one of the oldest maybe—wild and unpredictable, as skittish as an untamed horse. I capture the spirit of it in my mind, and I envision the future I want: where Jamie is alive, where he gets to go back to San Francisco and walk through the doors of our house, and where Mama and Baba and Nainai get to fuss over him. They would be much happier with him there and me gone anyway. I see a reality where Jamie gets to go to med school, accompanied by Kai, and becomes a doctor. Where he gets to save lives over and over again. But he does all of this looking like me, because this would only work if I gave up my body for his soul to reside in.

There is a stirring inside me, a strange sensation as my soul begins to detach itself from my physical body, like a row of buttons being undone one by one. One button plucks free, then another, and another. This is the right thing to do. This is what Jamie deserves, a second chance at life. But instead of the peace I expected to feel, I feel sadness and, more surprisingly, anger. Part of me is fighting it with all its might. *I don't want to die*, a small voice inside me screams. I don't—I want to live. I want to feel the sharp, brilliant cold of the Bay Area winds hitting my cheeks. I want to play *Warfront Heroes* and feel that rush of endorphins when I defeat a particularly tough opponent. I want to feel the warmth of Kai's fur as she wraps herself around my neck. I want to hang out with my friends and laugh along with Namita as we tease Danny about his archery obsession. There is so much I want to do in my life.

I ignore the voice. It's right that I sacrifice myself for Jamie. It's right—I shouldn't be so selfish. I should—

"NO!" someone roars, and my soul is slammed back into my body. I crash painfully onto the ground. Jamie stands over me, his face scrunched up with anger. "What was that, Theo?" he hisses.

I sit up, rubbing my back and wincing. "I was—it's a spell to give you another shot at life."

"In your body," he says, his eyes burning, his eyebrows knitted together. "And what would have happened to you? To your soul?"

"I don't know—probably would've gone to Diyu," I mumble, finding it hard to meet anyone's eyes.

Danny's mouth drops open. Xiaohua twines a bit tighter around his shoulders. Namita gasps and shakes her head. They're all looking at me with a world of sadness written all over their faces.

"So you were going to give up your life for mine?" Jamie says. "Without telling me first?"

"You wouldn't have agreed to it," I mutter.

"Yeah, you got that right!" Jamie snaps. "I wouldn't have! Theo, you can't do that, you hear me?"

"No! You know what I can't do? I can't go on without you, Gege. I don't know how to be without you." I'm bawling again, and I don't even try to stop it. My nose is running freely, my tears hot on my cheeks. And I'm angry, so angry. "You left us! You left us and we're all broken without you, and I don't know how to piece it all together. Mama and Baba are barely—can I even call what they're doing living? You left us!" The last three words come out in a broken shout that leaves me shaking and empty. I hadn't realized that deep under the thick layers of sorrow, I was angry, too. Angry at Jamie for not telling us about Reapling, for not seeking help. I look up at him. "Please don't make me go home without you; don't make me go back and face Mama and Baba and everyone as an only child. I need you, Gege. We all do. Mama and Baba need you so much more than they need me."

"That's not even close to being true," Jamie says, his face softening. He places his hands on my shoulders and looks into my eyes. "Didi, they need you more than ever. You are their son, too. You deserve to live every bit as much as I did. More, actually, because you didn't go on a foolhardy quest to save a deity and get yourself killed in the process."

"And you're not alone," Kai says, hopping up onto my shoulders and curling around me. "I can't believe you were about to give up your body for Jamie." I can feel tiny tremors going through her paws, and it hits me how shaken she is by what I was just about to do.

"Yeah, you're not alone," Namita pipes up.

"You're stuck with us for good now," Danny says. Xiaohua nods solemnly.

"Speak for yourselves—I swear no fealty to any human," Fragrant Sausage grouses.

Something like joy unfurls in my chest, a small flame dancing in the heavy darkness of grief. I never realized it until now, but part of me did feel that because I'm the "worse" kid—the less obedient one, the less gifted one—that I somehow didn't deserve to live while Jamie died. But it was just me all along, my own grief and insecurities. Mama and Baba and Nainai and Kai, none of them wished that Jamie were the one alive instead.

As though reading my thoughts, Jamie smiles at me. "Never apologize for existing, Didi. I'm so thankful that you managed to survive the whole ordeal at Reapling. If anything had happened to you, I wouldn't have been able to forgive myself. You deserve to live. Not just live, but thrive. You've got such a long and amazing life ahead of you."

Jamie is right. As much as I hate to admit it, I am delirious with relief that I won't be dying today. But it feels so selfish to feel this way. To feel, even in the depths of my sorrow, grateful that I'm still alive. But I do. Because despite everything, despite the overwhelming weight of grief, *I want to live.*

I hug him tight. "What's going to happen to you?" I whisper.

"Ahem," King Qinguang says. We all look up to see him dabbing at his eyes. He clears his throat again, sniffles, and straightens up. "Right, enough of that. So. The human Jamie Tan does not, in fact, have a physical body for his soul to return to.

Therefore, he will be processed as per normal conditions, i.e., a dead person."

Even though I knew this was coming, the words still ring heavily, reverberating throughout my entire body.

Jamie stiffens, but he lifts his chin and meets King Qinguang's eye bravely. "I'm ready for my judgment, Your Majesty."

King Qinguang nods regally. "Here in Diyu, we practice the art of reincarnation. Though your physical body dies in the human world, your soul will be reborn into a new body. You will leave behind your memories of your past lives and start anew. What you are reborn as is determined by how well you have lived in your past life. Those who were cruel will be reincarnated as an animal, most likely an insect."

We all grimace. Jamie was one of the best people I knew, but who knows what standards King Qinguang uses to judge our souls? He might see Jamie's lies about practicing the violin as a huge transgression and choose to punish him for it. I look at Jamie's hand in mine and hope with all my being that he passes King Qinguang's judgment.

King Qinguang sits up straight, his voice booming across the vast space. "Jamie Tan, for your courage and your selflessness in your lifetime, you will be reincarnated as a human."

There's a collective sigh of relief.

"A human? Thank you so much, Your Majesty," Jamie says, bowing low.

Even though I know that this is the best possible outcome, sadness churns deep inside me, like a blunt axe cleaving through my heart. Jamie will be reincarnated, which is good, but he'll be forever gone from me.

King Qinguang must have seen the sorrow on my face because he smiles kindly and says, "Do you know what the beauty of reincarnation is, Didi?"

I shake my head, not daring to speak because the lump in my throat is too big, too knotted, and the weight on my heart crushing.

"Those who are reincarnated never truly leave us. Those who were close to you in a previous life will be close to you in the next. It will be a different relationship, of course, but Jamie will be close to you—he will be reborn as a neighbor's child or perhaps a cousin. Your paths are forever intertwined, and just because one life has ended, doesn't mean that the relationship has."

I look at Jamie, both of us crying and smiling at each other through our tears.

"I guess it's my turn to be the didi," Jamie says, laughing.

King Qinguang shrugs. "You might be a girl—I don't know."

"So I might be a meimei instead." He squeezes my hand. "But I'll be close to you—that's the only thing that matters."

I nod, hugging him tight. "I'll look for you," I promise. "I won't stop until I find you."

Jamie squeezes me before pulling away. "But you also have to live your own life, Didi. Don't derail your life to come looking for me, okay? You have to promise you'll live your life to the fullest extent."

"I'll make sure he does," Kai says. She hops from my shoulders and lands on Jamie's, licking his cheeks like a little dog. "I'm going to miss you so much."

"Take care of my brother, Kai."

"I will. You did good, kiddo," she says with a wink.

Jamie grins at her. "I'm so glad I chose you as a spirit companion and not a water dragon."

"Pfft, spot-on! What can a poxy dragon possibly do that I can't? Present company excluded, of course," Kai adds with a sheepish smile at Xiaohua.

Xiaohua merely rolls her eyes and blows a stream of smoke out of her nostrils.

"Are you ready to begin your next journey, Jamie Tan?" King Qinguang says.

It feels like my heart is breaking in two, and one half is being carried by Jamie. But Kai, Namita, Danny, Xiaohua, and even Fragrant Sausage crowd around me, their arms holding me tight so I don't fall apart, and somehow, I manage to stay on my feet. Somehow, as Jamie walks forward, ascending the steps until he is in front of King Qinguang, I keep breathing. King Qinguang places a gentle hand on Jamie's forehead. Jamie's eyes meet mine, and he opens his mouth and says, "See you, Didi." Light shines from King Qinguang's palm, enveloping Jamie's forehead, and somehow I keep breathing. The light expands to cover all of Jamie, becoming too bright to look at, and we all look away. When the light disappears, there is no one in front of King Qinguang.

Jamie is gone.

And somehow, I am still here. And somehow, I know that I will be okay.

THEO
30

I don't know how long I stand there, but I know that the entire time, I am surrounded by my friends.

After a while, King Qinguang clears his throat again. We all look up at him. "Now, we need to deal with the rest of you, then maybe we can finally have some peace in my court once again."

"Assign my chefs back to me and be done with it!" King Wuguan calls out.

King Qinguang shoots him a dirty look. "Silence! This is not a democracy. Theo Tan, Namita Singh, Danny Chang, none of you are technically dead."

At some point, Namita, Danny, and I find ourselves holding hands. Kai twines herself around my neck, and Xiaohua stays close to Danny while Fragrant Sausage stands between Namita's feet and yawns.

"You have willfully ignored the laws of the living and come down here and disrupted all of Diyu's courts. Do you have any idea how much trouble you've caused? We're going to have to work overtime hours to fulfill our quota for the season; otherwise we'll never hear the end of it from the Jade Emperor."

"Oh," I squeak. I wasn't expecting this much sternness from King Qinguang after the kindness he had shown Jamie. Now I have no idea what to expect from him.

King Qinguang picks up his gavel. "I charge you, Theo Tan, and you, Namita Singh, and you, Danny Chang, to be banished—"

Oh gods. Namita's and Danny's hands go slick in mine. I don't blame them; I'm sweating like—like Fragrant Sausage.

"—back to the human world, where you will live out the rest of your lives. You are not allowed to come back until after your human years have ended." The gavel slams down with a loud thud.

There's a moment of uncertainty because the sentence was delivered with such cold solemnity that my brain was expecting bad news. I stare at my friends, who are looking just as confused, then as one, the actual words sink in, and our faces clear. We all break into grins and hug one another, laughing and cheering.

"Do you mean it, Your Majesty?" I gasp, still hugging my friends.

"How dare you question His Majesty's decree!" the demon assistant squawks.

A corner of King Qinguang's mouth twitches with what looks suspiciously like a smile, but he quickly recovers and assumes his usual stern expression. "Yes. Now do not dally. We have much to do. Come, all of you." He raises a hand, his palm already glowing with a vibrant green light.

Hand in hand, we all approach. King Qinguang places his hand above us and mutters a few words. The lush green light swells out of his palm, flowing down over us, and I can smell grass and flowers and verdant greens. I can feel warmth on my skin, not the sickly heat of lava pools or pits of fire, but the gentle warmth of the spring sun. And with all my being, I am grateful to be alive. I miss the human world, and all of the mess and chaos that come with it. I am ready to go back. A smile spreads slowly across my face, like honey, and I close my eyes, letting the green light swallow me whole.

When I next open my eyes, we're in Muir Woods, surrounded by majestic redwoods and damp grass. We stand there for a moment in silence, just blinking and breathing in the earthy smell of leaves and brown soil and moist air around us.

"We're back," Namita breathes, and the sound of her voice breaks the spell. We all grin at each other.

"We are!" I laugh, and now we're all laughing and whooping and hugging one another.

Then Namita pulls a fist back and punches me in the shoulder.

"Ow, what the—"

Tears shine in her eyes. "I am SO mad at you, Theo. I can't believe you were going to sacrifice your own life, and you didn't even tell us, and—argh!" She is practically snarling at me.

"Yeah, seriously dude," Danny mutters. "That's messed up. You're not alone, you know?"

"We literally just went through hell and back for you," Namita says, jabbing a finger at my chest. "I hope you get once and for all that we're part of each other's lives for GOOD."

I can taste tears at the back of my throat. My entire body feels warm; even the hairs on my arms feel like they're singed. Namita and Danny are right. We've been through hell and back. There is no way that we're not going to be friends forever. I have an actual ride-or-die team. And I can't express how freaking amazing that feels.

"I can't believe it!" Danny half shouts, laughing through his tears as he wraps his arms around Xiaohua. Kai untwines herself from me and hops onto the ground and looks up at Danny.

"You did well," she says.

Danny beams down at her. "Never, not in a million, gazillion years, did I think I would be so glad to have you by my side in Diyu."

Kai preens. "I am rather an asset, aren't I?"

Xiaohua rolls her eyes, but Danny laughs. "Yes, Kai. You really saved the day, especially at King Wuguan's court."

To my surprise, Kai turns her head to one side, as if somewhat bashful. "You should give yourself more credit, kid. You're not as pathetic as you seem."

"Gee, thanks." Danny and Kai grin at each other, and I feel such a huge weight lifting from my heart because it's clear to me that Danny is fully recovered. He's standing as tall as ever, his chest puffed out, and his smile is sure and strong. He's back to the confident Danny I first knew him as, but better now because there is no longer the cruel glint in his eyes. He no longer feels the need to put others down because he's less insecure about himself. And Kai was the one who got him through that.

"I must admit," Xiaohua grumbles, "that in the end, perhaps the fox isn't so much a force of evil as much as . . . a force of chaotic good."

Kai preens.

"Unbelievable," I whisper to Kai as she slinks back to me, and she side-eyes me. "I know I am," I mimic at the same time as she says those exact words. We look at each other and laugh.

"It's been . . . rather a long and twisty journey," she says.

"Yeah, it really has." For a while, we don't speak. Not because there's nothing to say, but because there is just so much that can't be conveyed by words alone. We merely stand there, shaking our heads slightly and smiling through our tears, and I know she knows exactly what I'm thinking.

"Are you okay?" she says softly, her golden fox eyes roaming my face with concern.

I nod. "I will be. Are you okay?" Because it's not just me who has lost a big chunk of his heart. Kai was Jamie's companion. In some ways, she was even closer to him than I was.

She lowers her head, casting her eyes down. "He's gone. I can feel it. Before, there was this . . . weight that was tethering me to his memory. Our bond was broken, but a single thread remained, and I could always sense it, tugging at me, reminding me that I still had a job to do. But now, I feel free." She sighs, her pointy ears drooping slightly. "I miss him, but I know he's going to be all right, and that brings me peace."

"I know what you mean." I know exactly the heartbreaking freedom she speaks of, the empty weightlessness of it. It's sad and peaceful at the same time. I hold out my arm, and Kai uses it to hop up to my shoulders. I smile as she settles into her usual position, twining her warm, bushy tails around my neck like a scarf.

"Ugh, this place is way too chilly for my bones," a small voice grumbles.

We all look down. From behind Namita's legs, Fragrant Sausage peers at us. When she sees us staring, she frowns. "What are you all looking at?"

"Er . . . ," Kai mutters. "Why are you here? You are technically very dead. I mean, you couldn't be more dead than, you know, being ground up with spices and turned into a fragrant sausage."

Fragrant Sausage narrows her eyes at Kai. "I decided I've had enough of watching humans suffer in hell, didn't I? I'd rather watch them suffer here in the human world."

"And King Qinguang let you go, just like that?" Namita says.

"I told you: I'm special! He said I should come along and keep an eye on you lot."

"This pig has way too much sass," Kai says.

Xiaohua snorts. "Now you know how we feel around you."

Kai lifts her upper lip to show her fangs at Xiaohua, but the air between them isn't charged with tension the way it usually is. It must be because Xiaohua can sense the new bond between Kai and Danny and is no longer on edge, feeling like she has to protect Danny from Kai. Just as I think that, Danny reaches out a fist for Kai to bump.

Namita bends over and scoops Fragrant Sausage into her arms. "Fragrant Sausage! I'm so happy you got to come with us!"

"Don't be too happy—who knows if I'm staying? If you bore me, I'm out of here."

"I know," laughs Namita, squeezing Fragrant Sausage affectionately. "But you and I are going to have some wild adventures!"

Fragrant Sausage gives a cynical snort but accepts the cuddle grudgingly. We all smile at one another and start walking.

Danny grins at us. "Hey, you guys realize something? I was right about archery saving the day."

Everyone groans, even Xiaohua. Then we all start laughing.

"My head was in Niu Mo Wang's flesh," Kai grumbles through her laughter. "Buried so deep! Ugh!"

"And when you started wriggling away when they were trying to pull you out!" Namita giggles. "I thought I would die laughing."

Our stories flow as smoothly as rivers do. We're so eager to share all the details of our incredible adventure in Diyu. By the time we get out of the woods, the sun is rising. We stand there, overlooking the bay and the Golden Gate Bridge below us. Half the bay is still shrouded in dark purple, but as the sun rises, it's as though the blanket of darkness is pulled back and everything is awash in warm golden light. It feels like more than just a new day. It feels like a brand-new start.

Kai reaches down from my shoulders, and I put my hand up and clasp her paw. Our eyes meet and a world of empathy passes between us. I know without having to say a single word that she sees the shifting colors of every emotion I'm feeling. And though Jamie is gone, we both know that it won't be long before our paths cross his once again. And what a beautiful thing it is to realize that all of us are now and forevermore intertwined, our souls interlacing to make an endless, marvelous pattern that will go on and on and on until the end of time.

THE END

ACKNOWLEDGMENTS

This is the first time I have ever written the words "The End" on a series, and I have to say there is nothing quite like the bittersweet feeling that comes with closing the door on characters I've spent so much time with. I hope that one day I may revisit Kai's and Theo's beautiful, dangerous world once more, but for now, this is where we part ways.

Theo Tan and the Fox Spirit was the book that got me my agent, Katelyn Detweiler, and without Katelyn, I wouldn't have the career I have now. I have Theo to thank for Katelyn's wonderful presence in my life!

Katelyn was the one who found the perfect home for Theo and his friends at Feiwel and Friends, and I'm so grateful for the chance to work with my brilliant editor, Holly West. Holly's notes are always on point, and thanks to her, this story has been elevated so much more beyond the mess of a draft that I sent her way. And she does so with all the patience and grace in the world.

Thank you to all of my writing friends who have seen Theo's journey through from beginning to end, you know who you are. And most of all, thank you to my husband, Mike, whose confidence in me never wavered, even though it took me ten long years to get my first book deal. To Emmie and Rosie, I can't wait for the day to come when I will be able to read Theo and Kai's story to you.

AMBIGUOUS ANNIVERSARY

The Bicentennial of the International Slave Trade Bans

Edited by

DAVID T. GLEESON
and **SIMON LEWIS**

The University of South Carolina Press

© 2012 University of South Carolina

Published by the University of South Carolina Press
Columbia, South Carolina 29208

www.sc.edu/uscpress

Manufactured in the United States of America

21 20 19 18 17 16 15 14 13 12   10 9 8 7 6 5 4 3 2 1

Library of Congress Cataloging-in-Publication Data

Ambiguous anniversary : the bicentennial of the international slave trade bans /
  edited by David T. Gleeson and Simon Lewis.
       p. cm. — (The Carolina Lowcountry and the Atlantic world)
    Includes bibliographical references and index.
    ISBN 978-1-61117-096-2 (cloth : alk. paper)
    1. Slave trade—North America—History. 2. Slave trade—Great Britain—
History. 3. Slave trade—Atlantic Ocean Region—History. 4. Slavery—North America—
History. 5. Slavery—Great Britain—History. 6. Antislavery movements—North America—
History. 7. Antislavery movements—Great Britain—History. I. Gleeson, David T. II. Lewis,
Simon, 1960-
    HT1049.A43 2012
    306.3′62097—dc23

                                                                          2012011634

Portions of David Gleeson's essay are republished, with permission of the editors, from his article "Securing the 'Interests' of the South: John Mitchel, A. G. Magrath, and the Reopening of the
Transatlantic Slave Trade," *American Nineteenth Century History* 11 (November 2010): 279–97.

This book was printed on recycled paper with 30 percent postconsumer waste content.

CONTENTS

CONTENTS

FOREWORD

1807/1808–2007/2008

James Walvin

The bicentenaries of British and American abolition (2007–8) offered contrasting examples of historical commemorations. The 2007 British commemorations of the abolition of the slave trade involved an innumerable and varied round of events, culminating in a service in Westminster Abbey before the Queen and her senior government ministers. By contrast events in the United States the following year were relatively small scale and muted. In Britain institutions, from national galleries to local schools, commemorated 1807 in their own distinctive way. The British government lent its encouragement and help, the Palace of Westminster hosted its own exhibition, the BBC brought its unrivaled cultural influence to bear, and the Heritage Lottery Fund poured millions of pounds into supporting the commemorations. The end result was a quite remarkable year for anyone interested in British history and the way it is periodically celebrated in the public arena.

But why 1807–8? What was so special about ending the slave trade? How, for example, should we balance British abolition against Britain's dominance of the slave trade before 1807? And of equal significance, how do we measure the significance of 1807–8 against the continuing flow of enslaved Africans across the Atlantic after 1808?

In the slow buildup to 2007 in Britain, those keen to commemorate abolition raised these and many other historical questions in the committees and groups convened across the length and breadth of the nation to plan the commemorations. In the process serious, substantive discussion took place about the significance of 1807 and ensured that most of the commemorations emerged stripped of any sense of triumphalism. Conscious of the need to avoid accusations of merely organizing a "Wilberfest" (an event to honor, yet again, the work of William Wilberforce), most organizers of commemorations succeeded in offering thoughtful, judicious events. More than that, the commemorations were to have some long-term (and quite unpredicted) consequences. They helped, for example, to establish the history of the slave trade and its abolition as part of the nation's "National Curriculum" in English schools. They also prompted a number of important and continuing research projects into the links between regional and local British history and the world of Atlantic slavery.

The basic outcome of the 2007 commemorations, however, was an affirmation of the importance of the slave trade and slavery in British history (though the two were often confused in popular discussion in 2007). To scholars and specialists in the fields, this may seem merely to be stating the obvious. Yet it needs to be stressed that even in academic circles, Atlantic slavery was for too long thought to be a marginal specialist interest that belonged to the Africanists, oceanic historians, and students of the Americas. Looked at from Britain, slavery appeared exotic: overseas, in Africa and the Americas—over there—far removed from the ebb and flow of British historical experience. Yet the abundance of recent scholarship—and the events of 2007—confirmed in lavish detail that the world of Atlantic slavery was integral to British historical experience. Time and again a local library, a local school, or a major metropolitan public institution (the British Library, Parliament, the National Gallery, the Victoria and Albert Museum) offered their own distinctive view of the formative links between Britain and the world of Atlantic slavery. It could be traced through a single picture (a portrait of a famous figure whose eminence was shaped by slavery), via a single commodity (the British addiction to slave-grown sugar), or by telling a local story (Liverpool's rise to maritime greatness on the back of her slave ships).

This flurry of commemorative activity in 2007 was of a kind and a range that surpassed other historical commemorations, even though the British have a national penchant for celebrating certain aspects of their historical past. Popular commemorations tend so often to focus on great British victories and triumphs in the face of adversity: Nelson's defining victory over the French at Trafalgar, the Battle of Britain, royal anniversaries of various sorts, the death of the last surviving soldier from World War I. These and many more speak to a certain view of the past—and to a taste for a particular kind of British history. Yet 2007 opened up an entirely different appreciation of the past.

At first many might have felt that 2007 was, once again, merely a reprise of that familiar myth of the British at their virtuous best: bringing an undoubted evil (the slave trade) to an end. But how could one explain the massive British role in Atlantic slavery in the years before 1807? And if the Abolition Act of 1807 was worth commemorating, what about the many acts of Parliament, passed in the century before, that licensed, controlled, regulated, and encouraged the slave trade? The commemorations, then, raised difficult questions not only about historical commemoration, but also about the very nature of British history.

The American remembrance of the bicentenary of slave trade abolition in 2008 stood in sharp contrast to that of Great Britain. The American rejection of the slave trade in 1808, like the British, did not extend to slavery itself. Both nations felt they could thereafter refuse the commercial attractions of the Atlantic slave trade. But neither felt the need to end slavery itself, either in the British Caribbean or on the

American mainland. Moreover the emergence of cotton slavery in the expansive new South after 1800 actually strengthened the case for North American slavery. The new cotton plantations, however, did not require enslaved labor imported from Africa. The slave trade in the United States was overland, not oceanic. Thus it seemed easy to decry the Atlantic slave trade (because it was no longer required). The American slave trade consisted of local-born slaves, moved overland and by river to the booming cotton industry of the South. This apparent contradiction (ending the slave trade while supporting slavery) was similarly reflected in Britain. An abolitionist nation, fierce in its denunciations of the slave ships, nonetheless clung to its slaveholding sugar plantations for a full thirty years after abolition in 1807.

That both the United States and Britain distinguished abolition of the slave trade from emancipation of slaves has, for many scholars, undermined the moral foundations of abolition itself. Such critics, in their turn, have drawn attention to the economics, not the morality, of abolition. Did both nations turn against the slave trade simply (or even largely) because that trade had run out of economic steam? Needless to say, such simple questions mask a complexity of historical arguments that continue with unabated vigor to the present day.

American abolition in 1808 emerged from a totally different political and economic context than the British abolition of 1807. Likewise the U.S. bicentenary was utterly different—and low key. In many places it passed without notice or comment. On one level this may simply reflect the relative unimportance of the slave trade to the United States in 1808. Abolition made no great difference to North America. That could not, however, be said of Britain in 1807. (If in doubt, read the outraged squeals from Liverpool's merchants in the run-up to 1807.) Yet there seems to be much more than this to the muted American response in 2008. Here, however, we enter contemporary political culture. The cultural and political differences between a unitary Britain and a federal United States made it almost impossible to imagine a national commemoration of abolition in the latter in 2008. Regardless of ideological inclination, in the absence of a national curriculum and a national broadcaster, there was no mechanism in place to promote an integrated commemoration at the national level. Nothing in 2008 could begin to touch the national psyche as did the extraordinary television phenomenon of *Roots* in 1977. Instead the United States has responded to the history of abolition only piecemeal and sporadically—with stamps honoring such heroes of abolitionism as Frederick Douglass (1967), Sojourner Truth (1986), and Harriet Tubman (1978); a smattering of recent apologies by states for slavery; varied state educational requirements governing teaching about slavery and the slave trade; individual conferences and symposia sponsored by federal and state humanities councils; and so on.

For all that there are rich possibilities for serious comparative and transatlantic reflections on 2007–8. It was with those intellectual prospects in mind that the College of Charleston, as part of its continuing scholarly program, gathered together a

group of international scholars to discuss the complex transatlantic historical ramifications of abolition. Here in revised and edited form are the contributions to that
scholarly event. They offer, inevitably, a set of distinct studies. In effect they form
parts of a historical jigsaw that when pieced together provide a coherent shape and
begin to address some of the important intellectual questions raised by the events
of 2007–8. Those questions range far and wide, from the local to the general, from
the theoretical to the specific. They take us from the edge of American frontier settlement to the broad contours of contemporary slave-based economics and from
the minutiae of parliamentary arguments to considerations of gender and childhood. Considered in their totality, they offer a broad appreciation of the historical
challenges posed by the events of 2007 and 2008.

What follows is in effect an opportunity to explore the wider intellectual problems posed by historical commemorations and the current issues that lurk beneath
the surface of what seem, at first glance, straightforward historical anniversaries.
The essays also allow us to think more closely about the connections between the
academic and the popular, between the worlds of scholarship and public history.
In the process we might begin to appreciate the realities and mythologies of the
shaping of historical memory—on both sides of the Atlantic.

ACKNOWLEDGMENTS

This collection is the scholarly culmination of the Carolina Lowcountry and Atlantic World Program's commemoration of the banning of the international slave trade by the United Kingdom and the United Sates in 1807 and 1808, respectively. The commemoration involved broad and wide collaboration with a number of agencies, individuals, and institutions, all of whom we wish to thank.

We wish to express particular gratitude to the following agencies: the Avery Research Center for African American History and Culture, the Charleston County Public Library, Charleston County Park and Recreation Commission, the City of Charleston, the Convention and Visitors Bureau (Charleston), Drayton Hall, Friends of Sierra Leone, the Gibbes Museum of Art, the Gullah Geechee Nation, Middleton Place, the National Park Service, the Penn Center, the Pink House, the South Carolina African American Heritage Commission, the South Carolina Heritage Corridor, the South Carolina Historical Society, South Carolina Parks, Recreation, and Tourism, and the West Africa Council of South Carolina.

Among the many individuals who were associated with the project in various ways, we would like to express our thanks to the following: Jane Aldrich, Tony Burroughs, Nicholas Butler, John Carpenter, Toni Carrier, Kwame Dawes, George Estes, Rob Forbes, Rhoda Green, Harlan Greene, Bill Grimke-Drayton, Shawn Halifax, Lawrence Hill, Joseph Inikori, Joe James, Paul Lovejoy, the Reverend Christian King, George McDaniel, Wevonneda Minis, Carolyn Morales, Aspen Olmsted, Joseph Opala, Brenda Marie Osbey, Bing Pan, Bernard Powers, Dale Rosengarten, Tracey Todd, Craig Tuminaro, Leo Twiggs, Carolee Williams, and many more.

Funds to support the various projects came from the CLAW program and its Wachovia Foundation, and from the College of Charleston's Office of Institutional Diversity, as well as from the Post and Courier Foundation and the Humanities Council SC, which fully lives up to its motto to inspire, engage, and enrich. We wish to thank deans David Cohen, Sam Hines, and Cynthia Lowenthal for their continued institutional support of the CLAW program. We could not have coped with the logistics of such a wide-ranging commemoration without the remarkable skills and unflappable patience of Lisa Randle. Hope Watson provided additional enthusiastic and efficient assistance. College of Charleston graduate students Charles Wexler and Kate Jenkins helped enormously with the conference that spawned this book. Thanks, too, go to Maggie Lally for invaluable editorial assistance in preparing the final manuscript. Since he moved to England, David Gleeson has received great support from his colleagues at Northumbria University, especially the associate dean for research, Don MacRaild; department head David Walker; and history research lead Sylvia Ellis.

The volume's existence, however, depends on the scholarship, commitment, and patience of our contributors. We would like especially to thank James Walvin for offering valuable suggestions and comments on the manuscript and for providing his insightful foreword. We are similarly grateful to the University of South Carolina Press's anonymous reviewers, whose detailed and judicious comments on individual essays and on the shape of the book as a whole led to some valuable fine tuning. Alexander Moore shepherded us through the whole process with his habitual care and generosity of spirit.

For their ongoing support, the editors would also like to thank our families and friends on both sides of the Atlantic.

INTRODUCTION

Ambiguous Anniversary

DAVID T. GLEESON AND SIMON LEWIS

In 1807, on March 2 and March 25, respectively, the U.S. Congress and the British Parliament both passed laws banning the international slave trade. Despite having been passed into law some three weeks earlier than the British law, the U.S. law only came into effect on January 1, 1808, eight months after the British ban's implementation. Two hundred years later, in March 2007, there was worldwide commemoration of the bicentenary of the U.K. ban. Yet in the United States, the bicentennial of its ban was barely recognized. Indeed in an op-ed piece in the *New York Times* on December 30, 2007, noted U.S. historian Eric Foner commented on the irony that in a society "awash in historical celebrations . . . one significant milestone has gone strangely unnoticed: the 200th anniversary of Jan. 1, 1808, when the importation of slaves into the United States was prohibited."[1] Foner overstated his case, however. Had his ears been attuned to what was going on in Charleston, South Carolina, or had he literally been tuned in to the BBC World Service, he might have known that when the BBC came to Charleston on March 25, 2007, as a part of their year-long reporting on worldwide commemoration of the passage of the British ban, they found a "home-made but heartfelt" outdoor interfaith memorial service, the public curtain-raiser for Charleston's extensive and sustained commemoration of the U.S. ban.[2] While the service could not match the pomp and circumstance of the service in Westminster Abbey on the same day (participants in which included a delegation from South Carolina), it certainly had as much poignancy: held on the aptly named Liberty Square, a National Park Service site close to Gadsden's Wharf, where many enslaved Africans first disembarked on the continent of North America, it culminated in a procession (singing a South African freedom anthem) to the water's edge, where sprigs of rosemary were scattered into the harbor in memory of the unnumbered dead of the Middle Passage. Joining the BBC reporters, who came from both the Washington and London offices of the organization, were local Charleston print and television journalists. No reports, however, appeared in statewide South Carolina media, and there was similarly no national news coverage of the event.[3]

Why this discrepancy in commemoration and coverage? As demonstrated by the essays by Kenneth Morgan and John Oldfield that bracket this collection, the passage and enactment of the two laws by two of the most significant parties to the slave trade on either side of the Atlantic were, despite their near simultaneity, quite independent of each other. Although set broadly within a similar emergent discourse of human rights, each was driven by dissimilar processes. As the culmination of a popular abolitionist movement that had been building for well over twenty years, the British act might be seen as the world's first ever successful campaign for international human rights. Regardless of the economic calculus and consequences, the law's passage was ultimately the triumph of a movement propelled by a clear assertion of a moral imperative. The enslaved African was a brother and a man, and if Britons could not condone their own enslavement and forced transatlantic transportation, they could not condone the enslavement and shipment of Africans.[4]

In the United States, as Morgan and Mercantini show in the first two chapters, the moral temperature was somewhat lower, as numerous individual states had already banned the trade, and the signing of the federal act was the seemingly inevitable constitutional outcome of the twenty-year deferral agreed to at the Constitutional Convention of 1787. As Morgan writes, the passage of the U.S. act was a relatively "subdued process"; although voting "had been preceded by vigorous debates," the act was passed by an unusually clear, almost unanimous margin of 113 to 5. Even in Charleston, whence had come the Constitutional Convention's delegates most implacably opposed to federal action against the slave trade and where traders had brought in unprecedented numbers of enslaved Africans in the final years before the expected ban, public debate appears to have treated the issue as an economic rather than a moral one. An attempt in the South Carolina House of Representatives to allow legal entry of ships arriving after January 1, 1808, with cargoes of slaves who had embarked well before the deadline was voted down on December 18, 1807, by the solid enough margin of 46 to 32 votes. The *Charleston Times* of December 29, 1807, reprinted verbatim the resolution, which referred not to slaves or the slave trade but simply to "property of sundry merchants and others, good citizens of this state, who are interested in the African trade." From the wording of the resolution, the matter was of no more moral import than legislation concerning the trade in tea or sugar would have been.[5] Remarkably it does not appear to have been a hot-button issue.

These differences, added to the obvious difference that the full achievement of the abolitionists' goals came about gradually through further legislation in the case of the United Kingdom, but only through the violence and terror of civil war in the U.S. case, in part, perhaps, explain the massive discrepancy between the blanket commemoration of abolition in the United Kingdom in 2007 and the relative silence in the United States in 2008, where the bicentenary was, in Foner's words, "one significant milestone [that] has gone strangely unnoticed." Both the passage of the British law and its bicentenary commemoration touched the national psyche in the United Kingdom in ways that their U.S. analogues did not. And while it is clear why the half-century-long continuation of legalized slavery—including the legal buying and selling of enslaved people and their transportation within and between slaveholding states, followed by the national trauma of the Civil War—might have eclipsed the 1808 ban on international slave trading, nonetheless, as Foner argues, the passage and enactment of the 1807–8 ban is still "worth commemorating not only for what it directly accomplished, but for helping to save the United States from a history even more terrible than the Civil War that eventually rid our country of slavery."[6]

Commemorating the Abolition Act in Great Britain in 2007 in sites whose wealth had depended on the trade, and finding the appropriate mode and tone, was, as John Oldfield shows in the ending essay, complicated enough, and not without strong criticism whenever it veered toward self-congratulation and avoided issues of reparations. In Charleston, where the Carolina Lowcountry and Atlantic World (CLAW) program at the College of Charleston coordinated the most comprehensive public commemoration of the 1808 ban, the question of how to address the commemoration was also vexed. Charleston was the single most important port of entry for enslaved Africans into continental North America, and hence arguably the birthplace of African America. From the early eighteenth century through the Civil War, Charleston and the surrounding lowcountry had a majority or close to majority black population. After the war and into the twentieth century, despite the "Great Migration" of African Americans to the North, the region retained a sizable black minority. Currently in the tricounty area that includes the city of Charleston, African Americans make up 35.8 percent of the population of Charleston County, 28.1 percent of Berkeley County, and 35.3 percent of Dorchester County. The city of Charleston itself is 33 percent African American, while the black population of the city of North Charleston holds a slim majority, at slightly more than 50 percent.[7]

Slavery, its history, and its legacy are thus live issues here, felt in the skin that people are in. Yet very few locally had even heard of the 1808 ban, and many were confused to hear of it, being unable to disentangle the abolition of the slave trade from the abolition of the peculiar institution of slavery as a whole. Commemorating the banning of the international slave trade here in Charleston is not the same as doing so in England, Canada, West Africa, the Caribbean, or anywhere else: there are particular ramifications at this particular node of the Atlantic world that make this inquiry unique and perhaps uniquely important now as the United States has as its president a man whose father was African and his mother Euro-American, with families across multiple seas.

When the CLAW program first announced its conference that would be the academic centerpiece of Charleston's commemoration, initial announcements referred to the conference as "The 'End' of the Atlantic Slave Trade: A Bicentenary

Inquiry." The quotation marks around *End* were intended to do quite a lot of work, indicating the organizers' skepticism about the impact and significance of the ban, on this side of the Atlantic, at least. As plans moved forward, however, it became more and more apparent that to talk about the "end" of the trade, whether qualified by quotation marks or a question mark or any other trick of punctuation, was inappropriate and even in some ways misleading. Since we had been arguing that the ban on the international trade was a step in the long and painful process toward emancipation of black people in the United States and hence an essential step in the national story of liberation, we figured that it would be better to replace *end* with *ending,* using the present infinitive form to indicate our awareness of the fact that the international slave trade did not end in 1807 or in 1808, nor even at the end of the U.S. Civil War or when Brazil finally outlawed slavery in 1888—in fact the international trade in enslaved people, although universally illegal, still continues, and its continuation is frequently brought up by those who would rather not have us pay attention to the particularly racialized form of the transatlantic trade. Commemorating the 1807 and 1808 bans and celebrating the success of the intellectual, spiritual, and political movements that made them possible was and is not just an academic exercise, passively looking backward to history, but in some ways needed to be construed as an activist process inspiring a new generation of campaigners committed to the abolition of (illegal) slavery and the slave trade worldwide.[8]

The central ambiguity of commemorating an "end" of something that is not itself over (let alone of something whose legacies are still very much with us) is what led us to title this collection of essays *Ambiguous Anniversary.* In looking specifically at the U.S. ban in 1808, we are drawing attention to a whole range of attendant ambiguities. As we have already mentioned above, although the ban might be seen as a triumph for the abolitionist movements on both sides of the Atlantic, it did not in itself bring about the abolition of slavery. Neither was it enforced with complete commitment or success. David Brion Davis points out, for instance, that owing to the "high rate of natural reproduction" of the enslaved population in the United States, "the outlawing of the Atlantic slave trade did not weaken the system" of slavery in general. Davis also points out that the "Atlantic slave trade declined by only 5 percent" between 1826 and 1850, and that "some three million Africans, or about one quarter of the grand total exported, were shipped off to the Americas after 1807, despite the militant efforts of the British navy to suppress this mostly illegal commerce."[9] David Gleeson's essay shows how far from irrevocable the ban was considered in South Carolina especially and the Deep South generally, and how an Irishman committed to fighting for freedom from Britain could prove to be one of the strongest advocates for reopening the trade as late as the 1850s. The essays here by Peter Coclanis and Louis Kyriakoudes and by Gregory O'Malley show how the transatlantic trade was merely a portion of the American side of the trade as a whole, and as Steven Deyle reiterates in this volume, we know that the ban on the international trade stimulated the internal trade within the slaveholding states.[10]

Likewise while the abolitionist movement during the Age of Revolution drove the gradual expansion of the idea of freedom in the English-speaking Atlantic world prior to 1807,[11] the period between 1808 and 1860 in the United States saw the reverse effect. Thus between 1760 and 1860, we see on the one hand the foundation of Freetown and the colony of Sierra Leone and the rise of numerous black intellectuals and political leaders (whether we consider them African, African American, Afro-British, or Atlantic Creole), including Olaudah Equiano, Phillis Wheatley, Francis Williams, Ottobah Cugoano, and Toussaint Louverture;[12] but on the other hand we see stricter boundaries of nineteenth-century concepts of race reinforcing the racial aspect of U.S. slavery and hardening the battle lines between the free and the unfree. Similarly ambiguous processes occurred in parts of Latin America.[13]

Issues of race and racism, then, did not just dissipate with the banning of the transatlantic slave trade or even slavery itself. Key to the endurance of a system of racial supremacy was the memory of slavery. For many in the United States, its ugly side was ignored, and the myth of the "happy slave" burgeoned, along with the view that Africa was uncivilized and thus slaves had been done a "favor" in their removal from a "barbarous Africa."[14] Black scholars such as W. E. B. Du Bois challenged this view from its very inception, but it took the birth of anti-imperial movements in Africa and the civil rights movement in the United States to undermine it seriously. While academics have adjusted their views to post–civil rights historiography, changing public perceptions has been more difficult. In Charleston, for example, there is still an acknowledgment gap in the public memory of the city's history in general, and particularly when it comes to slavery.[15] The CLAW program and the Avery Research Center for African American History and Culture at the College of Charleston have attempted to fill this gap, as indeed the city has with its support of the Moja Arts Festival and the planned International African American Museum. These efforts do not, however, solve the issue of the acknowledgment gap or always explain fully the reason for its existence. Sometimes just acknowledging something that happened is not enough. Mere recognition may ignore deeper, more problematic, and more controversial questions. For example, owing to its popularization by Steven Spielberg, the *Amistad* affair stands out as an incident where the judicial system of the United States can be and has been invoked in national self-congratulation on the subject of slavery. During the late spring and early summer of 2008, two of Charleston's most high-profile cultural festivals included *Amistad*-related events. The annual Spoleto Festival USA featured as its headline opera only the second-ever run of *Amistad* by Anthony Davis, while the annual HarborFest featured the U.S. "homecoming" of the re-created vessel the *Freedom Schooner Amistad,* following its circum-Atlantic voyage from New Haven, Connecticut, that took in stops in slave trade–related ports in Canada, England, Portugal, Sierra Leone, and the Caribbean.[16]

A number of spin-off events were associated with these high-profile visits. Among these one in particular revealed the specific ambiguities involved in self-congratulatory commemoration of the U.S. Supreme Court's *Amistad* decision of 1841. On May 31, 2008, the Avery Research Center held a roundtable discussion titled "Expert Opinions" involving an impressive array of legal experts and historians, two black and five white, including South Carolina Supreme Court justice the Honorable Donald W. Beatty and South Carolina's first woman chief justice, Jean Toal. The audience, too, was mixed, both racially and between locals and out-of-towners. The panelists' presentations and their responses to audience questions were unanimous in their acknowledgment that the Supreme Court had made the right decision, both legally and morally, and the tone of the discussion was more than professionally civil; rather it was positively convivial, even lighthearted from time to time. One question, however, quite late in the proceedings created an immediate and jarring frostiness. A member of the audience—local, African American, identifying himself as a "native Charlestonian"—got to his feet and brought up the r-word, *reparation*. At that point, already quite well on into the event, Chief Justice Toal and the others on the panel sidestepped the question: the panel discussion had been about the *Amistad* case. Her effective ruling out of order of the question revealed that while we may indeed have come a long way in our ability to deal with issues such as slavery and race, a key ambiguity remains: although it is now widely accepted that the slave trade and slavery were a crime against humanity, they are apparently crimes without a perpetrator, or at least crimes whose perpetrators are beyond the reach of justice.[17]

In the face of these and other imponderables, therefore, it is clear that the present collection, while answering *some* questions relating to the 1807 and 1808 bans on the transatlantic slave trade, will also raise new ones for scholars, students, and the general public to grapple with in the continued debates over the meaning of history in people's lives. The whole subject is full of ambiguities. We have organized this book to acknowledge some of these. The first two chapters, "Proscription by Degrees: The Ending of the African Slave Trade to the United States" by Kenneth Morgan and Jonathan Mercantini's "'Most Contemptible in the Union': South Carolina, Slavery and the Constitution," examine the ambiguities in the creation of the American ban in 1808. Morgan's essay gives a good overview of the various twists and turns that led up to the 1808 ban, countering the view of it as purely a fait accompli when first hinted at with a twenty-year reprieve for the trade in Article I, Section 9, of the United States Constitution. Morgan highlights what a long and complex process it was and not just, as he puts, it a "Whiggish" march toward liberty. Mercantini's piece digs into the murky origins of the ban in the Constitutional Convention of 1787 and how and why South Carolina split from the upper

South and dug in its heels against an immediate ban and, indeed, continued to complain about any future ban. Yet in a seemingly contradictory fashion, the state itself had banned and would continue to ban the trade during parts of the early national period. Mercantini explains these ambiguities in white South Carolinians' attitudes toward the international slave trade.

The chapters by Wilma King and Inge Dornan, on slave children and on women in the slave trade, respectively, challenge what we typically think of the trade itself. Thanks to the Spielberg movie, the image of Cinque on the *Amistad* dominates the popular image of Africans in the Middle Passage. King and Dornan strongly counter this view and emphasize that issues of age and gender must be taken more seriously, both in the trade's impact and in the opposition to it.

Greg O'Malley's work on "continued forced migrations" in his essay as well as Louis Kyriakoudes and Peter Coclanis's work on the "M-Factor"—that is, migration—indicate clearly the ambiguities of the "Middle Passage." O'Malley makes a strong case that the Middle Passage did not end geographically at the harbor wall nor historically after the 1807 and 1808 bans. On the contrary the initial journey into slavery extended beyond the American and Caribbean ports when the trade was still legal; the trauma for enslaved Africans did not end when they had crossed the Atlantic. Even traders and owners recognized that the passage did not end with disembarkation, as they tried to spread the slave interest into the interior from its original bases in the tidewater and lowcountry areas.

Kyriakoudes and Coclanis make a case for considering continued forced migration of slaves as a key element in understanding the sectional economic differences of the late antebellum era. By focusing on the mobility of labor, forced and otherwise, they show that the movement of whites and blacks from the Atlantic states to the Old Southwest can be linked together much more closely. They emphasize that many white settlers brought slaves with them, rather than just moving and seeking slaves from the upper South to fulfill their labor needs. Thus slavery, through the forced migration of African Americans, was in the DNA of the white move West and settlement there. The fact that the 1808 ban did not stop the spread of slavery west challenges the view of it as a stepping stone to emancipation. In "An Ambiguous Legacy: The Closing of the African Slave Trade and America's Own Middle Passage," Steven Deyle examines this ambiguity in a broader perspective. Deyle acknowledges that the traumas of the "American Middle Passage" make commemoration of the 1808 ban a tricky one. Despite the ambiguities, however, he believes the ban was historically significant and should be recognized, as indeed it was by contemporary abolitionists, as the first serious step toward emancipation.

The continued slave trade after 1808 had serious physical and psychological implications, but it also created ideological ones. The ambiguous issues of "blackness" and "whiteness" can be studied in the slave trade context. In their respective essays, Jean-Pierre Le Glaunec and David Gleeson indicate that racial identities hardened after the slave trade ban. Noting that connections between racial identity and the ban on the African slave trade have gone largely unnoticed by historians, Le Glaunec goes out on a speculative limb to argue that the abrupt end of the African slave trade in January 1808 dramatically accelerated the formation of a shared sense of blackness in early American Louisiana. This shared sense of a black identity, Le Glaunec suggests, replaced earlier, narrower affinities based on place of birth (African or Creole), affinities that were further complicated by even narrower conceptions of ethnicity and colorism. Gleeson's interest, by contrast, is with a converse consolidation of whiteness. Arguing that the attempts to reopen the international trade in the 1850s give insight into the racial identity of Irish Americans, Gleeson looks at the actions and rhetoric of two community leaders in the South to highlight that rather than marking a beginning of the end to the racial ideology of slavery, the banning of the trade actually hardened definitions of white racial identity into which Irish immigrants could integrate easily.

We conclude where we began: with commemoration. The introduction to this essay highlighted how the commemoration of the bicentennial of the U.S. ban in 2008 was, to put it mildly, understated. Apart from our own efforts in Charleston, there were no major public events or press coverage. As James Walvin's foreword clearly shows, there was a huge contrast in the amount and scope of 2007 bicentennial events in the United Kingdom with the effort the following year in the United States. John Oldfield, in the final chapter, "2007 Revisited: Commemoration, Ritual, and British Transatlantic Slavery," recognizes the "unparalleled explosion of interest" in the bicentennial, but he also acknowledges how problematic, and indeed controversial, aspects of the U.K. commemoration were. New issues on how and why the ban occurred in 1807 arose, as did questions on how self-congratulatory the British could be over it. Indeed it seems that the public events and exhibitions of 1807 have opened up a whole new set of questions that have "forced Britons to examine the paradoxes embedded in national histories." We hope that the essays collected here will help all those who read them confront these paradoxes, too, and enrich their understanding of the resonance historical issues have in contemporary life.

Notes

1. Eric Foner, "Forgotten Step toward Freedom," *New York Times*, December 30, 2007. The *Boston Globe* carried a similar article on June 24, 2008, complaining that "celebrations surrounding the end of the slave trade in this country are muted compared to England's" but mentioned Charleston's efforts; Vanessa E. Jones, "Neglected: Some Say the US Is Ignoring the Commemoration of the Slave Trade's End," *Boston Globe*, June 24, 2008, http://www.boston.com/lifestyle/articles/2008/06/24/neglected/.

2. *The World Today*, March 25, 2007, BBC World Service.

3. There was no coverage in the *State* newspaper based in the capital in Columbia or in any of the national U.S. papers. There was coverage in the local newspaper, the *Post and*

Courier. See Jamie McGee's "Honoring the End of an Injustice: Interfaith Ceremony Marks Anniversary of Atlantic Slave Trade's Abolition," *Charleston Post and Courier,* March 26, 2007. See also Greg Hambrick, "Dark Days," *Charleston City Paper,* March 21, 2008, available at http://www.charlestoncitypaper.com/charleston/feature-zwnj-dark-days/Content?oid=11 09028 (accessed May 13, 2010).

4. The literature on the British ending of the slave trade and slavery is extensive. For more information, see Roger Anstey, *The Atlantic Slave Trade and British Abolition, 1760–1810* (London: Macmillan, 1975); Robin Blackburn, *The Overthrow of Colonial Slavery, 1776–1848* (London: Verso, 1988); Seymour Drescher, *The Mighty Experiment: Free Labor Versus Slavery in British Emancipation* (New York: Oxford University Press, 2002); James Walvin, *England, Slaves and Freedom, 1776–1838* (Jackson: University Press of Mississippi, 1968); Adam Hochschild, *Bury the Chains: The British Struggle to Abolish Slavery* (London: Macmillan, 2005).

5. For an excellent description of South Carolina's reopening of the trade in 1803 and the rush to import slaves before the January 1, 1808, ban, see James A. McMillin, *The Final Victims: Foreign Slave Trade to North America, 1783–1810* (Columbia: University of South Carolina Press, 2004).

6. Foner, "Forgotten Step."

7. For the importance of Charleston in the colonial and revolutionary slave trade, see McMillin, *Final Victims,* 33–38, 53–58, 88–90, 105–7, 124–31; Peter H. Wood, *Black Majority: Negroes in South Carolina from 1670 through the Stono Rebellion* (New York: Knopf, 1974), 333–41; W. Robert Higgins, "Charleston: Terminus and Entrepot of the Colonial Slave Trade," in *The African Diaspora: Interpretive Essays,* ed. Martin L. Kilson and Robert Rotberg (Cambridge, Mass.: Harvard University Press, 1976), 114–31; Elizabeth Donnan, "The Slave Trade into South Carolina before the Revolution," *American Historical Review* 33 (July 1928): 804–28. For the continued importance of African Americans in the Lowcountry, see Peter Coclanis, *The Shadow of a Dream: Economic Life and Death in the South Carolina Low Country, 1670–1920* (New York: Oxford University Press, 1989). For current census figures, see United States Census Bureau, http://quickfacts.census.gov/qfd/states/45000.html, accessed October 1, 2009.

8. In concert with the CLAW program's commemoration of the bicentenary, the College of Charleston's political science department chose human trafficking as the theme for its annual convocation, with a visit from Dr. David Batstone, leader of the Not for Sale campaign, as the keynote event (on the Not for Sale campaign, see http://www.notforsale campaign.org/). Other significant events in and around Charleston have resonated with the eighteenth- and nineteenth-century abolitionist movements, too, as local plantations have held family reunions for descendants of enslaved and of owners, frequently drawing on the respective groups' shared Christian faith to move toward reconciliation, apology, and forgiveness. In this latter regard, they were following in the footsteps of the venerable Anti-Slavery International, formed in 1839 by Thomas Clarkson and others as the Anti-Slavery Society (http://www.antislavery.org/English/what_we_do/our_history.aspx). For more recent organizations and Charleston's local responses, see, for example, the website of Drayton Hall, http://www.draytonhall.org/research/people/; Coming to the Table, http://www.comingtothetable.org/; *Traces of the Trade: A Story of the Deep North,* http://www.traces ofthetrade.org/; Tenisha Waldo, "Making a Connection," *Charleston Post and Courier,*

September 23, 2007, http://www.postandcourier.com/news/2007/sep/23/making_connection 16969/; Wevonneda Minis, "Noisette Family to Gather," *Charleston Post and Courier,* August 22, 2008, http://www.postandcourier.com/news/2008/aug/22/noisette_family_gather51651/; Brian Hicks, "Insight into Slave History," *Charleston Post and Courier,* May 5, 2007, http://www.postandcourier.com/news/2007/may/05/insight_into_slave_history/; Adam Parker, "Voyage to Freedom," *Charleston Post and Courier,* May 25, 2008, http://www.postand courier.com/news/2008/may/25/ama42036/; "Good Morning Lowcountry," *Charleston Post and Courier,* June 21, 2007, http://www.postandcourier.com/news/2007/jun/21/good_morn ing_lowcountry/ (all websites accessed May 14, 2010).

9. David Brion Davis, "The Universal Attractions of Slavery," review of *Abolition: A History of Slavery and Antislavery,* by Seymour Drescher, *New York Review of Books,* December 17, 2009, 72–74.

10. On the strengthening of the internal slave trade in the aftermath of the ban on the international trade, see Steven Deyle, *Carry Me Back: The Domestic Slave Trade in American Life* (New York: Oxford University Press, 2005); Adam Rothman, *Slave Country: American Expansion and the Origins of the Deep South* (Cambridge, Mass.: Harvard University Press, 2007); Walter Johnson, *Soul by Soul: Life inside the Antebellum Slave Market* (Cambridge, Mass.: Harvard University Press, 2001).

11. Davis comments that the Somerset decision of 1772 that set the precedent concluding that slavery was illegal in Great Britain (though not in the empire) was not matched elsewhere in northern Europe, where economic self-interest still overrode moral imperative even in the Age of Revolution. Davis, "Universal Attractions," 74.

12. Vincent Carretta, ed., *Unchained Voices: An Anthology of Black Authors in the English-Speaking World of the Eighteenth Century* (Lexington: University Press of Kentucky, 1996).

13. On the entrenchment of slavery and racial attitudes in the United States, see George M. Frederickson, *The Black Image in the White Mind: The Debate on Afro-American Character and Destiny, 1817–1914* (New York: Harper & Row, 1971), chaps. 1–6; Don E. Fehrenbacher, *The Dred Scott Case: Its Significance in American Law and Politics* (repr., New York: Oxford University Press, 2001); Reginald Horsman, *Josiah Nott of Mobile: Southerner, Physician, and Racial Theorist* (Baton Rouge: Louisiana State University Press, 1987); James Oakes, *The Ruling Race: A History of American Slaveholders* (New York: Norton, 1998); Lacy K. Ford, *Origins of Southern Radicalism: The South Carolina Upcountry: 1800–1860* (New York: Oxford University Press, 1991); *Deliver Us from Evil: The Slavery Question in the Old South* (New York: Oxford University Press, 2009). For Latin America, see, for example, Nancy Leys Stepan, *"The Hour of Eugenics": Race, Gender, and Nation in Latin America* (Ithaca, N.Y.: Cornell University Press, 1996).

14. For an example of this dominance, see the chapter on Africa in the book on slavery by the "dean" of Old South historians, Ulrich B. Phillips, *American Negro Slavery* (New York: Appleton, 1918; repr. with a foreword by Eugene D. Genovese, Baton Rouge: Louisiana State University Press, 1966). Even defenders of Phillips's academic reputation such as Genovese admit that this chapter, titled "The Early Exploitation of Guinea," is "close to being worthless" (Genovese, foreword, viii) because of its total acceptance of racist interpretations of African culture.

15. W. E. B. Du Bois, *The Souls of Black Folk* (repr., New York: Simon & Schuster, 2005). The most influential challenge to the traditional scholarly views on slavery came with Kenneth Stampp, *The Peculiar Institution: Slavery in the Ante-bellum South* (New York: Knopf, 1956). For the contested memory of history in the South, see W. Fitzhugh Brundage, *The Southern Past: A Clash of Race and Memory* (Cambridge, Mass.: Harvard University Press, 2005). For an excellent study on how Charleston has presented its history, see Stephanie E. Yuhl, *A Golden Haze of Memory: The Making of Historic Charleston* (Chapel Hill: University of North Carolina Press, 2005).

16. Davis's opera (with libretto by his cousin Thulani Davis) premiered at the Lyric Theatre in Chicago in 1998. For details on the goals of the *Freedom Schooner Amistad,* see http://www.amistadamerica.net, accessed February 6, 2012.

17. Article 4 of the United Nations Universal Declaration of Human Rights, passed in 1948, states, "No one shall be held in slavery or servitude; slavery and the slave trade shall be prohibited in all their forms," http://www.un.org/en/documents/udhr/, accessed May 14, 2010. On the reparations debates, see, for example, "A Roundtable on Reparations," special issue of *African Studies Quarterly* 2, no. 4 (1998), available online at http://web.africa.ufl.edu/asq/v2/v2i4.htm, or Charles J. Ogletree Jr. "Repairing the Past: New Efforts in the Reparations Debate in America," *Harvard Civil Rights–Civil Liberties Law Review* 38, no. 2 (2002): 279–320.

PROSCRIPTION BY DEGREES

The Ending of the African Slave Trade to the United States

Kenneth Morgan

homas Jefferson, presenting his annual presidential address to Congress on December 2, 1806, anticipated the time, just over a year thence, when legislators would have the power, under Article I, Section 9, of the United States Constitution, to take action over slave importation to the United States. "I congratulate you, fellow citizens," he wrote, "on the approach of the period when you may interpose your authority, constitutionally, to withdraw the citizens of the United States from all further participation in those violations of human rights which have been so long continued on the unoffending inhabitants of Africa, and which the morality, the reputation, and the best interests of our country, have long been eager to proscribe."[1] Whatever the inconsistency of his changing views on slavery, Jefferson had regularly advocated ending the slave trade to North America. In 1772 he and all other members of the Virginia House of Burgesses called for George III to abolish the British Atlantic slave trade. Jefferson repeated this view in *A Summary View of the Rights of British America* (1774) and in an initial draft of the Declaration of Independence (1776). He recommended abolishing the slave trade to Virginia in his drafts of a constitution for the Old Dominion in 1776. This was defeated in the state legislature but adopted two years later by the same body.[2] On March 2, 1807, just a few months after Jefferson made the remarks quoted in his address to Congress, the House of Representatives took a decisive vote, 113–5, in favor of a prohibitory act. This was the legal end of the transatlantic slave trade to the United States. The voting figures suggest that the decision was clear cut, even though the vote had been preceded by vigorous debates. Such unanimity by legislators over a slavery issue was rare in the nineteenth-century United States.[3] This was the first occasion in world history that a slaveholding nation ended the importation of enslaved Africans.[4]

On January 1, 1808, the prohibitory act came into effect only nine months after Britain had enacted its own legislation to end the slave trade in the British Empire.[5] But whereas the British abolition of the slave trade occurred after a long antislavery battle of twenty years, with much lobbying activity inside and outside Parliament and some dramatic twists and turns in the final couple of years before abolition was achieved, the end of the slave trade into the United States was a much more subdued process, and not the result of a sustained abolitionist crusade. In fact, as this essay will show, it was a matter of proscription by degrees, and in its final stages in 1806–7, it did not depend on a bitter struggle between abolitionists and anti-abolitionists. The eradication of the slave trade to the United States was a long-drawn-out affair that began in the 1760s. It made advances in individual colonies before the American Revolutionary War and continued to make an impact at the state level between the Declaration of Independence and the creation of the Constitution. Congress was prohibited from interfering with slave importation for twenty years after the Constitution was ratified, but further advances toward abolition occurred between the ratification of the Constitution in 1788 and the prohibitory act of 1807. This summary might imply a Whiggish sequence of events gathering momentum to end the slave trade to the United States. But this did not happen. Rather the issue of the slave trade was only partially connected to abolitionist ideas or campaigns; it also reflected considerations over the economy of individual colonies and states, the inability to end the slave traffic while Britain retained sovereignty in North America, the political complications in securing a ban created by the onset of a federal nation, and the way in which the slave trade was inextricably connected to broader matters concerning slavery on American soil. Political maneuvering was an essential component in the ending of the African slave trade to the United States.

The scale of the transatlantic slave trade to the thirteen North American colonies that became the United States was always smaller than to British territories in the Caribbean, and a minor part of the international slave trade as a whole, but it was still significant in numbers. Recent research has shown that around 389,000 African captives arrived in North America via the transatlantic slave trade, of whom 306,000 came on United States–owned vessels. An additional 66,921 slaves were brought from the Caribbean to the North American mainland.[6] The distribution of slave arrivals in North America was disproportionately concentrated in the staple plantation colonies and states, for obvious reasons. South Carolina and Georgia, producing mainly rice and, to a lesser extent, indigo as staples cultivated by slaves, but later adding cotton as an additional crop requiring black labor, took the lion's share of these imports, amounting to approximately 40,000 Africans before 1750 and over 160,000 thereafter. More than 90 percent of these captives disembarked at Charleston. The tobacco plantations of Virginia and Maryland absorbed nearly 100,000 Africans before 1750 and 38,000 subsequently.[7] The remaining saltwater slaves arrived in much smaller numbers at destinations north of the Mason-Dixon Line and in the Gulf States. Thus the Lower South dominated slave imports into North America, the Chesapeake was the next most significant region of slave importation, and other areas were marginal. Because of better slave reproduction rates in Virginia and Maryland compared with South Carolina and

Georgia, the number and proportion of slaves arriving in the Chesapeake declined over time in relation to those disembarking in the Lower South.[8] In the first decade of the nineteenth century, nearly 67,000 slaves arrived in the Carolinas and Georgia. Between 1804 and 1807, when South Carolina reopened its slave trade, U.S. ships brought 28,000 slaves to Charleston. The year 1807 was the first in the history of the Anglo-American slave trade in which more slaves disembarked in the United States than in the British Caribbean. When the United States banned African slave imports from January 1, 1808, it was therefore ending a thriving trade.[9]

Georgia, the last colony settled by Britain on mainland North America before the American Revolution, was the first of those colonies to ban the slave trade, but that proscription was eventually revoked. In 1732 Georgia's philanthropic founding trustees drew up a charter for the colony that excluded slavery: they wanted settlers to be self-sufficient and not dependent on enslaved workers. They were also concerned about the security threat posed by bringing in slaves. In 1735 the House of Commons supported this decision. The policy was reversed, however, in 1750 when planters, ambitious to exploit the commercial possibilities of rice production, successfully lobbied Parliament for the importation of Africans to Georgia for plantation labor.[10] Apart from the distinctive case of Georgia, the first serious action against the slave trade to British North America arose from the scruples of Quakers in the Delaware Valley. The Religious Society of Friends associated the slave trade with warlike activities and the taking of stolen property. By the Seven Years' War, Pennsylvania and New Jersey Quakers, convinced that slave trading was immoral, offered strong admonitions against the traffic among their members.[11] The Philadelphia Yearly Meeting ruled in 1758 that local Friends who imported, bought, or sold slaves should be brought "under discipline." In the following year, the New York Yearly Meeting followed suit. By the 1760s Quakers throughout North America were lobbying against slave imports. Their abolitionist ideas had more impact in the northern colonies than in the southern ones, though in the 1760s and 1770s Friends active in Virginia and Maryland spread the antislavery message. The activities of Quakers in New Jersey and Pennsylvania, notably the lobbying and publications of Anthony Benezet and the writings of the preacher John Woolman, were particularly influential in spreading antislavery ideas in North America and Great Britain. Benezet, in particular, was very active in contacting fellow antislavery sympathizers to take action to end this "unnatural and barbarous traffic."[12] Little discussion of slavery occurred before 1776 among other Protestant groups such as the Anglicans, Congregationalists, Lutherans, and Presbyterians, though some prominent members of these denominations, such as the Presbyterian doctor Benjamin Rush, attacked the iniquity of the slave trade.[13] Yet it was the Quakers, though relatively small in number, who had sufficient zeal, organization, and commitment to proselytize the abolitionist creed to a wide audience throughout the Anglophone world.[14]

The only way in which the slave trade to the North American colonies could be ended before the American Revolution was by parliamentary legislation, and that was out of the question at a time when an abolitionist movement in Britain had still to be formed. But a degree of proscription was available to individual colonies, either through import duties on incoming slave shipments or nonimportation of enslaved Africans. Colonial self-determination rather than antislavery opinion underpinned such proscription.[15] Import duties on slaves were implemented at various times by all British North American colonies, except for New Hampshire, Connecticut, Delaware, and North Carolina. Thus the Pennsylvania Assembly brought in a duty of ten pounds per head on imported slaves in 1761 and twelve years later raised it to twenty pounds. This helped to curtail the slave trade to the colony. Ultimately, however, colonial laws to restrict imported slaves could be overturned by the British Privy Council, and so their effect was muted.[16] The nonimportation agreements of 1769 and 1770 succeeded in bringing the slave trade to a halt for a year in South Carolina. Slaves were also included in the nonimportation agreements of 1769 and 1774 in Virginia.[17] Benezet was hopeful that restriction of slave imports could be extended: by the early 1770s the New England colonies had laws that virtually amounted to a prohibition of the trade, and possibly ten thousand to twenty thousand people in Virginia and Maryland could be expected to petition Parliament on this matter.[18] But his was too optimistic a view at the time. Efforts to curtail imports had a temporary effect because they only lasted for certain periods. Moreover, as Jefferson put it in 1774, "our repeated attempts to effect" the ending of slave imports from Africa "by imposing duties which might amount to a prohibition, have been hitherto defeated by his majesty's negative."[19]

Mixed motives are apparent in the various attempts to proscribe British slave imports at the colony level by law. Not all actions taken were given impetus by a sense of the immorality of the transatlantic slave traffic, though some were; others were connected with broader economic and political matters. In New Jersey and Connecticut, for instance, attempts to restrict slave imports in the 1760s and early 1770s arose not from a humanitarian concern for Africans but from the perceived deterrent to white immigrants posed by slave imports through labor competition.[20] Nevertheless some positive steps toward restricting slave imports to certain North American colonies were made on the eve of the American Revolution. In 1770 a bill drawn up by the Rhode Island Assembly to prohibit the importation of slaves was rejected. But local Quakers urged the colony's assembly to take action against the slave trade, and in 1774 an act to this effect was passed that pointed to the way in which the slave traffic contradicted natural rights ideology. It turned out to be ineffectual, however, because of significant loopholes.[21] In Massachusetts attempts to curtail the slave trade met with opposition. The lower house of the assembly debated the slave trade in 1767, but a measure for levying a duty on imported slaves failed. In 1771 the General Court of Massachusetts approved a bill to stop slave importation, but Governor Thomas Hutchinson refused to acquiesce because the sponsors of the bill included what he regarded as an unsubstantiated claim that slavery was unlawful. In 1774 another bill to prohibit slave imports into Massachusetts was passed easily by both legislative houses, but the governor refused to sign it. Hutchinson's action appeared to support British measures against the colony in the aftermath of the Coercive Acts of 1774. Two influential Connecticut Congregational clergymen, Jonathan Edwards Jr. and Levi Hart, wrote and preached against the immorality of the slave trade. Their views influenced the Connecticut Assembly to end slave importation in 1774.[22]

Moves to curtail the slave trade were evident particularly in the largest southern colony, Virginia, which unlike the northern colonies just discussed, had participated in the slave trade since the mid–seventeenth century and had a large slave population of 221,000 in 1780—easily the largest of any U.S. state.[23] In 1699, 1710, 1723, 1728, 1767, and 1769, the Virginia House of Burgesses voted for laws in favor of slave import duties. On the two latter occasions, it voted to double the duty from 10 percent to 20 percent, but the Privy Council vetoed these proposals.[24] The Virginians' actions raised revenue to defend their citizens but also limited slave importations. On some occasions this stemmed from fear of slave insurrections; on others from the desire to restrict slave imports to increase the value of slaves already living in Virginia.[25] Virginia had numerous indebted tobacco plantations on the eve of the War of Independence coupled with significant demographic growth among existing slave communities. The transition from tobacco to grain in the Chesapeake economy in the Revolutionary era meant that fewer imported Africans were needed for field labor, because cultivation of grain products did not require a plantation workforce. Raising import duties on Africans arriving in the colony seemed the solution to these economic problems.[26]

In the Virginia Assembly's debate on slave import duties in 1759, Richard Henry Lee argued that importing more Africans would deter Virginia from attracting skilled European immigrants needed for a diversifying regional economy.[27] This theme was frequently aired over the next fifteen years. Influenced by antislavery ideas and worried about the effects of slavery on white people, Arthur Lee, in his "Address on Slavery" (*Rind's Virginia Gazette*, March 19, 1767), attempted to persuade the House of Burgesses to end the slave trade to the colony. He argued that Britain and the American colonies would profit by an increase in free settlers instead.[28] At a June 1774 meeting of Prince George County freeholders, it was argued that "the African trade is injurious to this colony, obstructs the population of it by freemen, prevents manufacturers and other useful emigrants from Europe from settling among us, and occasions an annual increase of the balance of trade against this colony."[29] Around the same time, the Fairfax County Resolves, written by the planter George Mason, announced a stop to slave importation and asked for an end to "such a wicked cruel and unnatural trade."[30] Virginia planters sometimes condemned the slave trade while wanting to retain slaves as an essential part of their livelihood. Patrick Henry, who referred to the slave trade as "an abominable practice" but wanted to remain master of his slaves, was a prominent example.[31] Tidewater planters, in particular, opposed the slave trade at this juncture, for they had sufficient slaves already and did not want to see new supplies depress prices.

Overall Virginia politicians condemned the slave trade earlier than any other southern colony or state. On August 6, 1774, the Association of the Virginia Convention, the delegates of the freeholders in the colony, called for an end to the African slave trade. In 1778 the Virginia Assembly reversed British policy, without any public discussion, by ending further slave importation with immediate effect. This was influenced by an economic depression in Virginia, which reduced the need for new slaves. Jefferson, it should be observed, favored the Virginia law against slave importation but had no significant role in drafting or introducing the act. It is noteworthy that this law only came about after considerable delay and procrastination in the Virginia legislature: the whole House only approved it eighteen months after first considering the matter. This suggests that Virginia's politicians were uncomfortable in enacting anti–slave trade legislation. And of course the law did not mean that Virginians were yet willing to end slavery.[32]

South Carolina, the colony in British North America with the largest black majority by the Revolutionary era, also regularly imposed duties on slaves disembarked within its jurisdiction. But the colony's history of restricting slave imports was varied. The South Carolina Assembly imposed differential taxes on slaves imported from all areas from 1703, when the duty on imported Africans was ten shillings but double that amount for slaves brought from the West Indies. The duties were revised at frequent intervals down to 1776. Sometimes the South Carolina Assembly imposed very high duties on slave imports to protect the planter class and to maintain a manageable white-black ratio in the colony's population. Such duties amounted to a virtual ban on slave imports. This situation occurred in 1717 when an import tax of forty pounds per slave effectively stopped the trade for two years until the legislature reduced the tax to ten pounds for every new captive imported from Africa. It happened again between July 1741 and July 1744 in the aftermath of the Stono Rebellion of September 1739, the largest slave revolt in the British North American colonies. For part of this period, import slave duties were increased to twenty-five, fifty, and one hundred pounds. These taxes reflected the concern of white South Carolinians over the high ratio of blacks to whites in their colony's population and the need for internal security against further slave revolts. The prohibitory tax on slave imports also operated between 1745 and 1749. Under a South Carolina act of 1751, three-fifths of the proceeds of slave import duties were used to settle white Protestant immigrants in the colony. In 1760 South Carolina prohibited the slave trade because the colonists feared the growing number of African-born slaves, but the Privy Council disallowed the act, and the governor was reprimanded. Heavy slave import duties were reintroduced in South Carolina between 1766 and 1768 in the wake of extensive planter indebtedness in the colony. Once again these taxes effectively stopped the slave trade into South Carolina. Rising political conflict between Great Britain and the North American colonies led to South Carolina instituting outright bans on slave imports in 1770 and 1775.[33] This pattern of imposing and then rescinding import duties on slaves indicates that South Carolina used this device as a political tool to safeguard their staple economy.

By the mid-1770s the first attempt to ban the slave trade by the North American colonies as a whole came with a pledge from the First Continental Congress not to import or purchase another slave from December 1, 1774, "after which time, we will wholly discontinue the slave trade."[34] This was followed by a ban on imported slaves suggested by the Second Continental Congress in 1776. Both congresses included a delegation from South Carolina, which, of all the colonies and states, had the longest history of intransigence on banning the slave trade. The resolutions showed that delegates from various colonies could speak with a united voice. That the South Carolina delegates acceded to this proposed ban on slave imports is explained by the fact that both Continental Congresses acted within the broader context of nonimportation of British goods at this stage of the Anglo-American crisis. In both cases the decisions were influenced by widespread dislike of the traffic in enslaved Africans by many people in the northern colonies and the Upper South, though economic considerations—as outlined above in considering taxes on slave imports into Virginia and South Carolina—were much more important than moral scruples about the slave trade.[35] These resolutions were well observed initially in North America.[36] Yet they had no binding effect because neither the First nor the Second Continental Congress had the political authority to enforce its views: individual colonies were not required to bring their laws into line with the decisions of Congress, which could only signal its intentions.

Jefferson's insertion of a slave trade clause into the draft of the Declaration of Independence was aimed at King George III to justify the revolt against Britain by the American colonists. But it was straining the argument to blame the monarch for a trade in which Virginians and other American colonies had freely participated. The Continental Congress deleted the clause from the final document partly for this reason and partly because congressional delegates from the southern states considered it an indirect attack on slavery itself. As Jefferson noted, this was done "in complaisance to South Carolina & Georgia, who had never attempted to restrain the importation of slaves, and who on the contrary still wished to continue it."[37] The Continental Congress had already agreed to prohibit further importation of slaves in British ships on the basis that such captives were an item of trade, but the deletion of Jefferson's comments from the Declaration of Independence anticipated the way in which the matter of slave imports largely remained the prerogative of individual states for the next generation.[38] After 1776 North Americans were involved not just in the extensive war effort but in drafting and debating constitutions for the new states that made up the United States of America. In these circumstances it was difficult for them to focus on an effective ban to the slave trade. Disruptions to the transatlantic slave trade in the Revolutionary War meant that slave imports into North America were effectively curtailed in any case from 1776 to 1783, and the matter, for the time being, was not important on the political agenda of the United States.[39]

No clause in the Articles of Confederation and Perpetual Union, the governing constitution of the alliance of U.S. independent states, dealt with the slave trade; under those articles, ratified in 1781, the confederation government did not have the right to regulate commerce. John Jay's draft treaty of commerce with Britain, written during the Paris peace negotiations in June 1783, at the end of the American War of Independence, included a provision that Britain should not in the future carry or import slaves into the United States from anywhere in the world. He backed up this statement by stating that it was the intention of the American states "intirely to prohibit the Importation thereof." This, as he realized on reflection, was an overconfident prediction, and the clause was dropped from the final treaty.[40] Nevertheless criticism of the slave traffic continued in the American Revolutionary era. There were private protests, such as that by Benjamin Rush, who stated: "Let not our united republics be stained with the importation of a single African slave into America."[41] Even in South Carolina, a leading planter such as Henry Laurens, who had once imported large numbers of Africans, hoped his fellow citizens would prohibit further importations on grounds of conscience.[42] In 1779 North Carolina Quakers went to court to abolish slave imports, but the state legislature rejected their case.[43] There was also a group protest in the form of a Quaker petition to the Continental Congress on October 4, 1783, in which more than five hundred Friends prayed for the end of the slave trade to North America. Yet this had no effect on public policy. A congressional committee recommended that each state should deal with the slave trade in its own way, but southern congressmen voted against this judgment.[44] This is a reminder that sovereignty in the new United States remained with individual states before 1788, as there was yet no federal system of government, and that perceived infringements of states' rights affected the approval or disapproval of committee decisions.

Between the Declaration of Independence in 1776 and the Constitutional Convention of 1787, many states took action against the slave trade, in a variety of ways and for diverse reasons. Even though it was often impractical to abolish existing laws, passed while the thirteen colonies were under British sovereignty, state legislatures authorized new laws on slavery and the slave trade, and sometimes principles on these matters became part of the new state constitutions. Virginia's ending of the slave trade in 1778—through a statute rather than a clause in the state constitution—has already been noted. This was one of the first governments in the modern world to end the slave trade. Why the statute was enacted is not absolutely clear. But it may have been connected with an influx of new representatives into the assembly, combining with eastern representatives to stop slave imports to increase the profits on selling slaves they already owned; and possibly, too, the presence of potentially rebellious slaves during the Revolutionary War also persuaded Virginia planters to end the slave trade.[45]

Anti–slave trade resolutions were passed in various other states during the Revolutionary era. In 1776 Delaware's constitution prohibited slave importation. Pennsylvania's gradual abolition law of 1780 followed suit. In 1783 the Maryland state legislature enacted a law that ended the slave trade. In 1784 the Rhode Island Assembly passed a statute that prohibited future importation of slaves into the state but failed to specify any fines for violation. The New York legislature banned importing slaves for sale in 1785 and authorized substantial fines for those who did not comply. This was one of several measures in the immediate aftermath of the Revolutionary War in New York in which legislators sought to move toward the gradual abolition of slavery.[46] In 1786 Governor William Livingston of New Jersey, who regarded slavery as incompatible with humanity, Christianity, and the inalienable rights of mankind, was influenced by the petitions of the Quaker David Cooper and other Friends to oversee an act that banned slave imports and liberalized slave manumissions. However the slave trade clause of this New Jersey act was limited, because it imposed low fines on violators and did not authorize the freedom of slaves illegally brought into the state.[47]

Whatever the limitations of these initiatives, by early 1787 only three states— Georgia, South Carolina, and North Carolina—still allowed slave imports. The number of states importing enslaved Africans dropped from three to two when, on March 28, 1787, a couple of months before the Constitutional Convention, South Carolina's legislature passed an act prohibiting slave imports for three years. This measure was the culmination of contentious debates that began in late September 1785, with some legislators in the state's House of Representatives arguing that slaves had increased South Carolina's wealth and others countering this view by emphasizing the insufficiency of the state's current poor export values to pay for imports, including slaves. The prohibition act of 1787 produced further acrimonious debate among South Carolinians over whether to ban slave imports. This legislation, which originated as an amendment to an act regulating the recovery of debts, was supported by influential lowcountry planters concerned about poor economic conditions in the state. Despite division among South Carolinians over the continuance of the slave trade, they wanted to maintain their states' rights on this matter. No politicians in South Carolina desired a permanent ban on slave disembarkations; they expected to choose when, and for what reasons, they could restrict or open the trade.[48] Jefferson congratulated South Carolina's legislature for "suspending the importation of slaves, and for the glory you have just acquired by endeavoring to prevent it forever." Echoing his long-held view that the slave trade must be ended, he added that "there is a superior bench reserved in heaven for those who hasten it."[49]

The opportunity to secure wider prohibition of the slave trade into the United States came with the Constitutional Convention that met on May 25, 1787. Slavery was not high on the agenda of the fifty-five delegates who met in Philadelphia to agree a draft of a federal constitution. Over the course of the summer, however, slavery became a central issue. During August the convention considered the slave trade to the United States. A compromise emerged whereby some New Englanders supported South Carolina's and Georgia's insistence on their right to import slaves in return for the Lower South's aid for New England's demands that Congress be empowered to regulate all foreign commerce.[50] The Pennsylvania Abolition Society petitioned the convention to outlaw slave imports at the first opportunity after a federal government was established. The petition was sent by the society's secretary, Tench Coxe, to Benjamin Franklin, the society's president. In his old age, Franklin had assumed an antislavery stance, accepting that a new nation based upon the inalienable rights of man could not legitimately subject blacks to lifelong bondage.[51] But Franklin did not present the petition at the Constitutional Convention, which he attended daily as a Pennsylvania delegate, because he was worried that the southern states would take umbrage and that the petition would defeat "the wishes of the enemies of the slave trade."[52]

Franklin correctly judged the mood and disposition of the convention over slavery—a word not even mentioned in the Constitution owing to its sensitive connotations. For a time it seemed that the issue of slavery would lead to the breakup of the convention. Political compromises were reached to accommodate the views of South Carolina and Georgia, where slave importation was an important issue. The slave trade could not be separated in terms of the overall acceptance of the proposed Constitution from other aspects of slavery in the United States: all were intertwined. James Madison later acknowledged that there was more debate about slavery at the convention and in the ratifying conventions than was ever recorded. He claimed that "the States were divided into different interests not by their difference of size, but principally from their having or not having slaves."[53] When the convention adjourned on September 17, 1787, the draft document of the Constitution included explicit sanctions for slavery in at least five articles and indirect protection of slavery in several other clauses.[54] This is why some historians regard the Constitution as a proslavery document that abandoned an antislavery ethos encouraged by the ideals of the American Revolution and gave the South considerable protection for slavery.[55]

The Constitution made no attempt to prohibit the transatlantic slave trade. Thus it is incorrect to state, as Adam Rothman does, that "the delegates from the lower South . . . blocked the federal Constitution from immediately prohibiting the importation of slaves."[56] But it is also mistaken to suggest that the question of the slave trade was handled quietly at the Constitutional Convention.[57] On the contrary the importation of Africans was a contested issue in that forum. John Dickinson of Pennsylvania thought it "inadmissible on every principle of honor & safety that the importation of slaves should be authorized to the States by the Constitution." He did not believe that the southern states would refuse to confederate if they could not get their way on slave imports, especially as the power to limit such trade was "not likely to be immediately exercised by the Gen[era]l Government." Madison insisted, to no avail, that the provision was "dishonorable to the National character" and the new federal government and that "twenty years will produce all the mischief that can be apprehended from the liberty to import slaves."[58] Delegates from the Chesapeake argued for banning slave imports. Luther Martin of Maryland opposed the traffic on moral grounds, while George Mason of Virginia argued that the "nefarious traffic" of the slave trade would never wither away of its own accord because of the strong demand for slaves in western backcountry areas.[59]

South Carolina's delegates, however, proved uncompromising on this sticking point. Three of its four delegates—John Rutledge, Charles Pinckney, and Pierce Butler—had voted to close the slave trade at the state level a few months earlier.[60] But the prospect of federal jurisdiction over the slave trade was a different matter. Pinckney warned that his state "could never receive the plan if it prohibits the slave trade." It would be unequal, he argued, to require South Carolina and Georgia to confederate on these terms, because they could not flourish without saltwater Africans. Virginia, by contrast, would gain by stopping slave imports, because her existing slaves would rise in value. These arguments underscore the fact that South Carolina's delegates were not concerned about the morality of the slave trade; they regarded it entirely as a commercial practice that needed protection.[61] John Rutledge, who had been the first governor of South Carolina after 1776, summed up the Lower South's case: "If the Convention thinks that N.C., S.C. & Georgia will ever agree to the plan, unless their right to import slaves be untouched, the expectation is vain. The People of those States will never be such fools as to give up so important an interest."[62] Rutledge was among a minority of delegates at the Constitutional Convention who argued that the right of slave importation should remain untouched; but his words were direct and emphatic, representative of others who shared his position, and not phrased as if they were a bluff.[63]

It was eventually agreed that the Constitution should provide a cordon protecting slave imports from congressional interference for a further two decades. Article I, Section 9, of the Constitution, dealing with the foreign slave trade, stated: "The Migration or Importation of such Persons as any of the States now existing shall think proper to admit, shall not be prohibited by the Congress prior to the Year one thousand eight hundred and eight but a Tax or duty may be imposed on such Importation, not exceeding ten dollars for each person." At Madison's insistence the phrase "that there could be property in men" was deleted from this clause, thereby fending off the suggestion that slaves were being specified: "such persons" could include free immigrants.[64] Article V added that no amendment could be made to this clause before 1808. As Don E. Fehrenbacher succinctly stated, these statements "implicitly confirmed federal regulatory power while explicitly suspending it until 1808."[65] The Lower South, led by South Carolina, did well out of these clauses: they had argued against a ban on the slave trade and had achieved that as well as gaining explicit protection for the trade for a further twenty years. Article V forestalled any attempt that the Upper South and Middle States might make to combine to end the slave trade after ratification.[66]

Article I, Section 9, and Article V were only agreed upon through a compromise between South Carolina and New England over slave imports after South Carolina delegates had threatened to leave the Union unless they received protection of their right to control future slave imports to their state. At this juncture the northeastern states supported their claim, even though it was clear that South Carolina occupied an isolated position. A vote of seven votes in favor and four opposed confirmed the compromise. The measure was supported by New Hampshire, Massachusetts, Connecticut, Maryland, North Carolina, South Carolina, and Georgia and opposed by Pennsylvania, New Jersey, Delaware, and Virginia.[67] Several delegates —notably Luther Martin, James Madison, Charles Cotesworth Pinckney, and George Mason—made explicit remarks outside of the convention about the constitutional bargain struck between the New England states and the Lower South over slave imports.[68]

The New England states agreed with Charles Cotesworth Pinckney of South Carolina that no congressional action on the foreign slave trade could occur before 1808—rather than 1800, as originally suggested at the convention—in return for support over import duties to protect their regional commerce. Pennsylvania delegates Coxe and Franklin voted against extending the slave trade clause from 1800, to no avail.[69] William Livingston of New Jersey, who had earlier opposed slave imports to America, chaired the constitutional committee that selected 1808 as the date before which no congressional action over slave imports to the United States would be permitted; like many other delegates, he realized that a compromise was necessary among the states to secure the Constitution.[70] The compromise was possible because South Carolina and Georgia were much more committed to maintaining the right to import slaves than the other states cared about abolishing the trade.[71]

Gary B. Nash has argued that the northerners should have called the bluff of the Lower South, which was in no realistic position to secede from the Union, and that thereby the cause of abolitionism could have been given urgent emphasis. His interpretation blames northern abolitionists for losing their nerve in pressing the need to solve the problem of slavery at a crucial turning point in its political history.[72] This is an interesting line of interpretation. As suggested above in the quotations from Rutledge and Pinckney, there was no bluff in the South Carolina delegates' expressed views. Whether South Carolina's delegates feigned their intended actions is difficult to prove, as they never had to act upon their views. South Carolina's belligerence was unlikely to lead to secession, because delegates from the Lower South were mainly deeply committed to the Constitution whether or not they secured a compromise with New England.[73] But as argued above, the antislavery views of some northerners were less strongly put forward at the convention than New England's desire for a compromise with the Lower South to protect its own regional interests. It is this lack of nerve by northern antislavery sympathizers that Nash regards as a lost opportunity to tackle the problem of slavery in the new nation. On the other hand, the federal government had no jurisdiction over slavery as a result of the Constitutional Convention, nor was it intended that it should have such legal oversight of what became "the peculiar institution."

One should not underestimate the debate over slavery and the slave trade at the convention. Federalists and Anti-Federalists both used the issue of slavery to deal with broader political issues in the debates over the framing of the Constitution.[74] The libertarian language of the American Revolution was frequently used to debate slavery and the slave trade, because this was the political discourse that Americans understood and approved.[75] Even so this does not mean that they considered slavery and the slave trade as necessarily of lesser importance than matters of governance and the distribution of federal power: the specific issues were intertwined with the broader remit faced by the delegates. Nor does it imply that slavery and the slave trade—however euphemistically embedded in the Constitution—were merely rhetorical devices. Thus although slavery and the slave trade often featured as rhetorical or tactical strategies at the Federal Convention and in the ratification debates and public discussions of the Constitution, they also attracted partisan views depending on whether delegates and commentators regarded these institutions as morally reprehensible or commercially valuable.

That slavery and the slave trade were not a sideshow in the framing of the Constitution is apparent from the lengthy debates over ratification in a number of states. The ratifying conventions in Delaware, New Jersey, Georgia, Connecticut, and Maryland made no mention of the slave trade. There was also very little debate over Article I, Section 9, in New York. But the clause was discussed in Rhode Island, New Hampshire, North Carolina, Massachusetts, Pennsylvania, Virginia, and South Carolina. In each case it was the subject of highly differentiated views. The Massachusetts ratifying convention gave detailed consideration to the proposed rule over the slave trade. Comparisons with the Articles of Confederation, which omitted clauses on slavery and the slave trade, did not feature in the arguments; instead commentators focused on the slave trade in relation to Christian morality, republican notions of liberty, and the extent of congressional power over the traffic.[76]

Many opponents of the constitutional clause on the foreign slave trade attacked it on moral grounds. Thus the Anti-Federalist Quaker preacher James Neal, in the Massachusetts ratification convention debates, objected to the notion that the slave trade could flourish for another twenty years because it favored "the making merchandise of the bodies of men; and unless his objection was removed, he could not put his hand to the constitution."[77] Other New England commentators decried the brutality of the slave trade and argued that the Constitution preserved a miserable trafficking of black Africans that ran counter to the compassionate creeds of Christianity.[78] Possibly the moral and religious legacy of Puritanism in New England influenced the stance taken against the slave trade by many in that region.[79] In the Middle States, the slave trade also elicited criticism on grounds of conscience. It was attacked for "entailing endless Servitude on Millions of the human Race" and for ensuring that "poor Africans" were doomed to "endure a continuance of depredation, rapine, and murder, for 21 years to come."[80] The views of Pennsylvania Quakers were of particular importance given their avowed abolitionist stance. They had hoped that the Constitution would eradicate the slave trade in terms of equity and natural justice. The Pennsylvania Abolition Society, as noted earlier, petitioned the Constitutional Convention to suppress the slave trade on humanitarian grounds. But though Friends objected to the slave trade clause and other protection for the continuance of slavery, they mainly supported ratification because as a religious society they were not concerned with setting up or pulling down governments.[81] In the South there was less of an appeal to conscience in relation to the slave trade clause in the Constitution, notably in South Carolina and Georgia, but in the Chesapeake there were occasional attacks on the immorality of the slave trade using volatile language and appeals to the consciences of those involved.[82]

Other negative views about Article I, Section 9, emerged during the ratification process. In New England in particular, people complained that the South was authorized to continue slave trading for another twenty-one years without an opportunity to amend the constitutional clause.[83] A writer in Philadelphia's *Independent Gazetteer* worried that there was no guarantee that the clause would be dealt with thereafter. Another report in the same newspaper interpreted the slave trade clause as giving southern states the right to import enslaved Africans for a further twenty-one years "against the declared sense of the other states to put an end to an odious traffic in the human species."[84] Another line of attack laid emphasis on Congress's impotence to deal with the slave trade on a national basis over the next generation. The Reverend Samuel Hopkins, a prominent antislavery publicist from Rhode Island, thus argued that an asylum for slaves was prevented until 1808 "unless every individual state should suppress this trade."[85] Other critiques of the slave trade clause insisted it was immoral, inconsistent with the actions of the Continental Congress, and at odds with cherished republican principles of liberty and justice. As an Anti-Federalist put it succinctly in February 1788, "Can we who have fought so hard for Liberty give our consent to have it taken away from others?"[86] In the South idiosyncratic denunciations of the slave trade clause came from George Mason, an influential planter and Virginia delegate to the Constitutional Convention, and the elderly Charlestonian Rawlins Lowndes, the chief Anti-Federalist opponent to ratification in South Carolina. Mason's denunciation of the slave trade —while continuing to support slavery—was a wily attempt to protect the peculiar position of Virginia, with a surplus of slaves and a rapidly growing slave population. Lowndes criticized the slave trade clause because it was a compromise with the northern states that avoided any stipulation that they should pay duties on their shipping. Both Mason and Lowndes found their views overturned in their respective states.[87]

Negative views about Article I, Section 9, were counterbalanced by a good many positive views in the ratification process. James Pemberton, a Philadelphia Quaker, and James Iredell, leader of the North Carolina Federalists in the state constitutional ratification debates, both acknowledged that it was impossible to end the slave trade at the Constitutional Convention because of the position taken by South Carolina and Georgia. They favored adopting the Constitution, however, partly because it could then exercise firm central authority on the slave trade in due course. Pemberton argued that individual states were not inhibited from enacting laws restricting the traffic. Iredell noted that if the Constitution were not adopted, it would be within the power of every state to continue the slave trade forever.[88] Madison, who devoted considerable attention to the question of the slave trade in 1787–88, argued in the Virginia ratifying convention debates that the greater evil of the southern states not entering into the Union would have resulted if "temporary permission of that trade" had not been permitted. Under the Articles of Confederation, he reminded delegates, the slave trade could have continued forever; but Article I, Section 9, meant that it could be ended in 1808. "Is the importation of slaves permitted by the new Constitution for twenty years?" he asked, adding, "By the old, it is permitted forever."[89] In *The Federalist* Madison suggested that the slave trade would be strongly discouraged by government up to 1808 and might even be abolished by some states, an outcome that was supported by groups such as the Pennsylvania Abolition Society.[90] Thereafter, as some anti–slave trade advocates in the Middle States hoped, Congress would have the power to stop "that iniquitous traffic."[91]

That the ratification debates divided into pro– and anti–slave trade arguments about the Constitution reflected the battle between Federalists and Anti-Federalists over political sovereignty in the new nation, but they also pointed to the continuing contested issue of the slave trade. Though the Constitution specified that the federal government could not tamper with the slave trade before 1808 and also excluded the possibility of constitutional amendment on this matter, it gave

Congress delegated power to act on the slave trade thereafter.[92] Planters were all too aware of the threat to future slave importations after 1808, so many increased their slaving activities in the first two decades of the American Republic to counter this problem.[93] But they also realized that the rapid growth of slavery in the South after 1788 could lead to southern control of the House of Representatives and therefore that Congress would not necessarily prohibit slave imports after 1808.[94]

Between 1788 and 1808, the foreign slave trade was a matter of frequent debate both inside and outside Congress, in relation to overall U.S. policies toward trafficking in enslaved Africans and states' rights over this matter. The slave trade continued to be a contentious issue because of South Carolina's intransigence over the "Guinea" traffic and its links to other political goals, some connected directly with slavery, some indirectly. Some abolitionists, such as Moses Brown, a leader in the campaign against the slave trade in Rhode Island, feared that the twenty-year delay in dealing with slave imports might mean that individual states would retract from an anti–slave trade position. The jurisdictional uncertainty embodied in the constitutional clauses dealing with the slave trade—whether Congress had an exclusive power over the slave trade for twenty-one years, and whether state laws on slave imports remained valid—also kept the flame of controversy burning on the continuation of the slave trade to the United States.[95]

Rhode Island Quakers, notably Brown, petitioned the Rhode Island Assembly to prevent the slave trade. Both houses of the state's legislature passed a statute to this effect on October 31, 1787, six weeks after the end of the Constitutional Convention. In the following year, Rhode Island Friends pressurized Massachusetts and Connecticut to pass almost identical legislation. The slave trade laws of these three New England states all included firm penalties for violations, though enforcement was not an easy task.[96] By the early 1790s, nine of the fourteen states had banned slave importation. Apart from the three New England states just mentioned, the others were New York, New Jersey, Delaware, Maryland, Virginia, and South Carolina. In two others (Pennsylvania and North Carolina), prohibitive duties had been imposed; in Vermont slavery was banned in its constitution of 1777; and in New Hampshire the abolition of slavery in 1792 rendered further legislation over slave imports unnecessary.[97] That left Georgia as the one state where slave imports were still allowed. Despite the near unanimity achieved by individual American states in banning slave imports by the time the Constitution was ratified, controversies over ending the slave trade to the United States continued. It was, of course, within the purview of the governments of individual states to overturn laws proscribing the trade; this will be demonstrated for the period after 1788 in the case of South Carolina. More important, the possibility of a national ban on slave imports remained a pressing issue in the Federalist era.

The first time that the issue of the slave trade was raised in Congress after the ratification debates was on May 13, 1789, almost two weeks after George Washington became president of the United States. Josiah Parker from Virginia proposed that a duty of ten dollars per imported slave be added to a tariff bill. This met with a strong rebuttal from the Georgia planter and politician James Jackson, who insisted that the tax would discriminate against his state and should therefore be opposed. Madison asked Parker to withdraw his proposed amendment, which he did. Parker revised it four months later as an independent bill. The House of Representatives postponed consideration of it, no doubt recognizing that it could inflame opposing interests in Congress. Duty-free slave imports were therefore maintained for individual states.[98]

The issue of the slave trade was soon raised in petitions. Two such petitions reached the second session of the First Congress—convened in New York City—on February 11, 1790. One came from the Quaker Yearly Meeting of Pennsylvania, New Jersey, Delaware, western Maryland, and Virginia. It called for a "sincere and impartial inquiry" into "the licentious wickedness of the African trade for slaves" and for an immediate end to the slave trade from Africa to the United States. The other petition, submitted by Quakers from New York and western New England, had the more limited intention of seeking congressional help to maintain a policy of legal containment of slavery in New York. On February 12, 1790, another petition was presented to Congress by the Pennsylvania Abolition Society—endorsed by the elderly and frail Franklin, as president of the society—that urged Congress to disregard its constitutional limitations and to take action against the slave trade. James Pemberton provided the main leadership on the submission. The petitioners hoped that in due course Congress would also dismantle slavery within the United States.[99] This request for action was stymied by the constitutional barrier against amendment of Article I, Section 9.

The debates on the petitions on the floor of Congress were the fullest public exchange of views on slavery that had yet occurred in the new American Republic. They were reported in detail in two New York newspapers and in one Philadelphia newspaper.[100] Some congressmen from South Carolina and Georgia attacked Quakers and other northern emancipationists about the petitions. They focused not just on arguments dealing with Article I, Section 9, but on the entire abolitionist thrust on slavery. The slave trade was not always condemned separately; it was often attacked as the embodiment of all that was immoral about slavery.[101] Some critics also impugned the character of Quaker petitioners and charged them with Anti-Federalist motives, notably Franklin's support of the Pennsylvania Abolition Society's petition. Northerners, supported by some members from Maryland and Virginia, asked for a clearer definition of the Constitution's powers to regulate the slave trade.[102] Critics of the slave trade made the sectional argument that northerners who wanted to end imports of enslaved Africans to the United States were motivated by the desire to sell off their own surplus slaves to southern purchasers. Interestingly the anti–slave trade rhetoric deployed by some Virginians in the debates never extended to a definite call for action to prevent slave imports to individual states.[103] The congressional committee handling the petitions responded to them fairly blandly and suggested no action. Their report on March 8, 1790, echoing the evasive language used to avoid the word *slave* in the Constitution, reiterated the decision "that the General Government is expressly restrained from prohibiting the importation of such persons as any of the states now existing shall think proper to admit until the year 1808." It also implied that scruples about continuation of the slave trade would have to be dealt with on a state-by-state basis.[104]

George Washington privately wrote that the Quaker petitions were awkward and revived an issue that the Constitution had deferred until 1808: the presentation of the petitions interrupted congressional consideration of Alexander Hamilton's plan for federal funding of state debts.[105] Others shared his views, as the fate of other Quaker petitions sent to Congress indicates. Warned by politicians that an attempt to persuade Congress in 1790 to eradicate the slave trade would cause instability in the new nation, the petitioners from the Pennsylvania Abolition Society backtracked, abandoned further petitions in the same vein, and concentrated instead on laws to alleviate conditions in the slave trade. The failure of the Quaker submissions to Congress on the slave trade marked a watershed in attempts to influence government policy on this matter. They indicated that until 1808 any attempt to adopt a federal policy on the slave trade could be sabotaged by pro–slave trade congressmen. Thus in 1790 a suggestion from Rhode Island that there should be a constitutional amendment to the slave trade clause was unsuccessful: this simply was not feasible because of Article V of the Constitution. A Quaker petition in 1791 that made an "improper" request for federal intervention in the foreign slave trade was returned after representatives from the Lower South indicated their disapproval.[106] Nine Quaker petitions on slavery submitted to Congress on December 8, 1791, were buried in committee, and in the following year, the House of Representatives returned an antislavery petition put forward by the Delaware Quaker Warner Mifflin.[107]

After the clear defeat of the Quaker petitions submitted to Congress in 1790, the federal government accepted that nothing could be done to end the slave trade immediately because of constitutional limitations, but it showed concern to limit importations where possible. Clearly the abolitionist message had made a deep impression on many legislators, and abolitionists continued to attack the cruelties and injustice of the slave trade.[108] Though Congress could do nothing immediately to end the foreign slave trade, it could and did act over the carrying of slaves by U.S. citizens. Thus congressional acts of 1794 and 1800 forbade U.S. citizens and residents from carrying on the slave trade to foreign countries. The 1794 legislation was the first slave trade law passed by Congress, where it succeeded after little debate because it specifically disavowed any intention to abolish slave imports to the United States. It laid down a heavy penalty of $2,000 for anyone caught importing slaves but had no specific means for policing the traffic. The act included various loopholes, which made evasion relatively easy. Unresolved problems over the slave trade continued to make a mark in the early 1790s, notably many unproductive efforts to enforce anti–slave trade laws in New England.[109] The legislation was not completely ineffectual, however, because a number of prosecutions occurred, notably a federal court trial of the prominent Rhode Island slave trader John Brown (the brother of the abolitionist Moses Brown), who had illegally shipped slaves in an American vessel to Cuba. In 1797 he was found guilty of infringing the act of 1794. The second act of 1800 extended the scope of prohibition, increased the penalties to include imprisonment for a maximum of two years, and authorized U.S. naval ships to take slave vessels as prizes. These two acts therefore attempted to suppress American participation in the slave trade without having any authority to prohibit slave imports to U.S. ports.[110]

Proscription on federal intervention over the slave trade until 1808 meant that restriction of slave imports had still to proceed on a state-by-state basis. This remained the only way to tackle the problem in the Federalist era. Restrictions on slave imports to individual states came about through as many diverse factors as had been the case in the colonial era, except that now the specter of slave rebellion was more potent. In 1792 fears over slave insurrection—stimulated by the spread of rebellious ideas emanating from the massive Saint-Domingue slave revolt of 1791—induced South Carolina to close the slave trade.[111] In 1794 North Carolina finally prohibited the legal trade in slaves after seven years in which it first laid duties on slave imports (in 1787) and then (in 1790) repealed that statute. Tennessee adopted North Carolina's prohibition in 1796. In 1798 Congress forbade slave importation from abroad into the Mississippi Territory. This was extended in 1804 to a congressional ban on slaves imported to the Orleans Territory and to the rest of the Louisiana Purchase.[112] These actions imply that Congress wished to act to end the slave trade to the United States, but at this time it could only do so constitutionally for the territories rather than existing states. In 1793 Georgia passed an act prohibiting the slave imports from the West Indies, the Bahamas, and Florida, a statute inspired by fears of the spread of slave unrest from Saint-Domingue. Georgia permanently outlawed the slave trade from Africa in its new state constitution of 1798.[113]

After that decision all U.S. states were, in fact, closed to slave imports. But this did not mean that African arrivals ended at American ports, because there was the option, backed by the Constitution, for states to reopen their harbors to slave imports if they so wished. In other words proscription by degrees on a state basis could never fully end the African slave trade to the United States. Thus a petition by Philadelphia's black residents in 1800 calling for a ban on slave imports to the United States was doomed to failure. Introduced in Congress by Robert Waln, a wealthy Quaker representative from Pennsylvania, it drew indignation from opponents of slave trade restriction, notably John Rutledge Jr., former chief justice of South Carolina.[114] The growth and spread of slavery into the western federal territories, and the increased productivity of cotton production after the invention in 1793 of the cotton gin, meant that slaves were drawn away from states such as South

Carolina where economic circumstances might lead to their replacement by Africans. These imports might comprise illegal shipments of slaves or legitimate disembarkation of Africans in any state that chose to reopen its slave trade.[115]

In 1803 an act of Congress for the first time forbade the importation of "any negro, mulatto, or other person of colour" to states that banned the foreign slave trade. The wording, perhaps taking its cue from the Constitution, meant, but did not state, slaves. The act authorized government officials to intervene in instances where this occurred. It received firm southern support and was given impetus by fears of an influx of troublesome slaves and free blacks from the French West Indies. The implementation of enforcement immediately by the U.S. collector of customs at Charleston, by seizing a brig recently arrived with enslaved Africans, alarmed planters and played its part in South Carolina's reopening of the slave trade in late 1803, which brought around forty thousand Africans through Charleston in four years. These came from West Africa: a ban on importing slaves into the Palmetto State from the West Indies was retained because of fears that Caribbean slaves might bring with them the spirit of defiance demonstrated in the Saint-Domingue revolt.[116]

South Carolina reopened its slave trade for several reasons: the need to supply the state with new black workers to maximize cotton production; the intention that a legal supply of slaves would eradicate illegal shipments from the Caribbean; and the prospects held out by the Louisiana Purchase of 1803 to extend slavery to vast new western territories bought from Spain and France. This important land acquisition, which doubled the territory of the United States, was ratified in November 1803, just one month before South Carolina reopened its slave trade.[117] The fact that three thousand illegally smuggled slaves had arrived in South Carolina between 1800 and 1803 indicated a continuing demand for fresh supplies of African captives and helped sway arguments in favor of reopening the state's importation of slaves. A coalition of upcountry planters needing workers to meet the cotton boom and lowcountry planters recognizing business opportunities was instrumental in persuading South Carolina's legislature to reopen the trade, though some legislators opposed the decision.[118]

South Carolina's decision to reopen the slave trade was highly controversial both inside and outside the state. Within the state lowcountry legislators (supported by much public opinion) largely opposed reopening the slave traffic, while upcountry representatives favored a law to this effect. The governor of South Carolina wanted to close the slave trade, arguing that slave imports would increase "our weakness, not our strength."[119] But even with the governor's support, attempts to close the slave trade failed in 1804, 1805, and 1806.[120] The revival of the slave trade to South Carolina had a wider impact, too. Throughout much of the South, the fear of slave revolt was strong at this time. Reopening the slave trade ran the risk of adding to the numbers of slaves likely to rebel.[121] In South Carolina itself, the incorporation of large numbers of Africans into the existing slave labor force between 1804 and 1807 led to some collective acts of resistance.[122] Virginians attacked South Carolina for reopening the slave trade in 1803, but a notice in the *Charleston Courier* (January 22, 1806) replied that this was a disingenuous argument that neglected to point out that Virginia's interstate domestic slave trade would be harmed by admitting more Africans into Charleston.[123]

There were other implications, too. In January 1804 legislator David Bard of Pennsylvania introduced a resolution into Congress to impose a tax of ten dollars on every slave imported into any part of the United States. This revived a proposal made by Josiah Parker fifteen years earlier.[124] A vigorous debate on the floor of the House of Representatives ensued in the following month. Ostensibly it concerned the right of Congress to raise such an import tax, which was permitted by the Constitution, but contributions to the debate also reiterated the constitutional proscription on banning the slave trade to the United States before 1808. Rawlins Lowndes argued that the proposed tax would fall almost entirely on South Carolina, even though the resolution for the debate did not single out that state. Though he hoped Congress would legislate conclusively on the slave trade in 1808, which he supported, a tax on imported slaves would make it more difficult later for Congress to effect a full ban. Congressmen Andrew Gregg of Pennsylvania agreed: "Sanction the trade by imposing the tax," he stated, "and soon the traders will demand your protection." Northerners in the debate pointed out that a large number of people at the Constitutional Convention of 1787 opposed the slave trade. Congressman Joseph Stanton Jr. of Rhode Island went further by characterizing the slave trade compromise as "one of the most humiliating concessions made by that venerable Convention which framed the Constitution."[125]

After the debate Congress postponed a decision on the proposed tax on imported slaves to the second Monday in March. Most of those who voted for the postponement thought it would give the South Carolina legislature an opportunity to revoke the act that had reopened the slave trade to their state.[126] The last roll call vote supported the bill by rejecting a motion for indefinite postponement by 69 to 42. Nothing then happened to the measure, because Congress devoted most of its time to consideration of British proposals to restrict in wartime the goods that the United States could send to British Caribbean colonies. Congress failed to impose the tax, but the debates revealed that all eight South Carolina delegates, along with half the other southerners and many northerners, opposed both the ten dollar tax and the reopening of the slave trade by South Carolina.[127] South Carolina's reopening of the slave trade in 1803 gained widespread disapproval in several other states. The legislatures of North Carolina, Tennessee, Maryland, New Hampshire, and Vermont tried unsuccessfully to persuade their federal congressmen to request a constitutional amendment that would close slave imports on a federal level at once.[128]

When Louisiana became a U.S. territory in 1803, it already participated in the foreign slave trade. In 1804, however, Congress outlawed the international and domestic slave trades to Louisiana. A Senate vote of 21–6 supported the ban. This proscription was partly prompted by fears once again of a slave revolt. White Louisianans vigorously debated the pros and cons of the decision. One source claimed that Louisianans had "almost an universal sentiment in favour of this inhuman traffic, and the prohibition thereof is the great source of discontent." Francophone planters particularly wanted to keep the territory's slave trade open. But this was a one-sided, partisan view. Louisiana planters divided over whether banning slave imports would stymie any attempt at slave rebellion or whether it would cut off a supply of new slaves to Louisiana when plantation society there was growing. There was a particular fear of slaves being admitted from the West Indies "that have been concerned in the insurrections of St. Domingo."[129] The ban was ineffective, however, because in October 1805 the domestic slave trade to Louisiana was opened. Between 1805 and 1808, Louisiana took slaves from ships that had touched at Charleston—some from Africa, others from Cuba—as well as smuggled slaves from Texas and Spanish West Florida. Between seven thousand and eight thousand slaves arrived in Louisiana through New Orleans, from overland and overseas, in those four years. The 1805 Territorial Acts failed to close the South Carolina loophole. This allowed Louisiana continued access to African slave imports until 1808.[130]

South Carolina experienced much controversial debate as a result of the closing of the foreign slave trade to Louisiana while its domestic slave trade was allowed. In 1805 and 1806, planters and legislators fiercely contested whether South Carolina should keep its reopened slave trade. Opponents argued that the state's economy was in debt, that it was being drained of specie, and that the slave trade threatened public safety. Those who supported the status quo reiterated the prospects for business gain through providing additional African captives to meet the southwestern cotton boom. Among the arguments set out vigorously, the question of whether the slave trade to South Carolina should be banned on moral or humanitarian grounds was not a major issue. In 1805, after a contentious debate, South Carolina's House of Representatives voted 56–28 in favor of closing the African slave trade; but the Senate defeated this by a vote of 16–15. In 1806 the Senate again stopped the proposal to ban slave imports to South Carolina with a 16–16 tie vote.[131] The outgoing governor of the state disagreed with this decision. In the *Charleston Courier* (December 17, 1806), he argued that South Carolina "should cease to practice what every other state in the union discountenances."

The legal proscription of the foreign slave trade to the United States as a whole was a "quiet abolition."[132] Nevertheless it ended in a distinctive way. In December 1805 Senator Stephen R. Bradley of Vermont called for a law to be passed prohibiting slave imports from January 1, 1808, in line with the expiration of Article I, Section 9, of the Constitution. Two months later a Massachusetts senator reinforced this call. But opponents of the call considered it too soon for such a proposal to be drafted. The matter was particularly controversial, of course, for South Carolina.

An editorial in the July 10, 1806, edition of the *Charleston Courier* revealed the resentment felt by pro–slave trade people in the state against outside criticism of the slave traffic by northern states or even by those in the Upper South.[133] But Jefferson's call for such a law in his opening message to Congress on December 2, 1806—at the earliest point at which action could follow constitutionally—stimulated a swift change in the politics of the matter. It was immediately followed by a legislative attempt to end the foreign slave trade to the United States. Bradley introduced a Senate bill on the topic on the following day. A committee of seven charged with oversight of the bill discussed proscribing the slave trade to the United States. They agreed on the main points quickly and reported on December 15, 1806, the chief details encapsulated in the act of 1807.[134] No southerner in Congress was willing to defend the international slave trade at this juncture.[135]

The legislative history of the measure proscribing the slave trade to the United States was complex, because two bills on this issue were proposed—the Senate bill already mentioned and a different bill from the House of Representatives.[136] Congressional debates did not focus on proscription, for several reasons: all states except South Carolina had closed slave importations to their jurisdictions; the moral arguments over the slave trade had long been accepted even by many South Carolinians; and it was expected that the constitutional clause restraining Congress from acting over the slave traffic would expire in 1808 and be overturned. In addition stopping slave imports would benefit many Americans: northerners would increase their political power by slowing down population growth in the South; Chesapeake planters could request higher prices for the surplus sales they wanted to sell to the Southwest; slaveholders in the Lower South would lessen the risk of slave revolt by reducing the influx of slaves from the Caribbean imbued with a rebellious spirit.[137] Besides these points the Lower South, contrary to some expectations held in 1788, was too weak to prevent an abolition of slave imports: the North had grown faster than the South within twenty years, the new western territories did not support African slave imports, and the New England economy was not linked to a further influx of slaves.[138]

Contention over proscribing the slave trade during the congressional debates instead focused on the status of blacks illegally imported. In particular congressmen fiercely debated Section 4 of the proposed legislation, which stated that any "negro, mulatto or person of colour" found in the United States after December 31, 1807, would be forfeited. Discussion concentrated on whether *forfeited* meant that such persons would be free or slaves. There was also debate over whether penalties for those caught importing slaves in the future should be a fine or imprisonment and whether the crime constituted a capital offense. Eventually it was decided to strike out a clause that stipulated death as the punishment for owners and masters of vessels employed in the slave trade and to include a clause prescribing imprisonment for not less than five and not more than ten years for those who defied the law. The Senate bill eventually became law rather than the House of Representatives' bill.[139]

The congressional debate on the slave trade in 1806 revealed the sectional divisions between North and South over slavery. They foreshadowed the greater sectional tension over slavery that sparked strong controversy in the United States from the era of the Missouri Compromise (1819–21) through the Civil War.[140] The debates over the slave trade in Congress in 1807 avoided humanitarian rhetoric, indicating, as noted at the beginning of this essay, that the ending of the African slave trade to the United States was not the result of a moral crusade. It was not surprising that a moral tone was absent from the debates, because during the previous generation, stretching back to the first Federal Congress in 1789–90, there had been no general debate in the legislature or elsewhere in the public sphere pertaining to the morality of the slave trade.[141]

The slave trade act passed by Congress in 1807 had ten sections. Its regulatory framework was extended in further acts of 1818, 1819, and 1820. But none of this legislation fully stopped the slave trade. The end of the legal slave trade to the United States did not solve the problem of smuggling Africans into the nation, something that continued for many years thereafter.[142] Nor could it prevent the extensive internal slave trade within the United States (amounting to around seven hundred thousand people) in the period from Jefferson's presidency through the Civil War.[143] And ending the foreign slave trade did not, as in the case of the British Caribbean after the British act of abolition, lead to a diminishing slave population; on the contrary natural reproduction kept slavery in the United States flourishing into the antebellum era. Despite these continuing problems with North American slavery, beginning on January 1, 1808, when the U.S. act to abolish the slave trade went into effect, black leaders in the northern states gave annual sermons of thanks to mark the official end of the traffic in African captives to the United States.[144] On January 1, 1808, the day the trade legally ended, the black abolitionist preacher Absalom Jones gave a moving thanksgiving sermon in Philadelphia.[145] In the Lower South, slaveholders welcomed the fact that their slave population in future would mainly consist of acculturated creoles rather than African captives or potentially rebellious slaves imported via the Caribbean.[146]

In sum the abolition of the transatlantic slave trade to the United States was the result of proscribing the traffic step-by-step. It was determined by complex contingent factors and not by a wave of anti–slave trade campaigning. This was partly because the attack on the slave trade moved at different paces in various parts of North America; partly because of the location of political sovereignty; and partly because the issue of the slave trade was bound up with broader issues of slavery and politics in the transition from the thirteen British colonies in North America to the new federal nation. Quakers made significant inroads into banning the slave trade in Pennsylvania and New Jersey in the generation before the American Revolution, and their influence later spread throughout the northern colonies and states and into the Chesapeake by the 1780s. Numerous colonies tried to restrict slave imports by imposing import duties on Africans, but these moves were always subject to the veto of the British Privy Council and to the political sovereignty held by Britain before 1776. During the Revolutionary era, from the Declaration of Independence to the Constitution, lack of a central government meant that the United States as a whole had no political authority to ban slave imports. Anti–slave trade action nevertheless had an important effect on state legislation over the slave trade in this period. By 1787–88 the debates over the ratification of the Constitution revealed that the slave trade was a contentious issue. The congressional ruling on the slave trade stalled any federal action on this matter for twenty years, but in that period various other restrictions were made by Congress on the traffic in slaves.

When the legislature, at Jefferson's behest, debated the slave trade clause of the Constitution in 1806–7, very few delegates, even from the Lower South, supported the slave trade: South Carolina and Georgia had had twenty years since the constitutional clause in which to stock up slaves, and there was a widely held belief that Congress could, and would, act according to the Constitution and ban slave imports at the earliest opportunity. The resulting act of 1807 ending the slave trade to the United States concluded a battle that had proceeded as proscription by degrees. It occurred when the demand for slave labor was expanding in the cotton and sugar belts of the Deep South and when it was not crystal clear that reproduction of the existing U.S. slave population would meet this demand.[147] It can be seen as a delayed outcome of the American Revolution and as the first national success for antislavery forces in the United States.[148] The act has been characterized by William W. Freehling as "the most important slavery legislation that Congress ever passed."[149] Joyce Appleby has also summed up the broad implications of the legislation: "Jefferson's foreign policy in this one act did more to extend the realm of freedom than any deed of his contemporaries in the age of democratic revolutions." It was Jefferson's last public act against slavery.[150]

Though action over the slave trade had been delayed by contentious debates over slavery in the United States and by political divisions between South Carolina and the federal government, the end of the slave trade to the United States was only possible because a brief constitutional clause had separated congressional jurisdiction over its fate from other aspects of slavery. Paradoxically the proscription by degrees that characterized the American struggle to prohibit the slave trade was made necessary by the limits on congressional action for twenty years after 1788 but then was made possible on a federal level, and taken up with alacrity, precisely because it dealt with an aspect of U.S. slavery that could be politically siphoned off from other features of slavery. Jefferson realized the discrete political status of the African slave trade when he gave his presidential address to Congress in late 1806. Thus the American end of the slave trade, though achieved by degrees, succeeded because it compartmentalized a specific part of the problem of slavery that could, in 1808, lead to federal political action on constitutional grounds. The demise of the slave trade to the United States did not depend, as in the British case, on getting humanitarian arguments accepted by legislators, for the various reasons already explained. The protection given to slavery in the Constitution was a much more intractable matter to resolve, and in the case of the United States it took the bloodiest war on its own soil to lead to slave emancipation more than half a century after Americans had legally stopped importing enslaved Africans.

Notes

This was a keynote lecture at the conference "Rethinking Africa and the Atlantic World," organized by the British Group in Early American History, University of Stirling, September 2009. It was also presented at a seminar while I was a visiting fellow at the Robert H. Smith International Center for Jefferson Studies, Monticello, in April 2010.

1. 16 Annals of Cong. 241 (1806), available at http://lcweb2.loc.gov/ammem/am law/lwac.html.

2. David Brion Davis, *The Problem of Slavery in the Age of Revolution, 1770–1823* (Ithaca, N.Y.: Cornell University Press, 1975), 173–74; Woody Holton, *Forced Founders: Indians, Debtors, Slaves, and the Making of the American Revolution in Virginia* (Chapel Hill: University of North Carolina Press, 1999), 66; Julian P. Boyd et al., eds., *The Papers of Thomas Jefferson*, 38 vols. to date (Princeton, N.J.: Princeton University Press, 1950–), 6:298.

3. Don E. Fehrenbacher and Ward M. McAfee, *The Slaveholding Republic: An Account of the United States Government's Relations to Slavery* (New York: Oxford University Press, 2001), 136. For the text of the legislation, see 16 Annals of Cong. 1266–70 (1807). The debates on this matter and the voting figures in the Senate were not recorded.

4. Paul Finkelman, "Regulating the African Slave Trade," *Civil War History* 54, no. 4 (2008): 379.

5. For a summary of the campaigns to abolish the British slave trade, see Kenneth Morgan, *Slavery and the British Empire: From Africa to America* (Oxford: Oxford University Press, 2007), 148–71. The only comparative study of British and American slave trade abolitions is Seymour Drescher, "Divergent Paths: The Anglo-American Abolitions of the Atlantic Slave Trade," in *Migration, Trade, and Slavery in an Expanding World: Essays in Honor of Pieter Emmer,* ed. Wim Klooster (Leiden: Brill, 2009), 259–88.

6. David Eltis, "The U.S. Transatlantic Slave Trade, 1644–1867: An Assessment," *Civil War History* 54, no. 4 (2008): 4, 13; Greg O'Malley, "Final Passages: The British Inter-colonial Slave Trade, 1619–1807" (Ph.D. diss., Johns Hopkins University, 2007), 112. Eltis's total is based on the revised Trans-Atlantic Slave Trade Database, compiled by Eltis, Stephen D. Behrendt, David Richardson, and Manolo Florentino, available online at www.slavevoyages.org, accessed December 2, 2011. This compilation revises the double counting of data on slave imports to the United States found in James A. McMillin, *The Final Victims: Foreign Slave Trade to North America, 1783–1810* (Columbia: University of South Carolina Press, 2005).

7. Eltis, "U.S. Transatlantic Slave Trade," 357, fig. 2. These totals exclude the intra-American slave trade documented by O'Malley.

8. These demographic contrasts are explained in Philip D. Morgan, *Slave Counterpoint: Black Culture in the Eighteenth-Century Chesapeake and Lowcountry* (Chapel Hill: University of North Carolina Press, 1998), 81–95.

9. Eltis, "U.S. Transatlantic Slave Trade," 370; David Eltis and David Richardson, "A New Assessment of the Transatlantic Slave Trade," in *Extending the Frontiers: Essays on the New Transatlantic Slave Trade Database*, ed. David Eltis and David Richardson (New Haven, Conn.: Yale University Press, 2008), 48; Seymour Drescher, *Abolition: A History of Slavery and Antislavery* (New York: Cambridge University Press, 2009), 135.

10. Betty Wood, *Slavery in Colonial Georgia, 1730–1775* (Athens: University of Georgia Press, 1985).

11. For participation by Friends in the slave trade, see Darold D. Wax, "Quaker Merchants and the Slave Trade in Colonial Pennsylvania," *Pennsylvania Magazine of History and Biography* 86, no. 2 (1962): 143–59.

12. Anthony Benezet to Granville Sharp, May 14, 1772, in Prince Hoare, *Memoirs of Granville Sharp, Esq . . .* (London: Colburn, 1820), 98.

13. [Benjamin Rush], *An Address to the Inhabitants of the British Settlements in America, upon Slave-keeping* (Philadelphia: Dunlap, 1773).

14. Jean R. Soderlund, *Quakers and Slavery: A Divided Spirit* (Princeton, N.J.: Princeton University Press, 1985), 17–31; Gary B. Nash and Jean R. Soderlund, *Freedom by Degrees: Emancipation in Pennsylvania and Its Aftermath* (New York: Oxford University Press, 1991), 42; Arthur Zilversmit, *The First Emancipation: The Abolition of Slavery in the North* (Chicago: University of Chicago Press, 1967), 80.

15. Philip D. Morgan, "Ending the Slave Trade: A Caribbean and Atlantic Context," in *Abolitionism and Imperialism in Britain, Africa, and the Atlantic,* ed. Derek R. Peterson (Athens: Ohio University Press, 2010), 102.

16. Christopher Leslie Brown, *Moral Capital: Foundations of British Abolitionism* (Chapel Hill: University of North Carolina Press, 2006), 136, 144; Nash and Soderlund, *Freedom by Degrees,* 24, 71. For slave import duties at the colony level, see W. E. B. Du Bois, *The Suppression of the African Slave-Trade to the United States of America, 1638–1870* (Cambridge, Mass.: Harvard University Press, 1896), 9–38 and appendix A; Ruth Scarborough, *The Opposition to Slavery in Georgia prior to 1860* (Nashville: George Peabody College for Teachers, 1933), 99–101; Darold D. Wax, "Negro Import Duties in Colonial Pennsylvania," *Pennsylvania Magazine of History and Biography* 97, no. 1 (1973): 22–44, and "Negro Import Duties in Colonial Virginia: A Study of British Commercial Policy and Local Public Policy," *Virginia Magazine of History and Biography* 79, no. 1 (1971): 29–44; and Elizabeth Donnan, ed., *Documents Illustrative of the History of the Slave Trade to America,* 4 vols. (Washington, D.C.: Carnegie Institution of Washington, 1930–35), 3:72–73, 76–77, 289–90, available online at http://abolition.nypl.org/texts/us_slave_trade/.

17. Duncan J. MacLeod, *Slavery, Race and the American Revolution* (New York: Cambridge University Press, 1974), 31.

18. Benezet to Sharp, May 14, 1772, in Hoare, *Memoirs of Granville Sharp,* 100.

19. Thomas Jefferson, *A Summary View of the Rights of British America* (London: Kearsly, 1774), 29.

20. MacLeod, *Slavery, Race and the American Revolution*, 32; James C. Connolly, "Slavery in Colonial New Jersey and the Causes Operating against Its Extension," *Proceedings of the New Jersey Historical Society* 14 (April 1929): 189, 191.

21. Mack Thompson, *Moses Brown: Reluctant Reformer* (Chapel Hill: University of North Carolina Press, 1962), 81; Zilversmit, *First Emancipation*, 106.

22. Zilversmit, *First Emancipation*, 100–103, 107–8; George H. Moore, *Notes on the History of Slavery in Massachusetts* (New York: Appleton, 1866), 130–40; Bernard Bailyn, *The Ordeal of Thomas Hutchinson* (Cambridge, Mass.: Harvard University Press, 1974), 378.

23. For the figure cited and further data on the slave population of North American colonies and states, 1610–1780, see Susan B. Carter, Scott Sigmund Gartner, Michael R. Haines, Alan L. Olmstead, Richard Sutch, and Gavin Wright, eds., *Historical Statistics of the United States: Earliest Times to the Present. Millennial Edition*, vol. 5, pt. E, *Governance and International Relations* (New York: Cambridge University Press, 2006), table Eg1–59, 653.

24. Virginia statutes laying down duties on imported slaves are summarized in Donnan, *Documents*, 4:66, 102–3, 122–23, 127–31, 133–35, 137–42, 144, 150–56, 158–59.

25. Wax, "Negro Import Duties," 29–44.

26. Holton, *Forced Founders*, 66–67, 71.

27. Bruce A. Ragsdale, *A Planter's Republic: The Search for Economic Independence in Revolutionary Virginia* (Madison: University of Wisconsin Press, 1996), 120.

28. The text of Lee's address is reprinted in Gary B. Nash, *Race and Revolution* (Madison, Wis.: Madison House, 1990), 92–96.

29. Richard K. MacMaster, "Arthur Lee's 'Address on Slavery': An Aspect of Virginia's Struggle to End the Slave Trade, 1765–1774," *Virginia Magazine of History and Biography* 80, no. 2 (1972): 152.

30. Quoted in Eva Sheppard Wolf, *Race and Liberty in the New Nation: Emancipation in Virginia from the Revolution to Nat Turner's Rebellion* (Baton Rouge: Louisiana State University Press, 2006), 23.

31. Patrick Henry to a correspondent, January 18, 1773, in *Patrick Henry: Life, Correspondence, and Speeches*, ed. William Wirt Henry, 3 vols. (New York: Scribner, 1891; repr., New York: Franklin, 1969), 1:152–53.

32. Ragsdale, *Planters' Republic*, 135, 251; Wolf, *Race and Liberty*, 14, 24–25, 28.

33. W. Robert Higgins, "The South Carolina Negro Duty Law" (master's thesis, University of South Carolina, 1967); Du Bois, *Suppression of the African Slave-Trade*, 11; David Richardson, "The British Slave Trade to Colonial South Carolina," *Slavery and Abolition* 12, no. 3 (1991): 131; Robert M. Weir, *Colonial South Carolina: A History* (Columbia: University of South Carolina Press, 1997), 146, 165, 208; Finkelman, "Regulating the African Slave Trade," 380.

34. Worthington C. Ford et al., eds., *Journals of the Continental Congress, 1774–1789*, 34 vols. (Washington, D.C.: Government Printing Office, 1904–37), 1:77.

35. Davis, *Problem of Slavery*, 24.

36. Du Bois, *Suppression of the African Slave-Trade*, 47.

37. Thomas Jefferson's Notes of Proceedings in Congress, July 1–4, 1776, in *Letters of Delegates to Congress, 1774–1789*, vol. 4, *May 16–August 15, 1776*, ed. Paul H. Smith (Washington, D.C.: Library of Congress, 1979), 359. Jefferson preserved the deleted passages: see Thomas

Jefferson, "Autobiography," in *Thomas Jefferson: Writings*, ed. Merrill D. Peterson (New York: Library of America, 1984), 21–22.

38. Drescher, *Abolition*, 125.

39. Data on slave imports to revolutionary North America are available at Trans-Atlantic Slave Trade Database, www.slavevoyages.org, accessed January 2, 2012.

40. Richard B. Morris, ed., *John Jay: The Winning of the Peace: Unpublished Papers 1780–1784* (New York: Harper & Row, 1980), 15, 540.

41. Benjamin Rush to Nathanael Greene, September 16, 1782, in *Letters of Benjamin Rush*, ed. Lyman H. Butterfield, 2 vols. (Princeton, N.J.: Princeton University Press, 1951), 1:286.

42. Henry Laurens to Alexander Hamilton, April 19, 1785, in *The Papers of Henry Laurens*, vol. 16, *September 1, 1782–December 17, 1792*, ed. David R. Chesnutt and C. James Taylor (Columbia: University of South Carolina Press, 2003), 553–54.

43. Maurice Jackson, *Let This Voice Be Heard: Anthony Benezet, Father of Atlantic Abolitionism* (Philadelphia: University of Pennsylvania Press, 2009), 249.

44. Roger Bruns, ed., *Am I Not a Man and a Brother: The Antislavery Crusade of Revolutionary America, 1688–1788* (New York: Chelsea House, 1977), 494–501; Matthew Mason, *Slavery and Politics in the Early American Republic* (Chapel Hill: University of North Carolina Press, 2006), 28.

45. "A Bill to Prevent Importation of Slaves," in Boyd et al., *Papers of Jefferson*, 2:22–24; Michael A. McDonnell, *The Politics of War: Race, Class, and Conflict in Revolutionary Virginia* (Chapel Hill: University of North Carolina Press, 2007), 331–32.

46. Davis, *Problem of Slavery*, 24; Thompson, *Moses Brown*, 182; David N. Gellman, *Emancipating New York: The Politics of Slavery and Freedom 1777–1827* (Baton Rouge: Louisiana State University Press, 2006), 52–53; Zilversmit, *First Emancipation*, 152–53; Nash and Soderlund, *Freedom by Degrees*, 102.

47. Graham Russell Hodges, *Root and Branch: African Americans in New York and East Jersey, 1613–1863* (Chapel Hill: University of North Carolina Press, 1999), 169; Carl E. Prince, Mary Lou Lustig, and David William Voorhees, eds., *The Papers of William Livingston*, 5 vols. (Trenton & New Brunswick: New Jersey Historical Commission, 1979–88), 5:255.

48. Donald L. Robinson, *Slavery in the Structure of American Politics, 1765–1820* (New York: Harcourt Brace Jovanovich, 1971), 298–99; Donnan, *Documents*, 4:480–89, 492–94; Rachel N. Klein, *Unification of a Slave State: The Rise of the Planter Class in the South Carolina Backcountry, 1760–1808* (Chapel Hill: University of North Carolina Press, 1990), 131–32; Jerome J. Nadelhaft, "South Carolina and the Slave Trade, 1783–1787" (master's thesis, University of Wisconsin, 1961). South Carolina passed further acts prohibiting slave importation in 1788, 1792, 1794, 1796, 1800, and 1802. See Patrick S. Brady, "The Slave Trade and Sectionalism in South Carolina, 1787–1808," *Journal of Southern History* 38, no. 4 (1972): 601–20.

49. Thomas Jefferson to Edward Rutledge, July 14, 1787, in *Writings of Thomas Jefferson*, 10 vols., ed. Paul L. Ford (New York: Putnam, 1892–99), 4:410.

50. Paul Finkelman, "Slavery and the Constitutional Convention: Making a Covenant with Death," in *Beyond Confederation: Origins of the Constitution and American National Identity*, ed. Richard Beeman, Stephen Botein, and Edward C. Carter II (Chapel Hill: University of North Carolina Press, 1987), 195–217.

51. Gary B. Nash, "Franklin and Slavery," *Proceedings of the American Philosophical Society* 150, no. 4 (2006): 635.

52. Quoted in Richard S. Newman, *The Transformation of American Abolitionism: Fighting Slavery in the Early Republic* (Chapel Hill: University of North Carolina Press, 2002), 47.

53. Max Farrand, ed., *The Records of the Federal Convention of 1787*, 4 vols. (New Haven, Conn.: Yale University Press, 1937), 1:486–87.

54. Finkelman, "Slavery and the Constitutional Convention," 190–92.

55. Ibid.; William M. Wiecek, "The Witch at the Christening: Slavery and the Constitution's Origins," in *The Framing and Ratification of the Constitution*, ed. Leonard W. Levy and Dennis J. Mahoney (New York: Macmillan, 1987), 167–84; Staughton Lynd, "The Compromise of 1787," *Political Science Quarterly* 81, no. 2 (1966): 225–50; Jack N. Rakove, *Original Meanings: Politics and Ideas in the Making of the Constitution* (New York: Knopf, 1996), 72–75, 85–88; James Oakes, "'The Compromising Expedient': Justifying a Proslavery Constitution," *Cardozo Law Review* 17, no. 6 (1996): 2023–56.

56. Adam Rothman, *Slave Country: American Expansion and the Origins of the Deep South* (Cambridge, Mass.: Harvard University Press, 2005), 7.

57. See Larry E. Tise, *Proslavery: A History of the Defense of Slavery in America, 1701–1840* (Athens: University of Georgia Press, 1987), 78.

58. Farrand, ed., *Records of the Federal Convention*, 2:414–15.

59. Ibid., 2:364–65.

60. Lacy K. Ford, *Deliver Us from Evil: The Slavery Question in the Old South* (New York: Oxford University Press, 2009), 82. Charles Cotesworth Pinckney, the fourth delegate, voted on that occasion to keep the state's slave trade open.

61. Rebecca Starr, *A School for Politics: Commercial Lobbying and Political Culture in Early South Carolina* (Baltimore: Johns Hopkins University Press, 1998), 102.

62. Farrand, ed., *Records of the Federal Convention*, 2:370–73; Steven M. Deyle, *Carry Me Back: The Domestic Slave Trade in American Life* (New York: Oxford University Press, 2006), 23.

63. See Paul Finkelman, "The Founders and Slavery: Little Ventured, Little Gained," *Yale Journal of Law & the Humanities* 13, no. 2 (2001): 422.

64. Farrand, ed., *Records of the Federal Convention*, 2:530–32.

65. Fehrenbacher, *Slaveholding Republic*, 136.

66. Finkelman, "Founders and Slavery," 436–37.

67. Farrand, ed., *Records of the Federal Convention*, 2:408–9, 415; Richard Beeman, *Plain, Honest Men: The Making of the American Constitution* (New York: Random House, 2009), 327. Rhode Island was absent from the decision because it had not sent delegates to the convention. New York's delegates lacked a quorum.

68. For details, see David L. Lightner, "The Founders and the Interstate Slave Trade," *Journal of the Early Republic* 22, no. 1 (2002): 28–29.

69. David Waldstreicher, *Runaway America: Benjamin Franklin, Slavery, and the American Revolution* (New York: Hill & Wang, 2004), 234.

70. Davis, *Problem of Slavery*, 123–25; Prince et al., *Papers of William Livingston*, 5:302n1.

71. Beeman, *Plain, Honest Men*, 323.

72. See two works by Nash: *Race and Revolution*, 27–29, and *The Forgotten Fifth: African Americans in the Age of Revolution* (Cambridge, Mass.: Harvard University Press, 2006), 79–85.

73. Finkelman, "Slavery and the Constitutional Convention," 221.

74. Mason, *Slavery and Politics,* 32–33; Matthew Mason, "Slavery and the Founding," *History Compass* 4, no. 5 (2006): 943–55.

75. MacLeod, *Slavery, Race and the American Revolution,* 44.

76. Samuel Bannister Harding, *The Contest over the Ratification of the Federal Constitution in the State of Massachusetts* (New York: Longmans, Green, 1896), 71.

77. Massachusetts Ratification Convention Debates, January 25, 1788, in *A Necessary Evil? Slavery and the Debate over the Constitution,* ed. John P. Kaminski, Constitutional Heritage 2 (Madison, Wis.: Madison House, 1995), 88. For divisions between Federalists and Anti-Federalists in Massachusetts over the slave trade clause, see John Craig Hammond, "'We Are to Be Advanced to the Level of Slaves': Planters, Taxes, Aristocrats, and Massachusetts Antifederalists, 1787–1788," *Historical Journal of Massachusetts* 31, no. 2 (2003): 180–81.

78. *Northampton Hampshire Gazette,* February 6, 1788, and *Exeter Freeman's Oracle,* February 8, 1788, in Kaminski, *Necessary Evil,* 96, 98.

79. Jean Yarbrough, "New Hampshire: Puritanism and the Moral Foundations of America," in *Ratifying the Constitution,* ed. Michael Allen Gillespie and Michael Lienesch (Lawrence: University Press of Kansas, 1989), 245–49.

80. *New York Journal,* November 23, 1787, and *New York Morning Post,* April 11, 1788, in Kaminski, *Necessary Evil,* 150.

81. James Pemberton to John Pemberton, September 20, 1787, in Kaminski, *Necessary Evil,* 116; Timothy Meanwell in the *Philadelphia Independent Gazetteer,* October 29, 1787, in ibid., 120; the Pennsylvania Abolition Society Petition to the Constitutional Convention, *Pennsylvania Gazette,* March 5, 1788, as reprinted in the *Philadelphia Independent Gazetteer,* March 7, 1788, in ibid., 148; Owen S. Ireland, *Religion, Ethnicity and Politics: Ratifying the Constitution in Pennsylvania* (University Park: Pennsylvania State University Press, 1995), 81.

82. For examples, see Kenneth Morgan, "Slavery and the Debate over Ratification of the United States Constitution," *Slavery and Abolition* 22, no. 3 (2001): 45.

83. Massachusetts Ratification Convention Debates, January 25–26, 1788, and *Exeter Freemen's Oracle,* February 8, 1788, in Kaminski, *Necessary Evil,* 88–89, 98.

84. *Philadelphia Independent Gazetteer,* November 8, 1787, in Kaminski, *Necessary Evil,* 126.

85. Samuel Hopkins to Moses Brown, October 22, 1787, in Kaminski, *Necessary Evil,* 73.

86. *Exeter Freemen's Oracle,* February 8, 1788, in Kaminski, *Necessary Evil,* 98.

87. Morgan, "Slavery and the Debate," 47.

88. Ibid., 48.

89. Virginia Ratifying Convention Debates, June 17, 1788, in Kaminski, *Necessary Evil,* 141; *The Federalist* no. 38, January 12, 1788, in Kaminski, *Necessary Evil,* 187.

90. *The Federalist* no. 42, January 22, 1788, in Kaminski, *Necessary Evil,* 141–42; Davis, *Problem of Slavery,* 326.

91. Robert Waln to Richard Waln, October 3, 1787, in Kaminski, *Necessary Evil,* 118; Morgan, "Slavery and the Debate," 49.

92. Davis, *Problem of Slavery,* 126.

93. Allan Kulikoff, "Uprooted Peoples: Black Migrants in the Age of the American Revolution, 1790–1820," in *Slavery and Freedom in the Age of the American Revolution,* ed. Ira Berlin and Ronald Hoffman (Charlottesville: University Press of Virginia, 1983), 146.

94. Finkelman, "Founders and Slavery," 431.

95. Howard A. Ohline, "Slavery, Economics, and Congressional Politics, 1790," *Journal of Southern History* 46, no. 3 (1980): 340.

96. Jay Coughtry, *The Notorious Triangle: Rhode Island and the African Slave Trade, 1700–1807* (Philadelphia: Temple University Press, 1981), 205–6; Elizabeth Donnan, "Agitation against the Slave Trade in Rhode Island, 1784–1790," in *Persecution and Liberty: Essays in Honor of George Lincoln Burr* (New York: Century, 1931), 473–82; Charles Rappleye, *Sons of Providence: The Brown Brothers, the Slave Trade, and the American Revolution* (New York: Simon & Schuster, 2006), 248.

97. Robinson, *Slavery in the Structure*, 299.

98. Fehrenbacher, *Slaveholding Republic*, 137–38; Robin L Einhorn, *American Taxation, American Slavery* (Chicago: University of Chicago Press, 2006), 152–53.

99. Ohline, "Slavery, Economics," 340; Joseph J. Ellis, *Founding Brothers: The Revolutionary Generation* (New York: Knopf, 2001), 81–83; Waldstreicher, *Runaway America*, 236.

100. Ellis, *Founding Brothers*, 88; Nash, *Race and Revolution*, 38. For the congressional debates on the petitions, see 1 Annals of Cong. 1197–205 (1790), 2 Annals of Cong. 1413–17, 1450–74 (1790), and Helen E. Veit, Charlene Bangs Bickford, Kenneth R. Bowling, and William Charles diGiacomantonio, eds., *Debates in the House of Representatives. Volume XII. Second Session: January to March 1790* (Baltimore: Johns Hopkins University Press, 1994), 270–73, 282–92, 295–313.

101. MacLeod, *Slavery, Race and the American Revolution*, 36.

102. Edgar S. Maclay, ed., *Journal of William Maclay* (New York: Appleton, 1890), 196; Thomas E. Drake, *Quakers and Slavery in America* (New Haven, Conn.: Yale University Press, 1950), 102–5.

103. Einhorn, *American Taxation*, 154.

104. 1 Annals of Cong. 1465 (1790); Gellman, *Emancipating New York*, 95–99. For further analysis of the Quaker petitions to Congress in 1790, see Robinson, *Slavery in the Structure*, 302–10; Ohline, "Slavery, Economics," 355–60; Stuart E. Knee, "The Quaker Petition of 1790: A Challenge to Democracy in Early America," *Slavery and Abolition* 6, no. 3 (1985): 151–59; and Richard S. Newman, "Prelude to the Gag Rule: Southern Reaction to Antislavery Petitions in the First Federal Congress," *Journal of the Early Republic* 16, no. 4 (1996): 571–99.

105. George Washington to David Stuart, March 28, 1790, in *The Papers of George Washington: Presidential Series*, ed. Dorothy Twohig, 14 vols. to date (Charlottesville: University Press of Virginia, 1987–2005), 5:288; Waldstreicher, *Runaway America*, 237.

106. Newman, *Transformation of American Abolitionism*, 48–49, 57; Davis, *Problem of Slavery*, 326n68.

107. Drake, *Quakers and Slavery*, 107.

108. See, for example, an address given before the Connecticut Society for the Promotion of Freedom, dated September 15, 1791, and printed as Jonathan Edwards, *The Injustice and Impolicy of the Slave Trade and of the Slavery of the Africans: Illustrated in a Sermon*, 2nd ed. (Boston: Wells & Lilly, 1822).

109. Thompson, *Moses Brown*, 200–201.

110. Coughtry, *Notorious Triangle*, 93, 212–21; Fehrenbacher, *Slaveholding Republic*, 140, 382n25.

111. Ford, *Deliver Us*, 84–85.

112. W. E. Minchinton, "The Seaborne Slave Trade of North Carolina," *North Carolina Historical Review* 71, no. 1 (1994): 17–18; Robinson, *Slavery in the Structure*, 297, 299; Fehrenbacher, *Slaveholding Republic*, 136.

113. Scarborough, *Opposition to Slavery*, 108–10; Ford, *Deliver Us*, 86.

114. Nash, *Race and Revolution*, 79; Jordan, *White over Black*, 328.

115. Fehrenbacher, *Slaveholding Republic*, 141.

116. Ibid., 141–42; Rothman, *Slave Country*, 38.

117. Jed Handelsman Shugerman, "The Louisiana Purchase and South Carolina's Reopening of the Slave Trade in 1803," *Journal of the Early Republic* 22, no. 2 (2002): 253–90.

118. Ford, *Deliver Us*, 96–102, 105.

119. Quoted in Brady, "Slave Trade," 617.

120. Stephen J. Goldfarb, "An Inquiry into the Politics of the Prohibition of the International Slave Trade," *Agricultural History* 68, no. 2 (1994): 29–30.

121. Rothman, *Slave Country*, 37–38.

122. Michael P. Johnson, "Runaway Slaves and the Slave Communities in South Carolina, 1799 to 1830," *William and Mary Quarterly*, 3rd ser., 38, no. 3 (1981): 419.

123. Deyle, *Carry Me Back*, 24.

124. 13 Annals of Cong. 820 (1804).

125. Ibid., 991–92, 999, 1003–4, 1014 (quotation), 1017 (quotation), 1027, 1034.

126. Ibid., 1036.

127. Fehrenbacher, *Slaveholding Republic*, 143.

128. Ulrich B. Phillips, *American Negro Slavery: A Study of the Supply, Employment and Control of Negro Labor as Determined by the Plantation Regime* (New York: Appleton, 1918), 138–39; Herman V. Ames, *The Proposed Amendments to the Constitution of the United States during the First Century of Its History*, 2 vols. (Washington, D.C.: Government Printing Office, 1897), 2:208–9, 326–28.

129. William C. C. Claiborne to James Madison, July 5, 1804, and July 12, 1804, in *The Papers of James Madison. Secretary of State Series*, vol. 7, *2 April–31 August 1804*, ed. David B. Mattern, J. C. A. Stagg, Ellen J. Barber, Anne Mandeville Colony, Angela Kreider, and Jeanne Kerr Cross (Charlottesville: University Press of Virginia, 2005), 422, 445 (quotations); John Craig Hammond, *Slavery, Freedom, and Expansion in the Early American West* (Charlottesville: University Press of Virginia, 2007), 30, 37–38, 46–47, 187; Everett S. Brown, ed., "The Senate Debate on the Breckinridge Bill for the Government of Louisiana, 1804," *American Historical Review* 22, no. 2 (1917): 345–50; Ford, *Deliver Us*, 112–14; James Scanlan, "A Sudden Conceit: Jefferson and the Louisiana Bill of 1804," *Louisiana History* 9, no. 2 (1968): 152–55.

130. Hammond, *Slavery, Freedom, and Expansion*, 50, 188; Jean-Pierre Le Glaunec, "Slave Migrations and Slave Control in Spanish and Early American New Orleans," in *Empires of the Imagination: Transatlantic Histories of the Louisiana Purchase*, ed. Peter J. Kastor and François Weil (Charlottesville: University Press of Virginia, 2009), 214, 216.

131. Ford, *Deliver Us*, 121–23.

132. Robin Blackburn, *The Overthrow of Colonial Slavery, 1776–1846* (London: Verso, 1988), 286.

133. Donnan, *Documents*, 4:517–19.

134. Scarborough, *Opposition to Slavery,* 112.

135. Ford, *Deliver Us,* 125.

136. Du Bois, *Suppression of the African Slave-Trade,* 105–6.

137. MacLeod, *Slavery, Race and the American Revolution,* 156–57; Anthony A. Iaccarino, "Virginia and the National Contest over Slavery in the Early Republic, 1780–1833" (Ph.D. diss., University of California, Los Angeles, 1999), 126.

138. Finkelman, "Founders and Slavery," 432–33.

139. 16 Annals of Cong. 167, 170–72, 221–22, 240–44 (1806). For a summary of the debates, see Du Bois, *Suppression of the African Slave-Trade,* 96–108, and Robinson, *Slavery in the Structure,* 324–37.

140. Matthew E. Mason, "Slavery Overshadowed: Congress Debates Prohibiting the Atlantic Slave Trade to the United States, 1806–1807," *Journal of the Early Republic* 20, no. 1 (2000): 59–81.

141. Drescher, *Abolition,* 135–36.

142. This is a major theme in Du Bois, *Suppression of the African Slave-Trade.* See also Ernest Obadele-Starks, *Freebooters and Smugglers: The Foreign Slave Trade to the United States after 1808* (Fayetteville: University of Arkansas Press, 2007).

143. For the scale and characteristics of this form of slave trading, see Michael Tadman, *Speculators and Slaves: Masters, Traders, and Slaves in the Old South,* 2nd ed. (Madison: University of Wisconsin Press, 1996); and Deyle, *Carry Me Back.*

144. Nash, *Race and Revolution,* 199.

145. James Sidbury, *Becoming African in America: Race and Nation in the Early Black Atlantic* (New York: Oxford University Press, 2007), 135–37.

146. Ford, *Deliver Us,* 149.

147. Adam Rothman, "The Domestication of the Slave Trade in the United States," in *The Chattel Principle: Internal Slave Trades in the Americas,* ed. Walter Johnson (New Haven, Conn.: Yale University Press, 2004), 35.

148. Sidbury, *Becoming African,* 135.

149. William W. Freehling, *The Road to Disunion,* vol. 1, *Secessionists at Bay, 1776–1854* (New York: Oxford University Press, 1990), 136.

150. Joyce Appleby, *Thomas Jefferson* (New York: Times Books, 2003), 131 (quotation), 138.

"MOST CONTEMPTIBLE IN THE UNION"

South Carolina, Slavery, and the Constitution

Jonathan Mercantini

The rhetoric of South Carolina's leaders left no doubt regarding their commitment to slavery. That sentiment was something even those on both sides of the state's debate over ratifying the new federal Constitution could agree on. Rawlins Lowndes, the spokesman for the Anti-Federalist position in the state, proclaimed, "Without negroes this state would degenerate into one of the most contemptible in the union." He echoed Charles Pinckney, one of the state's delegates to the Philadelphia convention and a supporter of the new government, who had previously asserted that "whilst their [*sic*] remained one acre of swampland in South Carolina," he would oppose any restrictions on slavery.[1]

During the hot summer of 1787, the South Carolina delegation held steadfast to that commitment to slavery. In the debate over apportionment for the House of Representatives, when the infamous Three-Fifths Compromise was under consideration, John Rutledge declared, "the true question at present is, whether the Southern States shall or shall not be parties to the Union." When the other major issue regarding slavery at the convention arose, that of the continuation of the international slave trade, Pinckney stated the South Carolina position even more bluntly: "South Carolina can never receive the plan if it prohibits the slave trade."[2] Despite misgivings by some northern members of the convention, the South Carolinians were able to make their demands stick, as slaves would be considered in the total population for apportionment purposes and the slave trade continued for a minimum of twenty years. By successfully executing these brinkmanship practices, South Carolinians extended the international slave trade in America until 1808, thereby creating the "ambiguous anniversary" of the end of the trade.

For many years since, historians have taken the South Carolinians at their word. Recently, however, several historians have advanced dual arguments with regard to slavery and the Constitution: namely that South Carolina was in no position to secede from the new federal union in 1787 and could have been made to accept severe limitations on the institution of slavery. This argument has been pressed further, as the antislavery movement in the Revolutionary period has come to be portrayed as stronger than had been commonly accepted. There are, however, a number of problems when this thesis is applied to South Carolina, especially when a larger context than just the ratification of the Constitution is considered. Throughout the Revolutionary War, South Carolinians made it clear that their dedication to slavery was greater than their devotion to the Union and the cause of independence. Moreover South Carolinians had adopted a history of the war in which they had largely achieved independence on their own, with only limited help from their northern allies. Coupled with their belief in the importance of South Carolina's economy to the success of the new nation and a political culture in which brinkmanship dealings with central governments—be they in London or Philadelphia—was the norm, a pattern emerges where South Carolinians would not accept any outside interference into the most important of their local issues: the peculiar institution and its preservation and growth in the Palmetto State.

Gary Nash has put forth the most adamant statement challenging the conventional wisdom, asking, "Could slavery have been abolished?" in the second chapter of his book *The Forgotten Fifth: African Americans in the Age of Revolution.*[3] Nash complains that the argument that slavery could not be abolished in the late eighteenth century reeks of inevitability. He offers five broad reasons why the Constitutional Convention represents a missed opportunity to have begun the abolition of slavery in the United States: the strength of the northern abolition movement, previously underestimated, which saw slavery as anathema to the revolution's universal ideas of human rights; (most directly relevant to the ideas put forth here) that the Lower South was "most precariously situated and ill-prepared to break away from the rest of the nation";[4] there was less racism and a greater optimism of black equality in the Revolutionary era based on the ideas of "cultural environmentalism"; the opening of the trans-Appalachian West created the best opportunity for a federal program of compensated emancipation; and the growth of the abolition movement and the cessation of the African slave trade in Great Britain and the revolt of blacks on Saint-Domingue demonstrated the necessity of abolition. In general, then, Nash sees abolition as a means of unifying the new nation. He does not agree that northern states or even states in the Upper South were forced to accept slavery as the price of Union.

There are a number of problems with Nash's argument. First and foremost is that he frequently conflates the Upper South and Lower South. Although those two regions demonstrated considerably different sensibilities on the question of continuing the slave trade, the differences go much further. Despite the fact that they possessed the vast majority of the nation's slave population, these two regions can in no way be equated. While Virginia and Maryland were looking to rid themselves of their slaves, particularly as wheat, far less suited to gang slave labor, replaced tobacco, the Lower South hungered for slaves from both internal and external sources. This fundamental difference is an important part of the larger question that will be considered below.

On the larger issue, however, Nash has also missed the depth of the Carolinians' commitment to enslaved labor. Even if the abolition movement was stronger in the North than previously considered, as David Brion Davis and David Waldstreicher have ardently asserted, that position had no bearing in South Carolina, nor did northern notions of the potential for black equality.[5] While southerners did fear a slave uprising, and their acceptance of the new Constitution was in part based on the idea that the "eastern" (New England) states would come to their aid in the event of an internal revolt, they felt secure in their ability to control their slave population, especially as the white population in the backcountry grew rapidly. Moreover the idea of compensated emancipation fails to take into account that slavery represented more than just wealth and the area's primary form of labor and investment. First was the belief that rice could not be grown profitably in the South Carolina swamps and tidal basins with wage labor. Perhaps even more important are the myriad ways in which slavery served larger social and political purposes, which could not be accomplished via compensated emancipation. Slaves were a measure of status and wealth as well as of labor in this society. White South Carolinians were eager to demonstrate their success as well as to free their wives and children from the drudgery of field labor and to give their progeny the opportunity of education. They would not sacrifice these social achievements by selling their slaves to the federal government.

Throughout the Revolutionary War, most elite South Carolinians acted more concerned about preserving their own wealth than in making sacrifices for independence. When a raid of British soldiers threatened Charles Town, demanding its surrender in May 1779, a majority of the inhabitants agreed to accept neutrality and British occupation in order to prevent the invading British troops from pillaging the city. Only the determination of Christopher Gadsden and other government officials prevented the surrender of the city to what was later learned to be a relatively small number of British troops unprepared for the siege that would be necessary to take the city. The willingness to surrender so easily demonstrates the Carolinians' lack of commitment to the cause of independence.[6]

The following spring, when Charles Town was besieged by a large force of British troops before capitulating, the majority of the city's inhabitants agreed to surrender and accept British occupation in order to maintain their wealth and status. A majority in the capital had been nominally in favor of the Patriot cause until the British invasion in early 1780. After their capture in the surrender of Charles Town, most of the population agreed to sign a congratulatory address to the British, though neither side took that as an indication of loyalist feeling.[7]

These sentiments reflect the larger frustrations that South Carolinians felt toward their fellow states. William Moultrie asserted that the other states could offer no complaint should Charles Town surrender, "as they have not fulfilled their engagements to it [South Carolina] in giving it aid and assistance, from which promise that State came into the Union."[8] After the war South Carolinians would increasingly avow that they had won their independence because of their own actions during the war. This account of Charles Town's defending itself against invasion in June 1776 (against the orders of General Charles Lee), staving off the marauding British in 1779, and holding out against the British siege campaign for six weeks in 1780 points out the lack of assistance from the North and thus asserts that South Carolina had essentially won its independence by its own actions. Added to this narrative were rumors that spread through Charles Town and the countryside in 1780–81: "It is currently reported, & believed here, that G. Britain will offer America, the Independence of all the states except So. Carolina & Georgia—& perhaps even of No. C.—& that such a proposition will be accepted—I think it impossible, that Congress will leave us in the Lurch—but, pray, inform me candidly, & fully what may be expected on that Head."[9]

For their part northerners were frustrated by the South Carolinians' lack of commitment to independence. As one northern delegate to the Continental Congress wrote, "How can South Carolina expect we will send our men to their support, when they will do nothing for themselves?" James Lovell of Massachusetts made the point even more explicit and connected his unwillingness to support the campaign in the Lower South with that region's putting slavery ahead of independence: "The State of Sth. Cara. have *thought* we neglected them, we *know* they neglected themselves. They will not *draught* to fill up their Battalions, they will not raise *black regiments*, they will not put their militia when in camp under continental Rules."[10]

It is also important to recall that the Revolution in South Carolina was the most destructive and vicious in any state. Conditions in the South Carolina backcountry more closely resembled a civil war than anywhere in America. As General William Moultrie wrote during his travels in 1782 as he returned to his plantation, "no living creature was to be seen, except now and then a few camp scavengers." Livestock as well as the previously abundant population of deer, squirrels, and birds "was now destitute of all."[11] The scale of the ruin is even more remarkable given the limited means and capabilities troops had for such devastation in the late eighteenth century. In addition to the destruction of livestock and other productive resources, thousands of slaves ran away to British lines, encouraged by promises of freedom, and many, many more were seized by British forces and their Tory allies, who left Charles Town, for the West Indies in many cases, in December 1782.[12]

Because of widespread destruction, the recovery of the South Carolina economy proceeded slowly. Credit was tight, especially as British lenders who had previously dominated the market were, of course, not returning, though they expected to have their debts paid. Rice fields and irrigation systems took time to recover from wartime neglect, and the Carolinians needed new markets for their crops. Most important, as many as fifty thousand slaves had been lost. Still South Carolina's economy was on the road to recovery. In 1783 it was the only state to pay its full assessment to the Continental Congress. Moreover South Carolina had been the wealthiest colony before the war, and the most productive on a per capita basis; that economic power would not be forgotten by the other states that recognized they needed South Carolina to play an important role in the new nation's economy.

With regard to trade, South Carolinians also seemed to have suffered more than the Upper South for the American victory in the War for Independence. By the mid-1780s tobacco exports exceeded prewar levels, and producers also saw price increases. Rice and indigo production, however, was lower in the 1790s as the British found new sources, especially for indigo, and rice planters struggled to repair the damage from the Revolutionary War as well as to replace the lost slave population that was responsible for producing the crop. Overall South Carolina saw a drop not just in per capita production (which had been the highest for all of the rebelling colonies prior to the war) but in absolute production as well.[13] Thus South Carolina went from being the most productive colony in British North America to one whose economy was unable to keep up with its fellow states. Under these conditions South Carolinians, especially the most successful ones, cannot be blamed for seeking advantages to aid their economy and trying to recover their lost fortunes. For these men that meant access to slaves and the wealth and status they could produce.[14]

First of all the New England states who dominated the shipping industry recognized the potential in transporting rice and even indigo, the staple crops of the lowcountry. In addition New Englanders were increasingly willing to provide credit to South Carolina planters to enable them to rebuild. Virginia and Maryland saw in South Carolina a market for surplus slaves, while Pennsylvania eyed the state's expanding population, white and black, as an emerging market for its grain. These potential benefits encouraged the other states to agree to concessions they might not have liked on slavery in order to strengthen an important aspect of their own and the national economy.

Paradoxically, then, the American Revolution strengthened the institution of slavery in the Lower South. Although, as Ira Berlin and Ron Hoffman argue, the institution was transformed, and as Philip Morgan has famously shown, slaves demanded and received greater autonomy in the rice-growing regions under the task system, it remained the dominant social and economic system in the Lower South, and the South Carolinians' commitment to slavery, not to mention the rapid growth of cotton production, would push its expansion westward.[15]

In 1787 South Carolina eagerly supported the call for a national convention to discuss amending the Articles of Confederation. The state sent a distinguished group of delegates: John Rutledge, the only man to be present at the Stamp Act Congress, Continental Congress, and the Constitutional Convention; Charles

Pinckney; Charles Cotesworth Pinckney; and Pierce Butler. Henry Laurens, former president of the Continental Congress, was also selected but did not attend because of poor health. The South Carolinians supported a stronger national government, particularly one that would be able to provide assistance in the two areas they thought would most help their state: support against rebellion and foreign trade. Certainly both of these aspects of government power were of considerable interest to the Lowcountry. However the Carolinians were unwilling to pay any price to stay in the Union. Any effort on the part of the other states to limit slavery was hotly refuted. Indeed the Carolinians repeatedly used their influence to expand the federal protections for slavery. Much of this effort stemmed from the political culture of brinkmanship that had developed in South Carolina beginning with the legacy of conflicts with metropolitan authorities during the colonial period. This trend persisted with the new American government, as South Carolina had successfully protested to get rice exempted from the nonexportation agreement that had been ratified to protest the Intolerable Acts of 1774 and later to get the clause condemning slavery removed from the Declaration of Independence. Thus while it might appear from the outside that South Carolina was not in a position to bluster and to make demands upon the other states, the state's leaders had long experience in doing just that.[16]

Moreover South Carolinians had already proven themselves willing to make rash and unsound decisions to protect their local rights and privileges and in general their independence. Defending local rights, after all, had been one of the primary factors in their decision for independence, even though their ties to Great Britain and their vulnerability to Indian attack and slave revolt seemingly should have prevented or at least cautioned them from joining the Patriot cause.[17] This powerful political culture is an important part of what Nash and others who point to the weakness of South Carolina's bargaining position miss; while South Carolina might in fact have needed the Union more than the new nation needed them— a point that is not necessarily clear—they would still choose slavery and local control of the slave trade (foreign and domestic) over Union, as they had done on a number of previous occasions.

The Three-Fifths Compromise represented a victory for the Lower South, but perhaps a less dramatic one than is commonly assumed. First, in this compromise, unlike that over the slave trade the following month, South Carolina had the support of the Upper South states, particularly Virginia, which would see part of its national power checked if slaves were not counted. Moreover the convention delegates were able to apply the three-fifths ratio from the tax law of 1783, in which each slave was counted as three-fifths of a freeman in the apportionment of taxes. Predictably southern delegations, especially South Carolina's, initially demanded that slaves be counted equally with whites; after all, those whites who did not possess full citizenship, such as women, servants, and children, were still counted.

But in the ensuing debate, North Carolina's William R. Davie issued the ultimatum that his state would never agree to join the Union unless blacks were at least counted at the three-fifths ratio. It should also be noted, however, that slaves were not counted in any southern state for apportionment purposes.[18] In states such as South Carolina, counting slaves in determining representation would not have been necessary, as the lowcountry region, home to the vast majority of the state's slave population, was already greatly overrepresented in the state legislature; increasing that region's political power because of slave population would probably have antagonized the already restless backcountry region, which was clamoring for more representation.

The other southern delegations also pointed to classical notions that representation should be based upon wealth as well as population. Although some northern delegates sought to reject counting slaves at all, the Three-Fifths Compromise made sense in that it reasonably balanced the political power between the northern and southern states. As Albert Simpson argued in 1941: "The South demanded the counting of at least three-fifths of its slaves in the apportionment of representation as its price for uniting with the North under a strong, centralized government. The North paid that price in order to obtain a government that would protect its commercial, financial and industrial interests."[19]

Although the Three-Fifths Compromise did receive attention in the state ratification conventions, it was generally accepted with little controversy. Only one of the *Federalist Papers,* number 54, addresses this issue. In that essay Madison takes the perspective, unique among the entire collection, of "one of our southern brethren" to make the case. Madison proclaims that the federal Constitution "views them [slaves] in the mixt character of persons and of property. This is in fact their true character." Madison also argues that it was entirely proper for representation to be based upon both wealth and population, particularly because government was instituted as much for the protection of property as for the protection of the individual. He concedes that the reasoning was "strained in some points, yet on the whole, I must confess, that it fully reconciles me to the scale of representation."[20] As Don Fehrenbacher notes, "One can scarcely overstate the importance of the fact that in the three-fifths ratio delegates had available a packaged compromise already ratified by eleven of the thirteen states."[21]

Anti-Federalists in the northern and southern states took different approaches in opposing this aspect of the new government. "Brutus" asserted that if those held in bondage should be counted, then "the horses in some of the States, and the oxen in others, ought to be represented." He went on to note that because the slave trade was allowed to continue until 1808, the southern states could enlarge their share of federal power simply by importing more slaves. Southern Anti-Federalists made the opposite complaint, believing that slaves should be fully counted, in part because wealth, together with others such as women who were excluded from voting and other forms of political participation, had long been included in determining representation.[22]

The Committee of Detail, which drafted these elements of the Constitution, reflected the dominance of its chairman, John Rutledge. Rutledge presented a pro-southern package that included the compromise, contained no taxes on exports or capitation tax except in accordance with the three-fifths ratio, and required a two-thirds majority for navigation acts. Furthermore Congress was never to prohibit the importation of slaves or to tax those imports. This proposal was far more than Rutledge was able to get away with. Some of the more ardent antislavery men in the convention went so far as to renew the discussion of the Three-Fifths Compromise. However, a motion to base apportionment solely on free population was defeated 10–1. It was the prosouthern commerce clauses that were overturned, and of course, consideration of Congress's authority to halt the slave trade and impose taxes on slave imports gave rise to the second major dispute over slavery, that of continuing the international slave trade, at the convention.

The debate over the international slave trade proved to be far more complex, for a number of reasons.[23] One is that the issue created strange alliances among the delegates. Virginia, which supported counting slaves for apportionment, opposed any continuation of the slave trade, desiring to limit the Lower South's sources for slave purchases and increase the value of their own slaves. The Middle States joined Virginia in opposition, along both economic and moral grounds. Gouverneur Morris of Pennsylvania proclaimed that continuing what George Mason had called the "infernal traffic" would bring "the judgment of heaven on a country." James Wilson of Pennsylvania believed that because Georgia and South Carolina had both banned the importation of slaves at the state level, they would not "refuse to Unite because the importation might be prohibited."[24]

Unlike with the Three-Fifths Compromise, the Lower South was joined only by the New England states in supporting continuation of the slave trade. Roger Sherman and Oliver Ellsworth of Connecticut accepted the trade as necessary to keeping South Carolina and Georgia in the Union. Massachusetts, Connecticut, and New York (all of which were heavily involved in the shipping industry and stood to gain considerably from slave imports) joined the Carolinas and Georgia as well. The South Carolina delegation was not finished, demanding that the slave trade be continued until 1808, instead of 1800 as had been originally proposed. In exchange the South Carolinians agreed to allow Congress to pass navigation laws with a simple majority rather than a two-thirds vote.

These two main points, both of which benefited South Carolina considerably, along with other minor details such as a provision in the Constitution for returning fugitive slaves and ensuring that not even a constitutional amendment would prohibit the importation of slaves prior to 1808, give considerable credence to the notion that the U.S. Constitution was a proslavery document. That the word *slave* does not appear anywhere in the text supports the notion that the framers understood the power of that word and its inconsistency with the larger ideals they espoused. As Don Fehrenbacher states, "Slavery, as a brooding presence in the land, significantly influenced the deliberations of the Constitutional Convention, but the Convention made no calculated effort to affect the institution of slavery."[25] Paul Finkelman agrees that the northern delegates knew what they had agreed to, making major concessions to the South and winning little in return. The compromise was accepted with the expectation of future economic benefits from the alliance between the eastern (New England) states and the Lower South.[26]

In a speech supporting ratification, South Carolinian David Ramsay pointed to this new alliance, asserting that the New England states would be able to assist South Carolina much more quickly than its more immediate geographic neighbors such as Virginia. "The Eastern states, abounding in men and ships, can sooner relieve us, than our next door neighbors," in the event of either a foreign invasion or a slave insurrection.[27] This assertion may also reflect continued frustration with the lack of support South Carolina had received from Virginia and Pennsylvania during the revolutionary conflict. In a letter to Benjamin Lincoln of Massachusetts, Ramsay reiterated this theme, noting that "your delegates never did a more political thing than in standing by those of South Carolina about negroes." He added that Virginia had lost much popularity because of its opposition to allowing the foreign slave trade.[28]

Overall, then, the proslavery character of the Constitution is largely the result of the South Carolina delegates, who successfully used the brinkmanship tactics they had mastered over the preceding forty years to tremendous effect in the deliberations of the convention. As Finkelman concludes: "On every issue at the convention, slaveowners had won major concessions from the rest of the nation."[29] Northern delegates (with a few notable exceptions) did not consider the issue of slavery as worth dividing the fragile nation; in their view these compromises were an acceptable price to pay for strengthening the floundering Union.

Slavery was clearly the most divisive issue at the Constitutional Convention, one that precluded any easy solutions if the northern delegations sought to interfere with it where it already existed. Moreover, betting that slavery would only be further marginalized in the years and decades ahead would have been smart in 1787. The cotton gin, which would dramatically increase the demand for slaves, was still six years away. Virginia, which possessed by far the largest slave population, had legalized individual manumissions without the approval of the legislature and seemed eager to try to rid itself of its black population. The rest of the nation could anticipate a time when black slavery would be an archaic institution, present only in rice-growing regions of the Lower South. Even the convention's most ardent antislavery spokesman, Rufus King, acknowledged as much, writing that the Three-Fifths Compromise "was necessary of the establishment of the Constitution."[30]

David Brion Davis goes much further in his examination of the Constitution, asserting that it not only enabled slavery to exist and survive but also actually strengthened the institution by freeing southern slaveholders from various imperial restraints. Davis claims that southerners faced far fewer restrictions than did those in the British West Indies in the later eighteenth and nineteenth centuries. The Constitution, in Davis's reading, gave the South a disproportionate amount of federal power while at the same time shielding their local authority from interference. Davis adds that the experience in Philadelphia made it clear that the support of southern states for any issue on the national agenda requiring a broad consensus had to be bought at the expense of black slaves.[31]

Even after signing a document that was highly favorable to their state's interests, the pro-Constitution forces in South Carolina were not assured that the state would accept the new form of government. The debate over ratification occurred in two steps. The first occurred in the state legislature when it considered the call for a special ratification convention, and the second at the ratification convention itself. At the time of the convention, a majority of South Carolinians, particularly those in the backcountry regions, opposed the new government. This did not come as a surprise to the supporters of the document, who had stacked the ratification process with a majority of delegates from the lowcountry districts where support was the norm.

Rawlins Lowndes, who had occupied prominent leadership roles in South Carolina since the era of the Stamp Act, served as the chief spokesman for the opposition in South Carolina.[32] Lowndes feared that the new government, particularly northern interests, would enrich themselves at the expense of the southern majority. He accepted that the state's representatives in Philadelphia had done "everything in their power to procure for us a proportionate share in this new government; but the very little they had gained proved what we might expect in the future; and that the interest of the Northern states would so predominate, as to divest us of any pretensions to the title of republic."[33]

His first attack on the limits imposed by the northern states was directed against the potential of the slave trade being ended by the federal government in twenty years. Lowndes articulated an early vision of the "positive good" defense of slavery, arguing that the trade could be justified on the basis of "religion, humanity and justice; for certainly to translate a set of human beings from a bad country to a better, was fulfilling every part of those principles." Lowndes's solution was that restrictions on the trade should be made only with a two-thirds majority of the states.[34]

Advocates of the new government advanced a series of rebuttals to this opposition. In responding to Lowndes's fears about northern domination of the new nation, Edward Rutledge stated that while the northern states were already full and therefore unlikely to gain much additional power, the southern states, and South

Carolina in particular, still had considerable room to grow; thus the state could expect an increase in representation in the near future.[35]

David Ramsay, in an editorial published in February 1788, argued that it was not likely the federal government would abolish the slave trade twenty years hence. Indeed as the amount of rice produced by South Carolina increased, the eastern states would benefit from the carrying of it and join with South Carolina in opposing any new restrictions on the movement of slaves, just as they had supported continuation of the slave trade at the convention. He added that even if such a prohibition should pass, twenty years of imports, natural increase, and the influx from Virginia would afford a sufficient number of slaves to meet the state's demand for labor. Later, in an oration celebrating the state's ratification of the Constitution, Ramsay did not raise the issue of slavery at all, confining his remarks to the ability of the new government to provide security against enemies both foreign and domestic and to the economic and trade benefits of a more unified nation.[36]

However, as M. E. Bradford has asserted, it seems that the protection the new government afforded slavery helped the ratification effort in South Carolina. Bradford states that the inclusion of a Bill of Rights prior to ratification would have made South Carolina less willing to accept it, because a call for universal human rights could have been construed to include slaves, something that obviously would have been anathema to South Carolinians. In the end the document was highly favorable to South Carolina, as it protected slavery, benefited Charleston's merchant community, and provided increased security while acknowledging the limits of the federal government in infringing upon state authority.[37]

The South Carolina convention ratified the new government, despite the objection of the vast majority of backcountry delegates. It had also been the backcountry men who objected to the state's three-year ban on slave imports beginning in 1787. The apparent contradiction of demanding the continuation of the slave trade in the Constitution while prohibiting the trade at the state level was not difficult for lowcountry leaders to explain. Their point was that restrictions on slave imports should properly come at the state, not the federal, level. The state's delegates to the Constitutional Convention had supported the state ban but, as we have seen, were quick to demand that the trade not be prohibited by the federal government. Even Lowndes, who opposed ratification in part because it could potentially ban the trade in 1808, had supported the state's prohibition on the trade.

One additional reason for the ban was concern about slave insurrections during this period, a fear heightened by the slave revolt on Saint-Domingue in 1791. While less important in the state's prohibitions in the 1780s, the threat of revolt was an important reason for keeping the trade closed in the 1790s. In the end economic demands trumped security concerns when the trade was reopened from 1803 to 1807.[38]

Despite the prohibition on the external slave trade, domestic imports were not banned. And in fact the slave population of the state grew, particularly in the backcountry, with the majority of new settlers bringing slaves with them. But with the rapid expansion of cotton monoculture, as the cotton gin made that staple much more profitable, the demand for black labor reached a point where the trade could be safely reopened.

In his history of the final years of the slave trade, James A. McMillin estimates that slave imports from 1783 to 1810 may have been as much as 170,000. In his overview of the U.S. transatlantic slave trade, David Eltis has offered an estimate of about 103,000 during this same period. The majority of these foreign slaves were forcibly imported in the first decade of the nineteenth century, particularly after South Carolina reopened the trade in 1803. According to McMillin, South Carolina imported almost 100,000 of that total number, more than three times that of Georgia. Even if Eltis's lower numbers are used, slave imports from 1800 to 1807 far exceeded the number of slaves imported into the lowcountry in the 1770s. McMillin is highly critical of the protection granted to the international slave trade at Philadelphia, adding that the extension of that protection from 1800 to 1808 was especially detrimental, for it facilitated the expansion of slavery into the Old Southwest by keeping the supply of slaves high and prices low.

McMillin's numbers, almost three times earlier estimates, demonstrate the demand for slaves among South Carolinians and the Lower South's commitment to slavery, even in the face of increased opposition from the North. Even Eltis's numbers, about one-third less than McMillin's, demonstrate the strong demand for slaves in South Carolina. McMillin adds that the trade was encouraged not just by plantation owners but also by Charleston's middle-class merchant community, who both participated in and benefited from the trade. This widespread participation indicates a general acceptance not just of the institution of slavery but also of the slave trade itself among the state's white population.[39]

Economic historians add that not reopening the trade until 1803 was an economically rational decision on the part of the South Carolinians. Although slave prices increased immediately after the Revolutionary War because of the large reduction in the slave population, the state's struggling economy and the drop in rice prices led to a decline in slave prices in the 1790s, with the cost falling below that of slaves in the West Indies for the first time since before the Seven Years' War. Thus although much has been made of the legislature's ban on slave imports, the ban was not especially significant, because the high price of foreign slaves limited demand for slaves anyway. When slave prices rose back above those in the West Indies in the early 1800s, the South Carolina legislature quickly acted to reopen the international trade. Prices in South Carolina remained well above prices in the Chesapeake throughout this period, moreover, accounting for the increase in the internal movement of slaves from the Upper South to the Lower South. The persistence of low prices in the Chesapeake also accounts for the muted concerns the South Carolina delegation expressed over the federal ban of the slave trade in 1808, as they remained confident they could obtain enough slaves at reasonable prices to meet demand.[40]

Slavery was considered essential for the economic growth of the backcountry, especially as cotton became an increasingly viable crop for that region. It was, additionally, seen as important for unifying the state politically. The most important statement of this thesis comes from Rachel Klein, who argues persuasively that the lowcountry was willing to accept the backcountry as an equal political partner only when slave ownership was widespread enough to guarantee that the two regions in the state would have the same political and economic interests. This political unification occurred around both state and national issues. The reopening of the slave trade in 1803 generated the final increase in the slave population that would convince the lowcountry that the backcountry shared their same interests and goals. At the national level, the backcountry men were now Republicans but also slave owners, while the lowcountry Federalists found greater common ground with the Republicans through their support of the Louisiana Purchase—and the expectation of an increase in slave territory—and because of the party's refusal to confirm John Rutledge for chief justice of the Supreme Court and to appoint South Carolinians to national positions in general.[41]

Other recent work on the South Carolina backcountry further highlights how slavery was considered an essential ingredient for growth and development in that region. In his community study of the Waxhaws region, Peter Moore asserts that "slave ownership became a social imperative." Families did not purchase slaves solely for labor but because "slaves brought status and wealth, security and prosperity, and freedom from drudgery, ignorance, stigma and mutual obligation." Slaves freed the white children of backcountry families, for example, to pursue their education and further advance the family's fortune. Moore's analysis extends the findings of lowcountry scholars to the rest of the state, that slave ownership "represented success and defined achievement." Moore also finds that slave ownership in the backcountry was expanding rapidly in the 1780s, before the rise of cotton culture. His findings confirm the picture that many settlers to the South Carolina backcountry were bringing their slaves with them to take advantage of the economic opportunities there. Together slavery and the rise of staple crop production, first wheat and eventually cotton, made the backcountry "southern" and safe for lowcountry elites to join their backcountry fellows in a political union that rested first and foremost upon slavery.[42]

By 1787 South Carolina's political leaders had a long-demonstrated commitment to slavery first and everything else—independence, union, and equality—second. Moreover, they had capable, experienced leadership at the state and national level to push their proslavery agenda forward and a political culture of brinkmanship that succeeded in getting any opposition to accede to their demands. Their motivations for protecting the institution and future viability of slavery in their state were deeply rooted in the entire society. Rich and poor, lowcountry and backcountry, the vast, overwhelming majority of white South Carolinians were certain that their state and their society could survive only if the peculiar institution did likewise.

South Carolina stood out from its fellow states in this determination to make the Constitution a proslavery document. However, the rhetorical commitment to slavery was not mere bluster but rather a true reflection of the state's mentality regarding the central importance of slavery to South Carolina. In order to understand this commitment, it is important to recall the many differences that made the state distinct. Unlike Virginia and Maryland and even Georgia, slavery was introduced to South Carolina with the first white settlers. Similarly the challenges of producing the colony's staples of rice and indigo led most Carolinians to believe that their crops could not be produced with free wage labor.

The Revolutionary era set in motion efforts to end slavery outside of the Lower South. Northern states, including Connecticut, New Jersey, New York, and Rhode Island, began the process of gradual emancipation. In 1787 Rhode Island passed laws that prohibited the slave trade, and Connecticut and Massachusetts followed suit the following year. Moreover, the first new state in the region after independence, Vermont, banned slavery in its constitution. For all of these laws, as Joanne Pope Melish has argued, "abolition in New England was gradual indeed," and slavery would persist in New England well into the nineteenth century.[43] While they may have begun to prevent the further importation of slaves into the northern states and to ban participation in the slave trade, the New England states were unwilling to demand the same from South Carolina as the price of union.

This is not to say that the founders should be excused, nor is it to assert that a constitution so favorable to slaveholders was inevitable. That document, however, clearly reflected the prevailing opinions of the time. Far from being an anachronism, slavery was the norm, in the United States as elsewhere. By successfully demanding the continuation of the African slave trade until 1808, South Carolina accomplished the vital goal of maintaining local control over the trade. When economic and political interests dictated reopening the trade, South Carolina did so, further strengthening the institution of slavery there and throughout the South and securing the unification of the previously divided state on the basis of slavery. Thus when South Carolinians demanded representation based upon both slave and free population and the continuation of the slave trade for twenty years, they knew they had a good chance of success, and the other states knew that the Carolinians' place in the Union depended upon their agreeing to those demands.

Notes

1. "Rawlins Lowndes and Edward Rutledge Debate in the South Carolina Legislature," in *The Debates in the Several State Conventions on the Adoption of the Federal Constitution: As*

Recommended by the General Convention at Philadelphia in 1787, 5 vols., ed. Jonathan Elliot (Washington, D.C.: Printed for the editor, 1836–1845), 4:19–20.

2. James Madison, *Notes on the Debates of the Federal Convention of 1787* (Athens: Ohio University Press, 1984), 507, 503.

3. Gary Nash, "Could Slavery Have Been Abolished?" in *The Forgotten Fifth: African Americans in the Age of Revolution* (Cambridge, Mass.: Harvard University Press, 2006), 69–122.

4. Ibid., p. 72.

5. David Brion Davis, *The Problem of Slavery in the Age of Revolution, 1770–1823* (Ithaca, N.Y.: Cornell University Press, 1975); David Waldstreicher, *Runaway America: Benjamin Franklin, Slavery, and the American Revolution* (New York: Hill & Wang, 2004).

6. David K. Wilson, *The Southern Strategy: Britain's Conquest of South Carolina and Georgia* (Columbia: University of South Carolina Press, 2005), 113. For a discussion of John Laurens's plan to raise a regiment of black troops, overwhelmingly defeated by the South Carolina legislature, see Gregory D. Massey, "The Limits of Antislavery Thought in the Revolutionary Lower South: John Laurens and Henry Laurens," *Journal of Southern History* 63 (August 1997): 511.

7. Walter Edgar, *South Carolina: A History* (Columbia: University of South Carolina Press, 1998), 238–39.

8. William Moultrie, quoted in Wilson, *Southern Strategy*, 110.

9. John Rutledge to Delegates of South Carolina in Congress, May 24, 1780, in "Letters of John Rutledge," *South Carolina Historical and Genealogical Magazine* 17 (October 1916): 135.

10. James Lovell, quoted in David B. Mattern, *Benjamin Lincoln and the American Revolution* (Columbia: University of South Carolina Press, 1998), 90.

11. William Moultrie, *Memoirs of the American Revolution* (New York: New York Times & Arno, 1968), 355.

12. Robert M. Weir, "'The Violent Spirit,' the Reestablishment of Order, and the Continuity of Leadership in Post-Revolutionary South Carolina," in *An Uncivil War: The Southern Backcountry during the American Revolution*, ed. Ronald Hoffman, Thad W. Tate, and Peter J. Albert (Charlottesville: University Press of Virginia for the U.S. Capitol Historical Society, 1985), 71–72.

13. James F. Shepherd, "British America and the Atlantic Economy," in *The Economy of Early America: The Revolutionary Period, 1763–1790*, ed. Ronald Hoffman et al. (Charlottesville: University Press of Virginia for the U.S. Capitol Historical Society, 1988), 26–27, 32.

14. Russell Menard, "Slavery, Economic Growth and Revolutionary Ideology in the South Carolina Lowcountry," in Hoffman, *Economy of Early America*, 272.

15. Ira Berlin, introduction to *Slavery and Freedom in the Age of the American Revolution*, ed. Ira Berlin and Ronald Hoffman (Charlottesville: University Press of Virginia, 1983), xviii–xix; Philip D. Morgan, *Slave Counterpoint: Black Culture in the Eighteenth Century Chesapeake and Lowcountry* (Chapel Hill: University of North Carolina Press, 1998).

16. Jonathan Mercantini, *Who Shall Rule at Home? The Evolution of South Carolina Political Culture, 1748–1776* (Columbia: University of South Carolina Press, 2007), 244–49.

17. Robert Olwell, "'Domestick Enemies': Slavery and Political Independence in South Carolina, May 1775–March 1776," *Journal of Southern History* 55 (February 1989): 21–48.

18. Paul Finkelman, "Slavery and the Constitutional Convention: Making a Covenant with Death," in *Beyond Confederation: Origins of the Constitution and American National Identity*, ed. Richard Beeman, Stephen Botein, and Edward C. Carter II (Chapel Hill: University of North Carolina Press for the Institute of Early American History and Culture, 1987), 198.

19. Albert F. Simpson, "The Political Significance of Slave Representation, 1787–1821," *Journal of Southern History* 7 (August 1941): 318–19.

20. James Madison, "The Same Subject Continued with a View to the Ratio of Representation," in *The Federalist: The Essential Essays*, ed. Jack Rakove (Boston: Bedford/St. Martin's, 2003), 149–52.

21. Don E. Fehrenbacher and Ward M. McAfee, *The Slaveholding Republic: An Account of the United States Government's Relations to Slavery* (New York: Oxford University Press, 2001), 33.

22. "Brutus" [Robert Yates], Anti-Federalist Papers no. 54—accessed online at http://www.utulsa.edu/law/classes/rice/Constitutional/AntiFederalist, accessed January 17, 2008.

23. For a more detailed account of the debate over the international slave trade at the Constitutional Convention, see Paul Finkelman, "Regulating the African Slave Trade," *Civil War History* 61, no. 4 (2008): 384–94.

24. Fehrenbacher, *Slaveholding Republic*, 33–35; Mercantini, *Who Shall Rule*, 247.

25. Fehrenbacher, *Slaveholding Republic*, 36–38.

26. Finkelman, "Making a Covenant," 221–22.

27. "'Civis' [David Ramsay] to the Citizens of South Carolina," in Elliot, *Debates in the Several State Conventions*, 4:150–51.

28. David Ramsay to Benjamin Lincoln, January 29, 1788, in Elliot, *Debates in the Several State Conventions*, 4:117–18.

29. Finkelman, "Making a Covenant," 224.

30. Mercantini, *Who Shall Rule*, 248; "Rufus King in the United States Senate," in *The Records of the Federal Convention of 1787*, ed. Max Farrand, entry no. 327, 3:428–30.

31. David Brion Davis, "American Slavery and the American Revolution," in Berlin and Hoffman, *Slavery and Freedom*, 272–73.

31. It is interesting to note that Lowndes had been controversially deposed from his position as Speaker of the Commons House during the Stamp Act controversy in 1765. It is unclear whether his later opposition to the Constitution was somehow related to these earlier conflicts with other members of the South Carolina elite, including the Rutledges and Pinckneys, who represented South Carolina at the Philadelphia convention and strongly supported ratification.

33. "Rawlins Lowndes and Edward Rutledge Debate," 4:20.

34. Ibid. Of course even this protection would not have prevented the cessation of the trade in 1808, when only three dissenting votes were cast.

35. Ibid., 4:25.

36. "'Civis' to the Citizens," 4:152; "David Ramsay's Oration at Charleston, South Carolina," in Elliott, *Debates in the Several State Conventions*, 4:506–13.

37. M. E. Bradford, "Preserving the Birthright: The Intention of South Carolina in Adopting the Constitution," *South Carolina Historical Magazine* 101 (January 2000): 91–100.

38. Patrick S. Brady, "The Slave Trade and Sectionalism in South Carolina, 1787–1808," *Journal of Southern History* 38 (November 1972): 609–11.

39. James A. McMillin, *The Final Victims: The Foreign Slave Trade to North America, 1783–1810* (Columbia: University of South Carolina Press, 2004), 48; David Eltis, "The U.S. Transatlantic Slave Trade, 1644–1867: An Assessment," *Civil War History* 54, no. 4 (2008): 349–55, 62, 665–66.

40. Peter C. Mancall, Joshua L. Rosenbloom and Thomas Weiss, "Slave Prices and the South Carolina Economy, 1722–1809," *Journal of Economic History* 61 (September 2001): 629, 632–33, 637.

41. Rachel Klein, *Unification of a Slave State: The Rise of the Planter Class in the South Carolina Backcountry, 1760–1808* (Chapel Hill: University of North Carolina Press, 1990), 165–68, 258.

42. Peter N. Moore, *World of Toil and Strife: Community Transformation in Backcountry South Carolina, 1750–1805* (Columbia: University of South Carolina Press, 2007), 77; Menard, "Slavery, Economic Growth," 272.

43. Joanne Pope Melish, *Disowning Slavery: Gradual Emancipation and "Race" in New England, 1780–1860* (Ithaca, N.Y.: Cornell University Press, 1998), 64–76.

AFRICAN CHILDREN AND THE TRANSATLANTIC SLAVE TRADE ACROSS TIME AND PLACE

WILMA KING

Charlotte one of my fellow prisoners . . . did comfort me when I was torn from my dear native land.

Sarah Margru Kinson to George Whipple,
September 18, 1847

"Your image has been always riveted in my heart, from which neither time nor fortunes have been able to remove it; so that, while the thoughts of your sufferings have damped my prosperity, they have mingled with adversity and increased its bitterness," wrote Olaudah Equiano, also known as Gustavus Vassa, as he reflected upon the fate of his beloved sister and the strife that separated them. Although the veracity of Equiano's account of his birth and early childhood in Africa have been called into question, his narrative still offers a vivid representation of the experiences of boys and girls who endured abduction, sale, and involuntary removal from Africa to America.[1] Equiano's account squares with what we know of political instability in West Africa in the eighteenth century, when rivalry and even warfare among different ethnic and language groups was not unusual. In fact it probably intensified with the increased demands in the Americas for black laborers.[2]

Reconstructing the experiences of young Middle Passage survivors—whether legally before 1808 or illegally thereafter—presents numerous difficulties for historians of the transatlantic trade. The ostensibly straightforward task of combing through survivors' narratives, official records, ships' manifests, and journals kept by medical doctors and captains of ships is complicated by the absence of a clear definition of who was or was not a child. On the one hand, Dr. James Houstoun, chief surgeon at Cape Coast Castle in 1722, noted that several females under ten years of age were listed in Royal African Company books as "women." On the other hand, captains interested in increasing profit margins were just as likely to list men and women as "children" to achieve tax-free status or increase the size of the cargo. Additionally the designations "man boy" and "woman girl" appear in the records, making it even harder for researchers to make clear distinctions between adults and children.[3]

Definitions of *childhood* are similarly unstable. Based on his study of children in the transatlantic trade, historian Erik Hofstee writes that "many of the individuals taken on board a slaving vessel were children by physical or chronological definitions but had had first-hand experiences of the hardships of life that easily rivaled those of most adults. Many had, even before boarding the slaving vessel, suffered more and seen more suffering than many adults do in their entire lives."[4] A "singular blend of the child and the adult, with aspects of each being contained in the same individual," these youngsters, Hofstee continues, "had prematurely and irrevocably left their childhood behind them." If any of the girls and boys had enjoyed a protected period in their lives or a childhood as it is thought of today, that ended once they were incorporated in the international trade in human chattel.[5]

Despite the lack of clarity in historical records, there is ample evidence to show that boys and girls under sixteen years of age constituted a significant number of the Africans catapulted into the transatlantic trade in human beings. Paul Lovejoy estimates that 12.2 percent of the Africans in the transatlantic trade between 1663 and 1700 were children. The numbers increased significantly between 1701 and 1809 when they escalated to nearly 23 percent. In her study of children in the British trade in Africans, Audra A. Diptee affirms that between 1786 and 1792, 27 percent of the Africans transported from West Central Africa were children, while Lisa A. Lindsay, in an overview of the Atlantic slave trade published in 2008, puts the number of children at 28 percent.[6]

While it is impossible to determine the exact number of African children transported to the United States before or after 1808, the size of this population suggests that they were not taken haphazardly. In general the most marketable age appears to have been between ten and twenty-four years, and even a cursory review of the sources indicates that children were frequently the chattels of choice and explicitly mentioned in instructions to slavers. Consider the 1746 correspondence in which William Ellery, owner of the *Anstis*, told Capt. Pollipus Hammond, "if you have good trade for the Negroes . . . purchase forty or fifty Negroes. Get most of them mere Boys and Girls, some Men, let them be Young, No very small Children." Nearly twenty years later, entrepreneurs John Watts and Gedney Clarke discussed procuring Africans for sale in New York. "For this market," wrote Watts, the slaves "must be young the younger the better if not quite Children, those advanced in years will never do." And in 1764 Esek Hopkins, captain of the *Sally*, received similar directives from his employers, John, Moses, Joseph, and Nicholas Brown of Providence, Rhode Island. Hopkins was directed to "transact any and all business whatever" related to the voyage, but his employers added specific instructions to him to bring "four likely young slaves" for their own use. The "likely young slaves" were to be "about 15 years old."[7]

The 1799 instructions from the Liverpool entrepreneur Thomas Leyland to a captain he employed reflect the sustaining interest and expediency of buying and selling African children. Leyland advised: "We require the utmost exertion to finish your Trade in the shortest time particularly in the Congo where a long stay is always fatal to the Crew and may be the total ruin of our Voyage . . . [and] Not to buy slaves over 20 years and if females are scarce then buy boys in their places." Aside from their availability, especially near the coast, and interests in filling a ship's hold quickly, several other factors made children attractive to traders when compared with adults. Boys and girls were easier to seize, more malleable, and required less space aboard ships than adults. Furthermore children would potentially serve owners longer than their adult contemporaries. Nothing in the 1808 ban limited the life sentence of children once enslaved.[8]

While the primary focus of this essay is on children's experience of the Middle Passage, it is clear that many boys and girls were further subjected to involuntary relocations through the interstate, intrastate, and interregional trades in people of African descent, and that this trade actually increased after 1808 when the United States prohibited participation in the transatlantic trade in human beings. There were differences in the movement of children from Africa to North America and from one American household, city, state, or region to another, yet they shared a timeless commonality. They were separated from families, friends, and familiar surroundings. Such dislocations, temporarily or permanently, were among the most dreaded and loathsome aspects of bondage for those taken away involuntarily and for those who remained behind. In either case once apart, their chances for permanent reunions were nil.[9]

Researchers seeking narratives by youthful Middle Passage survivors are certain to encounter obstacles, including a paucity of published narratives by females, who were less likely to gain literacy and publish memoirs than the male survivors who outnumbered them. Additionally almost all enslaved youngsters lived under extremely harsh conditions without opportunities to record accounts in a timely manner and preserve them. As a result the extant records were created after survivors were no longer children, thus raising questions about the construction or reconstruction of the chronicles. Critics are likely to charge that such recollections are not representative of the whole, have been distorted by the authors' ages and emotions, or that the accounts, especially if written by amanuensis, are reflections of political agendas favoring abolition.[10]

The small cache of letters written in 1774 by the freeborn Little Ephraim Robin John and Ancona Robin Robin John is therefore especially important. Although their specific ages are never mentioned, data surrounding important events in their lives suggest they wrote the letters as adolescents and that they were not mature adults when enslaved. In 1767 the Robin Johns' elders, influential slave traders in the Bight of Biafra, had arranged for them to study in England. This decision was not unusual among elite Africans interested in preparing their male and female off-spring for future negotiations with Europeans. In the case of the Robin Johns, the plan went badly awry, however.[11]

Instead of transporting them to London, the captain of the *Duke of York,* a British slaver, clapped the Robin Johns in irons, transported them across the Atlantic Ocean, and sold them into slavery.[12] They remained together throughout their ordeal and wrote about their experiences as they occurred or within a rela-tively short period of time. Their correspondence is most relevant for investigating the actual mechanics of the transatlantic trade in general, and it shows how the Robin Johns freed themselves and returned home by way of England in less than a decade. Their oral and written English-language skills, acquaintances with Euro-pean traders, and tenacity weighed heavily in their success. It also appears that they were familiar with *Somerset v. Stewart* (1772), a landmark case involving a Virgin-ian, James Somerset, who had run away from his owner, Charles Stewart, two years after Stewart, a Boston customs officer, had carried him to England. After recaptur-ing Somerset, Stewart planned to send him to Jamaica, where he would be sold. British abolitionists and sympathizers supported Somerset, who won a favorable decision.[13] In all probability British abolitionists encouraged the Robin Johns to seek legal redress. Ultimately the court ruled in their favor, and they were reunited with their families in Africa.[14]

Unlike the Robin John letters, which focus specifically on their immediate indi-vidual experiences, several narratives by Middle Passage survivors are nostalgic and evoke an idyllic life in Africa. A brief memoir by the African-born Florence Hall for example describes her playing in an open field with peers when raiders abducted her and several of her playmates. Similarly Ottobah Cugoano recalled how as a young boy he and eighteen or twenty friends amused themselves before their abduction. Boyrereau Brinch, too, recalled his childhood as a time when he and his peers "could anticipate no greater pleasure, and knew no care." Life, as Brinch knew it, ended suddenly when he was "snatched away from [his] native country."[15]

Several autobiographies by Middle Passage survivors indicate that even as chil-dren they had a working knowledge or fear of potential dangers from raiders. The Guinea-born Venture Smith wrote about a 1729 assault when an army of raiders "laid siege and immediately took men, women, children, flocks, and all their valu-able effects." The raiders greeted the helpless boy with "a violent blow on the head with the fore part of a gun, and at the same time a grasp around the neck." After-ward Smith, who was six years old at the time, watched as raiders "closely interro-gated" his father before they "cut and pounded on his body with great inhumanity." "I saw him," Smith wrote, "while he was thus tortured to death." Years later Smith admitted, "The shocking scene is to this day fresh in my memory, and I have often been overcome while thinking on it."[16] Several survivors' narratives, including Cugoano's, affirm that African children attempted to evade kidnappers, almost

always to no avail. Cugoano recalled, for instance, "Pistols and cutlasses were introduced, threatening, that if we offered to stir, we should all lie dead on the spot." The
resistance of Florence Hall and her friends was similarly futile; Hall wrote, "cries
and screams were raised, but raised unheard, if heard, unattended."[17] Once
enslaved, Hall, Cugoano, Equiano, and other African girls and boys all faced similar adversities to those of the adults who were thrown into the transatlantic trade.

According to the well-known slave trader John Newton, the children and adults,
like immature and mature emotions confined in one body, were sometimes mingled together without distinction during the sales or negotiations on the African
coast. Newton mentions routine transactions on March 21, 1750, when a Mr. Tucker
came aboard his ship with "4 slaves, 2 men, 1 woman girl, and 1 woman with a small
child." Several days later Newton exchanged "No. 60, 61; 2 small boys (of 3 ft 4 in)
for a girl (4 foot 3 in) and No. 80, a small boy (3 ft 8 inches) for a woman." Similarly Stephen Hopkins, captain of the Rhode Island slaver the *Salley*, recorded a
December 1, 1764, purchase of "1 man & 1 man boy Slave" along with "1 woman," "2
galres & 1 boy."[18]

A glance at the account book for the *Salley* leaves the impression that Hopkins,
who acquired 196 Africans, of whom 32 were girls and 42 were boys, paid less for
the children than for the adults. A closer examination of the captain's records suggests, however, that it was not only size and maturity that determined prices. Supply and demand and the captain's negotiating skills compared to other Europeans
and Africans must also be considered. On November 15, 1764, Hopkins made his
first purchases, a girl and boy, exchanging 156 gallons of rum and "1 barel of flower"
with a Captain Hewet for the children. A December 1, 1764, purchase of a boy and
girl cost Hopkins 195 gallons of rum. Later in the same month, on December 26,
Hopkins exchanged 52 gallons of rum for a single boy and 28 gallons for a "small
garle" the following day. On January 6, 1765, Hopkins exchanged 160 gallons of rum
for "1 man & 1 woman Slaves."[19]

When considering Hopkins's purchases over this period, one must ask if the
difference in the price of a man and woman in January adequately reflects their
value when compared to what Hopkins paid for the two children in November.
Beyond that, what was the value of a barrel of flour? Was it worth four gallons of
rum? Clearly factors other than those ostensibly revealed in the account book influenced the trade, including African slavers' own fondness for European textiles,
iron, guns, and ammunition. In his 1732 "A Description of the Coasts of North and
South Guinea," John Barbot, an agent-general of the Royal Company of Africa,
noted that the "most staple commodities" for trade included "common red, blue,
and scarlet cloth, silver and brass rings, or bracelets, chains, little bells, false crystal,
ordinary and coarse hats; Dutch pointed knives, pewter dishes, silk sashes, with false
gold and silver fringes; blue serges; French paper, steels to strike fire . . . looking-
glasses in gilt and plain frames, cloves, cinnamon, scissors, needles, coarse thread

of sundry colors . . . Lastly, a good quantity of Cognac brandy." The "demand for this or that item shifted dramatically, often to the consternation of merchants who brought thousands of items only to find no demand for them." The vacillation in desires reflects the behavior of consumers who were responding to "changing fashions of nonessential commodities" rather than basic necessities.[20]

Thus far this essay has focused on the theft of childhood from individual African girls and boys by kidnapping and sale into the transatlantic trade in human beings before 1808. The essay also considers the economic and social impact of the theft of children from West Africa. While the detailed demographic and economic consequences of the slave trade on Africa remain topics of debate, most historians agree that they were catastrophic: the traffic in human beings robbed Africa of millions upon millions of girls, boys, women, and men whose energy, labor, and creativity was consequently prevented from contributing anything, physically or fiscally, toward the development of their homeland.[21]

Similarly the social impact of the international trade took significant personal tolls. Even the lives of the children *not* kidnapped were severely affected by the absence of loved ones. At the structural level, while the loss of a great number of men among people who practiced polygyny might have been offset by continued reproduction, and consequently women continued as caregivers with the assistance of other women, the quality and quantity of time women spent with their offspring changed. In regions where most of the Africans removed were males between twelve and sixty years of age, a disproportionate amount of work shifted to women. In the absence of able-bodied men, women's work in general increased, and women spent more time felling trees and clearing fields for cultivation and less time cultivating them. This resulted in less agricultural produce both for subsistence and for disposal as marketable surplus commodities. Additionally since there were fewer men to hunt, fish, and raise livestock, diets became restricted and contained fewer sources of protein.[22]

The loss of childhood for those thrust into the Middle Passage was just the beginning of their ordeal. Traders selected the able-bodied from those who were less able by examining males and females "even to the smallest member . . . without the least distinction or modesty" and branded them with the name or symbol of the trading company. William Bosman, chief factor of the Dutch West India Company at Elmina and author of *A New and Accurate Description of the Coast of Guinea, Divided into the Gold, the Slave, and the Ivory Coasts, etc* (1701), claimed branding seemed "very barbarous" but declared it was "followed by meer necessity" because it prevented African traders from switching healthy and hearty males and females with those who were not. Bosman writes that white traders took "all possible care" not to burn the Africans "too hard, especially the women, who are more tender than the men."[23] The factor's comment does not indicate if children, who were presumably "more tender" than the women, were branded. In any case while the actual pain from the sizzling iron subsided over time, branding made an indelible imprint on the slaves' psyche, and the scars upon the skin were visible reminders of the physical and mental pains they endured.

Descriptions of the Middle Passage all include accounts of horrendous conditions and treatment aboard the ships, with physical and psychic discomforts ever present. Augustino, abducted as a child after 1808 and taken to South America, recalled that "the clothes of all the negroes going on board ship were stripped off ... even to the last rag." One former crew member aboard a slaver claimed, "The Hollanders and other Europeans take no such care in transporting their slaves to America, but ship them poor and faint, without any mats, or other necessaries." The observer wrote, "It is pitiful to see how they crowd those poor wretches, six hundred and fifty or seven hundred in a ship, the men standing in the hold ty'd to stakes, the women between decks, and those that are with child in the great cabin, and the children in the steerage, which in that hot climate occasions an intolerable stench." Boys and girls sometimes walked about the deck and breathed fresh air but remained within earshot of "the shrieks of the women, and the groans of the dying," which an eyewitness said "rendered the whole a scene of horror almost inconceivable."[24] And even though some captains may have provided a few comforts, conditions aboard ships in the Middle Passage were never less than miserable.[25]

Much has been written about the Middle Passage, especially the crowded conditions aboard ships when adults were allotted more space than children. Young males were to fill no more than five feet by fourteen inches, and the space designated for young females was four feet six inches by twelve inches. Captains known as "tight packers" crowded large numbers of Africans into small amounts of space without regard for their health or safety. One particularly callous example is that of the *Wolf*, a sloop that sailed from New York in 1750. According to the ship's surgeon, William Chancellor, the *Wolf* did not have a quarterdeck or platform to accommodate the children of three and four years of age who were taken aboard. Without their own special space, said Chancellor, "They lie on Casks & it is no wonder we loose them so fast."[26]

The atrocious conditions aboard slavers were generally known and prompted Sir William Dolben, a member of Parliament and friend of the well-known British abolitionist William Wilberforce, to introduce the bill "An Act to Regulate the Carrying of Slaves." Dolben had gone aboard a slaver and was horrified to see the actual amount of space the Africans occupied. The act, effective August 1, 1788, was to prevent overcrowding. It established a proportion of five to three between the number of Africans carried and the ship's tonnage up to 201 tons and one person per ton thereafter. The act implicitly recognized the presence of children in the trade and set four feet four inches as a standard height for regulatory purposes. If more than two-fifths of the Africans were children under four feet four inches tall, every five such children over the two-fifths proportion were deemed equal to four adults. Although the 1788 act was unusual in recognizing that conditions for transporting children might need special amelioration and described by David Eltis and Stanley Engerman as "an opening shot in the British campaign to abolish the slave trade," its impact was not felt immediately.[27]

Consider the 186 Africans brought aboard the *Madam Pookata,* under the command of Thomas Brown between November 6 and December 5, 1788. Brown's journal indicates that 47 men and 30 women were aboard the *Madam Pookata.* Of the women 8 had "children at the breast." The other Africans were "boys" and "girls." The number of boys over four feet four inches was 24, and the number of girls in the same category was 12. There were 44 boys under four feet four inches tall, and 26 girls in the same category. Notwithstanding their heights, males outnumbered females consistently. Even more poignant, the girls and boys under four feet four inches, including the babies at the breast, outnumbered the total number of adults and taller, if not older, children.[28]

Two factors complicate the discussion about the boys and girls aboard the *Madam Pookata* and African boys and girls in general. First the journal uses the designations "boys" and "girls" to set them apart from men and women. Second it is hazardous to suggest that height is a clear indicator of who was or was not a "child." The designations "boys" and "girls" are used for males and females over four feet four inches tall as well as those under four feet four inches in height aboard the *Madam Pookata.* Obviously something more finite than height determined when males and females were considered as men and women or boys and girls.[29]

Regardless of regulations, and even after the British and American bans of 1807 and 1808, boys and girls occasionally made up the majority of captives aboard slavers. In 1734, for example, the *Margarita* left Africa with 93 Africans, 62 males and 31 females, aboard. The captives were between ten and eighteen years old, with fully 87 percent sixteen or younger. The largest cluster comprised 22 males and 17 females, all twelve years of age. The average age of the children was thirteen years and four months old. Similarly the British vessel *Maria* sailed in 1791 and disembarked 74 Africans, all of whom were children. Among them were 49 boys and 25 girls. Detailed information about the survivors aboard the *Wanderer,* which sailed in 1858 in violation of the 1808 ban, remains elusive; it is known, however, that the vessel's human cargo of 487 Africans consisted primarily of teenage boys.[30]

In such cases when children made up the majority of kidnapped Africans on slavers, their experiences must have differed from other occasions when they were in the minority. Because so few narratives speak directly about interpersonal relationships among children as they crossed the Atlantic, it is impossible to know if their actual numbers added to their comfort or compounded their despair and to gauge the extent to which children assumed positions of authority or fostered camaraderie among their peers. In the case of Olaudah Equiano, however, who wrote about more than one Atlantic voyage, association with "a number of boys" apparently mitigated, albeit temporarily, the pains of disengagement. In fact Equiano claimed that his life aboard a ship bound for England became "more agreeable" because of the boys, "for we were always together, and a great part of our time was spent in play." It is reasonable to think that other children crossing the Atlantic may have had similar opportunities to "play" and interact freely, however fleetingly, since they were unfettered.[31]

While Equiano developed friendships among shipmates, some African children were transported with relatives and friends. The presence of loved ones may have diverted attention and alleviated anxieties, albeit temporarily, from the children's foreboding situations. In the case of two sisters aboard the *Ruby* of Bristol in 1787, the older girl, nicknamed "Eve" because she was the first female aboard, had fallen into the hands of traders following the mysterious appearance of a goat in her family's garden. One of the great men in the village said their father had stolen the animal and demanded restitution. The father, a poor man, had to give up one of his three daughters, and he selected "Eve," a teenager. The disengagement from her family and sale into slavery must have been traumatic for the girl.[32] Three months later Eve's eight-year-old sister was brought aboard the *Ruby*. The circumstances of the younger girl's purchase are unknown, but they were together. Their reunion may have been reminiscent of a brief but joyous one Equiano describes with his sister. "As soon as she saw me," he wrote, "she gave a loud shriek, and ran into my arms." Neither child could speak but "clung to each other in mutual embraces" and wept. The "joy of being together" made them forget what Equiano called their "misfortunes." It is easy to imagine a similar reunion between Eve and her sister and the joy they shared at that moment.[33]

In the absence of relatives, many Africans established friendships with shipmates who then became fictive kinfolk based on common experiences and adversities. Sarah Margru, one of four Africans classified as a child aboard the Spanish vessel *Amistad* in 1839, described how important such relationships with shipmates could be. She explained, "*Charlotte* one of my fellow prisoners . . . did comfort me when I was torn from my dear native land." She "used to tell us," remembered Margru, "that one day we shall all see our native land."[34] What was the source of Charlotte's profound wisdom? Had she exuded such mature behavior before abduction in Africa and arrest in America? Was her apparent optimism simply aimed at pacifying the other children around her, or was it based on a genuine understanding of the judicial procedures surrounding their case? Either way her prediction came true in 1841 when the U.S. Supreme Court ruled in favor of the *Amistad* survivors, allowing them to return to West Africa.[35]

Unlike the *Amistad* survivors, the vast majority of Africans never returned to their native lands, and many had no shipmates to alleviate their fears. In testimony before the Select Committee of the House of Lords in 1849, Augustino, who was twelve years of age when abducted and taken to South America, remembered the extreme anxiety among the children. Of "the young ones," he said, "several of those jumped overboard, for fear they were being fattened to be eaten."[36] The fear of white cannibalism was widespread among Africans in the Middle Passage, and Equiano's narrative contains several comments about his fear of cannibals. Once Equiano was aboard the ship, he saw a "large furnace of copper boiling" surrounded by sorrowful-looking Africans in chains and imagined the "white men with horrible looks" planned to eat him. To dispel such ill-founded notions, Equiano claims whites, crew members or potential buyers, brought enslaved Africans from the local area to tell the new arrivals that they would not be devoured. Perhaps such explanation alleviated the specific fear of cannibalism, but other challenges remained.[37] Whether Equiano's narrative is based on actual experience, research, or enduring folklore, it is a reflection of the Africans' failure to understand what awaited them in the New World, and it added to their psychological torment and contributed to debilitating emotions.

Not even adults could have been prepared for the rampant sexual exploitation surrounding them before and after boarding the ships. Boyrereau Brinch wrote about "common sailors" ravishing "women in the presence of all the assembly" and claimed parents sometimes witnessed their "daughters being despoiled."[38] Similarly Ottobah Cugoano mentioned sexual exploitation in his narrative, saying, "It was common for the dirty filthy sailors to take the African women and lie upon their bodies." The veteran slave trader John Newton concurred and admitted that on some ships "the license . . . was almost unlimited." It was not a universal practice, but it was "too commonly, and, I am afraid, too generally prevalent," acknowledged Newton.[39] He confessed that he too "not only sinned with a high hand . . . but made it [his] study to tempt and seduce others on every occasion." Despite his own admissions, the captain, who had traveled a "zigzag course to Christian belief," was irate on January 31, 1753, when open sexual abuse occurred aboard the *African*. He noted that William Cooney, one member of his twenty-two-man crew, seduced "number 83," an African of unknown age, "down into the room and lay with her brutelike in view of the whole quarter deck." Newton punished Cooney by clapping him in irons. "I hope this has been the first affair of the kind on board," wrote the captain, "and I am determined to keep them quiet if possible."[40]

Newton's phrase "to keep them quiet" is not entirely clear. Did his determination to "keep *them* quiet" refer to the "first affair of this kind"? Or did *them* refer to the women on the quarterdeck who probably created a commotion in response to the "brutelike" assault? In either case Newton objected to Cooney's behavior and was anxious about "number 83." "If anything happens to the woman," he wrote, "I shall impute it to [Cooney]." Newton's language overlooks the fact that something had *already* happened to "number 83": she had been separated from her family, removed from her place of birth, and raped in the process. The captain's concern, however, was located elsewhere—in something that was yet to come. "Number 83" was "big with child."[41]

Newton's concern with the gestating "number 83" introduces yet another complexity in discussing the transatlantic trade and children. The captain may have asked himself if the "brutelike" assault would endanger the woman's fetus. Would it cause premature labor? If "anything happened" to "number 83" or her unborn child, destined to become a productive worker over time, what were the economic costs to Newton? The questions could be recast to focus on "number 83" and others. "If anything happen[ed]" to "number 83," what did it mean to her psychological health and to that of the children who may have witnessed the rape?

And how could such brutality fail to shape their attitudes and that of their offspring about the whites who claimed to own them? Hatred of their tormentors and rebellious behavior were not unusual. In fact resistance to the exploitative nature of slavery and all of its manifestations were continuous themes, whether Africans young or old were fighting their abductors while in their villages or while moving overland to the shore. Once aboard the ships, refusing to eat and committing suicide were commonly reported acts of resistance. Crews countered rebelliousness by forcing the recalcitrant to eat and flogging others into submission. Since the Africans appeared more affected by pain than by fear of death, crews used nets or rigs to stop them from throwing themselves overboard.[42]

Other acts of defiance included mutinies or insurrections. In the essay "Shipboard Revolts, African Authority, and the Slave Trade," based on data collected about transatlantic slavers between 1650 and 1860, David Richardson estimates that mutinies occurred on as many as 10 percent of the voyages, with up to 10 percent of those on board losing their lives. Considering the relatively large percentage of children crossing the Atlantic Ocean, a great many girls and boys must have witnessed such bloody tumults.[43]

One case in point involved a mutiny on the Newport, Rhode Island, sloop *Little George* under the command of George Scott. On June 1, 1730, he sailed from the Bannanas, south of the River Sierra Leone, on the Windward Coast of Africa with ninety-six Africans aboard, including thirty-five men and an unspecified number of "Young Slaves." At 4:30 A.M. on June 6, when approximately one hundred leagues from the shore, Scott heard a commotion and realized a rebellion was underway. The Africans had removed their irons and killed several members of the crew.[44]

During the uprising the Africans gained control of the ship and forced Scott along with three men and a child, approximately ten years of age, identified only as "the boy" into the cabin below. Captain Scott described the situation as a state of consternation and hopelessness. To break the stalemate, he "sent up the boy in order if possible to Bring them [the Africans] to terms." That the captain, seemingly without concern for safety, employed the child as a negotiator raises questions about the youngster's position and potential. Scott's phrase "bring them to terms" reflects his belief that the boy was capable of effecting a compromise and that language was not a barrier.[45]

What terms could Scott offer through the boy that the Africans yearned for or coveted? Anything less than their liberty and safe passage back to their homes and loved ones was not likely to persuade them to negotiate with an emissary designated by a man whose primary mission had been to transport them across the Atlantic and sell them into a lifetime of bondage. "The Africans but little Regarded our Message," said Scott, and he realized he was in no position to dictate terms or stop them from sailing the ship back to Africa. According to Scott, "in four days" the Africans "maid land" and disembarked.[46]

The "Young Slaves" aboard the *Little George* observed activities on the deck but left no recorded impressions of the boy who was linked to the ship's captain. Without accounts from the young slaves, it is impossible to know if they saw him as a peer or pondered why leaders of the rebellion did not rescue the ten-year-old boy. It is also impossible to know if the young slaves saw the boy as Scott's emissary. Did they believe his movements into and out of Scott's cabin placed him in a position of importance? Or did they think he had received his just deserts when the Africans put him in irons or when they left him behind? Clearly further research is needed to develop a full account about the boy and the young slaves as the mutiny unfolded.[47]

Boys and girls were in the midst of the mutiny aboard the *Little George,* but active participation as insurrectionists was a different matter. While historical records sometimes raise unanswerable questions about young rebels in the Middle Passage and the extent to which they participated in mutinies, evidence suggests that even very young Africans were sometimes viewed as potential threats. For example when the *Henrietta Marie* sailed from London to the Bight of Biafra in 1699, she carried more than eighty pairs of iron shackles of various sizes, some of which would only fit very small wrists. Among other evidence attesting to the rebelliousness of boys and girls is a 1734 warning issued by Samuel Waldo, owner of the Massachusetts slaver *Affica,* to Capt. Samuel Rhodes. "For your own safety as well as mine," wrote Waldo, referring both to physical and to fiscal security, "you'll have the needful Guard over your Slaves, and putt not too much confidence in the Women nor Children lest they happen to be Instrumental to your being surprised which might be fatall." Such advice was worth heeding.[48]

The captains were vigilant in guarding against mutinies, but they could not prevent them entirely. William Snelgrave, commander of the London-based *Henry* in 1721, observed that the crew secured the Africans "very well in Irons, and watch[ed] them narrowly." Yet, they revolted. When asked, through an interpreter, "what had induced them to mutiny," the Africans explained that they had been carried away from their homes by "a great Rogue" and were "resolved to regain their Liberty if possible."[49]

The veteran slaver John Newton concluded, "It is always taken for granted, that they [Africans] will attempt to gain their liberty." In December 1752 the captain discovered a mutinous plot as two Africans attempted to remove their irons. Three boys divulged information about their plans, causing Newton to locate a cache of weapons, including knives, shot, and a "cold chissel." Four other boys were responsible for supplying the weapons. For their parts in the plot, Newton put them in irons and used thumbscrews, turned "slightly," as a way of urging them "to full confession." Captain Newton rounded up and punished additional "rebels" by putting them in collars or neck yokes. He had resorted to tough measures of restraint against the would-be insurrectionists and stopped them, but only for the moment. "It is not to be expected," wrote Newton with confidence, that the Africans "will tamely resolve themselves to their situation."[50]

Newton's observation conforms to the conventional wisdom of the time, but Marcus Rediker's *The Slave Ship* contains an account of "resistance" that suggests that fear of rebellion could prompt extraordinary and irrational violence against children. In 1765 Thomas Marshall believed an African child aboard his ship, the *Black Joke,* was challenging his authority by refusing to eat. As initial punishment Marshall used the cat-o'-nine-tails one day and fastened a log nearly two feet long and weighing more than ten pounds around the putative rebel's neck the following day. As neither method proved successful, the captain resorted to further chastisement and used the "cat" again. Death relieved the supposed "rebel"—in this case a suckling babe—of further punishment, yet the captain's anger was still not assuaged, and he commanded the child's mother to toss her offspring into the "watry grave."[51]

Rather than deliberate defiance, the child's refusal to eat was probably a sign of illness; yet the cost of "resistance" was its life. Whatever the child's immediate cause of death, it is significant to note that the captain believed he could not let the "rebel" go unpunished for fear that other Africans aboard the *Black Joke* would imitate him. The captain's behavior speaks volumes about his determination to make any rebel-in-the-making fear for his or her life and to instill the notion that resistance would not be tolerated. In the process he used one of the most vulnerable and least economically valuable of his chattel to demonstrate his authority.

Ultimately such heavy shows of force did not cause Africans and their descendants to "tamely resolve themselves to their conditions," enslavement, in the Middle Passage or elsewhere.[52] The African-born poet Phillis Wheatley, for instance, asserted the innate and unquenchable resistance to enslavement when she wrote, "In every Breast God has implanted a Principle, which we call Love of Freedom, it is impatient of oppression and pants for Deliverance." There are striking similarities between Wheatley's writing and that of George Tucker, a contemporary, who concluded: "The love of freedom, sir, is an inborn sentiment, which the God of nature has planted deep in the heart: long may it be kept under by the arbitrary institutions of society; but, at the first favourable moment, it springs forth, and flourishes with a vigour that defies all check." Both Wheatley and Tucker were aware of the thirst for freedom among British colonists who were rebelling and claiming the Crown was enslaving them.[53]

While the rhetoric of the Revolutionary War era was powerful, it could not mask the fact that most American citizens did not demand freedom and equality for people of African descent as they did for themselves, nor did the citizens demand an immediate end to the participation in the transatlantic trade of Africans. However, Thomas Jefferson was not completely silent. As a young planter, he opposed the international trade in humans and listed it in the initial draft of the Declaration of Independence among the "long train of abuses and usurpations" committed by the king. Without naming George III in the drumbeat of grievous "facts . . . submitted to a candid world," Jefferson claimed "He" was responsible for "captivating & carrying" a distant people "into slavery in another hemisphere, or to incur miserable death in their transportation thither." This allegation against the king does not appear in the Declaration of Independence as signed on July 4, 1776. After all, the Founding Fathers could hardly claim it was he who insisted upon the vile trade when it was they who were intent upon maintaining it. Afterward several states banned participation in the international trade in Africans, but it was not until the drafting of the Constitution of the United States in 1787 that lawmakers agreed not to pass any legislation interfering with the trade before 1808.[54]

The Founding Fathers' decision regarding the transatlantic trade was related more to building a republican nation—the agreement assured South Carolina's and Georgia's support of the Constitution—than to saving African children from the devastating effects of removing them involuntarily from their loved ones, communities, and cultures. Even when the ban was enacted in 1808, the legislation had no effect on the status of persons enslaved in the United States, and there was no change in their unrelenting work regime whether kidnapped into slavery in Africa or born enslaved in North America. Children of African descent in North America followed the status of their mothers and, with few exceptions, were destined to a lifetime of unfree labor. Exceptions occurred during the Revolutionary War era, when states north of Delaware either abolished slavery or made provisions for its gradual demise. The gradual abolition laws specified dates upon which children born after passage of the statutes were to be freed but left the status of the parents unaffected. Until that time the *post nati* children were to "serve" or work for "temporary owners" or other persons responsible for them until they came of age.[55]

Both before and after 1808, persons owning, indenturing, or hiring children in the United States used boys and girls initially to complement workers, but as they grew older, boys and girls became experienced substitutes for aging laborers and finally replaced them. After 1808 the majority of enslaved children were agricultural laborers in the production of tobacco, rice, cotton, and sugarcane.[56] "The rigors of a field," remembered Frederick Douglass, "less tolerable than the field of battle, awaited me." A child's entry into the labor force made an impact upon the wider community since it meant additional hands, however small, performing house-wifery, husbandry, industrial, or agricultural chores. Enslaved youngsters accomplished many tasks that any adult could complete, but it often took two or more children.[57]

Regardless of the kind of work performed, children learned to work satisfactorily from older experienced workers, and examples of such associations are boundless. The former slave Clayton Holbert remembered that his owner "always had a man in the field to teach the small boys to work," and William S. Pettigrew, a North Carolina slaveholder, hired Eli Moore, a free man, to show youngsters how to use the scythe efficiently and safely. In other instances children learned to work while in "trash gangs," agricultural units made up of children, pregnant women, and older workers. Sometimes children learned craft skills by working with their own relatives. John Matthews said, "I had to help my pappy in de shop when I wus a child," adding, "I learnt how to beat out de iron an' make wagon tires, an' make plows." Still other children were apprenticed, as in 1802 when the twelve-year-old boy April Ellison began training with William McCreight, a gin maker. Children's labor contribution to the local, state, and national economy across the centuries was invaluable, becoming even more precious over time as they replaced older workers.[58]

In addition to having no immediate impact on the condition of enslaved children already in the United States, the 1808 ban on the international slave trade did nothing to stop the buying and selling of enslaved children internally. Indeed children who had been transported from Africa, as well as their contemporaries born in North America, were subjected to further relocations prompted by the economic ambitions of owners or persons who hired or apprenticed them. After 1808 potential owners relied even more heavily upon sales within the United States. Sometimes owners migrated to new locations and took their human chattel in tow. At other times they scattered them about from one farm to another within their own estates or sold them off to different locations. The shifting supply of and demands for enslaved laborers inextricably linked the North American slave trade with the birth of the nation.

When considering the reasons for selling boys, girls, men, and women, the scholar Michael Tadman cautions against the line of argument that slaveholders sold slaves only because of the "need to discipline troublesome slaves" or as a result of emergencies or indebtedness. If these factors alone were indeed responsible for the massive scale of trading, the institution of slavery must have been in "chronic disorder," Tadman writes. "In reality, the great traffic in slaves stemmed, not from special emergencies, but instead from the fundamental racist insensitivity of masters, and from their receptiveness to the temptation of making extra profits through sales."[59] As Walter Johnson argues, "There were probably almost as many reasons given to justify the selling of slaves . . . as there were slaves sold."[60]

Notwithstanding the reasons and regardless of differences in distances traveled, the nature of the North American trade in human beings, interstate, intrastate, or interregional, was identical to the transatlantic trade in the sense that both totally disrupted the lives of laborers when moving them to new work sites. The contours of human trafficking in the United States follow the declining tobacco economy in the Chesapeake and the expansion of the cotton culture in the Lower South. Unfree laborers transformed the new region, and their lives were transformed in the process. In his monograph *Soul by Soul: Life inside the Antebellum Slave Market,* Johnson says that two-thirds of those who migrated to the Deep South were transported there by men in the business of buying and selling human beings.[61]

More than two million slaves were sold at public and private sales within the United States between 1820 and 1860, a number far larger than the number of Africans sold into the United States before 1808, when the United States ended its legal participation in the international trade in Africans. This figure is more meaningful when presented from the perspective offered by Herbert G. Gutman in 1975: "Once every 3.5 minutes, 10 hours a day, 300 days a year, for 40 years," wrote Gutman, "a human being was bought and sold in the antebellum South." Contemporary scholars argue that Gutman's estimates are actually too low, but while debate over the accuracy of the estimate continues, it is evident that between 1820 and 1860, the chances of children in the Upper South being sold into the Lower South by 1860 approached 30 percent. Knowing that children would probably be sold as they grew older placed parents and adoptive families in a precarious position.[62]

The ever-present threat of being sold away from loved ones became a part of the slaves' psyche and African American culture. The Works Progress Administration interviews conducted in the 1930s provide an abundance of recollections about sales and the threat of sales. One interviewee, for example, said, "Babies was snatched from deir mother's breasts and sold to speculators. Chillens was separated from sisters and brothers and never saw each other again. I could tell you about it all day, but even den you couldn't guess de awfulness of it." Another former slave said, "Most folks can't remember many things happened to 'em when they only eight years old, but one of my biggest tribulations come about that time and I never will forget it! . . . I was took away from my mammy and pappy." Yet another slave-born interviewee recounted the day when "de speculataws" came, after which she "ain't never seed nor heared tell o' my Ma an' Pa, an' bruthers, an' susters from dat day to dis."[63]

The buying and selling of children and adults seeped into the vernacular and into musical lyrics. Hampton Normal School and Fisk University's students, some of whom were slave-born, sang "Is Master Going to Sell Us To-morrow?"—a "characteristic favorite" for black and white audiences at late nineteenth-century fundraising concerts. The lyrics reminded listeners of the dread-filled days with that question. The query, ostensibly posed by a child, is directed toward the representative enslaved "Mother," whose response is "Yes, yes, yes!" The line "He is a going to take *us* down to Georgia" is ambiguous and suggests that the word *us,* also in the title, refers to the mother and child as a family unit. But by the song's end, it is clear that *us* refers only to the child, who urges: "Mother, don't you grieve after me." The consoling words are lost in the song's last lines, which underscore the finality of the sale. "Mother," says the child, "I hope to meet you in heaven."[64]

The song conveys the lamentations of a mother and child, but its bitterness is controlled by the musical score and falls short of the account by Solomon Northup, a freeborn man who was kidnaped and enslaved in 1841. Northup met Eliza and her children, Randall and Emily, in a Washington, D.C., area slave pen. Knowing that they were destined for sale, the mother was inconsolable. Northup wrote: "Language can convey but an inadequate impression of the lamentations to which she gave incessant utterances." The weary mother displayed unbounded grief when her son was auctioned off. Her owner threatened to give her a hundred lashes if she did not stop the lugubrious weeping. The mother could not control herself as she "embraced him passionately; kissed him again and again, and told him to remember her—all the while her tears falling in the boy's face like rain." Randall, like the child in the song, tried to comfort his mother when he said, "Don't cry, mama." As if to reassure her, he added, "I will be a good boy." He was ten years old.[65]

Perhaps indicating the beginning of recognition that children—even enslaved children—require different treatment under the law than adults, several of the southern states prohibited separate sales of children before they reached ten years of age. In spite of these extenuating factors, separations occurred, and slaveholders sold children who were too young to manage on their own. Charles Ball opened his narrative with the claim of separation from his mother at an even younger age— less than five years old. The parting made a profound impression: "My poor mother . . . saw me leaving her for the last time," he wrote, "and wept loudly and bitterly over me," incurring the wrath of the slave driver, rawhide whip in hand.[66]

The separation of children from parents could be devastating, and Northup, who had witnessed mothers kissing their dead children before putting them into the grave, believed that the emotion Eliza displayed when the trader sold her daughter was beyond comparison. "Never," wrote Northup, "have I seen such an exhibition of intense, unmeasured, and unbounded grief, as when Eliza was parted from her child." Emily was two or three years younger than Randall and less capable of managing on her own. To further complicate the emotional separation, Eliza heard the trader suggest that "there were men enough in New-Orleans who would give five thousand dollars for such an extra, handsome, fancy piece as Emily would be." In short the trader planned to sell her where she would fetch a high price as a "fancy girl" and become a concubine for the highest bidder. The trafficking in women, "fancy girls" or ordinary females, for sexual purposes was a lucrative business. Eliza, who understood that her daughter would be exploited sexually, as she had been, "became absolutely frantic."[67]

In all its horror and variety, the internal trade generated a vast amount of money. Steven Deyle asserts: "In the late 1850s, Richmond and Charleston each had annual slave sales totaling more than $4 million, and it has been estimated that the figures for New Orleans were larger than the two cities combined. However, the trade probably played an even greater economic role in some of the region's small towns.... In 1860, the *Natchez Courier* reported that $2 million worth of slaves were sold in that city annually—a rather large sum for a town whose population totaled only 6,600."[68] While economists may calculate the profits and losses from the sale of human beings in the transatlantic trade or the trade within the United States, the emotional or psychological costs for the children or adults who were torn away from familiar persons and places are incalculable. For Americans of African descent, the ban of 1808 could do nothing to mitigate that cost.

Most of the people sold in the Upper South traffic were teenagers and young adults. Between 1850 and 1860, an estimated 111,136 out of 269,287 slaves exported from the selling to the buying states were under nineteen years of age.[69] As with the sale of kidnapped African children, the sale of enslaved children in the United States caused the breakup of family life as well as the loss of individual freedom. The 1846 *Charleston Mercury* contains numerous advertisements for the sale of children and "Slave families," a phrase referring more often than not to women and children. For example an advertisement for the thirty-two-year-old "Mary Ann," an "excellent Meat and Pastry Cook," appeared on November 7, 1846. The woman's four children, ranging in age from eleven months to eleven years old, were also for sale. They, unlike many children transported from Africa or across regions within the United States, remained together. That the mother and children were not separated is a significant mitigating factor, but it should not overshadow the fact that the woman's partner or the children's father is not with them.[70]

Adjustments to the loss of loved ones and experiences in enslavement were likewise not monolithic occurrences for children born in Africa or North America. Solomon Northup, who had fallen prey as an adult to traders and was enslaved for twelve years, wrote: "There may be humane masters, as there certainly are inhumane ones—there may be slaves well-clothed, well-fed, and happy, as there surely are those half-clad, half-starved and miserable; nevertheless, the institution that tolerates such wrong and inhumanity . . . is a cruel, unjust, and barbarous one."[71] All too often the slaveholders' sense of family differed from that of the individuals they owned. All enslaved boys or girls who lost a family member because that individual was sold, hired out, or ran away from slavery endured the harshest side of paternalism—separation. And the effects of that brutality lasted well beyond the end of slavery.[72]

Enslaved girls and boys, whether imported from Africa or transported from one North American household, city, state, or region to another, may have experienced differences in owners and treatment, but all were "strangers in a strange land" and faced great physical and psychological difficulties. The passage of the 1808 ban on the international slave trade may have spared some African children from kidnapping and violent uprooting, but African American children had a long time to wait before they were treated with common decency and could begin to enjoy that phase of life called childhood.

Notes

An earlier version of this essay, "Africa's Progeny Cast upon American Shores," appeared in Wilma King, *African American Childhoods: Historical Perspectives From Slavery to Civil Rights* (New York: Palgrave Macmillan, 2005), 9–22.

1. Olaudah Equiano, *The Interesting Narrative of the Life of Olaudah Equiano: Written by Himself*, ed. Robert J. Allison (Boston: Bedford, 1995), 51; Vincent Carretta, *Equiano, the African: Biography of a Self-Made Man* (Athens: University of Georgia Press, 2005); Vincent Carretta, "Olaudah Equiano or Gustavus Vassa? New Light on an Eighteenth-Century Question of Identity," *Slavery and Abolition* 20, no. 3 (1999): 96–103; Paul E. Lovejoy, "Autobiography and Memory: Gustavus Vassa, alias Olaudah Equiano, the African," *Slavery and Abolition* 27, no. 3 (2006): 317–47; Vincent Carretta, "Response to Paul Lovejoy's 'Autobiography and Memory: Gustavus Vassa, alias Olaudah Equiano, the African,'" *Slavery and Abolition* 28, no. 1 (2007): 115–19.

2. Michael L. Conniff and Thomas J. Davis, *Africans in the Americas: A History of the Black Diaspora* (New York: St. Martin's, 1994), 41–44; John Thornton, *Africa and Africans: In the Making of the Atlantic World, 1400–1680* (Cambridge: Cambridge University Press, 1994), 98–101. See also Augustino, "'It Was the Same as Pigs in a Sty': A Young African's Account of Life on a Slave Ship (1849)," in *Children of God's Fire: A Documentary History of Black Slavery in Brazil*, ed. Robert Edgar Conrad (University Park: Pennsylvania State University Press, 1984), 37–38; Belinda [Royall], "Petition of an African Slave to the Legislature of Massachusetts (1782)," in *Unchained Voices: An Anthology of Black Authors in the English-Speaking World of the Eighteenth Century*, ed. Vincent Carretta (Lexington: University Press of Kentucky, 1996), 142–44; Boyrereau Brinch, *The Blind African Slave, or Memoirs of Boyrereau Brinch, Nicknamed Jeffrey Brace. Containing an Account of the Kingdom of Bow-Woo, in the Interior of Africa; with the Climate and Natural Productions, Laws, and Customs Peculiar to That Place. With an Account of His Captivity, Sufferings, Sales, Travels, Emancipation, Conversion to the Christian Religion, Knowledge of the Scriptures, &c. Interspersed with Stricture on Slavery, Speculative Observations on the Qualities of Human Nature, with Quotations from Scripture* (St. Alban's, Vt.: Whitney, 1810), http://docsouth.unc.edu/neh/brinch/brinch.html, accessed July 12, 2011; Ottobah Cugoano, "Thoughts and Sentiments on the Evil and Wicked Traffic of the Slavery and Commerce of the Human Species," in *Three Black Writers in Eighteenth Century England*, ed. Francis D. Adams and Barry Sanders (Belmont, Calif.: Wadsworth, 1971), 43–106; Philip D. Curtin, ed., *Africa Remembered: Narratives by West Africans from the Era of the Slave Trade* (Madison: University of Wisconsin Press, 1967); James Albert Ukawsaw Gronniosaw, *A Narrative of the Most Remarkable Particulars in the Life of James Albert Ukawsaw Gronniosaw, an African Prince, as Related by Himself* (Bath, U.K.: Gye, 1770), http://docsouth.unc.edu/neh/gronniosaw/gronnios.html, accessed July 12, 2011; Florence Hall, "Memoirs of the Life of Florence Hall," unpublished manuscript, c. 1820,

Powel Family Papers, Historical Society of Pennsylvania, Philadelphia; Jerome S. Handler, "Survivors of the Middle Passage: Life Histories of Enslaved Africans in British America," *Slavery and Abolition* 23, no. 1 (2002): 23–56; Jerome Handler, "Life Histories of Enslaved Africans in Barbados," *Slavery and Abolition* 19, no. 1 (1998): 129–41; Vernon H. Nelson, ed., "John Archibald Monteith: Native Helper and Assistant in the Jamaica Mission at New Carmel," *Transactions of the Moravian Historical Society* 21, no. 1 (1966): 29–51; Venture Smith, *A Narrative of the Life and Adventures of Venture a Native of Africa, but a Resident above Sixty Years in the United States of America. Related by Himself,* in *Five Black Lives: The Autobiographies of Venture Smith, James Mars, William Grimes, the Rev. G. W. Offley, James L. Smith,* ed. Arna Bontemps (Middletown, Conn.: Wesleyan University Press, 1971), 1–35.

3. Elizabeth Donnan, ed., *Documents Illustrative of the History of the Slave Trade to America,* 4 vols. (Washington: Carnegie Institute of Washington, 1930), 2:289, available at http://abolition.nypl.org/texts/us_slave_trade/, accessed July 12, 2011; Paul Lovejoy, "The Children of Slavery—the Transatlantic Phase," *Slavery and Abolition* 27, no. 2 (2006): 198–99; David Eltis, "The Volume, Age/Sex Ratios, and African Impact of the Slave Trade: Some Refinements of Paul Lovejoy's Review of the Literature," *Journal of African History* 31, no. 3 (1990): 365–94; David Eltis, "Fluctuations in the Age and Sex Ratios of Slaves in the Nineteenth-Century Transatlantic Slave Traffic," *Slavery and Abolition* 7, no. 3 (1986): 258; Erik J. W. Hofstee, "The Great Divide: Aspects of the Social History of the Middle Passage in the Trans-Atlantic Slave Trade" (Ph.D. diss., Michigan State University, 2001), 66; Gwyn Campbell, Suzanne Miers, and Joseph C. Miller, "Children in European Systems of Slavery: Introduction," *Slavery and Abolition* 27, no. 2 (2006): 165.

Esek Hopkins, captain of the *Sally,* purchased a "woman garle Slave" April 3, 1765, and exchanged goods valued at £108 for her. The following day Hopkins purchased a "Woman Slave" and exchanged goods valued at £126. See *Brig Salleys* Account Book (hereafter cited as *Brig Salleys* Account), April 3, 1765, John Carter Brown Library, Brown University, Providence, Rhode Island, http://dl.lib.brown.edu/catalog/catalog.php?verb=render&id=1161038 386638650, accessed July 12, 2011.

4. Hofstee,"Great Divide," 67. It is not the intent of this essay to argue that African children did or did not enjoy a childhood in the modern sense but to note the presence of black boys and girls in the international and domestic trade before and after 1808. Furthermore the contemporary literature on childhood as an historical concept generally ignores African children as well as those of African descent. See David Archard, "The Concept of Childhood" in *Children: Rights and Childhood* (London: Routledge, 1993), 15–28; Hugh Cunningham, "Review Essay: Histories of Childhood," *American Historical Review* 103, no. 4 (1998): 1195–208; Willem Koops, "Imaging Childhood," in *Beyond the Century of the Child: Cultural History and Developmental Psychology,* ed. Willem Koops and Michael Zuckerman (Philadelphia: University of Pennsylvania Press, 2003), 1–18; Roger Cox, *Shaping Childhood: Themes of Uncertainty in the History of Adult-Child Relationships* (London: Routledge, 1996).

5. Hofstee, "Great Divide," 67.

6. Campbell, Miers, and Miller, "Children in European Systems of Slavery," 168; Paul Lovejoy, "The Children of Slavery—the Transatlantic Phase," *Slavery and Abolition* 27, no. 2 (2006): 200–204; Audra A. Diptee, "African Children in the British Slave Trade during the Late Eighteenth Century," *Slavery and Abolition* 27, no. 2 (2006): 187; Lisa A. Lindsay,

Captives as Commodities: The Transatlantic Slave Trade (Upper Saddle River, N.J.: Pearson/ Prentice Hall, 2008), 4; "Thomas Clarkson's Efficiency of Regulation of the Slave Trade," in Donnan, *Documents*, 2:571–72; Hofstee, "Great Divide," 66.

7. Donnan, *Documents*, 3:138, 457; Charles Rappleye, *Sons of Providence: The Brown Brothers, the Slave Trade, and the American Revolution* (New York: Simon & Schuster, 2006), 60; Hofstee, "Great Divide," 68.

8. Paul Lovejoy, "Children of Slavery," 204; G. Ugo Nwokeji, "African Conceptions of Gender and the Slave Traffic," *William and Mary Quarterly*, 3rd ser., 58, no. 1 (2001): 62.

9. See Solomon Northup, "Twelve Years a Slave: Narrative of Solomon Northup," in *Puttin' On Ole Massa: The Slave Narratives of Henry Bibb, William Wells Brown, and Solomon Northup*, ed. Gilbert Osofsky (New York: Harper & Row, 1969); Charles Ball, *Fifty Years in Chains: The Life of an American Slave* (New York: Dayton, 1859; repr., Detroit: Negro History Press, 1971); James William McGettigan Jr., "Boone County Slaves: Sales, Estate Division and Families, 1820–1865," 2 pts., *Missouri Historical Review* 72 (January 1978): 176–97; 72 (April 1972): 271–95; Sojourner Truth, *Narrative of Sojourner Truth, a Bondswoman of Older Times, Emancipated by the New York Legislature in the Early Part of the Present Century, with a History of Her Labors and Correspondence Drawn from Her Book of Life* (New York: New York Times & Arno, 1968), 44–46; Nell Irvin Painter, *Sojourner Truth: A Life, a Symbol* (New York: Norton, 1996), 32–37; Michael Tadman, *Speculators and Slaves: Masters, Traders, and Slaves in the Old South* (Madison: University of Wisconsin Press, 1989); Walter Johnson, *Soul by Soul: Life inside the Antebellum Slave Market* (Cambridge, Mass.: Harvard University Press, 1999); Erskine Clarke, *Dwelling Place: A Plantation Epic* (New Haven, Conn.: Yale University Press, 2005), 319, 393–94, 411, 430.

10. Handler, "Survivors of the Middle Passage," 26–36.

11. Ephraim Robin John and Ancona Robin Robin John to Charles Wesley, August 17, 1774, Charles Wesley Papers, Special Collections, John Rylands University Library, University of Manchester, Manchester, England (cited hereafter as Wesley Papers). See Randy J. Sparks, "Two Princes of Calabar: An Atlantic Odyssey from Slavery to Freedom," *William and Mary Quarterly*, 3rd ser., 59, no. 3 (2002): 555–83; Randy J. Sparks, *Two Princes of Calabar: An Eighteenth-Century Odyssey* (Cambridge, Mass.: Harvard University Press, 2004); Gomer Williams, *History of the Liverpool Privateers and Letters of Marque with an Account of the Liverpool Slave Trade* (New York: Kelly, 1966), 535–66; Daniel L. Schafer, "Family Ties That Bind: Anglo-African Slave Traders in Africa and Florida, John Fraser and His Descendants," *Slavery and Abolition* 20, no. 3 (1999): 4–5, 13; Carol P. MacCormack, "Slaves, Slave Owners, and Slave Dealers: Sherbro Coast and Hinterland," in *Women and Slavery in Africa*, ed. Claire C. Robertson and Martin A. Klein (Madison: University of Wisconsin Press, 1983), 278; Bruce L. Mouser, "Women Slavers in Guinea-Conakry," in Robertson and Klein, *Women and Slavery in Africa*, 323–24, 326.

12. Robin Johns to Wesley, August 17, 1774; Sparks, "Two Princes," 567–68; Williams, *History of the Liverpool Privateers*, 535–37, 541–42.

13. Robin Johns to Wesley, August 17, 1774; Sparks, "Two Princes," 568–83. See also William M. Wieck, "Somerset: Lord Mansfield and the Legitimacy of Slavery in the Anglo-American World," *University of Chicago Law Review* 42, no. 1 (1974): 86–146; James Oldham, "New Light on Mansfield and Slavery," *Journal of British Studies* 27, no. 1 (1988): 45–68.

14. For discussion of Africans who succeeded in returning to Africa, see Terry Alford, *Prince among Slaves* (New York: Harcourt, Brace, Jovanovich, 1977); Howard Jones, *Mutiny on the Amistad: The Saga of a Revolt and Its Impact on American Abolition, Law, and Diplomacy* (New York: Oxford University Press, 1987); J. C. Furnas, "Patrolling the Middle Passage," in *Readings in American History, 1607–1865*, ed. Robert M. Spector (New York: American Heritage Custom, 1993), 155–62.

15. Hall, "Memoirs of the Life"; Ottobah Cugoano, "Narrative of the Enslavement of Ottobah Cugoano, a Native of Africa; Published by Himself, in the Year 1787," 120, http://doc south.unc.edu/neh/cugoano/cugoano.html, accessed July 12, 2011; Brinch, *Blind African Slave*, 14, 68–71; Sylvia Diouf, *Dreams of Africa in Alabama: The Slave Ship Clotilda and the Story of the Last Africans Brought to America* (New York: Oxford University Press, 2007), 43. See also Kevin Dawson, "Enslaved Swimmers and Divers in the Atlantic World," *Journal of American History* 92 (March 2006): 1327–55, for a discussion of recreational swimming among people of African descent.

16. Smith, *Narrative of the Life*, 8, 9; Robert E. Desrochers Jr., "'Not Fade Away': The Narrative of Venture Smith, an African in the Early Republic," *Journal of American History* 84 (June 1997): 40.

17. Cugoano, "Narrative of the Enslavement," 120; Hall, "Memoirs of the Life."

18. John Newton, *The Journal of a Slave Trader (John Newton): With Newton's Thoughts upon the African Slave Trade,* ed. Bernard Martin and Mark Spurrell (London: Epworth, 1967), 41; *Brig Salleys* Account, December 1, 1764. See Diptee, "African Children," 188–89, for a discussion about trading children.

19. See *Brig Salleys* Account, November 15, 1764; December 1, 1764; December 26, 1764; January 6, 1765.

20. Donnan, *Documents*, 1:282–83; Frances Fitzgerald, "Peculiar Institutions: Brown University Looks at the Slave Traders in Its Past," *New Yorker*, September 12, 2005, 72; John Thornton, *Africa and Africans in the Making of the Atlantic World, 1400–1800*, 2nd ed. (Cambridge: Cambridge University Press, 1998), 52–53; Gronniosaw, *Narrative*, 9; Darold Wax, "A Philadelphia Surgeon on a Slaving Voyage to Africa, 1749–1751," *Pennsylvania Magazine of History and Biography* 94 (October 1968): 483; Ira Berlin, *Many Thousands Gone: The First Two Centuries of Slavery in North America* (Cambridge, Mass.: Belknap Press of Harvard University Press, 1998), 22. For discussions focusing upon motives for engaging in the Atlantic slave trade, see George Metcalf, "A Microcosm of Why Africans Sold Slaves: Akan Consumption Patterns in the 1770s," *Journal of African History* 28, no. 3 (1987): 377–94, and Robin Law, "Dahomey and the Slave Trade: Reflections on the Historiography of the Rise of Dahomey," *Journal of African History* 27, no. 2 (1986): 243–47. See also Diouf, *Dreams of Africa*, 25; *Brig Salleys* Account; Stephen D. Behrendt, "Markets, Transaction Cycles, and Profits: Merchant Decision Making in the British Slave Trade," *William and Mary Quarterly*, 3rd ser., 58, no. 1 (2001): 171–204, for references to trade goods.

21. See David Eltis, "The Volume and Structure of the Transatlantic Slave Trade: A Reassessment," *William and Mary Quarterly*, 3rd ser., 58, no. 1 (2001): 29, 30, 35; Eltis, "Volume, Age/Sex Ratios, and African Impact," 485–92; Lindsay, *Captives as Commodities*, 4, 5; Paul E. Lovejoy, "The Impact of the Atlantic Slave Trade on Africa: A Review of the Literature," *Journal of African History* 30, no. 3 (1989): 365–94. See also Thornton, *Africa and*

Africans, 72–74; James A. Rawley, *London: Metropolis of the Slave Trade* (Columbia: University of Missouri Press, 2003), 17.

22. John Thornton, "Sexual Demography: The Impact of the Slave Trade on Family Structure," in *"We Specialize in the Wholly Impossible": A Reader in Black Women's History,* ed. Darlene Clark Hine, Wilma King, and Linda Reed (Brooklyn: Carlson, 1995), 58–59; Nwokeji, "African Conceptions of Gender," 57.

23. Donnan, *Documents,* 1:293, 402, 442.

24. Ibid., 1:459; Equiano, *Interesting Narrative,* 56; Augustino, "Same as Pigs," 38; Conrad, *Children of God's Fire,* 33. See also James A. Rawley, *The Transatlantic Slave Trade: A History* (New York: Norton, 1981), 283–306; Daniel P. Mannix and Malcolm Cowley, *Black Cargoes: A History of the Atlantic Slave Trade, 1518–1865* (New York: Viking, 1962), 104–30.

25. Although a full discussion of the morbidity and mortality rates aboard slavers is beyond the scope of this essay, useful sources for such a study include *Brig Salleys* Account; David Eltis, "Mortality and Voyage Length in the Middle Passage: New Evidence from the Nineteenth Century," *Journal of Economic History* 44 (June 1984): 301–8; Philip D. Curtin, "Epidemiology and the Slave Trade," *Political Science Quarterly* 83, no. 2 (1968): 190–216; Joseph C. Miller, "Mortality in the Atlantic Slave Trade: Statistical Evidence on Causality," *Journal of Interdisciplinary History* 11 (Winter 1981): 385–423.

26. Wax, "Philadelphia Surgeon," 468; Hofstee, "Great Divide," 88.

27. David Eltis and Stanley L. Engerman, "Fluctuations in Sex and Age Ratios in the Transatlantic Slave Trade, 1663–1864," *Economic History Review* 46, no. 2 (1993): 314, 317; John Pollock, *Wilberforce* (New York: St. Martin's, 1977), 82–83; Carretta, *Equiano,* 255–56; Sheila Lambert, ed., *House of Commons Sessional Papers of the Eighteenth Century,* vol. 68, *George III, Minutes of Evidence on the Slave Trade 1788–1789* (Wilmington, N.C.: Scholarly Resources, 1975), 73–76; Donnan, *Documents,* 2:584; Hofstee, "Great Divide," 72, 78; James W. LoGerfo, "Sir William Dolben and 'The Cause of Humanity': The Passage of the Slave Trade Regulation Act of 1788," *Eighteenth-Century Studies* 6 (Summer 1973): 431–51; "Anno vicesimo octavo George III. Cap. LIV: An Act to regulate, for a Limited time, the shipping and carrying Slaves in *British* Vessels from the Coast of *Africa,*" William Loney RN: Victorian Naval Surgeon, http://www.pdavis.nl/Legis_21.htm, accessed July 12, 2011. See also Campbell, Miers, and Miller, "Children in European Systems," 165; Lovejoy, "Children of Slavery," 199–200.

28. Lambert, *House of Commons Sessional Papers,* vol. 67, *George III, Minutes of Evidence on the Slave Trade, 1788–1790* (Wilmington, N.C.: Scholarly Resources, 1975), 282. The *Brookes* (sometimes spelled *Brooks*) served as the epitome of "tight packing" and was known to transport between 609 and 740 Africans without attention to size. The committee printed thousands of diagrams of the *Brookes* and circulated them widely. The diagrams were literally and figuratively the most recognizable anti–slave trade "poster" of the nineteenth century. See also Adam Hochschild, *Bury the Chains: Prophets and Rebels in the Fight to Free an Empire's Slaves* (Boston: Houghton Mifflin, 2005), 155–56.

29. See Robert A. Margo and Richard H. Steckel, "The Heights of American Slaves: New Evidence on Slave Nutrition and Health," *Social Science History* 6 (Fall 1982): 516–38.

30. Colin A. Palmer, *Human Cargoes: The British Slave Trade to Spanish America, 1700–1739* (Urbana: University of Illinois Press, 1981), 121–22; Anne Farrow, Joel Lang, and Jenifer Frank, *Complicity: How the North Promoted, Prolonged, and Profited from Slavery* (New York:

Ballantine, 2005), 131; Erik Calonius, *The Wanderer: The Last American Slave Ship and the Conspiracy That Set Its Sails* (New York: St. Martin's, 2006), 107, 110–24; Hofstee, "Great Divide," 72, 78; Lovejoy, "Children of Slavery," 203–4; David Eltis, Stephen D. Behrendt, David Richardson, and Herbert S. Klein, eds., *Transatlantic Slave Trade: A Database on CD-ROM* (Cambridge: Cambridge University Press, 1999), #18076.

31. See Equiano, *Interesting Narrative,* 65; Marcus Rediker, *The Slave Ship: A Human History* (New York: Viking, 2007), 279.

32. George Francis Dow, *Slave Ships and Slaving* (Westport, Conn.: Negro Universities Press, 1970), 172–73. See also Walter Rodney, *West Africa and the Atlantic Slave-Trade,* Historical Association of Tanzania, no. 2 (Nairobi: East Africa Publishing House, 1967), 10–11; Diptee, "African Children," 189–90.

33. Equiano, *Interesting Narrative,* 50; Dow, *Slave Ships and Slaving,* 173.

34. Sarah Margru [Kinson] to My Dear Mr. [George] Whipple, September 18, 1847, American Missionary Association Archives, Tulane University, New Orleans (emphasis in the original). See also John W. Barber, *A History of the Amistad Captives: Being a Circumstantial Account of the Capture of the Spanish Schooner Amistad, by the Africans on Board; Their Voyage, and Capture Near Long Island, New York; with Biographical Sketches of each of the Surviving Africans; Also, an Account of the Trials Had on Their Case, before the District and Circuit Courts of the United States, for the District of Connecticut* (New Haven, Conn.: Barber, 1840), 15.

35. Jones, *Mutiny on the Amistad,* 188–94.

36. Augustino, "Same as Pigs," 39; Hofstee, "Great Divide," 100–102.

37. Equiano, *Interesting Narrative,* 54, 57. See also William D. Piersen, "White Cannibals, Black Martyrs: Fear, Depression, and Religious Faith as Causes of Suicide among New Slaves," *Journal of Negro History* 62 (April 1977): 147–59; John Thornton, "Cannibals, Witches, and Slave Traders in the Atlantic World," *William and Mary Quarterly,* 3rd ser., 60, no. 2 (2003): 273–94.

38. Brinch, *Blind African Slave,* 103 (emphasis in the original); James Pope-Hennessy, *Sins of the Fathers: A Study of the Atlantic Slave Traders, 1441–1807* (London: Weidenfeld & Nicolson, 1967), 99, 100; Newton, *Journal of a Slave Trader,* 75. See also Daniel L. Schafer, *Anna Madgigine Jai Kingsley: African Princess, Florida Slave, Plantation Owner* (Gainesville: University Press of Florida, 2003) for insight about a long-lasting, intimate relationship between a slave trader and African woman that began when she was a teenager.

39. Newton, *Journal of a Slave Trader,* 75. See also Pope-Hennessy, *Sins of the Fathers,* 100; and Quobna Ottobah Cugoano, "Thoughts and Sentiments on the Evil and Wicked Traffic of the Slavery and Commerce of the Human Species," in Carretta, *Unchained Voices,* 149.

40. Newton, *Journal of a Slave Trader,* 75, 105. See also Pope-Hennessy, *Sins of the Fathers,* 100; Rawley, *London,* 111; and Dow, *Slave Ships and Slaving,* 174.

41. Newton, *Journal of a Slave Trader,* 75; Pope-Hennessy, *Sins of the Fathers,* 100.

42. Equiano, *Interesting Narrative,* 54; Donnan, *Documents,* 3:376. See also Leonard Shengold, *Soul Murder: The Effects of Childhood Abuse and Deprivation* (New Haven, Conn.: Yale University Press, 1989); Nell Irvin Painter, "Soul Murder and Slavery: Toward a Fully Loaded Cost Accounting," in *Southern History across the Color Line* (Chapel Hill: University of North Carolina Press, 2002), 15–39.

43. David Richardson, "Shipboard Revolts, African Authority, and the Atlantic Slave Trade," *William and Mary Quarterly,* 3rd ser., 58, no. 1 (2001): 72, 74. See also Donnan,

Documents, 2:355; Eric Robert Taylor, *If We Must Die: Shipboard Insurrections in the Era of the Atlantic Slave Trade* (Baton Rouge: Louisiana State University Press, 2006); *Brig Salleys Account,* August 28, 1765.

44. "I George Scott the Subscriber of New Port Rhode Island," Rhode Island Historical Society, Providence; Donnan, *Documents,* 3:118–21; *Boston Weekly News-Letter,* April 29–May 6, 1731, 1; Jay Coughtry, *The Notorious Triangle: Rhode Island and the African Slave Trade, 1700–1807* (Philadelphia: Temple University Press, 1981), 151, 157.

45. "I George Scott"; Donnan, *Documents,* 3:119. For discussions regarding a lingua franca, see Thornton, *Africa and Africans,* 206–18; Ira Berlin, "From Creole to African: Atlantic Creoles and the Origins of African-American Society in Mainland North America," *William and Mary Quarterly,* 3rd ser., 53, no. 2 (1996): 255, 258.

46. "I George Scott"; Donnan, *Documents,* 3:119.

47. See Equiano, *Interesting Narrative,* 61–62, for a discussion of interactions between the author and a white boy on board a ship.

48. Donnan, *Documents,* 3:45; Hofstee, "Great Divide," 97; Rawley, *London,* 1. See also Antonio T. Bly, "Crossing the Lake of Fire: Slave Resistance during the Middle Passage, 1720–1842," *Journal of Negro History* 83 (Summer 1998): 178–86; Richardson, "Shipboard Revolts," 69–92; Taylor, *If We Must Die.*

49. Donnan, *Documents,* 2:354–55.

50. Newton, *Journal of a Slave Trader,* 71, 72, 77, 103.

51. Rediker, *Slave Ship,* 286.

52. Newton, *Journal of a Slave Trader,* 103.

53. Phillis Wheatley to the Rev. Samson Occom, February 11, 1774, in *Am I Not a Man and a Brother: The Antislavery Crusade of Revolutionary America, 1688–1788,* ed. Roger Bruns (New York: Chelsea House, 1997), 306; Ira Berlin, *Slaves without Masters: The Free Negro in the Antebellum South* (New York: Oxford University Press, 1981), 15. See also Bernard Bailyn, *The Ideological Origins of the American Revolution* (Cambridge, Mass.: Belknap Press of the Harvard University Press, 1967).

54. See Alfred Hinsey Kelly and Winfred A. Harbison, *The American Constitution: Its Origins and Development,* 5th ed. (New York: Norton, 1976); William Cohen, "Thomas Jefferson and the Problem of Slavery," *Journal of American History* 56 (December 1969): 503–26; Edwin Gittleman, "Jefferson's 'Slave Narrative': The Declaration of Independence as a Literary Text," *Early American Literature* 8 (Winter 1974): 252.

55. See Arthur Zilversmit, *The First Emancipation: The Abolition of Slavery in the North* (Chicago: University of Chicago Press, 1967); Joanne Pope Melish, *Disowning Slavery: Gradual Emancipation and "Race" in New England, 1780–1860* (Ithaca, N.Y.: Cornell University Press, 1998); Leslie M. Harris, *In the Shadow of Slavery: African Americans in New York City, 1626–1863* (Chicago: University of Chicago Press, 2003); Gary B. Nash and Jean R. Sunderlund, *Freedom by Degrees: Emancipation in Pennsylvania and Its Aftermath* (New York: Oxford University Press, 1991).

56. See Wilma King, *Stolen Childhood: Slave Youth in Nineteenth-Century America,* 2nd ed. (Bloomington: Indiana University Press, 2011), 71–106, for a discussion of work performed by enslaved youth in the United States.

57. Frederick Douglass, *My Bondage and My Freedom* (New York: Dover, 1969), 206, 219.

58. George P. Rawick, ed., *The American Slave: A Composite Autobiography,* 2nd ser., vol. 16, *Kansas Narrative* (Westport, Conn.: Greenwood, 1972), 1; George P. Rawick, ed., *The American Slave: A Composite Autobiography Supplement,* 1st ser., vol. 9, pt. 4, *Mississippi Narrative* (Westport, Conn.: Greenwood, 1977), 1452; Michael P. Johnson, "Work, Culture, and the Slave Community: Slave Occupations in the Cotton Belt in 1860," *Labor History* 27 (Summer 1986): 325–55; William S. Pettigrew to Moses, June 12, 1857, Pettigrew Family Papers, Southern Historical Collection, University of North Carolina, Chapel Hill, North Carolina; Charles L. Perdue Jr., Thomas E. Barden, and Robert K. Phillips, eds., *Weevils in the Wheat: Interviews with Virginia Ex-Slaves* (Bloomington: Indiana University Press, 1980), 26; Michael P. Johnson and James L. Roark, *Black Masters: A Free Family of Color in the Old South* (New York: Norton, 1984), 6, 11–15, 16, 17, 67, 78, 106; Norman R. Yetman, ed., *Life under the "Peculiar Institution": Selections from the Slave Narrative Collection* (New York: Holt, Rinehart & Winston, 1970), 48, 49.

59. Tadman, *Speculators and Slaves,* 111, 113, 117.

60. Walter Johnson, *Soul by Soul,* 27; Steven Deyle, *Carry Me Back: The Domestic Slave Trade in American Life* (New York: Oxford University Press, 2005), 17–24, 27. For other ways in which enslaved families were separated, see Brenda E. Stevenson, *Life in Black and White: Family and Community in the Slave South* (New York: Oxford University Press, 1996), 209–12; Richard S. Dunn, "A Tale of Two Plantations: Slave Life at Mesopotamia in Jamaica and Mount Airy in Virginia, 1799 to 1828," *William and Mary Quarterly,* 3rd ser., 34, no. 1 (1977): 32–65.

61. Johnson, *Soul by Soul,* 215.

62. Daina Ramey Berry, "'In Pressing Need of Cash': Gender, Skill, and Family Persistence in the Domestic Slave Trade," *Journal of African American History* 92 (Winter 2007): 23; Deyle, *Carry Me Back,* 172–73; Tadman, *Speculators and Slaves,* 25–26, 45.

63. Dorothy Sterling, *We Are Your Sisters: Black Women in the Nineteenth Century* (New York: Norton, 1984), 10–11. For scattered references to separation of children from loved ones by sales, see George P. Rawick, ed., *The American Slave: A Composite Autobiography,* 19 vols. (Westport, Conn.: Greenwood, 1972); George P. Rawick, ed., *The American Slave: A Composite Autobiography: Supplement,* 1st ser., 12 vols. (Westport, Conn.: Greenwood, 1978); George P. Rawick, ed., *The American Slave: A Composite Autobiography: Supplement,* 2nd ser., 10 vols. (Westport, Conn.: Greenwood, 1979); Frederic Bancroft, *Slave-Trading in the Old South* (Baltimore: Furst, 1931).

64. See *Jubilee and Plantation Songs. Characteristic Favorites, as sung by the Hampton Students, Jubilee Singers, Fisk University Students, and Other Concert Companies. Also a Number of New and Pleasing Selections* (Boston: Ditson, 1887), 51.

65. Northup, "Twelve Years a Slave," 245, 264, 265.

66. Ball, *Fifty Years in Chains,* 10–11; Bancroft, *Slave-Trading in the Old South,* 22, 133–34n, 144, 197, 239.

67. Northup, "Twelve Years a Slave," 267–68. See also Catherine M. Hanchett, "'What Sort of People and Families . . .': The Edmondson Sisters," *Afro-Americans in New York Life and History* 6 (July 1982): 21–37; Edward E. Baptist, "'Cuffy,' 'Fancy Maids,' and 'One-Eyed Men': Rape, Commodification, and the Domestic Slave Trade in the United States," *American Historical Review* 106 (December 2001): 1619–50; Melton A. McLaurin, *Celia: A Slave*

(Athens: University of Georgia Press, 1991); Richard Wrightman Fox, "Performing Emancipation," in *The Problem of Evil: Slavery, Freedom and the Ambiguities of American Reform*, ed. Steven Mintz and John Stauffers (Amherst: University of Massachusetts Press, 2007), 298–311.

68. Deyle, *Carry Me Back*, 155.

69. Tadman, *Speculators and Slaves*, 25–26, 44. For relevant information regarding the slave trading business in the United States, see Edmund L. Drago, ed., *Broke by the War: Letters of a Slave Trader* (Columbia: University of South Carolina Press, 1991).

70. *Charleston Mercury*, February 3, 1846; February 21, 1846; March 3, 1846; March 23, 1846; April 4, 1846; April 9, 1846; July 1, 1846; July 16, 1846; August 5, 1846; August 25, 1846; October 1, 1846; October 17, 1846; October 20, 1846; November 3, 1846; November 7, 1846; November 26, 1846, contains advertisements for the sale of children.

71. Northup, "Twelve Years a Slave," 338.

72. Eric Perkins, "Roll, Jordan, Roll: A 'Marx' for the Master Class," *Radical History Review* 3 (Fall 1976): 47–48; Norrece T. Jones Jr., *Born a Child of Freedom, yet a Slave: Mechanisms of Control and Strategies of Resistance in Antebellum South Carolina* (Hanover, N.H.: Wesleyan University Press, 1990), 7, 26–30, 196–206; James D. Anderson, "Aunt Jemima in Dialectics: Genovese on Slave Culture," *Journal of Negro History* 41 (January 1976): 99–114.

"MADDA! MADDA! YIERA! YIERA!"

African Women Slaves and the Abolition
of the British Transatlantic Slave Trade

Inge Dornan

The status and experiences of African female slaves formed a prominent part of parliamentary debates on the ending of the transatlantic slave trade. The West India faction in Westminster highlighted the role of slave women in the British West Indies to insist that the survival of the colonies depended on a continuous supply of slaves from Africa. Whereas the abolitionists pointed to the treatment and experiences of women in the Middle Passage and on West Indian plantations to condemn the African slave trade, in the words of William Wilberforce, as "utterly unnecessary" and a "waste of life."[1] This chapter explores why and how the subject of women slaves provoked such political controversy and why this debate in particular played such a crucial part in dividing political opinion on the trafficking of Africans to the New World.

Locating the ways in which slave women featured in the parliamentary debates on the slave trade reveals how gender became an important part of the political discourse on abolition in Britain. Hitherto the historiography has been dominated by two competing theories on the abolition of the slave trade: on the one hand, that the decision to abolish the slave trade in 1807 was principally the result of economic and political imperatives, in large part prompted by a perceived decline of the West Indian sugar colonies in the years following the American Revolution; on the other that it was the successful conclusion of a widespread and long-running humanitarian campaign, driven by reformist and evangelical fervor in Britain and America. Examining the ways in which gender was deployed in the parliamentary debates to argue the case for and against the slave trade suggests that economic and humanitarian arguments, most especially those presented by the abolitionists, rather than being treated as discrete and unconnected, often overlapped.[2]

It was through the construction of both the pro- and antislavery discourse in Parliament that the voices and experiences of slave women acquired a degree of political importance thus far overlooked by historians. Both sides of the debate relied heavily on eyewitness testimony to drive home their political message. But it was the abolitionists in particular who depended on firsthand accounts of the treatment and responses of African slaves to the Middle Passage and to West Indian slavery to counter the arguments of their opponents. When Parliament finally introduced the 1807 Abolition Act, the abolitionists celebrated their achievement as the most "glorious measure" ever to be adopted by any legislature in the world. Nevertheless focusing on the gendered nature of the slave trade debates in Parliament, as well as the role that women slaves played in the case presented by the abolitionists, indicates that the legacy of the Abolition Act is more ambiguous than the abolitionists' tributes at first suggest.

I

In May 1787, spearheaded by Granville Sharp and Thomas Clarkson, a group of twelve like-minded men, most of whom were Quakers, gathered to form the Society for Effecting the Abolition of the Slave Trade (also known as the London Committee). Antislavery sentiment had been expressed by individuals on both sides of the Atlantic long before this date, but it was only once the London Yearly Meeting banned Quaker ownership of slaves in 1761 that a formal and official stance of opposition toward slavery and the slave trade was adopted by any one particular group in Britain. Henceforth, the Quakers became prominent activists in the transatlantic campaign to abolish the slave trade. In the 1770s and 1780s, opposition to the British slave trade gained momentum on the back of several high-profile court cases—most famously *Somerset v. Stewart* (1772), which appeared in spirit if not in theory to ban slavery in Britain, and *Gregson v. Gilbert* (1783), commonly known as the *Zong* case, which brought the horrors of the Middle Passage to the British public's attention, when the owners of the slave ship *Zong* were exposed for filing an insurance claim for the deaths of 133 slaves, who were deliberately thrown overboard by the captain and crew. Granville Sharp, an activist, reformer, and self-taught student of law, advised on these and other such cases on behalf of the slaves involved. It was Olaudah Equiano, perhaps the most famous black abolitionist of the period, and himself a former slave, who brought the *Zong* case to Sharp's attention. Two years after this, in 1785, Thomas Clarkson, a divinity student at Cambridge University, won the Members' Prize for a Latin essay on the subject of the slave trade and therein sealed his lifelong passion for and commitment to abolitionism. By the time he and Granville Sharp formed the London Committee in 1787, they not only commanded the support of the Quakers on both sides of the Atlantic, but also, crucially, of William Wilberforce, an evangelical Christian and a member of the House of Commons, and the prime minister, William Pitt the Younger. The London Committee's first major political breakthrough came in February 1788, when, after receiving a flood of antislavery petitions to Parliament, George III called for Britain's first formal hearing into the abolition of the slave trade. It was the first official inquiry of its kind in the world to investigate the status and nature of trafficking Africans to the New World.

In North America, by comparison, although abolition sentiment was building in both public and political circles, the abolition of the American slave trade was neither the result of an extensive public campaign nor of a prolonged and dedicated political enquiry of the kind witnessed in Britain. It was instead set in motion during the War of Independence, when nonimportation agreements included slave imports, and was finally decided upon in 1787, when state delegates gathered in Philadelphia to discuss the formation of the U.S. Constitution. Overall the decision to end the foreign slave trade was the result of a relatively contained political debate (compared with Britain), albeit one that sparked divisions between delegates and stopped short when it threatened to upset the progress of the Constitution. In the end the Americans agreed to delay the abolition of the slave trade until January 1, 1808.[4] In Britain the act to end the slave trade was, by way of contrast, the product of almost twenty years of public and political campaigning and parliamentary inquiries and debates, during the course of which an enormous body of eyewitness testimony was collected and scrutinized on the roles and experiences of Africans in the transatlantic slave trade.

Under the king's instructions, a committee of the Privy Council was first tasked with conducting this investigation. In April 1789, after more than a year of interrogating dozens of eyewitnesses on behalf of each side of the political divide, the committee submitted its mammoth, 850-page report to Parliament. Proponents of the slave trade immediately condemned it as "insufficient, defective, and contradictory," "manufactured," "hearsay," and "false."[5] The prime minister, William Pitt the Younger, who sided with the abolitionists, was reportedly "irritated" by efforts to discredit the evidence. Nonetheless given the controversy it aroused, it was agreed, albeit reluctantly by the abolitionists, to allow a select committee of the House of Commons to conduct its own inquiry into the slave trade—later, the Lords, too, instigated their own investigation.[6] From the outset eyewitness testimony was important to the arguments of both supporters and opponents of the slave trade— indeed it was an essential weapon in the hands of the abolitionists. Needless to say, though, firsthand accounts of the slave trade proved to be a problematic source for building a solid case for or against the slave trade, since the subjective nature of the testimony made it relatively easy for each side to contest the arguments of the other and ultimately hard for any one side to secure a quick and resounding victory.

Defenders of the slave trade premised their arguments against its abolition on the impact that such an action would have not only on the progress of the British West Indian colonies, but also on Britain's economic and political status and on the livelihoods of West Indian planters and landowners. Sir John Dalling, a former planter in Jamaica, summed up the case presented by the West India interest in Parliament: "it would be the ruin of every proprietor, and produce beggary to his descendents; and by degrees also, I am afraid, commercially speaking, [bring] bankruptcy, in this country."[7] Members of Parliament for the City of London charged that it would bankrupt the capital.[8] Lord Penrhyn argued that the planters would be ruined as a result of the loss of upward of seventy million pounds worth of mortgaged land in the West Indies.[9] Other MPs made a strong case to suggest that such a decision would pave the way for other European nations, namely France, to take Britain's place in the slave trade, thereby costing her both economically and politically.[10] Some also predicted that it would ignite mass slave rebellions in the British slave islands—such scaremongering seemed well founded when news reached Britain of the slave rebellion in Saint-Domingue in 1791.[11] Britain's West Indian islands, too, sent resolutions to the Commons spelling out how they would be ruined if and when slave imports ceased.[12]

During the course of deliberating the economic and political outcomes of ending the slave trade, the West India faction repeated their position that it had to be preserved on pragmatic grounds, irrespective of moral or humanitarian arguments. Their reasoning was founded on a conviction that the British West Indian slave populations could not be sustained (and certainly not expand) without continuous supplies of slaves; in the event that the slave trade was abolished, slavery too was likely to collapse—resulting in heavy economic and political losses to both the colonies and Britain. It was arguments based upon a predicted decline in the West Indian colonies that persuaded the West India interest to turn to the gendered dynamics of the slave trade and slavery as a convincing rationale for opposing the end of Britain's involvement in the transatlantic slave trade.[13] And it was the importance attached to this line of argument by the West India interest in Parliament—much more than was necessary, according to Pitt—which led the Commons and Lords select committees to examine the status, conduct, and treatment of African women in the slave trade.[14]

The parliamentary committees thus concentrated part of their agenda on the demographics of the slave trade—in particular on discovering the percentage of women and girls trafficked from Africa to the New World. Both eyewitness testimony and data produced on the slave trade confirmed that the sex ratio of African captives was heavily weighted in favor of males. Overall women and girls amounted to roughly a third of all Africans trafficked to the New World.[15] When asked why the slave populations struggled to increase naturally, many of those interviewed blamed uneven sex ratios. Robert Lambert, a former resident of the Windward Islands and Jamaica, when asked why he thought it was impossible to maintain "the stock of Slaves" without importation, answered bluntly: "The disproportion of females to the males." He then proceeded to speculate that "the females cohabiting promiscuously" and "the diseases which they bring with them from the Coast of Guinea, and contract by living together in this promiscuous manner" were also likely contributing factors.[16] Gilbert Francklyn, too, blamed the "disparity of the sexes," but like Lambert he also pointed the finger of blame at African women themselves, citing their "dissolute life" and the common practice of "suckling their children for a great length of time."[17] That a large burden of responsibility for the poor rates of natural increase should be shouldered by African women slaves was a view shared not only by other eyewitnesses but also by managers and planters throughout the British West Indies.[18] Committee reports sent to Parliament from both Barbados and Tobago went so far as to downplay the influence of unequal sex ratios on the natural growth of the slave population. Barbados speculated that "perhaps excessive Labour, and other Excesses and Indiscretions of the Female Slaves" were to blame.[19] And Tobago submitted a long and detailed narration of the loose sexual morals, poor maternal instincts, and low levels of care provided by slave mothers to their children.[20] Testimony on the numbers of women captives in the slave trade sat alongside firsthand accounts of slave women's sexuality and poor maternal instincts to substantiate the West India interest's case that the sugar islands were doomed if not for the continued importation of slaves.

Fixating on unequal sex ratios and the immoral conduct of African women was dangerous territory for the abolitionists. At several points over the course of the slave trade debates, several MPs suggested that the simplest solution to the problem would be to increase the imports of African females.[21] To counter this suggestion, the abolitionists developed an argument that allowed for the natural increase of the slave population without importing more slaves but also dealt with the uneven sex ratios and deleterious effects alleged to be caused by slave women's promiscuity and apparent lack of maternalism. They built their rebuttal on the grounds that the slave population would begin to increase if the planters adopted a concerted policy to "breed" their slaves. Slave merchants typically preferred female captives to be young and healthy and not beyond childbearing age, but hitherto there had been no deliberate agenda to increase their numbers as part of an effort to "breed" slaves in the British slave colonies.[22] Indeed Thomas Clarkson thought that "the object of keeping up the stock of slaves by breeding had never been seriously attended to" in the West Indies.[23] When questioned on the practice of "breeding," a number of eyewitnesses alleged that deliberate efforts to "breed" slaves had taken place on some estates in Jamaica and that in some such cases it had been shown to increase the numbers of slaves, but most agreed that it was not undertaken as a matter of course and certainly not pursued to any extent elsewhere in the slave islands.

Abolitionists also argued that the slave population would increase through better treatment of slaves. Abundant eyewitness testimony was presented to the Commons and Lords revealing the degree of wanton violence inflicted upon slaves by plantation owners and managers.[24] In particular examples of widespread sexual abuse of women and girls, forced prostitution, and complete disregard for family bonds and marital unions were highlighted as major impediments to the natural growth of the slave population. The Commons committee was particularly disturbed by eyewitness testimony of the torture of female slaves by white women.

What especially shocked them was that such incidents were perpetrated by "elite" white women; that they frequently took place in public view; and that such women were rarely if ever held accountable for their behavior.[25] Testimony of the torture and violence inflicted on slave women and girls was highlighted by the abolitionists to shift the terms of the debate away from the immoral behavior of slave women (and uneven sex ratios) to the treatment of women slaves as a determining factor in the demographics of the slave population. From this platform it seems that the abolitionists hoped to overturn arguments for the necessity of slave imports by instead suggesting that if planters and managers only treated their slaves better, then the slave population would start to rise naturally. Clarkson considered this argument essential to the abolitionists' case: the "better treatment of the slaves in the colonies," he averred, was the "foundation of the abolition of the Slave Trade." If marriage between slaves was encouraged and children and the infirm properly cared for and not "over-worked" or "worn down by the weight of severe punishments," then the slaves "would necessarily increase, and this on an extensive scale."[26] Why did the abolitionists present a case that allowed for the continuation of slavery in the colonies? When the London Committee first formed, it weighed the odds of the likely success of a campaign to abolish the slave trade or a crusade to bring down the institution of slavery. It was decided that the former was more likely to attract public and political support—though secretly many abolitionists clung to the belief that once the slave trade ended, slavery too would eventually cease to exist (a line of argument that was not lost on the West India interest).[27] To maximize support for their cause, or at the very least to minimize damage to it, they therefore adopted a politically pragmatic position that sought to steer clear of arguments that openly pronounced the end of slavery. Nevertheless their calls for a commitment to "breeding" (alongside better treatment of slaves) clearly threatened to expand rather than halt the spread of slavery in the colonies— these developments would have important ramifications for the status and experiences of women in slavery in both the West Indies and North America.

In the House of Commons debates on April 18–19, 1791, William Pitt summed up the importance of the "population question" to the outcome of the parliamentary battle over the abolition of the slave trade: "almost every one he believed, appeared to wish, that the farther importation of slaves might cease, provided it could be made out that the population of the West Indies could be, by any means, maintained without it."[28] Thomas Clarkson, listening to Pitt's speech, suggests that it was "the impracticability of keeping up the population there [that] appeared to operate as the chief objection" to its abolition.[29] Pitt proceeded to note that he "could not help thinking, there was an over great degree of sensibility among those gentlemen, on this particular point, and that their alarm was excited in a degree which the occasion by no means justified."[30] Hitherto the abolitionists had focused their case on demonstrating how the West Indian slave populations would rise without further importations of slaves. Now Pitt delivered an alternative argument: basing his case on data gathered on slave births and deaths in the British West Indies, he argued that there was in fact no hard evidence to prove that the West Indian slave populations were struggling to increase or indeed would even do so once the slave trade was brought to an end. All previous figures denoting the lack of natural increase among the British West Indian slave populations had, he insisted, been founded upon misleading calculations, since they had failed to take into account the numbers of slaves who died as a result of the "seasoning process" (the period after the Middle Passage when Africans first arrived on the slave islands and were introduced—and thereafter adapted or succumbed—to their new environment and living and working conditions). If the slave trade ended, those deaths would decrease or cease altogether, the sex ratios would even out, and the creole slave population would rise, he reasoned. The abolitionists were hopeful that if Pitt's calculations could "show that the abolition would not be ruinous, it would be enough" to tilt the balance of parliamentary opinion in their favor.[31]

Crucial headway was made by the abolitionists in the wake of Pitt's speech, as the tide of political opinion shifted from *if* to *when* the slave trade should be abolished and whether this should be done immediately or gradually. On the other hand, "the great subject of population" refused to die. If anything the change in the direction of the debate breathed new life into this line of argument. In 1792 a Commons majority proposed gradual rather than immediate abolition of the slave trade on the grounds that it was necessary to continue slave imports until the slave populations had begun to rise in the British Caribbean islands. In the meantime, some MPs suggested, planters and managers ought to pursue policies designed to help increase the slave population. Mr. Jenkinson, later Earl of Liverpool, recommended that planters should be granted premiums to promote "the increase of slaves by birth"; that every slave woman who reared five children to seven years old should be emancipated; and a five pound bounty should be given to every slave ship captain importing more females than males under the age of twenty-five years.[32]

The abolitionists fiercely denied the practical basis and moral righteousness of gradual abolition of the slave trade. Lord Mornington, noting that he would "not repeat those enormities out of the evidence, which had made such a deep impression on the House," was nonetheless alarmed at how long Britain might be allowed to "persevere in the crime of its continuance." Mr. Smith was even more pointed in his criticism. He rejected the suggestion of limiting the importation of slaves to those under twenty-five years of age on the basis that it would "only operate as a transfer of cruelty from the aged and the guilty to the young and innocent." And he demanded of the House "whether, if it related to their own children, any one of them would vote for it."[33] Over the course of the next few years, one motion after another was submitted to Parliament calling for an end to the slave trade. No matter how many times Pitt's calculations were repeated in the Commons and

Lords and no matter how many times the abolitionists called for better treatment of slaves or insisted upon greater attention to "breeding" to increase the slave population, a majority of Parliament remained opposed to abolition. Clarkson blamed such steadfast opposition on the spirit of the times: "under a combination of effects, arising from the publication of the *Rights of Man,* the rise and progress of the French revolution, and the insurrection of the negroes in the different islands, no one of which events was to do with the abolition of the Slave Trade, the current was against us," he concluded.[34]

By small degrees the winds of political change moved in favor of abolition. Precisely how and why nonetheless remains a subject of fierce debate among historians.[35] One factor generally overlooked by historians is the role and impact of eyewitness testimony in shaping and conveying the abolitionists' case in Parliament. Demography and reproduction formed only one part of the abolitionists' battleground; the inhumanity and injustice of the slave trade was another. To push this latter argument forward, the abolitionists drew heavily on the "tragical stories"[36] presented to Parliament by eyewitnesses involved in the slave trade. Of course these "tragical stories" alone did not persuade parliamentarians to pass the Abolition Act in 1807. Nevertheless they did play a recognizable part in the abolitionists' humanitarian crusade, which was intended to combat (and divert attention away from) political and economic arguments in favor of preserving the slave trade.

II

When William Wilberforce delivered his first speech to Parliament on the slave trade, on May 12, 1789, he deliberately evoked the responses of African men, women, and children to "the most wretched part": the Middle Passage. His aim was to challenge claims by some eyewitnesses, who spoke on behalf of the West India interest, that the trafficking of Africans via the slave ship was nothing short of "a comfortable conveyance." When proponents of the slave trade harnessed evidence of the slaves' dancing and singing on board the slave ships to suggest that they were happy to be removed from their homeland, Wilberforce struck back: "when they sung they were in tears," and their songs were a "lamentation for the loss of their country." He drew Parliament's attention to the violence of capture and enslavement and the slaves' reaction to this by reminding MPs of the captain who "threatened a woman with a flogging because the mournfulness of her song was too painful for his feelings." It was by pitching poignant examples of the slaves' humanity (and their innocence) against graphic and brutal images of the inhumanity of the Middle Passage that the abolitionists sought to drive home the message that the slave trade ought to be abolished not on the grounds of "policy, but justice."[37]

When eyewitnesses were asked to cast their minds back to the slave ship, captains and crew alike frequently remarked on the babel and din of slave voices,

sometimes protesting and resisting their enslavement and at other times express-
ing their suffering and despair. What especially unsettled and disturbed them were
the voices of the women captives. The frequency with which they commented
on the vigor of women's voices on board the slave ship contrasts with observations
that the men were sometimes "sullen" and "dejected." Capt. Ashley Hall was questioned as to whether slaves "usually appear dejected" when they first stepped onto
the slave ship, he responded: "Always; it soon wears off with the young Slaves, and
some of the women; but the men are dejected and appear unhappy in the extreme,
the whole voyage." Such testimony chimed with published accounts of slave ship
voyages that dated back to the early days of British slave trading. For example Capt.
William Snelgrave, who had a long history of involvement in the slave trade, considered slave women most especially vocal and difficult to manage on his ships; the
women "used always to be the most troublesome, on Account of their Noise and
Clamour," he observed.[38]

Slave women's voices—grieving and protesting—could be as disruptive to the
slave ship as a hurricane at sea. As James Arnold's testimony, presented on behalf
of the abolitionists, indicated, some captains preferred to dispense with grieving
slaves altogether rather than have them on board their ship. He described to the
Commons select committee the moment when one woman embarked in such a
"dejected State of Mind" that "some Times she cried excessively, at other Times she
laughed in the same Excess; at other Times she made a most dreadful Noise, so that
the ship was greatly disturbed . . . in consequence of which the Captain disposed of
her the next Day." Another eyewitness recalled that an Ebo slave woman, "after suffering much from sea sickness, and seeming to pine and waste, was sent on shore,
and left in charge of one of her own countrywomen," but it was later discovered
that "she hanged herself."[39] The sounds of grief and despair evoked by eyewitnesses
were presented as incontrovertible evidence that the captives were in fact far from
happy to be snatched from their homeland or, as some defenders of the slave trade
claimed, that their condition was preferable to slavery in Africa. Such testimony
provoked Lord Grenville to conclude of the Middle Passage that there was no
"greater portion of misery condensed within a smaller space, than ever existed in
the known world."[40]

It was vital that the abolitionists harness eyewitness testimony of the emotional
and psychological trauma experienced by Africans in the Middle Passage. First
since contemporaries rarely accepted that Africans shared the same human im-
pulses, attachments, and sentiments as Europeans, the abolitionists, in order to
convince MPs that the captives suffered at the hands of the slave trade, had to persuade them to recognize and appreciate the Africans' humanity. The ways in which
African women expressed their suffering on board the slave ship was highlighted
as proof of this. Second the abolitionists struggled to win sympathy and support
for their case on the grounds of slave demographics and reproduction alone.

Unlocking the humanitarian case for abolition by extracting compassion for the plight of the slaves was one of a number of strategies deployed to convert MPs to the cause of abolition.

Wilberforce had chosen to share with his parliamentary colleagues how moved he was by accounts of the slaves' songs during the Middle Passage. Eyewitness testimony revealed that these songs were frequently expressions of grief and despair. But they were also testimonials of the slaves' humanity—of their history and their identity as African people. Henry Ellison recalled: "At the time of their dancing they always sing to some tune or other in their own way; I have very often heard them sing mournful tunes when in their rooms in the night time."[41] When James Towne was asked if he had ever heard the slaves singing and if he knew what they sang about, he said, "I have. I never found it anything joyous, but lamentations." He added, "I made it my business to learn what the subject was, and from their information it was complaints for having been taken away from their friends and relations."[42] Ecroyde Claxton, a ship's surgeon, recollected that the slave songs expressed their fears and pain: "They were ordered to sing songs by the captain, but they were sad songs of lamentations. The words of the songs used by them were, Madda! Madda! Yiera! Yiera! Bemini! Madda! Aufera! That is to say, they were all sick, and by and by they should be no more; they also sung songs expressive of their fears of being beat, of their want of victuals, particularly the want of their native food, and of their never returning to their own country—I could mention their own words."[43] The captives' songs were a direct response to capture and enslavement, as they were also a means of collectively recording and making sense of their experience. On this point James Arnold's testimony is instructive: "At other Times when the women were sitting by themselves below, he had heard them singing: but also at these Times in Tears. *Their Songs then contained the History of their Lives,* and their Separation from their Friends and Country. These songs were very disagreeable to the Captain, who has taken them up, and flogged them in so terrible a Manner for no other Reason than this."[44] David Henderson, too, was struck by the slaves' songs, and by their meaning, which he said "usually contained *the History of their Sufferings,* and the Wretchedness of the Situation." He learned this from a boy aboard the ship, since "he did not understand the Language enough himself."[45] These accounts were intended to drive home to parliamentarians that the slave ship's cargo was packed not full of commodities but of human beings—human beings defined by their show of suffering as they confronted the magnitude of loss that stretched before them. At the same time, examples of the violence inflicted on the captives—because they sang songs that disturbed the crew—provided a staggering indictment of just how brutal and dehumanizing the Middle Passage was.

The recollections of the seaman William Butterworth underscored the significance of slave women's voices aboard the slave ship. Writing about his experiences on the slave ship *Hudibras,* he recalled how one slave woman in particular was "'universally esteemed' among the bondwomen and especially among her own 'countrywomen.' She was an 'oracle of literature'—an 'orator' and a 'songstress' and her main purpose was to 'render more easy the hours of her sisters in exile.'" When she died, he noted, the women and girls on board the ship grieved loud and hard.[46] Just as eyewitness accounts of the slaves' songs recognized the powerful effect of the Africans' voices on the slave ships, so Butterworth in his narrative recognized the importance of the storyteller as a source of comfort and strength to her fellow captives. She was, moreover, the guardian of her people's history and heritage, so that when she died a part of the captives' past died with her.

Eyewitness testimony delivered before the parliamentary committees amplifying the voices of slaves suffering during the Middle Passage and chronicling their protest at capture and enslavement became interspersed with descriptions of the violence inflicted on female captives during the Middle Passage. The sexual assault of women and girls on board slave ships was not a subject matter that many witnesses felt keen to discuss with the select committees. Indeed it was a line of inquiry that tended to generate awkward silences and prickly responses. The Reverend John Newton was quite explicit about the molestation of slave women and girls aboard slave ships, but he too shied away from disclosing too much information on the subject, as he explained in his *Thoughts upon the African Slave Trade* (1788): "When the women and girls are taken on board a ship, naked, trembling, terrified, perhaps almost exhausted with cold, fatigue, and hunger, they are often exposed to the wanton rudeness of white savages. The poor creatures cannot understand the language they hear, but the looks and manners of the speakers are still sufficiently intelligible. In imagination, the prey is divided, upon the spot, and only reserved until opportunity offers. Where resistance or refusal would be utterly in vain, even the solicitation of consent is seldom thought of." Newton steeled himself from being more outspoken, by declaring: "This is not a subject for declamation." Although he did not wish to elaborate, he admitted that such horrors inflicted on slave women and girls were "little known *here*."[47] Interviewed by the Commons committee on May 12, 1790, Newton was put on the spot when he was asked: "Were the sufferings of the Negro Women on board ships aggravated by their being exposed to the brutality of the crew?" He replied: "In many ships they were, if we allow Negro Women to have any degree of sentiment."[48] To make the argument in favor of abolition on the grounds of justice persuasive, it was vital that parliamentarians be coaxed to empathize with the plight of the captives on board the slave ships; in this respect they had to be made to believe that African women owned the same degree of "sentiment"—the same innocence—as their own wives and daughters.

James Field Stanfield, who in 1788 published an account of his experiences on a slave ship as a series of letters addressed to Thomas Clarkson, was also wary of exposing the brutality of sexual violence visited upon female captives. He described how he witnessed an attack "practised by the captain on an unfortunate female slave, of the age of eight or nine" so horrific in nature that it left him speechless: "I cannot express it in any words," he said. Although he could not face describing the crime committed against the child, he nevertheless made a point of saying that it was "too atrocious and bloody to be passed over in silence."[49] That Stanfield was unable to find the words to describe what he saw was in itself testimony of the horrors of the Middle Passage. As Lord Grenville smartly observed: "the suffering here was so great, that neither the mind could conceive, nor the tongue describe, it."[50] James Arnold, speaking before the Commons committee, corroborated Stanfield's written account by explaining how futile it was for women captives to resist sexual assault. He recalled that the captain of the *Ruby* sent for a slave woman "and ordered her to come by herself; he attempted to sleep with her in the Cabin, but on refusing to comply with his Desires, she was severely beaten by him and sent below." It was the "general practice with the captain of the *Ruby*, on the receipt of a Woman Slave, to send for her into his Cabin for the same Purposes," he noted, and he remembered seeing "several who resisted his Attempts beaten in the same manner."[51] While such accounts alerted Parliament to the systemic nature of sexual violence on the slave ships, other eyewitnesses were far more reluctant to be drawn on the subject. Robert Norris, a witness for the West India interest, was asked, "Is there any Care taken to prevent any Intercourse between White Men and the Black Women?" His response was curt: "Orders are generally issued for that Purpose."[52] The sexual assault of women and girls on the slave ships was yet more evidence of the endemic violence and brutality of the Middle Passage. But it was also proof that the slave trade destroyed the morals and humanity of all those involved in it. As Lord Henry Petty remarked about the slave trade, "After spreading vice and misery all over this continent, it doomed its unhappy victims to hardships and cruelties worse than death. The first of these was conspicuous in their transportation. It was found there, that cruelty begat cruelty; that the system, wicked in its beginning, was equally so in its progress; and that it perpetuated its miseries wherever it was carried on. . . . Nor had we yet done with the evils which attended it; for it brought in its train the worst of all moral effects, not only as it respected the poor slaves, when transported to the colonies, but as it respected those who had concerns with them there. . . . It depraved the nature of all who were connected with it."[53]

That the horrors of the slave trade were too great for some captives to bear was made abundantly clear to Parliament. The committees were informed that upon boarding the slave ship, some Africans attempted to starve themselves to death, for which they were beaten and force-fed with instruments designed to unlock their jaws (Clarkson presented Parliament with a collection of instruments of torture used against slaves); other captives, they were told, jumped overboard and drowned or, as some eyewitnesses described, were eaten alive by sharks; and some died deaths so sorrowful that ship's surgeons found no other way to attribute the cause of death than that of "melancholy." Suicide was not particular to women, but the separation of families was cited as a reason for suicide in a number of the cases presented to Parliament.

Eyewitness testimony introduced by the abolitionists generally portrayed the captives as helpless and powerless victims of the slave trade. This characterization made sense given the abolitionists' insistence upon the "injustice" of the slave trade as an argument for its abolition; the Africans were thus presented as "innocent" victims. Other lines of inquiry pursued by the committees, such as the alleged kidnapping of Africans and the encouraging of wars between Africans by Europeans in order to increase the stock of available slaves, underscored the innocence of its victims and fueled arguments that the slave trade was "unjust"—or more to the point, "criminal." The futile efforts of women and girls to defend themselves against sexual assault by captains and crewmen reinforced this portrait of helplessness and innocence. Further eyewitness testimony suggested that the vulnerability of slaves to violence and abuse flowed from the slave ship to the plantation, as legislatures in the West Indies reportedly failed to protect slaves from the wanton cruelty of slaveholders and managers. The weight of testimony pointing to the slaves' powerlessness is underscored by the relatively few instances in which witnesses were questioned about slave revolts on board the ships or in the Caribbean islands. Did the abolitionists deliberately sidestep this issue? Certainly evidence that could be deployed by the slave interest to play upon prejudice and stereotypes of the Africans' savagery and propensity for rebellion would have cut across abolitionist arguments regarding their humanity and, in turn, may well have fanned arguments to suggest that abolishing the slave trade would unleash a wave of slave revolts across the West Indian colonies. Notwithstanding the abolitionists' characterization of the African captives as, for the most part, helpless and defenseless victims of the slave trade, it was the captives' voices, resurrected by eyewitnesses of the slave trade, that were deployed as evidence of the Africans' humanity and their suffering during the Middle Passage. Did the abolitionists hope that such testimony would win over the hearts of MPs and convert them to the cause of abolition? After all, it was the voices and experiences of African captives rendered before Parliament that the abolitionists turned to when they delivered their final motion to the Commons and Lords to end the slave trade in 1807.

III

It is hard to say precisely how MPs in Westminster responded to descriptions of the captives' suffering and their voices of grief and despair. It is even more impossible to say how much, if at all, such testimony influenced the final decision to abolish the slave trade. Nonetheless several MPs openly acknowledged the enormous impression that eyewitness testimony made on Parliament and its importance to the abolitionists' case. "It was impossible to read the evidence, as it related to this trade, without acknowledging the inhumanity of it, and our own disgrace," Lord Grenville remarked. What most especially troubled him, he added, was that Parliament had grown "so much accustomed to words, descriptive of the cruelty of this traffic, that we had almost forgotten their meaning." Most disturbing, he thought, was the fact that after almost twenty years of detailed inquiries and debates into the slave trade, it "had rendered cruelty familiar to us; and the recital of its horrors, had been so frequent, that we could now hear them stated without being affected as we ought to be." In this way on January 2, 1807, Lord Grenville introduced the Slave Trade Abolition Bill to the House of Lords. He concluded his opening argument by entreating the Lords "to conceive the hard case of the unhappy victims of it."[54]

Over the course of the parliamentary debates on the slave trade, other MPs besides Grenville also emphasized the power of eyewitness testimony to shape the direction of the political contest. Charles James Fox described Mr. Smith's firsthand account as "tragical stories which had made such an impression upon the House." Laying down the gauntlet to his opponents, Fox charged: "if any gentleman, after reading the evidence on the table, and attending to the debate, could avow himself an abettor of this shameful traffic in human flesh, it could only be either from some hardness of heart, or some difficulty of understanding, which he really knew not how to account for." History (and God), he warned, might well judge his colleagues harshly: "if the House, knowing what the trade was by the evidence, did not, by their vote, mark all to mankind their abhorrence of a practice so savage, so enormous, so repugnant to all laws of human and divine, they would consign their character to eternal infamy." He dismissed all talk of the "incredibility" of eyewitness accounts as "idle," noting, "never did he hear of charges so black and horrible as those contained in the evidence on the table." And if the House voted for its continuance, "they must have nerves of which he had no conception." Speaking of evidence of the brutal treatment of slaves in the West Indies, he said he was "glad to see that these tales affected the House. Would they then sanction enormities, the bare recital of which made them shudder?" Humanity, he declared, "did not consist in a squeamish ear."[55] Mr. Jenkinson, who opposed abolition, remarked that descriptions of cruelty toward slaves had "shocked the feelings of all who heard them." But he was not convinced that this was grounds for abolishing the slave trade or that it was sufficient evidence that all slaves were treated so badly.[56] Supporters of the slave trade occasionally attempted to contest and discredit eyewitness testimony of the horrors of the slave trade, as they had done with the first inquiry into the slave trade led by the Privy Council. But by and by even opponents such as Jenkinson struggled to contest the weight of testimony depicting the cruelty of the slave trade.

When Lord Grenville read the final motion to abolish the slave trade to the House of Lords, the first resolution he thus referred to was not the practicability of ending the slave trade but the fundamental inhumanity of it. It was the mountain of eyewitness testimony that had been laid before Parliament, over nearly two decades of public and political campaigning, which the abolitionists turned to in order to support the bill.

The second resolution pointed to the "injustice of the trade," which, it contended, "was not confined to the bare circumstance of robbing them [Africans] of the right to their own labour. . . . It was conspicuous through the system," through the "crimes" committed to obtain slaves "and when they possessed them, of all the crimes which belonged to their inhuman treatment." This resolution concluded by urging the Lords that they "owed it to their Creator, if they hoped for mercy, to do away with this monstrous oppression."[57] The third resolution addressed "the impolicy of the trade," or "the great subject of population," which had attracted so much controversy and debate. Pitt's calculations were briefly revived and his conclusions repeated, but little more was said on the subject, except to conclude that "whatever was inhuman and unjust must be, impolitic."[58] After the motion was read, the Lords and Commons fell back into debate. A majority in favor of abolishing the slave trade was at long last reached, and the king's signature was given to the Act on March 25, 1807. Grenville congratulated the House for completing "the most glorious measure that had ever been adopted by any legislative body in the world."[59]

The following year, on March 26, 1808, the Duke of Gloucester gathered together five hundred "Friends to the Abolition of the Slave Trade" to mark the first anniversary of the Abolition Act. In addition to toasting the achievements of parliamentarians, the abolitionists celebrated the coming to an end of the horrors of the Middle Passage. Lord Erskine's speech conjured an image that, he said, had converted him to the cause of humanity: "He had seen the parent weeping over her offspring, and the child over its parents, the next instant to be snatched from its society and protection forever!"[60]

The legacy of the Abolition Act is, however, more ambiguous than either Grenville's adulation or the anniversary tributes led by Gloucester and his friends suggest—most especially in regard to slave women. For the significance of the Abolition Act was quickly overshadowed by developments that undermined its humanitarian impulse. In 1807 and 1808, the respective years the act was introduced by Britain and America, the slave trade remained legal in other parts of the world; the institution of slavery persisted in the British West Indies and North America, as elsewhere; the internal slave trade in the United States swelled, and it grew apace, too, in the West Indies; and where the foreign slave trade was banned, illegal human trafficking commenced. All of these developments fell especially hard on women slaves, to paraphrase the ex-slave Harriet Jacobs.[61] A more or less constant feature of slave women's experience of slavery was their vulnerability to sexual violence and the suffering that attended their dual roles as "producers" and "reproducers." In the British West Indies, despite legislation enacted throughout the islands to ameliorate the slaves' condition and incentives and rewards offered to slave women to "breed," the slave populations did not markedly increase once the slave trade ended (as the abolitionists had argued it would). In North America, by contrast, the slave population boomed, and the institution of slavery expanded. In spite of the important role of slave women to the survival and expansion of slavery, both regions failed to engender a respect or reverence for slave motherhood. In fact the violent physical and sexual assault of slave women and the separation of mothers from children stand at the heart of almost every female slave narrative published in the antebellum era. Despite the myriad ways in which women adapted and survived enslavement, it is the cruelty and dehumanization that carried forth from the slave ship to the institution of slavery that lodged in their historical memory.

This chapter has shown how the parliamentary debates on the ending of the slave trade brought to the fore the politics of trafficking African female captives to the Americas. Hitherto the status of women in the slave trade had attracted comparatively little attention from politicians, slave merchants, and planters, but when the ending of the slave trade threatened to destroy the system of slavery, their status as "breeders" and their treatment and conduct in slavery attracted considerable political scrutiny in Parliament. In the eyewitness testimony introduced by abolitionists to push the moral argument in favor of abolition, center stage was given to the particular experiences and reactions of African women in the Middle Passage. Distressing as these accounts are, they reveal how and why the abolitionists considered testimony of women's experiences and responses to the slave trade an important part of their political battle. In order to counter the economic and political arguments put forward by the West India interest, predicting a decline in the slave colonies and British economic and political power if the slave trade were abolished, the abolitionists highlighted the treatment and status of slave women to argue that through "breeding" and amelioration of their conditions and treatment, the West Indian slave population would flourish without further slave imports. This line of argument juxtaposed (and often overlapped with) the humanitarian case for abolition. Historians have not jumped to scrutinize the relationship between these two corresponding arguments. The abolitionists' openly moral stance against the slave trade—and its treatment of slave women in particular—sits awkwardly with their promotion of a policy of "breeding" slaves in the West Indies (and simultaneously their strenuous insistence upon the better treatment of slaves). "Breeding," both in theory as well as in practice, stood at odds with the abolitionists' calls for an appreciation of the slave woman's humanity; indeed it reinforced the African woman's dual status as both a productive and reproductive commodity in slavery. Setting aside such tensions in the abolitionists' argument, there were, undeniably, MPs such as Lord Grenville, William Wilberforce, and Charles Fox who were shocked and disturbed by the eyewitness testimonies delivered to the parliamentary committees. To these men eyewitness reports were compelling evidence that the slave trade had to be abolished on moral grounds. When all is said and done, however, the extent to which these testimonies helped, in the final hour, to persuade the vote in favor of abolition is impossible to determine.

The bicentenary of the Abolition Act is an opportunity to restore to public memory the human tragedy of the slave trade. It is also a chance for the historical spotlight to fall on the voices of African captives in the slave trade and the ways in which those voices contributed to the politics of abolition in Britain. Hitherto these have been largely silent in historical studies on British abolitionism and the transatlantic slave trade.[62] Ultimately the 1807 act did not end the trafficking and enslavement of women. Instead it marked the beginning of a long and historic—and still ongoing—international crusade to end the exploitation and suffering of women in slavery throughout the world.

Notes

I am grateful to Kenneth Morgan, Mark Neocleous, and the two anonymous reviewers for their valuable comments and guidance on this chapter.

1. Report of William Wilberforce's speech to Parliament, May 12, 1789, in Thomas Clarkson, *The History of the Rise, Progress and Accomplishment of the Abolition of the African Slave Trade by the British Parliament* (London: Parker, 1839; repr., Whitefish, Mont.: Kessinger, 2004), 288.

2. There is a rich and long-standing debate on the factors that led to the abolition of the slave trade; see Lowell J. Ragatz, *The Fall of the Planter Class in the British West Indies, 1763–1833: A Study in Social and Economic History* (New York: Century, 1928); Eric Williams, *Capitalism and Slavery,* preface by D. W. Brogan (London: Deutsch, 1964); Roger Anstey, *The Atlantic Slave Trade and British Abolition, 1760–1810* (London: Macmillan, 1975; repr., Aldershot, U.K.: Gregg, 1992); Seymour Drescher, *Econocide: British Slavery in the Era of Abolition* (Pittsburgh: University of Pittsburgh Press, 1977); Seymour Drescher, *Capitalism and Antislavery: British Mobilization in Comparative Perspective* (London: Macmillan, 1986); Seymour Drescher, *The Mighty Experiment: Free Labor Versus Slavery in British Emancipation* (New York: Oxford University Press, 2002); Selwyn H. H. Carrington, *The Sugar Industry and the Abolition of the Slave Trade, 1775–1810* (Gainesville: University Press of Florida, 2002); David Beck Ryden, *West Indian Slavery and British Abolitionism, 1783–1807* (New York: Cambridge University Press, 2009);. On the role of gender in British abolitionism, see Clare Midgley, *Women against Slavery: The British Campaigns, 1780–1870* (London & New York: Routledge, 1992); Henrice Altink, *Representations of Slave Women in Discourses on Slavery and Abolition, 1780–1838* (New York: Routledge, 2007).

3. Steven M. Wise, *Though the Heavens May Fall: The Landmark Trial That Led to the End of Human Slavery* (London: Pimlico, 2006).

4. W. E. B. Du Bois, *The Suppression of the African Slave-Trade to the United States of America, 1638–1870, Vol. 1* (New York: Longmans, Green, 1896; repr., Charleston, S.C.: BiblioBazaar, 2007), chaps. 6–7.

5. Clarkson, *History,* 303; Adam Hochschild, *Bury the Chains: The British Struggle to Abolish Slavery* (London: Pan, 2006), 153–61.

6. Clarkson, *History,* 305–6.

7. "Extracts from the Minutes of the Joint Committee of Assembly and Council of Jamaica, 3 December, 1789," in *Minutes of the Evidence Taken before a Committee of the House of Commons, Being a Select Committee, Appointed on the 29th Day of January 1790 for the Purpose of Taking the Examination of Such Witnesses as Shall Be Produced on the Part of Several Petitioners Who Have Petitioned the House of Commons against the Abolition of the Slave Trade* (N.p., 1790), 431, *Parliamentary Papers on the Slave Trade*, 1790, Bodleian Law Library, University of Oxford (hereafter BLL, Oxford).

8. Clarkson, *History*, 300.

9. Ibid., 294.

10. Ibid., 295–96.

11. Ibid., 346.

12. "Extracts from the Minutes," 485–92.

13. Both David Richardson and Seymour Drescher have argued for the critical role that the subject of reproduction and demography played in the abolitionists' argument in the parliamentary debates from 1791. However, neither employs a gender framework to conceptualize this debate, nor do they connect the "population question" to the importance of eyewitness testimony on the status and experiences of slave women in the slave trade. Drescher, *Mighty Experiment*, chap. 3; David Richardson, "The Ending of the British Slave Trade in 1807: The Economic Context," in *The British Slave Trade: Abolition, Parliament and People*, ed. Stephen Farrell, Melanie Unwin, and James Walvin (Edinburgh: Edinburgh University Press, 2007), 127–40.

14. William Pitt's speech to Parliament, 1791, in *The British West Indies at Westminster, Part 1: 1789–1823, Extracts from the Debates in Parliament*, ed. Eric Williams, Publications of the Historical Society of Trinidad and Tobago (Port of Spain: Government Printing Office, 1954), 7.

15. There is an extensive literature on the demographics of the slave trade. On the ratio of female and male captives in the transatlantic slave trade, see, for example, David Eltis and Stanley L. Engerman, "Was the Slave Trade Dominated by Men?" *Journal of Interdisciplinary History* 23, no. 2 (1992): 237–57; David Eltis and Stanley L. Engerman, "Fluctuations in Sex and Age Ratios in the Transatlantic Slave Trade, 1663–1864," *Economic History Review*, n.s., 46, no. 2 (1993): 308–23; Herbert S. Klein, *The Middle Passage: Comparative Studies in the Atlantic Slave Trade* (Princeton, N.J.: Princeton University Press, 1978); Herbert S. Klein, *The Atlantic Slave Trade* (Cambridge: Cambridge University Press, 2005), chap. 7.

16. Robert Lambert Testimony, March 23, 1790, in *Minutes of the Evidence*, 422.

17. Gilbert Francklyn Testimony, March 13, 1794, in *Minutes of the Evidence*, 157.

18. Kenneth Morgan, "Slave Women and Reproduction in Jamaica, c. 1776–1834," *History* 91 (April 2006): 231–53; Jennifer L. Morgan, *Laboring Women: Reproduction and Gender in New World Slavery* (Philadelphia: University of Pennsylvania Press, 2004).

19. "Head of Information on Barbados," in *Barbadoes: Report of a Committee of the General Assembly, upon the Several Heads of Enquiry, &c. Relative to the Slave Trade* (London, 1790), *Parliamentary Papers on the Slave Trade, 1790*, BLL, Oxford.

20. *Report by a Committee of Both Houses of Legislature of Tobago Appointed by the House of Commons on 6 April 1797 Relative to the Increase of Negroes and the Melioration of Their State, Presented to the House of Lords 23 May 1799* (London, 1799), *Parliamentary Papers on the Slave Trade, 1799*, BLL, Oxford.

21. Clarkson, *History,* 426–27, 373.

22. See correspondence of Henry Laurens, Charleston merchant and slave trader, to John and Thomas Tipping of Barbados, December 4, 1764, in Elizabeth Donnan, *Documents Illustrative of the Slave Trade to America,* vol. 4, *The Border Colonies and the Southern Colonies* (New York: Hein, 2002), 408; "Letter of Instructions to the Master, Charleston 24th July 1807," in Donnan, *Documents,* 4:568; "The South Sea Company, Minutes of the Committee of Correspondence, October 10, 1717," in Elizabeth Donnan, *Documents Illustrative of the Slave Trade to America,* vol. 2, *The Eighteenth Century* (New York: Hein, 2002), 215.

23. Clarkson, *History,* 355.

24. See, for example, Mr. Davison's Testimony, March 4, 1791, in *House of Commons Sessional Papers of the Eighteenth Century,* ed. Sheila Lambert (Wilmington, N.C.: Scholarly Resources, 1975), 82:179–181 (hereafter *House of Commons*); Captain Cook's Testimony, March 7, 1791, *House of Commons,* 82:201–5.

25. Robert Forster Testimony, February 23, 1791, *House of Commons,* 82:132. The clergyman's wife at Port Royal was known to several eyewitnesses for her "wanton cruelty" toward her slaves; see Lt. Baker Davison, February 25, 1791, *House of Commons,* 82:152. On public knowledge of violence and no legal action taken, see Mr. Thomas Woolrich Testimony, March 26, 1790, *House of Commons,* 82:269–70, and Mr. Henry Hew Dalrymple Testimony, March 25, 1790, *House of Commons,* 82:305.

26. Clarkson, *History,* 149.

27. Ibid., 148.

28. William Pitt's speech, April 18–19, 1791, in Williams, *British West Indies at Westminster,* 6.

29. Clarkson's commentary on William Pitt's speech, April 18–19, 1791, in Clarkson, *History,* 385.

30. William Pitt's speech, April 18–19, 1791, in Williams, *British West Indies at Westminster,* 7.

31. Clarkson's commentary on William Pitt's speech, April 18–19, 1791, in Clarkson, *History,* 388.

32. "The great subject of population" is a phrase coined by Thomas Clarkson; Clarkson, *History,* 473. Mr. Jenkinson's speech, ibid., 433; debate on gradual or immediate abolition, ibid., 443–48.

33. Ibid., 445–46.

34. Ibid., 347.

35. See note 2. The historical debate has hinged on the degree to which the decision to abolish the slave trade by Parliament was the result of humanitarian consensus or economic and political forces that forced the winds of change in Westminster in favor of abolition.

36. Phrase reportedly used by Mr. Fox to describe the evidence from eyewitness testimony; in Clarkson, *History,* 391.

37. William Wilberforce's speech to Parliament, May 12, 1789, in ibid., 284–86.

38. Capt. Ashley Hall Testimony, 1790, *House of Commons,* 72:230; Capt. William Snelgrave, "A New Account of Some Parts of Guinea and the Slave-Trade in 1730," in *A New General Collection of Voyages and Travels Consisting of the Most Esteemed Relations, Which Have Hitherto Been Published in Any Language: Comprehending Everything Remarkable in Its Kind in Europe, Asia, Africa and America* (London: Astley, 1745), 500.

39. James Arnold Testimony, 1789, *House of Commons,* 69:126; Testimony of Mr. Fraser, 1790, *House of Commons,* 71:42.

40. Clarkson, *History,* 476.

41. Henry Ellison Testimony, 1790, *House of Commons,* 73:376.

42. James Towne Testimony, 1791, *House of Commons,* 82:22.

43. Ecroyde Claxton Testimony, 1791, *House of Commons,* 82:36.

44. James Arnold Testimony, 1789, *House of Commons,* 69:127 (emphasis added).

45. David Henderson Testimony, 1789, *House of Commons,* 69:139 (emphasis added); also see Captain Ashley Hall Testimony, 1790, *House of Commons,* 72:231.

46. William Butterworth, quoted in Marcus Rediker, *The Slave Ship: A Human History* (London: Viking Penguin, 2007), 280.

47. John Newton, *Thoughts upon the African Slave Trade* (London: Buckland & Johnson, 1788), quoted in Rediker, *Slave Ship,* 241.

48. Reverend John Newton Testimony, 1790, *House of Commons,* 73:143.

49. James Field Stanfield, quoted in Rediker, *Slave Ship,* 152.

50. Lord Grenville speaking on the final motion presented by the House of Commons to abolish the slave trade, 1807, in Clarkson, *History,* 476.

51. James Arnold Testimony, 1789, *House of Commons,* 69:126.

52. Robert Norris Testimony, 1789, *House of Commons,* 68:9.

53. Clarkson, *History,* 472.

54. Ibid., 477.

55. Mr. Fox's speech to Parliament, 1791 session, ibid., 391–94.

56. Mr. Jenkinson's speech to Parliament, 1793 session, ibid., 431.

57. Ibid., 477–78.

58. Ibid., 478.

59. Ibid., 498.

60. *Times* (London), March 26, 1808.

61. Harriet Jacobs, *Incidents in the Life of a Slave Girl,* ed. Lydia Maria Child, new introduction and notes by Walter Teller (New York: Harcourt Brace, 1973).

62. James Walvin observes that "the British have much preferred to discuss British abolition rather than British slavery" and refers to Britain's "historical amnesia" regarding its involvement in the slave trade and slavery; James Walvin, *Britain's Slave Empire* (Stroud, U.K.: Tempus, 2007), 197.

SLAVE TRADING ENTREPÔTS AND THEIR HINTERLANDS

Continued Forced Migrations after the
Middle Passage to North America

GREGORY E. O'MALLEY

By the mid–eighteenth century, European settlers in North America pushed well away from the Atlantic Coast to colonize interior regions, and their settlements filled in most coastal areas between the major port cities.[1] As they spread these settlers brought the institution of slavery with them. In the Chesapeake the quest for arable land to cultivate with slave labor prompted greater numbers of settlers to venture to the Piedmont. By the 1760s many Piedmont counties saw Africans and people of African descent accounting for well over half of their populations, and with more than 100,000 slaves in the Piedmont by 1782, more of Virginia's slaves resided in that region than in the Tidewater. Many westward-bound slaves had previously worked Tidewater plantations, but African-born slaves were also prominent in the Piedmont slave population. As scholars of Virginia's backcountry note, "it is not too farfetched to speak of the Africanization of the Piedmont during the third quarter of the eighteenth century."[2]

Lowcountry planters also ventured inland, especially with the introduction of indigo as the region's companion crop to rice. Meanwhile the slave population in the colony's backcountry grew from 2,417 in 1760 to 6,548 in 1768 and continued to grow rapidly thereafter, leading some scholars to assert that most slaves imported after 1780 were bound for the backcountry. As Charleston merchant Peter Manigault described slave imports to Charleston in the early 1770s, "Upwards of two thirds that have been imported have gone backwards." The invention of the cotton gin only accelerated backcountry development at the century's end, facilitating cotton cultivation in noncoastal areas.[3]

While historians are well aware that the slave regime expanded outward from coastal population centers in the eighteenth century, little attention has been paid to the mechanics of delivering slaves to regions distant from the ports of importation (or forced immigration). For the period when the transatlantic slave trade remained open, stories of slavery tend to start at the plantation while stories of the slave trade end in ports, with little attention to how people moved from one to the other. In contrast scholars are well aware of the importance of the overland trade for slavery's expansion in the antebellum period, after transatlantic importations ceased. This U.S. domestic slave trade had an important precursor in the colonial period, though it was smaller in scale. Perhaps the slave migration to the North American interior needs to be conceived of in two phases—first a dispersal trade of Africans from the Atlantic entrepôts from the mid-eighteenth to early nineteenth centuries, and second the forced migration of American-born slaves from the older plantation areas to the burgeoning Southwest, starting in the late eighteenth century and reaching unprecedented levels in the antebellum period.[4]

Just how slaves and slaveholders bridged the gap from port to plantation is an important question given the considerable distance emerging between them. To be sure some American-born or acculturated slaves migrated inland with plantation owners seeking new lands for themselves, but many landless colonists moved westward as a strategy for acquiring land, which was increasingly unavailable in coastal areas. Many backcountry planters owned few slaves, if any, prior to acquiring interior land. As a result these pioneers often sought "new negroes," slaves recently arrived from Africa.

Little is known about their journeys from port to plantation. For all the exciting advances in historical knowledge of the Atlantic slave trade in recent decades, there remains a pronounced tendency to depict the trade (and implicitly African journeys) as ending at the American port where transatlantic slave traders delivered their African captives. This tendency oversimplifies the migration experiences of many African captives. For instance of roughly 2.6 million Africans shipped across the Atlantic to British ports in the Caribbean and North America from the mid-seventeenth to the early nineteenth centuries, approximately 15 percent of them—well over three hundred thousand forced migrants—promptly boarded other ships for export from their place of arrival to other colonies.[5] Distribution of slaves after the Atlantic crossing occurred within the colony of arrival as well. Especially by the mid–eighteenth century, many arriving Africans continued their journeys overland after the Middle Passage to reach rapidly growing interior regions. Other slaves transferred to smaller vessels that ferried them to minor ports up and down the coast from an entrepôt. These dispersals within colonies are the focus of this essay. Such movements of Africans after the Atlantic crossing not only linked far-flung plantations to the Atlantic slave trade, but also put this human commerce on display across the American landscape—inspiring many Americans to become slaveholders but perhaps inspiring others to turn abolitionist.

Of course there are reasons why slave trade scholars focus less attention on such localized movements. For one, the Middle Passage was indeed the most significant and dramatic phase of Africans' journeys to American slavery, but perhaps equally important, the transatlantic trade is much more thoroughly documented. Movements of slaves by sea can be more systematically studied, because such movements were monitored and documented by port officials. Furthermore seaborne trade typically required more coordination between merchants on either end of a voyage, leading to extensive correspondence, not to mention documentation of the comings and goings of ships by newspapers and insurers. Movements within colonies left far fewer traces in the historical record. As a result rigorous quantification of Africans' further migrations within colonies is not feasible, and even more anecdotal sources often only hint at the experiences of African immigrants between the Middle Passage and the plantations where they settled. Yet these journeys were of major importance to many who endured them. What follows is an attempt to recover some of that elusive experience from a fragmentary and unsatisfactory record.

The journeys would have been rugged ones. For settlers in the British North American interior of the eighteenth century, communications and transportation to and from the entrepôts—which served as social, commercial, and political centers—was a constant challenge and concern given the underdeveloped transportation infrastructure, not to mention the spotty postal or shipping services. As a result the movement of Africans outward from the entrepôts was a haphazard, makeshift endeavor. Buyers of slaves from the hinterlands often traveled to entrepôts to make purchases and bring slaves home themselves, but this sometimes proved unfeasible, leading buyers to employ an amalgam of methods for delivering slaves. Some relied on agents to purchase slaves for them and then trusted those agents or other acquaintances to deliver the slaves. Others waited for merchants to bring slaves to their area for sale. For slaves this arrangement meant that their journeys after the Middle Passage were varied affairs that posed a range of challenges and, sometimes, opportunities. The first section of this essay seeks to uncover how merchants and planters organized the dispersal of slaves from the Atlantic entrepôts, while the second section questions how these journeys affected the overall migration experience of the captives who endured them. The conclusion considers some implications of this traffic for both the abolition of 1808 and the persistent growth of American slavery thereafter.

I.

The slave dealings of Charleston merchant Henry Laurens in the summer of 1764 highlight the varied methods for moving incoming Africans from entrepôts to hinterlands. In the wake of the Seven Years' War, demand for slaves was high throughout South Carolina, and to capitalize on this need Laurens imported slaves directly from Africa and via transshipment from the Caribbean. Recognizing that Charleston and its vicinity accounted for only part of the colony's demand, Laurens pursued sales in the hinterland through at least five channels.

First, Laurens courted remote buyers to sales in Charleston through direct correspondence and advertising. He wrote to William Frierson, in the Williamsburgh Township, sending him broadsides for the sale and asking him "to disperse the

Advertisements as quick & as generally as you can & I wish it may suit you & many others of my old friends in your Quarters to attend the Sales." He sent a similar invitation (without extra advertisements) to Daniel Heyward in "Indian Land." Apparently these appeals drew results, as Laurens later noted that "people come from all quarters" to buy slaves. Second, for those planters who could not travel to Charleston, Laurens fulfilled requests if they were willing to trust his judgment and integrity. For William Thompson, who lived on Black Mingo Creek, west of Georgetown, Laurens purchased "two Young Negroes, a Male & a Female," in accord with Thompson's request. He did not record how he planned to send Thompson the slaves.[6]

Third, perhaps encouraged by these sales to far-flung customers, Laurens became a buyer of slaves to send to outlying areas for resale to planters who did not travel to the entrepôt. With William Price, a Georgetown merchant, Laurens speculated on a "parcel of Negroes" imported by other transatlantic traders. Price then transshipped these slaves to Georgetown, a smaller port up the coast, for resale. Fourth, as a selling agent for slave traders to Charleston, Laurens occasionally sent slaves inland for sale. In August he was offered commissions to sell a group of slaves "which came in most wretched plight" from St. Kitts. Laurens "sold Three Men & three Women . . . & one Boy" in Charleston but explained to their owners that "as to the other eight I could not get them off here at any tolerable rate." Instead, he continued, "I have sent them a little way in the Country where I think there is a better chance of Selling them than here." He later reported that "those 8 Negroes sent into the Country have yielded at least 50 per Cent more than they would here." Finally, not satisfied to be only a slave merchant, Laurens purchased "Eleven New Negroes" for himself and shipped them up the Ashley River to his Mepkin Plantation on the schooner *Baker,* under Capt. John Gray and a crew of slaves.[7]

Of these varied strategies for moving slaves from port to hinterland, the most typical arrangement was probably slaves traveling in the company of the purchaser after a transaction in the entrepôt. The purchase of a slave was a major investment, so many planters preferred not to delegate the selection of slaves to friends or merchants who served as their agents in other types of transactions. Such an important purchase could draw remote planters to town when other transactions might not. In fact slave trading merchants in Charleston considered attracting such remote planters to slave sales as vital to their success. In 1756 the Charleston firm of Austin and Laurens explained the logic, while absolving themselves of blame for the slow sales of fifteen Africans whom Law, Satterthwaite, and Jones of Barbados had transshipped to Charleston for resale. "'Tis much more difficult to run off these small parcells than a Cargo of 3 or 400," Austin and Laurens explained. "When such a [large] Number are for Sale it draws down the People from every part of the Province & one bids upon the other. Very often they, in their hurry, take hold of very ordinary Slaves as prime overlooking their imperfections which in a small parcell scarse ever escapes notice." Slave traders relied on distant planters swarming to town to create a frenzy for slave purchasing and to generate fear among their peers that hesitation would send them home empty handed. Fortunately for Law, Satterthwaite, and Jones, their Charleston agents saw an opportunity for such excitement on the horizon. After explaining the slow sales, Austin and Laurens noted that "yesterday a Brigantine arriv'd to us with 140 [more Africans] from your Island which will bring down our friends from the remote parts of the Country & enable us to run off yours."[8]

Merchants hoping to attract these "remote" planters did not simply keep their fingers crossed, but actively marketed Africans in the backcountry. Newspapers in the eighteenth century circulated widely, so advertisements in periodicals reached planters close to town and in outlying areas. To ensure that distant readers had an opportunity to attend sales, merchants typically advertised well in advance. In Charleston, for example, a quarantine law required all arriving African captives to wait ten days at Sullivan's Island in the harbor to ensure any contagions were under control before entering port. Merchants routinely advertised the slaves as soon as the ships entered the harbor, so that planters could learn of a sale and travel to town during the quarantine period. For instance when the brigantine *Two Friends* arrived in Charleston Harbor at the end of October 1752 with slaves transshipped from Barbados, the merchants Glen and Cooper placed an advertisement in the *South Carolina Gazette*'s October 30 issue, informing readers that "on Thursday the 9th Day of November next, will be sold at Auction at the usual Place in Charles-Town, about Sixty very likely new NEGRO Men, Women, Boys and Girls." An advertisement in the following week's issue would have been more proximate to the sale, but giving potential buyers ten days of warning increased the likelihood that distant planters would travel to the sale.[9]

Some advertisers targeted backcountry planters more directly. In their account for a sale of slaves from Sierra Leone in July 1756, Austin and Laurens listed a charge of fourteen pounds (South Carolina currency) for "Printed Advertisements, hire of a Man & Horse to disperse them thro' the Country & Expences at the Sale." Clearly enticing backcountry buyers was a priority, although Austin and Laurens doubted the effectiveness of their marketing in this case because news of the declaration of war with France had just reached the colony. As a result they noted, "We are afraid Our advertisements will Scarce bring a Single person out of the Country to the Sale."[10] Such attention to drawing remote planters to the entrepôt suggests that many planters attended sales in person, meaning that after the Middle Passage Africans often made the journey to a plantation in the company of their new owner.[11]

In other cases planters chose not to travel to the entrepôts, preferring to appoint an agent to make purchases for them. Given the difficulty and expense of overland travel in the eighteenth century, backcountry planters routinely relied on friends and acquaintances to make smaller purchases for them on visits to larger towns, as Richard Winn of South Carolina's Fairfield District did in 1798. He wrote to a neighbor, S. W. Yongue, having heard that "you are going to Columbia I will take it a favour if you will be so good as to git me One P'd. of Good Tea. At this time I have Not as Much Small Money as will pay for it but Shortly after your Return Shall."[12] Given the financial risk involved in buying slaves, not to mention the logistics of such an expensive transaction, relying on an agent for the purchase of slaves could not be undertaken so casually. Nonetheless some remote planters relied on surrogates to purchase slaves in port cities. In one 1807 bill of sale for a slave, LeRoy Hammond and Charles Goodwyn acknowledged the receipt of $450 from a Beaufort planter named John Cheney, who was the "trustee nominated and appointed for that purpose by Mary Dayley of Edgefield District." It is possible that Dayley engaged Cheney to buy the slave for her due more to gender than geography, potentially viewing it as advantageous to have a male agent in the marketplace, but given her location in the backcountry Edgefield District and Cheney's residence in the coastal district of Beaufort, it also seems likely that Dayley employed Cheney because he had better access to slave markets.[13]

Allowing an agent to select slaves to purchase on one's behalf made trust vitally important, underscoring the need for personal ties connecting planters in the hinterland to people in the entrepôts. In 1786 Joseph Clay of Savannah sent a young man named Mr. Faning to Charleston to purchase "three new Negroes from the Windward Coast" on his behalf. (Devastated by the war, Georgia struggled to attract transatlantic slave shipments in the years immediately following the American Revolution.)[14] Faning was intimidated by the responsibility, however, so Clay also sent a letter of introduction to Daniel Bourdeaux, a mercantile correspondent in Charleston, stating that Faning "not being willing to depend intirely on his own Judgement in procuring them has Requested I wou'd get a Friend to see them before he finally purchased & sent them here in Order to have their Approbation." Thus Clay relied on two agents to purchase slaves on his behalf—perhaps trusting one more to keep Clay's interest at heart and the other more for his experience in trade. Each of the agents could take comfort that if something went wrong, their concurrence in the decision would minimize suspicions of negligence or fraud.[15]

To cultivate the trust of people for whom he purchased slaves, Henry Laurens sometimes offered a choice from among slaves he bought for his client and himself. When Elias Ball—a plantation owner up the Cooper River—asked Laurens to purchase six slaves for him, Laurens purchased eight. He sent them to Ball with a letter explaining that "if 8 is more than you want please to draw out two for me & send them when a convenient opportunity offers to Wambaw [one of Laurens's own plantations] or back again to Charles Town. I shall be glad to have them." Through this strategy Laurens offered his client a degree of choice and perhaps peace of mind from knowing that Laurens was willing to purchase the two least desirable of the slaves for himself.[16]

When agents purchased slaves for a distant owner, Africans presumably traveled from port to plantation either with the purchasing agent or in the company of another traveler who oversaw the delivery of the slaves for payment or as a favor. Unfortunately details are particularly sketchy for such arrangements. In a 1794 account, James and Edwin Penman and Co. described two slaves as "delivered to John Kendall." This note on delivery may indicate that the Penmans paid someone to take the slaves to Kendall, since other entries in the account do not use that language, but the record is by no means clear, especially since Kendall's location is not noted. Similar language also appears in William Ancrum's account book for 1758, which lists the receipt of £260 from Fesch and Guignard on January 14 for "a new Negro Woman Sold & deliver'd to them in September last," but again precisely what *deliver'd* means in this context is unclear.[17]

Absentee owners of backcountry plantations who resided in an entrepôt avoided the dilemma of whether to travel to town for slave sales, but delivering new slaves to their distant plantations still presented a challenge. In the 1770s Ancrum resided mainly in Charleston, while owning several plantations in the South Carolina backcountry, and the challenge of moving both people and goods between his plantations and the coast was a constant theme in his letters. He often noted slave purchases (of both recently arrived Africans and American-born slaves), and he hinted at varied methods for delivering these slaves to the interior. In January 1777 he wrote to the overseer of his Red Bank plantation near Camden to report that he was sending him "a Negro Woman named Ruth & her female Child by Mr. Rose's wagon."[18] Ancrum offered no details on Mr. Rose's identity or the terms of their agreement, but at times he appears to have paid for such transport of slaves. In an account for 1778, for example, he noted £8,200 paid "for 5 Negroes bo't" for his Roundabout plantation on the Congaree River near Columbia, plus an additional £10 spent for "Carriage up" of the slaves. Unfortunately Ancrum offered no further details on who supervised these slaves or by what mode they traveled, but it is nonetheless interesting that he paid for their delivery.[19]

Ancrum did not always pay for this service, however, since he owned several wagons, which were crucial for transporting his indigo to the coast. In December 1777, having just received several loads of indigo from his plantations, he wrote to Joseph Kershaw, a merchant friend in Camden, to thank him for overseeing the indigo shipment and to report having purchased seven "Negroes to settle at the Congarees" estate. Ancrum noted that he "sent Frank with them as far as Mr. Porckins plant[ation] Amelia." Frank was operating a wagon bound for Ancrum's Camden plantation, but the route to the Camden plantation and the Congaree plantation would have been the same—along the Cooper River—for the first three-quarters of the journey. Ancrum planned to catch up with the slaves himself at Mr. Porckin's plantation to take them the rest of the way to their destination while Frank and the wagon continued to his other estate. (Presumably Ancrum could outpace the wagon on horseback.) Frank's identity is elusive but tantalizing. He was likely a slave. In the same letter to Kershaw, Ancrum describes arrangements made to pay the various wagon operators for the delivery of the indigo, stating that he "paid Tomlinson the Carriage of what he brought. Mr. Russley's I shall either settle with him or you." No mention is made, however, of payment to Frank either for bringing the indigo down or sending the slaves and goods up, possibly because Ancrum owned him. The use of only a first name for Frank also hints at his being a slave, given the other names in the letter: "Mr. Porckin," "Tomlinson," "Mr. Loocock," "Mr. Russley." In fact the need to settle an account with Russley, while Tomlinson could be paid on the spot, may suggest that a slave operated the wagon that Russley owned as well. The idea that slaves drove these wagons must remain speculative but would not be terribly surprising.[20]

Such travel was not always by wagon either. Like Ancrum, Laurens was also an absentee plantation owner, and he shipped recently purchased slaves upstream to his plantations by riverboat on several occasions. For instance on January 1, 1763, Laurens wrote to his overseer at Mepkin Plantation, up the Cooper River, informing him that "I now send you by Mr. Dick's Schooner 25 Negroes," noting that "they are all well Clothed & I have put a Barrel of ordinary Rice in the Schooner which will serve for provision on the Passage & some time longer." He followed these slaves just days later with "Rinah, a Negro Wench big with child in Mr. Broughton's Boat." Peter Broughton was another planter up the Cooper River, so Laurens had clearly arranged for the vessel to stop by his plantation. Whether he paid for this service or simply called in a neighborly favor is unclear.[21]

Another arrangement for slave travel from entrepôt to hinterland was in the company of merchants—either selling agents in the transatlantic trade or colonial speculators who purchased slaves for resale outside the entrepôts. While most slave traders seemed content to attract backcountry planters to the entrepôts for slave sales (and let the buyers worry about the logistics of moving slaves inland), some traders pursued backcountry sales more aggressively. Drawing buyers to entrepôts for slave sales worked best in colonies such as South Carolina, where the slave system was most entrenched (making backcountry demand relatively high) and where the backcountry was not so distant that trips to port by plantation owners became infeasible. A different pattern emerged for smaller markets and deep interiors.

For instance merchants who imported slaves to Pennsylvania typically did not wait for buyers to come to them. With slave labor not so predominant, perhaps merchants feared that demand would not draw enough buyers to port. Whatever the reason, Pennsylvania merchants often took slaves into the countryside in search of buyers. In the 1730s and 1740s, Robert Ellis was the most prolific slave importer in Pennsylvania—mainly via intercolonial trade. He advertised numerous slave sales in Philadelphia newspapers, but he also distributed slaves throughout the region for sale by his agents. In September 1736, for example, he wrote to a Mr. Shaw, who was either up or down the Delaware River from Philadelphia, to inform him that he had "sent [him] four Negros, Two Garls and Two Boys, which I Desire you will Dispose of them if you can, [for] not Less than Twenty Six Pounds Each." Ellis sold other slaves from the same shipment in Philadelphia but apparently sought to spread slaves around to avoid glutting the small market.[22] Likewise in January 1739, when Ellis managed the sale of two slave shipments, he sent some slaves to Jacob Kollock in Lewes, in what is now Delaware, for sale on commission. Ellis's partner in Philadelphia, John Ryan, later complained to Kollock about the high commission he charged for his "Sales of 16 Negroes." Lewes was not the only farther destination for slaves from these shipments. To underscore his complaint, Ryan pointed out to Kollock that "there are Others concern'd with us (Mr. Ellis & I) who have been at Vast Pains & Trouble in . . . Selling 'em up & down in Severall Parts of the Country . . . [who] cant pretend to Charge more than 5 P Cent Commission." Apparently Philadelphia merchants were more aggressive in pursuing buyers rather than drawing purchasers to them.[23]

In the early 1760s, the only period in which Pennsylvania regularly received direct shipments from Africa, importer Thomas Riche continued the strategy of dispersing slaves to the surrounding area for sale. When Riche served as selling agent for the schooner *Hannah,* which delivered one hundred Africans to Philadelphia in 1761, he informed Samuel Tucker up the Delaware River in Trenton that "I intend Sending 15 or 20 up to you for Sale, for which we shall Furnish you with advertisements by the Post on Monday." Two weeks later, hearing that Tucker had "sold most of the negros," Riche "furnish'd [him] with a fresh Parcell." Riche and Tucker continued to work together in slave distribution over the following years, but Riche also marched slaves about the countryside himself.[24] After he received shipments of slaves, several days would often pass without Riche noting any letters written in his letter book; these gaps were typically followed by apologies for his delay in responding to correspondents due to spending time "in the country." In most cases Riche did not explain the reasons for this travel, but when he received a shipment of slaves from Gambert and Heyman during a cold spell in late 1763, he reported that due to the chill "we Cannot move them about the Country for sale." That comment, taken with Riche's routine absences from Philadelphia after slave shipments arrived, suggests that he often marched slaves into the countryside in search of buyers.[25]

At times southern slave traders speculated on overland ventures as well. For instance in Virginia many Piedmont planters surely traveled to Atlantic entrepôts to purchase slaves for themselves—a paucity of evidence for a more systematic Piedmont slave trade suggests this—but some merchants also speculated on slaves in the entrepôts with an eye to reselling them in western counties. In 1772 Paul Carrington—a burgess for Charlotte County in the Piedmont—purchased 50 slaves from the slave ship *Polly,* which delivered 450 Angolans at Bermuda Hundred, the furthest port up the James River. "Considering the sum large and a Considerable Risque in the health & life of the Slaves," he brought three investors into the scheme and then "convey'd the Slaves to the Country" at his plantation in Charlotte County, from which he "made the Sales & Collected the Debts." Presumably his customers were Piedmont planters from Charlotte and surrounding counties.[26]

Other direct evidence of such trading proves elusive, but Carrington was probably only unusual for his case ending up in court, hence the documentary record. Sales records from transatlantic slavers suggest that other Virginia merchants purchased slaves for resale in the mid–eighteenth century. For instance when the brigantine *Eadith* delivered 154 Gambians to the York River in 1761, amid the typical small purchases made by individuals, two mercantile firms bought slaves in larger numbers. "Taylor & Snelson" bought 20 slaves (8 men, 4 women, 4 boys, and 4 girls), while "Samuel Gest & Co." purchased 58 individuals (10 men, 17 women, 15 boys, and 16 girls). While the records do not indicate the intentions of these buyers, both the large number of slaves purchased and the corporate (rather than individual) names of the buyers suggest that these were speculators rather than planters. Such speculation made little sense unless one intended to transport such slaves to another market for resale. In Virginia in 1761, the Piedmont offered by far the most likely market.[27]

At times South Carolina merchants organized such backcountry ventures as well. In 1765 when transatlantic slave traders flooded Charleston with African captives, importers Brailsford and Chapman sought to alleviate the glut by sending for sale sixty Angolan and Windward Coast slaves to Jacksonburgh in the Pon Pon district, offering an unusually generous eighteen months credit.[28] Austin, Laurens, and Appleby advertised similar inland sales on numerous occasions.[29] Circumstantial evidence suggests that such distribution of slaves to Charleston's hinterland for sale was not unusual. In the 1750s Charleston merchants William Woodrop and Paul Douxsaint regularly imported slaves to the colony, and during the same period they employed John Wilkins to operate a store at Pon Pon in the South Carolina backcountry. The store's primary purpose was undoubtedly a broader commerce selling imported goods and buying plantation produce and perhaps deer skins, but given Woodrop and Douxsaint's role as slave importers, backcountry slave sales may also have factored into the operation.[30] The mercantile firm of Clay, Telfair, and Co. occupied a similar position in Savannah after the American Revolution. The firm was "concerned with Mr. McLean in a House at Augusta for the purpose of securing the Country & Indian Trading business," and in the same period these merchants—Joseph Clay in particular—actively imported slaves. Direct evidence for transporting slaves to their inland location does not exist, but given the growth of the state's interior population in these years, such traffic was plausible.[31]

During the Revolutionary War, William Ancrum and Thomas Wade undertook such a speculation in slaves for overland distribution, with Ancrum buying slaves in Charleston and sending them to Wade in Cheraw—in South Carolina's indigo producing upcountry—for resale. The war disrupted their venture, with Ancrum complaining that he was "sorry to observe the late stoppage of the Circulation of . . . Dollars has frustrated our original plan in regard to the sale of the Negroes & that you [Wade] was under a Necessity of disposing of them on Credit." Despite this concern about offering loans "in these troublesome times," the venture was apparently profitable, for Ancrum argued that the "profits likely to be made on the Sale of the Negroes are a sufficient inducem't to have continued the plan, could Negroes have now been purchased at the rate the others were, [but] they are now considerably advanced in price" in Charleston, so Ancrum declined to make a further investment. Ancrum and Wade probably invested in seasoned or creolized slaves for this overland venture, since African imports virtually halted during the peak years of the revolutionary conflict, but presumably a similar venture would have been feasible during nonwar years (for which, inconveniently, Ancrum's letter books do not survive).[32] Mathias Seller, who lived near Stono, may have undertaken such a venture in 1764, when he purchased three hundred slaves from Henry Laurens on credit. The size of the purchase suggests the intention to resell at least some of the slaves for profit, but if so Seller did not live up to his name, since Laurens had to threaten legal action for nonpayment of the debt the following year.[33]

Merchants also transshipped slaves from Charleston for sale in the smaller ports up and down the coast. As a selling agent for slave traders to South Carolina, Laurens often sent small groups of slaves to Georgetown for sale. In the fall of 1764, he sent "8 New Negroes" to merchant Samuel Wragg for sale and later explained that for commissions in such cases he "usually paid only 2 ½ per Cent & [was] never asked [for] more in the Country for the Sale alone." Since Laurens, and other selling agents in Charleston, typically received 5 percent commissions on the slaves they sold for transatlantic traders, this suggests that entrepôt merchants split their commissions with more remote traders when bringing them into the business of dispersing slaves.[34]

Other merchants speculated on slaves in Charleston in order to resell them in the smaller ports of the colony. In the winter of 1765, Francis Stuart purchased "fifty Ebo Slaves" from Laurens in Charleston for transshipment and resale in Beaufort, but the sales may have been slow, as Laurens complained the following February and again in May about the slow remittances of payment. The Africans in this venture had reached South Carolina via St. Kitts, so they experienced a particularly convoluted journey to American slavery, changing hands at least four times after the Atlantic crossing and enduring at least two subsequent "passages."[35]

This range of possibilities for getting slaves to growing backcountry regions illustrates that the interior migration was a haphazard enterprise. Africans traveled inland after the Middle Passage with planters who purchased them to exploit their labor, with the agents or creolized slaves of such owners, or with merchants who speculated on their value as commodities—a value they hoped would increase in the interior, away from Atlantic markets. The growth of the colonies ensured steady demand for slave labor in the countryside away from the Atlantic entrepôts, but the poor transportation infrastructure prevented a systematic overland distribution system from developing. Instead arriving Africans traveled inland with all manner of people—planters, merchants, slaves, or other travelers who just happened to be going their way.

II.

So what did such outward journeys from the Atlantic entrepôts mean for those Africans chosen to undertake them? Unfortunately very few slave narratives survive to describe the slave trade experience firsthand, and those that do survive do not describe distribution within North America in any detail. In fact the only auto-biographical account that mentions movement to the North American interior after the Middle Passage does so in one simple sentence. Abduhl Rahhahman arrived in North America at New Orleans and described his further movement as follows: "Then they took me to Natchez."[36] It is dishearteningly little for historians to work with. But reading between the lines of trader and planter accounts allows recon-struction of some aspects of the experience and facilitates some useful speculation.

Most fundamentally for the Africans selected, an additional move after the arrival in a North American entrepôt meant that their journey was not yet over when they completed the Middle Passage. While the phrase "Middle Passage," for most twenty-first-century readers, conjures thoughts of the horrific experiences of African slaves in their forced Atlantic crossings, the transatlantic voyage was termed *middle* to reflect European, not African, experience. For European traders the voyage typically formed the second leg of a three-part journey: a first passage, from Europe to Africa with trade goods; the "middle" passage, from Africa to America with slaves; and a third voyage, from America back to Europe with colo-nial staples or in ballast. There were certainly variations from this "triangle" trade, but this three-legged journey gave the Middle Passage its name.

The irony is that despite these Eurocentric origins, the term "Middle Passage" fits the experience of the ocean crossing for many African migrants in ways that historians often fail to recognize. The journeys of Africans in the transatlantic slave trade did not typically begin at their port of embarkation for the ocean crossing, nor did they necessarily end when transatlantic vessels reached the Americas. His-torians of the slave trade within Africa show that people often fell captive deep in the interior and faced extensive journeys just to reach the African coast.[37] Likewise just as slaves funneled into the Atlantic slave trade from wide regions in West Africa, many spread outward from their ports of arrival in the New World. This dispersal took the form of both a seaborne intercolonial (and even transimperial) slave trade, and also the more localized movement of people from entrepôts to sur-rounding plantation regions.[38] Keeping all of these aspects of the slave trade in mind is particularly vital, because the abolitions of 1807 and 1808 outlawed only the "middle" phase of this three-part forced migration (and only for U.S. and British traders). The commerce in enslaved Africans continued legally both within Africa and in America.

For Africans arriving in North America in the slave trade in the eighteenth century, more than mere chance selected some of them for lengthy voyages into the backcountry. North American ports received captives both directly from Africa and indirectly via the Caribbean, but if Henry Laurens is correct in arguing that only the largest slave shipments attracted the planters from deep in the interior, it was captives arriving directly from Africa who faced the greatest likelihood of an extended voyage to the hinterland. By contrast the more than 15 percent of individuals reaching North America on smaller shipments from the Caribbean were more likely to find themselves purchased by slaveholders closer to entrepôts for whom the trip to the slave mart was less of a project.[39] Thus for the African migrants, escaping one form of lengthy dispersal after the Middle Passage (seaborne transshipment) increased the likelihood of enduring another (significant overland travel).

Likewise Morgan and Nicholls show a bias in the Virginia Piedmont migration toward both young and female slaves, and they suggest that backcountry planters selected such people primarily because they cost less than men, but also because planters sought to grow their workforce through natural reproduction.[40] Both factors may have been important, but backcountry planters also faced constraints on their selectivity. In 1755 the Charleston merchants Austin and Laurens struggled to sell a group of recently arrived Africans for Henry Weare and Co. of Bristol, reporting that they were a poor assortment of slaves, unhealthy and mostly children. Countering allegations that they sold too cheaply, Austin and Laurens insisted that these Africans would have garnered much less, but "we had abundance of poor industrious People attended that Sale which come from 70 to 80 Miles distance who were forced to take such as we had." Remote planters who incurred the cost of traveling to an entrepôt to purchase slaves could not afford to go home empty handed. As a result they may have purchased fewer adult males than the wealthy coastal planters.[41]

Some merchants in the entrepôts also moved slaves they considered less desirable away from the major markets, seeking buyers who had fewer options. In 1733 George Burrington, an ex-governor of North Carolina, noted that "great is the loss this Country has sustained in not being supply'd by vessells from Guinea with Negroes . . . [because] we are under a necessity to buy the refuse refractory and distemper'd Negroes, brought from other Governments."[42] Burrington suggests that merchants in the entrepôts only sent less desirable slaves to remote markets such as his. Though not often moving slaves to North Carolina, Austin and Laurens employed a similar strategy when selling slaves in Charleston proved difficult. In 1756 they reported to Gedney Clarke of Barbados, who had transshipped one hundred slaves to them: "Finding we could not sell the last of your Negroes in Town at any tolerable price, being much reduced and ordinary, we sent nine of them round to George Town . . . & we hope shall very speedily have a better Sale of them than could now be obtain'd here." Georgetown was a small port about sixty miles up the coast, where Austin and Laurens hoped that less frequent slave deliveries would mean less discerning buyers. Tragically this approach suggests that those captives who were least fit for an extended journey after the Middle Passage may have been most likely to move a considerable distance from their port arrival in North America.[43]

Some Africans, however, reached the entrepôts in such debilitated condition that their onward journey had to be delayed or canceled altogether. Indeed when Austin and Laurens transshipped Gedney Clarke's nine unsold slaves to George-town, they reported that "one Wench being very much swell'd & having Impostume on her Knee we could not send with them."[44] Likewise in 1775 Savannah merchant Joseph Clay received a shipment of forty or fifty slaves bound for the plantation of Benjamin Stead, an absentee planter living in England, but Clay reported that "the Scurvy was among them. . . . 5 that we kept in Town had it to a Violent degree, 2 of whom are Dead; the other three seem likely to do well. We have not made any further attempt to get them on your Land," Clay continued, "nor shall not till they are all Strong & hearty." The sad tale of these captives makes clear that even those fortunate enough to survive the Middle Passage still faced risks of mortality and had more trials to endure en route to the plantation.[45]

The distances Africans traveled in their dispersal from the entrepôts could be quite considerable. In 1755 Austin and Laurens vended a group of African slaves in Charleston for Thomas Easton and Co. of Bristol and reported a delay in resolving a dispute with Daniel Heyward, the buyer of several slaves, because "he lives near 100 miles distance & writes us there was a mistake of £200 in casting up the Sum total of his Slaves." Austin and Laurens had to wait for Heyward to return his receipt before they could assess whether they had indeed made a mistake. Heyward's plantation was southwest of Charleston on the Combahee River, so the Africans he purchased probably traveled with him by sea as far as Beaufort and then either up the river by boat or overland to the plantation—a journey of several days by any route.[46] In the 1770s Peter Manigault reported even more extreme journeys, arguing that some backcountry planters "come at the Distance of 300 miles from Chs Town, and will not go back without Negroes, let the Price be what it will."[47]

For slaves bound to the Virginia Piedmont, the overland journey must also have been considerable. Bermuda Hundred probably served as the most frequent point of disembarkation for Piedmont-bound Africans, as it was the port farthest up the navigable portion of the James River. From there the closest and most populous Piedmont county, Amelia, was a fifty-mile overland journey. To Charlotte County, where Paul Carrington marched his fifty slaves for resale, the trip was nearly one hundred miles, and these were hard, slow miles on eighteenth-century roads and trails.

Thomas Riche moved slaves to the southwest from Philadelphia perhaps as far as northern Maryland in the quest for buyers. In 1754 upon receiving a shipment of slaves from Francis Moore's brig *Africa*, Riche's clerk reported to a correspondent that "Mr. Riche is gone to Maryland with Capt. Moore" and was away for seven to ten days. It remains possible that Riche and Moore made this journey entirely by sea by sailing around the Delmarva Peninsula and into Chesapeake Bay, but Riche's routine journeys to the countryside upon receiving slave shipments suggest that the venture was at least partly overland.[48]

As for the lived experience of the overland dispersal from North American ports to interior regions, the slapdash nature of that phase of the migration dictated that captives faced varied conditions. It is plausible that some slaves marched inland in coffles—walking chain gangs, in which at least adult males were shackled to one another—but I have found no direct evidence for this practice in eighteenth-century North America. Coffles were common in Africa at the time, however, and were witnessed by English slave traders, as Thomas Clarkson reported in his abolitionist critique of the slave trade in 1789. He reported an English slave trader's description of how African traders moved slaves overland to the coast: "They come in droves of three or four hundred at a time. The women and boys are permitted to walk freely. The men, however, are confined; the arms of some of the latter are tied behind them. Two or three others are tied together by means of leathern thongs, or ropes of grass, at the neck. Two others are confined by means of a pole, at each end of which is a crutch to put the neck in. . . . Their two necks being placed in the crutches . . . are confined in them by leather thongs. . . . Such a body of slaves is called a *cauffle*."[49] Precisely when American slave traders adopted this practice for controlling slaves on overland marches is unclear, but coffles certainly appeared in the nineteenth-century United States, when the domestic slave trade became more systematic in response to abolition's cutting off international sources of supply.[50] Of course most Africans bound for the interior in the eighteenth century traveled in smaller groups, so if coffles were used at all, they were probably rare.

For those traveling in small groups with a new owner, or perhaps his emissary, wagon travel was common—and by no means a luxurious form of travel. Eighteenth-century roads were rough, and the wagons were designed for hauling produce and goods, not seating passengers. William Ancrum, who often sent slaves to his backcountry plantations from Charleston by wagon, cautioned his overseers to be wary of the poor roads. In 1778 he instructed an overseer to "charge the Waggoner to be particularly careful that [the indigo crop] does not get wet by Rain or the Badness of the Road," suggesting both that the wagons offered poor protection from the elements and that the roads were rutted and potholed enough to risk tossing a load in a puddle if one was not careful. This hints at an uncomfortable ride for the slaves sent back on the same wagon's return journey.[51] Indeed slaves sent overland with wagons may often have walked alongside rather than riding within, as planters often struggled to claim space for their goods in infrequent wagons headed to the backcountry. Joseph Clay's apology to a backcountry acquaintance was typical when he was "very sorry to inform you the [hogshead of] bottle'd Porter was left behind" by a group of wagons heading out of Savannah. "I try'd all I cou'd to get them to take it but they said 'twas impossible." Slaves did not travel with this particular caravan, but given the premium for space they often must have been forced to walk when trade goods filled the wagons.[52]

For journeys of more than one day, little direct evidence survives with regard to where slaves slept, but conditions must have been rugged for this part of the journey as well. Few restaurants and inns were available for eighteenth-century travelers in British America, and where such facilities were available, they were almost surely not afforded for slaves. The lack of infrastructure for travelers is demonstrated by instructions that James Sanders Guignard gave in 1804 to an employee assigned to assess the logistics of travel between Orangeburg in the South Carolina backcountry and Charleston. Guignard's main concern seemed to be finding care for horses along the route, and he made no mention of slaves, but his concerns suggest the difficulties of travel. Concerned that the closest place he knew to Charleston for spending the night, "Coburn's old place," was "rather too far from Charleston," he instructed his agent to "enquire at Dorchester & at all other Houses on the Road between Dorchester & Charleston." If this was the situation by 1804, one imagines even scarcer accommodations in the mid–eighteenth century. Travelers had to rely on friends and even strangers for accommodation, so those traveling with groups of slaves probably forced them to camp out or perhaps found space for them in someone's barn or the slave quarters of some plantation.[53]

Accommodations were not only a concern while traveling; in some cases slaves endured long delays before a final sale to a planter. While major ports maintained slaves either aboard the ships that delivered them or in merchants' "houses" or "yards"—which were more than single-family homes—slaves dispersed to outlying areas, or who took a long time to sell, were not so easily accommodated. In 1762 Thomas Riche managed a sale of slaves delivered from the Senegal River aboard the *Paragon,* and in his search for buyers he sent captives up the Delaware River to Samuel Tucker in Trenton, but Tucker struggled to sell the slaves. After about a month passed, Tucker complained of the difficulty of keeping the slaves so long, and Riche instructed him to board the slaves out if necessary. This suggests that the slaves had lived at Tucker's home for the first several weeks. Concerned about the cost of boarding them out, Riche also urged Tucker to sell the slaves quickly, at cost if necessary.[54]

In some cases such boarding out of slaves was done with free blacks. In 1751 John Strutton of Philadelphia advertised "A Parcel of likely Negroes," who he said "may be seen at a Free Negroe Woman's, in Chestnut-Street." In 1759 Strutton placed a similar advertisement for a "Parcel of likely Negroe Men and Women," noting that "the said Negroes are to be seen at Emanuel Woodbe's (Negroe) in Water street, a little below Chestnut-street."[55] Presumably Strutton paid for the boarding of his slaves, and it is interesting to note this ancillary free black participation in the trade. If these slaves were recently arrived Africans (and Strutton's advertisements were not explicit on this point), then it is interesting to speculate about what this exposure to the African American presence in North America might have meant to them. Captives shipped with black wagoners or riverboat sailors saw similar opportunities for interaction with African Americans, but such encounters are obscured by history.

Where slavery was more entrenched, the boarding out of slaves was likely less of a concern, because slaves could be housed on the slave quarters of a plantation. Indeed when Paul Carrington speculated on the fifty African slaves whom he marched to the Virginia Piedmont for resale, he housed the slaves at his own plantation while he found buyers for them all. This process took at least six months, since he purchased the slaves in May and then bought warm clothing for fourteen of the slaves who remained unsold that fall.[56] Instead of encountering urban free blacks, these recently arrived Africans were thrust among seasoned or American-born slaves while awaiting sale to the plantation where they would settle.

The need to house slaves during the migration and while awaiting sale raises the issue of the overall duration of the slave trade for the captive migrants who endured it. It was a far longer ordeal than the weeks it took to cross the Atlantic. There could be extended migrations, but also lengthy periods of awaiting sale or movement on either side of the Atlantic crossing. Philadelphia merchant Jonathan Dickinson drove this point home when he complained to a colleague about "a parcell of Negroes that lay on my hands a yeare."[57] Such extended delays were more likely in a smaller slave market, but they were by no means unique.[58]

While the journeys (and the waiting) after the Middle Passage added hardship to the migration, in rare cases the interval between slave ship and plantation offered opportunities to African immigrants. Given the lack of firsthand information about Africans' experiences moving inland, we can only imagine what they learned about the geography of their new environment or about the society they were entering. It is especially intriguing to ponder what might have been learned when arriving Africans traveled inland under the supervision of slaves or boarded on plantations or in the homes of free blacks. Unfortunately the fragmentary and racially biased archival record leaves this realm of African knowledge almost entirely veiled.

While one can only speculate on what African immigrants heard and observed on their journeys to plantations, there is more solid evidence that some Africans seized the opportunity of the overland journey as a chance to flee enslavement. Having escaped the confines of the slave ship surrounded by the moat of the ocean, and having often had several days of fresh food and drink to recover their strength

before sale, many slaves attempted escape shortly after arriving. Advertisements for
runaways rarely described the circumstances of a slave's escape, but a striking number of such announcements refer to African-born individuals who only recently
disembarked from the Middle Passage, especially in the second half of the eighteenth century, when overland journeys for arrivals from Africa were most common. The *South Carolina Gazette,* for instance, frequently published descriptions
of slaves brought to the "workhouse" in Charleston. These slaves had to be publicly
advertised, because their owners could not be contacted directly to reclaim them—
typically because the slaves were described as speaking no English and not knowing who their masters were. For instance in 1753 the *Gazette* reported the arrival at
the workhouse of "a lusty new negro man, can't tell his master's name, with a white
negro cloth jacket, and a new duffil blanket." The following year it reported the
arrival of "a new negro, about 5 feet 2 inches high, cannot tell his own or master's
name, has a large bump on his left hand, with his country marks on each side of
his temples, above and below his navel." Similar announcements appeared every
week or two. Of course some individuals may have played dumb in order to avoid
return to a particularly abusive master or overseer, but the workhouse cannot have
been a pleasant place, and the men placing the announcements in the *Gazette* were
probably not fools. Their routine description of slaves as "new negroes" probably
reflects slaves who truly had spent very little time in the colonies, an impression
reinforced by frequent descriptions of their clothing and blankets as "new."[59]

Advertisements for runaway slaves placed by their owners reinforce this picture
of Africans frequently escaping shortly after disembarking in North America. Of
eighty slaves advertised as runaways in the *South Carolina Gazette* in 1760, for example, sixteen (20 percent) were described as "new negroes," who spoke no English and
often who did not yet have names assigned by their masters. In 1765 the percentage
of "new negroes" among advertised escapees was slightly higher, accounting for
eleven of forty-six runaways (24 percent). Most advertisements did not specify precisely where slaves were when they made their bid for freedom, but in some cases
the last phase of the slave trade migration offered the opportunity. For instance in
1765 William Harris announced that "a New Negro GIRL, about 13 or 14 years of
age, was sent on shore at Hobacaw [Hobcaw], out of the ship *Elizabeth,* Capt.
McNeill," which had recently arrived from Africa, "from whence she has either lost
herself in the woods, or is taken away, and harboured, by some person or persons."[60] Why Harris assumes a teenage girl could not have fled is unclear. Later that
same month, Joseph Kershaw placed another advertisement that suggests a possible escape between the Middle Passage and the plantation: "RAN away from the
subscriber, on Sunday the 28th of July, four new negro men, lately purchased of
Brailsford & Chapman," who were frequent importers of slaves.[61] While overall the
continued migration of slaves after surviving the Middle Passage must be viewed
as an additional hardship—full of risks of mortality, abuse, and discomfort—these

advertisements suggest that solid ground provided some slaves with greater opportunities to resist their enslavement.

The inland journeys that many Africans endured after crossing the Atlantic added considerable danger and suffering to their forced migration. Experiences varied widely, depending on where an individual was headed, whether as part of a large shipment or small, and on an individual's gender, ethnicity, age, and state of health. But for all Africans who traveled onward after their arrival in British America, the journey meant additional days or weeks of travel after the exhausting Atlantic crossing. It increased the likelihood of illness and death. Dispersal also made separation from countrymen or companions more likely. Furthermore the experience of sale and distribution in America must have impressed many slaves with their new status as chattel property in the New World. Slaves purchased for distribution and resale in the backcountry confronted the dehumanizing experience of having their monetary worth publicly negotiated additional times. They never accepted their status as property, but the experience of repeated trade must have imbued them with a sense of their new society's view of them as chattel.[62]

Of course other members of American society also witnessed the slave trade's dehumanizing spectacle of human commoditization. By the late eighteenth century, enough observers reacted with outrage to give rise to abolitionism. It was no accident that antislavery activists targeted the slave trade first. The exploitation of enslaved Africans on American plantations could be rationalized as just one of many forms of bound labor, existing on a continuum alongside indentured servitude, apprenticeship, and convict labor. But the buying and selling of human beings in the slave trade—the marching of Africans through the countryside, the separating of mothers from sons and sisters from brothers—displayed the chattel principle for public view at its most heartless and cruel. The callous calculations of slave traders about where and how to move captives and whom to sell at what locations inspired abolitionist outrage. Such marketing of people also proved the most vulnerable aspect of slavery to abolitionist critiques, culminating in the 1808 abolition of the international trade.

But the relationship between abolitionism and the commerce dispersing enslaved Africans across the American countryside was entirely ambiguous. The traffic stirred up abolitionists, but it also laid the groundwork for the robust intra-American slave trade of the nineteenth century that allowed Americans' commitment to slavery to grow despite the end of forced African immigration in 1808. Just as eighteenth-century traders marched arriving Africans from Atlantic ports to backcountry regions, interstate traders in the nineteenth century would march African American slaves from older Atlantic states to the southwestern frontier of Mississippi, Alabama, and Louisiana. For every budding abolitionist that colonial slave traders inspired, they helped create greater numbers of devotees to the exploitative chattel system by spreading slavery outward from the Atlantic ports. For the colonists settling in North American hinterlands in the eighteenth century, the inland distribution of slaves marked their integration with the coastal elite and the Atlantic's market economy. As Rachel Klein shows for South Carolina, the development of a backcountry slaveholding elite began not with the invention of the cotton gin but in the mid–eighteenth century. This process of bringing back-country settlers into slavery eventually worked to unify political interests across states such as South Carolina. Instead of inland settlers embracing a Jeffersonian vision of independent yeomanry, backcountry and coastal elites shared a commit-ment to slavery. The dispersal of slaves from entrepôts to hinterlands facilitated this process, not only by providing the exploitable workers but also by fostering com-mercial connections between remote planters and coastal elites.

Not only did backcountry planters seek connections to Atlantic markets in order to acquire slaves, but their very desire for slaves reflects their market ori-entation—their dream of shifting the North American backcountry to large-scale staple-crop production for the Atlantic marketplace. Some historians have argued that the eighteenth-century backcountry was "precapitalist—or noncapitalist" because its move to slavery "inhibited the development of a labor market." But this analysis rests on a rather narrow definition of a labor market. To be sure slavery sti-fled the development of free wage labor, but in a certain sense—as study of the intercolonial slave trade shows—the slave system created a labor market par excel-lence. Instead of commodifying labor, European settlers in the Americas commod-ified the laborers themselves in order to maximize market production and profits. The price of laborers was routinely negotiated in American marketplaces, and mer-chants bought, moved, and resold slaves to capitalize on variations between prices for laborers. This was a market logic taken to the extreme, though an extreme that later capitalist thinkers would reject as antithetical to "free" market capitalism. Given the experiences of slaves in this trade and the vital role that slavery played in the growth of the hinterlands, the dispersal of slaves outward from the Atlantic entrepôts marked a crucial stage in the slave trade and an important step in linking the hinterlands of North America to slave society and the Atlantic marketplace.[63]

Notes

1. See D. W. Meinig, *The Shaping of America: A Geographical Perspective on 500 Years of History,* vol. 1, *Atlantic America, 1492–1800* (New Haven, Conn.: Yale University Press, 1986), 244–54.

2. The Virginia Piedmont slave population grew by nearly one thousand slaves per year between 1760 and the Revolution; Philip D. Morgan and Michael L. Nicholls, "Slaves in Pied-mont Virginia, 1720–1790," *William and Mary Quarterly,* 3rd ser., 46, no. 2 (1989): 215–22 (quotation on p. 215). Likewise Allan Kulikoff argues for the "Africanization" of the Pied-mont, asserting that by the 1760s "nearly all Africans who arrived in Virginia landed at

Bermuda Hundred," the best upriver access point for the overland march to the Piedmont; Allan Kulikoff, *Tobacco and Slaves: The Development of Southern Cultures in the Chesapeake* (Chapel Hill: University of North Carolina Press, 1986), 75, 323–36.

3. For data on the 1760s, see Rachel N. Klein, *Unification of a Slave State: The Rise of the Planter Class in the South Carolina Backcountry, 1760–1808* (Chapel Hill: University of North Carolina Press, 1990), 19–24; for the 1780s and 1790s, see Patrick S. Brady, "The Slave Trade and Sectionalism in South Carolina, 1787–1808," *Journal of Southern History* 38 (November 1972): 601–20; Manigault, quoted in Klein, 20.

4. For more on the domestic slave trade in the United States after abolition of the international trade, see Steven Deyle, *Carry Me Back: The Domestic Slave Trade in American Life* (New York: Oxford University Press, 2005); Walter Johnson, *Soul by Soul: Life inside the Antebellum Slave Market* (Cambridge, Mass.: Harvard University Press, 1999); Walter Johnson, ed., *The Chattel Principle: Internal Slave Trades in the Americas* (New Haven, Conn.: Yale University Press, 2004); Michael Tadman, *Speculators and Slaves: Masters, Traders, and Slaves in the Old South* (Madison: University of Wisconsin Press, 1989); Robert H. Gudmestad, *A Troublesome Commerce: The Transformation of the Interstate Slave Trade* (Baton Rouge: Louisiana State University Press, 2003).

5. Greg O'Malley, "Final Passages: The British Inter-Colonial Slave Trade, 1619–1807" (Ph.D. diss., Johns Hopkins University, 2006); see also Daniel C. Littlefield, "Charleston and Internal Slave Redistribution," *South Carolina Historical Magazine* 87 (April 1986): 93–105; Jean-Pierre Le Glaunec, "Slave Migrations in Spanish and Early American Louisiana: New Sources and Estimates," *Louisiana History* 46 (Spring 2005): 185–209; Morgan and Nicholls, "Slaves in Piedmont Virginia."

6. Henry Laurens to William Frierson, June 11, 1764; Laurens to Daniel Heyward, June 11, 1764; Laurens to William Thompson, June 18 and 19, 1764; Laurens to Joseph Brown, June 29, 1764, in *The Papers of Henry Laurens,* vol. 4, *Sept. 1, 1763–Aug. 31, 1765,* ed. George C. Rogers Jr. (Columbia: University of South Carolina Press, 1974), 281, 305, 314–15, 320–21.

7. Henry Laurens to Paul Trapier, June 25, 1764; Laurens to Joseph Brown, June 26, 1764; Laurens to Timothy Creamer, June 26, 1764; Laurens to Day & Welch, September 10, 1764, December 17, 1764, in ibid., 4:316–19, 412–13, 538.

8. Austin & Laurens to Law, Satterthwaite & Jones, January 12, 1756, in *The Papers of Henry Laurens,* vol. 2, *Nov. 1, 1755–Dec. 31, 1758,* ed. Philip M. Hamer and George C. Rogers Jr. (Columbia: University of South Carolina Press, 1970), 65–66; see also Austin & Laurens to John Knight, December 18, 1755, or January 3, 1756, in ibid., 2:45, 59.

9. *South Carolina Gazette,* October 30, 1752. For the South Carolina quarantine law, see *The Statutes at Large of South Carolina,* 10 vols., ed. Thomas Cooper and David J. McCord (Columbia: Johnston, 1837–41), 3:773–74.

10. Account of sale of slaves from the sloop *Hare* from Sierra Leone, July 17, 1756, in *Papers of Henry Laurens,* 2:257–59; Austin & Laurens to Richard Oswald, July 26, 1756, in ibid., 2:270.

11. Merchants also wrote letters to individual planters at times to encourage them to attend sales; see Littlefield, "Charleston and Internal Slave Redistribution," 94–95; *Papers of Henry Laurens,* 4:305–6.

12. Richard Winn to Mr. S. W. Yongue, September 4, 1798, Richard Winn Papers, 1786–1798, South Caroliniana Library (hereafter referred to as SCL), Columbia.

13. Secretary of State, Misc. Records (Columbia Series), S 213006, Vol. B, 1776–1875, 457–59, South Carolina Department of Archives and History (hereafter referred to as SCDAH), Columbia. Many widows or otherwise independent women quickly adapted to managing financial affairs generally considered the proper role of their husbands or fathers; see Mary Beth Norton, *Liberty's Daughters: The Revolutionary Experience of American Women, 1750–1800* (Ithaca, N.Y.: Cornell University Press, 1980), 132–38.

14. Darold D. Wax, "'New Negroes Are Always in Demand': The Slave Trade in Eighteenth-Century Georgia," *Georgia Historical Quarterly* 68 (Summer 1984): 215–16.

15. Joseph Clay to Mr. [Daniel] Bourdeaux, February 13, 1786, Joseph Clay Papers, vol. 5, Georgia Historical Society (hereafter referred to as GHS), Savannah.

16. Henry Laurens to Elias Ball, July 15, 1765, in *Papers of Henry Laurens*, 4:652.

17. J & E Penman & Co. daybook and account book, 1794, MS no. R 498, 10, SCL; William Ancrum Account Book, 1757–58, 1776–82, SCL.

18. William Ancrum to Marlow Pryor, n.d. [between December 23, 1776, and January 16, 1777], William Ancrum letter book, SCL.

19. William Ancrum Account Book, f.24, SCL.

20. William Ancrum to Joseph Kershaw, December 9, 1777, William Ancrum letter book, SCL. For more on the growth of wagon traffic between Charleston and the backcountry, see Klein, *Unification of a Slave State*, 13. On slaves as wagoners, see Philip D. Morgan, *Slave Counterpoint: Black Culture in the Eighteenth-Century Chesapeake and Lowcountry* (Chapel Hill: University of North Carolina Press, 1998), 56–57.

21. Henry Laurens to James Lawrence, January 1 and 7, 1763, in *The Papers of Henry Laurens*, vol. 3, *Jan. 1, 1759–Aug. 31, 1763*, ed. Philip M. Hamer and George C. Rogers Jr. (Columbia: University of South Carolina Press, 1972), 203–5. Ancrum probably sent slaves to his plantations by boat as well. His letters occasionally mention shipments of corn and other goods down to Charleston by boat, and small boats may have served as the primary mode of transport from his Liberty Hill plantation on the Pee Dee River to Charleston. Ancrum's letters include far less about the travel logistics to Liberty Hill, but that may reflect the relative ease of water travel, since the lack of discussion of wagons to Liberty Hill is in marked contrast to Ancrum's correspondence with the managers at Red Bank and Roundabout; see Ancrum to Marlow Pryor, January 23, 1779, March 5, 1779, and December 7, 1779; Ancrum to Mr. Gerving, October 17, 1778; Ancrum to Joshua Ferral, February 6, 1779 and November 16, 1779, William Ancrum letter book, SCL.

22. Ellis to Mr. Shaw, September 18, 1736, Am 9251, Robert Ellis letter book, 1736–48, 8, Historical Society of Pennsylvania (hereafter referred to as HSP), Philadelphia. The slaves Ellis was selling probably reached Philadelphia via transshipment aboard the sloop *Elizabeth and Lavenia*, which delivered twenty-eight "Negroe Boys and Girls" from Charleston; see *Pennsylvania Gazette*, August 5–12, 1736. For more on Ellis, see Darold D. Wax, "Robert Ellis, Philadelphia Merchant and Slave Trader," *Pennsylvania Magazine of History and Biography* 88 (January 1964): 52–69.

23. John Ryan to Mr. Jacob Kollock, January 25, 1739, Robert Ellis letter book, 1736–48, 170–71, HSP. In an earlier example of slaves sent from Philadelphia down to Delaware, in May 1715, Philadelphia merchant Jonathan Dickinson reported to John Lewis of Jamaica about "ye three Negroes ye Sent" to Dickinson for sale, noting that he had sold them to some

"Low'r Countey [now Delaware] men at Thirty Pounds P head," but Dickinson did not make clear whether he traveled to Delaware with the slaves or whether the "Low'r Countey men" had come to Philadelphia. Jonathan Dickinson letter book, 1715–21, Yi 2 / 1628: Alcove 4, Shelf 12, ff.21–22, Library Company of Philadelphia.

24. Riche to Mr. [Samuel] Tucker, August 1 and August 18, 1761, Am 9261, Thomas Riche letter book, vol. 1, 1750–1764, HSP. For other transactions with Tucker, see ibid., letters dated August 13 and 16 and September 2 and 14, 1762.

25. Riche to Gampert & Heyman & Co., October 21, 1763, Riche letter book, vol. 1, HSP. For an example of Riche referring to being in the country shortly after importing slaves, see ibid., Riche to Mr. Lewis, August 6, 1761.

26. Paul Carrington's 1801 deposition about the 1772 slave trading venture, Carrington family papers, 1761–1964, Section 4, Mss1 C2358 C5, Virginia Historical Society, Richmond. See also Morgan and Nicholls, "Slaves in Piedmont Virginia," 211–12. For more on the *Polly*, see David Eltis, Stephen D. Behrendt, David Richardson, and Manolo Florentino, Trans-Atlantic Slave Trade Database, http://slavevoyages.org/tast/database/search.faces?yearFrom=1514&yearTo=1866&voyageid=17792, accessed July 5, 2011.

27. Invoice book of the *Eadith*, 1758–61, DX/169, 23, Merseyside Maritime Museum, Liverpool, England. For more on the *Eadith*, see Eltis et al., Trans-Atlantic Slave Trade Database, http://slavevoyages.org/tast/database/search.faces?yearFrom=1514&yearTo=1866&voyageid=90873, accessed July 5, 2011.

28. *South Carolina Gazette*, July 27, 1765. See also *Papers of Henry Laurens*, 4:652n9.

29. See sales advertised at Jacksonburgh, *South Carolina Gazette*, August 23 and October 11, 1760; and at Dorchester, ibid., October 26, 1760; see also *Papers of Henry Laurens*, 3:43–44, 52. Other advertisements hint inconclusively at merchants delivering Africans to the backcountry for sale. In 1756, for example, Charleston lawyer James Grindlay advertised "about 25 healthy young slaves" for sale at Jacksonburgh, offering "12 months credit." Grindlay may have been managing an estate sale, but in such cases advertisements typically specified to whom slaves had previously belonged and sellers usually avoided selling on credit. Since Grindlay served as a lawyer for English merchant (and slave trader) William Higginson, it would not be surprising if he used this connection to speculate on slaves for resale in the backcountry. *South Carolina Gazette*, February 5, 1756; for Grindlay's connection to Higginson, see *Papers of Henry Laurens*, 2:181n7.

30. For Woodrop and Douxsaint as slave importers, see "General Duty Books" of the Public Treasurer, SCDAH; for their store at Pon Pon, see *The Papers of Henry Laurens*, vol. 1, *Sept. 11, 1746–Oct. 31, 1755*, ed. Philip M. Hamer (Columbia: University of South Carolina Press, 1968), 99n8.

31. Joseph Clay to James Seagrove, April 16, 1784, Joseph Clay papers, vol. 3, GHS.

32. William Ancrum to Thomas Wade, July 27, 1779, William Ancrum letter book, SCL. While slave imports stalled during the war, Ancrum nonetheless implied an interest to import them if possible by including their current prices in a letter to the English merchants Greenwood and Higginson that same year, August 16, 1779. Such internal distribution was not limited to the mainland. In 1790 former Jamaican colonist Hercules Ross testified in the House of Commons hearings on the slave trade that "there used to be in Kingston many people who bought [arriving Africans] on speculation . . . to carry them to the country, and

retail them." House of Commons of Great Britain, *Abridgment of the Minutes of the Evidence, Taken Before a Committee of the Whole House, to Whom It Was Referred to Consider of the Slave-Trade,* 4 vols. (London, 1790), 4:142–43.

33. Benjamin Perdriau Jr. [Laurens's clerk] to Mathias Seller, April 23, 1765, in *Papers of Henry Laurens,* 4:613.

34. Henry Laurens to Samuel Wragg, October 29, 1764, in *Papers of Henry Laurens,* 4:484–85.

35. Henry Laurens to John Knight, April 14, 1764; Laurens to Smith & Baillies, April 30, 1764; Laurens to Francis Stuart, February 6 and May 24, 1765, in *Papers of Henry Laurens,* 4:246–47, 255–58, 576, 631.

36. Abduhl Rahhahman, "Abduhl Rah[h]Ahman's History [1828]," in *Slave Testimony: Two Centuries of Letters, Speeches, Interviews, and Autobiographies,* ed. John W. Blassingame (Baton Rouge: Louisiana State University Press, 1977), 685.

37. On the journeys of slaves within Africa, see Femi J. Kolapo, "The Igbo and Their Neighbours during the Era of the Atlantic Slave-Trade," *Slavery and Abolition* 25 (April 2004): 114–33; Robin Law, *The Slave Coast of West Africa, 1550–1750: The Impact of the Atlantic Slave Trade on an African Society* (Oxford: Clarendon, 1991), 182–91; Robin Law, *The Oyo Empire, c. 1600–c. 1836: A West African Imperialism in the Era of the Atlantic Slave Trade* (Oxford: Clarendon, 1977), esp. 207–36; Phyllis M. Martin, *The External Trade of the Loango Coast, 1576–1870: The Effects of Changing Commercial Relations on the Vili Kingdom of Loango* (Oxford: Clarendon, 1972), esp. chap. 4; Joseph C. Miller, *Way of Death: Merchant Capitalism and the Angolan Slave Trade, 1730–1830* (Madison: University of Wisconsin Press, 1988), 105–26; Jan Hogendorn, "Economic Modelling of Price Differences in the Slave Trade between the Central Sudan and the Coast," *Slavery and Abolition* 17 (December 1996): 209–22; G. Ugo Nwokeji, "African Conceptions of Gender and the Slave Traffic," *William and Mary Quarterly,* 3rd ser., 58, no. 1 (2001): 47–68; Philip D. Morgan, "The Cultural Implications of the Atlantic Slave Trade: African Regional Origins, American Destinations and New World Developments," in *Routes to Slavery: Direction, Ethnicity and Mortality in the Transatlantic Slave Trade,* ed. David Eltis and David Richardson (London: Cass, 1997), 122–45; Douglas B. Chambers, "Ethnicity in the Diaspora: The Slave-Trade and the Creation of African 'Nations' in the Americas," *Slavery and Abolition* 22 (December 2001): 25–26; David Northrup, "Igbo and Myth Igbo: Culture and Ethnicity in the Atlantic World, 1600–1850," *Slavery and Abolition* 21 (December 2000): 1–20; Jerome S. Handler, "Survivors of the Middle Passage: Life Histories of Enslaved Africans in British America," *Slavery and Abolition* 23 (April 2002): 37–38; Robert A. Sargent, *Economics, Politics and Social Change in the Benue Basin, c. 1300–1700* (Enugu, Nigeria: Fourth Dimension, 1999), esp. 190–95; John Thornton, *Africa and Africans in the Making of the Atlantic World, 1400–1680* (New York: Cambridge University Press, 1992), 194; Charles Piot, "Of Slaves and the Gift: Kabre Sale of Kin during the Era of the Slave Trade," *Journal of African History* 37 (January 1996): 34, 47; Alexander X. Byrd, "Captives and Voyagers: Black Migrants across the Eighteenth-Century World of Olaudah Equiano" (Ph.D. diss., Duke University, 2001), esp. 15, 25–45.

38. Many studies of the Atlantic slave trade ignore dispersal after the Middle Passage, but David Eltis estimates that 5 to 10 percent of Africans arriving in the Americas "quickly moved to other parts of the Americas, as part of the intra-American slave trade." David Eltis,

"The Volume and Structure of the Transatlantic Slave Trade: A Reassessment," *William and Mary Quarterly,* 3rd ser., 58, no. 1 (2001): 17–46. For a higher estimate, see O'Malley, "Final Passages."

39. Gregory E. O'Malley, "Beyond the Middle Passage: Slave Migration from the Caribbean to North America, 1619–1807," *William and Mary Quarterly,* 3rd ser., 66, no. 1 (2009): 125–72.

40. Morgan and Nicholls, "Slaves in Piedmont Virginia," 221–33.

41. Austin & Laurens to Henry Weare & Co., August 30, 1755, in *Papers of Henry Laurens,* 1:326–28.

42. Elizabeth Donnan, ed., *Documents Illustrative of the History of the Slave Trade to America,* 4 vols. (Washington, D.C.: Carnegie Institution of Washington, 1930), 4:236; see also George Burrington's report on the ports of North Carolina, July 27, 1736, CO 5/295, ff.32–3, Public Record Office, Kew, England.

43. *Papers of Henry Laurens,* 2:123–24. These nine Africans sent to Georgetown by Austin and Laurens endured one of the more convoluted journeys to North American slavery. They crossed the Atlantic aboard a French vessel, which was captured upon reaching the Caribbean by the British naval fleet under Comm. Thomas Frankland in the hostilities leading up to the official outbreak of the Seven Years' War. Gedney Clarke purchased one hundred of the confiscated slaves in Barbados and transshipped them to Laurens, who then transshipped nine of them to Georgetown. For another example of Laurens sending less desirable slaves to a marginal port for easier sale, see Austin & Laurens to John Yeates, June 12, 1755, in *Papers of Henry Laurens,* 1:265–66. Laurens employed a similar dispersal strategy with "50 New Negroes" whom he described as "wretched" and "extreamly meagre & thin," transshipped to him from St. Kitts in 1764, sending them to a Beaufort merchant for resale; see Laurens to John Knight, April 14, 1764, and to Smith & Baillies, April 30, 1764, in *Papers of Henry Laurens,* 4:246–47, 255–58.

44. *Papers of Henry Laurens,* 2:123–24.

45. Joseph Clay to Benjamin Stead, September 16, 1775, Joseph Clay & Co. letter book, 1772–76, vol. 2, GHS.

46. Austin & Laurens to Thomas Easton & Co., July 13, 1755, in *Papers of Henry Laurens,* 1:306. At another sale that year, Austin and Laurens noted, "there were forty or fifty [buyers] that came upwards of Seventy Miles distance." Austin & Laurens to Henry Weare & Co., July 2, 1755, 1:281–82.

47. Quoted in Klein, *Unification of a Slave State,* 20.

48. [Riche's clerk] to Henry White, August 24, 1764, Thomas Riche letter book, vol. 2, 1764–71, HSP.

49. Thomas Clarkson, *The Substance of the Evidence of Sundry Persons on the Slave-Trade, Collected in the Course of a Tour Made in the Autumn of the Year 1788* (London: Phillips, 1789), 35.

50. Deyle, *Carry Me Back,* esp. 146–47; Robert H. Gudmestad, "Slave Resistance, Coffles, and the Debates over Slavery in the Nation's Capital," in *The Chattel Principle: Internal Slave Trades in the Americas,* ed. Walter Johnson (New Haven, Conn.: Yale University Press, 2004), 72–90; Tadman, *Speculators and Slaves.*

51. William Ancrum to Marlow Pryor, October 29, 1778, William Ancrum letter book, SCL.

52. Joseph Clay to [unknown], June 9, 1789, Joseph Clay papers, v. 4, 341–42, GHS.

53. James Sanders Guignard, "Directions for W. M. Jervaine," undated [April 1804], Guignard Family papers, letter-sized folder 4, SCL. Moncks Corner did emerge as a sort of travelers' town in the late eighteenth century, offering taverns and accommodations to voyagers to and from the backcountry; see Klein, *Unification of a Slave State,* 19.

54. Thomas Riche to Samuel Tucker, October 18, 1762, Thomas Riche letter book, 1750–64, HSP. Unfortunately only Riche's response survives, not the details of Tucker's complaint.

55. *Pennsylvania Gazette,* October 10, 1751, and May 17, 1759; parenthetical *Negroe* in original.

56. Morgan and Nicholls, "Slaves in Piedmont Virginia," 212.

57. Jonathan Dickinson letter book, 1715–21, f.12, LCP.

58. When Laurens transshipped slaves from Charleston to smaller South Carolina ports, he sometimes complained to his agents about slow sales; see his letter to Joseph Brown in Georgetown, June 29, 1764, in *Papers of Henry Laurens,* 4:320–21.

59. For the particular "workhouse" announcements mentioned, see *South Carolina Gazette,* November 16, 1753, and January 22–29, 1754.

60. *South Carolina Gazette,* August 3, 1765. Overall statistics compiled from advertisements cited in "Searchable CD-ROM transcription of runaway slave advertisements in Charleston newspapers, 1732–1785," compiled by Ruth Holmes Whitehead, call number P 900062, SCDAH.

61. *South Carolina Gazette,* August 26, 1765.

62. For the best discussion of slaves' reactions to being bought and sold, see Johnson, *Soul by Soul.* His work deals with nineteenth-century experiences, so most of the slaves involved were born in the Americas, but nonetheless the more extensive primary sources in slaves' own words for that time period allow for a deeper appreciation of the humiliation of the experience.

63. For "precapitalist," see Klein, *Unification of a Slave State,* 3–4. For other arguments describing African slavery in the Americas as a capitalist enterprise rather than a precursor to capitalism, see Johnson, *The Chattel Principle: Internal Slave Trades in the Americas,* esp. 7–9; Jeffrey Robert Young, *Domesticating Slavery: The Master Class in Georgia and South Carolina, 1670–1837* (Chapel Hill: University of North Carolina Press, 1999), esp. 4–5.

THE M-FACTOR IN
SOUTHERN HISTORY

LOUIS M. KYRIAKOUDES AND PETER A. COCLANIS

In an important 1962 essay, the American studies scholar George Pierson sought to explain the distinctiveness of the American experience to a group of European academics. Rejecting Frederick Jackson Turner's identification of the frontier or David Potter's emphasis on a "people of plenty," Pierson argued that the roots of American exceptionalism lay in what he termed the "M-Factor"—the American propensity to migrate. According to Pierson, mobility, migration, and movement reshaped American institutions, promoted individualism, and spurred individual initiative and, in so doing, provided the key to the development of the American character.[1]

While such broad generalizations have rightly fallen out of favor in historical discourse, we suggest that historians of the Old South can learn from Pierson's insights. In particular the antebellum South, too, had its M-factor, brought on in part by the United States' banning of the international slave trade in 1808. While Pierson envisioned the role of mobility primarily in cultural terms, we see something more fundamental and essentially material at work—the operation of markets, labor markets in particular.

Labor markets in the antebellum South have fascinated people for a long time, beginning with a host of illustrious contemporaries ranging from Frederick Law Olmsted to Daniel Hundley to Harriet Beecher Stowe.[2] Until fairly recently, however, those writing on such markets have been much less concerned with economic analysis than with description, which is hardly surprising in light of the fact that so many of these who participated in such markets did so unwillingly. That is to say, not everyone feels comfortable, even today, analyzing the economic workings of labor markets wherein most of the participants were enslaved. As a result of such concerns, noneconomic questions relating, for example, to the moral character of some of the principals involved (slave traders, most notably) and the often horrific psychosocial effects the workings of such markets had on some of the participants (African American slaves, most obviously) have received far more attention than the economic characteristics of such markets, much less their relative efficiency.

Over the past two decades, this situation has changed dramatically. Although excellent, in some cases truly exceptional work continues to be done on essentially noneconomic aspects of antebellum southern labor markets—the work of Walter Johnson on the internal slave trade comes immediately to mind in this regard—a good deal of innovative and exciting work has also been done explicitly on the economic aspects of such markets.[3] The new economic studies have been as varied as they are important.[4] Some have involved highly technical econometric methods and concerns: for example, the scholarly dustup between John Komlos, on the one hand, and Jonathan B. Pritchett and Herman Freudenberger, on the other, over selectivity and selectivity biases in slave cargoes arriving in antebellum New Orleans.[5] Other work has reframed old questions and/or opened up new ones. Daina Ramey Berry's work, which deals with the economic strategies and bargaining tactics slaves themselves employed to optimize outcomes at sales and auctions, is a good example in this regard.[6]

If many questions relating to the economic workings of southern labor markets are still unanswered or unresolved (in the latter case, think Komlos versus Pritchett), we nonetheless are now pretty clear about several aspects of these markets, to wit: (a) the macro trend informing antebellum southern labor markets, the westward movement of slaves, was due primarily to interregional differences in the productivity of slave labor; (b) most of the interregional movement of slaves resulted from slave sales rather than from the migration westward of slaveholders and their slaves; (c) the overall working of this market, this interregional transfer of labor from lower productivity to higher productivity areas in the South, was economically efficient—much more so, for example, than labor markets in the North during the same period.[7]

We are making great strides in understanding the institutions that mediated these movements, and their selectivity in certain contexts, as work on the New Orleans slave market has revealed. What we lack is a fuller picture of the complexity of slave mobility across the South and a measure of correlates that explain these movements. By taking a labor-market approach, we subsume all slave movements, be they through sale or planter-accompanied migration, under one overarching rubric of *forced migration*. From this perspective it matters little that a planter privileged land among his capital assets and sold slaves or privileged labor, sold land, and migrated. Each represented a reallocation of labor to some degree, and although not a transoceanic voyage as in the days of the legal transatlantic trade treated elsewhere in this volume, each forced move represented a traumatic event, removing slaves from family, community, and familiar locality.[8]

This paper presents our initial attempt to chart the determinants of forced slave migration—slave labor markets—at the intercounty level. We employ new data—the recently drawn individual-level samples of the 1850 and 1860 slave census. Broadly speaking, we ask which demographic characteristics among their slave labor force did slave owners select when they sought to sell or migrate. And just as important, how did patterns of slave resistance—both passive and active—influence selectivity of forced slave migration? Finally we consider the ways in which the slave trade, by efficiently allocating labor across the region, helped to maintain the economic viability of the institution.

Data and Methods

New quantitative sources provide the empirical basis for constructing a comprehensive portrait of county and plantation-level slave population characteristics. The principal data employed in this study are derived from the Integrated Public Use Manuscript samples of the 1850 and 1860 slave censuses produced by the University of Minnesota Population Center. Overall the samples are 5 percent samples, except for 1860, where approximately one-fifth of slave counties were oversampled at 100 percent. With weighting, both the 1850 and 1860 samples are representative.[9]

The slave-census enumerations suffer from some well-known shortcomings that limit what they can tell about the slave population. The enumerations tell very little about the registrants' characteristics beyond basic information on age, sex, and residence. The registrations are organized solely by slaveholder, and therefore, unlike the census of the free population, enumerators did not record the subjects' household or family relationships; indeed despite attempts by free-state politicians, the censuses did not even record the names of individual slaves, save for centenarians in 1860.[10]

There is, however, much we can learn about the characteristics of the slave population from these limited data. The data reveal local population patterns as well as local slaveholding characteristics. From age and sex data, we can infer much about slave populations at the county level. This study employs the forward-survival-rate method of calculating estimates of net migration for slaves at the county level. The method is straightforward, even if the actual data manipulation is not. Age cohorts by sex at the beginning of a decade are multiplied by a survival ratio derived from the entire population that reflects an estimated mortality rate. The resulting figure is then compared to the actual population of the corresponding age cohort at the end of the decade in each county. The difference between the actual population and the estimated surviving population is attributed to net migration, positive or negative. Survival ratios are calculated by dividing each national cohort population of slaves at the second census by the corresponding age cohort at the preceding census.[11]

The method assumes a "closed" population that is unaffected by immigration or emigration. This is a reasonable assumption for the American slave population in the 1840s and 1850s, given the abolition of slave imports in 1808. While smuggling of foreign-born slaves into the South persisted after the ban on slave imports, the volume was statistically insignificant in the 1840s and 1850s. As Robert Fogel's analysis of place-of-birth data from black Civil War regiments shows, the incidence of former slaves of African nativity was zero.[12] Philip Curtin offers the estimate of approximately twenty thousand slave imports between 1840 and 1860. Even the higher—and empirically unsubstantiated—estimates of the illegal slave trade of a half million slaves smuggled into the country during the period of 1808–1860 would not lead to statistically significant differences in our calculations.[13]

The chief challenge posed by the data is the issue of spatial compatibility of individual counties across the 1840, 1850, and 1860 census years. There were dramatic changes in county boundaries during this 25 period, as new counties were carved out of existing counties and the boundaries of existing counties were adjusted. For county-level migration estimates to be comparable over time, the spatial units must be similar. This problem can largely be overcome by the use of a longitudinal template developed by Patrick Moran and Peggy Hargis. The template creates larger, multicounty units to correct for changes in boundaries over time. While the template allows for an analysis of intrastate migration patterns, its method of county consolidations to correct for boundary changes unavoidably reduces the number of county units available for analysis, in some cases by as much as two-thirds.[14]

County-Level Variations in Slave Net Migration

What, then, have we found? Of course the general shift of slave population across the South during the antebellum period was from the older slave states and the slave states of the Upper South to the newer, faster-growing states of the Lower South. Nothing in this analysis will contradict this basic fact of the forced migration of slaves. Older slave states—Virginia, North Carolina, and South Carolina in particular—showed heavy net forced out-migration during the entire twenty-year period from 1840 to 1860, reflecting the power of the interstate slave trade to satisfy the labor demands of Lower South planters. Mississippi, Louisiana, Arkansas, and Texas, for example, showed heavy in-migration during this entire period as the plantation system in these states expanded dramatically. Other states showed more complex patterns. Florida lost slave population to migration in the 1840s but gained in the 1850s. Georgia followed an opposite pattern, experiencing heavy in-migration in the 1840s and heavy out-migration the following decade. Complex labor-market demands were creating incentives for slaveholders to reallocate their labor in complex ways.[15]

TABLE 1. FORCED MIGRATION OF SLAVES BY SUBREGION, 1840–1860
(Nat Migration Rate per 1,000)

Subregion	Males		Females	
	1840–50	1850–60	1840–50	1850–60
East Coast slave states	-75.41	-68.28	-77.06	-78.63
Central South slave states (Ala., Ky., Miss., Tenn.)	40.07	-11.17	44.03	-16.01
Trans-Mississippi West slave states	298.86	138.95	264.4	125.1

Source: Calculated from Census Data, IPUMS Samples

County-level net migration estimates reveal more complex patterns that are obscured by broad regional and state measures. Every slave state had within its borders regions that either gained or lost slave population in response to localized economic conditions. Our county-level net migration calculations show that state-level net migration estimates obscure what were significant variations in slave net migration within southern states. The intrastate patterns of forced slave migration indicate that slave labor markets were spatially complex and responsive to local and subregional changes in slave-labor demands. No matter whether states as a whole were net importers or net exporters of slaves, a sizable number of counties exhibited migration trends that ran counter to the overall state trend. For example, while Virginia experienced heavy net out-migration of slaves overall, about 30 percent of its counties showed in-migration of slaves in the 1840s and 1850s. Among the states experiencing heavy in-migration, the data show similar patterns of intrastate redistribution. In Mississippi, which in the 1840s experienced an estimated net in-migration of 33,755 slaves, ten of twenty-four standardized county units employed in this study showed net out-migration. Likewise in Alabama in the 1840s, ten of its eighteen standardized county units exhibited out-migration, while in the 1850s eleven of the twenty county units showed out-migration. As table 2 indicates, such variation in county-level slave migration occurred in all slave states, both in the Upper South and Lower South.

TABLE 2. COUNTY NET MIGRATION STATUS

	1840–50			1850–60		
	Net Out-Migration	*Net In-Migration*	*County Units (n)*	*Net Out-Migration*	*Net In-Migration*	*County Units (n)*
Alabama	10	8	18	11	9	20
Arkansas	2	8	10	3	12	15
Florida	6	8	14	7	10	17
Georgia	20	25	45	27	14	41
Kentucky	32	26	58	45	22	67
Louisiana	9	14	23	13	15	28
Maryland	11	5	16	11	5	16
Mississippi	10	14	24	7	19	26

NOTE: Standardized county units do not equal actual number of counties due to consolidation of individual counties in the data set to account for boundary changes and the creation of new counties.

Source: Calculated from IPUMS Slave Census Samples

These localized, intrastate labor markets operated within the context of the larger tide of movement to the more productive lands of the Lower South, creating an internal slave frontier in each slave state to which a significant portion of the state's slave population was redistributed. For example in North Carolina, which had heavy slave out-migration in the 1840s, the counties of the southeastern portion of the state—Columbus, Brunswick, and New Hanover—showed significant in-migration. A decade later, while most counties exported slaves, there was a sharp internal shift of slave population to piedmont counties of the state as cotton production increased, presaging postbellum economic and population patterns that resulted in sharp increases in cotton production and population in the southern upcountry. This intrastate forced migration represented a critical mechanism by which the southern slave economy sustained its economic viability by adapting to changing labor demands.

Indeed the willingness of slave owners to sell their slave property when it promoted their business and financial interests formed the foundation of the economic efficiency of slave-labor markets. Slave family relationships generally were of no concern to owners seeking to sell, and shorter-distance, intrastate moves were no less disruptive to the lives of the enslaved than longer, interstate moves. Former slaves recalled these shorter-distance moves with the same bitterness and anger as those who were forced to move greater distances. Lillie Williams, who was born in central Mississippi, recalled being separated from her mother-in-law, who was auctioned "on a tall stump" to a planter in Aberdeen, Mississippi, in the northeastern corner of the state. Rachel Gains remembered the degradation of being sold to a planter in Trenton, Kentucky, "jes lak dey sold cows en horses," while her sister was sold to another master in Bowling Green, some sixty miles to the northeast.[16]

Age and Sex Selectivity

Forced slave migration in the antebellum South through sale or planter migration, like all migrations, was a selective process. Much of what is known about the selectivity of slave trading comes from studies of the New Orleans slave market and the pioneering quantitative work of Richard Sutch and Michael Tadman. New Orleans was an important exchange whereby Upper South slaves were sold to planters in the lower Mississippi Valley region, indeed, but it was one that accounted for only a portion of the total interregional movement of slaves.[17] By examining the contours of net migration between the three broad regions of the South—the Eastern Seaboard states, the central southern states, and the trans-Mississippi states—we can compose a more focused picture of the age and gender selectivity of forced slave migration across the region.

Forced slave migration was dominated by young adults. Planters most often selected young adults in the prime of their working lives because such individuals tended to be in the highest demand. The well-known slave trader Isaac Franklin wrote to his partner, Rice Ballard, about slave buyers' preferences for young adult men: "but few men over 20 years of age [have been sold] as the planters appear not to like men above that age."[18] The preference for the young is supported by the net migration estimates for the 1840s and 1850s. As shown in figures 1 and 2, which

**Figure 1. Slave Net Migration Rates by
Sex and Age by Subregion, 1840–50**

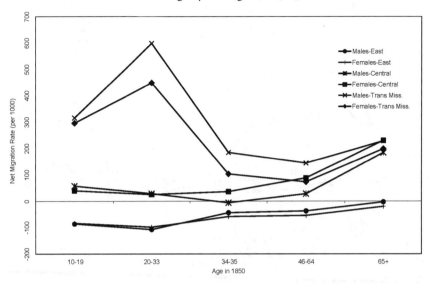

summarize net migration rates by age cohorts for the eastern, central, and trans-Mississippi South, the young were most likely to be forcibly moved from the eastern southern states, and they were most likely to be forcibly moved into the rapidly growing states of the trans-Mississippi South.[19] But the migration patterns are more complex than suggested by Franklin's observation. Our estimate of net migration rates by age cohort, as shown in figures 1 and 2, indicate that there were smaller but nonetheless significant net migrations of older slaves out of the eastern South and into the central and trans-Mississippi southern states. While forced migration was dominated by the young, older slaves formed a part of it, even on the cotton frontier.

Franklin observed that the slave market was dominated by the demand for male slaves. However, the broader perspective provided by our net migration estimates reveals that women made up a significant component of the forced migration, even on the newest regions of the cotton frontier of the trans-Mississippi South. Again, as the cohort net migration estimates in figures 1 and 2 indicate, slave purchasers showed a strong preference for balancing their slave labor forces with roughly equal numbers of young men and women. The data reveal a notable preference for males in the 1840s only in the states of the trans-Mississippi South. Remove the sugar

Figure 2. Slave Net Migration Rates by Sex and Age by Subregion, 1850–60

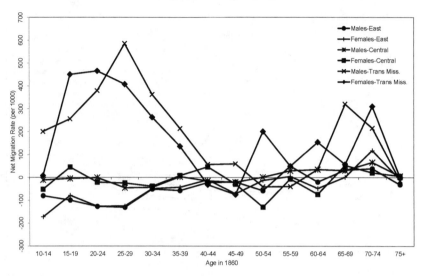

parishes of south Louisiana—an area with grueling labor requirements—and the male-female differential nearly disappears. In the Eastern Seaboard states and the central southern states, the forced migration rates for male and female slaves were nearly identical. In the 1850s the rates of male and female forced slave migration converged even further, especially on the frontier. This pattern diverges sharply from that of the transatlantic slave trade of the eighteenth and nineteenth centuries, where the sex ratio was generally close to two-to-one male. It also diverges sharply from the general patterns of frontier and long-distance migration, which had tended to be overwhelmingly dominated by males.[20] Everywhere in the South, slaves formed families and had children. As table 3 shows, there were no significant differences in fertility, as measured by the child-woman ratio, among the East Coast southern states, the central states, or the trans-Mississippi frontier.

TABLE 3. CHILD-WOMAN RATIO AMONG THE SLAVE POPULATION BY REGION, 1860

Subregion	Mean Child-Woman Ratio
East Coast South	1261.53
Central South (Ala., Ky., Miss., Tenn.)	1296.47
Trans-Mississippi South	1253.32

NOTE: Child-woman ratio is calculated as all children, age 0–5, per women, age 15–45, and multiplied by 1000.

Source: IPUMS Slave Census Sample

Why, then, did the forced migration of slaves to the newest sections of the cotton frontier reveal populations relatively balanced in age and sex? Why were the trans-Mississippi cotton regions not dominated to a greater extent by young slave men? We offer a possible explanation. It is likely that slave owners, especially those on the frontier, saw the slave family as an institution that tied slaves to their plantation and their locality. On the one hand, owners generally had no compunction about disrupting *preexisting* slave families with abandon to satisfy the demands of the market; that much is clear from even a cursory reading of the extant slave narratives, which are replete with stories of children sold from mothers and husbands sold from wives. George Womble, who was born into slavery in 1843, saw both his father and mother sold away from his Georgia plantation while he was still a small child. Tom McGruder, born in Virginia, passed through three different slave traders' hands before ending up in Georgia, separated from his mother and siblings.[21] In such cases the familial ties between husbands and wives, parents and children, and extended family members had little market, social, or cultural value to slave owners and were disrupted in a matter-of-fact, businesslike manner.[22] In fact recent research suggests that slave buyers in the West could often get "family discounts" if they were willing to take families intact, especially if such families included young children and/or weak or infirm members.[23]

That said, the data suggest that when assembling a plantation labor force, planters sought to create the potential for family formation by roughly balancing men and women of marriageable age.[24] An all-male plantation workforce was rare, and planters sought to situate their slaves in families. While demographic data offer no clear indication of motive, planters were likely driven by two considerations. Situating slaves in demographic environments conducive to family formation, even in a frontier environment where ostensibly there would be a productivity advantage to an all-male slave labor force, may have been motivated by the desire to earn a return on slave children. However, Richard Steckel's analysis of New Orleans slave manifests and other demographic data indicates that planters were reluctant to devote resources to the raising of slave children. They rarely provided adequate food for slave children. Slave child mortality reached astronomical levels. Birth weights were shockingly low, and measures of net nutrition derived from anthropometric data indicate that slave children were raised in an environment of privation and malnourishment. Planters may have promoted high fertility, but they invested little in the care and feeding of slave children until they reached an age where they could work.[25]

Another explanation is that slave resistance, both active and passive, influenced the selectivity of the slave trade, particularly on the cotton frontier. While the slave trade removed young adults from their families and communities, those forcibly removed still sought the opportunity to form families as they proceeded through the life cycle. The demographic contours of forced slave migration suggests that planters may have recognized this desire and sought to shape their labor force in a manner so as to offer opportunities for family formation as a means of accommodation to the demands of their bondmen and bondwomen.

Over the last two scholarly generations, a rich literature on the strength of the African American family under slavery has been accumulating. In this regard there is a good deal of evidence that for whatever reasons slaveholders in the Lower South encouraged slave marriages and family formation. One Mississippi planter, writing in almost stylized form in *De Bow's Review* in 1851, stated that he provided a nursery on his estate, encouraged marriages among his slaves, and "punished, with some severity, departures from marital obligation." In his travels in the area, Olmsted often (but not always) encountered planters with similar views. Certainly the child-woman ratio in the Lower South—and the adult sex ratio of both forced migrants and adult slaves in the antebellum South generally—were all consistent with social orders where marriage and family formation constituted the norm.[26]

The forced migration of slaves after the international trade ban drove population redistribution across the region. The "M-factor" of migration and markets shaped the fundamental operation of the slave system, revealing the mechanism that lay behind movements of slaves within states as well as between the Upper South and Lower South. Forced slave migration gave the system the economic flexibility necessary to keep slavery profitable for individual slave owners and viable across the region. It is notable that the westward migration of black southerners did not cease with slavery's demise. Once they were able to select themselves and move freely on their own accord, freedmen continued to head to western lands in the trans-Mississippi South and beyond. Similarly the internal cotton frontier continued to experience significant population movements, such as the settling of the Mississippi Delta in the 1880s and 1890s.[27] Similar fundamental economic incentives operated beneath the forced migration of slaves and the free migrations after abolition. As historians reevaluate the slave trade, focus on these complex networks of forced migration is needed.

As the slave trade is reevaluated in its totality, there is also a need to assess the similarities and differences among the complex networks of forced migration in all periods—when the international trade was still legal, between 1808 and the abolition of slavery in the United States, and after abolition—by looking at what stayed the same and what really changed in each of these eras. In doing so researchers will be able to provide more precise economic descriptions of the effects of abolition.

Notes

1. George W. Pierson, "The M-Factor in American History," *American Quarterly* 14 (Summer 1962): 275–89, esp. 283.

2. Frederick Law Olmsted, *A Journey in the Seaboard Slave States: With Remarks on Their Economy* (New York: Dix & Edwards, 1856); D. R. Hundley, *Social Relations in Our Southern States* (New York: Price, 1860); Harriet Beecher Stowe, *Uncle Tom's Cabin* (London: Routledge, 1853).

3. Walter Johnson, *Soul by Soul: Life inside the Antebellum Slave Market* (Cambridge, Mass.: Harvard University Press, 1999). Also see Edward E. Baptist, "'Cuffy,' 'Fancy Maids,' and 'One-Eyed Men': Rape, Commodification, and the Domestic Slave Trade in the United States," *American Historical Review* 106 (December 2001): 1619–50.

4. See, for example, Gavin Wright, *The Political Economy of the Cotton South: Households, Markets, and Wealth in the Nineteenth Century* (New York: Norton, 1978); Gavin Wright, *Old South, New South: Revolutions in the Southern Economy since the Civil War* (New York: Basic, 1986), esp. 17–80; Michael Tadman, *Speculators and Slaves: Masters, Traders, and Slaves in the Old South* (Madison: University of Wisconsin Press, 1989); Herman Freudenberger and Jonathan B. Pritchett, "The Domestic United States Slave Trade: New Evidence," *Journal of Interdisciplinary History* 21 (Winter 1991): 447–77; Joshua L. Rosenbloom, *Looking for Work, Searching for Workers: American Labor Markets during Industrialization* (New York: Cambridge University Press, 2002); Robert H. Gudmestad, *A Troublesome Commerce: The Transformation of the Interstate Slave Trade* (Baton Rouge: Louisiana State University Press, 2003); Lacy K. Ford, "Reconsidering the Internal Slave Trade: Paternalism, Markets, and the Character of the Old South," in *The Chattel Principle: Internal Slave Trades in the Americas,* ed. Walter Johnson (New Haven, Conn.: Yale University Press, 2004), 143–64; Adam Rothman, *Slave Country: American Expansion and the Origins of the Deep South* (Cambridge, Mass.: Harvard University Press, 2005); Steven Deyle, *Carry Me Back: The Domestic Slave Trade in American Life* (New York: Oxford University Press, 2005); Tomoko Yagyu, "Slave Traders and Planters in the Expanding South: Entrepreneurial Strategies, Business Networks, and Western Migration in the Atlantic World, 1787–1859" (Ph.D. diss., University of North Carolina, 2006).

5. Freudenberger and Pritchett, "Domestic United States Slave Trade"; Jonathan B. Pritchett and Herman Freudenberger, "A Peculiar Sample: The Selection of Slaves for the New Orleans Market," *Journal of Economic History* 52 (March 1992): 109–27; John Komlos and Bjorn Alecke, "The Economics of Antebellum Slave Heights Reconsidered," *Journal of Interdisciplinary History* 26 (Winter 1996): 437–57; Jonathan B. Pritchett, "The Interregional Slave Trade and the Selection of Slaves for the New Orleans Market," *Journal of Interdisciplinary History* 28 (Summer 1997): 57–85.

6. Daina Ramey Berry, "'We'm Fus' Rate Bargain': Value, Labor, and Price in a Georgia Slave Community," in Johnson, *Chattel Principle,* 55–71; Daina Ramey Berry, *'Swing the Sickle for the Harvest Is Ripe': Gender and Slavery in Antebellum Georgia* (Urbana: University of Illinois Press, 2007).

7. The above generalizations are based on our reading of the literature cited in note 4. On the relative efficiency of southern labor markets in the antebellum period, see especially Rosenbloom, *Looking for Work.*

8. Anthony E. Kaye, *Joining Places: Slave Neighborhoods in the Old South* (Chapel Hill: University of North Carolina Press, 2007) explores the importance of local neighborhood connections in the formation of slave communities.

9. Russell Menard, Trent Alexander, Jason Digman, and J. David Hacker, *Public Use Microdata Samples of the Slave Population of 1850–1860* (Minneapolis: Minnesota Population Center, University of Minnesota, 2004), http://usa.ipums.org/usa/slavepums.

10. The southern congressional delegation, led by South Carolina senator Andrew Butler, successfully opposed a proposed slave census schedule resembling the one used for the free

population that would record slaves' names and family relations. See Margo Anderson, *The American Census: A Social History* (New Haven, Conn.: Yale University Press, 1990), 39–42.

11. Richard Sutch used a similar method on state-level data in "The Breeding of Slaves for Sale and the Westward Expansion of Slavery, 1850–1860," in *Race and Slavery in the Western Hemisphere: Quantitative Studies,* ed. Stanley L. Engerman and Eugene D. Genovese (Princeton, N.J.: Princeton University Press, 1975), 173–210. A recent discussion of the method is Peter A. Morrison, Thomas Bryan, and David Swanson, "Internal Migration and Short Distance Mobility," in *The Methods and Materials of Demography,* 2nd ed. (San Diego: Elsevier Academic, 2004), 472–74.

12. Robert W. Fogel, "Problems in Measuring the Extent of Slave Smuggling," in *Without Consent or Contract: Evidence and Methods,* ed. Robert W. Fogel, Ralph A. Gallatine, and Richard Manning (New York: Norton, 1992), 50–52.

13. Philip D. Curtin, *The Atlantic Slave Trade: A Census* (Madison: University of Wisconsin Press, 1969), 74. The upper bound of estimates of slave imports for the 1840–1860 period is 350,000, but this estimate is not based upon any significant empirical foundation. See Peter D. McClelland and Richard J. Zeckhauser, *Demographic Dimensions of the New Republic: American Interregional Migration, Vital Statistics, and Manumissions, 1800–1860* (Cambridge: Cambridge University Press, 1982), 46–49, 123.

14. Patrick M. Horan and Peggy G. Hargis, *County Longitudinal Template, 1840–1990* [computer file], ICPSR06576–v1 (Ann Arbor, Mich.: Inter-University Consortium for Political and Social Research, 1995). We are currently in the process of creating county templates for the 1840–60 period that will result in far fewer county consolidations and, consequently, more cases. We gratefully acknowledge Prof. Peggy Hargis of Georgia Southern University for her generosity in sharing the research materials gathered for her county template database.

15. Estimates for state-level slave net migration can be found in McClelland and Zeckhauser, *Demographic Dimensions,* 159–64; Sutch, "Breeding of Slaves," 173–210; and Tadman, *Speculators and Slaves,* 12.

16. Lillie Williams interview, *Born in Slavery: Slave Narratives from the Federal Writers' Project, 1936–1938,* vol. 2, *Arkansas Narratives,* pt. 7 (Washington, D.C.: Library of Congress, 1941), 178; Rachel Gaines Interview, *Born in Slavery,* vol. 15, *Tennessee Narratives,* 18.

17. Pritchett, "Interregional Slave Trade," 58–60; Tadman, *Speculators and Slaves,* 22–31; Sutch, "Breeding of Slaves," 173–210.

18. Quoted in Yagyu, "Slave Traders," 153–56; quotation from p. 153–54.

19. The eastern southern states are defined as Delaware, Maryland, the District of Columbia, Virginia, North and South Carolina, Georgia, and Florida. The central southern states are Kentucky, Tennessee, Alabama, and Mississippi. Trans-Mississippi southern states include Louisiana, Arkansas, and Texas (for the 1850–60 period only). Missouri was excluded from the analysis due to the small number of slaves involved.

20. David Eltis and Stanley Engerman, "Was the Slave Trade Dominated by Men?" *Journal of Interdisciplinary History* 23 (Autumn 1992): 237–57. See also Everett S. Lee, "A Theory of Migration," *Demography* 3, no. 1 (1966): 47–57.

21. George Womble Narrative, *Born in Slavery,* vol. 4, *Georgia Narratives,* pt. 4, 179; Tom McGruder Narrative, *Born in Slavery,* vol. 4, *Georgia Narratives,* pt. 3, 77.

22. See, for example, Susan Eva O'Donovan, "Traded Babies: Enslaved Children in America's Domestic Migration, 1820–60," in *Children in Slavery through the Ages,* ed. Gwyn Campbell, Suzanne Miers, and Joseph C. Miller (Athens: Ohio University Press, 2009), 88–102.

23. Charles W. Calomiris and Jonathan B. Pritchett, "Preserving Slave Families for Profit: Traders' Incentives and Pricing in the New Orleans Slave Market," *Journal of Economic History* 69 (December 2009): 986–1011.

24. For evidence of fertility-based slave-selection criteria and pronatalist polices among frontier planters, see, for example, Johnson, *Soul by Soul,* 71, 91, 94, 144; Deyle, *Carry Me Back,* 28–29, 46; Yagyu, "Slave Traders," 110; Marie Jenkins Schwartz, *Birthing a Slave: Motherhood and Medicine in the Antebellum South* (Cambridge, Mass.: Harvard University Press, 2006), 9–31.

25. Richard H. Steckel, "Work, Disease, and Diet in the Health and Mortality of American Slaves," in *Without Consent or Contract: The Rise and Fall of American Slavery (Technical Papers),* vol. 2, *Conditions of Slave Life and the Transition to Freedom,* ed. Robert William Fogel and Stanley L. Engerman (New York: Norton, 1992), 489–507.

26. "Management of Negroes upon Southern Estates," *De Bow's Review* 10 (June 1851): 621–27, esp. 623; Frederick Law Olmsted, *A Journey in the Back Country 1853–1854* (1860; repr., New York: Schocken, 1970), 72–75, 89, 153–54. On sex ratios and adult sex ratios among African American slaves in the South from 1820 to 1860, see John W. Blassingame, *The Slave Community: Plantation Life in the Antebellum South,* rev. and enlarged ed. (New York: Oxford University Press, 1979), 150.

27. Robert Higgs, *Competition and Coercion: Blacks in the American Economy, 1865–1914* (Chicago: University of Chicago Press, 1977), 24–32; Clyde Woods, *Development Arrested: The Blues and Plantation Power in the Mississippi Delta* (New York: Verso, 1998).

AN AMBIGUOUS LEGACY

The Closing of the African Slave Trade and America's Own Middle Passage

STEVEN DEYLE

In a widely reprinted sermon given on January 1, 1808, in celebration of the official closing of the African slave trade into the United States, Philadelphia clergyman Absalom Jones gave thanks to God and the nation's leaders for ending the country's participation in this horrible traffic. According to Jones, God had finally *"come down to deliver* our suffering country-men from the hands of their oppressors." No more would American slaves be "exposed for sale, like horses and cattle," or would the nation "any more witness the anguish of families, parted for ever by a publick sale." Jones ended his sermon by proposing that "the first of January, the day of the abolition of the slave trade in our country, be set apart in every year, as a day of publick thanksgiving for that mercy."[1]

The sentiments expressed by Jones, and in similar sermons preached that day by African American ministers in New York, struck a responsive chord among free blacks in the North. By the following year, they were calling January 1 a day of "National Jubilee," and for the next two decades, African Americans in Philadelphia and New York celebrated that day with special sermons in their churches and parades through their streets. At the center of these celebrations was the belief among most free blacks, as well as many whites in the North, that the closing of the African trade would lead to the ending of slavery in the nation. For the most part, these New Year's Day sermons echoed this sentiment and followed the themes first set out by Reverend Jones. In his sermon in 1812, Russell Parrott called the closing of the African trade "a great and important event" that will "effect a total abolition of that shameful traffic in the bones and sinews of man." Ten years later Jeremiah Gloucester argued that this action had brought "a ray of genuine greatness and glory" to the nation.[2]

By the end of the 1820s, however, these slave trade commemorations had all but disappeared from northern cities, and African American leaders no longer spoke of a National Jubilee. Supporters of the closing of the African trade experienced a growing disillusionment with the significance of this event. There were several reasons for this transformation, including the blatant violation of the slave-trading laws by smugglers and the increasing public ridicule and violence by whites against blacks at their celebratory festivals. But the main reason for the decrease in public celebrations was the growing recognition that the closing of the African trade was not going to end slavery in the nation as many had hoped. In fact in those southern states that still retained the institution, slavery was becoming even more entrenched than it was before. Most important, the ending of the African trade in 1808 led to the creation of a terrible new middle passage within the United States. The number of American-born slaves forcibly transported from the Upper South to the Lower South in this new domestic slave trade would eventually exceed the number of African-born slaves brought to British North America. Instead of ending the public sale of humans like cattle or the tearing apart of families through sale, as Absalom Jones and others had predicted, such scenes were becoming more commonplace. The closing of the African slave trade did have a great impact upon American society; it was just not the one that most of the act's supporters had intended. The emergence of a new American slave trade ultimately had devastating consequences for the nation, and for most enslaved African Americans, it actually made their lives worse. No wonder supporters of the African trade's closing developed ambivalent feelings toward this event. Its unforeseen consequences dampened the nation's desire to celebrate this historic accomplishment and helps explain our continued preference to simply ignore its anniversary. The selective amnesia that began in the 1830s has continued to the present day, as can be seen in the nation's recent reluctance to embrace the bicentennial anniversary of this event in 2008.

By banning the African trade but not also simultaneously abolishing slavery itself, the United States had opened the door to the creation of this new American slave trade. In fact as long as slavery remained legal and there was a continued demand for slaves in the southern states, the closing of the African trade made a new domestic slave trade inevitable. Providing the fuel for the southern demand for slaves was the strong international demand for cotton. As more and more land was opened up in the Old Southwest or turned over to cotton production, planters in the new cotton states developed an almost insatiable demand for slaves. Because the nation had closed off all legal outside sources of supply, they could satisfy this demand only through a redistribution of the existing slave population. Recognizing that planters in the new cotton states were willing to pay hundreds of dollars more per slave than were owners in the older states, thousands of southern speculators transported hundreds of thousands of bondspeople from the Upper South and seaboard states to the markets of the Southwest.[3]

By transferring slave labor from parts of the South where there were excess slave populations to those areas where slaves were most in demand, this new American slave trade soon completely transformed southern society. From 1790 to 1860, Americans forcibly transported more than 1 million African American slaves from the Upper South to the Lower South; approximately two-thirds of these slaves arrived there as a result of sale. Twice as many individuals were sold locally within state lines. Slave sales occurred in every southern city and village, and coffles of slaves could be found on every southern highway, waterway, and railroad. This new domestic slave trade, in all its components, was the lifeblood of the nineteenth-century southern slave system. Without it the institution would have ceased to exist.[4]

The American slave trade brought great wealth to the South and the nation, but this wealth came with a terrible price. Nationally it resulted in long-term political changes that would eventually tear the country apart and culminate in bloody civil war. Because the demand for slaves was always greater in the Lower South than elsewhere, planters there drove up the price of slaves throughout the region. The rising prices made it increasingly difficult for those who wished to purchase slaves but played a crucial role in solidifying the white South's commitment to slavery. By 1860 price inflation had made slave property the most valuable capital asset in the slaveholding states, worth even more than the land the slaves worked. But it had also made slavery too valuable and too crucial a part of the southern economy for slave owners to ever give it up. When Abraham Lincoln's 1860 election threatened the security of this investment, slaveholding politicians—especially those in the Deep South, where slavery played a greater role in their economy—believed that they had little choice but to secede. Ironically by leaving the Union to protect slavery, the actions of these southern politicians resulted in a self-destructive war and the institution's ultimate demise.[5]

But for Absalom Jones and other African American leaders, the most inexcusable price that the nation had to pay for the American slave trade was the unconscionable pain and suffering that it brought to millions of this country's inhabitants. For American-born slaves the closing of the African trade now meant that sale posed a much greater threat to their lives and even more devastating and lifelong consequences. The selling of humans from one colonist to another had always taken place, but in the eighteenth century these sales usually involved either entire estates or the occasional individual sold to settle debts and balance accounts. After the African trade was closed off, all American-born slaves faced a greater possibility of sale, as anyone who wished to purchase slaves now had to do so from within the nation's existing supply of human property. This increased chance of sale proved especially true for those people living in the Upper South states neighboring the Chesapeake Bay, as this region was where most of the enslaved population lived. Moreover the region had a perceived surplus of slaves, so it supplied most of the commodities for the domestic trade, which carried these African Americans to the Southwest, where slaves were in greater demand. American-born slaves now also faced a greater probability of being forever separated from family and friends, as westward expansion meant that most individuals caught in America's new middle passage were being forcibly carried further and further from home. Not all black southerners became victims in this new domestic trade, but it was an ever-present reality of life for most African Americans in the South, and few families were untouched by it. It has been estimated that at least half of all enslaved families in the Upper South were broken through the long-distance trade through the sale of either a spouse or a child. Yet when combined with the even larger local trade, the percentage was almost certainly much higher, and sales destroyed countless families in both the Upper South and Lower South.[6]

The new domestic trade also impacted American-born slaves by accelerating changes that were occurring in white southerners' perceptions of their slave property. One especially demeaning example of this change was in slave owners' views of black women. During the colonial period, most southern slave owners valued enslaved women primarily for their ability to perform labor. By the late eighteenth century, this perception began to change as the importation of Africans tapered off during the American Revolution. After the supply of Africans was closed off in 1808, southern slave owners now began to value their female property for their ability to reproduce. Enslaved offspring had become a valuable commodity. Slave owners recognized the capital gains that each slave birth brought to their estates or the extra profits that the sale of these offspring could bring. While a slave woman's fecundity became important for owners throughout the South, this trait proved especially true in the slave-exporting states of the Upper South. Typical of the slave owners in this region was Thomas Jefferson of Virginia, who regarded "a woman who brings a child every two years as more profitable than the best man of the farm." Unfortunately in states such as Virginia, enslaved women who did not regularly reproduce often found themselves exported to the Deep South for this failure to be economically profitable for their former owners.[7]

This new perception of enslaved women as breeders likewise carried over in the way that they were treated while in the slave trade. Women had to confront embarrassing assaults upon their modesty and dignity, especially when sold at public auction. According to one visitor to an auction in Richmond, he had "never looked upon a more disgusting sight, young girls are put on the stand, & undergo the most indecent examination & questioning." Particularly insulting were the examinations to check a young woman's nursing ability. As one former slave explained, they would "take her by her breasts and pull dem to show how good she was built for raisin' chillun." While women were not generally examined in as intimate detail as men, they still had strange men grabbing their arms, legs, and breasts and sticking dirty fingers in their mouths to check their teeth. And if a potential purchaser desired, he could examine a woman's genitals, normally behind a screen, to check for venereal disease or a prolapsed uterus, both of which were common enough to elicit concern. Moreover slave auctioneers went out of their way to create a sexually charged atmosphere for their predominantly male customers. As one visitor to New Orleans noted when describing one of these men: "When a woman is sold, he usually puts his audience in good humour by a few indecent jokes."[8]

In addition to changing views toward women, the development of the domestic slave trade also altered the perception of enslaved children, who now came to be seen as commodities in their own right and were often the first individuals sold. The reason for this was simple. As one eighteenth-century Virginian explained when recommending such a sale: "The only objection to this scheme is, that it will be cruel to part them from their parents, but what can be done. They alone can be sold without great loss to you, and at present they are a charge." With the emergence of the American slave trade, more and more children began to be viewed as a quick source of cash, especially in the Upper South, where previously they had been seen as an expense.[9]

Many enslaved children found themselves being sold at an extremely young age. While most slaves sold into the interregional trade were between the ages of fifteen and twenty-five, young children were always present. Typical was the experience of Louis Hughes, who was born in 1832 and sold for the first time at the age of six. Within the next six years, he was sold three more times to different owners within his native state of Virginia before being placed on an auction block in Richmond and sold to a planter in Mississippi at the age of twelve. Young girls tended to be sold at an earlier age than young boys (they usually matured sooner), although young boys were frequently in greater demand and brought a higher price because of their labor potential. It was even more common to find very young children in the local trade. While owners generally sold toddlers with their mothers (they were easier to care for that way), they sometimes sold children as young as twelve, ten, or even two months old on their own. Newspapers regularly listed small children for sale, including one advertisement in Washington, D.C., for a "Negro boy, 4 years of age, well grown." When one Louisiana man asked his lawyer in New Orleans to be on the lookout for an orphan girl of eight or nine years of age, "he tellingly added that they are frequently offered."[10]

Many slave parents made special efforts to prepare their children for their eventual fate. Some emphasized the need to be stoic when faced with suffering and never to complain. Others were like the Virginia mother who advised her daughter before the girl's departure to "be good an' trus' in de Lawd." At such times parents frequently told their children to be polite and obey their elders in their new home. Laura Clark's grandmother counseled the little girl to "be er good gal, and mine bofe white and black." That way, "ev'body will like you." This advice was important for the six-year-old Laura, who was about to be taken from her home in North Carolina by a slave trader and sold in Alabama. Such young children needed to depend upon complete strangers, both black and white, for their survival.[11]

Despite their parents' best efforts to protect them, sale for the vast majority of young children was still a traumatic experience. This proved especially true for those who were sold at public auction. As one former slave recalled when describing her sale as a little girl: "I was scared and cried, but they put me up there anyway."

Sometimes when young people were too fearful, the crowd might ridicule them for their inability to handle their fate. According to one visitor to an auction in Washington, D.C., a sixteen-year-old boy "trembled all the while" before his sale, which resulted in "a good deal of laughing and talking amongst the buyers, and several jests." If youths could maintain the proper decorum on the stand, however, they might win over the respect of the bidders. Such was the case with a fifteen-year-old boy in St. Louis. As a visitor to this sale reported: "The little fellow appeared to realize his condition and when the big tear rolled down his cheek would meekly brush it aside and hold up his head with an air & manner which won him the sympathies of a great number of the spectators." Unfortunately this young man could hold his strong front only so long, for "as soon as he was sold, his feelings were vented in floods of tears."[12]

After the humiliation of the auction block, those boys and girls sold in the interregional trade were usually manacled to other slaves in a coffle and forced to march overland to their destination in the Deep South. While such a journey was difficult for most adult slaves, it was especially challenging for young children, who lacked the same physical strength to endure the long trek. Only the smallest children got to ride in the wagons along with others who required such assistance. In addition, at times they also had to defend themselves from other slaves who sought to take advantage of them by such actions as stealing their food or beating them.[13]

Upon their arrival in the importing states, enslaved boys and girls faced other painful challenges. As one former slave, Stephen Williams, recalled, he "was jes' a little chap" when he was placed with a hundred other slaves in a New Orleans slave pen, but he still remembered "like it happened yesterday" how "the dirt and smell was terrible, terrible." Moreover while most adult slaves from the Upper South considered sale into the Deep South a fate worse than death because of the region's frontier conditions, subtropical climate, rampant diseases, and extreme working conditions, for small children it likewise meant being exposed to potentially abusive adults, both black and white, without the protection of family and friends.[14]

While this lack of family protection was costly for all slave children, it proved especially so for young girls. Enslaved women throughout the South were routinely raped by white men; however, threats of retaliation by the woman's family or friends could, at times, offer some security from this violence. Young girls caught in the slave trade lacked even this minimal level of protection and were particularly vulnerable to sexual abuse, both by the enslaved men around them and by their new owners. After her sale in Missouri, a fourteen-year-old girl named Celia was raped on the way home by the sixty-year-old widower who had purchased her.[15]

Even as young children, southern slaves began to learn how to resist such sales as best they could. The former slave Henry Watson remembered that when a strange white man arrived on his plantation in Virginia, he "ran with the rest of the children to hide ourselves until the man had gone," while another former Virginia slave recalled that "young'uns fout an' kick lak crazy folks" when they were placed on the auction block. Some even learned how to use other ploys to negotiate a sale. At the age of fifteen, Ambrose Headen was forced to leave his family in North Carolina, walk fourteen miles to a slave market, and place himself upon an auction block before a crowd of five hundred people. After three hours of intense bidding, he was sold to a local planter who was known for his cruelty. Headen began crying and sobbing until the planter, at the urging of others, resold him to another buyer, just as he had hoped.[16]

Upon reaching adulthood most southern slaves continued resisting the domestic trade as best they could. At the extreme were those individuals who responded to an unwanted sale by violently attacking those whom they saw as responsible for their fate. After the owner of a slave in St. Louis sold the man's wife, the enraged man took a double-barreled gun and fired one shot each at his master and mistress in the middle of the night, killing his male owner. Others fought back while being carried to the Deep South for sale. In 1834 two traders, Jesse and John Kirby of Georgia, were attacked in Virginia by several Maryland slaves they were transporting south. As a local newspaper put it, in addition to robbing the two men of about $3,000, "their throats were cut, and the head of one cleft open with an axe." In addition to the slaves who lashed out violently against others, there were also some who responded to the domestic trade in more self-destructive behavior, including self-mutilation and taking their own lives or the lives of their loved ones. In Louisiana a recently sold woman named Agnes drowned herself and her infant daughter "in a deep water hole" rather than live with her new owner, while a newspaper in Nashville reported that another woman there jumped into the river with a child in each arm. According to the report, "Her master had threatened to sell her, and she was determined not to be sold." While most slaves did not respond to sale with violent resistance, for some it seemed the only choice available.[17]

A far more common form of resistance to sale was flight. All across the South, thousands of enslaved men and women fled their owners because of sale, the threat of sale, or the sale of a loved one. It was arguably the most prevalent reason for running away. Even one former slaveholder in Alabama later acknowledged that the separation of families through sale was "the cause of about half of the runaways." Slaves frequently ran away after being told that they were going to be sold, and some left at just the possibility of such an event. As one Missouri owner noted when advertising for his absent man, he believed "that nothing but the fear of being sent to New Orleans induced him to run away." Others absconded not long after sale, with some even disappearing before the new owners could get them home. Enslaved men and women also managed to get away from professional slave traders, both during transit and in their depots. After a woman named Angeline successfully escaped from a Richmond jail, the trader who advertised for her believed that she would return to "where she was raised, either by the Canal or

Central Rail Road." While it is common to think of runaway slaves as fugitives heading north, the vast majority remained in the South, with many crisscrossing the region, trying to reunite with family and friends. Some attempted to return home, others fled in an attempt to find family members who had been sold away. Flight was a relatively common response to sale, but as with violent resistance, the prospect for success was not very promising. The trip was filled with hazards, and those recaptured faced punishment for their actions. Still, despite the dangers and risks, thousands of enslaved men and women did flee their owners, and many were successful in their efforts.[18]

Bondspeople could also sometimes influence a sale to their liking. Those being sold at public auction frequently made their desires known through signals, both subtle and overt. Usually such influence entailed looks of encouragement or open pleas for a particular member of the audience to buy them, but it could also be conveyed in blunt expressions of displeasure. According to one British visitor, a woman prevented her sale to an undesirable bidder by warning him: "Buy me if you please; but I tell you openly, if I become your slave, I will cut your throat the first opportunity." Enslaved southerners had an even greater chance of affecting a sale when sold out of a slave dealer's depot. Given the longer time that most individuals spent in these facilities, they had a better opportunity to evaluate purchasers and do what they could to acquire an acceptable owner. According to John Parker, a young man who found himself in a New Orleans depot, "I made up my mind I was going to select my owner, so when anyone came to inspect me I did not like, I answered all questions with a 'yes,' and made myself disagreeable." Finally some men and women sought to prevent sale entirely by feigning illness or physical disability. Owners understood that their property could deliberately sabotage a sale and often took action to prevent it, usually in the form of a beating. Despite all of the efforts by sellers to get their human property to "talk right" and make a good sale, many of these enslaved people managed to manipulate these transactions and sometimes prevent them entirely.[19]

While many men, women, and children were able to mitigate, and sometimes even prevent, the harsh realities of sale, most had little choice but to accept the consequences of an unwanted sale, however unpleasant. Thousands, if not millions, of African American slaves were forcibly separated from their families and loved ones. Still, many of these people made valiant efforts to keep their families together, even if only in memory. One practice for remembering loved ones was naming newborns after those who had been recently sold. Others encoded family memory by naming their children after important relatives, especially fathers, who were more likely than mothers to be sold away. Such naming practices helped to sustain family memory across generations and across geographical space. Individuals transported to the Deep South also educated their children about the larger kinship group they had left behind. Many years later former slaves in Louisiana were able to recollect stories of family members in the Upper South, some of whom they had never met. Even when forced into other living arrangements, some slaves kept their families alive in memory. In Georgia, Frances Kemble encountered a woman who had had nine children and two miscarriages with a man named Tony. When asked, however, she made it clear that "he was not her *real* husband." The man whom she continued to think of as her real husband had been sold from the estate many years before for running away.[20]

In addition to keeping a family alive in memory, several men and women made efforts to stay in contact through the mail. Some managed to get word back to their loved ones while still in the hands of a trader. Others got in touch with family members after reaching their final destination, usually through the assistance of their new owners. While only a small number of enslaved southerners were able to communicate with loved ones who had been torn away through the domestic trade, a few managed to correspond with one another for years. One such couple was an elderly Virginia man and his sister (appropriately named Memory), who had been sold away to Tallahassee, Florida. After a silence of several years because of illness, the man once again contacted his sister, informing her of his recent heart troubles, as well as all of the news about her family and friends in Virginia. But it was obvious that he had thoughts of mortality on his mind. In a passage that conveyed the love and fondness that the two still maintained for one another, this enslaved man concluded: "I ardently long to meet you in Heaven, may it be our happy lot. Write to me soon and I will answer your letters. Affectionately, your brother Lenn."[21]

Despite these efforts to resist the worst aspects of sale, for most American-born slaves, little could be done to prevent this terrible reality, and they lived under a continual fear of being sold. Thomas Jones recalled that he and his wife "constantly dreaded a final separation," and Lewis Hayden noted that "the trader was all around, the slave-pen at hand, and we did not know what time any of us might be in it." The consequences of sale could be devastating for those sold and those left behind. As one former slave in South Carolina, Susan Hamlin, put it, "People wus always dyin' frum a broken heart." Many never got over this loss. After his entire family was sold, Charles Ball remembered how his "father never recovered from the effects of the shock, which this sudden and overwhelming ruin of his family gave him." Some responded by shielding themselves from the inevitable pain that a sale would produce and refused to get married or have children. But the majority of enslaved African Americans were able to live with this ever-present fact of life, and they maintained meaningful family relationships in spite of it. Still, the consequences of sale were more than a few could bear. Solomon Northup reported that after the two children of his companion, Eliza, were sold, she constantly talked "of them—often *to* them, as if they were actually present," while a woman in Arkansas who lost her children through sale continued to "make clothes and knit for them."

One Kentucky woman who was sold away from her children and taken to Louisiana once stripped off all of her clothing and threw it into a fire. As one witness testified: "She was melancholly [*sic*], dejected and always weeping, and speaking of her children from whom she was separated."[22]

Unfortunately for many enslaved African Americans, the pain and suffering caused by the domestic slave trade did not end with Emancipation. After the war men and women throughout the South sought to reunite families torn apart by sale. Some wandered the countryside, trying to get back to their former homes or to locate family members. Others flooded to the Freedmen's Bureau, seeking aid in finding their relatives. As one bureau agent explained, "In their eyes, the work of emancipation was incomplete until the families which had been dispersed by slavery were reunited." The bureau did the best it could, writing letters and acting as a clearinghouse for information. But in most cases the time and distance gone by was simply too great. Many placed advertisements in the "Information Wanted" section of African American newspapers, seeking knowledge about individuals who had long been sold away. While hundreds of these notices appeared in the years immediately following the war, they could still be found as late as the 1890s. Still despite all of their persistence and optimistic hopes, the sad reality was that most of these searches resulted in failure, and thousands of people were forced to accept that they would never see their loved ones again.[23]

Not surprisingly some never forgave those who had caused them so much suffering, and the consequences of the domestic slave trade would affect race relations in the United States for decades. After being reunited with her former husband at a contraband camp during the Civil War (both had since remarried), one woman proclaimed, "White folk's got a heap to answer for the way they've done to colored folks!" Even as late as the 1930s, another Virginia woman, Anna Harris, declared: "No white man ever been in my house. Don't 'low it. Dey sole my sister Kate. I saw it wid dese here eyes. Sole her in 1860, and I ain't seed nor heard of her since. Folks say white folks is all right dese days. Maybe dey is, maybe dey isn't. But I can't stand to see 'em. Not on my place." Recalling their experiences under slavery, elderly blacks frequently commented on the lingering anguish from such events. According to one Texas man, William Hamilton, "The only thing I remember about all that is that there was lots of crying when they took me away from my mammy. That's something I will never forget." Another woman, Patience M. Avery, stated simply: "Chile, it gives you de creeps up yo' spine to think 'bout it."[24]

Instead of ending slavery and putting a halt to the selling of men, women, and children like cattle, as many of the supporters of the African slave trade ban had hoped, this important national accomplishment in 1808 ironically ended up having an opposite effect upon the country. By not abolishing slavery at the same time, the closing of the African trade unfortunately led to a solidification of slavery in the southern United States and the rise of a terrible new middle passage that eventually tore the country apart and caused horrific pain and suffering to millions of this nation's inhabitants. No wonder African Americans stopped commemorating the anniversary of this event. Later on, January 1 would once again be celebrated by former American slaves, as it was the date when the Emancipation Proclamation went into effect in 1863. But others would choose to observe another liberation anniversary, "Juneteenth," in memory of June 19, 1865, the day when slaves in Texas were supposedly first told about the ending of slavery—two and a half years after it actually was abolished.

Over the years the anniversary of the closing of the African trade has also been ignored by most white Americans. In large part this has been because of their uneasiness in general about the subject of slavery. Prior to the Civil War, most white people avoided the topic whenever possible, because they knew how divisive it could be, and following the war there was simply no place for grim reminders of what life had really been like in the Old South if the nation was ever going to be reunited again. So instead of confronting the real cause of that terrible war, over the years white Americans have generally chosen instead to focus on the bravery and sacrifices of the fighting men on both sides. And if white Americans have always been uncomfortable with the subject of slavery, they have especially gone out of their way to forget about the American slave trade. In their celebrations of the nation's past, this horrific traffic never existed, despite the essential role that it played in the creation of so much of this country's wealth, not to mention all of the appalling heartache and pain that it inflicted upon so many of their fellow Americans.

This nation's failure to confront fully its slaveholding past also helps to explain why in 2008 the United States allowed the bicentennial anniversary of its banning of the African slave trade to pass by relatively unnoticed. True, there were a number of academic conferences, such as that sponsored by the Program in the Carolina Lowcountry and Atlantic World at the College of Charleston, and several cities held special events. But nationally no major commemorations took place. Congress did establish a commission to pursue events to honor the occasion but granted it no funding, and no national remembrances ever came out of it. The biggest public event was a one-day scholarly symposium at the National Archives. This lack of ceremony was in striking contrast to other recent national anniversaries, most notably the bicentennial of the Lewis and Clark Expedition that began in 2003. Its absence was also remarkable when compared to the celebrations that took place the previous year in Great Britain for its bicentennial anniversary of the outlawing of the African trade. The British government allocated the equivalent of $40 million for its celebration. There were national conferences, special events, new school programs, special coins, stamps, and the building of a new international museum on slavery. The BBC devoted hours of programming retracing Britain's involvement in the African trade, and every major museum staged a bicentennial-related event. The main reason for this difference between the two countries was because of the differing outcomes to their similar actions taken back in the early nineteenth century. Most British citizens in 2007 felt proud about their nation's accomplishment in 1807, because when their government banned the African trade it set in motion a series of events that eventually led to the abolition of slavery throughout the British Empire by the 1830s. Conversely when the United States passed its anti–slave trade act in 1808, it led to the emergence of one of the most powerful and dehumanizing race-based slave systems the world has ever known.[25]

Despite the eventual outcome of this action, the outlawing of the African slave trade on January 1, 1808, is an event that should be commemorated as "a day of publick thanksgiving" and remembrance, as Absalom Jones and others had originally intended. The African slave trade truly was a great crime against humanity, and the decision to end it is something in which all Americans should take pride. It was also the first time that the American government ever said that at least some part of human slavery was wrong. By preventing more Africans from populating the southern states, the closing of the African trade kept the southern slave power from getting even bigger and more powerful than it did. Still none of these developments would have brought much comfort to those American-born slaves who were forced to pay the price for their nation's failure to abolish slavery in 1808. Thanks to the new American slave trade, they had to experience needlessly more pain and suffering than any human should ever be forced to endure. Commemorating the abolition of the African slave trade would allow the American people to celebrate the courage that it took to stand up to one of the world's greatest evils. It may also finally force them to confront, acknowledge, and learn from the fact that for far too long, theirs was a nation that sanctioned, and profited from, a terrible evil of its own.

Notes

1. Absalom Jones, *A Thanksgiving Sermon, Preached January 1, 1808, in St. Thomas's, or the African Episcopal Church, Philadelphia; on Account of the Abolition of the African Slave Trade, on That Day, by the Congress of the United States* (Philadelphia: Fry & Kammerer, 1808), 12–14.

2. "National Jubilee of the Abolition of the Slave Trade," *New York Mercantile Advertiser,* January 2, 1809; Russell Parrott, *An Oration on the Abolition of the Slave Trade, Delivered on the First of January, 1812, at the African Church of St. Thomas* (Philadelphia: Maxwell, 1812), 3; Jeremiah Gloucester, *An Oration, Delivered on January 1, 1823, in Bethel Church: On the Abolition of Slave Trade* (Philadelphia: Young, 1823), 5. For a sampling of the many other sermons and speeches in celebration of the African trade's closing, see Peter Williams, *An Oration on the Abolition of the Slave Trade; Delivered in the African Church, in the City of New-York, January 1, 1808* (New York, 1808); Henry Sipkins, *An Oration on the Abolition of the Slave Trade; Delivered in the African Church, in the City of New-York, January 2, 1809* (New York, 1809); William Miller, *A Sermon on the Abolition of the Slave Trade: Delivered in the African Church, New-York, on the First of January, 1810* (New York, 1810); George Lawrence, *An Oration on the Abolition of the Slave Trade, Delivered on the First Day of January, 1813, in*

the African Methodist Episcopal Church (New York, 1813). For a further discussion of these celebrations, see David Waldstreicher, *In the Midst of Perpetual Fetes: The Making of American Nationalism, 1776–1820* (Chapel Hill: University of North Carolina Press, 1997), chap. 6; and Mitch Kachun, *Festivals of Freedom: Memory and Meaning in African American Emancipation Celebrations, 1808–1915* (Amherst: University of Massachusetts Press, 2003), chap. 1.

3. On slavery's spread into the Old Southwest, see Adam Rothman, *Slave Country: American Expansion and the Origins of the Deep South* (Cambridge, Mass.: Harvard University Press, 2005).

4. The classic and still important work on the domestic slave trade is Frederic Bancroft's *Slave Trading in the Old South* (1931; repr., New York: Ungar, 1959), which first argued that the domestic slave trade was a pervasive factor in antebellum American life. After 1931 little was done on the topic until Michael Tadman gave a statistical analysis for the magnitude of the interregional slave trade, showing most slave owners' active participation in it. See Tadman, *Speculators and Slaves: Masters, Traders, and Slaves in the Old South* (Madison: University of Wisconsin Press, 1989). There has since been an outpouring of new work on the domestic trade. Walter Johnson examined the meaning of a slave sale to all the parties involved. See Johnson, *Soul by Soul: Life inside the Antebellum Slave Market* (Cambridge, Mass.: Harvard University Press, 1999). Robert H. Gudmestad studied white southerners' evolving attitudes toward and acceptance of the interregional slave trade. See Gudmestad, *A Troublesome Commerce: The Transformation of the Interstate Slave Trade* (Baton Rouge: Louisiana State University Press, 2003). I examined the interregional and local slave trades and the effects of this traffic on the entire nation, including the North. See Steven Deyle, *Carry Me Back: The Domestic Slave Trade in American Life* (New York: Oxford University Press, 2005). For newer work being done on the domestic slave trade, see the essays in Walter Johnson, ed., *The Chattel Principle: Internal Slave Trades in the Americas* (New Haven, Conn.: Yale University Press, 2004).

5. For an expanded discussion of how the domestic slave trade led to rising slave prices and the creation of southern wealth, as well as the role this development played in southern secession, see Deyle, *Carry Me Back,* chaps. 2–3; and Steven Deyle, "An 'Abominable' New Trade: The Closing of the African Slave Trade and the Changing Patterns of U.S. Political Power, 1808–60," *William and Mary Quarterly,* 3rd ser., 66, no. 4 (2009): 833–50.

6. Tadman, *Speculators and Slaves,* 146–54. For an expanded discussion of the effect that the domestic slave trade had on African Americans in the South and the many ways that they attempted to resist its devastating impact upon their lives, see Deyle, *Carry Me Back,* chap. 8.

7. Thomas Jefferson to John W. Eppes, June 30, 1820, in *Thomas Jefferson's Farm Book,* ed. Edwin M. Betts (Princeton, N.J.: Princeton University Press, 1953), 46.

8. [C. Abner?] to E. Kingsland, November 18, 1859, [C. Abner?] Letter, Virginia Historical Society, Richmond; interview of Robert Williams in *Weevils in the Wheat: Interviews with Virginia Ex-Slaves,* ed. Charles L. Perdue, Thomas E. Barden, and Robert K. Phillips (Charlottesville: University of Virginia Press, 1976), 325–26; Thomas Hamilton, *Men and Manners in America,* 2 vols. (Edinburgh: Blackwood, 1833), 2:216–18.

9. Peter Randolph to William Byrd III, September 20, 1757, in *The Correspondence of the Three William Byrds of Westover, Virginia, 1684–1776,* 2 vols., ed. Marion Tinling (Charlottesville: University of Virginia Press, 1977), 2:628.

10. Louis Hughes, *Thirty Years a Slave: From Bondage to Freedom* (Milwaukee: South Side, 1897); *Washington, D.C., National Intelligencer,* November 28, 1837; Edward Stewart to John W. Gurley, December 19, 1858, Gurley Papers, Louisiana State University, Baton Rouge.

11. Herbert G. Gutman, *The Black Family in Slavery and Freedom, 1750–1925* (New York: Pantheon, 1976), 219–20; interview of Delia Garlic in *The American Slave: A Composite Autobiography,* 19 vols., ed. George P. Rawick (Westport, Conn.: Greenwood, 1972), 6:130–31; interview of Laura Clark in Rawick, *American Slave,* 6:72–73.

12. Interview of Sarah Ashley in *The Slave Narratives of Texas,* ed. Ronnie C. Tyler and Lawrence R. Murphy (Austin: Encino, 1974), 7; Basil Hall, *Travels in North America, in the Years 1827 and 1828,* 3 vols. (Edinburgh: Cadell, 1829), 3:34–40; Nathan Brown to Mary H., January 13, 1838, Brown Letter Book, Missouri Historical Society, St. Louis.

13. For a good account of the difficulties an enslaved eight-year-old boy faced while on an overland coffle to the Deep South, see "John Parker Memoir," 5–6, Rankin-Parker Papers, Duke University, Durham, N.C.

14. Interview of Stephen Williams in *Bullwhip Days: The Slaves Remember,* ed. James Mellon (New York: Grove, 1988), 290.

15. Melton A. McLaurin, *Celia, a Slave* (Athens: University of Georgia Press, 1991), 20–22.

16. Henry Watson, *Narrative of Henry Watson, a Fugitive Slave* (Boston: Marsh, 1848), 7; interview of Charles Crawley in Perdue et al., *Weevils in the Wheat,* 79; John W. Blassingame, ed., *Slave Testimony: Two Centuries of Letters, Speeches, Interviews, and Autobiographies* (Baton Rouge: Louisiana State University Press, 1977), 743–44.

17. *Boston Liberator,* November 9, 1849; *Farmville (Va.) Chronicle,* quoted in *Boston Liberator,* May 10, 1834; appeal, February 14, 1860, *Walker v. Hays,* No. 6606, 15 La. Ann. 640 (1860), University of New Orleans (hereafter, UNO); *Nashville Gazette,* quoted in *Boston Liberator,* February 11, 1853.

18. Interview of M. T. Judge, February 23, 1913, Nixon Papers, Alabama Department of Archives and History, Montgomery; *St. Louis Missouri Gazette & Public Advertiser,* March 29, 1820, quoted in Arvarh E. Strickland, "Aspects of Slavery in Missouri," *Missouri Historical Review* 55 (July 1971): 525; *Richmond Enquirer,* May 29, 1853.

19. Edward S. Abdy, *Journal of a Residence and Tour in the United States of North America, from April, 1833, to October, 1834,* 3 vols. (London: Murray, 1835), 3:350; "John Parker Memoir," 31.

20. Gutman, *Black Family,* chap. 5; Ann Patton Malone, *Sweet Chariot: Slave Family and Household Structure in Nineteenth-Century Louisiana* (Chapel Hill: University of North Carolina Press, 1992), 240; Frances A. Kemble, *Journal of a Residence on a Georgian Plantation in 1838–1839* (New York: Harper, 1863), 204–5.

21. Lenn to Memory, November 30, 1857, Elliot Papers, Florida State University, Tallahassee. For other examples of the letters that enslaved people sent to one another, see Deyle, *Carry Me Back,* 271–74.

22. Thomas H. Jones, *Experience and Personal Narrative of Uncle Tom Jones; Who Was for Forty Years a Slave. Also the Surprising Adventures of Wild Tom, of the Island Retreat, a Fugitive Negro from South Carolina* (Boston: Skinner, 1850s), 24; Hayden narrative in Harriet Beecher Stowe, *A Key to Uncle Tom's Cabin; Presenting the Original Facts and Documents upon Which the Story Is Founded* (Boston: Jewett, 1853), 305; interview of Susan Hamlin in

Rawick, *American Slave*, vol. 2, pt. 2, 235; Charles Ball, *Slavery in the United States: A Narrative of the Life and Adventures of Charles Ball, a Black Man* (New York: Taylor, 1837), 18; Solomon Northup, *Twelve Years a Slave*, ed. Sue Eakin and Joseph Logsdon (Baton Rouge: Louisiana State University Press, 1968), 60; Gutman, *Black Family,* 290; testimony of Dr. David Devall, May 17, 1852, *Buhler v. McHatton,* No. 3448, 9 La. Ann. 192 (1854), UNO.

23. Unknown agent, quoted in Eric Foner, *Reconstruction: America's Unfinished Revolution, 1863–1877* (New York: Harper & Row, 1988), 82; Leon F. Litwack, *Been in the Storm So Long: The Aftermath of Slavery* (New York: Knopf, 1979), 229–47.

24. Henry L. Swint, ed., *Dear Ones at Home: Letters from Contraband Camps* (Nashville: Vanderbilt University Press, 1966), 124; interview of Anna Harris in Perdue et al., *Weevils in the Wheat,* 128; interview of William Hamilton in Tyler and Murphy, *Slave Narratives of Texas,* 10; interview of Patience M. Avery in Perdue et al., *Weevils in the Wheat,* 15.

25. Among the many interesting commentaries that discussed the differences between how the United States and Great Britain both observed their bicentennials of the closing of the African slave trade, see Eric Foner, "Forgotten Step toward Freedom," *New York Times,* December 30, 2007; Eric Foner, interview, National Public Radio, January 10, 2008; Scott Horton, "The Forgotten Bicentennial," *Harper's Magazine,* December 31, 2007; and Te-Ping Chen, "Tracing Slavery's Past," *Nation,* March 14, 2008. "Ending the International Slave Trade: A Bicentenary Inquiry," a conference sponsored by the Program in the Carolina Lowcountry and Atlantic World at the College of Charleston, March 26–29, 2008, was the academic centerpiece of one of the most sustained attempts at a local commemoration of the anniversary.

BLACKNESS WITHOUT ETHNICITY

Some Hypotheses on the End of the African Slave Trade in 1808,
Race, and the Search for Slave Identity in Early American Louisiana

JEAN-PIERRE LE GLAUNEC

As part of a new, developing historiography on the history of race and the conditions of formation of slave communities in colonial and early national Louisiana, this chapter proposes possible avenues of discussion and research into the relationship between the banning of the international slave trade and the construction of race and identity in early American Louisiana. One of the challenges in the current redefinition of the history of Louisiana slavery is to integrate Louisiana into a complex, fragmented Atlantic as well as into a no less complex American South. To do so, and to break away from some of the founding myths of Louisiana history, we historians must engage in duly empirical reexamination of primary sources, no doubt, but also in the proposition of new paradigmatic threads that, in the absence of primary sources, can only be suggested in stark, theoretical, and inferential forms—in the full expectation that these speculative conclusions will be questioned and replaced in due time by other historians. This chapter, therefore, should not be read for what it cannot provide: although my inferences are based on the examination of many primary sources and should therefore be taken in earnest, I do not pretend to have full supporting evidence for all my hypotheses.[1] Both in form and content, what follows is aimed to raise questions as much as to provide answers.

The connections between the end of the African slave trade in 1808, race and the construction of race, and slave identity in early American Louisiana have so far, to a great measure, escaped the historian's attention. Yet I believe their interrelationships to be highly significant, both from an epistemological and from an analytical perspective, and as such research into the connections should occupy its due place in the new, fast-developing historiography of the region—heralded notably by the work of Shannon Lee Dawdy, Nathalie Dessens, Cécile Vidal, Emily Clark, Jennifer Spears, and Guillaume Aubert, among the most prominent.[2]

My basic intuition is that the abrupt end of the African slave trade in January 1808—and the start, or the new beginning, of a lucrative southern trade in its stead—had one important, and yet understudied, consequence in lower Louisiana.

Central among other effects, the 1808 ban may have dramatically accelerated the formation, and in the end favored the crystallization, of new, *peculiar* racial identities among the slave communities of lower Louisiana: racial identities with what I imagine to be a universalist twist. The year 1808 put an end to an Atlantic trauma but opened the door to a new form of traumatic cultural experience, namely that of southern displacement to Louisiana. Slaves responded to this new traumatic experience, I propose, by elaborating a shared sense of blackness that transcended ethnicity, gender, and class.

There is no doubt, of course, that Louisiana society had been thoroughly racialized before 1808, when the U.S. Congress banned the African trade. It is possible that something dramatic changed, however, at the time of the abolition—and in its immediate aftermath. The longtime opposition among slaves, whether seen from the slaves' or the whites' perspectives—between Creole (that is, born in Louisiana) and African, an opposition that faded and revived several times over the course of the colonial period—and the many ethnic subdivisions among the two groups, may have rapidly given way, if not entirely disappeared, because of a shared sense of blackness or black collective identity. This change may have been caused by a peculiar cultural encounter in early national Louisiana among three groups: (1) the last new Africans of the nineteenth century; (2) Francophone Creole slaves—at least nominally Catholic, through their exposure to baptism and the last sacraments,[3] to local farmers, planters, and town-dwellers; and (3) the masses of mostly Anglophone slaves, possibly Protestant (in particular Methodist and Baptist), arriving from the Upper South and Lower South, especially the Chesapeake.[4] This encounter brought together diverse but complementary threads of memory, interpretations of race, and visions of physical and cultural resistance that favored a new collective identity.

Along the way an ill-defined sense of fragmented blackness based on, and secondary to, the existence of multiple constructed ethnicities ("Creole," "Creolized," "Congo," "Bambara," "mulattoes," "quadroons," "francisés," "American," "English," etc.) appears to have been replaced by a shared understanding of what it meant to be "black"—this time, in great part at least, without ethnicity. In turn, and in response, it is possible that a new sense of common whiteness developed, strengthening in the process the new, post-1808 planters' world.[5]

Whites and blacks, as categories of collective identification, had existed in Louisiana ever since the arrival of the first African slaves in 1719. Clear dividing lines of racial difference had been internalized early on with the promulgation of the 1724 Code noir in New Orleans, notably as it referred to the ban on interracial unions.[6] It is clear that whites and blacks saw each other in terms of their phenotype right from the beginning and all through the course of the colonial period. *Blackness,* however, as a form of collective identity and a possible source of universalist solidarity, may have taken shape only out of the peculiar medley of cultures characteristic of post-1808 Louisiana, a reality that I view not as something fixed but as an ongoing process. At that juncture or thereabout, a number of factors coincided to erode the proximity between slaves and whites and thereby to prompt the rewriting of slave codes so as to make the color line clearer to all: the nature of plantations changed as sugar and cotton took hold; the size of plantations grew larger and larger; and there was a continuous flow of new slave arrivals—a stark departure from the erratic patterns of the African trade in the colonial period.[7] Consequently whiteness, as in how whites transcended their ethnic and class differences, may likewise only have materialized in the aftermath of 1808—with whites facing a surging black community, with sugar and cotton remaking the white world, and with Francophones and Anglophones intersecting in ways that stressed commonalities more than differences.

One can reasonably add that the situation in Louisiana was exceptional to the South—vastly different, for example, from the neighboring Mississippi Territory that also attracted scores of Anglophone slaves from the Upper South and Lower South after 1808. It differed in at least three ways. (1) Slavery in Louisiana predated the abolition of the Atlantic slave trade and the start of a massive internal slave migration by almost a century. In 1808 and shortly thereafter the coincidence of the end of one trade circuit and the beginning of another resulted in a human web of cultural interactions of unknown complexity in the Deep South, and possibly the entire South. (2) The Louisiana slave trade had been mostly Caribbean oriented for the preceding thirty years—centered on Jamaica and Dominica first, then Saint-Domingue and Martinique, and finally Cuba—in effect making Louisiana a vital part of a Caribbean trade system.[8] The ban of January 1, 1808, played a significant role in integrating formerly Caribbean Louisiana into the early Republic, maybe in more symbolic ways than statehood did four years later. (3) Louisiana had finally turned into, or returned to being, a slave society (as opposed to a society with slaves), based on the production of two new staple crops, developed on a large scale in the last years of the eighteenth century.[9]

In short, in comparison with other slave societies in the Deep South, Louisiana in 1808 already had a peculiarly mixed slave population, inherited from the French and Spanish periods of dominance. This particularly complex demographic situation and the economic landscape in the region therefore could, I propose, have favored the rapid emergence of a new sense of blackness.

To some extent the ad hoc construction of this new blackness—which may have played a critical role in bridging the gap between the slaves' conflicting senses of Africanness, Americanness, and what it meant to be from Louisiana, Saint-Domingue, or any other place in the slave Atlantic—may parallel the way French-ness, as a form of transethnic identity, was invented in colonial Louisiana by planters and officers who would not have defined themselves as such in metropolitan France. As Cécile Vidal has recently put it, "Dans les sociétés nouvelles des

Amériques, l'identité nationale était . . . le seul dénominateur commun entre des migrants volontaires originaires de diverses communautés et provinces du royaume de France, alors qu'une identité locale ne pouvait évidemment se mettre à exister immédiatement" (In the new societies of the Americas, national identity was . . . the only common denominator between voluntary migrants originating from diverse communities and provinces in the French kingdom, whereas a local identity could not, naturally, be made to exist immediately).[10] A sense of common blackness without ethnicity may have served similarly useful purposes in terms of how slaves, *involuntary* migrants, chose to devise their survival strategies in the immediate post-1808 period. Eventually local identities would develop, whether Louisianan, centered on a particular parish, southern, or based on religious differences. In the meantime, however, a sense of shared black identity probably served special social needs. Blackness may have served as an imaginative, creative, and permeable middle ground uniting slaves—whether "blacks" or mulattoes, "blacks" and "not so blacks"—in a new concept of race, before taking diverging paths once more as the antebellum period unraveled.

The second inference of my intuitive soundings is that, in time, these new and peculiar racial identities, forged in the crucible of Louisiana slavery in the immediate aftermath of the abolition of the Atlantic slave trade, reverberated back across the entire South, to help shape the way blackness came to be defined and used by slaves as a social and cultural category in the history of the antebellum United States. To put it differently, it is possible that the general shift from ethnic to racial identities in the South—a phenomenon that has been studied by Michael Gomez, among others—originated in Louisiana shortly after 1808—much earlier, that is, than the mid-1830s, as proposed by Gomez.[11] In short to look at race, the slave trade, and to search for the boundaries of slave identity in Louisiana around the time of the abolition also means to look in a forward fashion at the historical evolution of race and race relations in the entire Old South.

I propose here that we should look at Louisiana and the South as forming a complex dialectic and dialogic knot that allows us to examine how Louisiana became more southern, and vice versa: the processes whereby slavery in the South became more Louisianan. Of course in proposing such paradigmatic change, I do not mean that ethnicities stopped mattering after 1808. I imply, rather, that they should be seen primarily as social and cultural constructions that were under constant strain as January 1, 1808, opened the door for dramatic change in lower Louisiana—a change no one had imagined, whether slaves in the sugar fields, planters in their Creole houses, slave merchants in Charleston and Baltimore, or legislators in New Orleans and Washington.

This second phase of the argument is proposed here only as a tentative model of interpretation; part of my hesitation comes from the fact that, compared to the colonial period especially, and with the recent exception of Richard Follett's *The*

Sugar Masters, there is a glaring lack of scholarship in the history of antebellum Louisiana slavery.[12] The slave experience of that period clearly calls for a reexamination.

To conclude what has become a long, but necessary, exposition of my soundings, I would simply add that in my opinion, January 1, 1808, marks the beginning of a crucial social and cultural experiment in community formation in the history of Louisiana, in terms of how blackness and whiteness served as new common denominators. I argue further that this social and cultural experiment can be seen as a watershed that, in the end, made Louisiana southern and the South Louisianan. Two analogies would probably help make the point. I have in mind Shannon Lee Dawdy's 2008 work on French colonial New Orleans and Sylvia Frey's 2009 article on the American Revolution and Pan-Africanism. Dawdy insists on the fact that "colonies [like Louisiana] were key sites of production for political modernity."[13] In 1808 Louisiana was no longer a colony and not quite a state; yet it may well have been a key production site for racial modernity in terms of how whiteness and blackness were made to define the slave South. The issue of modernity has also been analyzed by Frey from the angle of Pan-Africanism—the catalysts of which she sees in the participation of blacks in the American Revolution and in the spread of Afro-Protestantism. "The era of the American Revolution played a seminal role in the development and spread of pan-Africanism," she says, before arguing that "an essential first step in the development of pan-Africanism was the emergence of a corporate African or racial identity in place of numerous ethnic identities."[14] Post-1808 Louisiana may well have been at the forefront, within the South, of such a complex process of identity creation.

Despite the possibly avant-garde role played by Louisiana in this process, the 1808 ban and the period around it have figured marginally in Louisiana historiography. Why? What can be inferred from this silence? How is one to proceed in light of it?

Central as it may have been, the end of the African slave trade in Louisiana has suffered from a certain obscurity, exemplified in a recent exhibit put together by the Historic New Orleans Collection on the topic "Between Colony and State: Louisiana in the Territorial Period, 1803–1812." As often occurs in such events aimed at a general public, the emphasis rested on political affairs, with a particular stress on 1803, marking the Louisiana Purchase, and 1812, when Louisiana acceded to statehood. Occurring between those two events, the ban on the African slave trade was nowhere to be seen.[15]

Such obscurity makes sense in light of the major themes that have been covered by historians of Louisiana in the past twenty years. Before Gwendolyn Midlo Hall broke new ground with the publication of her book *Africans in Colonial Louisiana: The Development of Afro-Creole Culture in the Eighteenth Century* in 1992, a study based in good part on the colonial records of Pointe Coupée parish, the history of

Louisiana slavery was very much marginal to the rest of the discipline, with the exception of the pioneer works of Paul Lachance and Thomas Fierher.[16] Since the publication of *Africans in Colonial Louisiana,* the historiography of slavery in the region has been dominated almost exclusively by two themes. Though it might seem a little specialized to some readers more accustomed to other regional historiographies, it does not seem unwarranted to detail briefly these two themes, considering the often acrimonious debates that have opposed historians of this complex region.

The first concerns the French and Spanish periods of colonization and the question of race and racial order in the context of a Catholic "frontier" colony evolving at a distance from Protestant colonies and states. Was Louisiana slavery in the French and Spanish eras based on a more fluid racial construction than other slave societies in North America? Was it more fluid than in the early American period when the so-called Anglos may have brought their more rigid and binary conceptions of race? Was French Louisiana—which has been the focus of most historians—a strictly ordained and policed society or another Babylon marked by racial and social confusion?

As is now well known among specialists of Louisiana, Daniel Usner and Gwendolyn Hall have both stressed what they see as the unusual fluidity of racial relations in the French period.[17] At the opposite end of the spectrum, Thomas Ingersoll, and more recently Guillaume Aubert, have argued that French Louisiana was in effect no different from Metropolitan France, or other slave societies in North America: namely a society plagued by strict racial barriers right from the onset.[18] Somewhere in between those two extremes, Cécile Vidal has argued that Louisiana was a racialized society right from the start, though race may not have determined all human relationships. She has argued further that the rapid racialization of slavery in Louisiana originated in the long French experience in the Caribbean, in particular in Saint-Domingue. Indeed according to her, Saint-Domingue and Louisiana shared "a common imperial racial culture."[19]

Shannon Lee Dawdy and Jennifer Spears, in books published respectively in 2008 and 2009, have tended to side with Gwendolyn Midlo Hall and Daniel Usner, though trying at the same time to distance themselves from this hotly contested historiographical debate.[20] According to Spears any strict codification of race would only have taken place late in the eighteenth century. Black-white unions were abnormally numerous in the French and Spanish colonial period and widely tolerated, she argues. She sees a watershed, not in the ban that went into effect on January 1, 1808, but in the racial baggage that Anglos brought with them in the early nineteenth century as they seemingly flooded the streets and plantations of early American Louisiana. In stressing the cultural and political impact of white Americans passing through New Orleans, a host of topics are, by the same token, pushed to the margins, including the complete overhaul of the plantation world with the cultivation of sugar and cotton, the subsequent arrival of new slaves, and the creation of a new equilibrium—or rather a new, brutal political asymmetry necessary to protect whites. In Spears's work, which culminates in the 1850s, race was transported south to Louisiana, as though the planters who remade race in the early American period were all Anglophones from the seaboard states. The possibility that new racial identities could have been forged in Louisiana out of the encounter of old and new slaves, old whites, and new whites does not seem to be considered.

Dawdy brings an interesting new twist to the debate as she looks not just at race but at what the inner workings of French New Orleans might tell us about patterns of colonialism in the early modern period. Race is nonetheless the pivotal axis on which her work revolves. Echoing Spears, as well as Hall and Usner, Dawdy insists on the gap between a supposedly strict royal theory about race and the informal, fluid local practices of New Orleanians. She contends notably that "another element of the social design that did not take off as planned [in Louisiana] was the imposition of a black/white racial code and elaborate segregationist policies governing public space."[21] In other words there may have been "developing boundaries of race" in the late French period, but fluidity prevailed. Any "emerging racial divide," as she puts it—a phrase that postulates once again that racial thinking was imposed following a top-down logic by whites gradually learning how to become racist—would come later in the eighteenth century.[22]

The fact that most historians of Louisiana have focused on the French period in the past twenty years, and only secondarily on the Spanish era, has pushed January 1, 1808, and early American Louisiana in general, to the sidelines. The same process of marginalization can be said to have taken place with the popularization of the second major theme in the historiography—the ethnicization of Louisiana slavery—following the work of such historians as Paul Lovejoy and Michael Gomez.[23] The beacon of this trend is another book by Gwendolyn Hall, *Slavery and African Ethnicities in the Americas: Restoring the Links,* published in 2005.[24] This important work, based on a slave database put together under Hall's supervision in the 1990s—from records found in the different parishes of Louisiana—stresses the many patterns of African continuity from one side of the Atlantic to the other. In the process Hall puts the African slaves brought to Louisiana on a diasporic pedestal, so to speak. "Bambara" and "Congo" slaves in Louisiana, and the many other slaves identified by their "national" appellations, are represented by Hall as the consummate experience of the black world. Louisiana slavery stands as a microcosm for the entire African American Atlantic.

Other historians who have adopted this perspective include Gomez and Kevin Roberts.[25] The ethnicity debate has centered on an argument that is now well known to specialists of the black Atlantic, namely the ethnic homogeneity or heterogeneity of the New World slave communities and the related questions of Africanization, re-Africanization, and Creolization as models of interpretation.

This debate has opposed, often in fierce terms, Gwendolyn Midlo Hall and Thomas Ingersoll.[26]

It is of course no surprise that January 1, 1808, and the period that immediately followed the abolition of the African slave trade have figured marginally in much of this discussion. The abrupt end of the trade, and the start of a large internal trade in its stead, sheds doubt on the possibility of ethnicizing slavery in the long term. Strangely enough much of the debate on ethnicizing slavery has usually taken place, anyway, in the absence of clear data about the African slave trade and slave purchasing patterns—whether African or not—in the French, Spanish, and early American periods.[27] A similar gap between theory and practice exists in terms of how historians have described the overall social, demographic, and economic evolution of farms and plantations in Louisiana over the course of the colonial and early national period.

It follows from this brief discussion that it is necessary to refocus some of the attention on the period hinging on the abolition of the African slave trade—which so far has been marginalized by a discussion of race in the French period and by an obsession with African ethnicities, especially in the late Spanish context. However, in order best to explore the impact of the abolition of the African slave trade on the making of race—both by slaves and by planters—it is important to frame this shift in attention in the *longue durée*. I propose here to view January 1, 1808, and its role as a catalyst in the formation of a new sense of blackness—that is, one not postulated on the existence of essentialized ethnicities—as one important marker among others, though an outstanding one, as will be seen.

This question relates, in fact, to the possibility, or maybe the necessity, of rethinking the evolution of slave identities and cultures away from national categories—whether French, Spanish, or American. This trend of thought is particularly well entrenched among historians of Louisiana. Daniel Littlefield, for example, in an article titled "Slavery in French Louisiana: From Gallic Colony to American Territory," has proposed to "follow [the history of slavery] in the region from initial settlement to American acquisition, noting some of the changes that occurred *under each administration*."[28] A slight variation on this purely administrative pattern is the separation proposed by Ira Berlin in his *Many Thousands Gone*, a separation postulated on economic terms.[29] In Berlin's view Louisiana evolved from a slave society in the early French period to a society with slaves around the middle of the French era; the reason for the switch did not depend on changes in the slave/white ratio but on changes in agricultural practice as Louisiana stopped being structured around a set of clearly identifiable staple crops. Louisiana became a slave society again late in the Spanish colonial era as it cultivated indigo, and then cotton and sugar, requiring new shipments of Africans to do so.

In contrast to Littlefield's and Berlin's periodization, I would propose to rethink the chronology around six major watersheds, each of them having to do with the ebb and flow of slave migrations into the region, with January 1, 1808, as the pivotal watershed. Hence instead of having three neatly defined periods—until 1763 (or 1769, when the Spaniards actually took control); between 1763 (or 1769) and 1803; and finally from 1803 onward with a pause in 1812—it is possible to delineate six broad periods that do not overlap exactly with national administrations:

1) 1719–1731: The first period starts in 1719 with the arrival of the first African slave ship in French New Orleans and ends in 1731, when the African slave trade was in effect halted due to the severe economic difficulties faced by the young colony following the Natchez revolt. Slaves in that short period of time were almost all of African origin, a majority originating in Senegambia, where the French slave trade was centered. Any sense of blackness would have been rooted in the African diasporic experience and would most likely have had clear ethnic undertones. New ethnic identities such as "Bambara" or "Bamana," as Gwendolyn Hall has recently argued, were constructed and negotiated in Louisiana as group survival strategies, sometimes surfacing in violent acts of rebellion.[30] The priority for slaves was not to define a putative blackness—such a thing would probably have made no sense in the context of their arrival—but to reform African links after the Atlantic crossing.

2) 1731–1776: The second period takes us into the first ten years of the Spanish period, roughly to 1776, when the African slave trade was gradually reopened in Louisiana by the Spanish authorities, though on a modest scale, via French and English free ports. Between 1731 and around 1776, slave migrations to Louisiana were minimal at best—one African slaver in 1743 and a trickle of slaves from the French and English Caribbean otherwise—and often null for a variety of causes: various prohibitions, the economic difficulties of the Company of the Indies, Atlantic turbulence such as the Seven Years' War, the lack of credit of early Louisianians, and the isolated location of the New Orleans market. Most slaves in Louisiana were Creoles—that is, born in the colony—and defined as such. By 1741, only ten years after the arrival of the last African ship, it was remarked that two-thirds of all slaves in the colony were indeed Louisiana born.[31] Thirty years later Africans would have been rare indeed along the Mississippi and its tributaries. Slave families would have had time to develop, as testified by many notarized records.[32] At the end of this phase, any sense of blackness would have been rooted in the Louisiana Creole experience. It would have had clear ethnic undertones, but ethnic solidarity would have become only minimally African. Slaves, though a majority, were scattered across the territory and only rarely settled in large groups. Any sense of corporate black identity would have to wait another thirty years.

3) 1776–1796: The next period coincides with the reopening of the African slave trade in the mid-1770s. In an article published in *Louisiana History* in 2005, I

calculated that between around 1776 and the mid-1790s, approximately ten thousand Africans were taken to lower Louisiana, then sold in its different parishes.[33] Slaves arrived from Africa via Jamaica, Dominica, Martinique, Saint-Domingue, and Cuba as part of the thriving re-export trade in slaves then in existence in the Caribbean. Most of them arrived from Jamaica and Dominica, two important islands in the English African trade. With the reopening of the transatlantic trade—it peaked in 1789 and then dwindled again—the slaves' sense of blackness may have been increasingly fragmented along two ethnic lines, one Creole, the other African. However, these two lines may not have been insurmountable boundaries, as Africans often arrived in the colony in small numbers before being sold individually or in pairs. Creoles and Africans, at this juncture, must have been engaged in intense processes of negotiation as to what elements of their cultures and identities would prevail, fuse, or disappear.

This period has often been seen by historians, first among them Gwendolyn Hall, as one of "re-Africanization." I have recently disputed this thesis in another article arguing that conditions on the ground were not favorable to a profound cultural re-Africanization of slave communities.[34] For one thing the slave trade never brought enough slaves to Louisiana to ensure the continuous transfer of African practices to already established Creole families and family networks— the trade was stopped as early as 1795 as Spain and France were at war.[35] Moreover African slaves were widely dispersed in small numbers across the land, and plantations were usually small and marked by a noted black and white proximity. In short, Louisiana in the period looked much more like early colonial Virginia than contemporary Jamaica, Saint-Domingue, or South Carolina.

4) 1796–1803: The fourth period starts in February 1796 with a ban on the African slave trade—in reaction to both a slave insurrection attempt in Pointe Coupée and the revolutionary events of Saint-Domingue—and continues until its timid reopening in late 1803. In the absence of new slave arrivals, except for a trickle starting in 1801, it may be postulated that Africans and Creoles continued exchanging ideas and values in order to find ways to survive together and form new kinship patterns. Most of them lived and worked on small farms or plantations in close proximity with whites. The two groups would have been engaged in an active search for hybrid, modern, and complex forms of ethnic and social identities. Phase 4 resembles phase 3 in many ways.

5) 1803—ca. 1808: The final years of the African slave trade, reopened under American rule, constitute the fifth period. It started with modest slave arrivals in the first ten months of 1804, was interrupted for most of 1805, and then peaked in 1806–7 when the Louisiana trade became dependent on transshipments from Charleston. Slave cultures and identities were probably infused with a new sense of Africanness as more than seven thousand Africans arrived in this

period, often in large groups.[36] New, possibly more rigid ethnic lines may have been reformed, opposing Creoles and Africans. Within the African group, slaves from Central Africa, known as "Congo," may have played a distinct part in this new ethnicization process.

6) ca. 1808–1811: The final, pivotal period starts with the ban of the Atlantic slave trade and covers approximately the first three years of an internal deportation of slaves that would last for the entire antebellum period. This trade hinged not only on Charleston but also on Baltimore and Norfolk. I hypothesize here that the constant influx of new slaves, often arriving in large groups and families, put a rapid check to the renewed ethnic divide between Creoles and Africans as well as among Africans themselves. (No clear data exist about how many arrived and from where.) Newspaper advertisements for slave sales bear testimony to this important and still understudied phenomenon that may have started a little earlier than 1808. For example the *Moniteur de la Louisiane* of January 31, 1807, advertised the sale of 103 slave men, women, and children, all in families, originating from only two plantations from Maryland. A comprehensive study of slave sale advertisements between 1802 and 1815, currently underway, will help elucidate the matter fully.[37] A new, possibly universalist-driven sense of blackness may have emerged out of this period of intense encounters; a new color line may have been traced along and through the plantations lining the Mississippi River as well as within New Orleans. The year 1811, when a group of slaves apparently decided to revolt in the parishes of Saint John the Baptist and Saint Charles, closes this phase—for reasons to be discussed briefly below.

We can fully understand the impact and importance of the ban of the African slave trade in 1808 only if we see it from such a broad perspective. What these six phases have in common, I hypothesize, is the strong probability that after 1731 lower Louisiana was never thoroughly re-Africanized again due to its erratic and often minimal slave trade. African slaves never really "poured" into Louisiana the way they did in Saint-Domingue, Jamaica, Cuba, or South Carolina, for example— so much so that a thriving re-export trade existed in those societies.[38] Unlike most slaves in the New World, whose lives "continued to be molded by the rhythm of ships returning to deposit more bodies," in Louisiana one could at times almost completely "escape the saltwater." In Spanish and early national Louisiana, "every cargo that left a slave ship in the Americas was [not] closely followed by a trail of others."[39] Excluding smuggling, which has often tended to be exaggerated, I have calculated in a separate article that Louisiana "only" received twenty thousand to twenty-two thousand Africans between 1763 and 1812—and perhaps another four thousand to five thousand non-Africans, slaves born in Jamaica and deported to Louisiana for repeated misconduct or crimes (as was often the case), for example, or born in Saint-Domingue or other Atlantic seaboard states.[40] If one could escape the "saltwater" in the history of Louisiana, it was never possible to escape the internal flow of southern slaves after 1808.

To some extent, although this periodization is based on conjectures that will need to be validated over the course of my current research, the five to six phases previously delineated may be regrouped into just two:

1) Before 1808 the black and white dichotomy may have existed as a filter over ethnic groups in a constant flux of cultural and social negotiations. Slaves may have defined themselves and may have been defined as *blacks,* but it is possible that more narrowly defined identities based on "Creole"/"Creolized"/"African"/ African "national" ancestry, etc., usually took precedence.

2) After 1808 the black and white dichotomy probably took center stage in Louisiana. This new racial construction did not emerge exclusively out of the planters' world; slaves too must have played a key role in the process, by defining a new corporate sense of blackness, thus urging whites to reinvent their own common whiteness, a necessary step for transcending their national, regional, or class differences. The slaves' new blackness would not have effaced secondary differences entirely, but these may have been principally linguistic, regional, or parish- or class-based from then on. With the advent of the southern slave trade, which sealed the inclusion of Louisiana among the large plantation societies of the South, the moderate, but real, degree of proximity that had characterized the slave/master relationship for most of the colonial period faded to the background as plantations were greatly enlarged and slave/master interactions were codified with more brutality.

Between 1803 and 1808, Louisiana planters clamored for more and more African slaves as the only way to develop the region's economy. However no one seemed to have regretted January 1, 1808, as soon as it became clear that a regular flow of new slaves would continue arriving by way of the southern trade. Merchants specializing in the transatlantic business simply adapted to the new market.[41] Louisiana planters and merchants stopped stipulating preferences for slaves on ethnic grounds when they realized that slaves already in America from the Atlantic seaboard and interior states would do the job just as well as Africans, whether "Congo," "Bambara," or of any other "nation." At this juncture planters and merchants, and whites in general, may have increasingly looked at slaves as blacks— quickly adapting to a new racial vocabulary. Looking at slaves in this new way also spoke about the planters' new survival strategies. Faced with increasing black majorities, a slave mobility that threatened their power, and a perception of increased slave resistance, planters in and around 1808 probably defined blackness as the main threat to contain.[42]

In particular, planters used the burgeoning press, in English and French, to set down their new racial preconceptions in print. Printed space, as in runaway slave or slave sale advertisements, was a medium through which Louisiana planters could construct and share a new discourse about the skin color and, more generally, the bodies of their slaves. It was a medium through which they could spell out their supposed racial superiority.[43]

TABLE 1. HOW THE 1808 BAN FITS IN THE *LONGUE DURÉE* OF LOUISIANA SLAVERY, 1719–CA. 1808

Before 1808: A color line shrouded in ethnic differences. Phase of intensive social and cultural negotiations

Phase 1: 1719–31	African slave trade opens; African, ethnic identities prevailing, in particular from Senegambia.
Phase 2: 1731–76	End of the African trade. Fast formation of Creole communities.
Phase 3: 1776–96	African trade reopened, then banned, and reopened again
Phase 4: 1796–1803	with severe limitations. Phase of creative contention between long-established Creoles and new, often dispersed Africans.
Phase 5: 1803–8	After slow start, African slave trade finally flows into Louisiana. Africans sold in large groups and less scattered. Possibly more rigid ethnic lines between Creoles and Africans.

After 1808: A new color line relegating ethnic differences to the background

Phase 6: 1808–11	Ban of African trade. Louisiana becomes a destination for thousands of new slaves arriving from the Upper South and Lower South. Ethnic divides starting to be replaced by a sense of shared blackness.

I should repeat here that this attempt at periodization in *black and white* is based on speculative claims and may not stand the full test of primary sources. Nonetheless the inferences are based on a long examination of sources, primary as well as secondary, and this chapter, proffered as one building block in a new historiography, simply charts one way in which we might rethink and reimagine the history of Louisiana slavery in the *longue durée* using the 1808 ban as a key vantage point from which to look backward and forward.

Looking forward from 1808, one inevitably stumbles upon the January 1811 slave insurrection in Saint John the Baptist and Charles parish, usually known as the "Charles Deslondes insurrection." This little-known event, which remains so despite all the hustle and bustle that has accompanied the publication of Daniel Rasmussen's undergraduate honors thesis, *American Uprising: The Untold Story of America's Largest Slave Revolt*, helps close this chapter and find a way out.[44] There are several ways to look at this insurrection, whether in the Louisiana, southern, or Atlantic contexts. One choice—as evident in Robert Paquette's 2009 article or in Rasmussen's much-hyped book—is to emphasize the "greatness" of the short-lived insurrection and to stress the heroic character of the rebels, thereby integrating them into the classic revolutionary narrative of the early Republic. In terms of slave blood spilled, Paquette writes that the 1811 insurrection is far "greater" than the Nat Turner rebellion of 1831.[45] Another option, which I favor, is to propose the broad and rough outline of a new historical explanation and to suggest the possibility of new causalities. At least symbolically for now, I would like to link the 1811 slave insurrection to the 1808 ban of the African slave trade in New Orleans and its consequences, and to see the former as a possible sequel to the latter. This possible link was alluded to briefly, though indirectly, by William Claiborne, the governor of the Orleans Territory, on January 20, 1811, in a letter to Colonel Ballinger: "I hope also [the late insurrection] will induce the Legislature . . . to interpose some check to that indiscriminate importation of Slaves from the southern States."[46] This "indiscriminate importation," as Claiborne put it disapprovingly, only started because of the end of the African commerce. My hypothesis, simply put, is that the insurrection revealed—and was, at least partially, motivated by—a new, emerging understanding of what it meant to be black and slave, a shared understanding made possible starting after 1808.

The 1811 insurrection has often been linked to the arrival of about three thousand slaves from Saint-Domingue in 1809, but never to the 1808 ban and the social and cultural transformations that ensued. The formulation of this link serves at least two purposes.

First, it is one way to break free from a startling overreliance on the records left by the planters and authorities who repressed the revolt[47] and a host of surprisingly omniscient—but anonymous—eyewitnesses whose sensational accounts were published in northern and southern newspapers between mid-February and the end of March 1811.[48] These records, in particular newspaper accounts, variously describing "insurrection of blacks," "bloody news," "insurrection in Orleans," and "Louisiana Insurrection," have so far never been analyzed in terms of their political conditions of creation and the rumors they participated in starting. And yet I strongly believe that they stand more as reflections of the desire for unity on the part of the emerging planter class and its fear of destruction than actual records of a slave insurrection.[49] Also at issue in these sources are the modalities of integration of the new territory into the Union. For example, in one newspaper account published in the Boston Repertory, under the title "Order Reestablished in the Mississippi Territory," the emphasis was not put on slavery and slave resistance. Actually the words slave and slavery were never used in the story. The emphasis was put instead on Republican order and the importance of reassuring potential settlers interested in relocating their slaves down south in the future state of Louisiana: "Let monthly musters and trainings restore general confidence, *and shew those who would wish to emigrate to our territory that we are prepared for every exigency from within and without* [emphasis added]."[50] If these sources do reflect, moreover, on the tensions then developing between "Anglo" and "French" Louisianans—the former criticizing the latter for their brutality and implicit lack of American paternalism, the latter reassuring the federal authorities that they were good citizens of the early Republic[51] as well as strong advocates of the southern slave system—it is unclear what truthfulness they may contain about a plot they may have witnessed but also surely imagined.

By linking 1808 to 1811, I would like secondly to call for research that would step back from the insurrection per se in order to reconstruct instead the way race was remade in early nineteenth-century Louisiana, a period marked by increased racial tensions, confrontations, and fears that produced what I see as a radicalization of white-black relationships.[52] Examples of such a phenomenon abound in the archives. In the records of the Conseil de Ville, for example, one finds a recurrent language of entrapment as though runaway slaves and other black rebels surrounded the city.[53] In notarial records one finds dramatic white testimonies about the fear of black rape, one of the greatest fantasies of the South.[54] Other records shed light on the black/white confrontation through narratives of slave suicides.[55]

To look at a possible connection between 1808 and 1811 is to envisage, I think, the possibility of a society suddenly transformed, both from the white and black perspectives: from the margins of the slave Atlantic to the center of the slave South, from a white/black proximity to threatening slave majorities, from small rice farms to large sugar and cotton establishments. In this process of change, planters feared that Louisiana might become a new Saint-Domingue, a fear reinforced by the perceived impossibility of mapping and controlling the new spaces of slavery in the territory. Whites could accommodate and control free blacks and mulattoes as long as the latter accepted the new racial rules,[56] but they feared slaves as the slave system took on a drastically different turn.

The new, raw, black and white reality of Louisiana slavery seemingly struck the territory, the South, and the nation with dramatic effect a mere three years after the abolition of the Atlantic slave trade came into effect. On January 8, 1811, a sizable number of slaves from the parishes of Saint John the Baptist and principally Saint Charles—that is, immediately above Orleans parish and the capital—rose up against their masters and, for two days, threatened the planters' new cotton and sugar world as they marched along the east bank of the Mississippi, first downriver, then upriver. On the third day, the revolt was brutally repressed, arrested slaves were interrogated, and most of them executed. In the two months that followed, newspapers across the nation reported the event with much sensationalism, putting the blame largely on the nefarious influence of Saint-Domingue—just two years earlier, about three thousand Saint-Domingue slaves had arrived in New Orleans, along with about three thousand whites and as many free people of color. One man, in particular, a certain Charles, belonging to the widow Deslondes—supposedly of Saint-Domingue origin but actually born in Louisiana—was referred to as the leader of the whole affair.[57]

Despite its undeniable importance, the revolt is still veiled in many mysteries—even more so as the primary sources, most of them written in French, have often been read and translated with a certain liberality.[58] Questions about the event remain unanswered. Out of the maybe one hundred or so insurrectionists, how many participated of their free will? Reports of slaves being brutalized by Charles, or others, exist, though these records have hardly surfaced so far in accounts of the event. Was there indeed one leader, as whites wrote in their letters to the governor and to the press, or was it a decentralized revolt? The slave interrogations, when looked at carefully, rarely mention Charles Deslondes—a compound phrase coined by whites at the time—but point toward the existence of multiple chiefs, in particular Dagobert, Romeo, or Amar, the last one being described as "chef de brigand, dénoncé comme tel par tous les autres brigands" (chief of the brigands and denounced as such by all other brigands). Did slaves really want to march on to New Orleans, as is today memorialized, and did they say so? Did they utter the words "Liberty or Death," which are usually ascribed to them? The sources would tend to deny both claims, in particular the "Liberty or Death" quotation, more reminiscent of Patrick Henry or Jean-Jacques Dessalines than anything else. Did the slaves march clothed in military garb and with full colors displayed, as one of the planters involved, Manuel Andry, asserted in a self-serving letter to the governor? Or could it have been a discursive strategy used by Andry to impress Governor Claiborne and to hide the simple bestiality that Andry and his troops manifested in repressing the revolt.

Three interpretations of the event have dominated up to now. One is that the insurrection was an outgrowth of the Saint-Domingue slave revolt—according to this theory, maroons were greatly involved in the preparation of the plot, a fact that does not appear in the records. Another asserts that the year 1811 was just another episode in the fight of the oppressed of the New World to liberate themselves. And the final interpretation is that it was simply a reaction to the new, harsh work conditions imposed by sugar planters.

More recently Adam Rothman has advanced the very interesting possibility that the insurrection was the end point of major political and commercial changes in Louisiana. As he puts it, "during the early years of the sugar boom in lower Louisiana, commercial development and political turmoil increased opportunities for individual and collective resistance by slaves, which in turn provoked new responses from local authorities," and "ultimately all the tensions of commercial and political development in lower Louisiana overflowed in January 1811, when enslaved people in the sugar plantation districts above New Orleans rose in the largest slave rebellion in the history of the United States."[59]

Rothman has probably proposed the most promising hypothesis so far, and I would like to build on it here. Indeed what he sees as "commercial development and political turmoil" was in my opinion predicated on—or went hand in hand with—race and dramatic changes in the racial foundations of Louisiana. There were commercial developments and political changes because there were major racial transformations, and vice versa. Interrogated as to the insurrectionists' objectives, Jupiter, one of the slaves supposedly involved in the revolt, responded that the rebels wanted "to destroy white men" (*détruire les blancs*).[60] As opposed to previous slave rebellions or insurrection attempts—for example the Natchez revolt of 1728, when Africans and Native Americans banded together; the Bambara revolt of 1731; or the 1795 Pointe Coupée plot, in which Africans played a defining role[61]— the 1811 insurrection was apparently motivated by a simple racial motive, "to destroy white men."

One thing is certain. As testified by compensation records filed by the planters who had lost slaves in the revolt, the insurrectionists were a motley group and their varied origins do not point toward the existence of an ethnic plot. Attempts at recreating ethnic solidarities are evident in other sources such as runaway slave advertisements or in lists of arrested slaves kept in the New Orleans police jail. The records of the insurrection show a different picture, one in which several slave drivers participated, as well as skilled sugar slaves, ploughmen and field slaves, "blacks," and "mulattoes." Skilled and mobile carpenters joined with domestic servants and other "nègres de confiance" (negroes that can be trusted). "Congo" slaves and two other Africans banded with Creoles, some from Louisiana, some from Jamaica, and possibly others from the American states and territories further north. Of course the slaves' show of black solidarity was a fragile one, and many slaves actually refused to take part in the action. True, it seems the insurrection included a multiplicity of "chefs des brigands," but it is not impossible that their attempt at "destroying white men" was predicated on a budding corporate blackness, a shared understanding of a new racial identity born of the peculiar encounter of people that took place in the aftermath of January 1, 1808—a peculiar encounter incarnated by the heterogeneity of the insurrectionists' group.

Armed with this modern type of identity, it may be that slaves forced whites to respond with the utmost brutality and, in so doing, to put on a dramatic show of their emerging whiteness for the first time in the early American period. As Governor Claiborne put it to the secretary of state six days after the start of the insurrection: "the arduous activity and firmness of the Militia have made an impression upon the Blacks that will not . . . for a long time be effaced."[62] In a sense the objective of the repression of the insurrection was both to impress blacks with white, glowing force as well as to perform whiteness, an idea developed by one of the generals involved in the repression, Wade Hampton. The show was directed to blacks *and* whites, "The prompt display & exhibition of a regular Military force all along the Coast (the river) by land & water, has had a most happy effect, *as well upon the blacks, as the Citizens, who by this countenance have been enabled to use & feel their own strength.*"[63]

In other words the 1811 slave insurrection may represent a dual expression of emergent black *and* white solidarity. If slaves may have expressed their new budding blackness without ethnicity by revolting, the new, emerging Louisiana planter class may have expressed its patriotism and attachment to the slave system by repressing the revolt, and by doing so manifested its new whiteness, too, without ethnicity.

Notes

1. This article is part of a Social Sciences and Humanities Research Council (Canada) project that takes the slave insurrection of 1811 in Saint John the Baptist and Saint Charles parishes as a pivotal moment in the evolution of slave cultures, slave identities, and racial relations from the beginning of the Spanish period to the early American period.

2. Shannon Lee Dawdy, *Building the Devil's Empire: French Colonial New Orleans* (Chicago: University of Chicago Press, 2008); Nathalie Dessens, *From Saint Domingue to New Orleans: Migration and Influences* (Gainesville: University Press of Florida, 2007); Cécile Vidal, "Francité et situation coloniale: Nation, empire et race en Louisiane française (1699–1769)," *Annales HSS*, no. 5 (2009): 1019–50; Emily Clark, *Masterless Mistresses: The New Orleans Ursulines and the Development of a New World Society, 1727–1834* (Chapel Hill: University of North Carolina Press, 2007); Jennifer Spears, *Race, Sex, and Social Order in Early New Orleans* (Baltimore: Johns Hopkins University Press, 2009); Guillaume Aubert, "'Français, Nègres et Sauvages': Constructing Race in French Colonial Louisiana" (Ph.D. diss., Tulane University, 2002). This new historiographical phase marks the end of the Gwendolyn Midlo Hall period, in which her *Africans in Colonial Louisiana: The Development of Afro-Creole Culture in the Eighteenth Century* (Baton Rouge: Louisiana State University Press, 1992) dominated all debates and acquired the status of paradigm. See also Peter K. Kastor and François Weil, *Empires of the Imagination: Transatlantic Histories of the Louisiana Purchase* (Charlottesville: University of Virginia Press, 2009).

3. Emily Clark with Virginia M. Gould, "The Feminine Face of Afro-Catholicism in New Orleans, 1727–1852," *William and Mary Quarterly* 59, no. 2 (2002): 409–48; Jean-Pierre Le Glaunec, "À la re-découverte des esclaves catholiques de Louisiane: Naissance et formation d'une communauté afro-catholique autour de la Cathédrale Saint-Louis, 1790–1830" (postgraduate thesis, Université Paris 7, 2001).

4. This aspect of the history of Louisiana slavery—the migration of Anglophone, Protestant slaves in the early nineteenth century—has hardly been touched by historians. See Alan Kulikoff, "Uprooted People: Black Migrants in the Age of the American Revolution, 1790–1820," in *Slavery and Freedom in the Age of the American Revolution*, ed. Ira Berlin and Ronald Hoffman (Charlottesville: University of Virginia Press, 1983), 143–71; Adam Rothman, *Slave Country: American Expansion and the Origins of the Deep South* (Cambridge, Mass.: Harvard

University Press, 2005). On interstate commerce within the United States, see Michael Tadman, *Speculators and Slaves: Masters, Traders, and Slaves in the Old South* (Madison: University of Wisconsin Press, 1989); Lacy K. Ford, *Deliver Us from Evil: The Slavery Question in the Old South* (Oxford: Oxford University Press, 2009); Walter Johnson, *Soul by Soul: Life inside the Antebellum Slave Market* (Cambridge, Mass.: Harvard University Press, 1999); Walter Johnson, ed., *The Chattel Principle: Internal Slave Trades in the Americas* (New Haven, Conn.: Yale University Press, 2004).

5. The phrase "blackness without ethnicity" refers to Livio Sansone's book *Blackness without Ethnicity: Constructing Race in Brazil* (New York: Palgrave Macmillan, 2003). Sansone reexamines the central Brazilian paradigm of a nation of racial and ethnic mixture in which ethnicities were considered almost nonexistent until very recently. In *Blackness without Ethnicity,* Sansone proposes a new way to ethnicize race relations in Brazil, stressing the fact that ethnicities are social constructions that serve a purpose and not essential categories.

6. Guillaume Aubert, "'To Establish One Law and Definite Rules': Race, Religion, and the Transatlantic Origins of the Louisiana *Code Noir,*" in *Louisiana and the Atlantic World in the Eighteenth and the Nineteenth Centuries,* ed. Cécile Vidal (forthcoming).

7. Jean-Pierre Le Glaunec, "'Un nègre nommè [*sic*] Lubin ne connaissant pas Sa Nation' —or How to Start Re-Thinking and Re-Historicizing the Formation of Slave Cultures and Communities in Lower Louisiana, ca. 1780–ca. 1812," in Vidal, *Louisiana and the Atlantic World.*

8. Jean-Pierre Le Glaunec, "Slave Migrations in Spanish and Early American Louisiana: New Sources and New Estimates," *Louisiana History* 46 (Spring 2005): 185–209 and 211–30; "Slave Migrations and Slave Control in Spanish and Early American New Orleans," in *Empires of the Imagination: Transatlantic Histories of the Louisiana Purchase,* ed. Peter K. Kastor and François Weil (Charlottesville: University of Virginia Press, 2009), 204–38; Greg O'Malley, "Beyond the Middle Passage: Slave Migration from the Caribbean to North America, 1619–1807," *William and Mary Quarterly, 3rd ser.,* 66 (January 2009): 125–72.

9. On the distinction between a slave society and a society with slaves, see Ira Berlin, *Many Thousands Gone: The First Two Centuries of Slavery in North America* (Cambridge, Mass.: Harvard University Press, 1998).

10. Vidal, "Francité et situation coloniale," 1028–29.

11. Michael Gomez, *Exchanging Our Country Marks: The Transformation of African Identities in the Colonial and Antebellum South* (Chapel Hill: University of North Carolina Press, 1998).

12. Richard Follett, *The Sugar Masters: Planters and Slaves in Louisiana's Cane World, 1820–1860* (Baton Rouge: Louisiana State University Press, 2005).

13. Dawdy, *Building the Devil's Empire,* 11.

14. Sylvia Frey, "The American Revolution and the Creation of a Global African World," in *From Toussaint to Tupac: The Black International since the Age of Revolution,* ed. Michael O. West, William G. Martin, and Fanon Che Wilkins (Chapel Hill: University of North Carolina Press, 2009), 48.

15. Another example of this obscurity is a recent article by Daniel Littlefield in which he attempts a synthesis of the history of slavery and race relations in Louisiana from the French period to the slave insurrection of 1811, an event that will be discussed below. According to him the "watershed" in the history of Louisiana slavery occurred in the 1790s, namely in the

rise of sugar and cotton. No mention is made of 1808. Daniel Littlefield, "Slavery in French Louisiana: From Gallic Colony to American Territory," in *Louisiana Culture from the Colonial Era to Katrina*, ed. John Lowe (Baton Rouge: Louisiana State University Press, 2008), 92.

16. Paul Lachance, "The Politics of Fear: French Louisianians and the Slave Trade, 1786–1809," *Plantation Society* 1 (June 1979): 162–97; Thomas Marc Fiehrer, "The African Presence in Colonial Louisiana: An Essay on the Continuity of Caribbean Culture," in *Louisiana's Black Heritage*, ed. Robert R. MacDonald and John R. Kemp (New Orleans: Louisiana State Museum, 1979), 3–31.

17. Daniel H. Usner, *Indians, Settlers & Slaves in a Frontier Exchange Economy: The Lower Mississippi Valley before 1783* (Chapel Hill: University of North Carolina Press, 1992); Hall, *Africans in Colonial Louisiana*.

18. Thomas Ingersoll, *Mammon and Manon in Early New Orleans: The First Slave Society in the Deep South, 1718–1819* (Knoxville: University of Tennessee Press, 1999); Aubert, "Français, Nègres et Sauvages."

19. Cécile Vidal, "The Language of Race and Ethnicity: The Use and Appropriation of Ethnic and Racial Categories in French Colonial Louisiana," paper presented at the Southern Historical Association, October 2008.

20. Dawdy, *Building the Devil's Empire*; Spears, *Race, Sex, and Social Order.*

21. Dawdy, *Building the Devil's Empire*, 209.

22. Spears, *Race, Sex, and Social Order*, 217.

23. Paul Lovejoy, "The African Diaspora: Revisionist Interpretations of Ethnicity, Culture, and Religion Under Slavery," *Studies in the World History of Slavery, Abolition, and Emancipation* 2 (1997), http://www.yorku.ca/nhp/publications/Lovejoy_Studies%20in%20the%20World%20History%20of%20Slavery.pdf, accessed February 7, 2012; Gomez, *Exchanging Our Country Marks.*

24. Gwendolyn Midlo Hall, *Slavery and African Ethnicities in the Americas: Restoring the Links* (Chapel Hill: University of North Carolina Press, 2005).

25. Gomez, *Exchanging Our Country Marks*; Kevin D. Roberts, "Slaves and Slavery in Louisiana: The Evolution of Atlantic World Identities, 1791–1831" (Ph.D., diss., University of Texas at Austin, 2003).

26. Hall, *Africans in Colonial Louisiana*; Ingersoll, *Mammon and Manon.*

27. As far as the Spanish period is concerned, it was until recently postulated that the slave trade records had disappeared. Yet most of the records are available in Spain and the United Kingdom. Uninformed comments about the Louisiana slave trade still abound. In her recent book, Jennifer Spears has argued that from the mid-1770s, "Euro-Louisianan planters could finally, after eighty years, purchase as many slaves as they needed or could afford." As a matter of fact, the slave trade was very limited, if not completely halted, until the mid-1780s. In the five years that followed, the Louisiana slave trade indeed reached important proportions, but planters and authorities never stopped complaining about the difficulties of providing for slaves. Spears, *Race, Sex, and Social Order*, 307n4. See also the recent article by Douglas Chambers, "Slave Trade Merchants of Spanish New Orleans, 1763–1803: Clarifying the Colonial Slave Trade to Louisiana in Atlantic Perspective," in *New Orleans in the Atlantic World: Between Land and Sea*, ed. William Boelhower (London & New York: Routledge, 2009), 335–46. The article's intent (one of clarification) is marred by the fact it is not based on Spanish and British records.

28. Littlefield, "Slavery in French Louisiana," 77 (emphasis added).

29. Berlin, *Many Thousands Gone*.

30. About the importance of the "Bambara" or "Bamana" minority in early Louisiana and its tendency to resist slavery, see Hall, *Africans in Colonial Louisiana*, 96–118, and *Slavery and African Ethnicities in the Americas*, 96–100. On the use of the word *Bambara* and its meanings, see Peter Caron, "'Of a Nation Which the Others Do Not Understand': Bambara Slaves and African Ethnicity in Colonial Louisiana," *Slavery and Abolition* 18, no. 1 (1997): 98–121.

31. Ingersoll, "The Slave Trade and the Ethnic Diversity of Louisiana's Slave Community," *Louisiana History* 37, no. 2 (1996): 137–38, 151.

32. See Gwendolyn Hall's Afro-Louisiana History and Genealogy Database, http://www.ibiblio.org/laslave/, accessed on April 26, 2010.

33. Le Glaunec, "Slave Migrations."

34. Le Glaunec, "Nègre nommè Lubin."

35. Lachance, "Politics of Fear," 166.

36. Le Glaunec, "Slave Migrations."

37. See also bills of sales such as those in the John McDonogh Papers, Tulane University, Special Collections, New Orleans.

38. An evocative comment on the state of the Louisiana slave trade in the Spanish period is that of Martin Navarro in June 1786: "El comercio de negros, no obstante la carencia de plata, continua, *bien que lentamente*" (emphasis added). "Oficio de Don Martin Navarro al Marques de la Sonora," Collección de documentos sobre Luisiana, folio 130, Spanish National Library.

39. Stephanie Smallwood, *Saltwater Slavery: A Middle Passage from Africa to American Diaspora* (Cambridge, Mass.: Harvard University Press, 2007), 5, 191.

40. Le Glaunec, "Slave Migrations," 185–209, 211–30.

41. Jean-Pierre Le Glaunec, "The Lost World of Jean-Michel Fortier, Citizen, and Merchant of Louisiana, as Seen through His Correspondence," in *Haïti: Regards croisés*, ed. Nathalie Dessens and Jean-Pierre Le Glaunec (Paris: Manuscrit de l'Université, 2007), 95–117.

42. Le Glaunec, "Slave Migrations."

43. Jean-Pierre Le Glaunec, "Lire et écrire la fuite d'esclaves dans le monde atlantique: Essai d'interprétation à partir des annonces pour esclaves en fuite publiées dans les journaux de Louisiane, Jamaïque et Caroline du Sud entre 1800 et 1815" (Ph.D. diss., Université Paris 7, 2007).

44. Daniel Rasmussen, *American Uprising: The Untold Story of America's Largest Slave Revolt* (New York: Harper, 2011).

45. Robert Paquette, "'A Horde of Brigands'? The Great Louisiana Slave Revolt of 1811 Reconsidered," *Historical Reflections* 35, no. 1 (2009): 72–96.

46. Dunbar Rowland, ed., *Official Letter Books of W. C. C. Claiborne, 1801–1816* (Jackson, Miss.: State Department of Archives and History, 1917), 109. The real concern, in Claiborne's opinion, was not so much the formation of new racial identities following the start of a massive southern slave trade but the "bad" characters of the slaves shipped south. See his address to the territorial legislature on January 29, 1811: "To guard however more effectually against occurrences of this kind for the future, some further, and stronger preventive to that indiscriminate importation of slaves, should be devised. It is a fact of notoriety that negroes of Character the most desperate and conduct the most infamous.—Convicts pardoned on

condition of transportation, the refuse of jails, are frequently introduced into this Territory" (123).

47. In particular, newspapers, official correspondence, and territorial papers.

48. See Paquette, "Horde of Brigands." See also Thomas Marshall Thompson, "National Newspaper and Legislative Reactions to Louisiana's Deslondes Slave Revolt of 1811," *Louisiana History* 33, no. 1 (1992): 5–29.

49. On writing about slave revolts, see Michael P. Johnson, "Denmark Vesey and his Co-Conspirators," *William and Mary Quarterly*, 3rd ser., 58, no. 4 (2001): 915–76; and Sibylle Fischer, *Modernity Disavowed: Haiti and the Cultures of Slavery in the Age of Revolution* (Durham, N.C.: Duke University Press, 2004).

50. *The Repertory*, February 22, 1811.

51. See, for example, Governor Claiborne to Mr. Dubourg, January 14, 1811, in Rowland, *Official Letter Books*, 99. See also Claiborne to Col. Vilerae [*sic*], January 16, 1811: "Assure my fellow Citizens of my confidence in their patriotism and bravery, and tender to them my best thanks for the services they have rendered the Territory," 101. Also Claiborne to Judge St. Martin, January 19, 1811.

52. See, for comparison, James Sidbury, *Ploughshares into Swords: Race, Rebellion, and Identity in Gabriel's Virginia, 1730–1810* (Cambridge: Cambridge University Press, 1997).

53. Le Glaunec, "Slave Migrations and Slave Control."

54. See, for example, case 52 in Saint Charles Parish Courthouse records, "Procès du nègre charles appartenant à Alexandre Chopin, Jugement, Exécution et estimation du dit nègre," October 6, 1808.

55. See Saint Charles Parish Courthouse records, "Procès-verbal par le sindic [*sic*] Dn Carlos Masicot [*sic*] sur laffaire [*sic*] d'un nègre de Mr. F^{cs} S^t. Amand qui avait voulue [*sic*] se tuer," April 15, 1799, 104–6. Other cases of slave suicides are reported in *Le Moniteur de la Louisiane*.

56. See, for example, how Governor Claiborne praised the support of free blacks in repressing the revolt, explaining by the same token that free blacks were put under the orders of a white officer. Claiborne to the Secretary of State, January 14, 1811, in Rowland, *Official Letter Books*, 100.

57. About the revolt, see Paquette, "Horde of Brigands." See also Herbert Aptheker, *American Negro Slave Revolts* (New York: Columbia University Press, 1943); Nathan Buman, "'To Kill Whites': The 1811 Louisiana Slave Insurrection" (master's thesis, Louisiana State University, 2008); Robert Paquette, "Revolutionary Saint Domingue in the Making of Territorial Louisiana," in *A Turbulent Time: The French Revolution and the Greater Caribbean*, ed. David Barry Gaspar and David Patrick Geggus (Bloomington: Indiana University Press, 1997), 204–25; Robert Paquette, "The Drivers Shall Lead Them: Image and Reality in Slave Resistance," in *Slavery, Secession, and Southern History*, ed. Robert Paquette and Lou Ferleger (Charlottesville: University of Virginia Press, 2000), 31–58; Junius Rodriguez, "Rebellion on the River Road: The Ideology and Influence of Louisiana's German Coast Slave Insurrection of 1811," in *Antislavery Violence: Sectional, Racial, and Cultural Conflict in Antebellum America*, ed. John R. McKivigan and Stanley Harrold (Knoxville: University of Tennessee Press, 1999), 65–88; Albert Thrasher, *On to New Orleans! Louisiana's Historic 1811 Slave Revolt* (New Orleans: Cypress, 1996).

58. A recent example of this approach to the sources is Rasmussen's *American Uprising*. The author never thought it useful to go back to the original sources written in French. Instead he trusted the English abstracts and translations proposed by Glen Conrad and Albert Thrasher. See *American Uprising*, 263.

59. Adam Rothman, *Slave Country: American Expansion and the Origins of the Deep South* (Cambridge, Mass.: Harvard University Press, 2005), 74, 95, 109.

60. Case 17 in Saint Charles Parish Courthouse records, February 20, 1811, "Interrogatoire et Jugement rendu contre le nègre Jupiter appartenant à Manuel Andry."

61. Hall, *Africans in Colonial Louisiana*, 96–118, 316–74.

62. William Claiborne to the secretary of state, Rowland, *Official Letter Books*, 100.

63. Wade Hampton to the Secretary of War, January 16, 1811, in *The Territorial Papers of the United States*, vol. 9, *The Territory of Orleans, 1803–1812* (Washington, D.C.: Government Printing Office, 1940), 918 (emphasis added).

IRISH AMERICAN IDENTITY AND THE REOPENING OF THE ATLANTIC SLAVE TRADE

David T. Gleeson

U pon arrival in the United States in 1853, the Irish patriot John Mitchel immediately took up the politics that had gotten him arrested at home in Ireland and sentenced to penal servitude. He founded a newspaper in New York City, the *Citizen,* and continued his vitriolic attacks on British policy in Ireland as well as his strong advocacy of Irish independence. A run in with the Catholic Church and the bitterness of Irish politics in the city eventually persuaded Mitchel to move south to avoid as he called it, "the blatherskite" of New York. He decided to take up farming in East Tennessee but found it to be too demanding and isolating. He missed the sophistication and conversation of town life and eventually moved into the nearest city, Knoxville. He quickly returned to the political scene and refounded his newspaper but now as the *Southern Citizen.* He continued his interest in Irish politics, but the paper's new title indicated a new cause for Mitchel, the South. Indeed the more specific raison d'être of the *Southern Citizen* was to campaign for the reopening of the transatlantic slave trade, which had been banned in the United States in 1808.[1]

Mitchel's endorsement of reopening put him on the extreme end of American and even southern politics in the 1850s. The call for the repeal of the 1808 ban was led by L. W. Spratt of Charleston, who had founded the *Charleston Standard* in 1854 to push the issue. Spratt and others who supported him tried to get the South Carolina state legislature to endorse the plan but failed. To many it brought back memories of the infamous middle passage, while for others it was another attempt to provoke a sectional crisis that would lead to the secession of southern states. Despite its lack of success, it was, as one scholar describes it, a serious effort in the proslavery advocates' "counter-revolution of slavery."[2] The slave trade issue can tell us about more, however, than just the politics of the 1850s. It can give insight into racial, class, and national identity. The campaign to reopen the trade highlighted a hardening of racial ideology as racism moved into a "scientific" mode. Researching and writing in the 1840s and 1850s, men such as Josiah Nott of Mobile, Alabama, began to "classify" human beings along strict racial lines. Defining people as distinct races became fashionable and a vital element of any national project. John Mitchel had been a member of the Young Ireland movement, founded in the 1840s to create a cultural Irish nationalism. Its newspaper, the *Nation*, indicated clearly its aim to create a new sense of Irish unity built around an imagined community of Irish people that had deep roots and transcended the deep religious divisions in Ireland. The movement then defended the Irish people, poor and rich, Catholic and Protestant, as an ancient nation with a long history of civilization. The defined "other" to this new Irish identity was the greedy and crafty English "Anglo-Saxon." Ireland needed to break free from connection to "perfidious Albion" and take its proper place among the nations of the earth.[3]

Mitchel was one of the strongest advocates of Irish freedom and had a democratic vision for it once the country had gained its independence. It seemed surprising then that Mitchel would become an advocate of African slavery and see black Africans not as anticolonial allies but as much "others" as the English in defining what the Irish were both at home and in America. Mitchel's first encounter with slavery had occurred during his transport to Australia in 1848 when his ship stopped in Brazil, and here he took it as an opportunity not to condemn Africans but instead the "Anglo-Saxons." Slaves apparently manned boats resupplying his ship, and Mitchel surmised them to be "African-born"; he "surveyed them long and earnestly, for before this day I never saw a slave in his slavery—I mean a merchantable slave, a slave of real money value, whom a prudent man, will in the way of business, pay for and feed afterwards." He wrote that "these slaves in Brazil [were] fat and merry, obviously not over-worked nor under-fed, and it is a pleasure to see the lazy rogues lolling in their boats, sucking a piece of green sugar-cane, and grinning and jabbering together." Mitchel continued that the slaves in Latin colonies seemed better treated than they had been under the English or were in the United States, adding, "To the exercise of power this Anglo-Saxon race always adds insolence." Ultimately he asked a ringing rhetorical question whose implied answer echoed the sentiment of many Irish in America: "Is it better then, to be the slaves of a merciful master and just man, or to be serf to an Irish Land–appropriator? God Knoweth."[4]

Despite his praise for slavery in Brazil, he still declared in 1848, that "I do not pretend that I altogether like the sight of these slaves. If I were a rich man I would prefer to have my wealth in any other kind of commodity or investment—except, of course, the credit funds."[5] On the benefits of slave ownership and American slave owners, he would revise his original opinions. According to Mitchel himself, he changed his mind on the rightness of slavery in 1854 because of his dealings with the social reformers of the North. He disliked their "British" style of opposing slavery. They, he believed, were "apostles" of "human progress," something he had always opposed in Ireland because it had led to the famine. An admirer of Thomas Carlyle, *despite* Carlyle's anti-Irish and pro–Oliver Cromwell opinions, Mitchel had been consistent in his critique of laissez-faire capitalism. Having already witnessed the "beneficial" nature of slavery in Brazil, he responded to one critic who had charged him with being a participant in slavery: "as far as being a participator . . . we for our part wish we had a good plantation well stocked with healthy negroes in Alabama."[6] Within six years Mitchel had come to the conclusion, in theory anyway, that not just slavery but personally owning slaves was "right." Initially, however, he usually based his support of slavery in antiabolitionist rather than proslavery rhetoric. In a response to a critical and beseeching letter from abolitionist Henry Ward Beecher, Mitchel declared that abolitionism was "treason," based on a British plot "to drive a wedge between North and South." He asked rhetorically, "Do you believe that the Exterminators of Ireland, the roughshod riders of India, the armed speculators in Guinea lives, sincerely wish for the liberty of any being, anywhere under the Sun?" He continued, "Englishmen come over here as [abolitionism's] apostles, and it has upon it the slime and trail of Exeter Hall" (Home of British abolitionism on the Strand in London). Mitchel and other Irish nationalists had long pointed out that the same evangelicals who endorsed abolitionism had seen the Irish famine as the benign work of an "all-wise Providence" directing the progress of the world by dragging the premodern Irish peasant into the modern era.[7]

Whatever his reasoning, Mitchel's defense of slavery quickly made him popular throughout the South. As a result he became even more enamored with southerners and their racial identity. Invited to speak to legislatures, public meetings, and universities, he came to the conclusion that white southerners had a "peculiar gentleness of demeanor and quiet courtesy" that he believed was "attributable to the institution of slavery." This gentility existed because the "unquestionable possession of great power, involving great responsibilities—which responsibilities are fully recognized by public opinion—trains a man to habits of self restraint." Also, he believed, "Southern society, wherever its elements are in equilibrium or nearly —that is where the slaves are numerous enough to occupy the field of toil—is the most perfect form of social polity now existing anywhere in the world."[8]

Mitchel then took this belief in the slave system to its logical conclusion in his new newspaper, which despite its focus on Irish news and distribution throughout the Irish centers of population in the South, he considered primarily "a *Southern* [his emphasis] journal."[9] He became particularly interested in the efforts to endorse the reopening of the trade at the annual Southern Commercial Conventions. After their failure in the legislature, Spratt and his allies, both inside and outside South Carolina, focused instead on these conventions. They had been established in 1852, mainly at the instigation of James D. B. De Bow of New Orleans. Their goal was to advance the economic aims of the South, a region that seemed to be slipping behind the rest of the nation. While interested in modernizing and industrializing the South, the conventions recognized the unique importance of the plantation economy and the slave system that underpinned it. As sectional tensions

increased through the 1850s, these conventions increasingly became more belliger-
ent in their sectionalism.[10] At the 1856 convention in Savannah, Spratt broached the
issue of reopening the trade. The convention voted to table the motion but also
allowed it to come up again at the 1857 convention in Knoxville, Mitchel's new city
of residence. Although Knoxville was not a hotbed of southern radicalism, the slave
traders had their greatest success to date. There was a major debate on the issue
along with a motion to repeal part (article 8) of the Webster-Ashburton Treaty
(signed in 1842), that had committed the United States to supporting the Royal
Navy's blockading of the African slave trade. This motion passed but the pro–slave
trade men did not have enough votes to call for an actual reopening of the trade.
They did manage, however, to have a committee formed to present a report on the
issue at the 1858 convention in Montgomery, Alabama.[11] Mitchel was not a delegate
at the Knoxville convention, but William Swan, his close friend and newspaper
partner, was. As a former mayor of the city, Swan was an organizer of the event.
A slave owner, Swan was also a strong advocate of reopening the trade. Mitchel and
Swan were neighbors in Knoxville in the summer of 1857, and less than three
months later the two had founded the *Southern Citizen*.[12]

Mitchel's support for the cause was recognized at the 1858 Montgomery convention, when the delegates voted to give him a seat, on the motion of one "Mr.
Warren of South Carolina," to welcome "John Mitchell [*sic*] . . . the distinguished
Irish patriot." He performed some secretarial duties at the event, but the minutes
do not reflect his having made a speech. He did, however, admire the speech
of famous Alabama fire-eater William Lowndes Yancey. Although L. W. Spratt
attended again and presented the report commissioned from the year before calling for repeal of the laws prohibiting the foreign slave trade, it was Yancey who led
the charge in the debate. He defended the motion on constitutional grounds—that
is, that the 1808 prohibition was unconstitutional—but also on class grounds.
Reopening the trade, Yancey charged, would help poorer whites in the South by
giving them a chance to buy slaves: "We need to strengthen the institution; and how
better can we do that than by showing the non-slaveholding class of our citizens
that they can buy a negro for $200, which, in a few years, by his care and instruc-
tion, will become worth a thousand dollars? Teach the poor white man, who cannot buy a negro, that by this means he can buy one, you secure him to the interests
of the South." His main opponent on the issue, Roger Pryor of Virginia, disagreed
on a number of grounds but used Mitchel as an example of how even foreigners
could see the importance of slavery and become a supporter of the "peculiar institution" without actually owning slaves. Indeed Pryor noted how Yancey had been
"proud to pay the tribute of his admiration" to Mitchel. Mitchel himself was not
impressed, embracing Yancey's logic instead. (He would eventually describe himself as a "disciple" of Yancey's). Mitchel wrote in his newspaper that the South could
not hope to expand slavery, into Kansas, Cuba, Nicaragua, or wherever, without

more slaves. For the South to compete with the industrializing North, it had to exploit its agricultural assets to the fullest and it could only do this with more slaves. To Mitchel it was logical, because, as Yancey had stated in his speech, "the great distinction between North and South is to be found in our peculiar institution." Ultimately Spratt's report was tabled, but Mitchel was glad that the issue was now "before the southern people" and that it would eventually be passed not by the U.S. Congress but by an independent southern nation.[13]

In the meantime reopening the trade would help the South achieve its full economic potential. Mitchel had always been a practical nationalist, not just interested in Ireland's cultural heritage and mythic past. He left that to the poets such as Thomas Davis (the founder and spiritual guide of Young Ireland and founder of the newspaper the *Nation*). Despite his criticism of "progress," he was always far more concerned with the present and the future than the distant past and took a keen interest in economics. Through his friendliness and consultation with "a Louisiana planter," probably the Irish-born Maunsel White, he did believe, however, that reopening the trade would be good for the South. Thus despite his opposition to the liberal industrialization, his booster rhetoric would have made any bourgeois proud. On a major trip through the South, in early 1858, while passing through north Alabama in the fertile Tennessee Valley, he noticed "the teeming soil not half cultivated, the wilderness not half tamed." Mitchel explained this by also noting that "the assiduous overseers [were] too evidently short-handed in the fields, the unpicked cotton flaunting in the winter wind." He lamented that this lack of agricultural development would hurt the nearby town of Tuscumbia, which had pretensions of growth with "ambitiously laid-out rudiments of stately streets." This underdevelopment was doubly annoying because of "the millions of negro slaves at this moment for sale by the enterprising kings of Dahomey, Ashante, and Yoruba." Mitchel had similar feelings when traveling down the Mississippi and, on observing the Arkansas delta, tried to convince planters on board the steamboat of the need for reopening the trade and tapping the "million or two negroes" available in Africa. The planters were reluctant to agree; Mitchel believed it was because they were averse to increasing sectional tensions. This reluctance frustrated him, because it handicapped the "southern labor system from full development and fair play" and stopped the South from maintaining "Southern institutions and interests against the North." From early on during his life in the South, Mitchel believed that the region was in full competition with a different system in the North.[14]

Mitchel was sure of the origins of this difference. Writing an open letter to his nationalist friend back in Ireland, Father John Kenyon, Mitchel defended his stance on the slave trade in the *Southern Citizen*, declaring that the British "form of civilization," industrialization and laissez-faire capitalism, which he had also observed in the northern United States—representing "the spirit of the age," as he liked to call it—would lead "to ruin," as it had ruined the peasantry of Ireland. In the South he saw hope for an alternative, more "civilized" system. Thus his aim was "to promote the success of one and the ruin of the other." Once he had endorsed what Eugene Genovese has described as the South's "alternative World view," he went for it wholeheartedly. He easily linked it with his passion for Irish nationhood.[15]

This trait and Mitchel's deep hatred of Britain along with his personal experience of the South and southerners perhaps explain his enthusiasm for slavery. But there was something else motivating Mitchel: race. Increasingly through the 1840s and 1850s, defenders of slavery used not only cultural, religious, and economic arguments to defend slavery, but also "scientific" ones. Josiah Nott had in 1854 developed his taxonomy of humanity with whites at the top and blacks at the bottom. But within the white genus he subdivided again, with the Anglo-Saxon and Teuton at the top, ahead of southern Europeans and the Celts. As a romantic nationalist since the early 1840s, Mitchel had already believed in the essential nature of a national people. In his first defense against charges of inconsistency with respect to his support of slavery, he played this ethnic/national card. In his reply to Henry Ward Beecher, he denied that there was a natural right to liberty: "I am not aware that every human being, or any one has an 'inalienable right to life, liberty, and the pursuit of happiness.' People often forfeit life and liberty; and as to 'happiness' I do not even know what it is. On the whole I fear that this is jargon." The liberty that Mitchel spoke of for Ireland, he explained, was "the sort of liberty—no better, no worse—which . . . the slaveholding Corinthians fought for against the Romans, and the slaveholding Americans wrung from the British. It was National Independence."[16]

Thus nations, not individuals, were entitled to liberty. The Irish were a nation, and Africans were not. Mitchel therefore thought that only certain races were national in nature and thus fit for independence. In his critiques of British imperialism, for example, he had spoken up for the rights of Indians. In vivid terms he criticized the crushing of the Indian Rebellion of 1857 and specifically "Queen Victoria who robs the people of India of their land and because they try to regain them prefers to sell or give them away than fire them out of a cannon's mouth." The "Hindoos [*sic*] or the dominant people of Hindu-stan are of the Caucasian race," Mitchel believed, "of the same Semitic family, according to the ethnologists, from which sprung King David and the mother of Jesus Christ." India had been ruined by British intervention and could only be restored through Indian national resistance.[17] Of course the Irish were also from a "distinguished race." Mitchel had been very aware of nativist criticisms of the Irish in America and had fought hard against their charges. He worried that some of his new southern friends, who on the whole he had found not to be nativist, might have absorbed some of the Know-Nothing propaganda. He told his southern "friends" that "the white laborers of Europe are of the highest and choicest breed and blood of men," whose "depressed" condition was because of the "accident of position." This station they might soon

change and make "highest heads of Europe . . . sleep on an uneasy pillow." Ultimately the white people of the South might soon suffer as the poor whites of
Europe, as Ireland suffered under England's rule. "The North is England; the South
is Ireland," and "in national character the North is more English, the South more
Irish," Mitchel declared. He continued, "The actual descent and affinity of the
Southern population is in far the greatest part Irish, French, Welsh, Spanish—in any
case *Celtic.* Perhaps Southerners would be but little obliged to me (seeing they are
crammed with Anglo Saxon 'literature') for this averment. Nevertheless it is a com-
pliment. The Celtic is the superior breed; of finer organization, more fiery brain,
more a passionate heart—less greedy, grabbing, griping and groveling. The greatest
nations that modern Europe has yet seen—greatest in every sense—have been
France and Spain; Celtic both."[18] The Irish were just as good as the English—
actually better. He was effectively declaring the essential whiteness of Irish men and
women as well as all the "poor whites of Europe." Why then would he not as an
Irishman consider owning a "plantation" and "negroes"? Why would any "poor"
man not buy slaves if they were cheap enough? Mitchel therefore saw reopening the
slave trade primarily not as a way to control poor whites, but as a way to spread the
benefits of this alternative, slavery-based civilization. In the process this broadening
of slave ownership would challenge the alternative civilization, the one based on
"British commercialism" that seemed to dominate the nineteenth-century world.

One African American critic had noticed early on that the real basis of Mitchel's
support for slavery and the slave trade was not opposition to British imperialism
but race. In an open letter from one who signed himself "A Colored man," he
accused Mitchel of hypocrisy for supporting Irish freedom while arguing for
African slavery. What a contrast with "our Wards, Douglasses, Penningtons, Smiths
and Garnetts, true champions of freedom," he continued, who "would at one blow
strike the fetters from off the limbs of the oppressed from the people of every hue
or clime of the earth." The base of Mitchel's support for slavery was race, he concluded, because Mitchel saw blacks "as not fit for the privileges" of freedom.
Although written in 1854, this "colored man's" observation was very astute. While
Mitchel defended slavery on all kinds of grounds, in the *Southern Citizen* and elsewhere, he often defended the reopening of the slave trade explicitly on racial
grounds. Africans, he believed, were "barbarous," and slavery would thus be good
for them: "negro slaves are in a greatly better and higher position upon [the] plantation than any African negro in Africa ever was; and [the] luckiest, jolliest, and
freest [his emphasis] on the face of the earth are the four millions in these States."
On his trip through the South in 1858, when he advocated the economic development of the South through the reopening of the African slave trade, he pointed out
that the "millions" of Africans for sale by the "Kings of Dahomey, Ashante" needed
to be purchased "by reasonable people, who know the use of a slave." These millions were "crying aloud" to be brought to the South as chattel and rescued "from

a too probable death to ornament a mat palace with their skulls to propitiate a divine monkey, or merely to furnish forth as a solemn feast with their brains." Ultimately in light of this scenario, Mitchel wrote, "Does not Ethiopia stretch forth its hand to Alabama?" Here Mitchel fully endorsed and propagated the racist and ignorant view of Africa as a barbaric place with no worthwhile civilization. Ultimately then, for these explicitly racial reasons, "the cause of negro slavery is the cause of true philanthropy, so far as that race is concerned," and the only thing stopping "philanthropic" southerners from buying slaves "in the cheapest market" and thereby "rescuing [Africans] from brutal barbarism, cannibalism, fetishism— and elevating them to the comparative dignity of plantation hands" was the prohibition of the international slave trade, something that needed to change as soon as possible. Slavery, Mitchel believed, was the only condition fit for Africans. When Louisiana tried to introduce new African labor, but legally, through an "apprentice" scheme in 1858, Mitchel saw it as dishonorable "subterfuge" and the introduction of the "ruthless British system of *coolieism*." He also stated, however, that "to introduce barbarous Africans on any other footing [than that] of slaves and property [would] revolutionize the whole social structure."[19]

Unlike George Fitzhugh, for example, the infamous southern proslavery theorist and advocate for the slave trade, Mitchel, as a supporter of the European masses, did not support slavery "in the abstract," that is, as applicable and necessary in all societies. Slavery to Mitchel was not meant for white people, even very poor ones. Racial and national unity trumped class interests.[20] Here Mitchel was indicating his confidence in his own and his countrymen's whiteness. He, and they, did not have to "become white." They already were so and indeed came from a "superior" branch of the "master" Caucasian race. The debate over reopening the slave trade had given him the opportunity to define that whiteness very clearly. If he was successful in this debate, the Irish and other poorer whites would be able to participate fully in slave ownership.[21]

But how representative was John Mitchel? Most Irish Americans did not endorse his position on the slave trade. They remained national Democrats, opposed to the trade because it would destroy the party that had befriended them and ultimately the Union that had given them opportunity. Even though his newspaper circulated in both sections, North and South, the Irish community ignored Mitchel's calls to abandon the Democratic Party and become "disciples" of William Lowndes Yancey. Their church too had condemned the African slave trade, if not slavery itself. Presbyterian divines such as John Bailey Adger, Charleston born but the son of a Irish immigrant, took the lead in opposing the trade in South Carolina.[22] The practicalities of actually gaining Irish American support for the reopening are not relevant here. Mitchel's view of Irish racial and national identity is what really matters. Did other Irish in America have the same confidence in their own racial identity as white?

Opposition to reopening the slave trade, however, does not necessarily mean that more moderate Irish Americans rejected Mitchel's racial ideology. In fact in public, anyway, they accepted that slavery was the best condition for Africans. One of these opponents of reopening the trade was Irish American leader Andrew Gordon Magrath. Magrath was a moderate national Democrat in Charleston. He was not a supporter of reopening the trade in the mid-1850s, seeing it as an attempt by southern extremists to break up the Union. Yet Magrath was the federal judge who, in 1860, played the key role in destroying federal attempts to enforce the prohibition on importing slaves. In a decision dealing with the captain of the notorious slave ship the *Wanderer,* he chose to overturn an 1820 law that had declared breaking the slave trade embargo as "piracy." Even though he had upheld federal regulation of the international slave trade in an 1858 case, Magrath decided in 1860 that almost forty years after its passage, this law was unconstitutional and that slave trading was merely a "misdemeanor." This decision put official approval on the local reluctance to enforce the slave trade prohibition. Ultimately it was the culminating element of "Carolina planter politicians' equivocal position on the issue," which, as a result, created "a shield for slave traders' illegal activities."[23]

Though born in Charleston, Magrath was not a typical South Carolina politician. He had been an attorney before his appointment to the federal bench in 1856. He owned ten slaves in both 1850 and 1860, and it seems that he speculated in them. But he was not a fire-eater—far from it. He had opposed immediate secession in the early 1850s, when South Carolina radicals such as Robert Barnwell Rhett had pushed for it in response to the issue of slavery in the western territories. This stance drew the ire of the Rhett faction. Magrath was accused of being a traitor to his state and a place seeker. When Magrath received the nomination to a judgeship from President Franklin Pierce, his opponents saw it as a payoff. The criticism reached its height in 1856 when Magrath accepted a drafting to run for the U.S. Congress from Charleston. The *Mercury,* Rhett's mouthpiece, published a piece attacking Magrath in public for faults they had privately accused him of for years, namely of being a disreputable place seeker with no honor or patriotism. The piece was so vitriolic that the dispute eventually led to a duel between Magrath's younger brother and Rhett's nephew with Rhett's relative dying from a bullet to the head. As a result of the duel, Magrath withdrew from the candidacy and retained his judgeship, the position from which he made his decision.[24]

Magrath had always been active in the Irish community. The son of a 1798 United Irish Rebellion refugee, he was an avowed Irish nationalist as well as an active member of the Hibernian and St. Patrick's Benevolent Society. He had also commanded the Irish Volunteers in the 1830s and led them in the Seminole War in Florida. Often called on to speak at Irish events, he described in great detail the wrongs committed against Ireland by Great Britain. "Might triumphed over right" was a phrase he was fond of. Magrath also stood up for the Irish in America. When some South Carolina politicians began to flirt with the nativist Know-Nothings,

Magrath wrote a pamphlet defending the rights and loyalty of foreign and Catholic Americans, which was published in Charleston. He declared Know-Nothingism to be un-American and particularly detrimental to the South, stating that, unlike foreigners and Catholics, the Irish included, the Know-Nothings were abolitionists. He noted sarcastically that "[Wendell] Phillips, [William Lloyd] Garrison, [Charles] Sumner, and [William Henry] Seward, fit expositors of what is right and proper for the citizens of the Slaveholding States, pronounce such men [Irishmen] dangerous to the Republic; and we, forsooth! are asked to cry amen, to this patriotic ordinance."[25] The foreigners were better Americans than the likes of Phillips and others.

Magrath had positioned himself as a friend of the less fortunate, the Irish immigrant. He did not take the same stance toward the forced "migrants," African slaves. The *Wanderer* had been commissioned by the Georgia adventurer and fire-eater Charles A. L. Lamar. Lamar was young and ambitious and from a prominent and wealthy family. He saw reopening the trade as a way to make money (he estimated the profit of one expedition at $480,000). He decided to force the issue by deliberately and openly breaking the prohibition. In December 1858 Lamar transferred 170 African slaves, recently landed on Jekyll Island, Georgia, from the *Wanderer* to a steamboat and brought them up the coast to Savannah. His brazen act in the face of customs officials in the Georgia city led to the seizure of the *Wanderer* and to the arrest of some of the crew. The captain of the ship, William Corrie, was arrested in Charleston and came before Judge Magrath's court. Initially, on instructions from the attorney general of the United States, the local federal prosecutor, James L. Conner, tried to get the case transferred to Georgia, where the crime had been committed, and into the court of Justice James M. Wayne, who was on record supporting the strong prohibition on the foreign slave trade. Magrath, however, refused to make the transfer, and when Conner offered a motion of *nolle prosequi* (not to proceed; that is, to drop the charges), Magrath dismissed it. He seemed keen to try Corrie in his court, even giving the grand jury a second chance to indict the accused, something they had been disinclined to do. (Jury nullification of the prosecution of slave trade lawbreakers had become common in the 1850s and led, for example, to Lamar's escape from justice). A failure to indict would have led to Corrie's release but also to his rearrest and transfer to Georgia.[26]

Magrath felt his opinion so important that he had it published locally (by the agent of John Mitchel's *Southern Citizen* in Charleston, S. G. Courtenay). A major part of the opinion deals with the jurisdictional issue and highlights the legal hoops he jumped through to retain jurisdiction. When he finally got to the constitutionality of the 1820 law, declaring the breaking of the African slave trade prohibition as piracy, he first attacked it on technical grounds. Magrath read the law as one that made the enslavement of Africans in Africa piracy. But, he pointed out, the Africans brought on the *Wanderer* were already enslaved. In other words the crew of the *Wanderer* had not enslaved anyone, and thus they had not committed piracy but had merely broken a trade law, which was a misdemeanor, not a capital offense:

"To infer that the slave trade is piracy because seizing and decoying on a foreign shore a negro or mulatto, with intent to make him a slave, is so declared; is not, in my mind, recommended by a rule of reason, or consistent with any previous legislation." If all slave trading was piracy, the act should have explicitly said so. Also the fact that "there have been verdicts of acquittal rendered by juries . . . [which] have been regarded as indicative of a purpose on the part of juries not to enforce its provisions," Magrath surmised, was a sign of the incongruousness of the law. As to the argument that the intent of the original lawmakers, from the context and debate of the 1820 law, was to increase penalties against illegal slave trading, Magrath stated, quoting a Chief Justice Roger Taney opinion in a different case, that "'the judgement of the Court cannot in any degree be influenced by the construction placed upon it by individual members of Congress in the debate which took place on its passage; nor by the reasons assigned by them when supporting or opposing amendments.'"[27] In other words the "original intent" of the lawmakers was not relevant here.[28]

Magrath also, however, put forward reasons beyond his (rather contorted) interpretations of law and precedent. He offered a class argument, declaring it unfair that sailors were the only ones held accountable under the law, while the men who commissioned the slaving expedition, and who benefitted directly from it, were not liable under the 1820 law. He asked rhetorically, "But with what show of reason is it to be urged that an Act is intended for the suppression of the slave trade, as a trade or business; which imposes its penalties only on those persons who may be fairly presumed never able to engage in it as a trade or business?" The ship's crew were merely the conveyors, not the traders. Magrath provided a hypothetical to strengthen his case: "If a passenger shall land, with intent to sell one hundred negroes, purchased by him in Cuba, he is subject to fine and imprisonment. But if the captain of the vessel purchases but one, and lands him on the same intent, he would then be considered a pirate, and must suffer death. . . . Surely, the statement of such a consequence would be of itself, sufficient to show that the construction which leads to it, must be alike irrational and illegal."[29]

Similarly he emphasized race throughout the opinion. He always referred to Africans as "negroes" or "mulattoes" and implied that their condition on the coast of Africa was that of slaves. Slave traders usually bought their slaves rather than kidnapping them. Indeed under Magrath's logic, kidnapping a "negro or mulatto" was not piracy if the person kidnapped had already been a slave in Africa. He admitted that "personal freedom" on the sea was guaranteed and that robbery on it was "piracy," but for Africans the "right to freedom" only existed "when the servitude recognized by the Constitution and laws of the United States is proved *not* [emphasis added] to exist in the particular case. . . . Then the intent to make a slave or rob him of his right to freedom cannot be sustained; for he cannot be robbed of that which he did not possess." With virtually all slaves unable to speak English and at the mercy of the slave traders' word regarding the condition in which they were bought, Magrath had made it impossible for any international slave trader to be charged with piracy in the United States. The navy would literally have to catch a ship's crew kidnapping slaves in Africa to charge them with piracy. If the traders managed to get the Africans to the United States and were apprehended there by authorities, they were subject only to fine and/or imprisonment for breach of trade regulations. With southern juries unwilling to convict slave traders, the piracy law voided, and the price of slaves rising, the rewards far outweighed the risks of breaking the 1808 prohibition of the trade.[30]

Magrath had been the friend of the stranger and the refugee, but only if they were white. While obsessed with the plight of the Irish, he felt no sympathy for the plight of Africans. As a result of his decision, he received the praise of his former nemesis, the *Mercury.* He also received the approbation of his community when he pointedly resigned the bench after Abraham Lincoln's election in November 1860. For his efforts Charleston elected Magrath to the secession convention, far ahead in the vote count of Mr. Fire-Eater himself, Robert Barnwell Rhett. Serving as a Confederate judge, Magrath became governor of South Carolina in 1864. He remained a favorite of the Irish community too and was often asked to speak on its most important occasions. Magrath, like Mitchel, was a symbol of Irish America's essential whiteness, in both their own eyes and, despite certain stereotypes, in native white eyes too. Both Mitchel and Magrath were unique individuals in the Irish American milieu, but they were very popular in that milieu. Their own Irish American constituents did not object to their positions, because they too were confident in their own whiteness. For all the talk of "God Knoweth" whether the slaves were better off than the Irish peasants, everybody knew that Irish immigrants were in a much more favorable position to that of slaves.[31]

These case studies highlight how, on racial matters, the Irish always considered themselves white and did not have compunctions about participating in slave trading. The Ryans of Charleston, for example, were major slave traders, of the legal kind, and pillars of the Irish community in that city. Others had no problem with dealing in the illegal trade, especially when it seemed that white southern juries and some judges refused to enforce the full effects of the law. Timothy Meaher of Alabama, for example, smuggled Africans into his state in the late 1850s purely to make money. Indeed he and his brother had moved to Alabama from New York and adapted quickly to the slave economy. Meaher had begun life in the South as a deckhand on a steamboat in 1835 but had quickly risen to the rank of captain.[32] By 1860 he had become a successful lumber merchant and steamboat operator, to which occupations he added that of slave trader. This Irish American saw an economic opportunity, which, although risky, was quite lucrative. Maunsel White, a Louisiana sugar planter and friend and supporter of John Mitchel, also had a personal interest in reopening the trade—he wanted more slaves to work his numerous plantations. White, although one of the richest sugar planters in the state (he owned more than 230 slaves in 1850), saw the reopening as beneficial for more than just him. Somewhat distinctive among the sugar elite, he supported the party of the "common man," the Democrats. He was well aware of his own humble background, as he had come to the United States at age thirteen. A friend of Andrew Jackson, under whom he had fought at the Battle of New Orleans in 1815, he remained a Democrat throughout his life even though his sugar neighbors supported the Whigs and its high tariff policies. He was not a conservative trying to preserve the status quo but a booster looking for expansion and growth. He was a believer in "Southern equality" and believed the southern economy had to grow or it would die. He attended the commercial convention in Montgomery, for example, wrote articles for economic journals, and offered to sponsor a chair in economics and business statistics at the state university. Slavery's continued expansion through the import of slaves from Africa was compatible with his idea of the overall growth of the South. It would be good for the whole region, not just the large planters. The institution had been the key to his success and could be for others.[33]

The reality of slave ownership, however, was that the majority of Irish never owned slaves or had the opportunity to buy them. Nevertheless those who did not participate directly in slavery rarely attacked the racial reasoning behind it. They did not see slavery as degrading to white labor or necessarily detrimental to their interest. They defined themselves as white, different in tradition and class perhaps, but nonetheless white in the fullest sense, and if the slave trade had been reopened, they would have purchased slaves if they had, like the Ryans, Meaher, and White, the means to do so. The effort to reopen the international slave trade thus highlights how race was a crucial element of Irish identity in America. The supporters of the bans of the trade in the United States saw their efforts as part of an attempt to end slavery and in the process lance the boil of racial tensions that could lead to servile insurrection and race war. Thomas Jefferson, the president who signed the ban into effect in March 1807, believed that it would help end the American dilemma of "holding the wolf by the ears" and aid his country's aim to continue being an "Empire of Liberty." Ironically, as Adam Rothman and Steve Deyle have highlighted, the ban actually strengthened the institution of slavery within the United States.[34] It also, however, strengthened the racist ideology behind it too. Increasingly as the divide between black slavery and white liberty hardened, America became more a "white man's republic" than one that promised "life, liberty, and the pursuit of happiness" to "all men." Irish immigrants arriving in the United States quickly adapted to this growing racialization of American identity, added it to their own sense of Irishness, and helped create a hybrid Irish American one that was fully part of the white American mainstream. Leaders such as Mitchel and Magrath then could easily endorse the continued enslavement of Africans without fear of antagonizing the racial sensibilities of their Irish American constituents or indeed white Americans in general. Thus the story of these two men and their involvement in the attempt to reopen the international slave trade tells as much about antebellum American identity as it does of the effort to create an Irish American one.

Notes

1. John Mitchel to "Matilda," 6. Aug. 1855, D.107/M/1, Pinkerton Papers, Public Record Office of Northern Ireland, Belfast, Northern Ireland.; David T. Gleeson, *The Irish in the South, 1815–1877* (Chapel Hill: University of North Carolina Press, 2001), 69–70. The best biographies of Mitchel are William Dillon, *Life of John Mitchel*, 2 vols. (London: Kegan, Paul, Trench, 1888), and Bryan P. McGovern, *John Mitchel: Irish Nationalist, Southern Secessionist* (Knoxville: University of Tennessee Press, 2009).

2. Ronald T. Takaki, *A Pro-Slavery Crusade: The Agitation to Reopen the African Slave Trade* (New York: Free Press, 1971); Manisha Sinha, *The Counterrevolution of Slavery: Politics and Ideology in Antebellum South Carolina* (Chapel Hill: University of North Carolina Press, 2000), 125–52.

3. See Reginald Horsman, *Josiah Nott of Mobile: Southerner, Physician, and Racial Theorist* (Baton Rouge: Louisiana State University Press, 1997). For Young Ireland and creation of Irish identity, see Niamh Lynch, "Defining Irish Nationalism and Anti-Imperialism, Thomas Davis and John Mitchel," *Eire-Ireland* 42 (Spring–Summer 2007): 82–107, and Patrick Maume, "Young Ireland, Arthur Griffith, and Republican Ideology: The Question of Continuity," *Eire-Ireland* 34 (Summer 1999): 155–74.

4. John Mitchel, *Jail Journal* (Dublin: M. H. Gill and Son, 1921), 153–54.

5. Ibid., 154.

6. Quoted in the *Savannah (Ga.) Morning News*, January 19, 1854. For Mitchel and Carlyle, see *Jail Journal*, 204; Thomas Carlyle to Lord Clarendon, 26 May 1848, in *The Carlyle Letters Online*, ed. Kenneth J. Fielding, vol. 23, available at http://carlyleletters.dukejournals.org /cgi/content/full/23/1/lt-18480526-TC-LC-01, accessed January 21, 2008. For Carlyle and slavery, see James D. B. De Bow's *Commercial Review of the South and West* 2 (April 1850): 527–38.

7. Quoted in the *Boston Liberator*, February 17, 1854. For more on ideology of British evangelicals toward the Irish Famine, see Peter Gray, *Famine, Land and Politics: British Government and Irish Society, 1843–1850* (Dublin: Irish Academic Press, 1999).

8. *Jackson Mississippian and State Gazette*, April 11, 1854; *Boston Liberator*, April 28, 1854, July 16, 1858; *Savannah (Ga.) Daily Morning News*, December 31, 1856; John Mitchel to "Matilda," 6. Aug. 1855, D.107/M/1, Pinkerton Papers, Public Record Office of Northern Ireland, Belfast, Northern Ireland.

9. *Knoxville Southern Citizen*, January 21, March 18, 1858.

10. Sinha, *Counterrevolution of Slavery*, 133–35; Takaki, *Pro-Slavery Crusade*, 146–59. The commercial conventions began in 1845 but became annual events after 1852. Vicki Vaughn Johnson, *The Men and the Vision of the Southern Commercial Conventions, 1845–1871* (Columbia: University of Missouri Press, 1992), 1–15.

11. Takaki, *Pro-Slavery Crusade*, 150–51, 154–55; W. E. B. Du Bois, *Suppression of the African Slave-Trade to the United States of America, 1638–1870*, (Mineola, N.Y.: Dover Publications, 1970), 170–71; *De Bow's Review* 23 (September 1857): 316–19.

12. Dillon, *Life of John Mitchel*, 2:100–101; Seventh Census of the United States, 1850: Slave Schedule, Knox Co., Tennessee.

13. *De Bow's Review* 24 (June 1858): 580–87; *Washington, D.C., National Intelligencer,* June 23, 1860; *Knoxville Southern Citizen,* June 3, 1858. Yancey's biographer considers his speech at the convention a major element in the fire-eater's rise to notoriety. Eric H. Walther, *William Lowndes Yancey and the Coming of the Civil War* (Chapel Hill: University of North Carolina Press, 2006), 216–21.

14. *Dublin Irishman,* January 11, 25, 1862. Mitchel's 1858 letters were reprinted here to enlighten Irish readers on his pro-Confederate stance during the American Civil War. Lynch, "Defining Irish Nationalist Anti-Imperialism," 86–87. For more on Davis, see Helen F. Mulvey, *Thomas Davis and Ireland: A Biographical Study* (Washington, D.C.: Catholic University of America Press, 2003).

15. Quoted in Dillon, *Life of John Mitchel,* 2:106, and *Charleston Mercury,* August 4, 1859. For a succinct view of Genovese's thesis, see his *The Slaveholders' Dilemma: Freedom and Progress in Southern Conservative Thought, 1820–1860* (Columbia: University of South Carolina Press, 1994).

16. Elizabeth Fox-Genovese and Eugene D. Genovese, *The Mind of the Master Class: History and Faith in the Southern Slaveholders' Worldview* (New York: Cambridge University Press, 2005), 216–17; Horsman, *Josiah Nott of Mobile.* See also George M. Fredrickson, *The Black Image in the White Mind: The Debate on Afro-American Character and Destiny, 1817–1914,* 2nd ed. (Hanover, N.H.: University Press of New England, 1987), 71–96. Mitchel, quoted in the *Boston Liberator,* February 17, 1854.

17. *Knoxville Southern Citizen,* February 4, 1858.

18. Quoted in *Jackson Mississippian and State Gazette,* March 10, 1858 (emphasis in original).

19. *Rochester Frederick Douglass' Paper,* January 27, 1854; *Jackson Mississippian and State Gazette,* March 10, 1858; *Knoxville Southern Citizen,* March 11, 1858. For more on the Louisiana apprentice scheme, see Takaki, *Pro-Slavery Crusade,* 170–74.

20. *Knoxville Southern Citizen,* March 11, 1858. For Fitzhugh's theories, see Harvey Wish, ed., *Antebellum Writings of George Fitzhugh and Hinton Rowan Helper on Slavery* (Cambridge, Mass.: Harvard University Press, 1960).

21. For whiteness and the Irish, see Noel Ignatiev, *How the Irish Became White* (New York: Routledge, 1995), and David Roediger, *The Wages of Whiteness: Race and the Making of the American Working Class* (New York: Verso, 1994), esp. 133–63. For strong critiques, see Peter Kolchin, "Whiteness Studies: The New History of Race in America," *Journal of American History* 89 (June 2003): 154–73; Eric Arnesen, "Assessing the Whiteness Genre: A Reply to James Barrett, David Brody, Barbara Fields, Eric Foner, Victoria Hattam, and Adolph Reed," *International Labor and Working-Class History* 60 (Fall 2001): 81–92.

22. *Washington, D.C., Daily National Intelligencer,* June 23, 1860; David T. Gleeson, *The Irish in the South, 1815–1877* (Chapel Hill: University of North Carolina Press, 2001), 137–38; Manisha Sinha, *Counterrevolution of Slavery,* 165–66; *Letters of the Late John England to Hon. John Forsyth* (Baltimore: John Murphy, 1844), iv–vi.

23. Sinha, *Counterrevolution of Slavery,* 135–36, 153, 167–73.

24. Seventh and Eighth Censuses of the United States, 1850 and 1860: Slave Schedule, Charleston County, South Carolina; William C. Davis, *Rhett: The Turbulent Life and Times of a Fire-Eater* (Columbia: University of South Carolina Press, 2001), 349–50; *Charleston (S.C.) Mercury,* September 24, 1856, September 30, 1856, October 1, 1856; *Columbia Daily South Carolinian,* October 2, 1856.

25. David T. Gleeson, "Smaller Differences: 'Scotch Irish' and 'Real Irish' in the Nineteenth-Century South," *New Hibernia Review* 10 (Summer 2006): 73–75; [A. G. Magrath], *Three Letters on the Order of the Know-Nothings Addressed to Hon. A. P. Butler* (Charleston, S.C.: Burke, 1855), 10.

26. Takaki, *Pro-Slavery Crusade*, 201–16; Sinha, *Counterrevolution of Slavery*, 168–70; *The United States vs. William C. Corrie, Presentment for Piracy: Opinion of the Hon. A. G. Magrath* (Charleston, S.C.: Courtenay, 1860), 6–7, 26–27. For more on the whole story, see Eric Calonius, *The Wanderer: The Last American Slave Ship and the Conspiracy That Set Its Sails* (New York: St. Martin's Griffin, 2008).

27. *United States vs. William C. Corrie*, 14–18.

28. The debate over original intent in American jurisprudence is a long one. Of course Taney had used selective original intent in the notorious Dred Scott decision. See Don E. Fehrenbacher, *Slavery, Law and Politics: The Dred Scott Case in Historical Perspective* (New York: Oxford University Press, 1981), esp. 189–90. For more on the general debate, see Keith Whittington, *Constitutional Interpretation: Textual Meaning, Original Intent, and Judicial Review* (Lawrence: University Press of Kansas, 1999).

29. *United States vs. William C. Corrie*, 17–18.

30. Ibid., 22; Takaki, *Pro-Slavery Crusade*, 208–11.

31. Gleeson, "Smaller Differences," 75–76; Sinha, *Counterrevolution of Slavery*, 170–73; Takaki, *Pro-Slavery Crusade*, 109; Nini Rodgers, *Ireland, Slavery and Anti-Slavery, 1612–1865* (New York: Palgrave Macmillan, 2006), 297, 331.

32. Slave Sale Broadside, 1852, South Carolina Historical Society, Charleston; "Catalogue of Negro Slaves of the Estate of the Hon. William McKenna Deceased," January 21, 1861, Archives of the Catholic Diocese of Charleston; Sylviane A. Diouf, *Dreams of Africa in Alabama: The Slave Ship Clotilda and the Story of the Last Africans Brought to America* (New York: Oxford University Press, 2007), 7–30, 72–90.

33. Maunsel White to Richard Maunsell, January 28, 1844; White to Andrew Jackson, January 26, March 12, 1845; White to Isaac Hayne, August 23, 1847; White to Board of Administrators, University of Louisiana, February 8, 1848; White to Editor, *Economist*, September 14, 1849; Deer Range Memorandum, May 3, 1858; August 7, 1858; June 4, 1860; August 15, 1860; Maunsel White Papers, Southern Historical Collection, University of North Carolina, Chapel Hill; Seventh Census of the United States, 1850: Slave Schedule, Plaquemines Parish, Pointe Coupée Parish, Louisiana; Richard Follett, *The Sugar Masters: Planters and Slaves in Louisiana's Cane World, 1820–1860* (Baton Rouge: Louisiana State University Press, 2005), 24–28, 34, 43.

34. John Chester Miller, *The Wolf by the Ears: Thomas Jefferson and Slavery* (Charlottesville: University Press of Virginia, 1991); Steven Deyle, *Carry Me Back: The Domestic Slave Trade in American Life* (New York: Oxford University Press, 2006); Adam Rothman, *Slave Country: American Expansion and the Origins of the Deep South* (Cambridge, Mass.: Harvard University Press, 2005).

2007 REVISITED

Commemoration, Ritual, and British Transatlantic Slavery

JOHN OLDFIELD

F ew could have anticipated the unparalleled explosion of interest in commemorating the bicentenary of the abolition of the British slave trade or, indeed, the level of activity associated with the anniversary. Major new exhibitions were opened in Liverpool, Bristol, Hull, Birmingham, and London. Smaller exhibitions also were put on in many other towns and localities, many of them not usually associated with slavery or the slave trade: for example, in North Wales, Guernsey, East Anglia, Derbyshire, Stroud, Fulham, Edinburgh, and Enfield. The BBC threw its weight behind the anniversary, as did two of the United Kingdom's leading heritage organizations, English Heritage and the National Trust.[1] There were similar initiatives in the schools, where the most significant development was the integration of slavery into the National Curriculum, ensuring that all children in the United Kingdom between the ages of eleven and fourteen would be introduced to the subject, either as part of the history curriculum or through classes in citizenship. The 2007 bicentenary also produced a rush of books and articles on slavery and abolition, from William Hague's biography of William Wilberforce to more specialized studies of transatlantic slavery and cultures of abolition. The public's enthusiasm for abolition seemed insatiable, as evidenced by the host of events (lectures, debates, conferences) sponsored by historical societies, community groups, and local television and radio stations.[2]

What did all of this interest signify? And what sense, several years later, can we make of the 2007 commemorations? To answer these questions, we need to place the bicentenary in some sort of context. As I have argued elsewhere, Britons have tended to view transatlantic slavery through the moral triumph of abolition. According to this sentimental discourse, abolition of the slave trade in 1807, followed twenty-six years later by the abolition of British colonial slavery, gave the country a unique advantage over its rivals. Such selfless actions, it was believed, legitimized Britain's role in the world, the country's stewardship over countless millions in Africa, India, and the Caribbean, and, no less important, its particular claim to speak for those who were too weak to speak for themselves. This way of remembering (or forgetting) Britain's experience of slavery was already established by 1850, if not before. (Perhaps we can trace it back to Thomas Clarkson's *History of the Rise, Progress and Accomplishment of the Abolition of the Slave Trade by the British Parliament*, published in 1808.) The British abolitionist George Thompson spoke for many when he argued in 1859, on the twenty-fifth anniversary of the abolition of British colonial slavery, that "even should our political economy be false, the principle on which the anti-slavery cause was based would stand unshaken, for that principle was that emancipation from bondage was the right of the slave, and that his enslavement was a crime to be abolished, not an evil to be mitigated." Echoing these sentiments, the London *Morning Star* heralded "Emancipation" as "one of the greatest events in the history of England" and one that "exalted this nation high above all the other civilised nations of earth."[3]

Over the years this moral argument came to dominate public discourse on emancipation (and hence transatlantic slavery). As the *Times* put it in 1884: "There is no nobler chapter in the history of English freedom than that which ended fifty years ago in the emancipation of every slave within the Imperial dominions of the British Crown."[4] Similarly throughout the celebrations that marked the centenary of emancipation in 1933–34, Britain's decision to free its slaves was variously described as a "sublime" or "disinterested" act and, as such, a sign of the nation's moral strength and superiority. The Oxford historian Reginald Coupland told a meeting in Kingston-upon-Hull that the abolition of British colonial slavery was "a striking example—perhaps the most striking example one can think of in modern history—of a power of pure idealism in a practical world." "It may be that politics is often no more than a mask for the strife of rival interests," Coupland conceded, aiming his sights at postwar cynics. "But the lives and works of Wilberforce and the 'Saints' are certain proof that not merely individuals but the common will, the State itself, *can* rise on occasion to the height of pure unselfishness."[5]

In other words Britons substituted for the indignity of transatlantic slavery—and its role in transforming Britain into a major mercantile and military power—what might be described as a "culture of abolitionism." Wilberforce was a key figure here. He was cherished first and foremost as a "statesman-saint" whose career seemed to exemplify what could be done by "moral power inspired by religion." His was quintessentially an "English story." As the historian George M. Trevelyan explained, emancipation, like the slave-trade agitation that had preceded it, "was pre-eminently a result of our free institutions, our freedom of speech and association, and all that habit of voluntaryism and private initiative which distinguished the England of Pitt and Fox, Castlereagh and Canning, from the Europe of Napoleon and Talleyrand."[6] The attorney general, Sir Thomas Inskip, went a step further when in 1934 he hailed Wilberforce as "the begetter of the principle, happily revived in recent years, that [Britain] was the trustee for helpless millions," adding significantly that this principle was "the true basis of the Empire."[7] In this way Wilberforce came to embody a certain kind of British philanthropy and, just as important, a certain type of Britishness characterized by justice, compassion, and fair play.

As the theorist Maurice Halbwachs reminds us, however, every realm of memory is also a realm of contest.[8] If, in the case of transatlantic slavery, challenges to the dominant (white) discourse were slow to emerge, at least with any force, in the last thirty or forty years they have grown apace, stimulated in large part by societal changes, as well as broadly political and cultural forces, among them debates about diversity and multiculturalism. Another impetus has come from below. In the English-speaking Caribbean, for instance, the years following independence witnessed the emergence of alternative versions of the slave past, many of them shaped by the work of black intellectuals such as Eric Williams and C. L. R. James. Similarly in Britain and the United States, blacks started to reclaim their history, aided in many cases by white scholars who took it upon themselves to revise traditional accounts of slavery and the transatlantic slave trade. Determined to unravel and document "the world the slaves made," scholars on both sides of the Atlantic increasingly turned their attention to what had hitherto been neglected areas of slave life: language, personality, culture, and community. The result was a revolution in slave studies that in many ways reflected developments in other fields, notably women's history.[9]

These influences, in turn, prompted a reappraisal of the black diasporic experience. Three related themes were important here. The first was the attempt to reimagine Africa not as a place where Europeans went to get "slaves" but as a rich and diverse continent capable of producing artifacts of the most stunning originality and complexity. Linked to this attempt was a growing emphasis on black agency, that is, the ability of enslaved Africans to shape their own lives, not least by resisting white oppression, either "passively" or, more violently, through acts of rebellion. And finally there was a much greater willingness to recognize the indignity of transatlantic slavery and its damaging impact on diasporic blacks, especially through the troubling legacy of racism. These themes were particularly evident in many of the new slave museums and galleries that appeared in Britain during the 1980s and 1990s, among them those at Hull (Wilberforce House Museum) and Liverpool (Transatlantic Slavery Gallery). I will have more to say about museums later, but it is worth stressing at this point that since the 1980s museums have emerged as key sites of memory in relation to transatlantic slavery, providing fresh perspectives, challenging comfortable ideas, and, on occasion, provoking passionate responses.

As the bicentenary approached, therefore, and thoughts turned to marking it in some way, Britons were faced with a number of awkward challenges, chief of which was: who and what should be remembered? Debates surrounding 1807/2007 were further complicated by another set of potentially divisive issues. One of these was the demand from church leaders, political activists, and some members of Parliament for the government to make an apology for British involvement in the transatlantic slave trade. Another, led principally but not exclusively by black pressure groups, was the call for reparations, a highly explosive issue that then, as now, divided political opinion in the United Kingdom.[10] Equally contentious in some quarters was the proposal for a national slavery remembrance day; that is, a permanent commemoration (on August 23 of each year) that in the words of MP Louise Ellman, one of the proposal's leading proponents, would recognize the inhumanity of transatlantic slavery, "celebrate slaves' rebellions and the resistance that played such a part in the emancipation," and emphasize the inextricable links between slavery and racism today.[11]

Despite these tensions there seemed to be understandable concern both inside and outside Parliament to improve awareness of British involvement in the transatlantic slave trade, however uncomfortable that knowledge might be. As Gary Streeter, Conservative MP for South-West Devon, told the House of Commons in the 2004 debate on the then forthcoming bicentenary of the abolition of the slave trade: "there must be an acknowledgment of the part that the country played in this appalling atrocity; that what we did was wrong; that it is a scar on our history, and is only partially redeemed by the fact that we led the way in the abolition of the trade and then the abolition of slavery."[12] Similarly Jeremy Corbyn (Islington North, Labour) urged his fellow MPs to remove themselves from "the English and European feeling of self-satisfaction that we did a good job for the world 200 years ago. The reality is that Britain and Europe made a vast amount of wealth from the slave trade, and that wealth is still with us." Many other MPs voiced similar sentiments, fueling a sense that 2007 was an opportunity not simply to confront the inhumanity of transatlantic slavery but also to "ensure that we learn the lessons of the past."[13]

In response to these and other demands, the government eventually threw its weight behind the bicentenary, committing itself to an ambitious initiative aimed at tackling poverty and inequality in the Caribbean and Africa, racism in the United Kingdom, and contemporary slavery in all its forms. The Heritage Lottery Fund also made available 20 million pounds to fund community-based projects inspired by the bicentenary.[14] In making these commitments, however, Tony Blair's Labour government imposed its own shape on the 2007 bicentenary, perhaps best summed up in the slogan "Reflecting on the past and looking to the future." As his critics had feared he might do, Blair neatly sidestepped the question of an apology, limiting himself to an expression of "regret" that something bad had happened. The message he and his ministers wished to convey, it seemed, was rather different, namely, that 2007 offered an opportunity for *all* Britons (the emphasis was important) to reflect on "the spirit of freedom, justice and equality that characterised the efforts of the early abolitionists," "the same spirit that drives our determination to fight injustice and inequality today."[15]

In terms of commemoration, this message was reinforced via an adaptive process that ironically breathed new life into Britain's "culture of abolitionism." Perhaps the best example of this was the series of six postage stamps produced by the Royal Mail to commemorate 2007. As Marcus Wood has observed, "British commemorative stamps constitute a semiotic environment that has always been, and remains, heartily and unapologetically, celebratory."[16] The commemoration of 2007 was no exception. All six stamps produced by the Royal Mail focused on specific individuals, among them Granville Sharp, Wilberforce, and Thomas Clarkson. To this extent the stamps evoked a well-established and essentially white heroic paradigm. But in adopting this celebratory stance, the Royal Mail was also careful to extend its frame of reference to include two black figures, Olaudah Equiano and Ignatius Sancho. Significantly it also included one white woman in the shape of Hannah More, who in this context is best remembered for her *Slavery: A Poem* (1789). Equally revealing was the deliberate pairing or "twinning" of these stamps in ascending monetary value: Wilberforce with Equiano (34p), Sharp with Clarkson (50p), and More with Sancho (72p).[17]

Essentially the same set of considerations was evident in the planning and orchestration of the special service of commemoration held in Westminster Abbey on March 27, 2007, which was attended by the Queen and Prince Philip, Tony Blair and members of his cabinet, and MPs, foreign dignitaries, community groups, and civil rights activists. Here again there was a deliberate attempt to accommodate black perspectives, most obviously through music and performance. Hence the involvement in the service of the London Adventist Vocal Ensemble, the Percussion and Mmenson Players of Efiba Arts (U.K.), and the U.K. Freedom 200 Chamber Orchestra. Also striking (and this was to become a familiar trope of the bicentenary) was the pairing of Wilberforce and Equiano, both in Archbishop Rowan Williams's address and in the presentation and blessing of key abolitionist texts, among them Equiano's *Interesting Narrative* (1789). Similarly the prayers included petitions for Ottobah Cugoano, Ignatius Sancho, and Mary Prince, all of them prominent black abolitionists, in addition to petitions for members of the Clapham Sect and those who used their influence in politics and society, among them Wilberforce and Henry Thornton.[18]

What these events emphasized, in other words, was a more inclusive or popular view of abolition. As the Very Reverend John Hall put it in his "bidding" in Westminster Abbey: "We have come here to remember the commitment and courage of a group of abolitionists, black and white, male and female, who gave much and risked much to end the cruelty of the transatlantic trade in slaves."[19] The same point was made in the 2007 exhibition "The British Slave Trade: Abolition, Parliament, and People," in Westminster Hall, adjoining the Houses of Parliament, where the organizers put on display the 1806 Manchester petition against the slave trade, linking it to a searchable database containing the names of all of those who signed the petition.[20] Of course there are good grounds for seeing abolition in this way. Largely as a result of growing interest in the "public sphere" and history from below, we have become accustomed to seeing abolition less as a movement that took place in Parliament than as a grassroots movement involving thousands of activists who were willing to distribute tracts, organize committees, and sign petitions. But what is interesting is how these ideas were taken up by government spokespersons, among them David Lammy, then the minister for culture, in order to emphasize the inclusive nature of abolition and therefore the idea of a shared legacy.[21]

Recently Catherine Hall has argued that organized activities of this kind should be seen in the context of a shift on the part of government ministers away from multiculturalism and toward "social cohesion," the implication being that multiculturalism has led to "social fracturing and increased separation" and is thus increasingly seen as a failed project.[22] Certainly a lot of what happened in 2007—at least at an official level—can be interpreted in this light. But attempts to use the bicentenary for wider political purposes did not go unchallenged. One of the fiercest critics of the official 2007 commemorations was the black activist Toyin Agbetu, who memorably disrupted the Westminster Abbey service and, in doing so, drew attention to a radically different interpretation of what 2007 meant, not least for black Britons. What Agbetu had to say is as follows:

> The "Wilberfest" abolition commemoration had eradicated any mention of resistance, rebellion and revolution instigated by millions of African people.
>
> I stood up with my arms raised in a gesture of nonviolence and said "Not in my name" to Dr Rowan Williams who was attempting to lead the congregation, including a number of African people, to their knees to beg God's forgiveness for slavery. . . . I went to the Queen and told her that in the history of the Maafa, the British are the Nazis. . . .
>
> I then turned to Tony Blair and told him he ought to feel ashamed for his behaviour. Blair quickly averted his gaze. The rest of what I said was directed to members of my own community who were present. I don't believe it was right for us to have remained in a venue in which the British Monarchy, Government and church—all leading institutions of African enslavement during the Maafa—collectively refused to atone for their sins.
>
> Then a gang of men attempted to drag me out through the back door on my knees. I strongly asserted that I would be walking out of the front door, on my feet, as an African.[23]

Several things are interesting about this text, not least its emphasis on black pride and the demand for some form of atonement. Equally revealing is what Agbetu says about Wilberforce ("Wilberfest") and resistance. Agbetu was not alone in questioning the public's preoccupation with Wilberforce in 2007. Reactions to Melvyn Bragg's hagiographic portrait of Wilberforce on BBC Radio 4 divided many critics, as did the film *Amazing Grace*.[24] Despite attempts to widen the frame of reference (and *Amazing Grace* did at least recognize figures such as Equiano), there was an uncomfortable feeling in some quarters that nothing really had changed. We can put Agbetu's point a different way. Despite the growing emphasis on black resistance, not least within academic writing about slavery, "official" narratives sometimes seemed at odds with these perspectives, preferring instead to fall back on what many, particularly black Britons, regarded as Eurocentric perspectives on slavery and abolition. More often than not, black agency was repackaged as black abolitionism; hence the emphasis on Equiano, who, for the most part, was reassuringly and somewhat patronizingly represented as Wilberforce's coworker.

Some, such as Marcus Wood, have gone further, highlighting the passivity of much of the black imagery surrounding 2007 and contrasting what happened in Britain with some of the imagery (postage stamps, for instance) produced in the Caribbean, where themes of resistance were much more evident.[25] These arguments have some merit, but they do not tell the whole story. Take museums, for instance. Since the 1980s museums have emerged as key sites of memory in relation to transatlantic slavery. There are a number of reasons for this development. The language of diversity, and more inclusive notions of Britishness, placed new demands on museums and galleries. National Lottery funding, launched in 1994, also underlined the message, articulated by many black and Asian community groups, that museums had a "public duty to make provision for all parts of society." These pressures, not to mention new technologies and new approaches to the interpretation of texts, led in the 1980s to a radical reappraisal of the role of the museum in modern society. In many museums today, visitors expect to find, and will find, discovery rooms, hands-on exhibits, film, interactive video, and audio recordings. Similarly greater emphasis is placed on "enactive" and "experimental" modes of learning, whereby visitors acquire knowledge through demonstration, role playing, or handling objects. "New" museums are also more user friendly in the sense that they quite openly seek and encourage the involvement of their "customers" through consultative groups, outreach programs, and dialogue with those who might have been ignored or neglected in the past (minorities, for instance).[26]

The result in the case of transatlantic slavery was the opening of exhibitions in Hull, Liverpool, Bristol, and London that were highly innovative, not least in their emphasis on black perspectives.[27] Interestingly most of these exhibitions, including those at Liverpool and Hull, were either replaced or refurbished ahead of the bicentenary. At the same time, new exhibitions were organized to coincide with the 2007 commemorations, some of them temporary and small scale (for example "The Wickedest of Cargoes" at the Old Town Hall in Stratford, London), others larger and much more ambitious. There is not space here to discuss all of these exhibitions. Instead I want to focus on just three: "Breaking the Chains" at the British Empire and Commonwealth Museum in Bristol; the International Slavery Museum in Liverpool; and finally "London, Sugar and Slavery" at London Docklands Museum.

The curators of "Breaking the Chains," which opened in 2007 but is now closed to the general public, were obviously keen to embrace a more inclusive view of

British abolition, noting the importance of petitions and petitioning, for instance, as well as highlighting the role of blacks in the movement, among them Equiano and Cugoano. The exhibition also included an interesting section on poetry and the relationship between abolition and women's writing. Though revisionist in tone (this was categorically not an exhibition about Wilberforce), "Breaking the Chains" again reinforced a view of abolition as a grassroots movement and, to that extent, was all of a piece with the "official" narratives favored by the press and government spokespersons. But at the same time, the exhibition was at pains to stress the importance of black resistance. Visitors were told that African communities developed tactics, including fortified villages and alarm systems, to defend themselves against the slave trade. Similarly the exhibition noted that on the Middle Passage there was one slave rebellion on every ten ships, an estimate based on some four hundred known incidents, although the actual figure may have been higher.[28]

"Breaking the Chains" also contained a large section on slave resistance in the Caribbean, highlighting both the significance of passive resistance (language, culture, going slow, and so on) and slave rebellions. Particularly striking was a display case containing a drum, machete, conch horn, and British government papers relating to slave insurrections in the British West Indies, which was framed by a graphic (really a transparency) showing the major rebellions against slavery in the region between 1650 and 1840. Another case dealt with the Baptist War in Jamaica (1831–32), which involved more than twenty thousand slaves and is said to have caused more than one million pounds in damage. Significantly the exhibition posited an indirect link between slave revolts and action by the imperial Parliament. "British forces crushed these [rebellions] forcefully," visitors were told. "But this brutality helped turned public opinion in Britain against slavery." The result was an extremely nuanced interpretation of "Abolition," one that remembered "the courage and strength of *all* those who fought and campaigned against slavery—in Africa, Britain, *and* the Caribbean."[29]

The curators at the International Slavery Museum, which also opened in 2007 and continues to attract large numbers of visitors, decided to take a different approach.[30] Here abolition is mentioned but never really explored, at least not as a popular movement. Instead it is wrapped into a much broader narrative charting the progress of human rights struggles from the late eighteenth century through the American Civil War, the civil rights movement, and Anti-Slavery International's campaign against modern slavery. Again the exhibition is at pains to highlight the importance of black resistance. To emphasize the point, a separate display charts the history of slave revolts in the Americas, from Black Spartacus in Brazil (circa 1695) through the First Carib War in St. Vincent (1773) and the final wave of rebellions (1830–32) in Virginia, Barbados, and British Guiana. But while the evidence for resistance is compelling, the museum's international focus arguably raises more questions than it answers. Here as elsewhere there is a tendency to use the successful Haitian revolution, which began in French Saint-Domingue in 1791, as a surrogate for unsuccessful risings in the British islands, just as there is a tendency to view what happened in the Caribbean as a model or template for the rest of the Americas, even when the evidence—certainly in the case of the American South, which experienced relatively few slave rebellions—would appear inconclusive at best.[31]

Also significant, given the context, was the heavy emphasis that the curators placed on the indignity of transatlantic slavery. Turning their backs on the mock-up of the interior of a slave ship, which had been a feature of the Transatlantic Slavery Gallery, opened in 1994, they came up with the idea of a panorama, a jarring series of sights and sounds that envelops visitors and seems to take its cue from Steven Spielberg's film *Amistad*. The clear intention is to shock and provoke. This part of the museum is dimly lit, all of the interpretation boards are black, instruments of torture are prominently displayed, and the sounds from the Middle Passage display provide a constant backdrop, reminding visitors of the inhumanity of the slave trade. This is a much more intense exhibition than "Breaking the Chains" and one obviously intended to unsettle visitors, challenging them to reflect upon the inhumanity of transatlantic slavery and white complicity in this "foul iniquity."

A third and final attempt to "imagine" transatlantic slavery can be found at London Docklands Museum, which again opened in 2007. Here the decision was made to embed slavery very firmly in the local experience. Visitors enter "London, Sugar, and Slavery" through a series of galleries devoted to the history of London as a port and, once inside, are constantly reminded of the city's heavy involvement in transatlantic slavery. More often than not these prompts are material objects such as the West India Dock Company's mace, which is made from sugarcane, with a silver "head" depicting a West Indiaman on a globe. At other times, however, the exhibition makes innovative use of interactive displays. Particularly effective are two London maps, one depicting the "business of slavery," the other charting the African presence in London, as well as patterns of "enslavement" and "resistance." The history of London's black population is an important theme running through the exhibition, which begins with a display describing the life experiences of Equiano, Francis Williams, George Augustus Bridgetower, and others. Later "London, Sugar, and Slavery" also draws attention to the work of black abolitionists in and around London, noting that "nothing worked as powerfully as the words of Africans themselves."[32]

In these and different ways, the exhibition reinforces the point that "an incalculable proportion of London's wealth, business, and buildings was founded on the profits of slavery." Similarly "London, Sugar, and Slavery" explores the history of London as a "home" for countless migrants from "colonized societies," who arrived in the metropolis with high expectations, only to experience "exclusion, personal assault, and violence." Yet at the same time the exhibition is also keen to stress the contribution that blacks made, not simply to the abolitionist movement, but also to London life in general. Tellingly the exhibition makes the point that Wilberforce would have "achieved little" without the help of Clarkson, Sharp, and Equiano. Equally revealing is the use "London, Sugar, and Slavery" makes of Robert Wedderburn, a black abolitionist who was a prominent figure in radical circles in London during the early nineteenth century. Central to the gallery's intention to challenge visitors is the juxtaposition of two full-length portraits: the first by Thomas Lawrence of George Hibbert, a West Indian merchant and slave owner, set against views of West India Quay; the second, a "reconstructed" contemporary portrait of Wedderburn, which contains references to Wedderburn's fight *against* colonial slavery, among them a liberty cap and a copy of the *Poor Man's Guardian*.[33]

The curators take a similarly independent line when it comes to the related themes of slavery and resistance. Here again visitors are told that "Africans resisted enslavement constantly, ranging from sabotage to armed uprising, [which] destabilised the slave economy." But while the exhibition draws attention to slave rebellions in the Caribbean and explores in some detail the linkage between resistance and abolition, it does not dwell on resistance or give it undue prominence. Similarly, while "London, Sugar, and Slavery" stresses the importance of the abolitionist movement, it also makes room for other explanatory models, chief among them being the arguments put forward by Marxist historian Eric Williams, whose work is explicitly acknowledged by the curators. A section entitled "A Question of Economics?" introduces visitors to the notion that "the West Indian trade's privileged status was under attack from British manufacturers who found that trade restrictions and monopolies were beginning to impede their own industrial development and wealth." This is an interesting intervention and one that is clearly intended to open up the debate over emancipation in the British West Indies. The problem, however, is that visitors are given very little help in evaluating Williams's arguments or in reconciling his ideas with those presented elsewhere in the exhibition.[34]

More innovative and ultimately more successful is the exhibition's handling of slavery as a lived experience. From the outset visitors are invited to reflect on the meaning of slavery. A short introductory film, for instance, explores the different ways in which slavery dehumanizes human beings, before bringing visitors up short with the statement, "I hope the slave trade will be abolished." But perhaps the exhibition's most effective innovation is a simple device that again demands that visitors "consider slavery and what it is." At regular intervals throughout the day, the lights in the gallery dim and a disembodied voice proceeds to run through a list of abuses that together define or describe slavery; for instance, "you will not speak your own language," "you will be taken from your family," "you will be someone's property," "you will have no privacy," and, finally, "you will not be free." The effect created by this device is powerful. When I visited the exhibition, most if not all of the visitors stopped moving round the displays when the lights dimmed. For the few moments that followed, the large gallery was eerily silent, except for the disembodied voice and our own (unvoiced) thoughts and reflections.

What does all of this add up to? Simply that what was said about slavery in 2007 was often a good deal more challenging and reflective than critics sometimes like to suggest. It was merely a question of where one chose to look. Certainly, on the basis of the evidence presented here, museums and galleries were only too ready to confront the deeper meaning of the slave experience, as well as the overriding importance of black agency and/or resistance. Perhaps just as important, these museums set out to inculcate a sense of black pride and achievement. The reimagining of Africa is important here. In Bristol, for instance, there was a deliberate attempt to overturn negative images of Africa (AIDS, famine, genocide) and replace them with more reassuring images of stable family life, vibrant modern city landscapes, and ancient civilizations.[35] These exhibitions also emphasize the achievements of the black diaspora— in music, sports, politics, and religion. Perhaps the best example of this is the Black Achievers Wall at the International Slavery Museum in Liverpool. Academics are sometimes nervous or skeptical about such "contributionist" histories, fearing that they tend to belittle or obscure the wrongs that black people have suffered in the past, but the Liverpool exhibition shows how successful they can be when they are embedded in a deeper sense of the legacy of slavery and how it has affected the development of all the countries involved.[36]

Finally the 2007 bicentenary also produced a number of slave trade memorials, chief among them being the Captured Africans monument in Lancaster. Lancaster does not usually figure prominently in histories of British transatlantic slavery, but for much of the eighteenth century it was the country's fourth largest slave port. Between 1745 and 1806, in fact, over two hundred slave ships left Lancaster, which, in turn, were responsible for transporting twenty-five thousand Africans across the Atlantic and into slavery.[37] It was in an effort to recover this history that in 2002 the Lancaster City Council, the Lancaster Museums Service, the County Education Service, and Globalink set up the Slave Trade Arts Memorial Project (STAMP). Formally launched in 2003, STAMP was responsible for a number of different initiatives, including an ambitious education and outreach program led by the black British performance poet SuAndi. It was also the driving force behind a project to create a "permanent commemorative art piece" on the quayside in Lancaster that would acknowledge the city's involvement in the transatlantic slave trade. To this end, in 2004 the Manchester-based artist Kevin Dalton-Johnson was commissioned to design an appropriate memorial, which was officially unveiled on October 10, 2005, in the presence of the mayor, 150 school children, and the black American civil rights activist Preston King.[38]

By his own admission Kevin Dalton-Johnson was keen to design a memorial that would contest Eurocentric views of the slave trade,[39] and his Captured Africans is rooted very firmly in the black experience of transatlantic slavery. The base, for instance, consists of a colored mosaic of the triangular trade, and scattered across it are six figures, some kneeling, some lying down, that explicitly commemorate black loss. Above the mosaic (the sea) is fixed a ship, and here Dalton-Johnson's memorial evokes the eighteenth-century "description" of the slave ship *Brookes*, in this case represented three-dimensionally. Each deck represents a specific cargo, organized in order of importance, with the slaves at the bottom and wealth at the top. Read as a whole, Captured Africans attempts not only to memorialize Africans but also to put the slave trade on show, as if it too was an exhibit. Not everyone has welcomed the appearance of Captured Africans, some preferring to throw a veil over Lancaster's slave past, as if it were best forgotten.[40] Nevertheless it represents a bold and innovative visual statement that emphasizes remembrance rather than celebration, that has less to do with the moral triumph of British abolitionism than with voices of the forgotten, the slaves themselves.

It is too easy to be negative or cynical about what happened in 2007. Above all it is important to place the bicentenary in its appropriate historical context. Thirty—or even twenty—years ago it was still possible to view transatlantic slavery by focusing on the moral triumph of abolition, as was evident in 1983 when Britons marked the 150th anniversary of the abolition of colonial slavery.[41] But 2007 provoked a very different set of responses that, taken as a whole, not only improved awareness of the indignity of transatlantic slavery and its role in securing Britain's rise to global power in the seventeenth and eighteenth centuries, but also emphasized the importance of black resistance in bringing the Atlantic slave system to an end. It is true that some of what took place in 2007—at an official level, at least—was evasive, manipulative, and even misleading. At the same time, there was undoubtedly a tendency to draw a line under 2007, as if all of that was now safely in the past, the undeniable effect of which was to encourage forgetting rather remembering. But it may be that what happened in Westminster Abbey in March 2007 or what was represented on the nation's postage stamps was less important than changes to the National Curriculum or than exhibitions like "London, Sugar, and Slavery" or than the countless community projects that were set up under the Heritage Lottery Fund. One thing is certain. The old consensus, the one that focused almost exclusively on Britain's tradition of humanitarianism, has broken down. It may be too early to predict what will take its place, but we should underestimate neither the extent to which the 2007 bicentenary altered perceptions of British transatlantic slavery nor the extent to which it forced Britons to look again at the paradoxes embedded in national histories that first enslaved and then liberated persons of African descent.

Notes

An earlier version of this essay was delivered at the Wilberforce Institute for the study of Slavery and Emancipation, Kingston-upon-Hull, in February 2009. I am most grateful to those present for their comments and to Dr Joel Quirk and his colleagues at WISE for this opportunity to revisit "*Chords of Freedom*."

1. The BBC commissioned thirty hours of programs relating to slavery during 2007, including Moira Stewart's award-winning *In Search of Mr. Wilberforce*. For English Heritage and 2007, see http://www.English-heritage.org.uk/discover/people-and-places/the-slave-trade-and-abolition/, accessed July 4, 2011. For the National Trust, see *National Trust Magazine*, Summer 2007, and http://www.reinterpretation.co.uk/, accessed July 4, 2011.

2. For changes to the National Curriculum, see http://curriculum.qcda.gov.uk/key-stages-3-and-4/assessment/exemplification/standards-files/history/level-5/transatlantic-slave-trade.aspx, accessed July 4, 2011. For books published to coincide with the 2007 bicentenary, see, for example, William Hague, *William Wilberforce: The Life of the Great Anti-Slave Trade Campaigner* (London: HarperPress, 2007); Richard Reddie, *Abolition! The Struggle to Abolish Slavery in the British Empire* (London: Lion Hudson, 2007); Stephen Tomkins, *William Wilberforce* (London: Lion Hudson, 2007); Brycchan Carey and Peter Kitson, eds., *Slavery and the Cultures of Abolition: Essays Marking the Bicentennial of the British Abolition Act of 1807* (Cambridge: Brewer, 2007).

3. Quoted in J. R. Oldfield, *"Chords of Freedom": Commemoration, Ritual and British Transatlantic Slavery* (Manchester: Manchester University Press, 2007), 1, 89–90.

4. *Times* (London), August 2, 1884.

5. Quoted in Oldfield, *"Chords of Freedom,"* 99–100 (emphasis in original).

6. G. M. Trevelyan, "Wilberforce: The Centenary of a Warrior," *Times* (London), July 29, 1933.

7. *Anti-Slavery Reporter and Aborigines' Friend*, October 1934, 106.

8. Maurice Halbwachs, *On Collective Memory*, edited, translated, and with an introduction by Lewis A. Closer (Chicago: Chicago University Press, 1992), 183.

9. For these "revisionist" perspectives, see, in particular, Ira Berlin, *Generations of Captivity: A History of American Slaves* (Cambridge, Mass.: Harvard University Press, 2003); Peter Kolchin, *American Slavery* (London: Penguin, 1995); James Walvin, *Black Ivory: A History of British Slavery* (London: HarperCollins, 1992); and Eugene Genovese, *Roll, Jordan, Roll: The World the Slaves Made* (New York: Pantheon, 1974). For a recent challenge to the revisionists, see Wilma Dunaway, *The African-American Family in Slavery and Emancipation* (Cambridge: Cambridge University Press, 2003).

10. For demands for the government to make an apology, see "UK Slavery Apology 'Needed,'" BBC News, March 25, 2007, http://news.bbc.co.uk/1/hi/uk/6492291.stm, and Ethan Cole, "Church Head Urges Clear Apology for European Slave Trade," *Christian Post*, March 22, 2007, http://www.christianpost.com/news/church-head-urges-clear-apology-for-european-slave-trade-26464/. For reparations, see Mark Oliver, "Archbishop Urges Church to Consider Slavery Reparations," *Guardian*, March 26, 2007, http://www.guardian.co.uk/world/2007/mar/26/religion.race/, and Dan Garland, "Anti-Slavery March Demands Reparations for Slave Trade," Indymedia UK, March 24, 2007, http://www.indymedia.org.uk/en/2007/03/366019.html.

11. *Hansard*, 6th ser., vol. 425, col. 159–62WH. August 23 is the date chosen by UNESCO as the International Day for the Remembrance of the Slave Trade and Its Abolition. Significantly it marks the successful uprising by slaves in French Saint-Domingue in 1791.

12. *Hansard*, 6th ser., vol. 425, col. 149WH, October 14, 2004.

13. Ibid., col. 149WH (Corbyn) and col. 143WH (Fiona Mactaggart, Slough, Labour).

14. For the Heritage Lottery Fund's "Remembering Slavery" initiative, see http://search
.hlf.org.uk/hlf/themes/index.html, accessed July 5, 2011. The HLF funded hundreds of local
projects commemorating 2007, as well as larger initiatives such as the International Slavery
Museum in Liverpool.

15. Government Press Notice, January 22, 2007. See also Department for Culture, Media
and Sport, "Reflecting on the Past and Looking to the Future: The 2007 Bicentenary of the
Abolition of the Slave Trade in the British Empire," PP889, March 2006. This paper, which
was signed by David Lammy, then the minister for culture, and Paul Goggins, minister for
communities and race equality, stresses the "clear links between the concerns for justice that
were present 200 years ago, and our current concerns to tackle present-day forms of slavery,
such as people trafficking."

16. Marcus Wood, "Significant Silence: Where Was Slave Agency in the Popular Imagery of
2007?" in *Imagining Transatlantic Slavery,* ed. Cora Kaplan and John Oldfield (Basingstoke:
Palgrave Macmillan, 2010), 180.

17. All six stamps were also sold in a special commemoration pack, "Abolition of the Slave
Trade," complete with short biographies and illustrated essays on the "triangular trade" and
the campaign to abolish the slave trade.

18. "Abolitionists Remembered in Westminster Abbey Ceremony," March 28, 2007, http://
www.anglicancommunion.org/acns/news.cfm/2007/3/28/ACNS4271, accessed January 2,
2012.

19. Ibid.

20. For the exhibition in Westminster Hall, see "Parliamentary Archives Puts Documents
about the British Slave Trade Online," Federation of Family History Societies, June 14, 2007,
http://www.ffhs.org.uk/news/news070614.php, and the accompanying collection of essays,
The British Slave Trade: Abolition, Parliament, and People, ed. Stephen Farrell, Melanie
Unwin, and James Walvin (Edinburgh: Edinburgh University Press, 2007).

21. See, for instance, Lammy's remarks in January 2006 at the launching of the government's plans to mark the bicentenary, "2007 Bicentenary of the Abolition of the Slave Trade:
Honouring the Past and Looking to the Future," Government News, January 20, 2006,
http://gov-news.org/gov/uk/news/2007_bicentenary_abolition_slave_trade_honouring
/54034.html. For popular abolitionism, see J. R. Oldfield, *Popular Politics and British Anti-
Slavery: The Mobilisation of Public Opinion against the Slave Trade, 1787–1807* (Manchester:
Manchester University Press, 1995), and Adam Hochschild, *Bury the Chains: Prophets and
Rebels in the Fight to Free an Empire's Slaves* (New York: Houghton Mifflin, 2005).

22. Catherine Hall, "Britain 2007: Problematizing Histories," in Kaplan and Oldfield, *Imagining Transatlantic Slavery,* 195–96.

23. Toyin Agbetu, "My Protest Was Born of Anger, Not Madness," *Guardian,* April 3, 2007,
http://gu.com/p/xvvhc. See also the *Independent,* March 28, 2007.

24. Bragg's tribute was broadcast in the BBC Radio 4 series *In Our Times* on February 22,
2007.

25. See Wood, "Significant Silence," 180–86.

26. Oldfield, *"Chords of Freedom,"* 120–21.

27. Ibid., 120–36. The exhibitions in question were the "Wilberforce" and "Slavery" galleries, which opened in 1983 at Wilberforce House Museum, Hull; the Transatlantic Slavery

Gallery, which opened in 1994 at Merseyside Maritime Museum, Liverpool; "A Respectable Trade? Bristol and Transatlantic Slavery," which opened in 1999 at Bristol City Museum and Art Gallery and was later moved to Bristol Industrial Museum; and finally the "Trade and Empire" gallery, which opened in 2001 at the National Maritime Museum, Greenwich, London.

28. See Joseph E. Holloway, "Insurrections on Board Slave Ships," http://www.slavery inamerica.org/history/hs_es_insurrection.htm, accessed October 30, 2009.

29. My emphasis. All of these quotations are taken from the display boards in the museum.

30. For visitor numbers at the International Slavery Museum, see Stephen Bates, "British Tourist Attraction Visitors Figures: Who's Up and Who's Down?" Datablog, *Guardian*, March 30, 2011, http://www.guardian.co.uk/news/datablog/2011/feb/23/british-tourist -attractions-visitor-figures.

31. See Douglas Hamilton, "Representing Slavery in British Museums: The Challenges of 2007," in Kaplan and Oldfield, *Imagining Transatlantic Slavery*, 137–38.

32. Particularly striking here is the determination to get away from the seeming obsession with Equiano, who in the past has dominated displays of this kind. Francis Williams (1702–1770) was a black scholar and teacher who was privately educated in London before returning to Jamaica, circa 1735. See www.vam.ac.uk/collections/periods_styles/hidden histories/object_stories/francisblackwriter/index, accessed July 11, 2009. Bridgetower (1780–1860) was a black violinist and composer who was also an original member of the Royal Philharmonic Society, founded in 1813. See http://chevalierdesaintgeorges.homestead.com /bridge.html, accessed July 4, 2011. This part of the display at London Docklands Museum features eight early black Britons in all: Equiano, Williams, Bridgetower, Charles McGee, Joseph Johnson, Dido, Elizabeth Belle, and William Ansah Sessarakoo.

33. For Wedderburn and radical politics, see Iain McCalman, ed., *The Horrors of Slavery and other Writings by Robert Wedderburn* (Edinburgh: Edinburgh University Press, 1991), 8–35.

34. All of these quotations are taken from the display panels in the exhibition. For Williams and responses to Williams, see Eric Williams, *Capitalism and Slavery* (1944; repr., Chapel Hill: University of North Carolina Press, 1998); Seymour Drescher, *Econocide: British Slavery in the Era of Abolition* (Pittsburgh: University of Pittsburgh Press, 1977); and David Beck Ryden, "Does Decline Make Sense: The West Indian Economy and the Abolition of the Slave Trade," *Journal of Interdisciplinary History* 31, no. 3 (2001): 347–74.

35. At London Docklands Museum, too, the curators are keen to stress the sophistication of African arts and material culture, seeing the past neglect of these artifacts as yet another example of European racism.

36. For critiques of contributionist history, see Evelyn M. Simien, "Black Leaders and Civil Rights: Transforming the Curriculum, Inspiring Student Activism," *PS: Political Science and Politics* 36, no. 4 (2003): 747–50; Leslie Alexander, "The Challenge of Race: Rethinking the Position of Black Women in the Field of Women's History," *Journal of Women's History* 16, no. 4 (2004): 50–60.

37. For Lancaster and the slave trade, see Nigel Tattersfield, *The Forgotten Trade: Comprising the Log of the* Daniel *and* Mary *of 1700 and Accounts of the Slave Trade from the Minor Ports of England, 1698–1725* (London: Cape, 1991), 324–25; David Eltis, Stephen D. Behrendt,

David Richardson, and Herbert S. Klein, eds., *Transatlantic Slave Trade: A Database on CD-ROM* (Cambridge: Cambridge University Press, 1999).

38. *Lancaster Guardian,* October 14, 2005.

39. See http://www.Lancaster.gov.uk/whatson/NewsRM.asp?id=SXDF14-A7805D92&cat =529, accessed July 16, 2009.

40. Ibid. For local responses to Captured Africans, see *Lancaster Guardian,* January 7, 21, 28, February 18, and October 28, 2005.

41. See Oldfield, *"Chords of Freedom,"* 105.

CONTRIBUTORS

Peter A. Coclanis is associate provost for international affairs at the University of North Carolina at Chapel Hill, where he is also the Albert R. Newsome Distinguished Professor of History. His many publications include *The Shadow of a Dream: Economic Life and Death in the South Carolina Low Country, 1670–1920* (1989).

Steven Deyle is an associate professor of history at the University of Houston, where he specializes in nineteenth-century U.S. social and political history, with a particular interest in slavery and the Old South. He has won numerous fellowships, including the 2009 Joyce Tracy Fellowship from the American Antiquarian Society in Worcester, Massachusetts. Professor Deyle's first book, *Carry Me Back: The Domestic Slave Trade in American Life* (2005), won the Southern Historical Association's Bennett H. Wall Award and was a finalist for the Frederick Douglass Prize.

Inge Dornan is a lecturer in history at Brunel University in West London, where she specializes in the history of slavery and the slave trade in British America, the West Indies, and Africa. Her forthcoming book, *The Politics of Silence: Slavery and the Slave Trade in Britain's Slave Colonies,* historicizes the mechanisms of violence and control that were key to the development of slavery in British America.

David T. Gleeson is reader in American history at Northumbria University. His most recent book was the edited volume *The Irish in the Atlantic World* (2010). Dr. Gleeson's first book, *The Irish in the South, 1815–1877* (2001), won the 2002 Donald Murphy Prize for Distinguished First Book in Irish Studies.

Wilma King is Arvarh E. Strickland Distinguished Professor of History at the University of Missouri. She specializes in African American history with a focus on the experiences of women and children during slavery and on the high tide of abolitionism. Her book *Stolen Childhood: Slave Youth in Nineteenth-Century America* received the 1997 Distinguished Book Award from the National Conference of Black Political Scientists.

Louis M. Kyriakoudes is associate professor and director of the Center for Oral History and Cultural Heritage at the University of Southern Mississippi. A specialist in the social and economic history of the nineteenth- and twentieth-century United States, Dr. Kyriakoudes is the author of *The Social Origins of the Urban South: Race, Gender and Migration in Nashville and Middle Tennessee, 1890–1930* (2003).

Jean-Pierre Le Glaunec teaches American history at the University of Sherbrooke in Canada. His research focus is on the history of slavery in the Atlantic world, with a particular emphasis on cultural identity in Louisiana.

Simon Lewis is associate director of the Carolina Lowcountry and Atlantic World program at the College of Charleston. A teacher of African literature, his most recent book is *British and African Literature in Transnational Context* (2011).

Jonathan Mercantini teaches history at Kean University in Union, New Jersey. His research focus is on late colonial and revolutionary America with an emphasis on South Carolina. His monograph *Who Shall Rule at Home: The Evolution of South Carolina Political Culture, 1748–1776* was published in 2007 by the University of South Carolina Press.

Kenneth Morgan is professor of history at Brunel University in West London, where he is a member of the Centre for Caribbean, American and Transatlantic History (CATCH). A Fellow of the Royal Historical Society, Professor Morgan has a special teaching and research interest in slavery and the slave trade. He has published six books and has edited or coedited six collections.

John Oldfield is professor of modern history at the University of Southampton. He is the author of *'Chords of Freedom': Commemoration, Ritual and British Transatlantic Slavery* (2007) and *Popular Politics and British Anti-Slavery: The Mobilisation of Public Opinion against the Slave Trade, 1787–1807* (1995). He is the editor of *The British Atlantic Slave Trade*, vol. 3, *The Abolitionist Struggle: Opponents of the Slave Trade* (2003) and has written extensively on the American South, U.S. race relations, and slavery and abolition in the Atlantic world.

Gregory E. O'Malley is assistant professor of history at the University of California, Santa Cruz. He is working on the manuscript of his first book, "Final Passages: The British Intercolonial Slave Trade, 1619–1807."

INDEX